THE NEW REPUBLIC:
TWILIGHT OF THE GODS

PART THREE OF A THREE-VOLUME TAVISH STEWART
ADVENTURE

K.R.M. Morgan

K.R.M. Morgan

MADBAGUS BOOKS

ISBN: 978-1-9164472-5-7

Cover design by MadBagus

Footnotes

Based on reader feedback, I have adopted footnotes in this third Tavish Stewart adventure to provide the equivalent of an optional "director's cut" version of the story. Those who do not desire such additional information will be able to read the simplified version of the tale and perhaps save the footnotes for any subsequent revisits to the story.

Acknowledgements

The author wishes to acknowledge the help and support of his wife, Maddy, without whom this book would not have been possible.

Statement on AI

This story is a product of the author's imagination, research, and personal insights. It was written **without** the use of Artificial Intelligence. The author meticulously crafted the text and performed the background research, ensuring a human touch in every aspect of this work.

Social Media

If you enjoy reading this book, please share a review on social media or Amazon so others can discover Tavish Stewart's adventures.

K.R.M. Morgan

Summary of the previous book

Antiquarian and Scottish army veteran Tavish Stewart is
forced into a confrontation with powerful high adepts from a
malign esoteric order. Consequently, the Scotsman and his
friends face their greatest challenge as the world they know
collapses.

Extract from the closing section of The New Republic: THE
QLIPHOTHIC GATES:

Back in the refined Swiss Resort of Grindelwald, a violent
storm raged, repeatedly striking lightning into the remains of
ancient wooden churches and mountainside shrines. Inside a
sealed boardroom deep within one of the peaks of the
Bernese Alps, a group of corrupt men congratulated
themselves. The hedging bets they had placed against the
financial resources and reputation of the United Kingdom
had paid off handsomely. They were now discussing
ramping up their blackmail and extortion over the current
leaders of the European Nations before they too were ousted
from power.

These corrupt men who had gathered around what had been
the Maelstrom boardroom were eagerly anticipating the
advancement that would surely accompany their control over
the continent of Europe. As they toasted each other with
the finest Dom Pérignon champagne, vaporous clouds began
to form in the room, and it became bitterly cold. Several
champagne bottles and the fluted glasses shattered as the
wine inside them froze, and the room was plunged into
darkness.

The chairman of the meeting, Colonel Jaree, who had only
recently taken over from Major General Smegett, announced,

"Gentlemen, please remain calm and seated. The emergency generator will come on momentarily."

Unseen by anyone, behind Jaree, the full-length picture of the late Dr Nissa Ad-Dajjal became increasingly lifelike. Thick, white ice tendrils formed around the edges of the image. Then slowly, like a butterfly emerges from a chrysalis, a perfect female form, with raven black hair and striking green hypnotic eyes, pulled itself slowly from the picture, finally stepping seductively from the portrait, unseen into the complete darkness of the board room.

After what felt like an eternity, the backup generators finally kicked in, and the red emergency lights came on from the ceiling. Jaree looked in shock as he saw the assembled men around the table all standing and looking aghast at something behind him before rushing in terror from the room.

Within seconds, he was the only person remaining. He wondered what could have caused such dread in these most ruthless men. As the icy cold air in the deserted board room became filled with the highly distinctive intoxicating musky scent of the Ghost flower of the Mojave Desert[1], he turned, saw that the canvas of the infamous portrait behind him was empty, and then, with a start, noticed that standing beside him was the tall, raven-haired, Dr Nissa Ad-Dajjal; involuntarily he exclaimed,

"Jesus Christ!"

A sultry voice corrected him, "Guess again...."

---

[1] This unique perfume was distilled exclusively by the Sultan of Oman's own perfume house, Amouage for only one person.

ULTIMATE EVIL

"To prefer evil to good is not in human nature; and when a man is compelled to choose one of two evils, no one will choose the greater when he might have the less." – Plato

4800 feet above Lake Skadar,

Montenegro.

4:55HRS (GMT+2), 14th Sept, Present day

The inky black night sky surrounding the tiny[2] white fibreglass plane was suddenly filled with hundreds of small flashes, followed milliseconds later by a series of explosions that violently shook the Cessna - shattering the relative calm of the past three-and-a-half-hour journey. A series of bright flashes illuminated a castellated tower far below. These were followed seconds later by more air bursts around the aircraft, each coming closer until, on the third occasion, the cabin's fuselage became filled with dozens of coin-sized holes[3] that punched clean through the aircraft's fibreglass cabin walls.

Stewart patted the steering column as he spoke calmly to the aircraft, as one would to a startled animal, "Come on, old girl. We will be fine, just so long as they don't..."

The instant that Stewart had spoken, he regretted it as the single propeller stuttered. Then, the constant loud vibration that had been the unnoticed background over the past hours abruptly stopped. The aircraft was filled with an eerie silence as the plane transformed from purposeful transport into nothing more than a poorly shaped glider. The illuminated altimeter dial began to tell a sad story, confirmed by the slight downward angle now being assumed by the aircraft.

---

[2] This aircraft has a 36-foot wingspan, is 24 feet long and weighs 1600 pounds.
[3] Caused by a Turkish KORKUT-FCS anti-aircraft gun firing a 35mm low altitude airburst ammunition shell.

Yet another bright flash issued from the ground, followed by more significant impacts on the fibreglass bodywork and, more alarmingly, flames that began dancing along both wings. Stewart immediately switched off both fuel lines, but the fire was already spreading, filling the air with a choking acrid smell of burnt plastic and a more ominous odour of leaking aviation fuel.

Years of military training kept Stewart calm as he pulled the red cylinder-shaped fire extinguisher from its fixing beside him. Directing the hose nozzle towards the spreading flames, he struck the central knob only to discover that years of neglect had dissipated the CO2 canister that powered the extinguisher.

The Scotsman exclaimed something under his breath as he threw down the empty canister in disgust and grabbed the Velcro pull-release tabs on a grey canvas container labelled "Paracadute di Emergenza" (Emergency Parachute). Stretching the canvas holder open revealed that the nylon shoulder straps had rotted through, and the parachute nylon had been used by numerous generations of rodents for their nesting materials, leaving a shredded mess of urine-soaked nylon.

"Bloody vermin!" Stewart exclaimed, although it was unclear if he was referring to the maintenance staff or the rats that had nested in the parachutes.

As the Scotsman looked around the cabin for some improvised solution that might save him from being incinerated, he thought how different his situation had been only minutes earlier.

In the profound darkness[4] of the early morning, Stewart's intelligent grey eyes had spent the past three hours

---

[4] In order to fly undetected, Stewart had disabled the running lights and Cessna ARC RT-359A transponder on the plane before take-off.

reflecting the nine illuminated dials that comprised the instrument panel of the "Bacio Volante", a twenty-year-old, four-seat Cessna[5]. The dimly illuminated figure of the solitary Scotsman had been seated on the left front side of the cockpit, enveloped by a deep and constant thrumming and powerful vibration from the Lycoming[6] engine that drove a single propeller that danced in front of the split windscreen. Looking around the cramped space, it was clear that the passing decades had not been kind to the Cessna, as evidenced by the numerous splits in the grey plastic seating and stains that decorated the aircraft's exposed surfaces, the sources of which were best left unimagined.

Stewart had been glad for the light grey Timberland fleece he wore over his polo shirt to compensate for the temperature inside the aircraft, as it was significantly cooler at altitude than it had been on the ground in Sicily[7] when his journey had started. Stewart reflected that the cooler temperature had, at least, reduced the strong smell of stale cigarettes, body odour and wet seawater permeating the small plane.

Towards the end of his journey, the small, single-engine Cessna had started to become buffeted in the turbulent airstream above Lake Skadar, over four thousand feet beneath him. From that moment, Stewart's strong hands had firmly held the plane's black plastic yoke controls to keep on course. Over the past three and half hours and four hundred miles, the Scotsman had frequently consulted the aircraft's compass dial and the luminous oversized hands on the dashboard clock, comparing the readings against the

---

[5] A Cessna 182a Skylane plane.

[6] A Lycoming O-540 – an air cooled, 250 horse power, 8874 cc, six-cylinder engine.

[7] It is 3.6 degrees Fahrenheit cooler with each additional 1,000 feet of altitude.

pencil-marked course on an Aeronautical chart duct taped to the right-hand armrest of his seat in order to correct his bearings towards Fortress Grmožur.

After his midnight meeting to organise cutting the electrical supply for the Meri-Isfet ceremony, Capomandamento Donne's men had driven Stewart to the Pio La Torre airfield, where they had acquired the ancient Cessna. The aircraft was owned by "Super-Premium Experiences", a local Sicily-based tour agency that provided wealthy tourists with skydiving and wingsuit experiences over the clear blue seas of the Northern Mediterranean.   The livery on the side of the plane and the advertising materials on the seats promised an experience that was "akin to a fighter pilot experience day". From his British Army parachute training, Stewart was an experienced jumper, so he was familiar with most of the discarded gear left in the cabin from the previous day's tourist trips. The equipment was soaked with seawater, showing the tell-tale salt stains that Stewart knew would require extensive cleaning before they would look pristine enough for the kinds of customers willing to pay for these Super Premium Experiences. In addition to such cleaning, the soaked parachutes would require a lengthy damage assessment before being repacked for any subsequent jumps.

As he had moved the soaking wingsuits and parachutes into the rear of the cabin, the Scotsman had briefly been intrigued by the Touch Tandem System[8] harnesses on the wingsuits, as he had not seen a tandem wingsuit in commercial use before. There was only one standard (non-tandem) wingsuit[9] that Stewart surmised must be used by a cameraman to record the all-too-short descent before the parachute deployed for a landing in the ocean. The

---

[8] Manufactured by the French company X-Sky.
[9] A Freak 4 wingsuit from Squirrel.

Scotsman could vividly imagine the challenges of maintaining control of the suit with the additional drag caused by a second person and the risk of movement by the passenger, causing a catastrophic loss of control. His assessment of the danger was confirmed when he saw the liability waiver forms required for each customer. The death rate cited of "one fatality per five hundred jumps" was probably a conservative estimate, given the complexity of a tandem wingsuit jump.   As the Scotsman dragged the soaking equipment to the rear two seats, he was thankful that his use of the Cessna should be far less dangerous. His clearing away of the skydiving equipment was to make room for a specialised Skydio infrared surveillance drone[10] that the Mafia deployed to assist them in various nefarious night-time activities. However, tonight the burglary that occurred after the drone had scanned its target property was undoubtedly going to be even more violent than usual Mafia operations.

The plan that the Scotsman had dreamt up with the help of Donne's Capos was to fly over Fortress Grmožur and launch the Skydio so that it could record details of the fortifications. The drone would wirelessly relay its infrared picture data to the controller in the Cessna before Stewart landed at a prearranged clearing two miles north of the Godinje settlement. At the landing strip, the Scotsman would rendezvous with the Mafia from the surrounding areas to storm the Meri-Isfet Grmožur stronghold at first light. In their planning, it had been assumed that the complete loss of power to the Fortress would incapacitate any air defences.

That assumption had been wrong as, even without searchlights or radar, someone had managed to hit the unilluminated aircraft in total darkness. Stewart did not dwell

---

[10] Skydio X2™ Color/Thermal Drone with black bodywork and four propellors with an operational ceiling of 10,000 feet and a 3.7-mile wireless control range.

on the astronomic odds against an unassisted anti-aircraft gun hitting its target in such conditions[11]. Instead, he focused on how to extend his life expectancy. He had learned from long experience dealing with the uncertainty of war and disaster that those who survived the longest had often benefitted from radical and unforeseen changes in their situation.

While the Scotsman searched the Cessna for a means of escape, three-quarters of a mile beneath him, the human form that had once been the French magical adept, Madeleine Mathers, strode confidently away from the Turkish-made anti-aircraft gun. As she walked over the wet cobblestones, the air was permeated with a heady mixture of scents, including nutmeg and gardenia, which are the keynotes of one distinctive French perfume[12]. Mathers wore a close-fitting bespoke black Crye Precision[13] combat uniform, which she had donned shortly after completing the midnight ritual, that had exalted her to become the Imperatrix of the Meri-Isfet, one of the world's most ancient and powerful left-hand path occult societies.

As supreme leader of the organisation's esoteric and paramilitary branches, she would never be expected to involve herself personally in combat. However, tonight, she opted to wear similar equipment to the Wolfsangel special forces who protected her, but with some enhancements to

---

[11] In complete darkness, with no means of measuring the target, range, height or speed it is close to impossible for an unaided anti-aircraft gun to hit a target. Such a task is similar to trying to hit a mosquito in a dark room with a peashooter.

[12] Organza by Givenchy.

[13] Crye Precision G4 FR combat uniform. The FR indicates a Flame Retardant material.

reflect her exalted position. For example, instead of the standard black polymer Glock 17 with biosensor modifications, Mathers wore a steel[14] Wilson pistol[15] strapped to her right thigh in a black Flyye[16] drop leg holster. In preference to the German-engineered KM2000 combat knife issued to Wolfsangel operatives, Mathers had selected a blade that more accurately reflected the kind of combat in which she specialised: quick, dirty and traitorously unexpected. Such tactics call for a particular type of blade - either a traditional stiletto dagger or, as Mathers had selected, a Finnish-made filleting knife[17] which adorned her left ankle in a bespoke leather quick draw sheath. She wore a blackened titanium version of the Apple Watch Ultra on her left wrist, modified in Cupertino specifically for military applications[18].

This device synchronised wirelessly with a military-specified pair of integrated augmented reality glasses, a high-definition camera, earpiece and throat microphone, and tactical gesture gloves[19]. These specialised gloves permitted users to communicate silently in complete darkness with their other team members using hand gestures. The state-of-the-art augmented reality system included a real-time

---

[14] 416 Stainless Steel rated 45 on the Rockwell C scale of metal hardness.

[15] A Wilson Combat Tactical Supergrade Professional pistol, chambered for 45 ACP (Automatic Colt Pistol) ammunition with an 8-round magazine. Regarded by many gun aficionados as one of the world's finest hand pistols. Certainly, one of the most expensive.

[16] A Flyye Specops SEALS drop leg holster.

[17] A Marttiini Martef filleting 23 knife. This ultra-thin 7.5-inch Scandinavian steel blade pierces effortlessly through the rib cage. It is also long enough to penetrate deep into the heart. Ideal for any world-class backstabber.

[18] Classified DOD project code named "SmartForce".

[19] Marketed as "IKill" and "IKill Pro" in numerous weapons trade shows (trademarks and patents pending, of course).

combat AI functionality that predicted an opponent's position and actions. Combined with the heads-up display of all fellow team members' positions and their biometric physiological readings, it provided an operational unit with what was advertised as "an unbeatable advantage[20]" over conventional forces. The only limiting factor with this ground-breaking system was its reliance on a heavy battery power supply that slowed the operator's movement and required lengthy recharging after mere hours of continuous use.

In stark contrast to her tactical clothing, Mathers also wore an antique silver brooch on her right breast, denoting the mythological wolf from the Viking Sagas, Fenrir. She believed she now personified this Ultimate Evil—the entity prophesized in the Sagas, who would bring about the destruction of all creation.

After the ritual, Mathers had gathered Regio's initiates ring, adze[21], skull[22] and flag[23], along with the Rauðskinna[24], the grimoire of grimoires for the Nordic dark art of Galdr. She vowed she would keep these items close to her to ensure that no other adept would ever gain control of them and

---

[20] No doubt qualified by some extensive terms and conditions.

[21] That Mathers had used to slay her fellow Ipsissimus.

[22] Belonging to one, Alois Hiedler (you know him by another name).

[23] The Blutfahne or Blood Flag, is a Nazi Party flag carried during the attempted Beer Hall Putsch in Munich, on November the ninth 1923

[24] Literally "Red Skin" – This unusual name is derived from the colour of the binding and pages, that were made from the skin of Saint Veiðimaður; one of the Christian settlers of Iceland when the Vikings took possession of the Icelandic islands around 873 CE. The Rauðskinna, also known as "The Book of Power", is alleged to provide the procedure to summon and control the manifestation of ultimate evil, the giant wolf of destruction described in the Viking Sagas, Fenrir.

have the power to overthrow her from her destiny, to rule and destroy all.

Mathers wore the adept's rings from Regio and Pederson[25] around her neck, threaded through a Chanel silk[26] scarf. Her own initiates ring remained on her right ring finger, with the pentagram inverted, to symbolise her devotion to the Left-Hand Path (LHP) of magick.

To the disbelief of the six Meri-Isfet adepts, who had accompanied their leader to the top of the Fortress tower, their new Imperatrix had sensed an aircraft flying above them. Without radar or the sophisticated computer AI systems embedded in her wearable technology, Mathers had closed her hazel-coloured eyes in concentration and spun the large anti-aircraft guns two setting wheels to the correct elevation and direction necessary to achieve a direct hit on the plane.

None of them had been aware of this unidentified aircraft when they gathered around Mathers in the fortress meeting room, watching body cam footage from a four-person Wolfsangel detachment on a seek-and-destroy mission in the nearby village of Godinje. This gruesome task of supposed vengeance had been commissioned by their new leader moments after she had emerged from the OTTG[27] ritual.

As all six junior adepts gathered around Mathers on the top of the fortress tower, they were granted more graphic insight into the death and destruction instigated by their leader in

---

[25] Pederson's ring was collected from his dead body by Mathers as she made her way to the Fortress prior to the OTTG ritual.
[26] Silk limits astral influences. Ritual objects are often wrapped in this material to prevent them from becoming contaminated between ritual uses.
[27] A ritual called The Opening of the Ten Gates (OTTG).

revenge for the villagers' assistance to the Meri-Maat[28]. The hypocrisy associated with the fact that the Meri-Maat adept who the wine grower, Pavel Ivanović, had helped was none other than Mathers herself when she was in human form was utterly irrelevant to the parasitic entity who now inhabited the French adept's body and astral essences. From the entity's perspective, assisting the one force on earth that could challenge the domination of the Meri-Isfet deserved the most vindictive punishment imaginable. Somewhere, buried deep within the French adept, the few remaining threads of Mathers' original consciousness recoiled with disgust at how far her morals had become corrupted. But, for the moment, she was powerless to resist the obscene compulsions that flowed through her.

The smell of smoke from burning homes and farms, combined with gunfire, cries of suffering animals and human screams of anguish, filled the night air - bringing to life the full horror of the destruction. Mathers was relishing the misery. Her entire body exhibited signs of arousal that verged on sexual release. Her preternatural senses vicariously enjoyed the suffering from the mayhem taking place so nearby. Technically, it was more accurate to say that the MUŠ.ŠÀ.TÙR[29] soul parasite that now indwelt within the physical and super-physical bodies of the French adept was exalting in the astral energy released by the suffering and pain that were occurring nearby at her instigation. The

---

[28] The Meri-Maat - beloved of Maat - are devoted to harmony, order and truth. Principals that are abhorrent to the rival ancient occult order, the Meri-Isfet - beloved of Isfet – who glorify chaos, pain and destruction.

[29] An ancient Mesopotamian creature described as looking like "a horned snake with two forelegs and wings." This multi-headed semi-immortal soul parasite was the basis for the Greek tale of the Hydra.

creature's astral form hummed at an inaudible frequency beneath the sounds of violence filling the night air.

As was the custom for Meri-Isfet adepts, each of Mathers' acolytes tried to emulate the reactions of their Imperatrix— all except one, the most senior of the group, a middle-aged man with a shaved head and a distinctive goatee beard that he had cultivated to mimic his previous mentor, Magister Ironheart.

Mathers sensed the man's acute discomfort and, approaching him, gently pulled the adept's face towards her as one might coax a petulant child. When the man's startled face looked deeply into her burning hazel eyes and became more subdued, Mathers addressed him quietly,

"What is it that disquiets you, Brother?"

The man stammered, clearly nervous about the new leader's reaction to his compassion,

"Imperatrix, I can sense the rape of the village women and the murder of their children..."

Before he could continue, Mathers interrupted him mid-sentence and smiled, "Yes, isn't it delightful?"

Then, seeing the growing shock in the faces of some of the other five adepts, Mathers turned towards the doorway that led back down to the control room, announcing,

"Since our esteemed Brother is so... disquieted by the atmosphere here, let us return to the meeting room below."

"Thank you, Imperatrix!" the man exclaimed, clearly relieved at his mentor's unexpected understanding.

Mathers waved off the man's appreciation. She gestured for him to lead the way down the spiral stone staircase visible in the dimly illuminated emergency lighting that had been on since the electricity supply had been cut. As the distressed adept started towards the steep steps, Mathers smiled cruelly as she exactly mimicked the man's gait[30]. When he reached the start of the stairwell, Mathers stumbled. While the French adept immediately recovered her stride, the man tripped and began to tumble out of control down the stairway. The man's cries of pain and distress reduced the further he fell until his twisted and broken body became utterly still and silent at the bottom of the steps.

The other adepts initially looked startled, but then, as their new leader led them down, they filed past the remains of their more compassionate compatriot and saw their Imperatrix laugh. With some disquiet, they realised they had witnessed yet another demonstration of Mathers' supernatural ability and abject cruelty.

Six Hundred and Thirty miles to the North West of Fortress Grmožur, inside an underground control centre concealed inside one of the higher peaks in the Bernese Alps, the newly resurrected form of Dr Nissa Ad-Dajjal glided silently and effortlessly through the long stone corridors. Her dark purple ritual robe flowed behind her like a bridal train, and her long raven black hair cascaded around her head, highlighting her flawless complexion and piercing green hypnotic eyes. Where this figure passed, the corridor walls, floors and ceilings became momentarily frosted with glistening surface hoar ice. Although these crystal formations were only momentary, it was noticeable that the columns, needles, plates and dendrite patterns formed by Ad-Dajjal's presence assumed shapes familiar to advanced

---

[30] This technique of mirroring the physical actions of a subject before influencing their behaviour is adopted within many magical systems and forms a vital part of charming animals and humans.

students of the Goetia[31]. Although it was penetratingly cold around this fearsome figure, there was no sign of air condensation typically formed by respiration in frigid climates; instead, the atmosphere was filled with the intoxicating aroma of the Ghost flower of the Mojave Desert.

The corpulent middle-aged men, who only moments earlier had been gathered around their boardroom congratulating themselves about their exalted status and invincibility under Cortez's imminent rise, were now scattering in terror from the visage that stalked their once ultra-secure complex. Fortunately for Colonel Jaree and his colleagues, Ad-Dajjal appeared utterly disinterested in them. Instead, she headed directly to the elevator leading to the complex's lowest levels. Entering the lift, she pressed her finger on the fingerprint recognition unit beside the floor selection buttons. Her icy cold touch frosted the mirrored surfaces on the panel and caused a momentary electrical overload, but the EMP-hardened systems compensated and quickly resumed functioning. After Ad-Dajjal's identity was confirmed, a secondary lock engaged on the double doors, and the lift descended well beneath what was officially indicated as the complex's lowest levels. As the elevator continued its descent, the unusual nature of Ad-Dajjal's resurrected form became more apparent. She cast a reflection in the lift's mirrored walls that intermittently flickered in and out of focus, like an ultra-high-definition video playback subject to rare moments of interference. For the most part, her reflections were of the flawless beauty of her human female form; however, the other images that momentarily appeared were more disturbing– a mangled body posed into grotesque and impossible positions, her skull set into a silent and unending scream of torment.

---

[31] The term Goetia refers to the evocation of evil spirits. It is derived from the Ancient Greek term for sorcery, γοητεία.

After the elevator doors opened, Ad-Dajjal slipped into the corridor, moving silently and as smoothly as a fluid flowing over a heated surface. It was noticeable that she no longer wore the inverted pentagram adept's ring on her right hand – an item she had once prized beyond all other possessions. Neither was her reanimated form infused by the MUŠ.ŠÀ.TÙR parasite that had permitted her to "cross the abyss[32]" and totally dominated her former existence. Nissa Ad-Dajjal was now a very different entity from the individual who so recently unleashed the red death plague to blackmail the nations of the world so she could perform the forbidden forty-ninth invocation of the Enochian magical system at the lost Citadel of the Djinn in the Gobi Desert.

The long corridor carved into the granite bedrock, through which the form of Ad-Dajjal now flowed, was interspersed by stone statues of specific deities[33] from the ancient world. Each figure marked a doorway to a particular ritual space dedicated to a different form of feminine power practised by Ad-Dajjal before her death. The last of these deities was a stone sculpture of the five-thousand-year-old Akkadian Goddess Ishtar[34]. After briefly contemplating the deity, whom many in the ancient world regarded as the Goddess of

---

[32] The transition from the second order degrees to the sublime magickal degrees of the third order.

[33] The statues included: Eris, Goddess of chaos, strife and discord. Hecate, Goddess of magic, the moon and terrifying entities of the night. Enyo, Goddess of destruction. Apate, Goddess of deceit who blinded mortals from the truth. And a group of three figures towards the end of the long passageway were The Erinyes, the three goddesses of vengeance (Alecto-endless anger, Megaera-jealous rage, and Tisiphone-vengeful destruction).

[34] The ancients who had carved this particular representation had focused on showing the many paradoxes present in a Goddess who was simultaneously responsible for violence and sexual pleasure, fruitfulness and decease, beauty and horror, and, finally, order and chaos.

Goddesses, Ad-Dajjal turned to the final figure at the very end of the long stone passageway. This female statue was portrayed in a brightly coloured leopard skin dress, with her head adorned with a silver, seven-pointed star that looked like a flower. The colours were as bright as when they had been painted millennia ago. This figure was Seshat, Goddess of libraries, called in many ancient papyri as Mistress of the House of Books. Some scholars believe Seshat was the feminine aspect of Thoth[35], the God of wisdom.

Ad-Dajjal pushed a sequence on the seven points on Seshat's silver crown, causing the statue to slide to one side, revealing the stone-framed entrance to a concealed area within the complex. Lights in the ceiling flickered on, showing a vast, air-conditioned storage space. As far as could be seen, row upon row of tall black stone racks were filled with books, documents, and historical artefacts of every size and description.

A series of framed images were set on the right-hand side wall. The first was a photograph of Ad-Dajjal's beloved ship, The Tiamat. This ship now lay at the bottom of the seventeen-thousand-foot-deep Hellenic Trench[36] after being blown apart by Tavish Stewart's close friend, Mohammed Sek, who ran the Istanbul branch of Stewart's Antiquarians.

The picture of the majestic ship was alongside four formal portraits, showing the senior leadership of the Meri-Isfet. Señor Edwardo Salvador and Cardinal Regio looked resplendent in their ninth-degree Magus[37] robes, while Oscar Pedersen (Magister Ironheart) merely looked resentful in his eighth-degree Magister[38] robes. Finally, in Ad-Dajjal's

---

[35] Creator of writing and God of magic.
[36] Where the African tectonic plate slides under the Aegean Sea plate.
[37] Master of Magic Arts.
[38] Magister Templi (Master of the Temple).

picture, she was posed like an empress on the high podium of the Berlin Meri-isfet lodge room, dressed in her tenth-degree Ipsissimus[39] regalia.

To those imbued with the necessary esoteric prowess, these pictures gave clear signs that their subjects had passed beyond the mortal realm. The first three images had started fading in a way that normally occurs to photographs after decades of exposure to the environment. Ad-Dajjal's picture remained untarnished, but the image was impossible to hold in the eye for any length of time. Almost as if the body was being subjected to enormous forces tearing it apart. This was, in fact, not far from the truth, as Karmic justice had determined that, unlike most tortures, even death would not end her torment. Ad-Dajjal's physical body was preternaturally destined to be attached for all eternity to an imperishable fig[40] wood torture rack called the "Sen No Yorokobi No Tēburu" or "Table of a Thousand Delights[41]".

The raven-haired figure briefly touched the portrayal of the suffering of her mortal remains before gliding past into the seemingly endless rows of cabinets.

As Ad-Dajjal progressed through the storage facility, she passed ever more ancient artefacts, ranging from printed,

---

[39] Meaning of being one's true self. The ultimate enlightenment and mastery possible in ritual magic.

[40] This infamous table was constructed from a two-thousand-five-hundred-year-old fig tree, ritually felled during a dark lunar cycle, that had originally stood in the Mahabodhi Temple grounds in Bodh Gaya.

[41] According to ancient occult records, this device had been assembled according to plans dictated by Dakini-Ten, esoteric Shingon Buddhism's discarnate Principle of Evil, during the fourteenth century at the infamous Shinseina Iki monastery. It prevented the soul from escaping the body that was attached to the table, allowing infinite torture.

bound books to loose-leafed handwritten manuscripts and scrolls and then to collections of papyri and cuneiform clay tablets. At the very end of the room, there was an extensive collection of carved stone frescos and a selection of cave and rock paintings. These precious items had each been carefully removed from their original locations and brought to form the oldest parts of Ad-Dajjal's personal library. Each item was priceless, and most were utterly unknown to art or archaeology. The exhibits were suspended in titanium frames set onto ceiling and floor rails that allowed the displays to be stacked horizontally, side by side, for storage and pulled from the storage rack for selective viewing.

The raven-haired figure knew the specific items she wanted to examine because, within a few moments, she had pulled a selection of the wall exhibits into a row in front of her. She then moved back a couple of paces to view them under the rows of spotlights directed towards this area, clearly to view and appreciate the exhibits.

The frames selected by Ad-Dajjal were stone frescos taken from the remains of a temple at Göbekli Tepe[42]. They showed a series of large carved images. The first image portrayed tall rotating cylinders located in different places around the globe. Each cylinder was spinning with such force that they cracked the firmament. The next framed fresco showed flaming balls hurtling through a series of concentric solid spheres that circled an enormous central globe composed of fire. Subsequent frames on this fresco showed some of the blazing balls making massive impacts on the inner spheres, causing immense firestorms and, on the one blue, water-covered globe, substantial tidal waves wrapping entirely around the planet.

---

[42] A Neolithic archaeological site in the Anatolia Region of Turkey dated to around 9500 BCE.

The third fresco was the first to show living creatures and included a group of humans along with a single beast that was a strange-looking mix of more familiar organisms. This creature was a complex snake-like chimaera with a thick segmented body, like a rattlesnake, multiple eyeless heads that resembled modern-day lampreys, and a long trailing fibrous tail similar to plant roots[43]. In the background was an area of shoreline that some recent cataclysmic event had destroyed- trees were uprooted, and the ground was covered in the decaying remains of sea and land creatures of every description.

Next to this strange snake-hybrid creature was a small group of seven human figures actively venerating the creature. These worshippers wore short-sleeved, full-length pleated gowns, long braided beards, and broad circular hats, carrying highly distinctive long-handled bags in their right hands. The figures looked very similar to images of the Anunnaki[44] from the Sumerian civilisation but predated the Sumerians by four millennia. Near to these human figures was a badly damaged boat made of bound reeds, with primitive sails and oars, that had been run aground. The final image on the Göbekli Tepe frescos was of an axe-like tool[45], along with a detailed picture of the crown of the human head, including a clear representation of the skull and an open multi-petalled purple flower[46] that flowed from the top of the head into the surrounding space.

Beside and below all these images was text in a strange pictographic language, which Ad-Dajjal could clearly

---

[43] A portrayal of a MUŠ.ŠÀ.TÙR.
[44] Anunnaki ("offspring of An") is derived from "An", the Sumerian god of the sky.
[45] An adze.
[46] The Sahasrara Chakra.

understand[47], because she picked up a small A5-sized Moleskin notebook and a black Mont Blanc ball pen[48] from a nearby wooden stand and started making detailed notes.

Meanwhile, six floors higher and two hundred metres South of where Ad-Dajjal was studying the Göbekli Tepe materials, the six corpulent and breathless senior representatives of the Wolfsangel covert security and intelligence agency were gathered together outside the elevator. They were deciding how to deal with the unexpected and highly unwelcome visitation now roaming freely within their headquarters. The Wolfsangel representative from Germany proposed that they should approach Ad-Dajjal to discover the reason for her return. However, the rest of the group was so terrified of her reputation that they instantly rejected the idea. The French representative argued instead that they should inform Alpha and get his decision on the appropriate action. However, this idea was also quickly dismissed as many in the group felt Alpha might view this as a weakness and instantly replace them. Then, Col Jaree, the leader of the group, spotted a lone figure in a dark Hockerty tweed jacket and Jolliman cavalry twill trousers, walking along one of the nearby corridors, carrying a steaming coffee mug. This figure was the base Chaplin, Father Baumgartner, who was heading back to his chapel near the barracks section for the dozen Wolfsangel soldiers who were posted on six-week duty rotations to guard the centre.

"Father Baumgartner!" hailed Jaree towards the gently ambling figure with his coffee cup.

---

[47] Unlike our modern archaeologists.
[48] Meisterstück Platinum-Coated Ballpoint Pen.

Like all the troops stationed at the base, Baumgartner was seconded to Wolfsangel duties from the special forces of the many nations whose governments were under the covert control of the organisation. In the case of the Calvinist minister, he usually served as a "Padre" (Second lieutenant) within the elite Swiss Grenadier Command 1 of Kommando Spezialkräfte[49].

Once the amiable, open-faced minister was close enough, Jaree addressed him while the other five senior Wolfsangel leaders gathered around. In typical military form, Jaree leapt straight to the point, saying,

"Baumgartner, it seems we have an unwelcome spiritual problem that you need to resolve for us."

"Sir?" queried the padre, clearly thinking that one of the Wolfsangel operatives under his ministry was suffering from some moral dilemma. It was probably guilt from some recent operation where a colleague had died or a girlfriend who had become unexpectedly pregnant, speculated the twenty-seven-year-old minister to himself.

"Yes, Baumgartner. We need you to perform whatever intervention is usual to send an unwelcome spirit, or whatever you call them, back to where it came from."

The other five senior members of the Wolfsangel leadership who were gathered closely around nodded their agreement and full support of this idea.

However, the fresh-faced Second lieutenant looked confused.

"A spirit, sir? Can you be more specific?"

Jaree hesitated and then decided to be frank with the minister.

---

[49] Based at Rivera within the Swiss canton of Ticino.

"We have a demonic visitation in the lower levels," Jaree pointed to the lift before continuing, "that needs to be sent back to where it came from."

"A demon?!" the young cleric looked shocked, before remarking, "Gentlemen, this is not the Dark Ages. We must not believe in demons or demonic possession – these things are mental illnesses. You need a doctor, not a minister of the church..."

Jaree interrupted the outburst of the junior officer and pulled rank, saying,

"Second lieutenant, we assure you this is not a medical matter. I am ordering you to intervene. Is that clear?"

Baumgartner nodded but continued to resist the idea of an exorcism and the concept of demons.

"Col. Jaree, the Swiss Calvinist church does not have a rite of exorcism..."

the padre paused, seeing the desperation in these men's faces. He added,"

"But I can pray for and with this soul."

"Good," responded Jaree, "do you need to fetch any equipment?"

"Prayer and the Word of God were enough for our Lord...."

Jaree interrupted again. He did not want an explanation. He just wanted the problem resolved. Like any reasonable leader, he wanted to be sure his officer had all the equipment he needed.

"What about a book of some formal rite?"

"As I said," the padre continued, "we do not believe in Popish nonsense of repetitive chants, rituals or talismans such as beads or holy water."

At this point, there was a shared look of concern between the six members of the Wolfsangel board.

Baumgartner noted the collective expression and decided this was the time to get to work. He demanded, "Lead me to this troubled soul!"

Jaree responded eagerly by opening the elevator doors and using his pass key to override the security codes; he bustled the padre into the lift and pressed the key for the lowest level where Ad-Dajjal had gone. The descent seemed to take an age, but in reality, it was under a minute before Baumgartner emerged from the double doors of the elevator and stood at the start of the long corridor with its line of goddess statutes from the ancient world. A bright light cascaded from the entrance to a large space, partially revealed from behind a statue at the end of the gloomy passageway. The Calvinist Minister entered the passageway and walked towards the library, still carrying his coffee mug in his right hand.

Six floors above the nervous Baumgartner, the Wolfsangel leaders were busy congratulating Jaree for his quick-thinking solution to their problem. With luck, their unexpected visitation would soon be a distant memory, and Cortez would never need to know. The time seemed to pass excruciatingly slowly, but twelve minutes later, the group of men saw the elevator floor indicator start to show the lift was returning.

The six men gathered expectantly around the elevator as the opening warning pinged and the double doors slowly opened, revealing a dishevelled Baumgartner. Gone was the calm and dismissive demeanour that had been so evident. The coffee mug remained but was visibly shaking in his right hand. It was empty, its contents now all over the padre's clothing. His skin was ashen white and soaked with sweat, his pupils wildly dilated, and his breathing came in ragged gasps. As the air inside the open elevator flowed into the corridor, there was a distinct aroma of urine.

As the six Wolfsangel leaders backed away in dismay, Baumgartner gasped,

"Let me through! I have to phone the Roman Catholic Bishop. You need an exorcist!"

A NEW DAWN

"There are decades where nothing happens; and there are weeks where decades happen." - Vladimir Ilyich Lenin

*4400 feet above Lake Skadar,
Montenegro.*

5:01 HRS (GMT+2), 14th Sept, Present day

The only sounds inside the small Cessna 182a were the rushing air over the wings and the gentle crackle of electrical systems shorting out. The relative silence of the aircraft's gliding descent, combined with the lack of any visual cues due to the darkness outside, conspired to give the feeling that there was no immediate danger. This illusion would have been only too easy to believe, except for the acrid smell of burning plastic which dominated the cabin. Stewart's eyes streamed, and his chest wheezed with each burning inhalation of these fumes. But, however great the temptation was to get fresh air, the Scotsman kept the small sliding windows on either side of the cabin firmly closed[50].

The fuselage maintained its slight downward angle, but it was no longer possible to assess the rate of descent accurately. Most of the instrument dials were cracked or obscured behind dark carbon stains. Those few instruments that did remain visible all pointed to zero.

Giving up on making a distress call on the broken shortwave radio, Stewart turned away from the instruments, noticing as he turned that the soles on his grey Puma trainers were becoming tacky from the heat of the fire currently spreading under the fuselage. Such extreme heat would, within

---

[50] The increased oxygen in the fresh air would increase the rate of combustion.

minutes, cause the fibreglass floor to give way completely, casting the contents of the cabin out into the air nearly a mile above the ground. Reluctantly, Stewart was forced to the inescapable conclusion that the fire would soon reach the aviation fuel in the wings. The only remaining question was, would the Cessna burn up before or after it hit the ground?

Standing up, the Scotsman pulled the small black plastic flashlight, that had been illuminating the aeronautical chart, free from its duct tape fastening and pointed the tiny beam back through the smoky cabin. Stewart's eyes fell immediately on the discarded cameraman's wingsuit and goggles. He already knew there were no usable parachutes; those left in the cabin were soaking wet and had not been repacked. If they had been dry and the Scotsman had unlimited time, he would have repacked one, but that was no longer an option. He only had seconds, and a wet parachute will not open[51].

As Stewart pulled on the soaking-wet Squirrel wingsuit[52] over his clothing, he resigned himself to the brutal fact that only a handful of people had survived landing in a wingsuit without a parachute – although most of these fortunate few sustained severe injuries. But, remaining in the aircraft was certain death and while jumping without a parachute was close to suicide, there was just a sliver of a chance. Stewart's love of life and natural optimism meant he always looked for the best option, even when the odds were grim.

"Right, Old Girl, at least let's have you go out in style!" muttered the Scotsman to the old aircraft as he retrieved a small red Wenger[53] pocket knife he had noticed was lying on

---

[51] The fabric sticks together and does not deploy.
[52] Freak 4 Squirrel wingsuit.
[53] Wenger Evolution 511 Swiss Army Knife. Sadly, it is no longer made. Its ergonomic handle design was considered to be superior.

the dashboard shelving. Opening the knife, he began to stab systematically with the reamer[54] blade, where he knew the fuel lines flowed behind the cabin walls. Once this work was completed, he resumed the flow to the fuel lines. As aviation fuel began to cascade over the cabin's interior, Stewart temporarily resumed his seat at the aircraft controls. Grabbing the yoke[55], he directed the plane into a steep dive towards the Fortress that was becoming visible in the pre-dawn light and locked the yoke firmly into position.

One thousand three hundred miles North-West from where Stewart was plunging to almost certain death, Cynthia Sinclair was exercising her long legs on a NordicTrack[56] exercise machine in the Scheveningen[57] prison gym. Dressed in a standard prison-issue cotton grey marl jog suit and white Adidas trainers, Sinclair was nearing the end of her early morning run. The digital display showed an average of eight miles an hour over the past twenty-four minutes of exertion. Through the full-length armoured glass windows surrounding the gym, Sinclair could see extensive repairs underway from damage that had occurred during the previous evening's storms and violent earth tremors.

The prison buildings had been constructed to withstand sustained terrorist attacks, so they were relatively unharmed, apart from the odd crack that had appeared in some of the grey and white[58] plasterwork in the endless corridors of the

---

[54] Reamer punch. You know, it's the pointy thing to get stones out of horse's hooves. Yes, that one.
[55] Aircraft's steering wheel.
[56] NordicTrack Commercial X32i running machine.
[57] United Nations Detention Unit
[58] Blue and White in the UNDT parts of the prison.

main prison. The perimeter fencing and wooden outhouses had fared less well. Several of the fence posts had fallen along with some of the floodlights. These were being raised by heavy lifting equipment in the pre-dawn light.

The extent of the recreation facilities at the UNDT facility in the Netherlands considerably improved on those at Belmarsh, where she had been held while under arrest in the UK for trumped-up terrorism charges. However, as one of the institution's highest-risk inmates, who was potentially facing the death penalty, Sinclair's exercise time was scheduled for when none of the general prison population would be active. Throughout her solo times in the gym, she was accompanied by three, heavily armed guards with MP5[59] machine guns, dressed in the smart grey-green trousers, jacket, dress shirt, tie and beret of the Royal Netherlands Army.

The rear of Sinclair's Adidas sweatshirt was soaked with patches of sweat that partially obscured the single word "Beklaagde" (prisoner) that was printed there. As she gradually slowed down from her five-mile run, she watched the early morning European regional news on a wide-screen television that was set up in front of the NordicTrack. The male and female announcers both shared the same blond, blue-eyed look that now dominated the European media.

The young female announcer started the summary, "There has been unprecedented damage to infrastructure around Europe. Reports continue to come in, but early estimates put the death toll from the global storm and earth tremors last night in the thousands. But this estimate will undoubtedly rise as emergency services complete their assessments. The winds, earth tremors and storm surges caused extensive damage to the major European ports."

---

[59] Heckler & Koch MP5 (Maschinenpistole 5).

The screen showed images of the severe damage in famous European ports, including Rotterdam, Piraeus, Valencia, Hamburg, and Antwerp. Shipping containers were scattered everywhere like discarded toys, and fallen cranes were lying over the sunken remains of massive container ships. Oil slicks and dead marine life were in evidence in all the pictures.

The next series of images showed some of the nuclear power stations in France. The TV announcer continued, "As a safety measure power stations in France have been closed down. Other nations are assessing if they should follow suit. Severe economic impacts are predicted with disruption to goods and supplies."

"No shit," exclaimed Sinclair as she slowed her pace further. The speedometer on the running machine now showed three miles an hour. Soon, she would begin her cool-down stretching routine. It was, she reflected, good to be back exercising after being confined for days in the tiny cell at Belmarsh. She secretly hoped that during one of her exercise sessions, she would catch a glimpse of Tavish Stewart, but so far, the guards had been scrupulous about keeping her segregated from all other inmates. All her requests to communicate with Stewart had been refused by the prison authorities on the grounds that it could prejudice their forthcoming trials.

The news coverage continued by showing more devastation, this time on the coastal regions, all the way from the Spanish Atlantic Coast to Cyprus. The damage seemed worst at the Eastern end of the Mediterranean around the coasts of Croatia and Albania.

The rugged-looking male announcer continued, "Coastal areas have been especially badly affected, with storm surge waves of over fifteen feet reported throughout the

Mediterranean region. An initial estimate of damage within Europe runs into the millions."

"Cities with old and historic buildings and monuments have suffered especially badly," stated the female news announcer. The scenes shown from London, Paris, Rome and Athens were shocking, with many of the older structures severely damaged with extensive areas of the capital cities reduced to rubble.

"Looks more like blast damage from high explosives," commented Sinclair to herself as she noticed that in many of the scenes, there were FF[60] troops in their highly distinctive white uniforms actively patrolling the affected areas.

The female reporter continued, "Hundreds of thousands of people have been made homeless."

Graphic scenes followed of families huddled in the streets begging for food from passers-by, most of whom ignored them and hurried on.

The male announcer came back on, "In the height of the storms and tremors last night, the heads of the national governments in Europe took refuge in undisclosed secure locations. Unfortunately, none of them has re-emerged this morning."

The female reporter assumed a serious but compassionate tone, "In response to this unprecedented humanitarian crisis, normal political governance mechanisms have had to be suspended. In the complete absence of any other form of leadership in Europe and the UK, overwhelming public opinion, as shown by the mass protests that have stormed the national seats of government in every nation this morning, demanded that Chairman Cortez lead the recovery process. Reluctantly, he has agreed, on the condition that he

---

[60] Freedom Force – Cortez's army.

surrenders control back to elected officials should they re-emerge."

Sinclair huffed, "I would not hold your breath."

The reporter continued, "Armies have therefore been placed under the direction of the FF forces to coordinate rescue and recovery operations."

"I bet that bastard Cortez had some hand in this whole bloody mess just to take control!" exclaimed Sinclair as she slowed to a plodding walk.

The broadcast continued, "But now an announcement from our sponsors."

A slick advertisement came on the screen, with white-coated doctors tending to tired and clearly stressed men and women. A professional male voice came on saying, "These worrying times have made us all feel overwhelmed. Most of us are suffering from panic attacks, sleepless nights and constant dread- such emotions impact our performance and risk serious damage to our health. Now we have the answer!

Developed in conjunction with leading specialists in Germany and Switzerland, WB is the all-new solution to today's psychosomatic challenges. This new wonder drug is guaranteed to make you a new person in no time. Ask your doctor or pharmacist for a free lifetime supply and find a new you, unencumbered from all that burden of stress that is holding you back."

A radically speeded-up narration that was incomprehensible unless replayed at a much slower speed closed the advert.

 "Wahrnehmungsblock is a German-manufactured neuro-inhibitory drug that stops specific, complex sensory and cognitive processes. WB can be highly addictive and may cause loss of critical judgement and induce submissive behaviour or unquestioning obedience to authority. High doses may induce permanent loss of conscious awareness. WB is a registered trade mark of the Wolfsangel group of companies."

The female reporter continued, "Now, back to the news headlines. The British Pound and Euro, along with the European stock market, came under extraordinary pressure last night. The two currencies lost over ninety-nine per cent of their value. Trillions were wiped from company values, causing all trading on British and European businesses to be halted on the London Stock Exchange and Euronext. In an emergency intervention that showed his usual courage and leadership, Chairman Cortez used his own financial resources to purchase all the stock from the affected companies, thereby saving British and European economies from complete ruin."

"And saving himself a fortune since their value was close to zero," commented Sinclair as she stepped down from the running machine and began some stretching exercises.

The news continued, "In a similarly bold move, our fearless Chairman announced that the valueless British Pound and Euro would be immediately replaced with a new cashless currency called the Crypto-Mark."

Sinclair's eyebrows raised in surprise as the reporter continued, "To speed up the efficient introduction of this cashless society, Chairman Cortez simultaneously announced that the existing UNITY barcode tattoos will provide all European and British citizens with a payment authorisation mechanism at barcode scanners that will be installed in all commercial premises and over the internet through credit payment systems. In addition, each legitimate citizen will have a basic universal income paid daily to their individual personal Crypto-Mark account."

Sinclair stopped stretching and gasped at the implication that the UNITY barcode tattoos had always been intended for such a pervasive impact. It was, Sinclair reflected, an ingenious way to have absolute control over every citizen. Cortez would know what people bought, where they went and what they did. More ominously, Cortez could also remove access for anyone or any groups that he felt were undesirable.

While Sinclair reflected on the genius of the plan, the news continued.

"For those who have had their homes destroyed or declared unsafe, residential camps have been set up at key locations throughout the region. Food, WiFi, streaming TV services, medical care, clothing and accommodation will be provided along with free education programmes for children up to the age of 21. These Care Camps will also provide employment opportunities for all residents who do not currently have work."

The news segment ended with a picture of one of the large Care Camps located just outside Manchester in the United Kingdom. Inside the tall wire perimeter fences, the images showed long rows of prefabricated houses. Happy families were gathered outside these homes, under large posters of a smiling Chairman Cortez.

"Utter bullshit!" remarked Sinclair to herself as she towelled her face dry and was led back to her cell at gunpoint by the three guards.

One hundred and twenty miles West from where Sinclair was being escorted back to her cell, in an elegant white tiled bathroom within a brick-fronted, Edwardian townhouse on

K.R.M. Morgan

Dean Ryle Street, London, Chairman Cortez was seated in his red leather barber's chair[61], receiving his customary morning hot towel shave. The tall, blonde barber expertly handled the long steel blade of a classic George Wostenholm[62] cutthroat, the tortoiseshell handle loosely held between her long fingers. The young woman's distinctive white cotton full-length apron showed a scattering of crimson drops of her own blood, from where she had tested the sharpness of the old nineteenth-century blade on her arms before commencing to remove the hot towels from Cortez's face. The numerous scar marks visible on her showed the extent of her devotion to duty.

The new overlord of Europe was wearing his grey Thai silk Armani dressing gown and was enjoying watching the unfolding drama taking place on a set of three portable 4k LG screens showing the live feed from underground bunkers in the UK[63], Belgium[64], and Germany[65]. Every few moments, Cortez raised his left hand, causing the barber to temporarily halt her work, as the silver-haired Argentinian was no longer able to contain his laughter at the antics taking place in the bunkers.

Gathered around the Chairman were his two blond-haired grandsons, who were dressed in the crisp white uniforms of the FF that now enforced the rule of Cortez throughout the region. The two younger men shared the aquiline features of their grandfather but wore their hair considerably shorter

---

[61] Hand made by Chelmsford for Cortez.

[62] George Wostenholm IXL Frameback 1850. Recognised as one of the world's classic cut throat razors.

[63] Code name, Pindar.

[64] Supreme Headquarters Allied Powers Europe at Casteau, Mons, Belgium.

[65] Ramstein Air Base in German Rhineland. It is NATO's central base & headquarters for United States Air force operations in Europe.

than the highly distinctive long silver hair of the older Argentinian. Their uniforms reflected their positions as leaders of the ground forces and intelligence services of New Europa, as the continent would shortly be proclaimed. Standing a respectful distance from these two leaders was the less than elegant figure of Major General Smegget- a short, fat man with thick gold-rimmed glasses and a badly miscoloured wig, who was the representative for the UK within the new army. Smegget had been summoned from the situation room in the top-secret Pindar[66] shelter just moments before the blue metal blast doors had been welded shut earlier that morning.

There was shared hilarity among the group as they watched the video feeds, except for the barber, who remained focused only on her work, as cutting the Chairman would be a deadly mistake[67].

The first video feed was from Belgium, where the EU elite and the NATO military leadership had taken shelter the previous evening. Like all the other three shelters being observed by Cortez this morning, they had originally been designed to house only the most essential individuals necessary to continue government or coordinate military responses after a thermonuclear war.

Over time, this mandate had become corrupted, so the bunker's mission became to provide shelter for the most influential people rather than the most essential. For example, radiation experts were replaced by merchant bankers, survival specialists with dot.com billionaires and agricultural experts with media celebrities. The bunkers

---

[66] Pindar is the UK's top-secret bunker, located one hundred and sixty-five feet under the Ministry of Defence building in London. You should tear this page out and eat it after reading these footnotes.
[67] Literally.

became filled with luxuries, and the accommodation became closer to a playboy penthouse than a military base.

The previous evening had seen a party atmosphere in all the bunkers, where the rich and famous celebrated their escape from the danger associated with the violent storms and earth tremors. However, this morning the canapés and Moët & Chandon had run out. The occupants rapidly discovered that all the entrances had been welded shut, the phones and radios disabled and the staff who had been tending to them were gone. Panic rapidly ensued. The rich and famous now found themselves haggard, hungry, hungover and trapped inside the very place they had thought was their refuge from the fate of the Plebs[68], who were excluded.

It was the antics of these dishevelled and desperate elites, as they fought each other for the few scraps of food and liquid that remained, that was so entertaining to the leaders of Cortez's New Republic.

At Casteau in Belgium, the EU president could be seen punching a globally recognised movie star to get the remaining dregs from a bottle of Evan mineral water. While in Ramstein, Germany, a senior NATO official was holding off a number of other armed senior generals with a loaded Beretta M9 pistol while he gnawed at the sole remaining discarded chicken leg that he had recovered from one of the metal waste bins.

The third LG display in front of Cortez was of Pindar, the British Government's top-secret bunker buried, one hundred and sixty-five feet under the Ministry of Defence building in

---

[68] Plebs is short for Plebeians – In ancient Rome these were citizens who were not of patrician, senatorial or equestrian class – they worked hard to support their families and paid taxes. If you enjoy Tavish Stewart adventures then you may be a Pleb, just like the writer.

London. The blue walls and high ceilings, with their metal air conduits, gave a backdrop of a scene of an epic struggle, as Sir Reginald Twiffers, the Prime Minister, Sir Johnathan Premble, the Foreign Secretary and Lord Jeremy Kenner, the Home Secretary, had barricaded themselves into the corner of the situation room using six upturned tables. The three senior cabinet ministers were using the tables to fend off a mass of wild-looking men in evening dress and women in what remained of their formal cocktail outfits from getting hold of the last Fortnum and Mason hamper. In a clear example of Premble's talents as the head of the diplomatic corps, he was throttling the Lord Privy Seal and Leader of the House of Lords while Twiffers held the last remaining half-eaten Jacob's cream cracker aloft above his head to avoid it being snatched by the clearly traitorous Kenner.

Cortez abruptly changed his mood.

"Enough of this frivolity; let us adjourn to the morning room for breakfast and commence the briefing," he announced as he dismissed the barber and, snatching the white towel that had been folded over her left arm, wiped his face clean of any remaining shaving foam. His two grandchildren followed the Chairman as he strode across the white marble bathroom floor and through a pair of double doors that led into a long, low-ceilinged room, dominated by a large mahogany table that was laid out for breakfast. The table was decorated with a crisp white Arthur Price linen cloth, antique[69] silver cutlery, Schott Zwiesel cut crystal glasses and white Limoges porcelain coffee cups.

Inside the breakfast room, was a single waiter dressed in a DAKS black livery coat, blue silk waistcoat and pinstriped trousers. The servitor had clearly been waiting for their arrival as he moved quickly around to the three men, pulled

---

[69] Sheffield 1900

back their chairs for them, and unfurled a linen napkin on each man's lap once they were seated. The efficient waiter then strode quickly to a heated trolley and started to unload three silver trays which he placed in front of Cortez and the two grandsons. With some flourish, he removed the silver cloche[70] from each plate and retired to the corner of the room, waiting for any requests. Like all servants, the waiter was completely ignored by Cortez and his two grandsons. Unless there was some action required, no social interaction was ever undertaken with the staff, not even eye contact. Human resources were, to these men, just to be exploited until they were of no further use and then discarded[71].

Before starting to eat, Cortez broke the cellophane on a new sealed packet of three Cohiba[72] cigars and, using a custom 9k gold Dunhill cigar cutter, piercer and matching gold Dunhill lighter, took a deep inhalation of the fine Cuban tobacco[73]. He then placed the unfinished cigar on a matching gold Dunhill cigar stand.

Everyone in the room had been waiting for Cortez before they started, so there was some relief when he began his breakfast of fresh medialunas[74] and picked up the large crystal glass of freshly squeezed Valencia[75] orange juice from his tray. The two grandsons started eating in a similar manner, aggressively consuming their tostadas (toast) and Tortilla Espanola (potato omelette), respectively.

---

[70] A covering for food items, to keep them warm and prevent insects.
[71] Yes, I think I have worked for these people as well.
[72] Cohiba Robusto – 3 pack. No, you can't afford it.
[73] As smoked by Fidel Castro, one of Cortez's heroes.
[74] Medialunas are a mix of a brioche and a croissant. They are made with many layers of sweet dough with flavours of lemon and vanilla.
[75] The best drinking orange juice in the world.

With his mouth full, Cortez gestured with his left hand for Major General Smegget to commence their morning briefing. Smegget looked nervous, and after clearing his throat and picking up his clipboard, he began reading from the prepared notes. He started with an update on the Care Camps.

"Construction of forty care camps in the United Kingdom has commenced with two hundred more underway in mainland Europe."

Cortez interrupted, "Get used to their new names, Smegget. They are called Britannia and New Europa. How many are operational?"

Smegget became flustered but soon found where the requested information was printed on his notes.

"Six are operational as of 04:00 Hrs this morning."

"Not good enough!" barked Cortez, "I have already started the social media campaigns to attract people to them. See to it that we have all forty camps in Britannia operational by the end of this week."

Smegget was about to say something about the number of people needed to speed up the construction work when one of the grandsons put down his black coffee[76] and intervened,

"Use the residents of the first operational camps to speed up the construction work on the others. Include the women and children. It will be good for them to get used to our expectations."

The piggy eyes behind Smegget's thick glasses reflected shock at using children as slave labour. For a moment, he contemplated mentioning the employment laws, but he

---

[76] Caza Trail Coffee, Breakfast Blend

quickly remembered the nature of who he was dealing with and thought better of it.

Cortez finished drinking the freshly pulped Valencia oranges from the fine crystal glass and turned to the grandson on his left, saying, "Corrado, once all the camps throughout New Europa are operational, we can commence genetic screening and segregation." Corrado nodded.

Cortez looked to the other grandson on his right.

"Hartman, how is Aspen progressing with the new media campaign to encourage the mass uptake of WB among the target demographics?" Cortez had very quickly and thoroughly adapted to the modern terminology and technology used by Beyond Facts Inc and was now the sole owner of the global new media company.

Hartman smiled before replying, "Better than one could hope, grandfather. Aspen has become a heavy WB user herself. When I met her yesterday afternoon, she was keen to help me in any way she could."

Hartman exchanged a knowing look with his brother.

"I would suggest you visit Ms Aspen yourself, Corrado. You will find her very *attentive*." The two young men laughed.

"Smegget, what is the situation with our uprising outside of New Europa?" demanded Cortez, ignoring the playful banter between the two younger men.

Smegget cleared his throat.

"As expected, there have been mass protests in most American states, demanding an end to repressive and wasteful democracy, but the President remembered his experience with the attempted Maelstrom takeover and refused to evacuate to the bunker we had prepared. He is hold up at Fort Liberty[77] and is using the USMC to maintain control over essential services. As you anticipated, Russia and China closed down their social media and the internet completely once the protests started there, so they have remained largely unaffected."

Cortez reflected for a moment.

"No problem. America will become the next to fall."

He turned to the grandson on his left. "Corrado, have our insiders get close to the president and make sure he has a change of heart." Corrado nodded his understanding.

Cortez was starting to find the meeting tedious. He looked to Smegget. "Anything else, Major General?"

"Yes, just a couple more items, Sir. Our Grindelwald base has reported a problem. A supernatural problem."

Cortez looked less than impressed. "This new chap, Colonel Jaree, is clearly not up to the job. Dispense with him and send a senior Meri-Isfet to deal with whatever bogeyman is bothering them."

"What else?" demanded Cortez, who was clearly becoming less sympathetic towards Smegget.

The Major General shuffled uncomfortably. "Shall we resume the search for Tavish Stewart?"

Cortez's mood instantly improved. "No, that will not be necessary. Release that priest O'Neill from the Hague and provide him with one of our people as a driver. He will lead us to Stewart. Have some Wolfsangel units follow them and eliminate the priest and Stewart once they have been found."

Cortez smiled cruelly, but if he was expecting the meeting to come to a close, he was disappointed. Smegget put a large

---

[77] Formerly Fort Bragg.

colour image of international terror mastermind Issac bin Abdul Issuin standing outside the Geneva headquarters of the Union Bank of Switzerland (UBS) in Geneva.

"This just came over the intelligence channels from Interpol. As a precaution, I have already tripled the protection detail covering you all," Smegget gestured to the three men.

The two grandsons sniggered and remarked, "Typical overreaction. We are more than capable of dealing with any threat ourselves. Anyway, look at this old fool,"

they pointed to the picture lying in front of Cortez, "he could not penetrate an old people's home, let alone our top-level security."

Smegget had read the terrifying details of Abdul Issuin's personnel file in Grindelwald, so he continued to try and mitigate the risk, "Shall we commence a search and destroy action for this target?"

Cortez pushed the image away from him on the table, saying, "Forget it, I agree, he is a washed up has been. He would never have allowed himself to be photographed if he was any good. Let Interpol deal with him. He is so incompetent that he is probably already locked up in some police cell."

At that instruction, Cortez abruptly stood and walked from the room with his two grandsons close behind. Following his three bosses, Smegget closed the two doors leaving the waiter to clear away the breakfast things. The servitor waited until he could hear the group move into another area of the building before walking over to the table and clearing away the plates to the trolly. When he had finished, he walked back to the table and sat quite deliberately in Cortez's seat. Ignoring the two unsmoked Cohibas, the waiter pulled a Montecristo Number 4 from his waistcoat's left front pocket. He then proceeded to use Cortez's gold Dunhill lighter to light it while he read Smegget's briefing notes that had been left on the table, along with the photograph from Interpol. As the Montecristo fully ignited, it illuminated the cruel smile that was spreading across the waiter's distinctive hawk-like features.

LEAP OF FAITH

"Attacking innocent people is always obscene." - Ayman Odeh

4200 feet above Lake Skadar,
Montenegro.

5:03 HRS (GMT+2), 14th Sept, Present day

Once Tavish Stewart was satisfied that the old Cessna aircraft was on a stable trajectory toward the inner ward[78] of Fortress Grmožur, he ran his hand over the thick carbon deposits forming on the cabin surfaces. Using the dark grey dust as improvised face camouflage, he rose from the left-hand pilot's chair, strode over to the sliding door inside the aircraft and pulled it open.   The icy cold blasted into the acrid fume-filled cockpit and lashed against Stewart's face. Relishing the fresh, oxygenated air, the Scotsman took some deep breaths before he braced himself against the door frame and leapt out into the semi-darkness, exclaiming fiercely through gritted teeth as he did.

"Here we are!! Here we are again[79]!!!"

As the Scotsman leapt fearlessly out into the pre-dawn sky nearly a mile above the Montenegrin countryside, eighteen hundred miles to the North West, lay a quiet Scottish glen at the Northern end of Loch Chon. The recent violent earth tremors and electrical storms of the previous evening had built up considerable seismic and piezoelectric potential in

---

[78] The fortified inner courtyard of a castle also known as a bailey.
[79] The British Army's battle cry

the ancient Archean gneiss, metamorphic beds and granite that form the region. A lingering string of dark cumulonimbus clouds that hung menacingly over the Loch suddenly unleashed a rumble of thunder and a flash of lightning. This lightning created a chain reaction between the oxygen and vaporised elements from the soil beside the Loch, which caused a discharge of the stored piezoelectric energy. This potential charge leapt from the bedrock to form a small luminous ball of plasma that flew up the length of the glen. The ball-lightning followed the stress lines within the bedrock, causing an earth tremor where it passed until it reached high above the ancestral Stewart Estate, where it burst like a massive firework. The discharge filled the air with the pungent odour of sulphur and scorched nearby foliage. Startled by the explosion, an enormous Emperor Stag rose from the ferns, raised a head adorned with massive antlers and issued a bellowing cry into the darkness of the pre-dawn.

A quarter of a mile further down the glen, the earth tremors disturbed the crypt at the site of the Stewart family cemetery. A fissure formed in the wall at the rear end of the vault. Old plasterwork fell to the floor, revealing the edges of a doorway concealed centuries before, that creaked open. Just visible inside, was a shield bearing the heraldic device of a pelican feeding its young from its breast[80].

Outside, the dying gusts of wind blew through the standing stones, causing a strange keening, not unlike a primitive bagpipe, to resound through the valley. Near Loch Chon, an

---

[80] This is the Stewart clan badge. Perhaps coincidently, it is also a symbol used by the Rosicrucian Order and some higher degrees within Scottish Freemasonry. This symbol has also been associated with a monastic order of Christian warrior monks who fled to Scotland after been declared as heretics.

old crofter tending his long-haired highland cattle[81] crossed himself and issued a quiet prayer for the Stewart clan member in distress.

Eighteen hundred miles South East of where the lone crofter was praying, Tavish Stewart extended his arms and legs as wide as possible to gain maximum lift from the soaking cameraman's wingsuit. Stewart had used Squirrel suits before with the British Army when training for clandestine approaches to target locations. However, the additional weight from the seawater and the special aero-acrobatic features of the modified Freak 4 made this suit feel very different. Stewart was used to travelling at slower speeds when using a wingsuit, around 95 knots (110 Mph), when trying to maximise the distance travelled or, as in this instance, the duration of the flight.

The duration was critical for the Scotsman on this flight because he was still hoping beyond hope to identify a landing site that could offer some chance of survival. However, the additional seawater weight made life more interesting for the Scotsman. Not only was he descending much faster than he would like, but he was also freezing from the wind chill, which was starting to form ice over the surfaces of the suit. Although Stewart did not have an altimeter, he could see through the borrowed goggles that he was descending much more quickly than he had wanted. He would hit the ground in less than three minutes, based on his estimate. The Scotsman's speed[82] was considerably faster than the gliding Cessna[83], and since he wanted the

---

[81] Bos taurus taurus
[82] 140 knots (160 mph).
[83] The Cessna was gliding at 65 knots (75 mph).

satisfaction of seeing the old plane give some payback to the bastards who had shot it down, Stewart banked. He circled the Fortress over the vineyard and towards the small settlement of Godinje. Although the lake's calm waters looked appealing as a landing site, Stewart knew that when objects hit water at high speed, the liquid did not have time to move its mass aside to accommodate the incoming projectile and became as hard as concrete.

Passing closer to the village square, Stewart saw the mayhem unfolding beneath him. The bright muzzle flashes from a semi-automatic rifle illuminated a long trench that had been dug close to the vineyard. Each subsequent bright flash showed more detail, even to a rapidly moving observer like Stewart. The Scotsman could see the outlines of men falling into the trench where they lay alongside a mess of arms, legs and torsos. Stewart's heart dropped. He had worked on peacekeeping operations in some of the world's most dangerous places, and after his retirement, he had hoped that he would never again have to witness such senseless murder. In addition to the sound of gunfire, the air was filled with the screams of women and the pitiful crying of children. Passing above this mayhem, Stewart vowed to take revenge on the men responsible for the massacre taking place below him if he survived.

Just over a mile away from the rapidly moving Scotsman, the old Cessna was coming to the final moments of its long and faithful service. Although no one could see through the aircraft's front windshield, if they could, they would have noticed a rapidly growing image of the courtyard within the walls of Fortress Grmožur. As this image grew, it was clear that the final destination for the burning aircraft would be a large, twenty-foot square, green-coloured metal container prominently labelled with a red diamond-shaped hazard symbol and the image of flames with the designation NFPA 704[84]. This large container was connected to the helipad outside via underground pipes to refuel visiting aircraft.

Due to the fuselage burning, the raging fires inside the small Cessna were moments away from reaching the autoignition temperature of the remaining Aviation kerosene[85] in the wings. Moments after this critical temperature was reached, the vapours in the Cessna's fuel tanks would ignite with explosive fury.

The final moments of "Bacio Volante[86]" ended abruptly. The small aircraft smashed front-first into the centre of the large green metal fuel storage tank, causing an impact that shocked the island's bedrock and the surrounding structures. Milliseconds later, the deafening sound of the impact reverberated around the walls and for some distance beyond the Fortress.

The small plane became embedded into the tank, rupturing the metal and releasing the fuel over the courtyard. Sixty thousand gallons of a straw-coloured liquid started flowing over the smouldering hot remains of the crashed Cessna and into the Fortress, cascading down stairways and through the interior passageways.

Inside the Fortress meeting room, the remaining five Meri-Isfet adepts were gathered around their Imperatrix. She relished the gruesome live body-cam footage from the Wolfsangel operatives completing their seek-and-destroy mission in Godinje.   The Imperatrix's pleasure was

---

[84] Aviation kerosene, also known as QAV-1
[85] Aviation kerosene has a flash point of 100 degrees Fahrenheit (when combustible vapour is released) and an autoignition temperature of 410 Fahrenheit (when the vapour ignites).
[86] Flying Kiss.

interrupted by a massive vibration that shook the bedrock and was followed moments later by a deafening bang that echoed through the Fortress.

"What the hell was that?" queried Mathers to her attending adepts. The astral parasite inhabiting the French adept's body began to feel a highly distinctive sense of impending doom. It instinctively knew it was facing some undefined but dangerous threat that could endanger its preternaturally enhanced physiology. However, before she could take action on these premonitions, the meeting room acquired the highly distinctive odour of hydrocarbons characteristic of kerosene.

Moments later, a straw-coloured liquid began flowing down the corridor from the Fortress courtyard, forming pools in the cracks between the flagstones. Within seconds, the thin, snaking flow of fluid had passed through the meeting room and poured down to the lower levels of the building. The trickle became a stream, and the Imperatrix's Magnum combat boots became soaked in the strange liquid. One of her youngest acolytes, a somewhat naïve young man with long dyed mauve hair, who was wearing open-toed sandals, remarked, "What a wonderful sensation. It's warm, like a hot bath!"

While the group tried to understand the strange liquid's nature, the kerosene odour's strength in the room grew stronger, as did the urge felt by the soul parasite that inhabited Mathers body to get as far away from the Meri-Isfet stronghold as possible. As the parasite searched for the source of this unusual sensation, the entity realised it was from its new human host. For some reason, the smell of this unknown substance was frightening.

The other five adepts looked helplessly toward their leader for guidance on how they should respond, only to see a growing look of terror form on the face of their Imperatrix.

The look of fear was because the soul parasite had just realised that the mysterious warm liquid flowing down the nearby stairway would soon reach her beloved Qliphothic Wheel[87].

The wheel was the ancient esoteric device which had, moments before, opened a gateway to previous creations[88] and the dark, magickal entities that resided there. These Qliphoth were consciousnesses who longed to destroy and replace our universe with their own. They prayed on those magicians foolish enough to listen to their promises of ultimate power and knowledge. The terrifying truth was, without the Trubka device, there could be no further communication with these all-powerful entities[89] who, the Imperatrix firmly believed, were her true teachers.

In a classic fear response, the French Adept dashed from the meeting room and flew down the steep stone stairs, taking them at inhuman speed, closely followed by her five confused assistants. When the acolytes finally caught up, their Imperatrix was standing at the top of the final five stone steps that led down into the room that housed the Trubka wheel. The floor of the generator room was awash with the strange liquid that flowed beside the eight massive HTS motors[90] and the six-foot-thick steel electricity conduits that had powered the rotation of the Trubka wheel during the recent ceremony that had exalted Mathers to become the Imperatrix. The exposed top of the opaline-coloured, Trubka cylinder was in the centre of the space. Its residual gravity

---

[87] The St Petersburg Qliphothic Wheel or as it was known by those adepts who had used it, "the Trubka" (трубка) or Tube.
[88] Called the "Sitra Achra" ' אחרא סטרא '.
[89] Qliphoth - קְלִיפוֹת - which literally means "Husks". The entities left from previous creations.
[90] 36.5-megawatt Northrop Grumman HTS (High temperature superconductor) ship propulsion motors.

fields were powerful enough to slowly cause the pool of liquid to rotate in an anti-clockwise direction

The huge HTS motors were still cooling down after running at full power during the recent ritual. These eight superheated generators had added considerably to the temperature of the mysterious liquid and caused it to emit a strange light. The slowly rotating fluid lapping at the bottom of the steps flickered with a light blue flame while the liquid's surface burnt a brighter yellow[91].

"How pretty!" exclaimed the young mauve-haired acolyte, "The fairies have taken residence!"

The soul parasite was not interested in these idiotic speculations about the fae nature of this substance. She was, instead, entirely focused on the classic black monogrammed Louis Vuitton leather bag[92] that was almost completely submerged near the Trubka. The bag contained Mathers' treasures[93] that she had recovered after the recent OTTG ceremony to be kept safe. However, now they were anything but safe.

"Fetch that bag!" she commanded the irritating mauve-haired acolyte who was delighting in the "fairy lights". The boy had been Ironheart's "sexual favourite", but his naïve behaviour was increasingly annoying to the MUŠ.ŠÀ.TÙR's current incarnation.

The young lad reluctantly stepped down the five stone steps and tentatively placed his foot into the glowing liquid, only to promptly scream and collapse on the two lowest steps, holding his foot in agony. As the boy cradled his badly scalded toes and cried, the unsympathetic MUŠ.ŠÀ.TÙR felt a wave of panic flowing through its body, again from its

---

[91] Caused by soot incandescence.
[92] Louis Vuitton KEEPALL BANDOULIÈRE 50.
[93] The adze axe, skull and flag, along with the Rauðskinna grimoire.

human host. Finally, accepting that the human part of her recognised some imminent danger from this strange liquid, she commanded the remaining four adepts,

"Gather close to me!" and she backed against the stone wall, pulling the confused acolytes to form a human shield all around her.

The rapidly flying Scotsman[94] was completing his pass over the ongoing massacre in the Godinje settlement when he saw his Cessna's slowly gliding white shape make its final approach before disappearing inside the Fortress walls. Exactly five seconds later, this was followed by the sound of an enormous impact. Stewart waited with anticipation for an explosion, but as seconds passed, nothing happened[95]. Sacrificing speed, Stewart gained height before resuming his two-mile circuit around the Fortress and village. The momentum of the soaking wingsuit rapidly[96] carried the Scotsman away from the town and towards the Meri-Isfet stronghold. Passing over the Fortress, he could look down and see fuel cascading from the ruptured storage tank and flowing into the Fortress's main building. A wicked smile grew on the Scotsman's face as he banked the wingsuit

---

[94] You must have known I would work that phrase in somewhere in this scene.

[95] Aviation safety experts have developed aviation fuel specifically to minimise the risk of an aircraft exploding during an accident. The flash point (when fumes are emitted) is well above usual ambient temperatures and there needs to be a significant build-up of these fumes along with a source of ignition and adequate oxygen before an explosion can occur.

[96] It takes 22.5 seconds to cover 1 mile at 160 mph.

around the castle's tower over Lake Skadar and flew back towards the senseless violence unfolding in the settlement.

One thousand four hundred yards from where Stewart was speeding over the calm lake water at over 150 miles per hour towards the settlement, a thin, thirty-something, former special ops National Guardsman was reacting to the impact of the Cessna into the Fortress. The former Guardsman, who went by the call sign "Striker" but whose real name was Saul, was the leader of the four-person Wolfsangel team. He remarked to his unit members through the throat mike, "Crap! Did anyone else see that?"

"Looked like an incoming TLAM[97] to me, Striker," replied BillyBob Jr., the unit's second in command, in a thick Southern drawl.

BillyBob's graduation from the US Army Ranger School made him the unit's self-appointed expert on weaponry. Although the two hundred and fifty pound giant of a man proudly wore the Ranger Tab[98] on his Wolfsangel uniform, he had never served in a Ranger unit, having moved into the "private sector" immediately after graduation. Strictly speaking, he had never been a US Ranger, but you would never guess this based on his constant bragging about his expertise.

"No," replied Saul dismissively, "if it had been a Tomahawk, we would have felt the blast wave by now."

The other two team members remained silent as they focused on brutalising the terrified women who had just witnessed the execution of their men. The brothers, husbands and fathers of Godinje now lay in a hideous tangle

------

[97] Tomahawk Land Attack Missile.
[98] Awarded on completion of the Ranger Training School.

of dead bodies. The dead lay in the mass grave they had been forced to dig after being dragged from their beds in the middle of the night- their mothers, wives and children had been forced at gunpoint to watch. These women were now being subjected to the rapes and beatings that are so frequent when adrenaline-filled men lose self-control and go on the rampage.

Saul regarded the readings projected inside the space age visor, which formed part of the cutting edge "IKill Pro" technology he and all his unit were wearing on this operation. The wide-angle tracking system showed something moving at high speed towards them over the lake, but it did not give off the heat signature[99] that would typically be associated with a drone; besides, it was travelling too fast for a human target.

Milliseconds after Saul dismissed the target as electronic noise in the tracking system, the fire in the old Cessna's fuselage finally reached the heated vapours in the plane's wings, just as the rising dawn caused the start of the daily temperature inversion of the vineyards. The warmer air on the land began to rise and draw in fresh, cooler, oxygenated air from Lake Skadar. This gust of oxygenated air fanned the flames in the Cessna fire- the additional oxygen creating a heat that rose well above the combustion threshold[100] of the QAV-1 aviation fuel. The resulting firestorm followed the path of the QAV-1 as it had flowed into the building, following the vapour trail deeper and deeper into the stone structure. The vapour cloud combustion then expanded at

---

[99] The soaking wet squirrel wingsuit has acquired a much lower surface temperature from wind chill.
[100] 410 Fahrenheit

5600 feet per second within the confined space inside the Fortress.

The massive stone walls and foundations acted to constrain the expansion so that, for six milliseconds, pressures in some places inside the building exceeded two hundred and thirty pounds per square inch, bursting the pressurised oxygen cylinders in the infirmary and further intensifying the blazing inferno. This heat, which reached over seven hundred degrees Fahrenheit, combined with the massive over pressure caused fractures to the reinforced structures supporting the masonry.

Concrete support lintels shattered as ten-foot-long flames burst from the Fortress doors and windows. Dislodged fragments of stonework, some as large as dustbins, flew a hundred and twelve feet into the sky above the castle and out into the surrounding lake at nearly one hundred miles an hour.

The noise from the massive explosion reached one hundred and thirty-six decibels, and the shock wave blew out windows in the nearby settlement. Milliseconds after this massive combustive expansion, there was a corresponding implosion, pulling all loose objects and broken building components into the vacuum formed at the source locations of the explosion. The entire event lasted twelve milliseconds but by the end of the blast, the once proud Meri-Isfet Fortress had been reduced to a pile of smouldering rubble. A massive blue-black cloud rose nearly three hundred yards into the morning sky and was visible for thirteen miles in all directions.

Back in Godinje, Saul's radio buzzed with a very satisfied-sounding Billy Bob,

"YeeeHaaa! Fucking told Ya so! It was a fucking Tomahawk!"

Saul remained professional, even though inside, he was bristling with irritation that his second in command was correct. He knew he would probably never hear the end of it. He reasserted his control over his unit.

"Guys, looks like we are under attack. Finish dealing with the remaining targets, and then let's get out of here."

Two miles away from where the women and children were being led under gunpoint to face their execution in the mass grave, twenty rough-looking men and women were standing beside various vans and pickup trucks. The group were surrounded by twelve, heavily armed Montenegrin Border Police officers, dressed in their distinctive dark blue uniforms, who had acted to arrest this group of vehicles as they headed towards Lake Skadar. Although the police had initially suspected that this group was involved with people smuggling from Albania, the weapons the group carried would have been better suited to starting a small war than picking up slave labour for Northern Europe.

Standing at the front of the assembled Mafia group, who had come to meet Stewart at this improvised landing strip, were two large, balding men who could have been brothers. Both men wore black leather jackets, blue jeans, and chain-smoked Russian Belomorkanal[101] cigarettes. The man on the left of the two was Antonio, the local Boss, while his colleague, Nico, the underboss, was more commonly known as "goldy" due to his prominent gold-filled front teeth. The two men looked at the large dark blue cloud of smoke visible over the hill that separated them from Godinje.

---

[101] Made by the Uritsky Tobacco Factory

Antonio turned to Goldy, "Stewart has started without us."

The Boss crossed himself and uttered a prayer. Goldy looked concerned and indicated towards the assembled criminals behind them.

"You want that we all pray for Stewart, Boss?"

Antonio looked at his Capo.

"I am not praying for Stewart. I am praying for those he is hunting."

TERMINAL VELOCITY

"Western society has accepted as unquestionable a technological imperative that is quite as arbitrary as the most primitive taboo: not merely the duty to foster invention and constantly to create technological novelties, but equally the duty to surrender to these novelties unconditionally, just because they are offered, without respect to their human consequences." - Lewis Mumford:

200 feet above the Godinje settlement, Montenegro.

5:06 HRS (GMT+2), 14th Sept, Present day

For the briefest moment, the massive fireball at Fortress Grmožur brightly illuminated the Godinje settlement. From the cast light Stewart identified a group of four men dressed in what he recognised as a high-tech variant of the Wolfsangel paramilitary uniforms he had encountered previously in London and Rome. These four men were holding the remaining village residents, that were exclusively women and small children, at gunpoint by a barn near the town square.

The crowd of around twelve women and six small children were in the process of being split into two groups. The larger group remained gathered under the control of two men by the barn entrance. These thugs were holding some smaller children at gunpoint to coerce and control the others. Another smaller group, of one woman and her child were being marched by the third gunman to a location next to the vineyard, presumably for execution. The fourth operative stood guard, scanning the surrounding area with his MP7[102] assault rifle, watching for any unexpected movement.

Stewart could see from the shadows near the vineyard that the four operatives had already forced the men from the village to dig a trench three feet wide and thirty feet long. This long pit was filled with a mass of twisted human-sized shapes that Stewart was all too familiar with from his time with UN peacekeeping forces in Rwanda and the former Yugoslavia. By the way that the third gunman was rough handling the woman with the small child, it was evident that he intended to force the mother to witness her own child's death before she, too, was executed.

The Scotsman had initially planned to try and stall his wingsuit from its terminal velocity speed of 120 mph[103] to around 50mph and then flat skim over the lake. It would probably be suicide, but it was a better end than having burnt to death in the slowly descending aircraft. However, seeing the brutality unfolding beneath him, Stewart modified his plan.

The Scotsman altered his glide path so that he headed towards where the third gunman had brought the woman and her child to a halt in front of the mass grave. Now that Stewart was considerably closer, he could see that the gunman's face was wrapped in a silver visor that cast a bright blue light over the man's face and upper body. Other digital equipment on the operative's wrist and waist threw a strange pattern of flickering light over the man's body.

The visor's backlight revealed that the operative was grinning as he pointed the barrel of his gun at the small child's head,

---

[102] The Heckler & Koch MP7 (Maschinenpistole 7) uses the proprietary HK 4.6×30mm armour-piercing cartridge.
[103] Stewart is grossly underestimating the speed of the soaking wet squirrel 4 wingsuit which is nearer to 160 MPH.

forcing the woman to plead loudly for her child's life. Clearly, the man enjoyed torturing his victims because the woman's begging only produced a broader smile on the gunman's face. The gunman demanded that the mother and small child should kneel and pray. Both did as the gunman commanded, kneeling in the cold, wet mud beside the open mass grave.

The small child closed her eyes and brought her palms together in a simple prayer,

A tear ran down the grubby face of the mother, who had already endured so much, as evidenced by her torn dress and facial bruising. The gunman raised his Glock and pressed the muzzle against the small child's head, taking the first pressure on the trigger.

At that precise moment, Stewart pulled up and flipped his Squirrel 4 wingsuit, so it slowed considerably, and the Scotsman's orientation changed 180 degrees, so his feet now led his forward momentum. It was in this position, at 52 mph, with his knees bent for impact, that Stewart landed directly into the shoulder blades of the third gunman. Stewart's velocity hardly changed as his impact against the back of the killer lifted the gunman's body from the floor, over the mass grave and into the first of nine consecutive wired vineyard trellises. The Scotsman held on to the shoulder and neck of the third gunman while his feet remained firmly planted on the killer's back as the two men smashed through row after row of vineyard trellises. The journey finally ended when the pair of men collided into a large cast iron pole with a bent top, like a fish hook, which marked the end of a section of the vineyard. The bent top of the pole pierced through the head of the Wolfsangel gunman, leaving his body hanging from the pole like some kind of macabre puppet. In contrast, Stewart was cast to the ground, where he lay motionless in the rich dark soil, smelling the distinctive scent of iron caused by the blood flowing onto the earth from the suspended body of the gunman. For a few moments, Stewart critically assessed his body for internal damage and broken bones – grateful to be alive. Thankfully, based on his brief initial analysis, his injuries were limited to a dislocated left shoulder, a couple of broken ribs on his right side and two black eyes from impacts to his goggles.

"Not bad for someone who just jumped from a mile high without a parachute." mumbled Stewart to himself.

Meanwhile, back at the edge of the open grave, one hundred yards West from the Scotsman, the small girl opened her closed eyes, saw that the gunman was gone and looked questioningly towards her mother.

"Mummy, what happened?"

The mother crossed herself.

"Our prayers were answered, little one."

Back at the end of the vineyard, Stewart remained lying on the ground and slowly placed his injured left arm ninety degrees from his body towards the metal pole supporting the dead Wolfsangel gunman. Stewart then wrapped his hand around the pole and simultaneously pulled and rotated his dislocated arm, resulting in a loud pop and immense relief for the Scotsman.

Two hundred yards North from where Stewart was treating his dislocated shoulder, the IKill Pro intelligent telemetric systems worn by the remaining three Wolfsangel operatives were going crazy, showing the flatline ECG alarm from one of their four-person team.

"What the fuck just happened to Ludvik?" demanded Saul.

Billybob took the initiative to answer the unit commander's question, addressing the third man of their team, "Hans, go forward and find Ludi."

Like the other Wolfsangel team members, Hans was a big man in his thirties who had completed a special operations training program for eligibility to serve in a part-time capacity in a branch of his nation's military. In Han's case, that had been the Danish Jaeger Corps[104]. However, the salary and benefits that were offered by the private sector for using the skills that he had acquired at taxpayers' expense proved irresistible, so he quickly joined Wolfsangel and enthusiastically embraced their ethos of ruthless savagery.

Following Billybob's command, Hans enabled his infrared scanning technology and automated response options on his IKill Pro and advanced cautiously towards the position being indicated by Ludvick's location transponder, directly South of him, hidden behind a tall row of toad green vegetation.

One hundred yards ahead, Stewart slowly hoisted himself to his feet, feeling his broken ribs far more acutely than he had while lying prone in the rich, dark soil. Each breath that he now took caused an all too familiar deep ache on his right side. It was noticeable that as the Scotsman made tentative

---

[104] The Danish Army's Jaeger Corps (Huntsmen Corps) located at Aalborg Air Base.

steps towards the dead operative, he hobbled slightly from impact stress in his ankles and knees, acquired during the repeated collisions against the rows of vines. After zipping up the wingsuit extensions, Stewart slowly limped around to the other side of where the dead operative was suspended to examine the strange digital equipment the killer was wearing. This technology was very different to what he had encountered in his earlier meetings with members of the Wolfsangel organisation. The most noticeable components included a wraparound semi-mirrored visor, gloves and a large glowing watch. As the Scotsman examined the dead man closely, he noted the copious amounts of blood and mucus that flowed from the cracked visor down the man's face, dripping from his chin, which rested on the dead man's chest.

As Stewart approached even closer so that his shoes came into direct view of the dead man's visor, the operative's gloved hands twitched towards him and attempted to pull the trigger of the Glock 17 gun that remained gripped by the man's motorised glove. The Scotsman instantly knocked the gun from the killer's hand and noted, with dismay, that the now empty glove continued to aim towards Stewart's feet and contract the trigger finger.

"Like the bloody Borg[105]!"

exclaimed Stewart as he picked up the dead man's discarded Glock 17 from the rich soil and noted the grip was full of the glowing bio-identification sensors he had seen in London. Realising that the pistol was useless, he ejected the magazine, putting it in one of his wingsuit pockets before throwing the gun to the ground. Ammunition was always useful.

---

[105] An aggressive cyborg species from the Star Trek franchise.

The soil and vineyard detritus around Stewart suddenly exploded from repeated high-velocity impacts, forcing the Scotsman to take cover by throwing himself to the ground. Grimacing from the pain from his complaining ribs, he explored the soil around him, his fingers quickly finding some red-hot spent cartridge rounds. After careful examination, he recognised the deadly armour-piercing rounds[106] that are custom-made for the MP7[107] - the standard assault rifle adopted by Wolfsangel.

"Not a very warm welcome when I just dropped in!"

joked Stewart as he pulled himself closer to the ground, and commando crawled in a Southerly direction, away from where the gunfire was being directed. However, the three round barrages inexorably followed Stewart's line of retreat, leading the Scotsman to mutter,

"Just my luck, another sodding Borg."

Continuing his low commando crawl, the Scotsman looked sideways and, in the gloom, saw the red targeting laser sight projected from the MP7 on some thick wooden blocks that were stacked directly to his left. Grateful for some cover, Stewart crawled around a tall pile of thick wooden slabs, each around eight feet long, one foot wide and six inches thick. Once around the other side of the wooden structure, it was revealed that there were, in fact, two similar wooden constructions laid out side by side with a gap of four feet between them. These two wooden assemblies were seven feet high and four feet wide. Quickly standing, Stewart looked over the top of the towers and came face to face with two bodies laid out on what were evidently funeral pyres. The Scotsman recognised one of the bodies as Cardinal Regio, the Meri-Isfet magician who he had last met in Rome

---

[106] HK 4.6×30mm
[107] Heckler & Koch MP7 (Maschinenpistole 7).

some days before. The other male figure looked like someone from a Viking diorama.

"Fancy meeting you two here. Ceremony not work out quite as you planned?"

remarked Stewart, as he dropped back down behind his improvised cover and discovered two large empty ten-litre containers of an odourless liquid, along with a large box of fire starter blocks and matches. Stewart touched the body of Regio and found it soaking wet. Someone clearly intended to cremate the two magicians, probably after they had finished brutalising the community.

Looking beyond the two funeral pyres, Stewart saw another human figure. This person had been suspended by his arms between two of the wooden funeral pyre blocks that had been buried vertically into the soil. Hurrying forward to see if the person needed first aid, the Scotsman found the figure was that of a big stocky man in late middle age, who had been tied to the wooden posts on either side of him and then had his back cut open into two long slits, which his lungs had been pulled through. Stewart was aware of the barbaric practice of the Viking, and Germanic tribes called "The Blood Eagle[108]" but had never seen it in real life- even in some of the most extreme genocides of recent history, this was a step too far. In this Germanic tribe punishment, the two lungs were pulled from the victim's back, so they inflated and deflated through the rear ribs and looked, for a period, like a pair of fluttering angel wings. The pain and humiliation of this method of death was exceptionally brutal, even for the dark ages.

---

[108] The Orkneyinga saga (1192 CE) describes the blood eagle as a sacrifice to Odin.

"Jesus, I wonder what you did to deserve this kind of treatment?" pondered Stewart to the corpse.

Nearby the poor soul who had suffered this horrific death was some vineyard equipment, including some six by three-foot black plastic sheeting nailed to wooden frames that the vineyard owner had obviously been preparing for the autumn frosts when he was caught and tortured. The Scotsman was convinced that this implementation of the Blood Eagle could not have been done by anyone other than Wolfsangel. His suspicion was confirmed when he found a black PVD KM2000 dagger beside the dead man's body.

"Bloody mad bastards."

muttered the Scotsman, as he looked back at the blue electric glow cast by the copious amounts of electronic gadgets worn by the operative who was coming ever closer to where Stewart was sheltering.

One hundred and ten yards away from the two funeral pyres, Hans gave his two comrades an update,

"I briefly saw a suppressed heat image moving through the undergrowth. I am pursuing."

There was a pause, and then Saul came on the communications channel, saying,

"How many of them are there, Hans? Assess if we are facing a SEAL team, as we will need to withdraw immediately!"

Billy Bob interrupted, "SEAL Teams do have infrared cloaking technology. Be careful of ambush or booby traps."

"Fuck," exclaimed Hans, "I had not considered booby traps."

The big Dane slowed his pace and began looking more carefully where he was walking.

Saul came back on the line, saying, "Guys, I am going up on the barn roof so I can see any heat images. I am not picking up any SEAL transponder identification signals. But we cannot be too careful."

As the Wolfsangel unit leader climbed the rickety wooden ladder that was attached to the right front side of the three-storey wooden barn, Billy Bob remained in front of the two, opened double doors and continued to use his MP7 to cover the small group of women and children who might now be required as hostages.

On the roof, Saul could see some indication of movement being registered on his IKill Pro, but nothing definite. Stewart's soaking, ice-covered wing suit continued to provide him with some protection from the advanced algorithms that were plotting his imminent and violent demise. Saul broadcast what he could see.

"There is some movement from behind the two funeral pyres where we sacrificed that traitorous bastard, Ivanović[109]."

"Confirmed, advancing toward that location." responded Hans as he continued to move closer to where Stewart was hiding.

Seeing the cast blue light from the smart technology on the Wolfsangel operative coming closer, the Scotsman moved behind one of the black plastic frost screens and used it to shield his thermal image from the scanning AI system that he

---

[109] Pavel Ivanović, the vineyard owner who assisted Madeleine Mathers, before she became infested with the soul parasite.

knew was attempting to track him. Stewart then threw the Glock 17 magazine he had unloaded onto Regio's funeral pyre and struck one of the large matches, throwing it close to where the gun magazine was now resting.

The fire started slowly but soon engulfed the pyre in a mass of bright yellow flames as the oil paraffin-soaked wood began to combust.

As Stewart had anticipated, the bright flames wreaked havoc with the advanced IKill Pro scanning software, overloading the thermal imaging algorithms.

"Fuck it, I can't see a thing!" exclaimed Hans as he lifted up his visor onto the top of his head.

Stewart meanwhile pulled up one of the four-foot-long stakes that had been holding the last row of vines in place and carried it in his right hand as he grasped both sides of the frost screen and advanced towards his stalker.

Saul's voice came over the Wolfsangel team's headphones. "I can still see him. He is... wait... yes, he is carrying a stick."

Billy Bob interrupted again, saying, "A stick? Are you sure, Boss? It could be a rifle."

Saul sighed. He was growing increasingly tired of his "know it all" second in command.

"Yes, I am sure. It's just a stick from the vineyard. Hans, use your torch. The man is there. Just shoot him."

Emboldened by this information, Hans threw his high-tech visor to the ground and pulled out a small black Fenix tactical penlight[110] from his left sleeve pocket. Slinging the MP7 rifle onto his back, the operative drew his Glock 17 and assumed a two-handed grip, with the torch in his left hand and the

---

[110] A Fenix LD12 AA Flashlight.

Glock in his right. As Hans advanced, he shone his thin beam of light into the thick foliage that surrounded him.

Suddenly, the air was filled with the sound of rapid gunfire. Instinctively, Hans discharged three rounds into the semi-darkness and addressed the unknown person who was hiding from him,

"Come out, you cowardly swine! I am going to make you beg for mercy."

A cultured, Scottish voice came from behind him, saying,

"Not going to force me to drink blended whiskey, I hope?"

Taken completely by surprise, Hans spun around to direct his gun and torch to where it sounded like the disembodied voice had come from. But the area was empty. All he could see was more of the toad green vines- it felt like being lost in a maze. Then his torch picked up the outline of an older man with short, cropped, greying hair and a light beard. This stranger was wearing a badly torn dark blue jumpsuit and carrying a thin metal garden stake as a walking stick. In the light from the Fenix, it was clear that this man was a mass of bruises and was limping. Saul, the unit commander, had been right. The man only had a stick, thought Hans.

Laughing, Hans addressed his target as he aimed his handgun towards the older man, who had hobbled much closer and was now within a few feet of him, saying,

"A stick against a gun. It's a totally unfair match, fuckwit!"

In the torchlight, it was hard to see the complete detail of what happened next, but there was a sudden blur of movement, followed by the sound of two loud impacts that emanated from Han's right kneecap and, almost immediately afterwards, Han's groin. Even through the extensive protective padding on the Wolfsangel's body armour, the pain from these two impacts was overwhelming and distracted Hans from his intended actions and forced him to drop to his right knee. The light from the torch that remained in the operative's hand showed that the circular motion of the vineyard stake carried by the stranger continued up and sideways before the older man in the jumpsuit smoothly altered his grip on the stake and thrust it violently down and diagonally into the right side of Han's neck- penetrating into the chest cavity, through the upper right lung, aorta, pulmonary artery and ending up in piercing into the upper left ventricle of Han's heart. As Hans collapsed face down into the rich dark soil, the ECG alarms blared on the IKill Pro systems of Saul and Billy Bob.

Looking at the dead gunman, who had so recently dismissed the combat potential of a simple stick, a cultured Scottish voice commented,

"Agreed, it was a totally unfair match."

The Scotsman then reached down and removed the black KM2000 knife from Han's ankle sheath and placed it, blade first into a zipped pocket on his left bicep. Leaving the body of the dead Wolfsangel operative where it lay, adding nitrogen to the vineyard soil, Stewart resumed holding the frost screen and slowly started heading North towards the two remaining Wolfsangel team members.

Meanwhile, on the barn roof, Saul was panicking, saying,

"We should withdraw."

Billy Bob sighed. He missed working with other Ranger-qualified operatives. They had more nerve when things went wrong.

"Boss, it is one man. All our weapons are biometric, so he is without a gun. He will be coming towards us. Let's split the hostages. I will take some of them to the pit and start executing them. You stay here on the roof, and when this prick comes to save the hostages, you take him out with your MP7."

As he was making the suggestion, Billy Bob secretly thought to himself; even a National Guardsman can't miss at two hundred yards with the IKill Pro making the aim and pulling the trigger. Not waiting for confirmation from his increasingly overwhelmed team leader, Billy Bob rounded up half a dozen of the traumatised women and children who were gathered in front of the barn. He corralled them towards the mass grave, following some six paces behind them, covering them with his MP7. Whenever the group slowed, he grabbed one of the smallest children and hit it severely.

Meanwhile, Stewart had reached the mass grave and lowered himself silently down among the tangle of dead bodies. It was certainly a grisly location, but in his time, the Scotsman had learnt that the most successful ambushes were from locations your target would never suspect.

From his vantage point, looking over the top of the edge of the pit, the Scotsman could see the tell-tale blue glow of the smart technology worn by one of the operatives as he advanced behind a group of crying women and their silent children. Satisfied that he had correctly guessed what the remaining two operatives would do, Stewart looked carefully to all the high vantage points and spotted the tell-tail blue glow of electronics from the second operative on the barn roof. Yes, that would be the sniper who would shoot Stewart once the first man had drawn the Scotsman to come and try and save these women and children, thought Stewart.

K.R.M. Morgan

The Scotsman lay down among the mass of bodies, many of which had brutal injuries, including swastika and Wolfsangel symbols carved into their exposed flesh.

"Fucking thugs," commented Stewart before becoming silent and unmoving.

His wet wingsuit was still retaining its cold temperature, which closely matched the post-mortem conditions of the bodies around him. Ignoring the strong smells of iron, excrement and fresh meat, Stewart pulled free the KM2000 dagger from his left bicep pocket and held it in his right hand before settling into as comfortable a position as he could, just in case he had to remain still for a prolonged wait.

Some twenty feet away, Billy Bob lined the pathetic-looking group of women in front of the pit, which already contained the dead bodies of their male family members. Shouting out towards the tangle of green foliage on the other side of the mass grave, Billy Bob challenged the unknown man who had so far killed two of his team members; his thick southern drawl carried over the length of the vineyard, stating,

"I am going to count from one to five. When I reach five, I will start shooting these innocents unless you surrender immediately!"

Billy Bob advanced to the edge of the open grave and looked out into the vineyard, his advanced IKill Pro software scanning for any unexpected movements.

"One!" Billy Bob paused and then continued,

"Two!" there was another pause as Billy Bob expected his target to emerge. Clearly, this must be an utterly heartless bastard he was facing.

"Three!"

"I am not bluffing, as you are about to see,"

"Four!" Billy Bob pulled one of the small children to him and placed the barrel of his MP7 against the child's head.

At that moment, Stewart rose from the darkness like a phantom in a single lightning-fast movement and stabbed the KM2000 blade up into Billy Bob's pericardium[111]. He then twisted the knife and then pulled the blade down the length of the left leg's femoral artery down to the ankle[112]. This long cut caused an uncontrolled mass of red arterial blood to pour down from the leg, over Billy Bob's left combat boot and form a cascading rivulet into the pit.

The concentrated burning pain from the deep knife penetration into the nerve plexus located between his legs was overwhelming. It caused the Ranger-trained operative to forget the child he was about to shoot- instead, he dropped his MP7 and grabbed his own groin with both hands, only to them covered in copious amounts of warm pulsing blood. An inhuman noise, half scream and half feral howl filled the air- it took Billy Bob a few moments to realise he was the one making it.

It took a moment more before the Wolfsangel operative realised he was mortally injured[113]. By that time, the

____

[111] In the soft tissue between his rectum and scrotum.

[112] William Ewart Fairbairn would approve. It is a safe bet that Stewart is fully familiar with Fairbairn's teachings which formed the basis of all commando training since the second world war. See Fairbairn "All-In Fighting, (1942) by Faber and Faber Limited (London). 132 pages. ISBN 9781783313419".

[113] Fairbairn's Timetable of Death for second world war allied special forces commandos indicate the bleed out times for strategic knife wounds, including his estimates for loss of consciousness and death. Modern authors dispute Fairburn's estimates but then again

Scotsman had grabbed Billy Bob's tactical belt and used it to drag the bleeding man down into the tangle of bodies. Stewart then finished his attack by ramming the now bloody KM2000 dagger deep into Billy Bob's chest. By the time the technique was completed, the hilt of the knife was all that remained visible from the big man's sternum[114]. The blue light from the dead man's IKill Pro visor and watch cast an eerie glow over Billy Bob's motionless body.

Stewart looked up at the gathered grimy faces of the women and children standing on the edge of the pit and made the universal silence gesture with the forefinger of his right hand. Seeing their understanding, the Scotsman then signalled for them all to come down into the grave, so they were no longer targets for the sniper on the barn roof. It was a gruesome place for sure, but at the moment, there was nowhere else they would be safer from the deadly MP7 rounds. Stewart helped the first two women down and then left them to complete the task.   Walking to the rear of the pit, Stewart rolled up over the edge to minimise his profile. He then picked up the frost screen and resumed his movement towards the barn and the one remaining Wolfsangel operative.

Back up on the barn roof, Saul was trying to come to terms with the terrifying reality indicated by the IKill Pro flatline alarm for Billy Bob. In a matter of ten minutes, he had lost his entire unit to a single unarmed man. Even from his high

---

very few modern "authorities" have as many certified unarmed hand to hand combat encounters (officially accredited as 55) as Lieutenant-Colonel William Ewart Fairbairn.

[114] Bullet proof vests are, typically, not stab resistant. Just as stab vests are not, typically, bullet resistant.

vantage point, with all his high technology assistance, he still could not see any evidence of his opponent. He did not even want to imagine what could have caused a hard man like Billy Bob to scream like he had, but Saul knew he did not want to die. Based on what he had seen so far, he decided to take the only remaining option. He stood up, pulled off his visor and shouted,

"I surrender! Here are my weapons,"

He then threw down his MP7, removed his Glock 17 pistol and KM2000 dagger and threw them off from the roof as well. He then continued, saying,

"I am coming down. As your prisoner."

Saul came slowly down the old wooden ladder just as the sun finally rose over the vineyard.

The National Guardsman stood in front of the open barn doors with his hands above his head. He shouted again,

"I surrender!"

There was movement from the darkness of the barn, and Stewart emerged, carrying a badly worn scythe that he had found hanging inside the building.

A cultured Scottish voice answered Saul's declaration, saying,

"Sit down slowly. Then put your hands on your head."

Saul was clearly startled to see Stewart. The way the Scotsman was holding the scythe and looking at him, it was abundantly clear that he was just waiting for an excuse to execute the last remaining Wolfsangel operative with what is termed in the special operations community "extreme prejudice".

As the National Guardsman slowly sank to the floor, four, dark blue police Opel Vivaro vans and two police Opel

Insignia[115] estate cars sped into the village courtyard in a cloud of dust. Ten, armed police officers quickly emerged and surrounded Saul and Stewart. The police officers began taking in the carnage around them. One older policeman, who was clearly in charge, spent some moments talking to the assembled women. After hearing their account of the evening's events, the police superintendent walked over and drew his Glock 17 service revolver and shot Saul in the temple, killing him instantly. The Wolfsangel operative looked stunned as his lifeless body fell forward into the dirt. The superintendent then turned to Stewart and said,

"Welcome to Montenegrin justice, Mr Stewart."

The superintendent gestured with his pistol.

"Please, put the scythe down and accompany me to the police station."

---

[115] Opel Insignia Sports Tourer estate.

THE BENBEN[116] LEGACY

*"Ten measures of magic (keshafim) were given to the world;
Egypt received nine while the rest of the world received one."
- Kiddushin 49a-b: The Talmud.*

*Ad-Dajjal's Personal Occult Library,
5000 feet beneath one of the highest peaks in the Bernese
Alps,
North of Grindelwald,
Bern, Switzerland*

14:23Hrs Sept 14th, present day

At the furthest end of the vast library[117], the frigid
atmosphere around the figure of Ad-Dajjal remained
permeated with the intoxicating aroma of the Ghost flower
of the Mojave Desert. The raven-haired beauty continued
examining some of the vast collection of carved stone frescos
stored in the enormous titanium storage racks at the rear of
the long library vaults. Her hypnotic green eyes exclusively
dwelt on a set of six, large stone fragments from Göbekli
Tepe, that were related to the strange snake-like creature
which the Assyrians would later call the MUŠ.ŠÀ.TÙR.

After four hours of intense work, Ad-Dajjal completed her
investigation of the Göbekli Tepe materials. Her Moleskin

---

[116] The benben stone (also known as a pyramidion) is the top of an
ancient Egyptian pyramid. Symbolically, it represented the first land
that rose above the primordial waters of creation by the creator
Atum. In Utterances 587 and 600 of the Pyramid Texts, Atum refers
to himself as this "mound". The top of pyramids were designed to
catch the reflection of the rising morning sun.
[117] There are no limits to what is possible when you have endless
funding from the collective quantitative easing of the world's central
banks.

notebook was now filled with detailed notes in English, about a mysterious complex of caves filled with ancient artefacts located beneath the neolithic Turkish site. She returned the large stone sections to their place in the titanium storage unit, placed her ornate Montblanc pen[118] on the study table and entered a small set of rooms offset from the main library.

The main area inside this restroom was around twenty feet long and fifteen feet wide, with grey matt-coloured walls decorated with various esoteric symbols from Levi's nineteenth-century works[119]. The ten-foot-high ceiling provided a diffused light from some concealed star-shaped holes embedded into the plasterwork. Apart from a single door at the far end of the small room, there was a coffee machine on the left and a steel computer workstation with a printer on the right-hand side. The air was cool and dry, with a slight scent of coffee.

From force of habit, once inside the restroom, she strode over to an exquisitely crafted Aequator[120] Coffee Machine in hand-finished walnut[121] , which perfectly complemented the rest of the simple décor of the small library restroom. After dispensing a steaming hot macchiato[122] in a white porcelain "UNITY" mug, Ad-Dajjal was genuinely shocked when the coffee immediately froze, causing the cup to explode violently. Broken ceramic fragments flew over the white-tiled floor, and semi-frozen coffee poured over the pristine purple ritual robes. Ad-Dajjal's irritation with herself at forgetting her changed reality was evident but only momentary. She

---

[118] Mystery Masterpiece by Montblanc and Van Cleef and Arpels.

[119] See - Levi, Eliphas (1896). Dogme et Rituel de la Haute Magi Part I: The Doctrine of Transcendental Magic. & The Magical Ritual of the Sanctum Regnum.

[120] An Aequator Peru ASD Swiss Made Coffee Machine. It grinds beans to perfection, but at a price.

[121] English Juglans regia walnut.

[122] Arabica Supremo Espresso and steamed milk.

left the fragments where they lay on the floor and strode into one of the two side rooms and disrobed in a large mirrored changing area. Objectively examining her flawless body, Ad-Dajjal looked carefully at the side of her face where in her physical incarnation, she had suffered significant withering on the left side of her face from a curse[123]. Now her features were utterly flawless. Her facial bone structures reflect a timeless beauty that would be the envy of Helen of Troy.

Whatever intelligence had brought her back to the physical world had relieved her of that disfigurement. Satisfied with what she saw in the mirror, Ad-Dajjal walked into a luxurious black Kohler LuxStone shower complete with Bader Hassoun and Sons soaps. The extreme cold surrounding her new incarnation caused so much steam and condensation that the normally super-efficient humidity controls within the underground complex could not cope. Red alarm lights on the walls came on momentarily but dimmed once Ad-Dajjal finished.

After drying herself with a pristine handmade Turkish[124] towel, she dressed[125] in a bespoke tailored, blood red, Thai silk Chanel trouser suit, complimenting her long raven black hair, white silk shirt and matching red leather flat-soled court shoes. Finally, she carefully applied a few sweeps of makeup from the long Louis Vuitton Malletier leather case that was placed outside the shower.

---

[123] The result of RHP Magus, Elizabeth Fitz-Glass's dying curse. See Bridge of Souls for more information on why Ad-Dajjal was cursed in this manner.

[124] A Coyuchi Cloud Loom™ Organic Towel.

[125] I do not *usually* describe what underwear my characters wear. But, since you are obviously interested in that kind of detail, I would suspect it would be something from Kiki de Montparnasse's latest Paris collection. No, you cannot afford it.

Ad-Dajjal exited the washroom, walked over to a thirty-two-inch 8k Apple Pro screen connected to a brushed aluminium Mac Pro unit and sat in front of the system. A few keystrokes on the Apple keyboard and a retina scan later and Ad-Dajjal had logged into the massive supercomputer array located directly beneath the library.

As she sat at the computer desk, her long dark hair cascaded around her head, highlighting her piercing green hypnotic eyes. Ad-Dajjal's long fingers flew over the keys, initiating complex Unix commands to access critical selected information from the combined databases of the world's premier intelligence networks to bring her up to date as to what had transpired since her earthly death two weeks earlier. The images and news items on the screen were read and understood at an inhuman speed.

First, there was the rise of Cortez and his New Republic, taking over Europe through concerted social media influences. Then there were confidential emails related to the acquisition and subsequent use of the St Petersburg Wheel by the two senior Meri-Isfet adepts, Edwardo Salvador and Cardinal Regio.

This information prompted an immediate search on recent severe weather and global geological activity, followed by access to discussions and shared images between astronomers and astrophysicists at NASA, Roscosmos[126] and the CNSA[127]. These confidential images and discussions showed some recent gravitational anomalies had caused significant disruption to the paths of near-earth asteroids. Graphics from NASA showed projected asteroid paths that

---

[126] The Russian State Space Corporation "Roscosmos".
[127] The China National Space Administration servers in Haidian, Beijing

involved substantial impacts on the inner planets of our solar system over the coming weeks.

The raven-haired beauty sighed at the stupidity of using the Qliphothic wheel devices that destroyed our creation without the certainty of becoming the supreme power of a new universe. The creators of previous existences would, she knew, never share power with fools stupid enough to destroy their creation just on the promise of forbidden knowledge.

Remembering her own design to perform the forbidden forty-ninth invocation of Enochian magic at the Citadel of the Djinn, her next search involved the people who had thwarted her plan. She saw that the rise of Cortez had radically affected the lives of Stewart, Curren and O'Neil, destroying their reputations and, in Stewart and Curren's cases, causing their incarceration at the UN prison at the Hague, facing the death penalty.

The raven-haired beauty then investigated the fate of her beloved general, the hawk-faced Abdul Issuin. Recent reports from within the Chinese MSS[128] talked about the activities of the international terror mastermind, successfully escaping from three elite FALCON commando teams and shooting down two jet fighters near the Gurvan Saikhen Mountain range.

For the first time since her return to the physical realm, Ad-Dajjal smiled as she remarked to herself,

"So, there is another way into the ancient Citadel without waiting for the one hundred and twenty-year cycle."

The raven-haired beauty's delight was short-lived as the next item that flew past her was confirmation from a PLA[129] investigation that Abdul Issuin had died in a motorcycle

---

[128] Ministry of State Security (MSS or Guoanbu).
[129] Chinese People's Liberation Army (PLA)

accident on his way to Beijing. After her perfect face showed momentary concern, Ad-Dajjal laughed delightedly at the classified NSA image of The Most Dangerous Man in The World looking up, deliberately, into a CCTV camera outside a Swiss bank in Geneva. Ad-Dajjal's icy touch frosted the high-definition screen as her fingers caressed the image, and she said,

"Not so easy to kill, are you, my beloved?"

Finally, there was a news flash related to a small plane crash in an area Ad-Dajjal had already indicated was of interest in her searches, near the Godinje settlement, in Montenegro. A quick array of commands accessed a replay from the United States 224 spy satellite. These recordings showed a Cessna plane crashing into Fortress Grmožur, followed some moments later by a massive explosion far greater than would be expected from such a small aircraft.

Ad-Dajjal quickly checked the live video feeds from the cell in the UN detention facility in the Hague supposedly containing Tavish Stewart, and smiled, exclaiming, "Ah, my Knight of the North, you are still a force to be reckoned with!"

One mile above where Ad-Dajjal was searching the world's premier intelligence databases, a strange-looking aircraft with USAF markings completed its approach to the secret location of the Wolfsangel headquarters. As the Bell Boeing V-22 Osprey came within eight hundred yards, the two Rolls-Royce AE 1107C turboprop engines tilted from horizontal to vertical, allowing the aircraft to hover like a helicopter. Fifty feet beneath the stationary plane, a large steel and asphalt landing pad extended from under the rocky outcrop on this unique Bernese Mountain.

Moments later, the V-22 landed and powered down the hurricane-force down-blast from its twin turboprops. As the roar of the turbine noise subsided, the rear access door lowered to the landing pad surface and a smartly dressed middle-aged man with short blond hair walked down the gangway. The man wore a dark blue United States Air Force Enlisted Honor Guard Uniform with a large badge on his sleeve showing the rank insignia of Chief Master Sergeant of the Air Force (CMSAF). A lone, dark-haired female USAF corporal walked two paces behind him, carrying a Dorr[130] aluminium case with a prominent cobra head symbol on its side.

The six leaders of the Wolfsangel headquarters, standing behind some transparent rotor down draft shielding at the perimeter of the landing area, scrutinised the man. Even though he was of a non-commissioned rank, the protocol stated that the CMSAF had precedence up to the rank of lieutenant general. More worryingly, they knew he represented Chairman Cortez, or as they knew him, Alpha.

The Wolfsangel leadership approached the newcomer, and the six saluted their visitor. The unit's leader, Col. Jaree, looked at the black plastic name badge on the CMSAF and addressed the newcomer, saying,

"Chief Booker, to what do we owe the pleasure of your visit?"

Booker looked at the assembled group and, before any introductions, stated,

"I have been sent to deal with your problems."

The emphasis in the statement was on the fact that there was more than one problem. The clear implication from the USAF Chief was that there should not be any problems that the assembled men could not solve themselves.

---

[130] Dorr aluminium medium case.

Jaree downplayed the implied criticism. "Problems? We only have one *challenge* that I am aware of." he looked to his colleagues for confirmation.

Booker grunted before continuing. He said, "I repeat that I have been sent to resolve **two** problems."

Before Jaree could respond, the newcomer removed his pristine white silicone "gripper" gloves[131], drew the chromed classic 1911 pistol from his gleaming black leather belt, slid back the gun's chamber and fired a massive .45 brass round into Col Jaree's forehead[132]. As the former leader crumpled to the ground, Booker looked directly at the shocked and blood-splattered faces of the five remaining men.

"Now, gentlemen, let us proceed to deal with your **second** problem. Kindly take me to the terror that is so frightening that you needed to call Alpha."

Without waiting for a response, Booker strode towards the series of four massive thermonuclear-resistant sliding doors that were recessed into the rocky mountainside. The USAF adjutant followed closely behind, carrying the large aluminium case.

One mile beneath where Col Jaree's exposed brain tissue was becoming the focus of numerous airborne scavengers, Ad-Dajjal had returned to her library. Having reached the furthest end of the long room, she opened the first in a series of seven motorised ten-foot square sliding doors on the rear wall. As these doors opened, strip lighting somewhere high above came to life, illuminating an annexe room around one hundred feet square with a thirty-foot-high ceiling. The air

---

[131] Part of the USAF Honor Guard dress uniform.
[132] Saves on complex resignation procedures.

smelt sterile and was of the same computer-controlled low humidity ambience of seventy-two degrees Fahrenheit as in the rest of the vast storage area. The walls were a light grey matt colour, and the floor was a clean, industrial-looking riveted metal. In addition to the strip lighting, numerous spotlights focused on a massive pyramidal-shaped stone edifice that filled the ample space.

This object was one of antiquity's most extraordinary missing artefacts, acquired at enormous cost by the Meri-Isfet back when the French conquered Egypt. Ad-Dajjal had moved the object from its long-term storage in Paris[133] to the Grindelwald location when the mountain base was constructed back in the late twentieth century.

The upper surfaces of the top third of the object were all covered with gold leaf[134], while the remaining lower surfaces were finished with a four-inch layer of highly polished white Tura limestone. Fissures revealed a base layer composed of massive, unpolished limestone blocks in a few places. The standard of masonry work in this inner central core was exceptional since, even after thousands of years, the stone blocks were so closely fitted that you could not slide a piece of paper between them. The only exceptions were in a series of rough breaks in the stonework where it had been necessary to have the blocks separated in order to be transported and reinstalled[135] in Ad-Dajjal's private sanctuary.

---

[133] This storage facility was in one of the original buildings built next to the Louvre by King Francis I in 1546 on the site of a 12th-century fortress built by King Philip II.
[134] To catch and reflect the rays of the rising sun each morning.
[135] You just cannot get the quality of workmen these days.

The highly polished white limestone on the lower two-thirds of the structure had a series of frescos carved deeply into each of the four triangular surfaces that formed this massive pyramidion capstone[136]. These carved images had originally been painted in vivid colours. The paint had faded from exposure to the atmosphere over time, but it retained much of its original splendour.

Ad-Dajjal stood in front of the vast, forty foot[137] long structure in front of her, the highly polished limestone and gold leaf shining almost as brilliantly under the spotlights as they had the day they were finished. The frescos on the surface in front of Ad-Dajjal showed the technical diagrams for constructing a complex set of monolithic structures on a vast, flat square plain[138].

At the Eastern side of the area portrayed on the schematic stood a giant stone effigy[139] of a massive female lioness[140], carved from the limestone bedrock representing the goddess Mehit[141]. This lioness goddess was facing the [142]rising

---

[136] Based on the angle and scale of this capstone the original pyramid beneath it would have been 481 feet high and the sides would have been 755 feet long.

[137] Yes, the ceiling is only 30 feet high but the pyramid is set at an angle of 51 degrees 52 minutes, so it just fits. Almost like the space was specifically designed for it, which it was.

[138] Almost a mile square, if the scale is correct.

[139] The Lioness statue was 240 feet from paw to tail, 66 feet from the base to the top of the head, and 62 feet wide at its widest part.

[140] The current human head is noticeably out of scale with the original size and scale of the lion body – this is the result of extensive re-carving by the old kingdom fourth dynasty pharaoh, Khafre in 2540 BCE to make the sculpture in his likeness.

[141] The earliest Egyptian writings describe this lioness as "the Distant Goddess" and represented the wild deserts of Nubia.

[142] The constellation of Leo rose in the East on the vernal equinox at 10,500 BCE.

constellation of Leo. Some adjacent hieroglyphs indicated this constellation was Mehit's consort, and the alignments depicted the vernal equinox.

Under the diagram of the Lioness were depicted three underground chambers, the largest of which was under the left paw, filled with stone tablets and papyri.

The diagram of the plateau also showed a large and complex tunnel system that led from the Sphinx, connecting to three pyramids of varying sizes. Depicted in the night sky above these three pyramids was the constellation of Orion. The diagram made it clear that the locations of these three pyramids aligned perfectly with the three stars that make up Orion's belt in the night sky[143].

Attached to the hidden tunnels between the Lioness and the largest of the three pyramids was a complex series of subterranean temples dedicated to some pre-dynastic gods. Finally, in addition to these formal temples was a vast waterway fed by the Nile that ran under the entire plateau width. The image of this mile-long underground canal was split into several sections, depicting the Mesektet barge's[144] progress and the challenges the sun faced to get from the West (setting) to the East (dawn).

Towards the end of the barge's night-time journey[145], a massive multi-headed serpent-dragon attacked the craft, trying to kill the occupants and prevent the sun from rising, plunging all creation into oblivion. A hieroglyph of five serpents stabbed with five large knives was directly under the

---

[143] This alignment of the pyramids with the positions of the stars in Orion's belt occurred in 10,500 BCE.

[144] The Ship of a Million Souls – the name given to Ra's solar barge when it passed through the underworld at night to (hopefully) re-emerge at dawn.

[145] The attack was shown as taking place in the tenth section of the barge's journey.

detailed carving of the multi-headed monster of chaos[146]. This representation of Apep included a depiction of some unknown force projected from the creature that held all but one of the occupants of the barge in thrall, so they could not resist the deadly attack made against them.

The one exception to this mesmeric spell was a lone figure who stood fearlessly at the front of the barge, thrusting a long spear with a brilliant shining orb at its far end[147]. This glowing tip shone like the sun god himself, and this heroic figure plunged it into the multi-headed creature's body.

Ad-Dajjal ran the long fingers of her right hand over the figure of this fearless hero. He had a dark animal head, two strange upright rectangular ears, and a long curved snout attached to a powerful human body. The raven-haired beauty began an invocation that had not been properly pronounced for over four thousand years. She spoke in the most ancient form of Egyptian that was lost millennia before the rise of the Greek and Roman civilisations.

"I am the slayer of gods, the shaker of the heavens, the wrath of the wilderness[148], the only hope against the ultimate darkness, I am the one, whose power is overwhelming[149]!"

---

[146] Apep – "The Enemy of Ra" and "The Lord of Chaos".
[147] The Spear of Ra or Heliokinesis.
[148] The Western desert, which we now know as the Sahara.
[149] Gaston Maspero (1894) "Les inscriptions des pyramides de Saqqarah" (Pyramid Texts). The oldest (publicly) known Egyptian magical writings.

As Ad-Dajjal made her invocation, the carvings on the pyramid surface suddenly became deeper and began to cast shadows on the polished limestone that were not present before. The air inside the vault was also noticeably changed, becoming considerably warmer and drier. Discrete red warning lights came on at several locations on the walls, indicating that the environmental controls were failing to keep the conditions at the ideal preservation temperature and humidity. Ad-Dajjal's breath ceased to be visible, and if anyone had been brave or stupid enough to touch her, they would have found that her skin no longer caused ice burns. The mysterious shadows on the benben's surface carvings grew more pronounced. They began to flow down from the white limestone, reaching the floor and slowly extending from the pyramid over the metal floor towards Ad-Dajjal's feet.

Two hundred yards from where Ad-Dajjal's invocation was causing strange changes to the benben, Chief Booker had hurriedly changed into his red silk ritual robes while coming down in the lift. Leaving the aluminium case containing his dress uniform beside the lift for collection on his return, he headed towards where the terrified Wolfsangel leaders had indicated the apparition was lurking.

The USAF senior NCO looked at his stainless-steel Rolex GMT Master as he strode confidently down the statue-lined corridor to Ad-Dajjal's library. He did not think this matter would take him long to "solve". He was already looking forward to a sumptuous dinner that evening as the guest of the acting[150] USAFE-AFAFRICA[151] commander at Ramstein Air Base, Germany, before returning Stateside on the red eye that evening. Hung from Booker's left sleeve was a thin rubber mat, and held in his right hand was a stick of carved rowan wood. This magical weapon was a treasure passed to Booker by his late father, who had been the Master of the Aaron Burr[152] Lodge in New Orleans.

One hundred yards away from where Chief Booker was contemplating the kind of dinner only base commanders[153] can enjoy, conditions surrounding the benben stone continued to become more esoterically charged. A growing static charge in the air made Ad-Dajjal's long raven hair begin to fly around her. Long shadows mysteriously cast from limestone carvings overshadowed her figure, obscuring her in such a way as to transform her appearance. Her head appeared longer, and her face more angular and pointed. The cast shadows also created the illusion that her height increased with each passing moment. These changes did not just apply to the raven-haired beauty. The metal floor in the annexe room was also transforming, the smooth surface breaking up into row after row of one-yard square blocks

Meanwhile, Chief Booker had entered the library and was close to the entrance to the rear annexe, visible through a set of wall-high sliding doors that had been pulled open.

---

[150] Booker is dining with the acting base commander because the substantive one remains in the underground bunker. Presumably fighting other VIPS for any remaining scraps.
[151] U.S. Air Forces in Europe - Air Forces Africa
[152] Traitors are heroes to the Meri-Isfet.
[153] Or senior politicians and civil servants.

Brilliant orange and red light and waves of warm air poured from the room and starkly contrasted with the darker and much cooler environmentally controlled atmosphere in the rest of the library. Booker unfurled the rubber mat on his arm to reveal a Goetic magic circle that was six feet in diameter and prepared to throw it to the ground and step inside it the moment he entered the room to confront the visitation.

Inside the brightly lit annexe, the effects of Ad-Dajjal's invocation continued. The shadow of the strange creature from the limestone carving now completely covered her, transforming her striking female form into a pitch-black silhouette of the strange hybrid creature that had been depicted defending the sun barge. When Ad-Dajjal's transfiguration[154] was complete, she no longer appeared human, and the carving of the entity on the barge had disappeared from the limestone. What had once been the resurrected form of Nissa Ad-Dajjal now appeared as an animated black silhouette of the tall and powerful creature. This shadow creature bowed, extending its arms into the air, its hands forming a triangle that encompassed the sun, which stood high in a clear blue sky above.

As Ad-Dajjal performed her adoration of the sun God Ra, Chief Booker came around the corner and entered the annexe. While his eyes struggled to adjust to the incredible brightness in the room, he threw down his mat and stepped into the magic circle. Based on over twenty years of magical practice, he was utterly confident of the protection afforded by the mighty god names and sigils surrounding its circumference. Gradually Booker's eyes started to get used to the bright light within the annexe, but he could not so

---

[154] In magical terms, Ad-Dajjal has made a god form assumption.

quickly adapt to the extreme heat. Booker's full-length ritual robes started to feel oppressively warm, and he hoped this exorcism would be over soon.

Booker could now see the phenomena that he had come to dispatch. The first thing that struck him was the entity's appearance. Whatever it was, it looked like a figure had been cut out of reality and replaced by pitch black.

There was also a powerful physical presence, not just its enormous size but the magical aura that the entity projected. This energy was more powerful than anything Booker had ever previously encountered. The shadow entity was over ten feet tall with a long face that bent gradually towards its body like an anteater[155]. However, based on its teeth and eye location, this creature was a predatory carnivore. It had long, square-shaped ears that stood proudly above its oddly shaped dark head. The outlines of the torso and dress were that of a warrior, with extraordinary muscular definition and heavy leather armour on its chest, arms and legs.

But the unusual appearance of the entity was not the only thing that struck Booker. Now he could look around him; he could see that the ground beneath his feet and his surroundings were definitely not those of the underground library annexe. Booker was standing on a small square artificial plateau at the top of a four-hundred-and-fifty-foot-high pyramid. The artificial mesa was made up of eighty-one blocks of limestone, laid out in a nine-by-nine pattern of one-yard square blocks. The view from this vantage point was disturbingly familiar, with the smog-covered modern city of Cairo in the distance and crowds of tourists on the Giza plateau beneath him. The dry heat of Egypt engulfed him and, as if to confirm this was not an illusion, a sudden gust of wind blew sand into Chief Booker's eyes.

---

[155] The original description of Anubis.

Believing this was some form of magical glamour that had been cast over him, Booker performed the classic Middle Pillar Technique followed by the Lesser Banishing Ritual of the Pentagram and that of the Hexagram. But still, the illusion remained. In exasperation, Booker performed the classic Rabbinical Kabbalistic exorcism on himself to remove an obsession by a Dybbuk[156]. By now, Booker was becoming increasingly frustrated, exclaiming, "What the hell is this?"

Taking a deep cleansing breath, Booker decided to step back outside the annexe to recentre his focus before re-entering and resuming his task. Repeatedly reassuring himself that everything he was experiencing was an illusion, Booker slowly and deliberately stepped backwards, only to find himself stumbling down to the upper steps of the large limestone blocks forming the structure's slope. Rubbing the numerous bruises that were now forming on his elbows and knees, Booker stood and stepped back up to resume his place inside his magic circle.

"This farce has gone on long enough!" Booker exclaimed, pulling out his chromed 1911 pistol and firing a single shot into the air, hoping to gain the entity's attention.

The enormous figure did not seem to notice. However, on the plateau below, several tourists heard the gun shot. They started shouting at some grey-uniformed tourism and antiquities police, who were sitting smoking and drinking coffee beside the historic landmark.

Booker ignored the growing commotion far below him and began a conjuration from The Book of Abramelin[157] to bind

---

[156] Unquiet spirit from the Jewish esoteric traditions.

[157] It is claimed by authorities that only the German original is imbued with magickal power. "Abraham eines Juden von Worms untereinander versteckte zum Theil aus der Kabala and Magia gezogene, zum Theil durch vornehme Rabbiner als Arabern un

any living creature. At the end of the long conjuration, all Booker had succeeded in doing was making his throat sore from shouting in the arid desert air. The strange entity continued what could only have been some form of lengthy adoration of the ancient sun god Ra.

In exasperation, Booker drew his 1911 again and fired four of the .45 calibre rounds into the centre body mass of the creature. If Booker was expecting to see the creature collapse and die, he was to be disappointed. However, he did succeed in finally getting the entity's attention as it turned its head and looked towards where Booker was standing. Seeing the opportunity to repeat the headshot that had successfully killed Col Jaree earlier, Booker discharged his last two remaining rounds into what must have been the creature's jet-black head.

The massive brass .45 rounds did not cause the entity any damage, but clearly, the bullets did annoy it. The massive thing strode over to Booker and, noticing the magic circle, made a deliberate step with its left leg across the circle boundary and placed one of its huge feet in front of the terrified Booker. In desperation, Booker pointed his father's wand at the black shadow thing that towered over him, but before he could utter a protective banishing, the monster opened its mouth and roared. The noise was deafening, carrying for miles across the Giza plateau and beyond the Cairo city limits. An unbelievably powerful stream of warm, damp, fetid air blasted into Booker's face, lifting him clean off his feet and starting him tumbling down the side of the massive pyramid.

---

anderen so wie auch von seinem Vater Simon erhaltene, nachgehend, aber meisten Theils selbst erfahrene un probirte, in diese nachfolgende Schrift verfaste und endlich an seinen jüngeren Sohn Lamech hinterllaßene Künste: so geschehen ud geschrieben circa Annum 1404. Wolfenbüttel Library, Codex Guelfibus 10.1."

By the time Booker recovered his senses, he was lying on a large limestone block, close to the bottom, surrounded by grey uniformed Cairo Tourism and Antiquities Police. As the USAF chief looked up towards the apex of the Great Pyramid, the strange shadow entity was nowhere to be seen. All that was visible were several armed police, searching for the source of the extraordinary sound everyone had heard just before a strange man tumbled down the pyramid. Booker looked back from the apex to the men surrounding him. He could see the police officers' lips moving, asking him questions, but he could only hear a high-pitched whistle.

Three thousand five hundred miles North West of where Booker was being led in handcuffs to a police-liveried Toyota classic Landcruiser 100[158], a long procession of black Mercedes SUV[159]s and BMW motorcycle[160] outriders surrounded a single black stretch, Mercedes Maybach[161] limousine. Vast crowds of cheering people lined both sides of The Mall in London as the procession of cars made its way through the capital.

Inside the ultra-luxurious leather interior of the armoured Maybach, Chairman Cortez was being briefed by Major General Smegget. Smegget read from a gold-plated iPad Pro, saying,

"Chairman, we have just received notification that a small aircraft has crashed into Fortress Grmožur, causing a massive

---

[158] 1999 model.
[159] Mercedes-Benz G-Class G 63 AMG 4MATIC.
[160] BMW R 1250 RT-P.
[161] Mercedes Maybach S600 Pullman guard limousine.

explosion. Initial reports indicate the stronghold may have been completely destroyed."

Cortez immediately responded, saying, "Survivors?"

"We do not know, Chairman. It is too early to tell, and we are completely reliant on local news for information."

"Not good enough!" snapped Cortez. "I want a Wolfsangel recovery team on site ASAP. And get rid of the locals. We do the search and rescue, understood?"

Smegget nodded as Cortez continued.

 "All survivors must be airlifted to our German clinic, understood?"

At that moment, the Chairman's mobile rang. Cortez nodded approval for the Major General to take the call. Smegget looked puzzled as he listened to the iPhone Pro.

"Yes, we will accept the charges."

The Major General looked towards Chairman Cortez.

"Sir, do you know a Chief Booker of the United States Airforce?"

Cortez nodded and gestured to be given the phone. After taking it, he snapped at the person on the other end of the line, saying, "I hope you did not disappoint me?" and then continued, "What do you mean problems? I thought you were one of the Meri-Isfet's leading lights? Col Jaree has been relieved of his duties? Good, so what is the problem?"

There was some further explanation on the other end of the line.

"Why are you in Cairo? I thought the supernatural problem was in Grindelwald?"

"You need a good lawyer?" Cortez gestured to Smegget for a pen and paper. The Argentinian spoke as he wrote on the Louis Vuitton jotting pad, "Yes, go ahead, Booker."

 "Cairo Antiquities Police Station,

El Khalifa, Cairo Governorate 4261235, Egypt."

"What's that? You want to speak to one of the senior authorities in the order? I may have some bad news there, Booker. You might be it!"

K.R.M. Morgan

THE MASK DROPS

"It must never be forgotten that nothing that is really great in this world has ever been achieved by coalitions, but that it has always been the success of a single victor." - Adolf Hitler

The Strand,
London WC2R 1LA

15.23HRS (GMT + 1), 14th Sept, Present day

The autumnal sun shone like a golden orb in the clear blue sky over the historic capital. This bright afternoon sunshine cast long shadows from the tall, five-storey buildings lining the famous central London thoroughfare. The broad pavements and even the central reservation, with its distinctive black cast iron street lights, were crammed with crowds eager to catch a glimpse of this afternoon's event.

The unseasonable warmth of an Indian summer prompted many to dress in light and colourful clothing, lending to a festival atmosphere. The entire length of The Strand was lined on both sides by vendors selling a wide range of takeaway meals and drinks. These stalls filled the air with an exotic mix of aromas from around the world, varying from designer coffees to candyfloss, curries, sauerkraut, bratwurst, pizzas and kebabs. A wide selection of the goods on sale had strong Nordic and German associations, especially the wines and beers. These beverages were served in distinctive paper cups that looked like lager steins and clear plastic wine glasses embossed with the now ever-present and popular Wolfsangel symbol.

Groups of small children lined the road, dressed in hurriedly constructed homemade approximations of the white FF uniforms worn by the goosestepping procession of weaponed FF soldiers, marching down the street in an

Easterly direction, clearing the way for the main procession that would follow. Their black leather calf-length boots, slamming into the ground in unison, filled the air with a resounding, frightening, and exciting cadence. The sound intimated extraordinary discipline and toughness, while the coordination provided a powerful visual impact from the sharp line of legs rising together in unison. The distinctive uniforms looked more sinister because the soldiers' faces were hidden beneath semi-mirrored iKill-Pro visors, and their arms were covered in various digital tools intended to augment their already deadly capabilities.

Noticeably, many of the crowd control officers from the Met[162] who lined the street had started to wear distinctive white armbands emblazoned with the Wolfsangel "FF" symbol to show their support for the new regime[163]. These white flashes on their left arm contrasted sharply with the more traditional dark blue uniforms.

All along The Strand, large high-definition LG screens were fixed to the buildings on either side of the road. These screens cycled through a series of images in a sequence. The most frequent pictures depicted a slightly younger Chairman Cortez wearing open-necked green military fatigues. His signature jewellery, the silver Wolfsangel slide symbol, was prominently displayed on the bolo tie[164] around his muscular neck. In these images, from his days leading the revolution in his Argentinian homeland, his long blond hair was tied in its standard ponytail and highlighted his piercing blue eyes. The Argentinian had his customary Cohiba cigar in his mouth and a classic stainless-steel Rolex submariner[165] visible from

---

[162] The Metropolitan police.

[163] Or they hoped to seek favour from the new bosses.

[164] Also called a shoestring necktie.

[165] A 1960s no date Rolex 5513 model diver's watch with a 26 jewel, calibre 1520 automatic movement. Seen in most classic action still

under his partially rolled-up left sleeve, in a pose that was reminiscent of Fidel Castro[166] and "Che" Guevara[167]. Under this picture ran the proclamation:

"A New Age of Freedom under our fearless leader, Chairman Cortez!".

These assertions were repeated on numerous static posters of all sizes plastered over the shop windows, that once displayed expensive designer goods, along the length of The Strand.

Other posters over doors showed FF forces in their distinctive white Hugo Boss uniforms helping the sick and old or repairing damage from the recent massive earth tremors and storms.

Interspersed with the propaganda images associating Cortez with famous revolutionaries of the twentieth century, the electronic displays along either side of The Strand ran a series of "Beyond Facts" adverts.

The first displayed information about the so-called "Cortez Care Camps". These showed happy families enjoying free meals from prominent fast-food providers in clean and modern cafeterias. In addition, images related to housing emphasised the free Wi-Fi and streaming television on offer. The same family who had enjoyed the free, fast food sat together, watching some sporting event while snacking. The Care Camp advertisement concluded by reminding the viewer that they would get a generous purchase and

----

pictures of "Heroes" of the 1960s. It has become the archetypal sports watch. In more modern times, the watch (and its numerous imitations) is favoured by the rich elites as a symbol of their financial status.

[166] Fidel Alejandro Castro Ruz – President of Cuba (1976 – 2008) .

[167] Ernesto "Che" Guevara – Argentine revolutionary in the Cuban Revolution.

compensation package for surrendering their property to take up residence at the thousands of camps under construction throughout Britannia and New Europa.

The second series of propaganda messages was related to the WB drug. These showed leading professional sports personalities and their glamourous partners living in luxurious settings and prominently consuming WB while attributing their success, recognition and lifestyle to the new wonder drug. The segment concluded with claims that a daily dose of WB would reduce stress while increasing performance. However, it was deliberately left unclear exactly what kind of performance was in question. To reinforce the WB promotion, a group of twenty attractive men and women with striking Nordic looks freely distributed supplies of WB to the people who lined the thoroughfare.

The final message in the never-ending repeated sequence on the giant electronic displays promoted the merits of getting a UNITY tattoo and registering for citizenship within New Europa. The video segment showed happy, smiling people and their children getting their unique tattoos and registering for all the lifelong benefits of "Cortez Care". Queues of applicants were shown in the United States, Canada and Australia getting tattooed so that they could come to New Europa to gain access to the promised free health care, housing, entertainment and meals. A section of legalise followed at such speed and in such small text that it was impossible to read. These unreadable conditions stated that applicants would be subject to genetic screening to determine the locations where they would be housed, the work they would be assigned, and the level of care they would receive.

Deliberately excluded from this live TV coverage of the support of the Cortez Revolution was a small group of around twenty people carrying banners that protested against the removal of democratic government, the unilateral seizing of assets and the forced relocation of the members of the Royal Houses of Europe to an undisclosed location. These twenty protesters were rapidly surrounded by white-suited FF officers, stunned with tasers, hogtied and roughly manhandled into one of many unmarked black Mercedes Sprinter vans patrolling up and down along the scheduled procession route. When a Metropolitan Police Officer intervened to question the grounds for this brutal treatment of the protesters, he was immediately tasered, hogtied with flexicuffs and bundled into the next passing Mercedes to share the unknown fate of the other protesters. If any of the Police officers working nearby noticed, they decided to ignore it.

Half a mile to the South West of the abduction of the prodemocracy protestors, at the end of the short drive down The Mall, Cortez's black Maybach Pullman Guard mounted the pavement on the southern edge of Trafalgar square through a gap in the protective bollards located around the pedestrian crossing on the A4 road. The security detail in the two black Range Rovers and four weaponed FF outriders on BMW motorbikes, with their iKill-Pro equipment integrated into their helmets, organised themselves strategically around the Maybach to provide cover and protection.

At all four corners of the historic square, the noise of pneumatic drills echoed off the surrounding buildings' Georgian facades. Thick dust clouds rose into the air as workers dismantled and removed the bronze statues of King George IV, General Sir Charles James Napier, and Major-General Sir Henry Havelock from their three plinths. Standing nearby were the statues that would replace them. The first

was Otto the Great, who founded the Holy Roman Empire[168] .
The second was Frederick the Great[169], who made Prussia the
foremost military power in Europe. The third was Bismarck,
who founded the 1871 German empire[170] and finally, the
famous empty pillar of Trafalgar square was to be occupied
by Alois Hiedler[171], founder of the Third Reich[172].

In addition, scaffolding surrounded Nelson's column, and a
Gottwald AK680 crane was removing the eighteen-foot-tall
statue of Lord Nelson[173]. A similarly sized figure of Chairman
Cortez, dressed in his revolutionary battle fatigues, as per his
publicity images being displayed on the large screens along
The Strand, stood near the bottom of the one hundred- and
sixty-nine-foot-tall column. Henceforth, the column would
become known as "Cortez's Column".

The area was now to be named "Freedom Square". Similar
monumental repurposing was underway throughout New
Europa, systematically reworking which individuals and
events would be celebrated, in a manner undertaken by
every new ideological revolution.

"History in the making, boys!" stated Cortez proudly,
gesturing to his grandsons Corrado and Hartman as the
three men stepped from the modern luxury and security of
the Maybach. The sound of Wagner's "Rienzi, der letzte der
Tribunen[174]" spilt out from inside the rear of the bespoke

---

[168] 10th century ruler of the first German Reich.

[169] Monarch of Prussia from 1740 - 1786

[170] The second German Reich which ran from January 1871 to
November 1918.

[171] He later changed his name to Adolf Hitler.

[172] January 1933 to May 1945.

[173] Vice-Admiral Horatio Nelson who led the victory at the Battle of
Trafalgar (21 October 1805) over the combined French and Spanish
navies at the cost of his life.

[174] Rienzi, the Last of the Tribunes.

leather interior of the limousine, along with the subtle scent of amber and florals that is so distinctive of Tom Ford's Soleil Brûlant cologne.

The two grandsons wore stylish black versions of the white FF uniforms that were now so frequently seen throughout New Europa. Over the past fifty-six hours, over seventy thousand FF troops and their equipment had been airlifted into bases in New Europa on a fleet of C-5M Super Galaxy[175] aircraft. This airlift continued alongside a systematic transformation of the existing European military forces to their new reality.

In contrast to his uniformed grandsons, Cortez wore a beautifully cut custom Brioni suit with a white Eton 80th Anniversary Dress Egyptian cotton shirt[176] and his signature bolo tie with its silver Wolfsangel symbol. He wore a pair of cashmere and silk socks on his feet inside gleaming black Stuart Weitzman leather dress shoes. Cortez continued to lecture his two grandchildren on the changes that were evident all around them.

"We have learnt from the mistakes of Napoleon and Urgroßvater[177], by starting our project for dominion over the world on this arrogant little island. Throughout history, we Europeans have sought to subjugate these pretentious British. Now they will learn what it is like to feel the yoke."

Cortez turned to Hartman, saying, "Make sure you assign the harshest tasks to these bastards to pay them back for their actions thwarting our last attempt at dominating Europe."

---

[175] The Lockheed Martin C-5M Super Galaxy has a payload of one hundred and thirty tons and can carry over three hundred and fifty soldiers.
[176] An Eton 80th Anniversary Dress Shirt.
[177] Great-Grandfather.

"Yes, Grandfather!" chuckled Hartman enthusiastically.

"I wish your father could have lived long enough to see this day!" said Cortez, wrapping his extended arms around the shoulders of his grandsons as the three men walked side by side towards a classic black open topped Großer Mercedes[178]. The ancient limousine's black bodywork gleamed in the autumn sun, as did the chrome on its two giant front headlamps, radiator grill and three-pointed bonnet decoration.

"Manufactured in the legendary Stuttgart works," Cortez stated as he ran his hand along the enormous bonnet before continuing, "Urgroßvater had this one fitted with steel armour plate in all the bodywork, two-inch-thick glass, nineteen-inch armoured wheels and bulletproof twenty-chamber tyres."

"It must weigh a ton!" chuckled Hartman.

Cortez smiled. "Over four tons actually, but the eight-litre supercharged engine can more than cope."

As Cortez opened the leftmost suicide door to enter, Major General Smegget hurried towards them, looking like a struggling penguin chased by a polar bear. The corpulent Smegget gasped for breath and waved his left arm to attract attention while holding his precious iPad in his right hand. The Major-General looked red in the face, and tiny beads of sweat had started to form on his brow.

"Chairman!" he gasped, "The Russians are making incursions into the Eastern borders of New Europa!"

---

[178] A Mercedes Benz 770, also known as the "Big Mercedes". This Series II - W150 (1943) was a gift to Hitler from Benito Mussolini of Italy, flown to Argentina in Feb 1944 in preparation for evacuation of the Fuhrer and his close associates

Cortez's face broke into a broad smile, making him look like the Cheshire cat. Given the man's usually icy demeanour, this was a disturbing look. He patted the shoulder of the hyperventilating Major-General.

"Calm yourself, Smegget. This is precisely what I would do. Revolutions are at their weakest when they begin, so it is the ideal time to attack. Now, what exactly is the nature of these incursions?"

No matter how cool and confident the Chairman sounded, Smegget could not feel calm. Even with the existing European NATO forces at its disposal, The New Republic had insufficient tanks and infantry to repel a full Russian invasion. Smegget stammered as he read from the briefing notes on his iPad.

"Tupolev supersonic bombers, escorted by MiGs."

"Tupolev Tu-160[179]s and MiG-31s?" enquired Cortez coolly as he stepped serenely into the eighty-year-old car and made himself comfortable on the well-worn, brown leather rear bench seat.

Smegget could not understand why the Chairman was responding with such calmness. Such an invasion had the potential to make The New Republic the shortest-lived revolution in European history. The Major-General again consulted his notes before responding, saying,

"Mostly, Chairman, but there are also reports of MiG-35s and Sukhoi Su-57[180]s escorting older Tu-95 bombers twenty

---

[179] Tupolev Tu-160 (Туполев Ту-160) Its Russian code name "White Swan". Its NATO reporting name is "Blackjack". It is a supersonic strategic nuclear bomber.
[180] The Su-57 (NATO reporting name Felon) is the first Russian multirole fighter to incorporate stealth technology and so called "supermanoeuvrability" (the aircraft can use intentional instability,

miles into New Europa's North Eastern airspace in Finland, Latvia and Estonia."

Cortez beamed with delight. "Excellent. The Russians have deployed their fastest and most powerful fighters and bombers[181]."

Smegget looked incredulous. "You are pleased?"

Cortez chuckled. "Indeed. As you will see, there is nothing like a real-world demonstration of our strength to inspire global respect."

"Chairman, shall I mobilise the air forces and armies of the respective nations?" enquired Smegget. Nervously, he wondered if he had enough time to get a flight to the United States before New Europa became a Neo-Soviet State.

"No, Major-General, you should invite the world's media to observe the Russian aggression." the Argentinian answered as he closed the massive steel car door after his two grandsons had joined him in the rear of the enormous Mercedes.

With that, the massive burble of the seventy-year-old eight-litre, straight-eight engine filled the air as the leviathan vehicle edged off the pavement and headed East towards The Strand. The enormous black limousine was rapidly surrounded by its supporting security escort of Range Rovers and motorcycle outriders, leaving Smegget scurrying to the

---

vector engines and fly by wire control to exceed the design limits of pure aerodynamic manoeuvrability).

[181] The Tu-160 is the fastest publicly acknowledged bomber in existence and is the largest publicly acknowledged variable-sweep wing airplane. The Mikoyan MiG-31 is one of the world's fastest fighter jets (2300 mph) and one of the few that can fire the latest Vympel R-37 (NATO reporting name Axehead) long range (250 miles) hypersonic (4800 mph) smart air to air missile.

small black Ford Focus he was assigned for the day's celebrations.

Three hundred yards to the South East of Smegget's old Ford Focus and one hundred and sixty-five feet beneath the grey Portland limestone Ministry of Defence building in Whitehall, conditions continued to deteriorate. Once the massive twin blast doors had closed, the guards gradually reduced airflow into the bunker[182]. Consequently, the carbon dioxide level increased, and the oxygen percentage dropped radically.

As if that was not bad enough, the temperature inside Pindar had also steadily risen, until now it stood at over ninety-five degrees Fahrenheit with one hundred percent humidity. The male VIPs had adjusted to this change by removing their dinner jackets, untying their ties and opening their shirts. Unfortunately, the females who had worn full evening gowns were less fortunate in their options to address the shifting climate. By mid-afternoon, most of the VIPs were not only wearing their underwear, but they had also started to contribute to a robust body odour smell that combined with the aromas unpleasantly emanating from the uncleaned toilets. Sadly, either through practice or principle, none of these highly privileged individuals attempted to conduct any form of cleaning of their cramped facilities in the underground bunker.

In response to these deteriorating conditions, Reginald Twiffers, Johnathan Premble and Jeremy Kenner had joined forces to try and use their extensive expertise in underhanded dealing to try and bribe the guard. In a rare

---

[182] As oxygen levels reduce so does activity and mental acuity. Ideal for keeping prisoners compliant.

moment of generosity, instigated by cerebral hypoxia destabilising their judgement, they worked together to get sufficient supplies for the entire group of former VIPs that Cortez had incarcerated in Pindar.

The trio of senior Cabinet Ministers assumed an uncharacteristically self-effacing behaviour towards the massive man who stood on guard inside the two blue metal blast doors. The guard's face was obscured behind a 3M full-face mask[183] connected to an oxygen bottle on his back. He was dressed in a black Kevlar-protected jumpsuit and readied a sinister-looking, fourteen-inch-long Xtreme Mega Legion stun baton[184] as the three senior ministers approached him. Obviously, the man anticipated that the three men might be thinking of rushing him as he caused the Mega Legion baton in his hands to emit a test charge that made a loud sizzling sound and filled the air with a strong smell of ozone.

"Get back!" he snarled in a thick East End[185] accent.

Twiffers raised his hands in a show of innocence and, reading the laminated white plastic name badge on the guard's jacket, addressed him in an uncharacteristically friendly manner, saying, "Mr Smith, or can I call you Jeff?"

Jeff grunted but still looked at the three dishevelled men, dressed in their grubby vests and boxers, with extreme suspicion.

"We have been watching how hard you work to protect us." Twiffers gestured to his two colleagues standing supportively on either side of him.

---

[183] A 3M™ Scott™ AV-3000 HT Face mask.
[184] A 125,000,000 Volt, Tiger-USA Xtreme Mega Legion 13.75" LED Stun Gun Baton 98M.
[185] The accent from the East End of London.

Jeff was considering if these three muppets[186] were being sarcastic[187] when Twiffers tried his first strategy, which worked so well on most of the Plebs[188] he needed to manipulate in some way.

Twiffers assumed a conspiratorial tone. "Men like yourself deserve some special mark of recognition. One that would raise you above the others."

"Like what, exactly?" queried Jeff, who was now more positively inclined to listen to whatever idea these three idiots had in mind.

Twiffers smiled in a manner familiar to second-hand car dealers who think they have a punter[189] who will buy the most highly overpriced and unreliable car in his stock. "Jeff, it is within our power to add your name to the New Years' honours list."

Twiffers looked closely into Jeff's face to see if he was getting the massive pupil dilation and rapid breathing exhibited by most individuals when offered the chance to add three meaningless[190] letters after their names on their junk mail and council tax bills. Shockingly, at least to Twiffers, Jeff showed none of the excitement generally associated with this gambit. The Prime Minster decided he needed to up the ante.

"Or, maybe even, **Sir** Smith. How does that sound? Have your pictures in the papers at The Palace[191] and everything."

Jeff looked amused. "You haven't heard then?"

---

[186] Idiots.

[187] Taking the piss, is how Jeff would have phrased it.

[188] More usually termed "gullible wide eyed loons" by politicians.

[189] Customer.

[190] To become a member of an empire that no longer exists.

[191] Buckingham Palace.

Twiffers raised his eyebrows.

"Heard what?" Twiffers, Premble and Kenner leaned in closer to hear what could have changed in what was one of the most lucrative[192] incentives they had to control and motivate the vainest members of society.

Jeff Smith paused, relishing the moment of revelation that would put these spoilt prigs into their place.

Then he announced, "The Chairman abolished the Monarchy and all its class-based snobbery this morning."

"What?! Cortez does not have the authority to do that. He is only the Chairman of the party, after all."

Smith chuckled. "He is a bloody sight more than that now, matey. He is the supreme leader of New Europa. He had the entire Royal Family, and the House of Lords rounded up this morning."

The colour had drained from the faces of the three senior ministers. Things were clearly worse than they had imagined. The blow from the announcement was worst for Kenner, who had been living off the prestige of his title since he inherited on the death of his father.   The Home Secretary sank to his knees, and tears ran down his face. Twiffers and Premble were made of sterner stuff, having fought their way up through the political landscape of rat-eat-rat.

Twiffers switched to his fallback plan. "Titles, well, they are just ego trips, aren't they?"

---

[192] There is, invariably, some financial or material "thank you" from the candidates for honours. Middle Eastern despots are especially generous. Often using unmarked notes delivered in Fortnum and Mason bags, allegedly.

He nudged Premble, who agreed, although his eyes lacked enthusiasm as he thought of the unsavoury things he had done to get his own Knighthood.

Twiffers continued. "But hard cash is always welcome,"

the Prime Minister paused to add a dramatic effect to his next statement.

"We do have access to considerable sums of money."

"Oh yeah, how much did you have?" asked Jeff.

Twiffers missed the significance of the burly guard's use of the past tense and continued his attempt to buy the cooperation of this arrogant upstart.

"Yes, we," Twiffers gestured to the distracted Premble standing beside him and down towards the floor, where Home Secretary, Jeremy Kenner continued to cry, "Made quite a killing with the COVID pandemic. Using emergency powers, we instilled mass panic and added a trillion to the national debt[193]."

Twiffers smiled, like a rat who has spotted a hunk of rotten meat down a sewer. "And most of that trillion went unaccounted for..."

The Prime Minister winked conspiratorially at Jeff.

"Nice gig," commented the burly guard, "But not much good now, is it?!"

"What do you mean?" stammered Twiffers, beginning to sense another bit of bad news coming.

Now, it was Jeff's turn to smile like a sewer rat.

---

[193] Politicians all think that emergency powers are wonderful – no tendering, no audits, no controls and certainly no transparency.

"There was a systemic meltdown of the financial markets overnight.   Chairman Cortez was forced to write off Europe's financial systems and replace them with his own new Crypto currency."

"No more cash?" asked the incredulous Twiffers, who was struggling to remember how much of his illegal stash from bribes and corrupt deals[194] were held in US dollars in the Cayman Islands and Panama.

In contrast, Premble looked like someone who had accidentally dropped his only set of Aston Martin keys down a fast-flowing drain.

The guard rolled his sleeve to show the UNITY tattoo on his left forearm.

"Now all we need are these tattoos. One scan, and we get whatever we need, within the limits set by the Chairman, of course."

This time it was Twiffers who turned ashen with shock.

"You mean it's all gone?"

Premble wiped his hand over his eyes, mopping away a tear. Twiffers was silent. But Jeff, the doorman, was not quite finished.

"I tell you what I could do. Those are nice Kettle and Hobs[195] the three of you are wearing. I could trade them for the contents of yesterday's cafeteria bins."

The big man gestured towards the Prime Minister, Foreign Secretary and Home Secretary's wrists.

---

[194] Organised criminal gangs are the most rewarding partners.
[195] Slang for a watch. Taken from the days when people wore pocket watches on a fob or chain. Fob = Kettle and Hob.

Reluctantly the three men exchanged dejected looks, realising that this would be the only way any of them would eat. One by one, they handed over their beloved 18kt gold Rolex day-date, 18kt gold Patek Phillipe Nautilus and a platinum[196] JLC[197] Reverso[198], respectively.

Jeff took the valuable timepieces in his fat hands before placing them in his uniform's trouser pockets.

"As they say, that will do nicely."

Twiffers, Premble and Kenner waited expectantly. After an awkward silence, Twiffers queried,

"Any idea when you will be able to bring the food, Jeff?"

Jeff could not help smiling as he gestured with the buzzing stun baton for the three men to back away and rejoin the other hungry and exhausted VIPs huddled in groups on the floors along the long corridor.

"See how I feel later."

While Jeff, the burly guard, was starting his classic watch collection, Clive Basildon, Director General of MI5, was making the most of his rare experience of sobriety by systematically testing each door in the rear of the underground complex in the hope of finding help. Unlike Cynthia Sinclair, Basildon had little field experience[199] so,

---

[196] Platinum looks like steel but that is half the fun for inverted snobs.
[197] Jaeger-LeCoultre.
[198] Reverso Tribute Gyrotourbillon.
[199] The policy of only promoting people with the "right" backgrounds means that British institutions are top heavy with Eton

rather than slumping down on the floor in the corridor like everyone else; he had asked himself what would Sinclair be doing in this situation. The answer, he had decided, was to explore what facilities were available that might prove of assistance in getting someone to release them from their confinement in Pindar[200].

Eventually, Basildon found a grey metal door with the words "Radio Room" stencilled in white paint. The grey colour of the steel entrance contrasted with the blue theme adopted within the rest of Pindar. Unlike the other doors, this one swung open, and after turning on the light switch, Basildon found himself inside a small, twelve-foot square room with the walls and ceilings covered in soundproofing wave-shaped black foam. Along one side of the room was a grey metal desk with outdated broadcasting equipment and a swivel chair that made the room feel and look like a nineteen-sixties radio station[201].

Sitting in the chair, Basildon powered up the old black plastic PYE[202] communications console. As the old equipment warmed up, the confined space of the small room began to fill with a strong smell from the decades of dust burning off from the hot thermionic valves that formed the basis of electronics before the rise of silicon.

---

and Oxbridge graduates with no real world experience but who are highly skilled in social networking and enriching their own lifestyles.

[200] The UK Government's Top Secret Crisis-Command Bunker.

[201] The infrastructure investment in Pindar has focused on luxuries for the "Metro Elites" and not its original core purpose, hence the museum like facilities.

[202] Founded by W.G. Pye in 1896 in Cambridge, the company supplied the UK government with communications equipment until 1996, when the Government sold them to the Dutch company Philips.

Basildon unplugged the heavily worn Koss[203] headphones, so the output went to two black Bakelite speakers and began talking into the old-fashioned PYE branded microphone. He began working through the call signs on a pinboard hanging on the wall beside the radio set for each of the remaining British Overseas Territories[204]. The two PYE speakers crackled and hummed as Basildon called out for the radio operators that once populated these airwaves before the advent of the internet.

"This is London. Any BOT[205] officers, please respond! We are in urgent need of assistance."

Anguilla (AI), Bermuda (BM), British Virgin Islands (VG), Cayman Islands (KY), Gibraltar (GI), Montserrat (MS), Pitcairn (PN), St Helena (SH), South Georgia (GS), and the Turks and Caicos Islands (TC) either ignored their radio call sign wholly or came on very briefly and expressed their delight at the fall of Britain.

The British Antarctic Territory (BAT) did respond, but the operator became belligerent when Basildon demanded they take some action to help the UK, saying, "What do you expect us to do? Send a brigade of fucking penguins?" and then abruptly went off the air.

Three very sorry-looking senior cabinet ministers entered the room during this final exchange. They slumped down to the floor behind Basildon with their backs sinking deeply into the black foam soundproofing. Twiffers, Premble and Kenner looked like broken men but perked up as suddenly, the crackle of the radio sparked up in response to Baslidon's generalised distress broadcast,

---

[203] KOSS PRO/4X PLUS Dynamic Headphones.
[204] Also known by some elites as "The Colonies".
[205] British Overseas Territories.

A highly distorted female voice came on the air. "FK Here."

"FK, where the fuck is that?" queried Premble.

Basildon pointed to the call sign chart on the wall before him. Near the bottom of the list was FK – the Falkland Islands.

"The Falkland Islands? I thought sheep just populated that." commented Kenner.

"And land mines." sniggered Premble.

Twiffers shushed the two giggling men as he rose and wheeled Basildon's chair sideways so he could control the microphone,

"Listen here! This is the Prime Minister! I must speak with the Ambassador immediately!"

A distorted female voice responded, "The Governor of the Falkland Islands and Her Majesty's Commissioner for South Georgia and the South Sandwich Islands is unavailable."

"Where is he?" Twiffers demanded officiously, resuming his normal arrogant behaviour now that he could boss someone around.

"She and her diplomatic team are drinking at The Rose in Drury Street," the voice answered through considerable static.

"What?" demanded the increasingly enraged Prime Minister.

The voice on the other end of the airwaves remained calm. Still, what she was saying remained highly distorted. "Ms Angela Swindon, CMG[206], has joined with the Argentinian army commander for a celebratory drink."

---

[206] The Distinguished Order of Saint Michael and Saint George. A diplomatic gong (award), for services rendered.

"Argentinian commander? Are the Argies visiting or something?" asked Twiffers.

There was a pause and what sounded like a sigh. Then the calm female voice continued. "No, Sir. The Argentinians were granted control of the islands by Chairman Cortez this morning as part of his reforms."

"Treason!" exclaimed Premble.

Evidently the Falklands operator overheard, as she corrected the Foreign Secretary, "No, it was a formal handover. The Union Flag was taken down and handed to the Argentinian commander along with the standard[207] of the island's defence forces[208]."

"But your unit remains loyal to the British Government?" asked Twiffers, clearly hoping that the person speaking to him commanded considerable forces who could launch a counter-offensive to retake the Falklands and, hopefully the British mainland.

There was a long pause then the female voice answered, saying, "Sorry to disappoint you. It's just me and my computer."

Twiffers still hoped for the best. "But it's a networked supercomputer, and you are an expert, am I correct?"

There was the sound of laughter. "Sir, I am just a C4[209] in the FCO. Before being demoted and transferred from GCHQ, I was a C1[210]."

---

[207] Flag.

[208] 1,200 infantry, engineers, signals unit and support staff.

[209] Higher Executive Officer (HEO) grade in the FCO Civil Service.

[210] Senior Executive Officer (SEO) grade in the MOD Civil Service.

Twiffers looked alarmed, but things were about to worsen as the woman continued. "My computer is a three-year-old Acer Aspire connected to SURE Falkland[211],"

There was the sound of typing. "which is currently running at.. " there was a pause and the sound of a mouse click, "seventy-six kilobytes per second, hence the poor quality of my transmission."

Twiffers realised that his hopes of salvation were lost, but he tried to remain professional.

"Thank you, my dear. I am sure you will do your best. By the way, what is your name? So, we can note your loyalty to Great Britain."

There was another pause before the voice responded, saying, "My name is Christine Twop. We met in Downing Street earlier this week when I warned you about..."

For the second time that afternoon, the colour completely drained from the Prime Minister's face, but decades of political life made him instinctively interrupt and divert blame, declaring, in a well-practised condescending tone,

"Best not to dwell on YOUR past failures, my dear, let's see what you can do now. We expect great things!"

Twiffers then reached over and turned off the radio, leaving Christine Twop alone in a small, dingy hostel bedroom in Port Stanley, wondering what she could do against the ruthlessly coordinated plans of Chairman Cortez.

---

[211] The internet provider for the islands.

K.R.M. Morgan

THE PRESIDENT'S DAILY BRIEF (PDB)

"The difference between a republic and an empire is the loyalty of one's army." - Julius Caesar

Fort Liberty (formerly Fort Bragg[212])
Cumberland, North Carolina
USA

10:32 HRS (GMT-4), 14th September, Present day

President (POTUS[213]) Wilson F. Jones, who preferred to be called just by his first name, looked tired. Dark rings were in evidence under his eyes, and, in contrast to his usual healthy glow, the former Governor of Massachusetts looked his full sixty-five years. A lack of sleep and the stress of the past twenty-four hours had taken their toll on a man who usually prided himself on his tanned, athletic looks.

He was wearing a well-worn grey marl cotton sweatshirt with a crimson shield in its centre with the word Veritas[214] at the top and then underneath the phrase, Lex et Iustitia[215]. Beneath the Latin phrase were eight overlapping curves inspired by the architecture of Austin and Hauser halls[216]. These halls formed Wilson's alma mater[217], where he had studied and later served as the Laurence H. Tribe Professor of Constitutional Law. After some years of lecturing about the

---

[212] Renamed on January 1st 2021, after the United States Senate renamed all US bases that had been named after Confederate army leaders.

[213] President of the United States of America and Commander in Chief.

[214] Truth.

[215] Law and Justice.

[216] HLS - Harvard Law School. The oldest law school in the United States, founded in 1817.

[217] The educational institution where someone studied.

malpractice so in evidence in American Society, he had felt morally compelled to give up his comfortable tenured position to, as his campaign had proclaimed: "Do something about it!"

In the intervening years since his election, first as Governor of Massachusetts and then the Presidency, Wilson had reduced bloated bureaucracy in government and simplified legislation. His policies on anti-corruption, insider dealing, reducing the national debt and tax had made him loved by most of the electorate. But these same policies made him reviled by the leaders of the military-industrial complex for reducing their control over the federal budget. Coming to the final year of his second term, with approval ratings running at over seventy per cent, he was resisting calls from Republicans and Democrats in the House of Representatives and the Senate for an unprecedented change to the Twenty-second Amendment[218]. His balanced response when dealing with the Red Death virus and Dr Nissa Ad-Dajjal's attempt at global domination had only boosted his popularity.

To match the informal nature of his sweatshirt, Wilson wore unbranded grey cotton marl jog bottoms and a pair of white leather Hersey walking sneakers[219]. Checking the time on his cream-dialled Shinola watch[220], Wilson strode the final few yards towards a two-storey wood-framed building. Following close beside and all around him were six, US Marines in pixelated urban camouflage BDU, with full body armour and Kevlar helmets, their M27[221] rifles covering the area

---

[218] Congress passed the amendment on March 1947 limiting any one individual to two terms in office.

[219] Hersey Custom Shoe Company walking sneakers. Made in Massachusetts.

[220] Shinola Runwell Chrono. Made in Detroit.

[221] The M27 Infantry Automatic Rifle (IAR) is a modified (Heckler & Koch) HK416 5.56mm select-fire assault rifle.

surrounding the POTUS. They had followed a similar formation escorting Wilson from the basic accommodation, where the President's wife and family had spent the night while massive storms, earth tremors, and tidal waves had battered the Nation. It was noticeable that one of the Marines was not holding her M27, instead she carried an innocent looking aluminium attaché case[222] that was handcuffed to her wrist.

Even now, ten hours after the strange phenomena had subsided, no one was entirely sure what had caused such massive damage to the infrastructure of Wilson's beloved country. Coastal areas, including Martha's Vineyard, where Wilson had been staying, had suffered considerable damage from unprecedented storm surges. The threat had been so significant that Wilson's security team had insisted that Marine One airlift him[223] to a safe location far away from coasts and geophysical fault lines[224].

The solar mass ejection that accompanied the phenomena had knocked out satellites and much of the technical infrastructure, but that was nothing compared to the ideological carnage that had simultaneously taken place. During the height of the natural destruction, highly organised groups stormed the government centres in Washington DC, taking over the buildings used by the House of Representatives, Senate, Treasury, FBI and The White

---

[222] This is a metal Zero Halliburton briefcase which carries the "nuclear football" that can launch America's nuclear weapons.

[223] This is "the call sign" of any United States Marine Corps aircraft carrying the president of the United States. It usually denotes a helicopter operated by Marine Helicopter Squadron One (HMX-1) "Nighthawks". Typically, a Sikorsky VH-3D Sea King. For security reasons flights containing the POTUS have three identical aircraft flying simultaneously to act as decoys.

[224] Cumberland County, NC has a very low earthquake risk. None having been recorded since 1931.

House. An angry mob had ransacked all these historic landmarks, the guards on duty mysteriously failing to defend the places that represented the constitution most had sworn to protect. In a series of globally televised events, the Stars and Stripes had been taken down and burnt outside of all the significant public buildings in the Nation's capital and replaced by the Wolfsangel flag. Most of the domestic broadcast networks had been seized by these populists and were now under their control. These stations were broadcasting nonstop, encouraging viewers and listeners to join what was being termed The New Republic.

Wilson suspected there was a coordinated plan guiding these supposedly spontaneous uprisings. Nothing could be proved, but a sinister intelligence was apparent to him in the systematic abduction of the five key figures in the US Government: the Vice President, Speaker of the House of Representatives, President pro tempore of the Senate, Secretary of State and the Secretary of the Treasury from their homes, offices and cars. Again, mysteriously and conveniently for the rebels, the secret service details had failed to stop these abductions.

To Wilson's highly analytical mind, the timing of these uprisings to coincide with the natural disasters was too convenient to be a mere coincidence. But he had been repeatedly reassured by Elaine Madden, his National Director of Intelligence[225] (NDI), that there was no evidence of any coordination between the various events. These reassurances had occurred six hours earlier, during a four AM phone call prompted by the breaking news about the riots, when Madden had forcefully insisted that the President resist his

---

[225] Established by the Intelligence Reform and Terrorism Prevention Act of 2004. The DNI has the power to control funding between different Intelligence Agencies. This gives the director of the DNI great influence over the Intelligence Community.

impulse to use the DC National Guard[226] to restore control over these critical institutions.   Reflecting on this badly flawed advice, Wilson recalled that his CIA Director, Mark Pimms, had frequently expressed severe doubts about Madden.

The President had initially attributed Pimms' remarks to professional jealousy, but now he was unsure. The decision not to use the DC National Guard had proved to be a serious error, as shortly after the mob had taken the buildings, Major General Arnold, in operational command of the DC National Guard troops, had declared allegiance to the uprising.

The whole situation left Wilson acutely aware that he was now the sole remaining member of the United States elected government in office and, therefore, exceptionally vulnerable. As if the uprisings and abductions were not bad enough, an increasing number of senior officers in the Military were following the example of the DC National Guard and declaring their unit's support for The New Republic. In addition, a growing number of State Governors publicly announced that they had joined the revolution. So far, these rogue states included Maine, Vermont, California, New York, Rhode Island, New Hampshire, Maryland, Oregon, California and, most painfully for Wilson, his home state of Massachusetts.

The President would learn more at the coming briefing, but while eating breakfast, he had seen the news coverage of running street battles in Las Vegas, Phoenix, and El Paso between supporters of the uprising and those who still respected the existing regime. All in all, this morning the POTUS was faced with the greatest threat to the Union since

---

[226] District of Columbia National Guard has just under 1400 troops.

1860[227].   Wilson hoped that this time diplomacy would prevail, but deep inside, he had doubts.

The six highly trained men who ensured that Wilson avoided the fate of the vice president and other legislature members were all from the Marine Raider Regiment[228] (MRR) based at Camp Lejeune, North Carolina[229]. Wilson had dispensed with his Secret Service detail after their recent betrayal[230]. He insisted on being protected by the man who freed him from captivity in the Cheyenne Mountain Complex[231], USMC Master Sergeant Jackson. By Presidential order, the modest and quietly spoken Jackson had been seconded from Camp Pendleton[232], promoted to the rank of Captain, and put in charge of protecting the POTUS.

As all these considerations ran through his mind, Wilson made a deliberate effort to appreciate the beauty of his surroundings and the fresh air before starting what promised to be one of the most important meetings of his career- one that could determine the future of the United States. He inhaled the beautiful lemon-scented aroma from an immaculately maintained grove of Southern Magnolia trees. The massive trees with their distinctive white flowers lined

---

[227] When the southern states seceded from the Union and prompted the American Civil War.

[228] An elite group of the Marine Corps tasked with Direct Action, Counterinsurgency & Special Reconnaissance. This unit had originally been designated as Tier One (elite spec op status) but alleged petty jealousy from the Army and Navy spec ops communities had forced the unit to lose this status.

[229] Home of the United States Marine Forces Special Operations Command (MARSOC).

[230] See The Bridge of Souls for more information on this diabolical plot.

[231] A defensive bunker operated by Space Force.

[232] Home to the 1st Battalion 1st Marines, which was Jackson's original unit.

either side of the gravel path leading up to a two-storey townhouse built in a style that was so popular in the late twentieth century.

At the bottom of the steps, he was greeted by Jessica Holmes, his grey-haired Personal Assistant, who had worked with him for the past twenty years of his political career. The depth of the crisis could be seen in her eyes as she held out her boss's briefing notes and his steel Parker pen, both attached to a plain wooden clipboard. Wilson took the clipboard and a large white insulated mug of Dunkin' Donuts coffee.

"Thank you, Jessica. Anything special I should know before I go in?" queried the President.

"Only that you need to keep an eye on those two women. Mark my words. They are plotting something. And whatever they are planning is not in your interests!" replied his trusted assistant.

Six thousand five hundred miles to the West of where Wilson appreciated the scent of the Magnolias, three elderly uniformed men, the operational heads of the three branches of the Russian Military, were sitting around an old-fashioned, black plastic Shadrinsk[233] branded Kazbek[234] communication system. The speaker rested on an old wooden table, covered in coffee stains and cigarette burn marks, in the centre of a gloomy grey concrete room around twenty-five feet square. The walls were undecorated, apart from a row of

---

[233] One of the major suppliers of field communication systems for the Soviet military.
[234] The Russian Nuclear Strike communication system.

six, Petrodvorets[235] branded mechanical clocks, only four of which were working, and only one was even close to accurate. Their ticking mechanical mechanisms were almost entirely drowned out by the regular thump from a single large, slowly rotating extractor fan located in the centre of the ten-foot-high ceiling. Two ancient fluorescent light bulbs thickly caked with dust, smoke and dead flies cast a rather gloomy light over the heavily stained table top. The inefficiency of the air extraction was attested to by the thick, sweet cigarette smoke that permeated the small room's atmosphere. The poor air circulation was partly due to the three hundred feet of reinforced concrete and soil above the communications room within the top-secret Amur Oblast[236] command and control centre for the Russian Nuclear deterrent.

Any doubts about the location of this underground bunker were dispelled by the distinctively tall peaked caps that are ubiquitous in former communist states. These particular caps were thick with the golden braid[237], that covered the shoulders, arms and lapels of the three men. Apart from their age, thick eyebrows and worried expressions, the three men were also united by wearing similarly styled uniforms[238], even if they were of different colours, notably black, green, and blue, denoting their respective services[239]. Although the original uniform design was stylish, by the time it reached production at North Korean labour camps[240], the numerous

---

[235] The Petrodvorets Watch Factory was a Soviet era clock manufacturer who supplied the military and space programs.
[236] 20 miles north of Belogorsk in the Russian Far East (in case you are a US submarine commander).
[237] Known as "scrambled egg" by those familiar with military service.
[238] Designed by Valentin Yudashkin.
[239] The Russian Navy, Russian Army, and the Russian Aerospace Forces, respectively.
[240] In violation of UN embargos.

cost-cutting exercises that had taken place meant that the nylon cotton mix material was rough, uncomfortable and unflattering in the extreme. Although the gold braid and medals worn by all three men distracted the eye enough that it was not immediately apparent. The three men consulted their cheap chrome-plated Sturmanskie, and Vostok watches as they prepared for their presidential briefing. Although, unlike Wilson's coming briefing, this communication would be entirely one-way and less of an exchange of ideas and more of a parade ground communication, loud, brief and with the expectation of immediate and unquestioning obedience.

As the appointed time came closer, the three men took different approaches to calm their nerves. One took a deep drag from a Golden Yava Classic and placed the partially finished cigarette into a tin foil ashtray full of spent butt ends. The other two men drank. One consumed a fortified RAF coffee[241] in a stained metal mug. The final man skipped the caffeine and instead downed a shot or three from another metal mug filled with an almost empty bottle of Belenkaya[242] that stood beside the foil ashtray. Notably, the vodka drinker did not refit the screw cap. Instead, he deliberately left it beside the bottle, presumably in case any of the three men became *thirsty* during the coming briefing.

Once the designated time arrived for the phone briefing, a shrill bell sounded, and three women officers, one for each Russian Federation military branch, entered the room with clipboards and pencils, each woman ready to note down the required actions for their particular service.

---

[241] Espresso with cream and vanilla sugar.
[242] Belenkaya Gold Vodka.

Three thousand three hundred miles to the West of the Russian Federation's most highly classified nuclear Command and Control centre, Demetri Zychopav, the Supreme Commander-in-Chief of the Armed Forces of the Russian Federation sat at the very far end of an extremely long table opposite the heads of the nation's Military: The Marshal of the Russian Federation (head of the Army), the Admiral of the Fleet (head of the Navy) and the Lieutenant General (head of the Air Force), respectively.

The room where this meeting was taking place could not have been in greater contrast to the dark and utilitarian setting of the communications room where the operational heads of the three branches of the Military waited to receive their daily instructions. The surroundings in Moscow looked like a royal residence, with gold leaf wall decorations, classical paintings, high ceilings and crystal chandeliers. The comparison with a royal palace is not far from the truth since the interior design of the Grand Kremlin Palace was closely modelled on Versailles[243].

The balding, former head of the FSB[244], Demetri Zychopav, who sat alone at the far end of the long table, was only five feet six inches tall[245] and weighed just one hundred and fifty-two pounds. But, like many people of small stature, he had a strong need to control everything in his world ruthlessly. Maybe this insecurity and overcompensation partially explained his need for over two thousand five hundred bodyguards[246]. Ten members of President Zychopav's

---

[243] Versailles is a former royal residence built by King Louis XIV near Paris.
[244] Previously known as the KGB. The Federal Security Service of the Russian Federation (FSB) is the infamous secret intelligence service.
[245] Maybe a little as five foot two inches, according to reports that mention four-inch lifts in his shoes.
[246] The Presidential Security Service.

protection detail lined the interior of the large meeting room. Each of the black-suited operatives carried a wicked-looking matte black machine pistol[247] and could be seen closely monitoring the three senior military leaders sitting opposite the President in case they launched any attack on their leader.

The former spymaster and undisputed ruler of the largest land mass on earth pulled up the sleeve of his immaculately tailored Dormeuil Vanquish II suit[248]. As the sleeve retracted, it revealed the white cotton cuff of a Gucci[249] shirt and exposed the time on the silver dial of an elegant platinum A. Lange & Söhne watch[250]. The dark blue colour of the Royal Qiviut[251] silk of the suit matched perfectly with his Louis Vuitton[252] dress shoes. President Zychopav's expensive taste in clothes[253] made a powerful statement of superiority when contrasted with the rough nylon fabric that made up the uniforms of his three most senior military officers sitting at the other end of the long table.

Although on paper, the three men sitting opposite the former intelligence chief were responsible for the three branches of the Russian Federation's Military, the President issued his speaker phone instructions exclusively to the three operational officers in the nuclear command and control

---

[247] The PP-91 KEDR machine pistol has a 30 round magazine and uses the 9×18mm Makarov round.

[248] One of the world's most expensive and exclusive bespoke suits. Known to be favoured by those who have an ostentatious need to show their wealth.

[249] Gucci Oxford GG shirt

[250] A. Lange & Söhne 1815 Up/Down. This model has a 36mm case, black alligator strap, an L051.2 calibre, argenté (Pure silver) dial and hands made of flame blued steel.

[251] The softest musk ox down, blended with lustrous silk.

[252] Louis Vuitton Manhattan Richelieu shoes.

[253] Tailored personally by Jules Dormeiuli.

bunker some three thousand miles away. This communication completely ignored the standard lines of command and starkly exposed that the sole purpose of the three most senior military officers sitting opposite was to act as scapegoats should the President's plans fail.

His commands were short and direct.

"Since no military opposition has countered our exploration of European airspace, our aircraft are to proceed deeper and commence bombing the military airbases in the nine nations[254] we originally liberated during the Great Patriotic War[255]. Our fighter jets will engage and destroy any and all resistance. Our goal is to achieve air superiority as rapidly as possible."

The three senior military officers sitting opposite the President shifted uncomfortably, but none dared to object[256]. The small man's speech became louder and more excited as he imagined his name immortalised alongside Stalin and Tsar Peter[257]as a bold visionary leader who restored Russia to its rightful position of global dominance.

The President continued his instructions, saying, "Simultaneously with our air offensive, the sixty-two armoured ground divisions posted along the European borders will immediately advance to seize as much territory as possible before any European reaction."

---

[254] Germany, Czechoslovakia, Hungary, Romania, Bulgaria, Albania, the Baltic states of Estonia, Latvia and Lithuania.
[255] The Second World War.
[256] The labour camps in Siberia are well known.
257 Peter the Great. Founder of the Russian Empire. (1682 to 1725).

"Finally, in anticipation of the response to our glorious action from the Pindos[258], raise our combat readiness[259] to FULL[260] and fuel up the Sarmat[261] and Avangard[262] weapons for immediate nuclear deployment[263]!"

Zychopav gloated to himself, clearly anticipating a quick and easy victory given the disorganisation caused by the recent natural disasters and transition to a new form of government in Europe. The former intelligence chief abruptly rose from his chair and, without saying a word, walked, with a slight limp, towards the ornate gold and white exit. The double doors opened for him and were held by the security detail waiting outside. He strode quickly through the seemingly endless corridors, eagerly making his way to his regular "rejuvenation therapy" session.

The former KGB head had always projected a robust masculine image to remain in power, but advancing age had started challenging his ego's need for strength. Over the past

---

258 A derogatory term for Americans.

259 The "combat readiness" scale is the Russian equivalent of the five DEFCON alert levels used by the United States.

260 Full is the equivalent of DEFCON 1. The four levels of the Russian war preparedness states are 1. CONSTANT, 2. ELEVATED 3. MILITARY DANGER and 4. FULL.

261 The Sarmat is called the 'Satan II' by Nato. This is a hypersonic (Mach 20, 15,000 mph) liquid-fuelled, multi warhead, thermonuclear intercontinental ballistic missile with a range of 11,000 miles. It is fitted with electronic and physical (flares and flak) countermeasures to make it "unstoppable".

262 The Avangard HGV – (Hypersonic glide vehicle) – is launched as one of a number of warheads from a single intercontinental missile (such as the Sarmat/Satan II). It exits the atmosphere and then glides at Mach 27 (20,000 mph) to its target with enhanced manoeuvrability.

263 The 15 warheads in the Sarmat/Satan II separate in flight. Each warhead produces an 800-megaton explosion, more than sufficient to destroy major targets.

five years, he had embraced any technique that promised to delay his body's natural physical decline. Testosterone and Anabolic steroids[264] had given him the illusion of slowing the inevitable loss of physical strength and muscle tone. But, as the years went by, he found the results from these substances less and less effective. So, he stopped following the guidance usually taken by athletes using such performance-enhancing chemicals to limit himself to weekly injections for a maximum of ten weeks before taking a break. Instead, he adopted a more radical regime of his own invention that combined traditional Russian shamanic therapies, such as drinking Wolf's blood[265], with prolonged regimes of strength and performance drugs. Inevitably, he began experiencing the well documented side effects from these drugs of increased aggression, anxiety, paranoia, hair loss, cough, and involuntary shaking of his hands and extremities. His close circle was the first to notice these changes, but the typical Russian fear of their leaders meant that no one dared advise him to stop a toxic regime that would fuel him with an ever-growing paranoia while it slowly killed him through hypertension and liver failure.

Back in the now empty palatial meeting room, the three military leaders who had sat opposite the President were ashen-faced from their understanding of the likely consequences of this full-scale attack. Their forces had already suffered unimaginable losses due to the badly judged invasion of Ukraine. Now, they were taking an action that would be certain to trigger Article five[266] of the NATO treaty and place not just Russia, but the whole world, at the risk of thermonuclear annihilation. The three men rose and,

---

264 The Anabolic steroid called Trenbolone.
265 An Alpha male wolf the president had stalked and shot himself in the Siberian forests.
266 "Any attack on a NATO member in Europe or North America shall be considered an attack against them all."

after collecting their previously surrendered mobile phones from the armed security officers, scurried from the room to seek ways to get themselves and their immediate families as far away from Moscow as possible.

PORRIDGE

*"I am not a number; I am a free man." - Patrick McGoohan,
The Prisoner*[267]

*Central Police Station
Centar Bezbjednosti Podgorica
C7V3+3C9, Podgorica, Montenegro*

16:35 HRS (GMT+2), 14th September, Present day

Lying on top of the dirty blue plastic mattress on the well-worn iron-framed cot bed, Tavish Stewart had just woken from nine hours of deep, dreamless sleep. Knowing that he faced a farcical show trial at the Hague before being publicly executed would have made most people too stressed to get any rest. However, years of military service had taught the Scotsman to grab any opportunity for sleep whenever and wherever he could. Stewart still wore the light grey Timberland fleece, light blue polo shirt, lightweight grey chinos and leather deck shoes that he had on during his long flight in the borrowed Cessna from Italy to Lake Skadar in Montenegro the previous evening.

As he lay, staring at the ceiling, he reflected on what had transpired since his arrest.

Eleven hours earlier, Stewart had removed his torn and blood-soaked Squirrel wingsuit after his arrest by the Montenegrin police outside the barn before facing an hour-long drive to the capital. The Scotsman had taken great care to note his route North from Godinje, across the M2 crossway bridge and along the M80 road to the Montenegrin capital, Podgorica. On arrival, the dark blue police Opel

---

[267] A 1967 British television series.

Vivaro vans had driven through a pair of open black steel gates leading into the courtyard surrounded by a modern grey concrete four-storey building. Stewart quickly realised this structure was the central police station for the Montenegrin capital.

Using the threat of three heavily armed police officers, one leading the way while the other two covered the Scotsman from behind, the Chief of Police separated Stewart from the Mafia members who were also travelling in the van. Behind the two rear gunmen, the Police Chief followed the Scotsman to an unknown destination located inside the western side of the building's car-filled interior courtyard. The guards carried what Stewart recognised as Gewehr 36[268] (G36) assault rifles. They would not have been the Scotsman's choice for such close prisoner escort work. Still, they were enough of a threat to take seriously, especially when the rear two guards knew military protocol well enough to keep more than twenty feet behind their captive. The green polymer G36 they were carrying had fallen from favour in most of Europe due to its predisposition to inaccuracy when overheated[269]. Still, Stewart had seen the weapon's deadly effectiveness first-hand during his UN peacekeeping service in the Yugoslavian civil war. Besides, in every likely failed escape scenario running through Stewart's mind as he walked, the weapons never had to fire for long enough to risk overheating.

During the journey from the large central courtyard to solitary confinement, Stewart continuously calculated North from the angle of the morning sunlight that streamed through corridor windows, counted the distances from each doorway, and the likely cover provided by every significant obstruction.

---

[268] Heckler & Koch G36 (Gewehr 36) is a 5.56×45mm assault rifle. Capable of 750 rounds per minute.
[269] Replaced by the more reliable Heckler & Koch HK416.

After seeing that the Scotsman was secure in a small single-person cell, the Police Chief gestured for the three officers to remain to guard Stewart. The Chief was a small man with short grey hair, wide eyes and a rather elegant moustache. Although he was dressed in the same black paramilitary uniform as his men, the quality and cut of the outfit were visibly superior. He checked the time on his Apple Watch before swaggering towards the entrance of cell number six, and addressing the Scotsman through the metal grille of the locked door.

"I suggest you make yourself comfortable, Mr Stewart. I am Glavni Nadzornik (Chief Superintendent), Marković, of the Podgorica Police division. My men will provide you with a meal and an opportunity to wash. Please do not attempt to escape."

He gestured again to the three guards.

"These fine men have instructions to kill you at the first sign of trouble. Remember, I get a substantial reward regardless of whether you are dead or alive. But I am a civilised man and do not wish you harm. Indeed, I sincerely regret the hours we will hold you here, but I need time to contact the Hague and then confirm receipt in my cryptocurrency account for the payment from Mr Cortez before I inform the UN Police where they can collect you. I am sure you understand."

Stewart nodded. "Fully. Don't hurry. I imagine it will take some time to transfer a billion Euros."

The Police Chief's wide eyes narrowed. "Not Euros, Mr Stewart. That currency ceased to exist earlier this morning. I will specify the equivalent Crypto-Mark payment of the one billion euro reward to my Bitcoin wallet." Marković unconsciously patted his left chest pocket where the top of his Apple iPhone Pro was just visible - evidently, a Bitcoin wallet app was installed on the police chief's phone.

During the hour-long drive to the police station, Stewart listened to the Mafia members discuss the revolution in Europe and how the change to the Crypto-Mark would negatively impact their black market business practices. The Scotsman could see that Marković distrusted Cortez so much that he wanted advance payment and a currency beyond the Argentinian dictator's control. A wise man, thought the Scotsman.

Addressing the three guards, who were regarding him with open contempt, Stewart said, in a friendly voice,

"Gentlemen, I have not eaten for nearly twenty-four hours, so that offer of a meal would be most welcome,"

Stewart then sniffed under the armpits of his fleece before adding, "And for all our sakes, I should take a wash."

Stewart's humour softened the guards' stern attitude. Thirty minutes later, after a warm shower and a shave, the Scotsman was finally rid of most of the deeply engrained sweat, soil, and blood he had accumulated while confronting the four Wolfsangel operatives.

When he returned to his cell, Stewart sat on the small cot bed and looked around his tiny room. The walls were that drab grey colour that only unfinished concrete could achieve. While some of the previous occupants had added insulting and offensive graffiti on most of the lower sections of the wall, the upper parts remained clean. The ceiling was composed of the same galvanised metal that covered the floor. The only visual breaks from the plain metal ceiling surface were from the light and a smoke detector. The light was a single seventy-watt bulb set inside a wire mesh cover. Years of grime and dust meant that considerably more light came into the cell through the iron bars of the locked door.

Apart from the bed, the other item in the ten-foot square room was a red metal latrine bucket that smelt and looked long overdue for a thorough cleaning.

The meal arrived just as Stewart had started reading some more humorous graffiti. One of the guards passed a tin foil plate, a plastic spork and a used plastic bottle of tap water through a meal opening in the white steel door- the meal comprised of that classic Montenegrin dish, Njegusi prosciutto. The cold sausages and smoked meats were well past their best, but after so many hours without food, they tasted magnificent to Stewart.

After eating, Stewart lay on the blue plastic mattress and instantly fell into a deep, dreamless sleep. He was woken nine hours later by the sound of the metal cell door being unlocked and opened. Standing at the entrance was the Police Chief, holding a single sheet of A4 laser printout in his left hand. He did not look like someone who had acquired a billion euros reward. He threw a spent cigarette butt to the cell floor and took a long swig after taking a steel hip flask from his right pocket. Superintendent Marković held up the A4 sheet to show Stewart. It was a grainy CCTV image of Issac bin Abdul Issuin standing outside the Geneva branch of the Union Bank of Switzerland (UBS), dressed in an immaculate Lufthansa pilot's uniform.

"Interpol circulated this image within the last five hours. Since your whereabouts have been well established for the past twenty hours, it is clear that you are innocent of the charges levelled against you for being this man."

The Police Chief continued, saying,

"Your Interpol warrant has, therefore, been revoked, as has the reward for your capture."

Stewart could not have heard better news, but he could see from the expression on the face of the Police Chief that things were not as simple as just letting the Scotsman go. The Chief pointed again to the video capture image.

"Odd that this skilled terrorist mastermind would risk himself to clear you. Someone with his skill sets would not make himself known by accident. Is there some connection between you two men?"

Stewart thought for a moment and decided to answer honestly, saying,

"Up until a moment ago, I thought he was a mortal enemy. But clearly, things are more complex."

"Indeed they are, Mr Stewart. Indeed they are." responded the policeman.

As Stewart wondered why Issac would have risked his safety by posing for this image, the Police Chief continued.

"The UN charges against you may have been dropped, but Mr Cortez still wants you dead. He has transferred ten million US dollars to my Bitcoin wallet to encourage me with that challenge. With the promise of another similar amount after proof of your death."

Stewart looked at the Chief, remembering how the head of police had abruptly executed the last Wolfsangel operative in Godinje with his Glock 17 service pistol.

"So, is it to be a bullet to the head right here?" queried Stewart as he calculated how he could overpower the Chief and the three, armed guards in the corridor.

"No, nothing so obvious, at least not in *my* police station, Mr Stewart. Even I cannot kill someone without getting unwanted international attention, especially after just getting off the phone with the UN about your case. But there are other options."

Superintendent Marković gestured for the armed guards to lead Stewart from the small cell along a corridor and out into the building's interior courtyard, adding.

"Come, I want you to enjoy the rich social life available to our detainees here at Podgorica Police Station."

Stewart noted the parked vehicles as they walked across the courtyard; one of them attracted his particular interest. It was a Volkswagen camper van with pre-2009 Paris number plates, metallic green bodywork and white paintwork on its upper sections. Attached to the rear of the split windscreen van was a carrying rack. Whatever was attached to the rack was concealed under a grey cover caked with road dust.   As the group passed closer to the parked cars and vans, Stewart saw that each confiscated vehicle had a set of keys left in the ignition to permit rapid removal if emergency access was ever needed.

The Scotsman continued his systematic observations as he passed through a pair of fire doors into a corridor that adjoined a large group holding cell twenty yards long and ten yards wide. The entire cell wall along the corridor had rows of closely spaced iron bars that gave the guards a clear view of the prison holding area. The interior was filled with rows of bunk beds and benches at one end, an exercise area in the centre with weight training equipment, and a basketball mini-court. At the furthest end of the room was a white tiled wall with overlapping segments that led to communal toilets and washing facilities. The entire area smelled strongly of cigarette smoke, garlic, sweat, and poorly cleaned bedding. Nearer to the washing zone, more pungent smells were added to the mix.

The Police Chief unlocked the double iron gates to the group holding area and led Stewart into the space, closely escorted by the three, heavily armed guards, who, for the first time, looked stressed and threatened. The Scotsman surmised that there must be some extremely dangerous men awaiting trial. Stewart looked around at the other men in the area. There were around fifty in total, some were lying on bunk beds, and others were lifting weights. A smaller group of four had been practising throwing and passing a basketball. All activity ceased, and there was an expectant silence as the Police Chief stood and addressed the hall in Serbian.

"Gentlemen, this is Tavish Stewart."

Superintendent Marković smiled as he gestured grandly towards Stewart.

"He is the man responsible for the arrest and prosecution of General Kolon Zeferski[270] and Surgeon Major Seff Razsof[271] to face trial at the International Criminal Tribunal[272] for the former Yugoslavia at The Hague[273]."

There were snarled comments from around the room. Only one voice was loud and distinct enough for the Scotsman to hear and understand. It was from a man who had risen from one of the bunk beds. He had enormous shoulders, a shaved head that sported a massive moustache and a swastika tattoo in the centre of his forehead. The man leered and pointed to his groin, exclaiming loudly,

"Направићу те својом кучком због онога што си урадио!"

---

[270] General Zeferski tortured and executed thousands of civilians including hundreds of women and children.

[271] The Sadist of Sarajevo, who was known for performing numerous unnecessarily cruel and painful procedures on captured civilians.

[272] For grave breaches of the Geneva Conventions, violations of the laws or customs of war, genocide, and crimes against humanity.

[273] Thanks to evidence collected by Stewart, both men were found guilty of their role in systematically killing over 7,000 civilians and the horrific torture of over 200 women and children. Although both men subsequently went mysteriously missing from their UN prison confinement and their whereabouts are unknown.

[I am going to make you my bitch for what you did!]

Stewart ignored the sexual threat and instead looked around him. There was a mixed reaction to the Police Chief's announcement. The strongest reaction came from a group of shaven-headed men covered with tattoos of red stars on their chests, shoulders and knees[274]. In addition to these red stars, some sported tattoos of spider webs[275], tigers, leopards and snarling dogs or wolves[276]. Many men, especially those looking with extreme hostility at Stewart, had numerous teardrop tattoos[277] on their faces.

The Police Chief motioned for silence and then continued.

"I know many of you served proudly with Zeferski and Razsof, but I want you all to treat Mr Stewart with the respect his conduct in the former Yugoslavia deserves."

A voice from the rear of the hall shouted, "Odjebi, Svinjo[278]!"

With that, the Chief smiled briefly at Stewart, saying,

"Nothing personal, Stewart. Try and embrace this as a new experience,"

before exiting the holding area with the three, armed guards who had been keeping the men under control.

---

[274] These are marks of rank for Eastern European organised criminals. Stars on the knees, mean that you will not kneel for anyone. Stars on the chest or shoulders show higher status.
[275] Denoting a thief.
[276] These aggressive animal tattoos are called "Oskals" (Big Grin). The symbols denote a person who enjoys inflicting extreme violence and is hostility to authority. The dog indicates a formal grudge against someone or some organisation.
[277] Each teardrop indicates a murder. Usually one committed while in prison against another inmate.
[278] Fuck off, Pig!

The guards on duty in the corridor outside the holding cell followed the Police Chief away from the area, leaving Stewart alone to face the extreme hostility of the murderous mob.

Within seconds of being left alone, Stewart's highly developed peripheral vision detected a fast-moving orange shape moving towards the left side of his head; instinctively, he grabbed a basketball and intercepted it before it violently impacted his face.   Stewart did not waste time turning to look towards the source of the basketball throw, as it was clear that the ball was intended merely as a distraction from what would be the real danger. Stewart cast the ball away and turned. Sure enough, from the opposite side of the court, the two massive men using the bench press frame were advancing directly towards the Scotsman. From the look of determination on their faces, it was clear that the plan was to rough Stewart up and then drag or coerce him to the washrooms, where more senior gang members would have the privilege of adding another tear to their face tattoos.

In a confirmation of the Scotsman's assessment, some twenty feet behind the two mountainous weight lifters walked one of the more senior gang members with a teardrop tattoo and red stars on his shoulders. This shaven-headed thug was carrying a red rubber band in his left hand and a well-used syringe full of a dark brown liquid in his right. Stewart knew the hypodermic would be full of a local variant of "Tar[279]". In some back room, a thirty per cent sample of pure heroin[280] would have been mixed with burned cornstarch[281] to produce a cheaper, rougher high for inmates desperate for a momentary escape from the hell of long-term incarceration.

---

[279] Black tar heroin.
[280] Imported into Europe through Albania, usually.
[281] Or some other form of lactose.

In a final signal of their plan for Stewart, the gang leader with the swastika tattoo and large moustache who had called out the sexual insult followed close behind. He grinned at the Scotsman as he rubbed the growing bulge within his trousers.

It was evident that once they had beaten and drugged him, Stewart's final humiliation would be to be raped as he died on the floor of the prison washroom. The inquest would declare death by misadventure from a heroin overdose with the added spice for the British tabloid press of homosexual activity. Such an outcome would give Cortez the public humiliation he so desired for Stewart, and Superintendent Marković would become twenty million dollars richer.

With such overwhelming odds, most men would plead for mercy. Instead, the Scotsman critically assessed the two bodybuilders rapidly closing in on him. When faced with multiple opponents, traditional Japanese martial arts teach that the practitioner should view the multiple attackers as a single entity and move to the outer edge of the group to avoid being surrounded. The other guidance is to deal with the most dangerous threat first and to make your response of such a violent nature that the other attackers become apprehensive for their safety.

In a response that surprised the two large men, Stewart began advancing towards them, looking as though he intended to pass in between them. At the very last moment, the Scotsman veered to his right. He looked sure to collide with the larger of the two weightlifters. The massive bodybuilder went to grab Stewart's polo shirt with both hands, but before he made contact, the Scotsman completed a lightning-fast snap kick targeting the large man's shin. The impact was so hard that there was a resounding crack as the hardened ball of Stewart's left foot caused a massive tibial shaft fracture in the bodybuilder's left leg.

There is a fundamental misunderstanding in popular culture concerning the so-called "softer" martial arts. The uninformed view them as being useless in real-world combat. This confusion is because lethal techniques, including strikes[282], were removed[283] when these arts were transformed into sports in the nineteenth and twentieth centuries[284].

Stewart could have killed both of the advancing bodybuilders silently and quickly. However, he wanted his attackers to make considerable noise and fuss in this situation. Before the neurological pain signals from the shattered shin bone fully hit the larger of the two bodybuilders, Stewart stamped violently down the big man's instep with his right foot. He then immediately thrust his right knee up into the bodybuilder's groin. As the huge man involuntarily bent forward in response to the groin attack, Stewart grabbed the man's shoulders and violently headbutted him on the bridge of his nose. The big man staggered backwards only to discover that his left leg was useless and unable to support his weight. The man collapsed to the floor on his back, screaming - unsure whether to hold his profusely bleeding nose, groin or broken shin.

With the floor space cleared of the larger of the two weightlifters, Stewart turned his attention to the second bodybuilder. To the credit of the big man, he did not back

---

282 Called Atemi (当て身).
283 Or more accurately, relegated to the teachings of the most advanced grades.
284 Without the initial use of a strike, many throwing techniques resemble a harmless dance between two highly cooperating partners. In their original form, these amusing dances invariably included strikes as part of a curriculum designed to provide a samurai with defensive and offensive capabilities in battlefield conditions against multiple fully armed opponents. The complete form of the technique is no longer practised because the mortality rates would make classes "unappealing".

away after seeing his friend go down. In truth, the attack had taken place so quickly that no one, apart from Stewart, was sure what had happened. Consequently, the second big man naively reached forward with his left hand, intending to grab the Scotsman and hold him while he punched him with his right fist.

Stewart wanted more noise, so his counter was a technique called "finger locks[285]". Usually, this technique places sufficient stress on the joints of the fingers so that the attacker experiences such levels of pain that they are forced to surrender. However, in his current situation, having this one person surrender would do little to save Stewart from his grizzly end. So the Scotsman continued the pressure grip on the fingers of the big man's left hand until he felt each finger bone joint extend beyond their mechanical limits. The weight lifter began to scream even louder than his bloodied associate on the floor and abandoned his attack on Stewart, instead bending over and cupping the broken fingers of his left hand in his right while he screamed.

The Scotsman backed away and took in the response from the gathered men. As he had anticipated, only the most determined men in the assembled group remained interested in continuing their planned assault on Stewart. The big man with the moustache and swastika tattoo had decided that his love for the Scotsman could wait. He had turned away and was returning to his bunk bed. The man carrying the syringe paused, clearly waiting for the Scotsman's next move.

Stewart decided that his best action would be to use the attacker's own plan against them. To the great surprise of the gathered men, the Scotsman turned and strode towards the washroom,

---

285 Yubi-waza (指技). Joint and ligament attacks on the fingers.

Predictably, two men were waiting for the Scotsman when he came around the concealed entryway to the washroom. Both were armed with improvised blades called shivs[286]. One of these shivs was formed from the sharpened handle of a toothbrush, while the other was a long shard of broken mirror embedded in expanding foam that had hardened to create an improvised handle. Since stabbing weapons are a greater threat to life than cutting weapons, Stewart first moved towards the toothbrush dagger. He deflected the stab, then took the attacker's right arm into a complex joint lock[287] that applied pressure against each of the major joints. The Scotsman then turned and, continuing the pressure on the man's arm, threw him backwards directly into the second attacker.

The entire move was blindingly fast. At the end of this technique, Stewart had taken the toothbrush Shiv off his first attacker, broken the two major joints of the attacker's wrist[288] and dislocated his wrist bones[289]. The second attacker pulled himself from under his unconscious compatriot[290]. He looked at how the Scotsman handled the improvised toothbrush blade and decided this would be an excellent time to leave the washroom.

As this second shiv attacker rushed from the washroom, his heroin-carrying accomplice strode calmly into the restroom. He expected to find Stewart dazed and bleeding on the grimy concrete floor. Instead, he found himself on the receiving end of a straight right punch to the jaw that would

---

286 The term shiv originates in criminal slang for a "knife," chive or chiv, which in turn is derived from the Gypsy word for a blade.
287 Katate dori shihonage waza.
288 Radiocarpal and Ulnocarpal joints.
289 The caphoid, lunate, and triquetrum.
290 The pain from destroying the wrist joints and dislocating the hand bones would overwhelm the consciousness within seconds.

have made Mike Tyson proud. A few minutes later, he woke to find himself with his hands and feet tied tightly together with the red elastic tubing he had been carrying. His tightly bound extremities were wrapped around a stinking steel toilet bowl riveted onto the floor. His mouth was so full of paper tissues that he could only issue the odd grunting noise. The expert way the drug dealer had been tied[291] forced his head to rest on the toilet rim directly above a bowl that had not been flushed for a considerable time. In some final unexplained twist, the Scotsman had draped his grey Timberland fleece over the drug dealer's head. The druggie could make out the reflection of the Scotsman in the white tile wall at the back of the toilet cubicle.

Tavish Stewart was some distance away and was putting a mass of partially dampened toilet tissues and paper hand towels into the wire-mesh waste bin. As footsteps approached the washroom entrance, Stewart concealed himself inside the toilet stall next to where the heroin dealer was so effectively tied up.

Superintendent Marković entered alone. His three, armed guards waited outside. Scanning the room, he immediately spotted Stewart's grey fleece draped over a body that the Police Chief surmised was in the process of vomiting as it died from a massive drug overdose. An overdose that Marković had personally organised and supplied to the Serbian gang members before escorting Stewart to the holding cell. In return for killing the Scotsman, the gang leaders would receive twenty thousand dollars. A pittance compared to the twenty million Marković would receive for the Scotsman's demise, but that was the reward for being in charge and having the courage to grab an opportunity when it arose.

---

291 Nawajutsu (縄術) - Rope Technique.

Marković pulled out his iPhone, ready for the photograph that would give him the remaining ten million dollars and grabbed the grey Timberland fleece.

"Jesus, this place stinks", he thought, "I will have a shower and a change of clothes once I have taken this picture."

As he pulled back the fleece, a momentary look of confusion came over his face, only to be replaced by a growing feeling of utter bliss, after he felt a small prick in his neck, followed by a spreading sense of warmth and pleasure. As Marković slumped, Stewart's strong arms caught him and removed the Police Chief's Glock 17, iPhone, vodka flask, wallet and BiC cigarette lighter.

Stewart emptied the flask over the waste bin after using the face of semi-conscious Marković to unlock the Chief's iPhone and reset the facial recognition to respond to Stewart's own rugged features. The Scotsman then used the Chief's lighter to alight the soaking paper. The damp tissue burnt slowly and began generating thick clouds of grey smoke, quickly filling the room and setting off the building's smoke detectors and fire alarms.

Outside the washroom, panic set in with the inmates and the guards. It was everyone's nightmare to be trapped in a burning prison. The cells were automatically unlocked, and the prisoners poured into the central courtyard. As the building's alarms continued to blare, thick smoke poured from the left side of the yard. In the resulting confusion, inmates snatched officers' weapons, and gunfire sounded in the confined space. In an increasing panic, the guards opened the main gates, and the sea of prisoners and police poured out into the street.

Inside the smoke-filled washroom, Tavish Stewart was in the process of leaving, only to find himself facing the shaven-headed gang leader with the swastika tattoo, large moustache and overactive libido. Somehow, this mob leader had acquired one of the green Gewehr 36A assault rifles and clearly knew how to use it based on how he handled the weapon.

There was a brief look exchanged between Stewart and the gang leader. Then, the Scotsman followed the gaze of the tattooed mobster. The thug was looking with unconcealed desire at the figure of the semi-conscious Police Chief slumped over the drug dealer's body, with his backside raised into the air.

The Scotsman raised his eyebrow and remarked,

"буди мој гост[292]," before exiting the washroom.

As Stewart came out of the building into the deserted courtyard, back in the smoke-filled washroom, the blissful smile on Superintendent Marković's face was matched by the expression on the gang leader's as he unbuckled his belt and advanced towards the recumbent Police Superintendent.

Minutes later, a classic 1967 green and white VW minivan exited the Police Station gates and powered away, down the road heading North.

---

292 Be my guest!

SHOCK AND AWE

"All warfare is based on deception. Hence, when we are able to attack, we must seem unable; when using our forces, we must appear inactive." - Sun Tzu, The Art of War.

Fort Liberty (formerly Fort Bragg)
Cumberland, North Carolina
USA

10:35 HRS (GMT-4), 14th September, Present day

President Wilson Jones waited beside his secretary, surrounded by a grove of majestic magnolias looking at the wooden two-storey townhouse where his daily briefing would take place. In front of the President were six broad wooden steps leading up to a short, open-fronted veranda and a pair of double full-length glass doors. A blue plastic sign with white text, located to the left side of the doors, proclaimed the building as the John F. Kennedy Special Warfare Center and School[293] (SWCS).

Since the other senior US government members had been abducted, the six Marines had agreed that it was almost inevitable that an attempt to remove the POTUS was imminent. In response, they raised their situational awareness and took every precaution to ensure no unpleasant surprises.

The blond-haired twenty-seven-year-old US Marine Captain, who led the POTUS' protection detail, used the light attached to the side rail on his FAST[294] helmet to examine under the wooden veranda for booby traps before he went up the six

---

[293] Informally known as the "Swick". This is the US Army's training centre for psychological and unconventional warfare (PSYOPS).
[294] Ops-Core Future Assault Shell Technology (FAST) Helmet by Gentex.

steps in a single, smooth motion. Moving silently across the porch, he gestured with his right hand to the two other Marines behind him to take positions on either side of the double doors. Within the blink of an eye, these soldiers had come up the six steps and reached their assigned positions, their M27[295] rifles ready. Captain Jackson's blue eyes were partially hidden behind a pair of tinted Oakley combat glasses[296] as he scanned the area around the doors. Seeing no signs of wires, lasers, or magnetic triggers, he pulled open the right side door and, upon entering, moved sideways into the corner of the long hallway so he had complete coverage of the room with his M27.

The room in front of him was twenty feet long and twelve feet wide, with a traditional wooden staircase on the left and an unfurnished area to the right. The walls were covered in framed photographs of notable visitors to the PSYOPS school over the past decades. A red light shone underneath a section of the wooden floorboards, where one of the Marines searched to ensure no unwelcome surprises awaited them.

Standing beside the staircase in the otherwise empty hall was a striking dark-haired woman talking on her black iPhone. Although she did not have that classic beauty often associated with famous and influential women, she excluded a powerful confidence many would have found intimidating.

The woman was in her mid-forties and dressed in a dark red linen business suit with a white cotton blouse and pencil skirt. If Jackson had been a fashion aficionado, he would hav been more appreciative of the fine materials and exquisite cut of the cloth, which accentuated the curves of the woman's body in the classy way that the Los Angeles-base designer, Aya Muse, is renowned for.

---

[295] A modified version of the HK416 by Heckler & Koch.
[296] US Standard Issue Prizm TR45 Radar by Oakley.

On the woman's lapel, next to a pin badge of the US flag, was a small golden brooch carved into the shape of a striking cobra's head, with two rubies for eyes and diamonds for fangs. Around the woman's neck was a thick gold chain with a distinctive pendant formed from a square of black onyx secured within a gold frame. Although it was nearly impossible to read the engravings on the surface because of centuries of wear, the gemstone had a series of carvings that formed a classic magickal talismanic word square. Written in a mix of ancient Hebrew, Aramaic, and Phoenician alphabets, the infamous "Alwib Allaasiq[297]" or "Sticky Web" talisman[298] channelled the power of the inverted Qliphothic force from the sixth sefira in the kabbalistic Tree of Life, namely Tiphereth[299] or beauty.   In the case of this ancient[300] talisman, the forces conjured were related to the demonic order Thagirion[301], ruled by the Archdemon Belphegor[302]. The choice of onyx was related not only to its powerful enhancement of the wearer's magickal will but also to the

---

[297] الويب اللاصق

[298] An esoteric artefact imbued with magickal force by means of ritual, intent and composition of materials.

[299] TIPHARAH (תפארה) - beauty or adornment. In the positive Tree of Life, it acts as a balance between the forces of Chesed (Kindness) and Gevurah (Strength). In the negative Qliphothic Tree of Death it destabilises judgement to reduce strength of will and makes victims prone to excessive generosity.

[300] Created by Zoroastrian mages in the third-century (CE) by order of Shah Ardashir for his use in his harem at Ardashir-Khwarrah (modern-day Firuzabad, Iran) in the Sasanian Empire.

[301] The order of Thagirion is known as "the disputers" there role is to create division and to limit progress. In some texts, this work is completed by demonic forms known as The Zomiel, who assume the shape of giants with a dark form to inspire conflict.

[302] Belphegor (בַּעַל-פְּעוֹר), literally "Lord of the Gap", is a demon who seduces with the promise of new knowledge or discovery but in fact leads people into procrastination and the sin of sloth.

stone's legendary ability to create and amplify conflicts. Finally, the woman wore a distinctive gold ring on her right hand with an inverted pentagram and the symbol 5=6[303].

Captain Jackson was unaware of any of this esoteric significance. He simply recognised that the woman contravening security regulations by using a mobile phone at a clandestine presidential briefing[304] was the Secretary of Defence, Jane L. Maskins.   Secretary Maskins was talking in hurried and hushed tones. She was concerned about some matter.

"Yes, tell me the moment there is *any* news regarding survivors from the fire at the Fortress, especially related to Magus Regio and Magister Ironheart. Listen, Hartman. I have to go. Wilson is coming!"

Captain Jackson lowered his M27 and approached the smartly dressed woman with his left hand outstretched for the offending phone. In his quiet southern drawl, he asked politely,

"Madam Secretary. You know the regulations regarding the use of a phone at briefings. Kindly surrender your phone."

A harsh and angry look came over Maskins' face. She looked as welcoming as a snowstorm at a Fourth of July parade and twice as cold. She snarled,

"Stand down, Soldier. Walk on and forget it, or I will have those two silver bars off your collar[305], and you will be cleaning latrines for what short time remains of your commission."

---

[303] An adepts ring - denoting the initiation grade Adeptus Minor - the first of the full adept grades in the Western Esoteric Tradition.
[304] The phone signal can be detected and used to triangulate the exact location of a target.
[305] Denotes the rank of Captain USMC.

Jackson ignored the deliberate provocation. Calling a US Marine "a soldier" will cause a bristle at the best of times[306]. The Marine waggled the fingers in his Kevlar glove to emphasise his demand for the phone. Jackson added, saying,

"Ma'am, you know the regulations regarding the use of cell phones at classified locations."

Maskins looked into Jackson's face, trying to judge if this man had the nerve to tackle the Secretary of Defense and take her phone by force. She pointedly looked at the Captain's sidearm[307] and then back into Jackson's cold blue eyes to see if she could provoke him to draw his weapon on her. Before snidely proclaiming,

"I will have you in a court martial and dishonourably discharged."

Concealed behind a wall of burly Marines, who had now filed into the hallway, President Wilson Jones had witnessed the inappropriate behaviour of Maskins. Wilson's voice announced,

"Not while I am in Office, Madam Secretary. Give Captain Jackson the phone, and you can explain later what was so urgent that you felt the need to break security protocols at this critical time."

Maskin's response was to hurriedly press a sequence on her screen that initiated an automated clean wipe procedure on her iPhone before passing the cell to Jackson. Smiling, she brushed her hair away from her face and, in doing so, surreptitiously rubbed the talisman around her neck. In a

---

[306] Marines do not serve in the Army.
[307] The M45A1 is the issued sidearm of the Marine Raider Regiment (MRR). It is a modified Colt 1911 .45 ACP pistol with reduced recoil and a desert tan "Cerakote" finish. It carries a seven round magazine and has three-point tritium sights.

transformation like a thousand-watt lightbulb had been turned on, suddenly Maskins radiated that indescribable something that defined Marilyn Monroe as a sex symbol. In a silky smooth and seductive tone, she stated,

"Mr President, I did not see you there. I was kidding around with the brave Captain, wasn't I, Captain?" she turned that thousand-watt presence directly at the Marine in front of her.

At that moment, Jackson felt an irrational compulsion to agree, but his highly developed willpower managed to resist. Instead, he just followed procedure and placed Maskins' phone in a Ziplock bag for later forensic analysis by Quantico[308] analysts.

With that, Maskins strode away with a walk that would have put Jessica Rabbit[309] to shame. While Jackson's men followed the exit of Maskins like dogs watching a squirrel, Captain Jackson spoke into his encrypted throat radio[310].

"Roof and ground units, double check the functioning of the HIMAD[311]."

"Anticipating trouble, Jackson?" enquired Wilson as he passed by, heading for the group of four Marines who had emerged from the lower levels of the building and were now guarding the stairs down to the basement.

"Just following protocols after a breach of communications silence, Mr President." assured Jackson.

---

[308] Home of the FBI Academy within the Marine Corps base in Quantico, Virginia.

[309] The highly sexualised cartoon character from Who Framed Roger Rabbit.

[310] A TCI TTMK III

[311] High to Medium Air Defense (HIMAD) system - known as the MIM-104 Patriot or "Phased Array Tracking Radar to Intercept on Target" (PATROIT) anti-missile and air defence systems.

"Very well, let's get to this meeting." said the POTUS.

At the bottom of two flights of stairs, Jackson's six men coordinated with the dozen Marines who had already swept meeting room Bravo[312] Two (2B[313]) for bugs and searched the attendees. Jackson and his men escorted the POTUS into a long, low-ceilinged classroom that had been laid out with the students' chairs stacked along the sides of the long room. The air in the basement retained the scent of the bleach that had cleaned every surface before the meeting.

Two trestle tables had been set up in the centre of the room with sufficient chairs for each attendee along both sides. A single chair stood at the head of the table next to two, thirty-inch TV screens and a large US flag on a seven-foot tall indoor flag pole. Fluorescent overhead lights illuminated a variety of PSYOPS training posters on the walls. In the centre of the table were insulated coffee dispensers, paper cups and plates of cookies.

As President Wilson entered the room, the Marines came to attention, and the attendees all stood. Wilson approached his chair and declared,

"At ease, everybody. It's going to be a busy day, so get a coffee and let's get started."

With that, he sat and looked at the men and women who would help him save his nation from its greatest threat for over seventy years.

On his right side was CIA director Mark Pimms. To Pimms' right were United States Marine Corps General Louis M. Arnold, United States Air Force General Cliff "Eagle" Smith,

---

[312] B for the basement.
[313] One of the larger basement classrooms at the Special Warfare Center and School (SWCS) in the two hundred and fifty square mile grounds of Fort Liberty.

United States Navy Admiral Peter G. H. Lorance and United States Army General Jeremy "Jim" H. Orne.

To the President's left side was his Secretary of Defence, the forty-three-year-old Jane L. Maskins, the dark-haired woman who had been on the phone. Next to her was the fifty-six-year-old, blonde-haired, blue-eyed, Director of National Intelligence, Elaine Madden. Both women were noticeably overdressed for the meeting, and based on the heady, musky scent that filled the air near them, both wore perfume that would be better suited to a cocktail party. The two were whispering and passing notes to each other rather like schoolchildren. Rumour had it that the pair had recently become lovers during frequent and highly mysterious trips to New Orleans. Wilson paid little attention to office scuttlebutt, but what was evident by looking at them was that the pair were close and shared a fascination with cobra-themed jewellery. Wilson hoped they would not provoke the senior military leaders sitting opposite them into another protracted argument, as they had on several recent White House meetings. The pattern had been for the pair to undermine assessments made by every military branch, especially the intelligence delivered by the CIA. Since Maskins had a supervisory role over the Military and Madden controlled funding to the US intelligence communities, their criticisms effectively stifled constructive discussion.   Wilson knew that if these two key cabinet members continued their aggressive style, he would have to find replacements.

Wilson turned to Pimms.

"Mark, can you give us a sitrep[314]?"

---

[314] A report on the current situation.

Pimms addressed the group without notes. While he talked, the two large TV screens beside the President showed images of the destruction around the United States.

"Mr President, last evening's violent storms and seismic events caused massive damage to coastal areas and major cities. Damage evaluations are ongoing, and all fifty states have declared a state of emergency."

The TV images switched to scenes of mobs overrunning significant government buildings and burning the Union flag. Pimms continued,

"Combined with these natural disasters, there has been enormous social unrest. The states of Maine, Vermont, California, New York, Rhode Island, New Hampshire, Maryland, Oregon, California and Massachusetts have formally ceded from the Union. They are forming a contra-federacy in opposition to the United States."

"Idiots." exclaimed the President, "We are back to the nineteenth century. Has none of these people," he gestured to the TVs, "heard of Abraham Lincoln and the bloodshed of our civil war?"

Maskins' silky voice interjected.

"But, Mr. President, it looks like the people's will is for radical change. Who are we to try to stop them? Have you considered that maybe we should embrace this as a moment to allow the people what they so clearly desire?"

There were enthusiastic murmurs of support from Madden sitting next to the Secretary of Defense.

Pimms commented, "Mr President, these people are being controlled, like puppets, through social media. We could slow the uprisings by closing down social media and public access to the internet."

"It would make us just like the totalitarian regimes we have long criticised. We assess that this radical action would only confirm the conspiracy theories feeding the uprising." Madden stated authoritatively, although in reality, she knew that her assessment was unfounded.

Wilson looked around the table, trying to get a feel for support for Madden's assessment. He commented,

"Very well, we leave the social media for the moment."

Madden and Maskins looked like cats with a bowl of the finest double cream.

Pimms disagreed but accepted the President's decision. He nodded and completed his assessment of the domestic situation by saying,

"The US situation is fluid, and it remains to be seen if there will be any further uprisings."

"What about outside the US?" asked Wilson.

"Coinciding with the global natural disasters, an antidemocratic movement arose using social media to coordinate the storming of government institutions globally, as they have here in the US. However, in Europe, Africa and South America, the uprisings appear to have successfully overthrown the established government with little or no resistance.

Mexico and Canada are in chaos. The Chamber of Deputies in Mexico City has fallen to the social-media-led mob, as has Parliament Hill in Ottawa. The Canadian Parliamentary Protective Service (PPS) surrendered control of the legislature, and the Canadian President has crossed the border into the US and is asking for asylum. All the Provinces have fallen, except Alberta, where The Premier of Alberta has mobilised the Reserve Reconnaissance Regiment[315] (RRR). Running gun battles are taking place on Jasper Avenue and outside the Alberta Legislature Building in Edmonton.

Outside of The Americas, satellite imagery shows Russia has mobilised its Army and Airforce along the borders of Europe."

"New Europa," corrected Maskins.

Pimms ignored the comment and continued, saying, "China has mobilised its forces and looks like it may attack Taiwan and Australia."

"Pure speculation, Mr President. I have seen these same intelligence reports. They could be military preparedness exercises." interjected Madden.

Mark Pimms sighed, "Mr President, our sources are confident Russia will invade the European nations. China is less certain, I admit, but it would be remiss of me not to mention it."

"Thank you, Mark. The purpose of our meeting is to review these events and decide on short and long-term policy implications for the United States," stated Wilson.

Pimms replied, "Sir, I would like to add that the timing of these social uprisings in Europe and even here in the US appear to be too perfectly coordinated with the natural disasters to be chance."

There was a loud snort of derision from Maskins.

"Not this paranoid nonsense again, Mark."

Pimms ignored the put-down from the Secretary of Defense and continued,

---

[315] The South Alberta Light Horse based at Canadian Forces Base Suffield near Suffield, Alberta.

"The uprisings were timed to perfection; Mr President, like someone, knew the storms and seismic events were coming. In fact, a credible source had been warning about a social media campaign for global revolution for some weeks."

The Director of National Intelligence, Madden, sighed and corrected Pimms,

"Mr President, we at National Intelligence have seen these same reports. They are just paranoid conspiracy theories from a discredited source."

Pimms looked desperately at the POTUS. Wilson raised his hand to silence Madden's interruption.

"I will hear it anyway. Go ahead, Mark."

The CIA director nodded his thanks to the President and continued.

"The NSA communicated with an operative at the British GCHQ, who believed they had uncovered evidence of massive coordinated social media campaigns to support an uprising identical to what we are experiencing."

"With respect, Mr President, these are just wild speculations," interjected Madden, who was now in a regular pattern of undermining everything the CIA Director suggested.

Wilson decided he needed to break her annoying pattern of behaviour.

"Madam Director, you will kindly let Director Pimms finish his answer to my direct question or leave this room."

"Yes, Mr President." Madden and Maskins exchanged a faked look of shock as though the President was making critical errors of judgement.

Wilson dealt with the two women's attempt to undermine him by stating,

"Without any clear data, I am open to wild speculation. When can we hear from this British asset?"

"She has been transferred to the Falklands, Sir." said Pimms.

There was a loud and deliberate snigger from the Secretary of Defense and the National Intelligence Director. Wilson let it ride. His secretary's warning about these two senior cabinet members was proving to be all too accurate. He would have to begin planning their replacements. He kept his focus on Mark Pimms, asking,

"Have the Falklands fallen?"

"Yes, Mr President."

Wilson turned to Admiral Lorance.

"Pete, can we extract this British Asset and bring them here to brief us?"

Lorance nodded and scribbled a note that he gave to one of the Marines for urgent action before saying,

"If Mark gives me the latest coordinates of the asset, I will have DEVGRU Red Team[316] on route within the hour with full logistical support[317]."

"Good." Wilson made a point of ignoring Maskins and Madden and turned back to the CIA Director.

"Mark, what do we have on the leader of this so-called New Republic?"

---

[316] Naval Special Warfare Development Group (DEVGRU) (prior to 1987 known as SEAL Team 6). DEVGRU and the Army's Delta are the US military specialists in hostage rescue missions.
[317] CV-22B Osprey tiltrotor aircraft and MC-130J Commando II for refuelling the Osprey.

Pimms pressed a remote control, and a video of the procession that had taken place in London began playing on the screens.

Cortez's cortege progressed down the Strand to a ticker tape welcome, then turned onto Waterloo Bridge and into Somerset House. The massive black Mercedes open-topped limousine stopped, and three men emerged. Pimms stopped the playback and highlighted each of the three individuals with a laser pointer.

"This is Chairman Cortez, and these are his two grandsons, Corrado and Hartman."

Captain Jackson's eyes narrowed at the mention of "Hartman", and he regarded Secretary of Defense Maskins with suspicion.

Cortez's hand-tailored Brioni suit fitted him perfectly and highlighted his lean and muscular physique. In contrast, the two grandsons wore elegant black Hugo Boss FF uniforms.

"Are the two grandsons aware of what their uniforms resemble?" asked General Orne with incredulity.

Pimms smiled. "Yes, Jim. We believe they are fully aware and are, in fact, making a statement to the world."

"Jesus." the Army general shook his head.

Pimms restarted the video playback. A TV reporter with a Beyond Facts company logo[318] on her microphone intercepted the group of three men as they proceeded to the entrance of Somerset House, which was adorned by red FF flags on either side of the door.

"Chairman, may we have a few words?"

---

[318] Now proud members of the Wolfsangel Group.

Cortez looked as if he was surprised by the intervention, although the script for this "impromptu" interview lay on his seat in the rear of the Mercedes limousine.

Cortez smiled like a genial grandfather. "Yes, of course."

The blonde TV reporter giggled nervously, asking,

"You were initially reluctant to take the leadership of the Unity Party, but you now seem to have embraced your new role as our supreme leader. What caused your change of heart?"

Cortez looked serious and locked his penetrating blue eyes on the camera lens like the consummate professional that he was. He looked like he was talking directly to each viewer.

"You are right. I was initially reluctant to take a leadership role. But when our elected leaders failed so singularly to respond in any way to the natural disasters befalling New Europa last night, as a man of the people, I was morally obligated to intervene. The failure of democratically elected leaders is, sadly, nothing new. The problems of the modern world, the introduction of slavery, segregation, poverty, hideous non-consensual experiments, two world wars, invasions of numerous nations and untold deaths and suffering have all been undertaken by democratically elected governments.

In hindsight, I am delighted that we, as a society, have finally reached a stage of maturity where New Europa is free from the restrictions enforced by democracy."

There were cheers from the crowds nearby, along with chants of "Democracy is mob rule!" and "Freedom from democracy!" Cortez waved at his supporters. The interviewer continued her questions.

"What are you here for today, Chairman?"

Cortez looked again into the camera lens.

"I am glad you asked, my dear. I have come to Somerset House to oversee a new group of weaponed FF officers who are seeking advancement to the highest honour available within New Europa."

"You mean advancement is possible beyond the elite weaponed FF, Chairman?" asked the dewy-eyed interviewer.

"Indeed. Those applicants who can prove their background to five generations and their exceptional martial prowess can travel to The Castle and undergo further trials to become Knights within The Order of the Black Sun. Unlike the honour systems that existed in the previous European nations, this one is based only on merit and ability.

Before I leave to oversee the first cohort of applicants for this highest honour, I wish to pass a message to the Presidents of America, Russia and China. For your safety, do not test our resolve. I especially make this clear to President Zychopav of The Russian Federation- withdraw the forces you have sent into our territory or face the consequences. Thank you."

Cortez then turned and strode towards the banner-covered entrance to Somerset House with his two grandsons. The video feed ended with a blank screen.

President Wilson turned to Pimms.

"I want everything we have on this man, Cortez."

Pimms nodded. "Mr President, to do so, I will need to break an executive order (EO) issued by one of your predecessors, President Harry S. Truman[319]."

Wilson's eyebrows raised.

"Under the circumstances, I think I need to know."

---

[319] The 33rd president of the United States. He served from 1945 to 1953.

K.R.M. Morgan

Pimms nodded and, reaching beneath the table, opened an attaché case and pulled out a waxed paper folder, which he then opened by tearing a seal, allowing him to remove an old, creased, buff letter-sized manilla file covered in signatures and dates.

At the top of the folder's front cover were the words in bold red ink

YANKEE WHITE[320] CATEGORY ONE

SPECIAL ACCESS PROGRAM (SAP) RESTRICTED DATA - PRESIDENTIAL EYES ONLY.

A SIGNATURE IS REQUIRED ON READING.

Underneath these sentences were two words in bold red ink

"UNHOLY SEED"

Wilson took the file and opened it so only he could read it. The rest of the Cabinet Members sat expectantly. Wilson read the single page in the folder, then closed it, signed and dated it before returning it to Pimms.

"He was his father? Are you sure about this?"

Pimms nodded. Wilson paused for a moment and then issued a series of commands.

"Disable the British Trident II systems."

"But they are our allies!" cried Maskins and Madden, almost in unison.

Wilson ignored the outburst and looked at Admiral Lorance.

---

[320] A security clearance for staff associated with The President and Vice President. There are three categories of Yankee White clearance with Category one clearance being the very highest.

"Hit the kill switch, Jim."

The admiral nodded and wrote a note, which another of the Marines promptly took and left the room.

The President then turned to Pimms.

"Mark, do we have people who can disable the French weapons?"

Maskins interrupted again, exclaiming, "Sir, we never act against our allies. Besides, we do not have any direct action agents active in friendly countries."

Pimms ignored the Secretary of Defense and quietly stated,

"Yes, Mr President. We do."

"Make it so." stated Wilson before turning to the group of military leaders.

"Take us to DEFCON 1 and get all our assets in Europe back home ASAP."

There was a flurry of activity, with urgent action notes issued by each cabinet member, which were taken away by Marines.

As Wilson was about to continue, another Marine hurried into the room and gave a note to the CIA director.

Pimms read the note and looked at President Wilson.

"Mr President, there are ongoing developments which impact our deliberations." He pointed to the screen and asked, "May I?"

Wilson nodded. Everyone turned to watch the two large TVs. The coverage from each of the major media outlets was identical. International news crews had been driven close to the Russian borders in Finland, Estonia, Latvia, Belarus, Lithuania, Poland and Norway. The footage from each location was similar, showing distinctively shaped long aircraft escorted by smaller delta-winged planes.

K.R.M. Morgan

Wilson turned to Air Force General Cliff "Eagle" Smith.

"Cliff, what are we looking at here?"

"Mr President, there is a mix of Tupolev supersonic and subsonic bombers escorted by a mix of MiGs and Sukhoi fighters." General Smith stood and came closer to the screen, before saying, "Yes, all the weapons pods are fully loaded."

"Could they be nuclear?" asked Wilson.

"They could be," answered Smith. He pointed to one of the long aircraft with a distinctive delta wing shape that was similar to the wings on the smaller escort fighters. "The Blackjack or Tu-160 is their supersonic nuclear bomber. But, I would expect them to use conventional weapons to take out the airfields so they can quickly gain air supremacy. That is what we would do. Using air-launched cruise missiles to destroy runways and hangars."

The camera angles shifted at that moment and showed large formations of camouflaged tanks and armoured cars, leading a more significant number of six-wheel trucks and SUVs fitted with mounted heavy machine guns.

"Christ!" exclaimed Army General Orne, "Zychopav's gone for a full invasion!"

He approached the screens and pointed to hundreds of vehicles rumbling at high speed over fields of unharvested wheat.

"Those are T-14 Armatas, their latest battle tanks. The other tanks are older designs, the T-72 and T-80. They are still formidable."

The General then pointed to some of the other vehicles. "Those are BTR-90s- their eight-wheeled armoured personnel carrier. And those are GAZ Tigrs - their clone of the HUMVEE. Mr President, judging by the hundreds of vehicles flowing over all these borders, this is a full-scale invasion of Europe."

Wilson ran his fingers through his greying hair. "Today just keeps getting better."

Madden and Maskins shared a not-so-secret delight at Wilson's distress.

By now, all four leaders of the respective military branches were standing beside the President, watching the unfolding Russian invasion on the two large screens.

Admiral Lorance pointed towards the leftmost screen showing a formation of six Russian planes, two bombers and four fighter escorts, approaching a large airforce base seventy miles inside the Polish border. The Navy Admiral asked,

"Cliff, what are those blobs hovering around the lead aircraft? Are they some part of their formation?"

Air Force General Cliff Smith looked closer. "I had not seen them earlier. If I did not know better, I would say they were digital camera artefacts."

At that precise moment, the mysterious flying blobs holding a pattern some two hundred yards in front gathered into a tighter formation, split into two and executed a classic close pass on either side of the lead bomber. The manoeuvre rocked the Russian bomber, but it quickly regained its stability and fired three cruise missiles[321] towards the airbase.

"Interesting," said General Smith, "whatever those blobs were, they were trying to force the Russians to back down

---

[321] Raduga Kh-55SM cruise missiles (conventional explosive warheads). Mach 0.6-0.78.

and call off their attack. Judging by the launch of those three AS-15 "Kents[322]", the Russians do not intend to stop."

At that moment, three of the strange blobs flew back past the speeding supersonic lead bomber and took off after the three cruise missiles. The mysterious blobs almost immediately reached the missiles and merged with them, disappearing.

"God, they are fast, whatever they are," commented Airforce General Smith. Just as he was about to try and provide an estimate of the speed needed to zoom past the bomber and catch the cruise missiles in mid-flight, the three projectiles unexpectedly dropped from the sky. They impacted the ground without any detonation, well short of the airfield.

"What just happened?" asked the mystified President.

Before Smith could answer, more blobs appeared and grouped around the lead bomber, which had launched the three cruise missiles. The blobs merged with the bomber's fuselage and disappeared.

"I think I know what that means." said Admiral Lorance.

Moments later, the large grey Tu-160 bomber fell from the sky like a toy discarded by a petulant child. It smashed into the wheat fields below without exploding.

"Interesting," stated Airforce General Smith, "The blobs must cause some massive EMP[323] that disables all aviation electronics. Even the emergency ejector seats don't appear to function."

"Would those blob things be able to do the same with our aircraft?" queried President Wilson, clearly thinking that the

---

[322] NATO name for the Raduga Kh-55SM
[323] Electromagnetic Pulse.

United States would have to face this new development in warfare at some point very soon.

"Almost certainly, Mr President," answered Secretary of Defense Maskins with an expression on her face which was unsettlingly positive, like she was enjoying the prospect of American defeat.

More blobs appeared around the remaining Russian aircraft in the lead formation. One of the fighters peeled away and accelerated towards them.

Airforce General Smith smiled, "Now we will see what those blobs things are made of! That is a MiG-31, made to take down our SR-71 "Blackbird" during the cold war. It is still the world's fastest combat aircraft."

"Publicly known combat aircraft," corrected Pimms.

"It's still a mean bird, and this one is carrying one of the latest Axehead[324] hypersonic smart air-to-air missiles. There! She has launched one!" exclaimed Airforce General Smith excitedly.

The missile flew after one of the blobs but could not get anywhere near it, as the blob took off vertically faster than the eye could see. The Axehead missile began to fly aimlessly around the sky after losing its target. Meanwhile, another blob had flown up to the MiG-31 and merged with it. Moments later, the MiG tumbled from the sky and crashed into the ground.

"What the fuck *are* these things?" exclaimed Airforce General Smith.

"They are UAPs General. We have a multi-agency task force trying to determine what they are and if they threaten our

---

[324] Vympel R-37

national security," said Director of National Intelligence Madden.

President Wilson remarked, "I think we can safely assume they do."

Before any Cabinet Members could comment further, the scenes they had witnessed over Poland repeated themselves throughout New Europa's invaded border areas.

As the cream of the Russian Air Force fell from the skies, the TV coverage focused on the Russian land invasion. The two screens showed several tanks and armoured columns hurrying to the crash sites of the downed aircraft.

Army General Orne pointed to a group of five vehicles shown on the right-hand TV screen, saying, "That's a single T-14 Armata accompanied by three, BTR-90 armoured personnel carriers and a GAZ Tigr SUV."

As dozens of men emerged from the personnel carriers to begin searching the crash site, the display seemed to suffer from interference that looked like rows of vertical lines. When the TV interference cleared, the tanks, personnel carriers and SUV were nowhere to be seen. In their place was a pile of steaming metal. Only when one looked closer could one see that the vehicles and the men had been crushed and pulverised by some unseen force.

Wilson became filled with an icy cold dread as he thought of the consequences of these weapons being used on American forces. Calmly, he instructed,

"Right, I want all of you to research what we have just seen, explain it and provide some ideas on how we could counter these weapons. We will resume our meeting three hours from now ."

He turned to Pimms. "Mark, have Marauder[325] and Black Star[326] ready for deployment."

---

[325] Ronald Reagan's 1987 allocation of 260 billion USD (over half a trillion USD in modern value) spending on the Strategic Defence Initiative (SDI) produced many top-secret weapons. None were as exotic as the magnetized target fusion system (code name MARAUDER). Developed from the high-powered pulsed power research device located at the Air Force Research Laboratory on the Kirtland Air Force Base in Albuquerque, New Mexico, this orbiting geostationary weapon generates compact streams of high-density plasma, that is ejected using a massive magnetic pulse destroying supersonic missiles in flight or strategic ground targets.
[326] The National AeroSpace Plane (NASP) project (code name BLACKSTAR), that resulted from Reagan's instruction to create a hypersonic space capable fighter bomber in his 1986 State of the Union Address, was a black budget project funded by NASA, DARPA, the US Air Force, the Strategic Defence Initiative Office (SDIO) and the US Navy. Boeing and Lockheed Skunk Works were the funded commercial partners.   The specification list of "Blackstar" (a weaponised version of the Lockheed Martin SR-72 "Aurora") made the NASA Space Shuttle, F-117 Nighthawk Stealth bomber and Lockheed Martin F-35 Lightning II fighter look like cracker toys. It was officially mothballed in 1995, although odd sightings continue to be reported near the Lockheed Skunk Works up to the current date.

K.R.M. Morgan

TIDES TURN

"There is a tide in the affairs of men. Which, taken at the flood, leads on to fortune". - William Shakespeare, 'Julius Caesar'

Blandings,
3a, Sandy Lane, Petersham
Richmond, Surrey, TW10

19:17 HRS (GMT+1), 14th Sept, Present day

The cloudless blue sky slowly acquired that beautiful golden orange hue that marks the close to a perfect late summer day. The celebrations in London switched to a carnival mood with street dancers, steel drums and floats representing every one of the diverse communities that make up the capital of New Britannia. Although it was getting cooler as the sun set over the tall buildings, the temperatures remained in the low 70s, permitting the participants in the evening celebrations to stay in their t-shirts and shorts, enjoying the many beverages and snacks offered by the numerous street-side vendors.

Out in the suburbs, it was much quieter. This peace was only broken by the odd passing car travelling through the country roads. Blandings was set back from one of these side lanes, a Dutch Gable-style Victorian detached home with a ten-year-old, light blue Subaru Forester parked at the end of a twenty-yard gravel drive. The old car was caked in mud around the lower parts of the wheel arches and sported several honourable battle scars from encounters with rocks and tree stumps.

The large house was surrounded by a beautiful sea of green, comprised of mature trees and shrubs that balanced seclusion with practicality. Whoever designed the garden had an expert awareness since they had ensured a pleasant leafy view from almost every room. Towards the rear of the beautifully secluded back garden was an old-fashioned wooden framed glass house filled with a mix of rare tropical plants from around the world.

Inside this hot house, the air was filled with a sweet and musky fragrance resembling the smell of baked goods. Beside an enamel sink inset to a wooden bench was a man in his mid-sixties with well-groomed grey hair and distinguished patrician features. Sir Fredrick Richards, the former Principal Private Secretary (PPS) for the Foreign and Commonwealth Office, gently hummed along to Op. 36[327] on Classic FM, broadcast from an old Grundig[328] radio. In his hands, a pair of sharp scissors[329] completed a delicate trim on a Gold of Kinabalu Orchid.

Richards' singing was interrupted by an attractive woman with long shoulder-length blonde hair and wire-rim glasses, wearing a grey art smock covered in oil paints. She called,

"Phone, darling,"

and then walked back to the house.

Moments later, Richards entered a large, classically designed hall with a red tile floor at the rear of the property. The tall walls were covered with rows of hooks filled with various coats and hats to match the numerous climates possible in England. Beside these coats was an oriental-style ceramic umbrella container that housed a range of umbrellas and walking sticks.

---

[327] Edward Elgar's variations on Op. 36, known as the Enigma Variations.

[328] Grundig Yacht Boy 80 World Receiver Radio.

[329] Sentei Garden Scissors.

K.R.M. Morgan

A grey-muzzled golden retriever dog hurried from its bed on the floor and nuzzled Richards, who called to his wife as he patted the dog's head,

"Did they say who it was?"

A female voice responded, "No, darling. Only that it was urgent and of national importance."

"It always is..." commented Richards dryly as he rolled up his shirt sleeves and wiped the perspiration from his eyes, spreading dirty smudges over his shirt and face.

As he reached for the handset of an old Bakelite dial phone resting on a small mahogany table, he wondered who would call him. It could only be someone who did not know he had retired, but surely everyone knew that, and they could hardly hold him to account for the bloody revolution.

"Yes, Richards here,"

 A smile spread over his face.

"Ms Twop? Christine, isn't it? Yes, of course, I remember you from your interview. You are a very talented young lady, as I recall. You got top scores on your Civil Service exams."

"GCHQ? Excellent choice. I am sure you will make an outstanding analyst."

He listened carefully.

"Moved to the Falklands? Whatever for? Do you like sheep, land mines and cold weather?"

Richards sat in the chair beside the phone table. As he listened, he patted the dog as it nuzzled into his lap.

"Ah, it was that idiot Twiffers. Yes, I can imagine he would find you very threatening. It is nice to hear from you, but I am sure you did not call just to tell me about your relocation. How can I help you?"

Richards listened, and a smile broke out on his face.

"Overthrow a revolution?

My, what fun! South Americans do it all the time, so I understand. But Ms Twop, it is a risky business overthrowing governments!"

There was a pause as Richards listened.

"Do I know how to start a revolution? It's not quite what the FCO[330] does or rather did, at least not officially. Of course, we did have Six[331] and other "sneaky beaky[332]" types, but on the whole, we held embassy parties and promoted British trade interests."

There was another pause.

"Well, yes, I might be able to tell you how, in theory. You need some key people.

Do I know such people? Ms Twop, this is hardly what one talks about over a public phone network."

Richards paused as his mind quickly thought about what he should do.

"Do you have a pen and paper? Good, then ring this number," he recited a long string of digits before continuing, "In," he checked his old Longines[333], "say 15 minutes?"

There were some more questions.

---

[330] The Foreign and Commonwealth Office.

[331] The Secret Intelligence Service (SIS) - otherwise known as MI6.

[332] The Increment was part of the SAS's Revolutionary Warfare Wing (RWW). It has been renamed E Squadron and is responsible for covert (deniable) intelligence and direct action against hostile targets.

[333] A white-faced, gold-filled (plated), 1970s Longines, conquest automatic, worn on a plain, brown leather strap.

"No, you are correct. It's not my normal number. It's a burner. Might I suggest you use whatever fancy security you have? Talk costs lives and all that."

One thousand three hundred miles South-East from where Richards was hanging up his old Bakelite phone, a rather shoddily dressed man with a bruised face, black eyes and blood-stained clothing was withdrawing the maximum[334] permitted amount of USD from one of Montenegro's few Bitcoin ATMs.

After escaping from the Podgorica central police station, Stewart used the Police Superintendent's iPhone to locate the nearest Bitcoin ATM[335] that dispensed foreign currency. After Cortez introduced the Crypto-Mark as a replacement currency for the Euro, the US Dollar became the de facto currency in the grey and black markets throughout New Europa. One emporium showing flexibility towards purchases that avoided the Cortez Crypto-Mark was the World Wines Shop in Podgorica. Having spent some years working in the region, first as a UN Peacekeeper and later in a semi-private capacity, hunting down the war criminals responsible for the numerous atrocities that had taken place during the Yugoslavian civil war, Stewart was familiar with Montenegro, its people, and its languages.

After withdrawing ten thousand USD[336], Stewart purchased one bottle of Glenfiddich and six bottles of Spirytus

---

[334] Ten thousand dollars.
[335] Run by BitCoinPay Trade.
[336] In a mix of twenties and one hundred dollar bills.

Rektyfikowany[337] vodka.   He bought a new Google Pixel phone in the nearby City Mall and several Telenor Montenegro prepaid tourist mobile sim cards.   Sitting in the appropriately named "Macchiato" cafe, he consumed a toasted cheese sandwich. At the same time, he used the complimentary wifi to set up his new phone with a Bitcoin wallet, which he then filled by transferring the funds remaining in the Police Superintendent's own Bitcoin wallet on the iPhone. Before returning to the VW camper, Stewart stopped in the city centre at New Yorker, a German clothing franchise, where he brought replacement clothes for the torn and blood-stained outfit he was currently wearing. The styles and brands were undoubtedly not what Stewart would typically consider wearing. Still, the black Calvin Klein cotton T-shirt, brown GANT leather bomber jacket, Levi 501s, Jockey underwear, unbranded black cotton socks and tan leather Docker boots were less conspicuous than the arterial blood spatter covering his fleece, polo shirt and chinos.

Once back in the VW, which still smelt of high-end French women's perfume and strong black coffee, Stewart delayed changing clothing. Instead, he checked Google Maps and drove South to the nearby "EKO Dahna" petrol station. He filled the camper's tank with petrol, purchased driving maps for Albania and Greece, and a large blue inflatable dinghy with a compressed air cylinder for rapid inflation. He paid for all these items in USD with a very generous tip. Once in conversation with the garage owner, the Scotsman asked for directions to the E762 road to Tirana in Albania and then onwards to Ioannina in Greece. Thanking the owner, Stewart headed South as though following the garage owner's directions.

---

[337] Spirytus Rektyfikowany is the strongest commercially-available alcohol in the world. It is distilled by the Polish Distillery, Spirytus. This vodka is 192 Proof or 96% ABV.

Some four miles further down the Southern route, Stewart pulled over into a sizeable unpaved layby occupied by numerous large trucks and some cars. He rapidly changed into his new, clean clothes before walking to a small, dirty, grey fibreglass stall serving food for travellers. The Scotsman made a point of engaging the cafe owner with questions about the route to Greece while he purchased a large coffee. Stewart made a point of paying in US dollars and including a substantial tip so he would be recalled as a highlight of the day. In the VW, he made two calls on his new Google phone. The first was to a number he had to read from a badly creased business card that he retrieved from his blood-spattered chinos, and the second call was to a number he had memorised decades before. Both calls were in English and lasted less than two minutes.

After hanging up, Stewart sipped his takeaway coffee and used his new Google Pixel to identify various shops, cafes and garages along the route to Ioannina in Greece. He rang each in turn and asked the staff to look for an item, such as a baseball cap, wallet or pen, which he claimed he had left at the location during a long fictitious journey South. The Scotsman gave each shop owner a detailed description of himself and his VW van and offered the superintendent's iPhone number as a contact. Stewart promised a hundred-dollar reward for the lost item, anticipating that the promise of compensation would make him more memorable. When questioned later, the shop owners would provide Stewart's description to any investigator tracing his route South.

As the Scotsman prepared to resume his journey, the Police Superintendent's iPhone rang. A deep male voice with a slight Spanish accent demanded,

"Where is my death picture of that damned Scotsman? Don't disappoint me, or I will withhold your final payment!"

Stewart instantly recognised Cortez's voice. Quickly calculating that he should delay the Argentinian's discovery that the Scotsman had survived, he smiled mischievously before answering in broken English with a thick and exaggerated Serbian accent,

"Chief Superintendent can't come to phone. He in bathroom." and then hung up.

After ensuring the Superintendent's iPhone's GPS location tracking was on, he exited the VW van. Stewart looked around him. Parked in front of the small snack kiosk was a blue, four-axil Mercedes-Benz Arocs transport lorry with an Ekol Greece livery on its sides. The Scotsman knew this Greek transport company from when he served in the region. Stewart walked close to the truck's rear, wedged the Superintendent's iPhone under the side tarps on the vehicle, and returned to his VW camper, knowing that when his escape was traced, the iPhone GPS tracking would be in mainland Greece, on its way to Athens.

With his diversion plans completed, Stewart returned to the VW, used the pressurised gas to inflate the blue dingy, and strapped the large boat to his van's roof to obscure the distinctive shape of his vehicle from aerial surveillance. Although the Scotsman knew that Cortez was not actively searching for the camper van now, it was inevitable that the surveillance footage from passing drones and satellites would be systematically searched within a few hours.

He then turned around the old VW and headed North on the M18 road for the four hours it took to cover the one hundred and forty miles[338] to Sarajevo. As the Scotsman had anticipated, Cortez's revolution had caused the traditional

---

[338] The VW camper can complete 620 miles between refuelling stops.

Montenegrin border crossing point in Hum[339] to be unstaffed, allowing Stewart to pass into Bosnia and Herzegovina undetected.

The old VW van arrived in the ancient city in darkness, and Stewart noticed enormous changes from the massive reconstruction after the conflict. Still, he recognised the airport, the Miljacka river and the other old landmarks[340] from when he served during the infamous siege[341]. Eventually, he saw the signs for the embassy district on the right-hand side of the M18 highway that travels through the centre of Sarajevo. Passing the Swiss and Turkish Embassies, Stewart finally arrived in front of a distinctive four-storey modern building with concrete and glass cleverly formed into a gigantic S shape with windows.   A sign on the large blue plastic placard beside the building proclaimed this as the UN House and the World Health Organisation centre.   Stewart pulled into the parking area for nine cars in front of the UN building and waited. Moments later, a large silver Opel Omega flashed its lights once. In response, Stewart flashed his lights twice, and the old Opel pulled into the empty parking lot some distance from the VW.

Six people emerged from the large car and scanned the immediate area. All were over fifty and dressed casually. Two of the four men had short hair and long beards, while the other two were clean-shaven. One of the women wore a dark-coloured head scarf, while the other had short blonde hair. Before moving away from the Opel, one of the women used a smartphone to scan the sky above them, checking

---

[339] Near Foča.
[340] Such as the Cathedral Church of the Nativity of the Theotokos, Vijećnica, Sarajevo cable car, Latin Bridge, Sebilj and the Sacred Heart Cathedral.
[341] The longest siege in modern warfare, lasting from April 1992 to February 1996.

there were no drones or surveillance satellites above them. All six moved with grace and caution, speaking of experience with urban warfare's harsh realities.

When the six newcomers approached the VW, four guards in distinctive blue UN uniforms emerged from their sentry hut beside the UN building. The UN officers loudly demanded identification and the purpose of the Opel and VW camper parking outside the UN offices well after official closing time. One of the men from the Opel presented his identification and explained something that prompted the two guards to salute and return to their posts.   Stewart embraced all six arrivals, and the group crossed the street to the late-night restaurant called "The Place". One of the newcomers from the Opel was well known to the restaurant owner, and the group of former UN war crimes investigators were soon seated together on one of the outdoor tables facing the UN building. By the group's unanimous decision, Stewart sat at the head of the table. It was noticeable that the group had left one of the seats vacant.

Thirty mins later, a black Volvo with Israeli diplomatic plates drove into a parking space between the Opel and VW van. Two large men emerged from the front and scanned the immediate area before the rear door opened, and an imposing grey-haired figure climbed out and strode across the broad street towards the restaurant. In his right hand, Mark Katz carried a small leather bag. As the Israeli intelligence[342] Operational Chief approached, an evening

---

[342] Mossad (HaMossad leModiʿin uleTafkidim Meyuḥadim) - Institute for Intelligence and Special Operations is the national intelligence agency for the state of Israel. Unlike many other national intelligence agencies, it is exempt from the laws of the State of Israel, making it a classic 'deep state' operation, free from political oversight.

breeze caught the jacket of his grey silk middle eastern[343] cut suit, revealing a massive brushed titanium pistol[344] in an old leather quick-draw holster[345] under his left armpit.   Katz smiled when he saw Stewart, and after the Scotsman shook the Israeli's hand and made introductions to the others, they all sat to discuss the future.

Eight hundred and sixty miles to the North West from "The Place" restaurant in Sarajevo, where Stewart and his friends were discussing Cortez's New Republic, Cynthia Sinclair was standing nonchalantly between two UN guards in the Commandant's office of the ICC[346] UNDU[347]. Sinclair wore one of the "Hague Penitentiary" grey marl polyester jog suits provided on her arrival. In contrast, the UN guards and Commandant were all dressed in the grey-green trousers, jacket, dress shirt, tie, and beret of the Royal Netherlands Army service dress uniform.

Standing close beside the two men, the former head of the British SIS was acutely aware of the deep earthy scent associated with cannabis consumption. Evidently, discipline

----

[343] Slightly wider lapels and a more generous fit to the thighs and upper arms.

[344] The Desert Eagle, Mark XIX, with a six-inch barrel chambered for the .429 DE cartridge, designed specifically for the Desert Eagle. This is a modified .50 AE with a 25% increase in velocity and 45% increase of energy when compared to a standard 240-grain, .44 Magnum.

[345] A chamois leather "Berns Martin Triple-draw" holster.

[346] International Criminal Court.

[347] The United Nations Detention Unit (UNDU) is an UN-administered jail. It is part of the Hague Penitentiary Institution's Scheveningen location, more popularly known as Scheveningen Prison, in The Hague, Netherlands.

among the UN staff was somewhat lacking. That was good news. Negligent supervision and smoking recreational weed might help in any escape attempts.

Seated behind his desk in the small office with its blue and white themed decor beside the UN Flag, Kaptian De Jong was feeling deeply uncomfortable. The recent radical changes in Europe were impacting the once scrupulous criminal justice system of the Netherlands and, more specifically, the ICC trial of Sinclair and Curren.   Within the last six hours, De Jong had learnt of the incredible CCTV footage of terror mastermind Issac bin Abdul Issuin emerging from a bank in Geneva. This photograph utterly discredited the allegations against Tavish Stewart. As a consequence, the Interpol warrants for the Scotsman had been revoked. Under normal circumstances, this fact alone would have raised serious doubts about the validity of the charges against Curren and Sinclair.

However, these were not normal circumstances. Chairman Cortez was now the supreme authority for all branches of the Military, Civil Service and Police within New Europa. The head of Netherlands Military Police had just informed the ICC that Cortez had commanded that the televised public trial of Sinclair and Curren would proceed immediately, without a jury or the usual panel of senior judges. Instead, as supreme leader, Cortez would adjudicate the trial himself. The lack of preparation time necessitated that the two defendants could act as their own legal counsel or plead guilty.

De Jong had the unenviable task of informing Sinclair of this drastic change. Curren's vegetative state meant that at least she would be spared the stress of the show trial. The UN prison Commandant had initially refused to assist with such a blatant miscarriage of justice. However, he was told that if he refused, he would be imprisoned and tried for treason alongside Sinclair and Curren. With a young family to support, De Jong had no option but to go along with this charade, and he had summoned Sinclair to his office. Due to his deep embarrassment at betraying his principles, he avoided the prisoner's gaze and was as brief and formal as possible.

"Miss Sinclair," De Jong gestured for Sinclair to sit as he picked through some papers on his desk,

"I regret that your trial and that of Miss Curren has been unexpectedly brought forward. It is now scheduled for ten AM, the day after tomorrow. With your execution, if found guilty, to follow immediately."

If Sinclair was surprised, she gave no indication. Instead, she asked,

"When do I see my legal counsel? By law, I have that right. We will demand an extension to provide enough time to prepare a proper defence."

De Jong continued to avoid eye contact. Instead, he looked at the papers in his hands as though they were the most interesting documents he had ever seen. After a delay, he answered,

"Yes, Miss Sinclair, that would be true under normal circumstances. However, these are not normal circumstances. The new authorities have decreed that you and Miss Curren must plead guilty or represent yourselves."

So, that was the game, thought Sinclair—a Soviet-style show trial. After a moment's thought, she picked up on another anomaly.

"You only mentioned Helen and me. Will Tavish Stewart face trial alongside us? Surely a classic show trial needs its star attraction?"

De Jong nodded, and for the first time, he made eye contact with Sinclair. There were tears in his eyes.

"Yes. I believe that would have been Cortez's original desire."

Sinclair immediately realised that the Kaptain was not a fan of the new regime or this latest development.

"So, what of Stewart? I saw on the news yesterday that you were celebrating his capture."

"A case of mistaken identity. Some Roman Catholic priest was arrested in Stewart's place. He will be released tomorrow morning."

"Is this priest's name Thomas O'Neill by any chance?" asked Sinclair.

"Yes. Why do you know him?" asked De Jong.

Sinclair began smiling as she realised that Stewart was still at large. There was hope, after all! Sinclair's spirits began to pick up.

"May I see Father O'Neill? For my confession before facing execution?"

"Sadly, no. My instructions are to keep him separate from you and Curren. But I can provide an alternative priest if you wish?" answered the Commandant.

Sinclair decided to try and exploit the unease that was clear on the unit commander's face.

"Kaptain, is Helen Curren fit to stand trial? The last I heard on the news, she was in a semi-vegetative state. Surely, even the most zealous prosecutor will not press charges against someone unaware of their surroundings?"

De Jong agreed, saying, "Under normal circumstances, Curren would be deemed unfit to stand trial. However, under this new regime...." The Commandant shrugged.

An hour later, De Jong was in the high-risk observation cell occupied by Father Thomas O'Neill. O'Neil was seated on his iron framed bed while Commandant De Jong stood with his back to the large glass wall that permitted round-the-clock observation of high-risk prisoners from the blue and white walled corridor outside. The priest had been assigned to this cell when he was admitted to the prison because it was believed he was terror mastermind, Tavish Stewart. It was inappropriate now O'Neill's true identity had been revealed and Stewart had been exonerated. For that reason, the cell door was now permanently ajar. De Jong had his hands behind his back as he addressed the priest. The prison Commandant anticipated this would be a much easier conversation than he had just completed with Cynthia Sinclair.

"Father O'Neill, we deeply regret your wrongful arrest and incarceration. I am pleased to inform you that you will be released from the Hague Penitentiary at 9 am tomorrow. The International Criminal Court has arranged for a driver and car to take you to your home in Rome on your release."

De Jong pointed towards the neatly stacked pile of new clothes wrapped in cellophane and a white paper envelope on the guard's table outside O'Neill's cell.

"We have also provided civilian clothes, shoes and some travel funds to help recompense you for the inconvenience of your detainment here at the UNDU."

O'Neill smiled. "Thank you, Kaptain, your guards have treated me very well, and the nurses you have provided have been most helpful in my post-operative care. So I have no complaints."

De Jong was relieved and turned to go before remembering something.

"Oh yes. I almost forgot. Something came for you by express courier this afternoon. It was lucky that they caught you before you left."

The Commandant gestured to the guard in the corridor, who brought in a small black moleskin notebook and a plastic DHL Express wrapping.

"Sorry that prison protocols necessitated our opening it."

O'Neill looked carefully at the address and customs declarations on the DHL wrapper.

"Grindelwald in Switzerland?"

O'Neill assumed it was related to his recent exorcism work in Geneva. But, as he opened the small notebook, he saw a neat copperplate roundhand script that looked like a nineteenth-century school book, except the contents were not just exercises in repeating letter shapes. Instead, the notebook contained details about a location which O'Neill recognised as the Neolithic site in the Southeastern Anatolia Region of Turkey, called Göbekli Tepe.

"This is very odd," exclaimed O'Neill excitedly, "If these notes are true, then someone knows considerably more than the current leading authorities about the oldest site known to humanity."

O'Neill sat on his bed and began reading the book page by page.

De Jong smiled. "I am glad you have something of interest to compensate you for losing your liberty. Good night, Father." With that, the Commandant left.

PROFIT AND LOSS

"Where profit is, loss is hiding nearby." - Japanese Proverb

*Basement Multimedia Centre
8b Duke of York St,
St James's Square,
St. James's, London SW1Y 6JX
23:00 Hrs (GMT+1) 14th September, present-day*

Chairman Cortez looked around the brilliant space surrounding him. There were no ceilings or walls, just an endless expanse of white. The Argentinian wondered if this might be similar to the afterlife. Momentarily intrigued, he considered if he should ask one of the Meri-Isfet about the nature of the post-mortem consciousness, that is of course if any of the senior Isfet adepts remained. Cortez dismissed the numerous concerns that now arose when he considered the recent massive explosion at their base on lake Skadar. He quickly quietened his mind. When he had heard back from the search and rescue teams he had dispatched to Fortress Grmožur, he would consider how he would proceed. If the only magickal resource left to him was that incompetent oaf, USAF Chief Booker, who was currently lingering in a Cairo police cell, he would have to adapt his strategy to reduce his reliance on magick. For now, he had core business to attend to - the business that would determine the use for the hundreds of Cortez Care Camps created throughout his dominions.

To the Chairman's immediate left and right in this strange, endless space were his two grandsons, Corrado and Hartman. Both were squinting as their senses acclimated to the peculiar setting for this late-night meeting. There were no familiar smells, just the clean, antiseptic scent of fresh plastic, given off by the state-of-the-art virtual reality equipment required to participate in the conference and the faintest hum from the supporting electronics.

Directly in front of Cortez was a perfect representation of a large black round table with seats around its enormous circumference. The only thing wrong with the image was that the table's surface was too perfect, smooth, and round to be anything that could have ever existed in the real, imperfect world in which we live. At each point around this virtual space was the CEO of one of the world's leading multinational corporations. There were only two prerequisites for inclusion in tonight's meeting. The first was that company revenue exceeded one trillion USD a year. The second was that the CEO had an insatiable desire to increase that revenue, regardless of ethical or environmental considerations.

The leaders of the handful of the world's multi-trillion-dollar corporations were grouped separately, showing that even in an artificial reality, the self-proclaimed "Overlords" who controlled hedge funds, defence, high-end technology and global merchandising demonstrated their superiority. Predominately male and aged over forty, these eight multi-trillionaires held over 80% of the world's known[348] wealth. Each had a vision for global commercial domination, and a few even had private space programmes. These four "SpaceOverlords" competed with each other to provide national space agencies with rockets, satellites, space stations and interplanetary probes.

The other lesser CEOs around the table represented various industries, including power generation, fossil fuels, health care, pharmaceuticals, steel, cars and chemical engineering. Seated together in another separate grouping were the CEOs

---

[348] Excluding the wealth of Chairman Cortez and his Wolfsangel organisation.

from the luxury brands[349], whose trademarks and logos graced and, in cyberspace, often defined the lifestyles of the uber-rich and famous.

Even in a virtual setting, Cortez's avatar exuded his unique charisma, part charm, part style and an unspoken but implicit menace. It was a mark of his global reputation that he could bring this gathering together tonight.   His digital persona was dressed in a classic Savile Row blue pinstripe suit with a contrasting red bolo string tie and his signature silver Wolfsangel holder. In contrast, his grandsons wore virtual representations of the Hugo Boss FF uniforms but in the more sinister black form associated with the Knights of the Black Sun. After Cortez's revelation about New Europa's highest honour earlier in the day, social media had become obsessed with the status and desirability of admittance to this secretive organisation. Even the global elite gathered around this virtual table recognised that the distinctive black outfits denoted an unusual purity of line and extraordinary martial prowess. Each of the CEOs knew that such people made formidable opponents, as demonstrated by the humiliation of the invading Russian forces that afternoon.

The exact tally of troops and assets lost by the Russian military in their attempted invasion would probably never be publicly disclosed. Still, conservative estimates were that the Russians had lost over a million soldiers and over two-thirds of their aircraft, tanks and equipment. And all of this was seemingly achieved with minimal intervention from the military of the New Republic. Rumours abounded of some secret technology, and these rumours prompted many of those involved in the defence industries and the technology sector to attend tonight.   While these thoughts and speculations filled the invitees' minds, Cortez looked

---

[349] Clothing, watches, jewellery, pens, luggage, sportswear and shoes.

dispassionately at the figures gathered around the table before him.

Cortez's augmented digital perspective of the meeting was unique among tonight's participants and included the company logos above each CEO and their GSR[350], BPM[351] and BP[352] readings. The Argentinian looked around the room and pressed a small button within his glove to ring a digital representation of a short, shrill bell sound which drew everyone's attention. Cortez began, saying,

"Colleagues, thank you for taking the time to participate in this gathering. When I sent each of you the specialised equipment needed to participate in this evening's event, I was confident that you would exhibit the curiosity and initiative you have shown throughout your professional careers. I am happy to see that none of you have disappointed me.

I am sure by now you are wondering about the purpose of this meeting. Put succinctly, I wanted to offer you and your organisations the opportunity to participate in what will become the most significant transformation in commerce since the Industrial Revolution."

There were mixed reactions from the men and women gathered in the virtual meeting. All of them were used to the overselling techniques used by salespeople when pushing a

---

[350] Galvanic Skin Response (GSR) is the change in electrical resistance of the person's skin. Often associated with a physiological or psychological stress reaction.

[351] Beats per Minute (BPM) is the heart rate. An indication of the blood volume being pumped around the body. Often the heart rate increases in response to stressful stimuli, like meeting Chairman Cortez.

[352] The Blood Pressure (BP) is a measure of the force of circulating blood on the walls of the arteries. It varies according to stress, exercise, illness and time of day.

new product or technology. Still, Chairman Cortez's reputation and recent track record made many of the group give him the benefit of the doubt. Of course, some participants were more cynical and openly laughed at the bold statement. Cortez carefully noted which individuals exhibited these adverse reactions and clicked another concealed button within his glove. He released a rapid-acting, odourless, colourless form of the WB compound within the VR suits of these sceptical participants and simultaneously disconnected them from the meeting. Many of the remaining participants registered surprise as several meeting members abruptly disappeared. The virtual meeting software instantly compensated for these missing avatars, removing the vacated space, so within a millisecond, the meeting did not look substantially different. Cortez smiled, knowing that in various locations worldwide, the concentrated overdose of WB released in the disconnected VR suits would already be causing disorientation. A catatonic state of mental collapse would follow within seconds, leaving the CEO a mindless body, much like the current Pope and Helen Curren. The Argentinian continued, safe in this knowledge, that he was now only addressing individuals willing to consider his proposal.

"That's better; now we only have the truly committed among us."

There were a few nervous laughs from the group. Cortez continued.

"My friends, your profits depend on an endless quest for the cheapest sources for your labour and materials. For decades, unionisation, health and safety regulations, increasing living standards, long holidays, shorter working hours, and generous sickness and pension schemes have systematically drained the potential out of your businesses."

There were nods and sounds of agreement from the audience. Cortez continued.

"The ever-improving living standards in the developed nations have driven all of you to outsource increasing amounts of your production to the developing world. This outsourcing trend has left your businesses increasingly vulnerable to disruption from various threats, including transportation, weather and natural disasters. There is also the risk of reputational damage to your brands from journalists discovering the real working practices adopted in many of your outsourced operations."

To emphasise Cortez's point, the augmented reality in the participants' visors showed banner headlines in the media reporting child labour, sweatshop conditions, and the use of political prisoners in production facilities for some of the most expensive and respected brands gathered in the virtual meeting. There were more murmurs of agreement. Cortez continued.

In addition, ever-increasing transportation costs are killing many of your businesses, especially those of you who have to maintain the pretence of your product being produced by skilled artisans in European craft settings instead of the reality of child labour in Asia.

There is also the harsh reality that China and India do not have the same respect for Intellectual Property (IP) law as the US or New Europa. Outsourcing your production often results in your IP being stolen and used against you with replicas and rival products that undercut your prices by orders of magnitude."

Cortez looked pointedly at some of the CEOs of US technology brands, high-end Swiss watches, and haute couture houses. These CEOs nodded and adopted grim expressions.

The VR screens then switched to bar charts of the average living standards for many nations used for outsourcing production compared to those in the developed countries. These showed comparative spending and income declining in the US and New Europa while radically increasing in Asia - especially in the newly emerging wealthy classes. Cortez waited for the implications of these charts to sink into his audience before resuming.

"The global dominance enjoyed by the Western nations over the past four centuries is in its final stages."

Some Western members of the group raised their voices in protest, which starkly contrasted with the nods of agreement from the Asian CEOs. Cortez waved his virtual hand to show he recognised the disquiet before continuing. The following virtual slide listed the world's wealthiest individuals.

"The reality is that looking at where the world's wealth is accumulating shows a clear trend towards the regions the West has been funding for its outsourced production. Cortez looked towards those CEOs from the West. For all your protestations, the reality is that Asia is quickly changing from being your source of cheap production to becoming your biggest luxury goods market.

Why? Because when people become rich, they want to show their wealth to everyone around them. How do you prove your wealth? Displays of unnecessary opulence. As you know, this is the basis of the luxury goods market."

Images on the VR presentation showed the value of luxury goods being purchased in the former emerging economies compared to those in the West. Cortez let the realisation of the profound changes sink in before hitting his listeners with his crucial point.

"However, with the recent transformation of society in New Europa and our other dominions, we can use the new economic reality to our mutual advantage. It is this new reality that I wanted to discuss with you all tonight."

The VR presentation switched to showing a map of the major population centres within New Europa. The map showed the fifteen major European cities with more than one million people. Cortez Care Camps in London, Birmingham, Istanbul, Berlin, Madrid, Rome, Bucharest and Paris were shown as examples. Each was close to completion and housed over a million workers. Each camp included massive warehouses and production plants that could be outfitted for any production, from processing raw materials to assembling cars, clothes, extremely small-scale microprocessors[353], or other goods. Alongside each camp's production plants, enormous highways, airports and goods train facilities were being erected. The final images showed details of the large and highly diverse skill sets possessed by the populations in New Europa. Skill sets that enabled any kind of production or manufacturing.

There were gasps of amazement and admiration from many of the audience, followed by solid murmurs of approval.

Cortez proclaimed,

"Now you begin to see the potential. These will be the new centres of cheap labour and production to supply the aspiring rich in Asia."

The VR presentation showed images of fathers, wives, and children working on a production line, making what looked like designer phones with a prominent logo. Other pictures showed similar camps, warehouses, and factories in Africa, with examples in Cairo, Kinshasa, Lagos, Luanda, and

---

[353] 2-nanometer (nm) chips house 50 billion transistors. Each the size of five atoms, in a chip the size of a human fingernail.

Johannesburg, producing a wide range of items, including sports goods, clothing, gold, and diamonds.

Cortez beamed proudly as the next slide showed his organisation's sources of raw materials in the Americas with a mix of facilities in Buenos Aires, Rio de Janeiro, Santiago, Sao Paulo, Bogota, Lima, Caracas and Cartagena. These included open-cast mines and tree felling in the Amazon, bottom trawling, cyanide and dynamite Fishing in formerly protected waters and massive expansions of the oilsands extraction in Alberta, Canada.

Seeing the proposed use of these techniques, one of the CEOs asked about the anticipated protests from environmentalist groups. Cortez nodded.

"Our complete control of global social media means we will quickly identify and deal with the sources of such protests before they start. Combining social media manipulation with the powerful psychoactive WB drug being laced into the food consumed by our populations means sustained protests are very unlikely."

Another CEO asked,

"Chairman Cortez, having a docile and obedient population is all very fine, but what about wars? We need constant conflicts to maximise weapons sales, development and military investment. Previous administrations worked with us to ensure there were always new conflicts that required military intervention. Will you do the same?"

Cortez nodded. "You do not need to worry on that front. Our FF forces will be very demanding regarding new weapons technology to deal with opposing forces to our revolution. We anticipate considerable resistance from those nations who have rejected the widespread use of social media."

As his audience eagerly accepted his proposals, Cortez concluded his presentation.

"Our new social reality is refreshingly free from restrictive working conditions and safety regulations. This will radically reduce labour costs and increase productivity to unprecedented levels. In addition, our freedom from all planning and environmental considerations means we will reduce your costs. Removing the democratic process will mean increased stability—no more changes to policy due to a change of government. And you will get all this for a percentage of your annual revenues. The exact percentage will be reviewed at the end of each financial year, starting at an introductory level which will be decided by competitive bidding. Bids for each industry and location will commence at dawn tomorrow and close at six pm, New Britannia time."

One of the CEOs asked, "Chairman, I do not see any provision for farming or animal husbandry in your Care Camps. How are you going to feed these millions of workers?"

Cortez nodded. "It is a good question. We will adopt the same methods that have proven effective within commercial farming- namely, using Category 1[354] material. We estimate our new working practices will result in an eight per cent loss of the original workforce each year. In addition, we will systematically remove the elderly, injured and sick from our populations. Selective breeding programmes will then only permit reproduction in the most healthy and productive stock of workers. Selective education programmes will prepare the future generations of our workforce. Our estimates show this to be an entirely self-sustaining model. The meat, fat and bones from the non-productive workers

---

[354] Category 1 permits the entire bodies or parts of the dead of the same species to become the food supply.

will be processed with appropriate flavourings into the fast food most popular with each camp population."

The CEO, who had asked the food question, countered.

"Category 1 material? You are proposing to start organised cannibalism!"

Cortez smiled. "That is a very theatrical way of expressing it. If you think about it objectively, burying or burning the dead, sick and unproductive wastes valuable resources. You will find we are not a wasteful organisation."

There was a murmur around the assembled group. Cortez ignored the disquiet.

One of the billionaires saw another unique business opportunity, and interjected,

"Chairman Cortez, as you are aware, many of us," he gestured to the other SpaceOverlords sitting on either side of him, "offer space tourism for very select customers."

Cortez nodded. He was well aware of these exorbitantly expensive vanity flights.

The Space-Overlord continued, by saying, "We believe there would be considerable interest from many of our existing clients in visiting your camps, under safe controlled conditions, to see for themselves exactly how these new worker classes exist. Will you be open to such camp tourism?"

The Argentinian smiled benignly. "Of course. If any of you want to explore such possibilities then include them in your bids. We will consider any proposal, provided it does not interfere with the main focus of our plants.

Now, ladies and gentlemen, we will leave you to discuss our proposal with your respective company boards before we open the bidding process in twenty four hours' time for the initial five-year contracts. Details of the bidding process have been sent to your respective offices."

Twenty minutes later, Cortez and his two grandsons, Corrado and Hartman, were seated in the opulent brown leather of three high-backed Chesterfield chairs in the third-floor reception room within the brick-fronted Edwardian townhouse in Westminster. The clothes their avatars had worn in the virtual environment were almost identical to those they wore now as they relaxed. The white linen blinds had been drawn on St James Square for the night, and the only light came from a set of six real candles in a seventeenth-century gold leaf chandelier set in the classic white plaster ceiling. These lights cast dancing shadows over the oak flooring, highlighting van Gogh's Sunflowers which, along with other art treasures, had been removed from the British National Gallery and Government offices to grace Cortez's home. The atmosphere was filled with dark sweet smoke from the evening cigars[355] enjoyed by the three men before they retired for the night. The crackling of black birch logs in the ornate iron fireplace filled the room with an ambience that enhanced the flavours of hazelnuts, honey and cinnamon in the rich golden cognac[356] that half-filled the enormous bulb-shaped crystal glasses[357] held in the three men's hands. The only sound was the chiming of the gold

---

[355] Ashton Aged Maduro No. 20 is an aged and hand-blended selection of tobacco from Dominica wrapped in Connecticut broadleaf by Arturo Fuente.
[356] Courvoisier XO Royal Cognac is a blend of Fins Bois de Jarnac and Grande Champagne eaux-de-vie, matured for thirty years in Tronçais and Limousin oak casks.
[357] Lalique 100 Points Cognac Glass in Clear Crystal.

K.R.M. Morgan

1960s Patek Philippe Cartel Clock that hung on the wall, proclaiming two AM.

The three Argentinians reflected on their achievements that day while they waited for their final briefing before bed. Cortez broke the silence.

"If only your father and beloved grandfather could have seen our victory parade through London today. The capital that defied them during their lives."

Before Corrado and Hartman could reply, a very tired-looking Major General Smegget entered the room and addressed the three seated men. Standing beside Smegget were a Fire Marshal and a Medic, their characteristic uniforms showing their professions.

Before the Major General could say anything, Cortez interjected,

"Before you begin, Smegget,"

the Chairman gestured to the space by the door that used to be occupied by a Servitor.

"Find me a replacement attendant – the last one seems to have disappeared, lazy bastard.

Now, what news about the Untermensch[358]?"

Smegget consulted his iPad.

"Chairman, the Russian incursion was repelled. As far as we can determine, there were no survivors."

The older Argentinian nodded while the two grandsons exchanged self-satisfied grins.

---

358 Untermensch is a Nazi term for non-Aryan "inferior people" who were often referred to as "the masses from the East", that is Jews, Roma, and Slavs – including the Russians.

"Excellent. Any follow-up from that madman in Moscow?"

Smegget shook his head. "Not as yet, Chairman. Our monitoring of his intelligence network suggests that he is still trying to determine what weapons we used."

If Smegget was hoping for some explanation of the nature of the strange weapons used that afternoon on the Eastern borders, then he was to be disappointed.

Instead, Cortez took a deep drag on his Maduro No. 20 before asking,

"And what about the Americans?"

Smegget cleared his throat and looked towards the grandsons for a response. The Major General had not received any intelligence about the Presidential daily briefing, but he knew that Cortez had some inner source of information and influence.

Hartman responded to the implicit request from Smegget. "Grandfather, our two sources in the Presidential cabinet indicate he is as mystified by the weapons as the Russians."

Cortez thought for a moment and then issued instructions,

"If Wilson is not convinced to surrender by the demonstration of our technical superiority today, we must take further steps to make him more amenable. He is a family man. Have Madden[359] take his family into our tender care. That breaks the will of even the most resilient opposition. However, if he still proves obstinate after we have his family, then Madden has authorisation to terminate him so that Maskins[360] can assume Presidential Authority."

Hartman nodded.

---

[359] Director of US National Intelligence, Elaine Madden.
[360] US Secretary of Defence, Jane L. Maskins.

Cortez smiled as he relished his subtle but irresistible power to corrupt, coerce and remove all opposition and blew out a perfect dark smoke ring high into the room above his Chesterfield.

"Excellent. That frees us to focus on more important issues. What news is there from the recovery work at the Fortress? Did you find our order's sacred relics?"

Smegget reflected on the ruthless nature of his boss, asking first about historical relics, not the human beings who had lived and worked in the Skadar complex serving his interests. Smegget pushed his concerns to the back of his mind and turned to the Fire Marshal to respond. The Major General had already decided that he did not want to be the one to give bad news. Cortez's reputation for brutality even made the big fire marshal stammer.

"Umm. No, Chairman. The combustion heat and the explosion's pressure wave effectively burnt and pulverised everything inside the structure."

"The box did nothing to protect the flag and skull?" asked Cortez.

The Fire Marshal shook his head. "Our teams on the site searched thoroughly for the items you described but found nothing other than small fragments of carbon."

Cortez frowned. The destruction of the relics was a significant loss to the history of his organisation. Still, they had served their purpose in the infernal Ten Gates ceremony last night, so he would have to move on.

"Everything was destroyed? What of the emerald coloured cylinder[361] installed in the basement? That is supposed to be virtually indestructible. Surely that remains?"

The St Petersburg Wheel [362]was critical to the next stages of his plans for world domination. The Argentinian did not fully understand the magickal process involved- only that the wheel was needed to change fate in his favour.

The Fire Marshal winced as he anticipated the wrath of the Chairman when he heard the answer to his query.

"It remains, Chairman, but under the extraordinary heat, it fragmented into three separate pieces. The weight was such that we could not move any of the three sections."

"Scheisse!" exclaimed Cortez. That was the worst news he could hear. Still, maybe Regio or Ironheart could provide an alternative.

"What of The Seniors? The Cardinal and the Viking?"

The Fire Marshall and Smegget both turned to look at the Medic. She flushed and addressed Cortez,

---

[361] An antediluvian esoteric device that opens portals to previous existences and the remnants of their gods. The devices break apart our current reality by propagating massive disruptions to the space/time/consciousness field. Sometimes referenced as "galgalim" גַּלְגַּלִּים (spinning fiery wheels) in the Abrahamic religions. The Vedic occult sciences call them Vinaash ke pahiye (नवनाश के पनिये) – "wheels of destruction". Tibetan Esoteric Buddhists know them as Niṣēdhita mēśinaharu (ननषेनित मेनशनिरु) - "forbidden machines". while Western Occultists are more familiar with the term, Qliphothic Wheels (מילגלג םייתפילק).
[362] The St Petersburg Qliphothic wheel is also known within esoteric lore as the Trubka cylinder (wheel).

"Chairman, the intense heat reduced everyone and everything to cinders."

"So, no one survived at all?"

The Medic shifted awkwardly.

"The recovery teams at Fortress Grmožur found the remains of a group of what we estimate to be between six to seven human remains in the basement. Buried in the centre of these cremated husks, we found one very badly burnt body that was barely alive...."

Cortez became much more animated and interrupted the doctor,

"Male? Could it be Regio or Ironheart?"

The Medic shrugged. "Chairman, the body was so badly burnt we cannot tell the gender. There is no chance they will survive. It is a miracle that they are alive at all. It will be a merciful release for them when they die."

Cortez did not care about suffering. He had heard about the strange powers of these Senior Meri-Isfet adepts. He needed to get to them before they died and find out what could be done about the loss of the St Petersburg Wheel.

"So, they are alive. Where are they?"

The doctor looked shocked.

"Chairman, they may be dead right now. No one can survive the level of burns they have suffered."

"Pha!" Cortez exclaimed, "I want them moved to the best burns unit in New Europa immediately with the utmost speed."

The Argentinian looked at Smegget. "And arrange the fastest way for me to get to their bedside. I need to talk with them if there is even the smallest chance they can communicate."

Cortez looked around and, after seeing that everyone was still standing open-mouthed in shock at his demand, added forcefully,

"Now!"

Smegget, The Fire Marshall and the Medic suddenly came to life and hurried from the room.

WUNDERWAFFE

"When WWII ended, the Germans had several radical types of aircraft and guided missiles under development. The majority were in the most preliminary stages, but they were the only known craft that could even approach the performance of objects reported by UFO observers." - Captain Edward J. Ruppelt, Head of Project Blue Book[363]

Fort Liberty (formerly Fort Bragg)
Cumberland, North Carolina
USA

13:50 HRS (GMT-4), September 14, Present day

Wilson F. Jones raised his eyes in a silent apology to his wife as an unscheduled phone call interrupted one of those increasingly precious moments of semi-private time with his family. His wife, Samantha, a mousey-haired forty-six-year-old former Harvard Librarian with dark-rimmed glasses, smiled half-heartedly. She coaxed her two small children, a blonde-haired boy and a dark-haired girl, to continue eating a picnic lunch on a wooden trestle table beside a range of children's toys as Wilson walked away from his family.

The air was filled with aromas from the various meals and BBQs being prepared around the hundred-yard-long picnic area outside one of Fort Liberty's numerous double-storey residential lodges for officers attending special forces training. The picnic clearing was surrounded by mature Southern Magnolia trees with distinctive white flowers that

---

[363] Project Blue Book was one of the many United States Airforce investigations into Unidentified Flying Objects (UFOS). It ran from March 1952 to December 1969. To save yourself some time reading the hundreds of pages of the report, pretty much everything is declared to be swamp gas or the planet Venus.

filled the area with a lemon scent and mixed with the BBQ smoke. Hidden discreetly around the area's perimeter were numerous members of Jackson's security detail in pixelated uniforms who constantly scanned the surroundings for any threat. Their M27 rifles systematically covered every possible entry and exit point, and they exchanged radio messages through their throat microphones. The only exception was around the First Lady and her children. To soothe some ruffled egos amongst the Fort Liberty camp leadership, Army Rangers provided protection for the President's family.

During this thirty-minute break from the serious preparation work for the resumption of the POTUS emergency briefing, the Senior White House staff made the best of the fresh air by eating lunch al fresco. Staff from each respective division, Intelligence, Army, Navy, Air Force, and Marines, were gathered on tables and benches, enjoying light-hearted banter, ice-cold beer, and excellent food. It was noticeable that CIA Director Mark Pimms was missing.

"Gathering some documents," was all Pimms had said before heading away from the relaxed picnic scene. The CIA Director could be seen greeting two dark-suited men who arrived in a grey Bell 429 helicopter that landed in a nearby car park. The other two members of the "intelligence" community, Secretary of Defence Jane Maskins and Director of National Intelligence Elaine Madden, did not seem to notice the CIA director's absence; both were deeply engrossed in a conference call on their iPhones. Madden watched as Maskins addressed whoever was on the other end of the brand-new replacement top-of-the-range iPhone the Secretary of Defense had retrieved from her bag after the morning briefing ended.

"Hartman, understand we do not take orders from Wolfsangel, but given the uncertainty after the fortress explosion, we will work with you on this time-sensitive issue."

There was a pause as Maskins listened to whatever Hartman replied.

"Understood. If he refuses to surrender, we will take his family. And what if that fails to bring him to his senses?"

A cruel smile came over the Secretary of Defense's face as she listened intently to her phone.

"Excellent." Maskins reached over and squeezed the other woman's hand. "Elaine will make me an excellent first lady." The two women smiled at each other as they simultaneously terminated the call and resumed eating their avocado salad.

Meanwhile, Wilson continued his conversation on his old iPhone as he strode into a clearing to get the nearest he ever got to privacy. Four Marines emerged from the undergrowth and took up strategic posts around the POTUS. The female Marine amongst the four was conspicuous for not carrying an M27 rifle. Instead, she kept close to the Commander-in-Chief in case the aluminium attaché case handcuffed to her right arm was needed. Wilson looked enviously at his staff consuming their meals, then checked his Shinola watch for the third time in as many minutes and interrupted whoever had called him.

"Demetri, yes, I saw what happened. The whole world saw it."

There was a pause. Then Wilson resumed.

"No, we have no idea what technologies were used. Our best people are working on it."

Another pause while the Russian President continued his complaints.

"No. I do not think a joint first strike against New Europa is warranted at this stage. No, I am not surprised that President Zi Fing refused. For one thing, what if the combined three superpowers failed? We would show ourselves to be impotent against Cortez. At least for now, he must wonder what we could do, which may stop him from launching a first strike himself."

Another pause.

"No, Demetri, we are not allied with this Cortez fellow. Yes, I give you my best assurance that we are as in the dark as you are about what happened. Thank you, Demetri, and again, the United States commiserates with you over the losses."

Wilson hung up and walked back to his wife and family, thinking, as he did, that he could grab a ham sandwich before they resumed what promised to be a long meeting.

Thirty minutes later, the picnic was over, and the whole group were seated in basement meeting room 2B in the SWCS[364]. Jackson's men had swept the low-ceilinged room for bugs again. They searched the attendees before the group resumed the same seating positions around the long trestle table as they had during their morning briefing with the POTUS. The odour of bleach that had been so pervasive in the morning had subsided somewhat and was replaced by the smell of Joffrey's Coffee[365] and warm fresh cookies from the nearest of the five base cafeterias.

The sixty-five-year-old Wilson took a long sip of coffee from his "Best grandad in the world" mug and resumed the meeting. The POTUS had no time to change, so he still wore his grey marl Harvard Law School cotton jog suit but had rolled up the sleeves to compensate for the humidity outside.

---

[364] The John F. Kennedy Special Warfare Center and School or SWICK.
[365] Supplied on US bases.

"Welcome back, everyone; grab yourselves a coffee and a cookie. I think we are in for another long one.   Before I ask each of you for your team's insights, I want to update you on a phone call I received from the Russian President."

There were exclamations of surprise from the military heads, and everyone sat up with interest.   Even the ordinarily sanguine Mark Pimms looked intrigued. Wilson continued, saying,

"Zychopav[366] was his usual abrupt self-"

"Steroids will do that." commented Elaine Madden. If Wilson heard the remark, he ignored it and continued.

"He wanted to know what we know. I told him, quite honestly, we did not know anything. Although."

Wilson looked around the table.

"I sincerely hope that by the end of this meeting, we will have a clearer idea of what happened in Eastern Europe this morning and, more importantly, our options when facing Cortez's war machine."

There were nods of agreement from the heads of the armed forces and an "Agreed, Mr President." from the Air Force and Army generals. In contrast, Madden and Maskins made an exaggerated sigh, signalling that they at least did not view Cortez as a threat to the United States.

Wilson took a bite of his chocolate chip cookie and then looked to the respective heads of each division.

"You have all had time to reflect and research. First, what do you think we saw? Jane and Elaine, why don't you lead off?"

Maskins and Madden smiled at each other. Maskins then stroked the strange black onyx pendant around her neck,

---

[366] Demetri Zychopav, President of the Russian Federation.

made eye contact with each military head, and then at the President. At least two of the generals exhibited a flush of embarrassment. Wilson was unmoved.

Madden made a big show of gesturing for Maskins to talk.

"Mr President. I will speak for both of us. After considerable research and reflection, we are certain we witnessed advanced technologies that render our defensive and offensive capabilities impotent."

There was a huff of dismissal from Army General Orne.

Maskins reached for a pile of papers titled "Assessment: Unidentified Aerial Phenomena." The front of the nine-page document was decorated with the Office of the Director of National Intelligence (ODNI) logo. Secretary Maskins passed copies of the report around the table to the other participants. Most skimmed through pages full of pictures of strange shapes in the heads-up displays from fighter jets or strange disc and tube shapes floating above nuclear silos. The exception to the group reading the report was CIA Director Pimms, who placed his copy to his left side unread. Maskins smiled condescendingly at the CIA director before addressing the group.

"Here are copies of the report that Director Madden and I prepared in response to the demand from the Senate to investigate these phenomena. We believe that we all witnessed Unidentified Aeriel Phenomena (UAP) this morning. Phenomena that credible witnesses have recorded since the last century. Our own Military has been researching these UAPs for the past decade."

Maskins looked pointedly at Admiral Peter Lorance, who looked gravely at the President and nodded before Secretary Maskins continued, saying,

K.R.M. Morgan

"It is within the realm of possibility, Mr President, that Chairman Cortez's regime is linked with unknown superior beings, perhaps even of extra-terrestrial or interdimensional origin."

There was a burst of laughter from Army General Orne. CIA director Mark Pimms merely smiled. The other participants looked stunned, clearly not knowing what to make of the assertion.

Maskins waited for silence before she resumed.

"We therefore strongly recommend that we open negotiations with Chairman Cortez to establish terms for peace between the United States and New Europa."

"Surrender?" exclaimed Marine Corps General Louis Arnold. "We never surrender, Mr President. We should attack!"

There were exclamations of support for the Marine General's position from the Generals of the Army and Airforce. Maskins looked furious. She turned to General Arnold and demanded,

"So what do you think they are, Louis? Cream puffs?"

President Wilson coughed and said,

"Last time I checked, Madam Secretary, I ask the questions here."

Madden mumbled, "For the time being."

Wilson turned to Captain Jackson and stated quietly, "Captain, kindly have some of your officers escort Director Madden and Secretary Maskins outside. Their presence is no longer required."

Jackson gestured to two of his men who came and stood beside the two women.

Maskins looked at the POTUS.

"Seriously? You are going to throw us out just for providing a summary of a detailed report on UAPs, which was, I will add, accepted by the Senate only a few weeks ago."

"It's your attitudes I can do without, Madam Secretary and Madam Director. Now kindly leave before I have these Marines frogmarch you to the camp guardhouse."

"We are going," the two women rose, and as they walked to the door, Maskins said, "You will regret this, Mr President."

"Maybe," said Wilson, "but right now, it is the right decision. Jackson, have your men keep an eye on these ladies; I will want to speak with each of them separately after this meeting concludes."

The blond-haired Marine Captain smiled and said, "Yes, Mr President."

Wilson then returned his attention to the heads of the Military.

"Now, gentlemen, let's hear what you all made of this morning's destruction of the Russian forces."

Army General Orne looked at the other three heads of the respective branches of the United States military, who nodded. Orne stood and addressed the POTUS,

"Mr President, we four have discussed what we saw, and frankly, we have no idea how the Russian forces were destroyed, but we all agree that we should take the initiative. With your permission, we will each summarise our proposed responses."

Wilson nodded. "Proceed, Jim."

General Orne remained standing. "Thank you, Mr President. We should initiate a first strike and remove the European and Argentinian sites that we know are Cortez's operation centres." Having said his piece, Orne returned to his seat.

Admiral Lorance then stood and addressed the POTUS,

"Mr President, we should send SEAL teams to assassinate the New Republic's leadership to destabilise the new regime."

Lorance sat while Air Force General Smith stood and addressed the group,

"Mr President, we should utilise our air supremacy and attack Russia while she is weakened. After neutralising the Russian threat that has dogged our nation for over seventy years, we can worry about Cortez."

Smith sat. There was a moment's silence, and then President Wilson looked to Marine Corps General Arnold.

"Louis?"

Marine General Arnold stood and addressed the President,

"Mr President, the Marine Corps stands ready to deploy to the rebellious states in our nation to restore civil order, with or without the assistance of the National Guard."

Wilson smiled at the loyalty of his military heads. Wilson then turned to the CIA director.

"Mark. Your turn. What is the CIA's analysis of what happened this morning?"

Pimms remained seated and replied,

"Mr President, what we have seen is classic intimidation[367]. A standard play to establish rapid dominance as we did in the two Gulf conflicts. It should not make us respond with either of the two extremes of surrender or attack."

---

[367] "The five basic military strategies are extermination, exhaustion, annihilation, intimidation and subversion" Bowdish, Randall Gregory. 2013. "Military Strategy: Theory and Concepts." Ph.D. University of Nebraska.

Wilson nodded his agreement to the assessment and stated, "Shock and Awe[368]."

"Yes, Mr President."

Army General Orne looked to his fellow military heads and stood after getting nods of approval.

"Mr President. We concur with Director Pimms' assessment. If you give us the funding, we can rapidly complete the development of our own super weapons that will give our beloved nation the best chance of defeating whatever these weapons are, regardless of where they come from."

Orne picked up a handwritten list in blue ink that had been scribbled onto the back of a white envelope with a United States Army logo on the front.

"With your permission, Mr President?"

Wilson nodded, and Orne read from the back of the envelope.

"Mr President, we believe that with emergency funding within six months, we could deploy weapons-grade lasers on our existing fighters. These would enable the Air Force to engage with these UAPS or whatever they are. We can also complete the development of the hypersonic drone program that could defend our ground troops and begin the deployment of drone ships for the Navy that are silent enough to track any water-based targets regardless of their technology. Finally, the Army needs the completion of the

---

[368] "Shock and Awe" also called "Rapid Dominance" uses displays of overwhelming power to distort an enemy's accurate perception of a battlefield and sap their will to fight. First proposed by Harlan Ullman and James Wade in 1996. It was adopted by the US Military after further development by the National Defense University of the United States.

smart bullet and smart armour programs that will equip our troops to match any ground-based forces."

Army General Orne sat, and everyone looked expectantly at the POTUS.

Mark Pimms coughed. "Mr President, these new weapons may not help us deal with the technologies we saw deployed by The New Republic this morning. Their EMP features will destroy modern smart technology instantly."

Wilson looked at the CIA Director.

"Come on, Mark, if you know what these mysterious UAPs are, we need to know."

There were sounds of solid agreement from the heads of the Military.

Navy Admiral Lorance, who had once been so sceptical[369] of the abilities of secret Cold War weapons held in reserve by the CIA since the 1980s, chided Pimms,

"Some more Level Seven[370] secret tech from the Regan and Gorbachev era? Come on, Mark. You already cleared us for Seven Level materials."

Pimms looked to the President. Wilson waved his hands expansively to give permission and stated,

"I agree with Peter. Everyone here already has Seven clearances, so let's have it. God knows we need this information."

Pimms nodded, saying, "Gentlemen, you have now all been authorised for level Ten materials."

---

[369] See the Bridge of Souls story for complete details.
[370] Officially, there are only five levels of secret materials in the United States government. Unofficially, there are obviously more.

There was a murmur of surprise from the heads of the Military, and Wilson raised his eyebrows as the CIA Director reached into the leather briefcase at his feet. He pulled out a large dust-covered folder and passed it to the POTUS.

Wilson scrutinised the outer folder while the Military leaders looked towards the head of the table with excitement. Pimms motioned towards Captain Jackson and whispered something to the Marine. Jackson nodded, and moments later, two old-fashioned 35mm reel film projectors were wheeled into the extended classroom and set up on either side of the table beside where the POTUS was seated. Simultaneously a large screen was set up at the far end of the room.

"Cold war secrets, Mr President?" queried General Orne with a knowing smile.

Wilson's face looked confused and surprised as he looked closer at the folder before he answered his Army general,

"Older Jim. Much older. They look like Project Files."

The President opened the folder and removed crumpled and worn manila envelopes. Each was covered in numerous different seals, signatures and dates indicating when they had been accessed. Many of the dates were over seventy years old.

Wilson picked up the first folder and stumbled over the German pronunciation of "Sonnengewehr", which was written in bold red capital letters on the front of the manila file.

Pimms quickly came to the President's aid.

"The English translation is "Sun-Gun", Mr President. It was a large parabolic mirror in earth orbit, designed to focus sunlight onto enemy targets to incinerate them."

"You mean, like a cruel child with a magnifying glass does with insects?" asked Wilson, before he took a deep breath and asked, "Is this what destroyed the Russian land forces?"

"No, Mr President," Pimms replied, "I believe the weapon that destroyed the Russian tanks and men this morning was something called "der Donnerkeil" or "The Thunderbolt." It is described in considerable technical detail in the green folder that contains what we learnt from recovered materials and the interrogation of former S.S. scientists in Operation Paperclip at the war's end."

Wilson leafed through the files and picked up the green one while Pimms continued, stating,

"Put simply, the Germans used balloons to get thousands of small heavy objects into a low Earth orbit, then used small thrusters to manoeuvre the payload over the enemy and release the objects. Newton's laws of motion[371] took care of the rest. The Germans experimented using rocks, and ball bearings before settling on long aerodynamic metal[372] spikes. From what we learnt, it proved a cheap method of deploying devastating force without the need for traditional munitions, which were in short supply in Germany by the war's end."

---

[371] The mass of the falling object, the drag coefficient, projected area, air density and gravitational acceleration. So, for a 20-pound arrow shaped projectile, with a 4-inch diameter, a drag coefficient of 0.294, air density of 0.0764 per pound/cubic foot and standard gravity (1 G), the terminal velocity of the object would be close to 1,000 mph. This single object travelling at 1,000 mph would produce kinetic energy of over 650,000 ft-lbs on impact. A rain of thousands of such objects would spoil your whole day.
[372] Made of depleted uranium or tungsten carbide, probably.

"Ingenious, in a very sinister manner," said Orne as he recalled the almost silent and instantaneous way the Russian land forces were despatched earlier in the day.

"Based on how those falling objects went through those heavily armoured tanks, they have evolved the technology considerably," remarked Marine General Arnold.

Pimms nodded. "We must anticipate that the weapons described in these files have seen considerable research and development over the past seventy years."

The President had picked up another of the files with a faded red cover and large black text. He looked towards Pimms and asked,

"Die Glocke?"

Pimms smiled.

"The Bell, Mr President. We know very little about it, and what we do know is, frankly, garbled supernatural nonsense. The recovered documents and S.S. interrogations read like something from a K.R.M. Morgan novel. We have dismissed "The Bell" as a Nazi misinformation campaign along with the "Schwarze Sonne" or "Black Sun", which was an alleged doomsday weapon that used fusion to create an artificial supernova that would destroy the entire planet. Even if the Black Sun weapon existed, no one would be crazy enough to use it. If I might suggest, we should focus on the remaining thick manila folder." Pimms gestured to the last of the folders that had come out of the envelope.

Wilson reached for what was the thickest of the old manila containers. The cover was smothered with official-looking stamps, seals and signatures, including the Lion and

K.R.M. Morgan

Unicorn[373], a large G.R.[374], and the seal of the President of the United States. The signatures beneath these seals were Winston Churchill[375], Franklin Roosevelt[376] and General Dwight Eisenhower[377].

It was dated December 13 1943 and had the title.

"Kraut fireballs" A/ka "Foo Fighters"

besides these typed titles, handwritten text was noted as having been added in Sept 1946.

"Projizierter Feuerbal[378]"

Beneath this was written in large red print the text.

RESTRICTED DATA[379] / ABOVE TOP SECRET[380]

EYES ONLY.

NOT FOR RELEASE.

REVIEW ONLY AFTER FORTY-FIVE YEARS[381].

---

[373] The Churchill War Ministry.
[374] George Rex (GR). George VI. King of The United Kingdom, the Dominions of the British Commonwealth and Emperor of India.
[375] Sir Winston Leonard Spencer Churchill was Prime Minister of the United Kingdom (1940 to 1945).
[376] Franklin Delano Roosevelt (FDR) - 32nd President of the United States from 1933 - 1945.
[377] Dwight David "Ike" Eisenhower - Supreme Commander of the Allied Expeditionary Force in Europe and five-star General of the US Army.
[378] Projected Fireball.
[379] The most stringently protected category of classified information in the United States.
[380] The highest war time security classification for the British war office.
[381] Winston Churchill was reportedly so concerned about war time encounters with UFOs and RAF bombers, that he ordered the incidents to remain secret for forty-five years to avoid mass panic.

Under that was the single title, "Addendums".

Addendum ONE: Paperclip and T-Force[382] 1946 debriefings of Sicherheitsdienst des Reichsführers-SS[383] officers. Added September 18, 1946. Signed by General Hoyt Vandenberg[384] and Major General Sir Stewart Graham Menzies[385]

Addendum TWO: Debris analysis July 8, 1947, Roswell Army Air Field. Added July 9, 1947. Signed Harry S. Truman[386], General Hoyt Vandenberg and John Edgar Hoover[387]

Beneath this were two short handwritten entries.

The first entry, dated November 20 1963, was an executive order by John Fitzgerald Kennedy[388] to "Permit urgent public disclosure of the nature of the flying discs being reported by the citizens of the United States". This entry was written in the highly distinctive blue ink[389] favoured by JFK.

The second entry was handwritten in black ink and dated November 22 1963. "Authorised SAD[390] for termination

---

[382] US Operation Paperclip and the British Operation T-Force (1945-1959) were the attempts by the Western Allies to gather the technology and secrets of the NAZIS at the end of World War Two.
[383] Sicherheitsdienst des Reichsführers-SS (Security Service of the Reichsführer-SS) or SD was the intelligence agency of the SS.
[384] Director of Central Intelligence (1946-47).
[385] Chief of MI6, the British Secret Intelligence Service (SIS) (1939-52).
[386] Harry S. Truman - 33rd president of the United States (1945-53).
[387] John Edgar Hoover - Director of the Federal Bureau of Investigation (FBI) (1924-72).
[388] 35th president of the United States (1961-63).
[389] Navy Blue ink from Mont Blanc.
[390] Special Activities Division (SAD) is the CIA's covert special operations team for deniable projects. Its operatives are called POOs (Paramilitary Operations Officers).

sanction at Parkland Health, Dallas". Signed by John Alexander McCone[391] and John Edgar Hoover.

Beneath these handwritten notes was the printed text

45-Year Security Review.

December 20 1986. Signed Ronald Reagan[392] and Margaret Thatcher[393]

VERDICT: CONTINUE RESTRICTION.

"Jesus, it's like a Who's Who of the last century!" exclaimed the POTUS. Wilson looked again at the entries for 1963, and his face went white. He looked at Pimms.

Pimms said nothing, merely nodding before adding, "Don't rock the boat, Mr President."

Wilson took a deep breath, tore apart the numerous red seals on the folder, and pulled out a number of sheets of brown paper of different sizes.

The President turned to Pimms, saying,

"Mark, please brief us."

Pimms nodded to Jackson, and the lights were dimmed. Seconds later, the first of the two ancient 35mm film projectors started. The clicking-clattering sound of the machine feeding through the film's sprockets filled the silent expectation that permeated the room as a bright light pierced the darkness like a searchlight.

The first images were of the classic counting clock, followed by a British War Office notice declaring the materials "ABOVE TOP SECRET". Pimms narrated,

---

[391] Director of Central Intelligence (1961-65).
[392] 40th President of the United States (1981-89).
[393] British Prime Minister (1979–90).

"The footage we are viewing, gentlemen, was taken using a hand-wound De Vry Standard[394] camera fitted into an Avro Lancaster[395] flying in close formation at 15,000 feet with a speed of 270 mph over Northern France at 03:00 HRS on Friday, September 17 1943."

The film focused on one of the other six bombers in the formation and showed a series of orbs of light coming alongside the bombers. These strange objects matched the bomber's course and speed with absolute accuracy.

"It's one of the UAPs!" exclaimed Airforce General Smith.

"Back then, they called them Foo Fighters," stated Pimms. "As allied bombing started in earnest, the RAF aircrews started reporting these strange lights flying beside and sometimes in front of their aircraft."

"Did they know what they were?" queried Wilson.

"Not at the time of this footage, Mr President."

The clip of the RAF encounter ended, and after some seconds of blank white screen, different footage followed. This film was smoother and had a better resolution.

Pimms resumed his narration, saying,

"This next sequence is from a U.S. Army Air Forces bombing strike against Nazi-occupied Europe on Wednesday, December 1, 1943, at 15:45 HRS. The footage was recorded

---

[394] The De Vry Standard was an all-metal hand wound newsreel cine camera. It used 33mm x 100ft film spools.
[395] The Avro Lancaster was a four engine British Second World War heavy bomber capable of carrying 14,000 pounds of bombs with a range of 2500 miles. Later versions carried the Dam Busting bouncing bombs, the 12,000 lb "Tallboy" and the 22,000 lb Grand Slam earthquake bomb. It carried seven crew.

using a Cunningham Combat Camera[396] carried on one of the aircraft and shows a formation of three Flying Fortresses[397]."

The footage was similar to the earlier clip, except it was taken during the day and showed Northern Europe's slate-grey winter skies. The B17s in the footage suddenly had mysterious light orbs appear beside them. Almost immediately, the U.S. plane opened fire on the spheres. Tracer rounds showed the devastating firepower of the U.S. aircraft.

"Atta boy!" exclaimed Airforce General Smith, "The B17 had .50 calibre Browning's. That should tear those orbs to pieces."

The grainy film showed direct hit after direct hit but without any noticeable effect on the orbs.

"Jeezus. What are those things?" pondered General Orne.

"We will come to that shortly," replied Pimms.

After some seconds of the B17's Browning machine guns blasting the orbs, four mysterious lights merged into the aircraft's engines. Moments later, the aircraft could be seen descending in a nose dive rapidly down towards the green fields beneath them[398]. The film abruptly cut back to the blank white screen.

"Did they survive?" asked Wilson.

---

[396] A magnesium-cased 35mm combat camera that served US forces in recording WW2.

[397] The Boeing B-17 Flying Fortress was a four engine US Second World War heavy bomber that could carry 6000 pounds of bombs with a range of 2000 miles. It carried ten crew.

[398] For further details on "Foo Fighters" inflicting damage on Allied aircraft see Chester, Keith (2007), Strange Company: Military Encounters with UFOs in WWII, Anomalist, ISBN 978-1-933665-20-7.

"Yes, but unfortunately, the crew were immediately captured by the S.S. who were waiting beneath them."

"Almost like the bastards knew where it would happen," pondered Wilson.

"Keep watching, Mr President," responded Pimms.

After a few seconds of blank white screen, the wartime footage resumed. This time, it was a much grainer image that shook, sometimes quite violently. The opening seconds showed a group of six Lancaster bombers a considerable distance beneath the camera. The footage panned up and showed a grey-coloured two-engine aircraft with enormous wings.

Pimms narrated, saying, "We are seeing British footage from Sunday, May 28 1944. A modified RAF Spitfire Mk 19[399] followed up on reports made by airmen who described an aircraft "high above them" on clear days" whenever the Foo Fighters appeared alongside them. The RAF responded by sending a highly modified reconnaissance Spit that could reach above 50,000 feet. Remember, gentlemen, the typical ceiling for most of our bombers was 20,000 feet."

The footage came closer and closer to the mysterious shape as the Spitfire climbed at what must have been an extraordinary rate of ascent.

"That's some kind of plane," remarked Airforce General Smith with respect.

The footage now showed the mysterious aircraft in much better detail. One could see it was a bomber with two

---

[399] The Spitfire Mk19 was the highest altitude aircraft during WW2 capable of reaching a height of 51,155 ft. This aircraft was also the fastest piston driven aircraft when it achieved Mach 0.96 (680 mph), and would probably have broken the sound barrier had the pilot not suffered from severe oxygen deprivation.

enormous wings, each with a single engine. There must have been a third engine inside the fuselage from the exhaust plumes.

Pimms commented, "This is a modified Henschel Hs 130[400]. It was an experimental German high-altitude reconnaissance aircraft. The third engine provided a supercharged air supply to keep the two external engines running."

The camera switched momentarily from the aircraft to show the Spitfire's altimeter, which read just under 50,000 feet. The footage then returned to the Henschel. A dark cloud obscured the sun, and for the first time, it was evident that two thin beams of light projected from either end of the German aircraft down towards the Lancaster bomber far below.

"Good God!" exclaimed Airforce General Smith, "The UAPs are the result of two intersecting projected beams. No wonder no one can catch them or shoot them down."

"But how does it cause the target aircraft to crash, Mark?" queried the President.

"For the entire duration of the war, our best brains could not figure that out, Mr President.

At the end of the war, we seized several partially burnt documents from the Fuhrer Bunker and interrogated a number of senior S.S. intelligence officers."

Pimms turned off the first film projector and played the reel on the second one. The screen was first blank and then, after a British War Ministry "Above Top Secret", a date of September 15, 1946, the title "T-Force debriefings of

---

[400] The Henschel Hs 130 had a maximum speed of 380 mph, a range of 1,861 miles and a service ceiling of 49,500 ft.

Sicherheitsdienst des Reichsführers-SS officers" and a signature of Stewart Graham Menzies.

The film cut to gloomy black-and-white coverage of a dark interrogation cell with a single bulb hanging over a metal table. Smartly dressed men in broad-lapelled suits sat on one side of the table while a tired, dirty-looking man chain-smoked on the other. In the centre of the table was an old-fashioned microphone connected to a huge reel-to-reel tape deck[401].

Pimms narrated, saying, "It was at these debriefings that we learnt the project's real name, "Projizierter Feuerball" or Projected Fireball. However, the details of the technology still eluded us. None of the scientists we captured had worked on the project, so they only knew it was some energy projection weapon. The entire project team and facilities for this particular weapon had been exfiltrated out of Europe before the German surrender."

Pimms paused to take a sip of coffee and then resumed. By now, the interrogation footage had switched to images of partially burnt schematic plans showing tantalising pictures of intersecting beams projected from multiple sources, sometimes two, but more often three or four. These early prototype projectors were shown mounted on trucks, ships and even railways.

The screen went blank for a second, and then a second spliced film reel started. Pimms continued his narration.

"Two years after these findings, we had a stroke of luck, although it did not seem like it then. On the night of June 13, 1947, one of our Project Mogul high altitude spy balloons

---

[401] The allies acquired the first reel to reel tape recorders from the Germans at the end of the war in 1945.

collided with an unknown aircraft over the New Mexico desert near the small town of Roswell."

There were some laughs from the Military leadership, who had already guessed what had happened on that fateful night. Pimms continued, saying,

"Intelligence staff from the nearby Roswell Army Airfield's 509th Composite Group collected the crash debris and found, mixed in with the balloon debris, were sections from a large aircraft."

By now, the film had resumed, and after the opening of U.S. Army Restricted notices, dates and location details, the footage showed the crash recovery. Army personnel could be seen cataloguing items before loading them into large U.S. Army trucks. Among the balloon debris were wing, tail and fuselage sections from a military aircraft. A close-up of the aircraft tail displayed a highly recognisable logo.

"Isn't that Cortez's symbol?" asked General Orne.

Pimms nodded. "The Wolfsangel was used by the inner members of Hitler's circle long before the Swastika."

Wilson laughed. "No wonder they hushed this up. Two years after telling Joe Public we had conquered the Nazis, the bastards fly aircraft over our airfields. There would have been riots."

The film switched to interior footage inside a large aircraft hangar. The recovered sections of the aircraft had been laid out in a reconstruction of the plane's shape.

"Don't tell me. It's a Henschel Hs 130," stated Wilson.

"Indeed, it is, Mr President," replied Pimms before he elaborated, "Sadly, the impact caused considerable damage to the aircraft, and the resulting fires destroyed most of the equipment, including the mechanism of the two large directional beams attached to the underside of the aircraft."

"So, we have no idea of what they are?" asked Wilson.

"Beyond confirming that they were some forms of particle beam that cause the manifestation of large light phenomena and EMP, we have no clear idea of their exact construction. A few years later, scientists at Lawrence Livermore[402] did find strong similarities between these recovered Roswell devices and the designs in notebooks of Nikola Tesla[403] recovered by the CIA after Tesla's death."

The projector spool abruptly ended, and Pimms called for the lights to resume.

There was silence for some time before the President eventually talked,

"Thank you, Mark," Wilson then turned to the Generals and Admiral.

"Right, now we know what we are facing, I want each of you to prepare your respective forces, so we can be prepared to counter this technology."

Wilson concluded by turning to Pimms. "Mark, disable social media. Claim it's a network outage. And announce that I will address the nation this evening at 6 pm EST."

Wilson stood. But before he could leave the room, an Army Ranger rushed in and conferred with Captain Jackson. Jackson approached Wilson and said,

---

[402] Lawrence Livermore National Laboratory.
[403] Nikola Tesla (1856-1943) was an inventor and engineer who discovered and patented the rotating magnetic field and alternating current that is the basis of modern electricity supplies. He also claimed to have developed a method to transfer and project almost limitless energy without wires or traditional conductors.

K.R.M. Morgan

"Mr President, I have just been informed that your wife and children have been taken. The six Rangers who were providing protection are all missing."

SUDDEN IMPACT

"If someone puts their hands on you make sure they never put their hands on anybody else again." Malcolm X

The ICC Detention Centre
Scheveningen Prison
Scheveningen 32 (entrance)
Pompstationsweg 32,
2597 JW Den Haag, Netherlands

09.30 am (GMT+2), 15th September, Present Day

The clear blue skies and summer temperatures that had favoured Northern Europe had given way to gun-metal grey clouds this morning. A sharp South Westerly wind from the North Sea exacerbated the distinct chill that filled the air. Occasional gusts brought a fine drizzle, making the lives of the numerous cyclists that filled the roads and cycle paths around The Hague miserable. But none of this mattered to Father Thomas O'Neill as he strode happily along the corridors of Scheveningen Prison, escorted by two UN guards dressed in their smart Royal Dutch army uniforms. In contrast, O'Neill had been provided with a sombre-looking black polyester off-the-peg suit[404], black leather oxford-style shoes[405] and, at his request, a black polyester shirt with an integrated white clerical dog collar. As he approached the reception desk at the front of the low prison building complex, he could smell the scents of salt, seaweed and iodine from the nearby ocean every time the door opened or closed. Since the odours marked his imminent freedom, few things in his life had ever smelt so sweet. As the two escorting UN military guards began the formal discharge

---

[404] By Suitsupply in Amsterdam.
[405] By Dutch shoe brand, Ecco.

process with the civilian prison officers in reception, O'Neill was instructed to sit in one of the orange-coloured plastic chairs that filled the room and await his release.

Sitting and facing out through one of the two expansive blast-protected windows that occupied the right side of the reception waiting area, O'Neill watched a supply van going through a complex security check. These checks included the use of under-vehicle mirrors and visual inspections before the vehicle was permitted into the covered driveway leading into the flat-roofed prison complex. The UN Captain had told O'Neill that a car and driver would be made available on his discharge, so he split his attention between looking at the large LCD wall clock and the entranceway to the prison. Secretly and because of his Jesuit training, guiltily, O'Neill was hoping for some luxurious big Mercedes to appear to whisk him back to his flat in Rome.

Time passed slowly, as it always does when eagerly waiting for an event. Then, precisely at 09.30, a small blue Seat Ibiza hatchback car drove slowly from right to left along the furthest of the two, tree-lined Pompstationsweg avenues. The vehicle was temporarily obscured behind the three tall white poles with their Wolfsangel flags that decorated the front of the prison before it turned into the twenty-yard accessway.

Since the car was not entering the prison complex, it avoided the detailed searches given to the van that O'Neill had watched moments earlier. Instead, it turned and entered the area designated for dropping off and picking up outside the prison reception. O'Neill could not see the chauffeur's face since he wore a peaked cap and sunglasses, which looked incongruous on such a grey day and with such a small car. Maybe he (the driver) was more used to driving high-end vehicles, thought O'Neill to himself.

The Seat parked next to numerous racks of bicycles and warning signs that threatened that motorised vehicles would be towed if left unattended. O'Neill stood, eager for his freedom. As his driver exited and walked towards the wired glass door, the priest was able to assess the man he would spend the next few hours with.

The driver was dressed in a two-piece black worsted wool suit that perfectly fitted his role as a driver, except for a pair of black rubber overshoes, which he wore over his classic black brogues- as if he expected the drizzle to intensify considerably. The two civilian security guards posted at the entrance checked the man's ID and paperwork, forcing him to remove his cap and dark glasses. Something vaguely familiar and deeply unsettling was triggered in O'Neill's subconscious by the man's face, but O'Neill could not place the hawk-like features. Dismissing the feeling that he had seen the man before, O'Neill exchanged a few pleasantries with the driver about last evening's European League football match before exiting the building. After days of incarceration, even the brisk wind and fine drizzle felt good, and O'Neill could not get away from the two-storey brick frontage of the prison quickly enough. As they walked to the car, O'Neill could hear the radio headphone in the driver's left ear burst to life in Dutch.

"De voorzitter heeft bijgewerkte instructies gegeven. U hoeft de priester niet meer naar Rome te vervoeren. Rij rechtdoor over de Pompstationsweg en ga het bos in. Parkeer op parkeerplaats Natuurspeeltuin en wacht op het busje en de volgende auto om de beëindiging van de priester te voltooien. Bevestigen. Over."

"Bevestigd," (Confirmed) replied the driver calmly into the microphone on his wrist.

O'Neill was fluent in many ancient languages but not Dutch, so it was not a surprise that he did not gather what had been said, but the priest was startled when the chauffeur stopped O'Neill from getting in the front. Instead, he insisted that O'Neill sat in the rear- even though the priest had no luggage and it was a small saloon, not the luxury limousine that O'Neill had originally hoped for. As he sat down on the left rear seat, O'Neill could not help looking over the partition into the rear of the hatchback. It was filled with trowels, bags of sand, cement, fertiliser and four large tubs of masonry nails.

"Looks like someone is a keen DIY-er," commented O'Neill, hoping to spark some conversation. The driver ignored the friendly enquiry, instead he asked,

"Do you understand Dutch?" he spoke in an accent that was a mix of Arab and Russian.

"No, none. Why?" answered O'Neill.

"It is good that you hear what I was just told. It will explain much of what is about to transpire."

The driver turned on the playback feature on his Samsung Galaxy Ultra phone. An automatic voice translation followed a static hiss.

"Chairman has issued updated instructions. You are no longer required to transport the priest to Rome. Drive straight across Pompstationsweg and proceed into woodland. Park at Natuurspeeltuin car park and wait for the vans and the following car to complete the termination of the priest. Confirm. Over."

"Termination? Are you going to kill me?" O'Neill could feel a wave of fear rising from within himself.

"No, I am not going to kill you, Fr O'Neill. But a small group of men and women are about to try."

Panic ran free through O'Neill's mind. He was about to run back into the prison when the driver's iron grip grasped O'Neill's right arm.

"Go back inside, and you will be found dead in your cell. Cortez controls everything now. Stay here, and I will get us both out of here alive."

O'Neill did not feel any better for the driver's reassurance.

"What use will you be against a team of assassins? I have seen you searched. You have no weapons, only some building supplies. You are as powerless against these people as I am."

The driver smiled, removed his cap and glasses and turned to look at the priest.

The recognition of the driver's identity suddenly came to O'Neill.

"Jesus Christ, you are Issac bin Abdul Issuin!"

exclaimed O'Neill, who instantly regretted having taken God's name in vain as he cowered into the corner of the rear passenger compartment. Then the implications of the instructions from Cortez suddenly registered.

"Cortez expected me to lead them to Tavish!"

The hawk-faced driver nodded as O'Neill continued his deductions.

"The fact he no longer needs me means Stewart is dead," O'Neill crossed himself and began a prayer but was interrupted by Abdul Issuin.

"Don't write Stewart off so easily. If I could not kill him on my last attempt, that arrogant shit Cortez and his goons could never succeed."

Their conversation was interrupted by a burst of angry words in Abdul Issuin's earpiece. The hawk-faced assassin gave a single-word response in his wrist microphone as he reached the dashboard, started the engine and turned the car's airbags off.

"Seat belt on, Dr O'Neill. It's going to be a bumpy ride."

With that, Abdul Issuin drove slowly through the prison barriers and down the short drive that intersected with the two tree-lined avenues that formed Pompstationsweg. A parked silver Audi A6 flashed its lights some distance to the right and pulled away from the curb, driving towards them. As the Audi approached, the three occupants inside became more visible through the tinted windshield. All three were wearing the same military fatigues O'Neill had last seen at the Colosseum in Rome some days before. The Audi had FF logos on its bonnet, doors and rear. Two of the three men inside held short, black polymer machine guns with the barrels pointed to the sky.

"I know those uniforms!" exclaimed O'Neill, "Mr Issuin, these men are dangerous."

The hawk-faced assassin smiled at the naivety of his passenger and commented,

"Shortly, I think, we will see exactly *who* is dangerous."

"Do you have any body armour I can put on?" asked O'Neill, remembering the machine gun fire back in the underground temple in Rome.

The hawk-faced driver looked into the rear-view mirror, assessed the weapons carried by the men and responded,

"Kevlar would not help. Those are Heckler & Koch MP7A2[406]s. They are designed to penetrate body armour. But look in the back. We have something better."

O'Neill looked behind the back seat again, saw numerous sandbags piled up, and smiled. Now, Abdul Issuin's pretence of building a garden wall made sense.

"Clever, but that means we will never be able to outrun them."

Abdul Issuin laughed. "Running away was never in the plan."

O'Neill gulped. He looked at the silver Audi and the small car he was sitting inside.

"Do you have a gun? Something concealed in this car, perhaps?" O'Neill asked optimistically.

The hawk-faced assassin shook his head, saying, "I couldn't risk it in case of a random spot search."

Abdul Issuin noted his passenger's growing concern.

"You worry too much, my friend. Let's see what they do when we head for the main road instead of the designated killing zone straight ahead in the woods."

The small Seat crossed the central reservation and turned left towards the main Van Alkemadelaan road. There was a sudden burst of speech on the earphone, followed by a loud siren noise. Behind them, the Audi's headlights came on full beam and bright flashing strobe lights illuminated from under the car's front radiator. Moments later, a concealed loudspeaker in the Audi broadcast a command,

---

[406] A revised variant of the HK MP7 machine gun with 4.6×30mm armour piercing rounds. Tests find it nearly five times more effective than the MP5 machine gun at passing through standard body armour.

"Trek nu over!" (Pull over now).

Abdul Issuin slowed and then stopped the car. Noticeably, he left the engine running and switched the gearbox into reverse. He reached over, pulled the front passenger headrest to its highest level, and lowered all the car windows. Gusts of wind and light drizzle blew into the cabin, spraying O'Neill's face. Behind them, the Audi stopped diagonally across the road ten yards behind the Seat, and a single operative emerged from the front passenger side of the FF vehicle. He was dressed in full body armour and carried a short polymer MP7 machine gun which he aimed towards the parked Seat. For a moment, he stood and assessed the area for additional threats.

To try and take his mind off his imminent violent death, O'Neill said the one thing that had been bugging him since he discovered the true identity of his driver.

"It was a good try, Mr Issuin, but it does not look like I will lead you to Tavish Stewart."

The hawk-faced assassin was busy adjusting the central rear-view mirror, but he raised one eyebrow in response to O'Neill's comment. When the killer spoke, it was noticeable that his attention remained fixed on the left side wing mirror where he could see the gunman that had emerged from the Audi.

"Please, Father O'Neill, don't flatter yourself. I already know where Stewart is located. I am here to add some spice to Cortez's plans. It is the least I can do."

O'Neill looked momentarily perplexed.

In the wing mirror, the hawk-faced assassin watched as the FF operative slowly walked towards the Seat. The barrel of the man's MP7 pointed towards Abdul Issuin as the approaching operative shouted,

"Blijf in het voertuig!" (Remain inside the vehicle!)

The loud command startled O'Neill but was entirely ignored by Abdul Issuin, who continued explaining his decision to intervene, saying,

"When Cortez accused Stewart of my achievements, it *motivated* me,"

Abdul Issuin spoke calmly as he pulled the headrest entirely from the passenger seat beside him and held it in his right hand out of sight. A wicked smile crept over the hawk-like face as he added,

"But my reaction will pale beside someone else's wrath at having her achievements attributed to a boring lawyer."

Before O'Neill could speculate as to who this other person might be, the Wolfsangel operative strode up to the small Seat and thrust the snub barrel of the MP7 through the open car window directly into the hawk-faced assassin's face. Abdul Issuin responded by begging pathetically, saying,

"Nee, nee, alsjeblieft, genade!" (No, No, please, mercy!)

The whimpering emboldened the Wolfsangel operative, who leaned closer and pushed his face through the side window, snarling,

"Prik! Daar had je aan moeten denken voordat je tegen ons handelde. Stap nu uit die verdomde auto, samen met die stomme priester."

(Prick! You should have thought about that before you acted against us. Now get out of the fucking car along with the stupid priest.)

In a calm, quiet voice that completely mismatched his begging, Abdul Issuin turned to O'Neill and said,

"Seat belt off and get down."

It took a moment for O'Neill to realise that the comment was meant for him. By the time he began to react, several things had happened simultaneously.

The Wolfsangel gunman was violently dragged into the front of the Seat by one of the long spikes from the detached headrest that Abdul Issuin thrust deep into the operative's windpipe and down into his trachea. As blood and sputum erupted from the man's throat, the hawk-faced assassin pulled the MP7 away from the dying operative and took control of the weapon in his right hand.

Simultaneously with this murderous attack, the hawk-faced assassin pulled himself sideways to lay down across the two front seats and out of sight. Using his right foot to flatten the accelerator and his free left hand to steer, he used the adjusted rear-view mirror to guide the car backwards at high speed towards the diagonally parked Audi behind them. The screaming noise from the three-cylinder engine was accompanied by loud cracks from MP7 fire directed from the parked Audi into the back of the accelerating Seat Ibiza. The bodywork of the small Seat resounded from numerous hammerlike blows, making the car shudder as it flew faster and faster backward. Huge holes opened in the cabin bodywork and both windshields. The safety glass shattered into thousands of tiny diamond-like squares, littering the rear seat where O'Neill was huddled down. The terrifying crescendo of thumping high-velocity bullets ended abruptly with an enormous impact that thrust O'Neill into the back of the rear seat and lifted the Seat and the parked Audi some inches into the air before both vehicles smashed violently into the road.

While O'Neill was still trying to gather his senses, Abdul Issuin had emerged like a feline predator from the front of the Seat. He dragged the gasping Wolfsangel operative by the headrest buried in the man's throat. After casting the gurgling body to the ground, the hawk-faced assassin discharged two MP7 rounds into the man's head. Grey matter and bone fragments mixed with the blood pouring from the man's throat onto the wet tarmac. Before the two loud gunshots had finished echoing off the walls of the nearby prison, Abdul Issuin had strode silently to the remains of the Audi. He discharged another four rounds, two into each of the Wolfsangel operatives, who were still recovering from the recent impact.

The back third of the smaller Seat Ibiza was embedded into the rear right side of the larger Audi saloon car, bursting open the fuel tank and collapsing the hatchback on the small Seat. The bags of fertiliser, concrete and containers of masonry nails had spilt into the open space inside the partially crushed Audi. Soaking the mix with high-octane gasoline and making the ammonium nitrate form massive clumps filled with embedded masonry nails.

Sixteen gallons of amber liquid spilt over the tarmac. The petrol poured over the black rubber overshoes worn by the hawk-faced assassin and formed large pools under the two cars. The air reeked of the heady smell of gasoline. In the distance, a siren broke the silence as two dark blue Ford Transit vans with riot grilles over their front windshields hurtled side by side at high speed towards the crash. Inside the Transits, heavily armed men dressed in black FF combat fatigues were preparing themselves for imminent action.

By now, O'Neill had recovered enough to sit up. The exorcist looked like a startled deer as Abdul Issuin wedged open the pulverised rear passenger door with the hilt of the MP7 and began shoving the priest from the car towards the side of the avenue. When they had reached the curb, O'Neill went to sit down to recover his senses but halted when the hawk-faced assassin pulled the silver weather cover off from a jet-black futuristic motorcycle. The bike was decorated with red text that said "Kawasaki Ninja H2[407]" over its frame and central fuel tank.

O'Neill looked at the bike and then at the two wrecked cars—the motorcycle was parked opposite the Seat's wreckage.

"You planned all of this?" asked a stunned O'Neill.

"I do this for a living," stated Abdul Issuin, as if that explained the perfect placement of the bike. He then passed the priest a thin metallic jumpsuit that had been folded on the rear seat of the powerful motorcycle, saying,

"Here, put this on."

O'Neill looked perplexed at the Velcro fastenings down the front and legs of the paper-thin material.

"It will block the tracking devices that they have placed in your clothing," explained Abdul Issuin as he got onto the bike and started the supercharged engine. The assassin looked expectantly at O'Neill, waiting for him to get on the tiny pinon passenger seat.

"It doesn't have any number plates!" remarked O'Neill as if this made the bike unsuitable as their means of escape.

"That's okay; it's not road legal," the assassin said as if that made it okay, "Besides, the FF are not interested in giving us traffic tickets."

To emphasise the assassin's point, the two dark blue Wolfsangel Transit vans, speeding towards them, sirens blaring, pulled up with a screech of brakes, stopping directly behind the smashed cars. Dozens of black-suited FF

---

[407] The Kawasaki Ninja H2R track-only variant is the world's fastest and most powerful motorbike. It is fitted with a variable-speed centrifugal supercharger, ram-air 326 horsepower engine with 50% more power than street-legal machines.

operatives poured out and began advancing towards the crash scene. Five of them began searching the wreckage for survivors. The remaining operatives took up covered positions behind the car wreckage and the tall poplar trees lining the avenue. Moments later, a volley of high-velocity rounds flew past O'Neill's head and buried themselves into a nearby tree trunk, prompting the exorcist to climb onto the back of the bike and exclaim,

"Go! Go! Before they kill us!"

To O'Neill's shock, the hawk-faced assassin reached slowly into his right jacket pocket, pulled out a narrow aluminium tube, and extracted a Montecristo No.4[408].

O'Neill watched with disbelief and exclaimed,

"How can you think of smoking when they are trying to kill us?"

The hawk-faced assassin smiled. "They are only trying to kill *you*, Father O'Neill. Their standard operating procedure will demand that they interrogate me, so they have to take me alive. These are just warning shots."

Abul Issuin placed the cigar in his mouth and then slowly opened a cardboard matchbook promoting something called "Vics Club[409]" and struck a match. The flame illuminated the cruellest smile that O'Neill had ever seen as Abdul Issuin ignited the Habano[410].

---

[408] A Cuban Montecristo No.4 Cigar. Favoured by The World's Most Dangerous Man.

[409] One of China's most famous nightclubs. Located in Beijing's Chaoyang District.

[410] Spanish for "from Havana" - denotes the very finest cigars handmade with tobacco grown in the rich mineral soils of the Vuelta Abajo near the Sierra de los Oraganos mountains.

Seemingly oblivious to the numerous high-velocity rounds flying ever closer, Abdul Issuin made several long draws on the cigar until the burn was fully established. Enjoying a deep inhalation, he casually cast the still-flaming match down onto the petrol-soaked asphalt beside him- only then did the hawk-faced assassin open the throttle on the world's fastest motorcycle.

As the Kawasaki accelerated, it triggered speed cameras positioned along Pompstationsweg. Later analysis of these pictures by Wolfsangel operatives showed the bike rising onto its rear wheel at speeds well over 100 mph. Numerous photographic analysts remarked that these blurred pictures of Abdul Issuin with his jacket flaring behind him on the superbike as it wheelied away resembled a Sheikh on a fine Arab stallion.

As the Kawaski exceeded 150 mph along the Van Alkemadelaan road towards the coast, the gasoline pools under the two crashed cars ignited into a wall of superheated fire. They quickly exceeded 410 Fahrenheit and triggered the congealed clumps of ammonium nitrate to start to melt, venting nitrous oxide, water vapour and nitrogen gas. The mix of concrete, fertiliser, gasoline and masonry nails compressed the normal expansion, bypassing the standard critical detonation diameter of ammonium nitrate.

The resulting 3000 feet per second explosion flattened the two transit vans, and two crashed cars into the poplar trees and embedded masonry nails into the frontage of the prison, some 200 yards away. The Dutch news coverage that evening described the incident as an unprecedented gas main rupture.

CAVE OF DREAD

*"Humans are thought to be at the top of the food chain...
But there are beings who hunt them..." - Sui Ishida*

*Two miles beneath Finsteraarhorn[411] Mountain,
Ten miles Southeast of Grindelwald,
The Bernese Alps,
Switzerland.*

14:00 HRS (GMT+2), 15th September, Present Day

The form of Nissa Ad-Dajjal flowed along a narrow, dimly lit stone corridor carved through the granite of the Bernese Alps that rose thousands of feet above her. The chill from the surrounding bedrock was intensified by the penetrating preternatural cold which had surrounded Ad-Dajjal since her return to the material realm. A wave of frost formations in the shapes of various Goetic sigils appeared momentarily on the walls alongside wherever she passed. The stone floor iced over in the pattern of her footsteps, only to melt away as the adept continued on her way. The only light in this claustrophobic space was from the flickering flame cast by a beeswax taper carried in Ad-Dajjal's right hand. The flickering light highlighted the strange patterns in the quartz seams flowing through the rock; pareidolia made some look like contorted faces, while others resembled demonic claws.

Since her encounter with the USAF adept[412] Booker on top of the great pyramid of Giza, the raven-haired Hierophant had changed into a close-fitting jet-black silk Chanel trouser suit decorated with a pattern of red oriental dragons which

---

[411] The Finsteraarhorn (14,022 ft) is located in one of the most remote areas in the Swiss Alps, surrounded by uninhabited glacial valleys.
[412] USAF Chief Booker.

complimented her red leather Jimmy Choo stiletto heel ankle boots[413]. The narrow corridor she travelled formed part of Ad-Dajjal's many private ritual temples contained within the Finsteraarhorn complex. However, this particular one was of special significance to Ad-Dajjal because it formed a ritual space dedicated to the spiritual path she had studied for over thirty years during her mortal existence. Nissa Ad-Dajjal's chosen esoteric training had been with the Tachikawa-ryu, the eleventh-century Japanese left-hand, magick school of Mikkyō, esoteric Shingon Buddhism. She had picked this school for a single reason; it was the only remaining esoteric school that had escaped persecution and disruption. Successive purges by Christian and Communist regimes over previous centuries had systematically extinguished the esoteric lineages of Europe[414], America[415], India[416], Tibet[417] and China[418]. Consequently, the Japanese Mikkyō, is the world's only remaining intact esoteric initiatory lineage. Ad-Dajjal's depth of study and numerous initiations at the Mount Koya and Hiei temples placed her among the most accomplished adepts in the long history of the ancient Tachikawa-ryu school. Even within the highly competitive and often critically dismissive Meri-Isfet hierarchy, she was acknowledged as the global expert on the most ancient occult arts of Asia.

This afternoon, the ritual temple she was approaching along the dark narrow rock passage was dedicated to the oldest

---

[413] Jimmy Choo Minori 85 Ankle Boots.
[414] Only the two oldest and most secretive orders survived in Europe, devoted to Good (Maat) and Evil (Isfet) respectively. You know their names but most do not.
[415] Waashat, Midewiwin, Earth Lodge, Ghost Dance, Crow and Mexicayotl.
[416] Vāmācāra and Dakṣiṇācāra.
[417] Nyingma, Kagyu, Sakya and Gelug.
[418] The Esoteric Buddhist tradition called the Mìzōng.

traditions to survive within the Tachikawa-ryu. Many of these rituals had, allegedly, been dictated by Dakini-ten[419] and transcribed in human blood onto scrolls made from the mortified flesh of disciples of the order as an act of devotion.

The volcanic rock that comprised this ritual space's walls, floor and ceilings had been transported from Mount Osore[420], known in Japan as Mount "Dread". This sacred Shingon Buddhist site is located in the caldera of an active volcano known within esoteric lore as one of the gates to the underworld. The extrusive rocks within the volcano are imbued with specific occult energy patterns[421] that dramatically enhance dark spiritual manifestations. This phenomenon accounts for the many horrific and terrifying occult phenomena encountered at Mount Osore over the centuries. When objects linked with violence, pain, suffering, death or supernatural evil are placed in proximity to these rocks, they manifest on the physical plane with phenomena typically only perceived by those with extraordinary psychic abilities.

At the end of the half-mile-long descending passage, the corridor opened into a space fifty feet square with ten-foot tall ceilings, called the Osore Tengu[422] temple or, as the staff

---

[419] Esoteric Shingon Buddhism's discarnate Principle of Evil.

[420] Mount Osore (恐山, Osore-zan), or Mount Dread, is in the remote Shimokita Peninsula of Aomori Prefecture, northern Tōhoku, Japan.

[421] A rare form of Telluric energy that enhances the natural life force (chi/prana) and transforms it into a very rarified form, called Uḍāna that is responsible for psychic manifestation within the chakras of the human material and immaterial bodies.

[422] Tengu (天狗) 'Heavenly Sentinel' are supernatural entities within the Japanese Shinto religion. The most ancient images of the Tengu depict them as large creatures with bird-like features (often Kites). The Egyptian Goddess Isis was depicted with the wings of a Kite, which she used to generate the breath of life for Osiris. See - Anne

at the Finsteraarhorn underground complex called it, "The Cave of Dread". Every surface in sight comprised the unique dark igneous rock transported from Mount Oscore. As the raven-haired adept paused to light two large candles on either side of the entrance from her beeswax taper, shadows flickered across the damp stone walls. A careful observer would notice that not all of these flitting shadows were cast by the lighted wax taper or the two candles; some showed independence and coordination unknown in inanimate objects.

After lighting the two, six-foot-tall black candles, Ad-Dajjal lit two, four-foot tall cones of dark incense[423] alongside them, filling the air inside the ritual space with a smoky mix of camphor, pine and mint.

A tall square red and black Torii[424] gate stood in front of the two lighted candles. The gate's horizontal twin top bars were decorated with unusual bird-like creatures representing one of the many forms assumed by the Kami[425]. These discarnate entities are traditionally summoned during Shinto ceremonies.

Ad-Dajjal bowed and picked up a long-handled ladle[426] from a rock cistern of mountain water that she used to ritually

---

Baring & Jules Cashford. The Myth of the Goddess Evolution of an Image. Penguin Books. 25 Mar 1993.

[423] Kyara, one of the finest agarwood incense, made specially for Ad-Dajjal's ritual work by Akiyoshi Tshami, grand master of Tachikawa-ryu.

[424] In the Shinto religion this gate separates the mundane world from that of the spiritual.

[425] The exact nature of the Kami is subject to some debate, even within Shinto. The range of invisible supernatural beings included under the label ranges from divine to demonic and includes the spirits of the deceased.

[426] Called the chouzubachi ladle.

wash her left and right hands before rinsing her mouth with her cupped left palm. After this, the raven-haired beauty rang a silver bell suspended from the ceiling and threw a thick wad of US bank notes, bearing the likeness of James Madison[427] to the wet stone floor of the room, where it lay beside numerous other similar offerings from her previous visits. After completing two brisk claps with her hands, Ad-Dajjal bowed again and advanced further into the sacred space.

The ringing of a consecrated bell, followed by an offering and two summoning claps, is designed to alert the Kami within the ritual space of the presence of a visitor. In everyday settings, the invisible beings remain unseen to all but the most spiritually gifted. However, the environment of this room was as far from ordinary as was possible in the material realm. Not only were all the surfaces made from rock that enhanced psychic manifestation, but the area had also been deliberately stocked by Ad-Dajjal with powerful esoteric artefacts with exceptionally dark provenance. On this occasion, the summoning had attracted the attention of numerous dark entities, who noticed the absence of initiatory sigils in the newcomer's aura and the lack of an initiate's ring.

These powerful malevolent energies were bound to this place by the presence of objects that shared one attribute; their dark histories would horrify any sane individual. But, for Nissa Ad-Dajjal, they were treasures of a secret universe of knowledge and power. That is not to say that Ad-Dajjal was insane, at least not by any recognised legal definition since she knew and understood the difference between harmful and beneficial action. She had complete control over her

---

[427] The $5,000 US dollar banknote is decorated with the face of James Madison, the fourth president of the United States.

behaviour and fully understood the likely consequences of her actions. It was just that she always chose malevolence.

Along the Northern side of the large room, stacked in rows of clear Perspex racks within a hermetically controlled environment, were Ad-Dajjal's most prized possessions. Every one had a dark history and provided some direct malign influence over material reality. The topmost row contained the Dakini-ten scrolls, the ultimate treasure of the Tachikawa-ryu. These ancient documents described the most arcane ceremonies, detailing techniques that defy modern physics.

Beneath the scrolls was the most powerful of the thirteen Dharmadhātu skulls[428]- the infamous skull of Devadatta[429], the so-called "Judas of Dharmavinaya", the disciple who tried to murder Buddha. The surfaces of this particular skull were covered with gold leaf and engraved with an obscene liturgy of Sanskrit sutras from the one hundred and nine blissful communions with Dakini-ten, the Principle of Darkness involved with the infamous Skull Ritual of Tachikawa-ryu. Beneath the skull was a container filled with blood-soaked linen-bound experimental log books and assorted vivisection equipment from Unit Tōgō[430] and Unit 731[431]- where the

---

[428] One of the most infamous relics within Tantric dark magic. The skull is used for necromancy that deliberately desecrates the sacred remains of a revered Hijiri (Japanese Holy Man) or, as in the case of Ad-Dajjal's skull, uses the remains of a powerful adept of the left-hand path to enhance their own powers. For more details of the ceremony see - Sanford, J. H. The Abominable Tachikawa Skull Ritual. Monumenta Nipponica, 46(1), 1-20. (1991)
[429] The disciple who was also the cousin and brother-in-law of Gautama Siddhārtha (the Buddha).
[430] A lethal human experimentation camp within Zhongma Fortress, Beiyinhe, sixty-two miles south of Harbin, China.
[431] Manshu Detachment 731 (Unit 731) was a biological and chemical warfare research unit that conducted experiments that

wartime Japanese[432] Army conducted some of the most horrific human experimentation ever recorded. These World War 2 memorabilia complemented the other items Ad-Dajjal had collected from Unit Togo- an operating table, interrogation chair and a chest containing restraints and other devices used within the more grisly vivisection studies.

Some ten feet in front of the Perspex storage racks, towards the centre of the room, was a raised platform of rocks constructed around a body of still, dark water[433]. The stones forming the structure had been transported from a deep water well installed in the courtyard at Uji[434] Palace, a residence allocated for the concubines of the twelfth-century feudal warlord, Minamoto no Yoritomo[435].

The "Uji Incident", as it is called, is well-known by serious students of Japanese paranormal history. Indeed, it is often cited as an example of the perils of summoning unknown discarnate entities. Spirit possession was common in feudal

---

resulted in the horrific deaths and suffering of over a quarter of a million people.

[432] Surgeon General Shirō Ishii and Lt. Gen. Masaji Kitano planned and led these horrific experiments.

[433] Originally, the water in this well was taken from the Seta River. It is recycled and filtered through the bones of the unfortunate "Uji Incident" victims.

[434] Uji (宇治市) is a small town between Nara and Kyoto. The location is renowned for having the oldest Shinto shrine and the remains of a haunted palace.

[435] Minamoto no Yoritomo (源 頼朝) founded the Kamakura shogunate (1185 to 1333).

K.R.M. Morgan

Japan[436] for prophecy[437] and healing[438]. For this latter purpose, one of the older dowager concubines, Lady Hisui Hasu[439], brought the renowned "Onmyoji[440]", Shitte Iru Hito[441], to the palace to help one of the younger women, Kichōna Hana[442] conceive. As was the practice, the shaman used a Catalpa Bow[443] to communicate with his familiar spirit[444] to determine the cause of the young woman's infertility. By all accounts, the ceremony went well, providing a prognosis and, probably more importantly, entertainment for the bored court members.

Only after the shaman had left the palace did things go awry. With hindsight, it is clear that the ceremony had permitted other discarnate entities to gain entrance to the material world. According to the few who survived the events of that fateful evening, it started when the subject of the spiritual intervention, Kichōna Hana, started behaving erratically. In the middle of the night, she woke the household by shouting obscenities in a rasping voice that was not her own. As the possession strengthened its hold over the young woman, she

---

[436] See - Iyanaga, N. Healing by Spiritual Possession in Medieval Japan, with a Translation of the Genja Saho. Religions, 13(6), 522. (2022).
[437] See - "Catalpa Bow": A Study of Shamanistic Practices in Japan" by Carmen Blacker (Japan Library, 1999).
[438] See the 11th-century Japanese Classic, "Tale of Genji", written by Lady Murasaki Shikibu, for details of how spirit possession was used for healing.
[439] 翡翠蓮
[440] An Onmyoji is a shaman trained in Taoist, Buddhist and Shinto magic.
[441] 知っている人
[442] 貴重な花
[443] A single-stringed musical instrument.
[444] The spirit guardian or helper of a shaman or magician.

began speaking in different voices and languages, some utterly unfamiliar to the court members[445].

As is often the case[446] with groups of young people confined together, the erratic behaviour rapidly spread to the other young concubines. Within hours, the entire household had become drawn into the supernatural infestation. The sixteen Samurai assigned to guard the palace tried to control the situation, but tragically, they also became targeted by the invading discarnate entities. During what must have been a terrifying night, the guards slaughtered the entire household they had been entrusted to protect before killing themselves with their Wakizashi short swords. The local servants who discovered the gruesome scene in the morning sent word to their feudal Lord, Minamoto, who ordered the bodies thrown in the well and the palace burnt to the ground.

To avoid damage to his reputation from such a scandal, Lord Minamoto expunged the "Uji Incident" from the official history of his reign. The story became one of those cautionary tales told in conspiratorial whispers on late nights around a blazing hearth in the mid-winter. The location of the accursed palace would have been lost, except that it lay by the bridge on the main routes between the regional cities of Nara and Kyoto. Consequently, it was a natural spot for travellers to stop overnight. Predictably, very few of these travellers had a peaceful night's rest. The lucky ones just suffered from terrible nightmares. The unlucky ones, probably more psychically aware, were visited by ghoulish forms. Others heard strangely compelling voices suggesting harm to their travelling companions or themselves. The number of murders and suicides reported at the site

---

[445] Ruling out Japanese, Chinese and Korean.
[446] See Hecker, J. F. (1844). The Epidemics of the Middle Ages (First ed.)

eventually forced the local Shichō[447] (authorities) to prohibit camping at or near the old Uji bridge.

It should not be thought for a moment, that Ad-Dajjal had gathered these macabre relics from mere idle curiosity or even some morbid interest in the darker aspects of Oriental history. The truth was that each item was a superlative example of how a demonic influence could drive an individual, or group of individuals, to exceed every rational boundary of cruelty to others or even to themselves. The residual energies associated with these horrific acts bound the spiritual power of the perpetrators to the objects stored in this dark cavern, where they were animated into heightened activity by the rock cladding from Mount Osore.

In the darkest ceremonies of the Tachikawa-ryu, the souls of the demonically possessed provide a potent weapon that, through concentrated will and specific ritual, can be directed to inflict harm on individuals and groups or even cause accidents and natural disasters. These vengeful spirits, called Onryō[448], are easier for a skilled sorcerer to control and direct than a true demonic form[449]. Therefore, Ad-Dajjal viewed the cave's artefacts as nothing more than an arsenal of weapons, each capable of inflicting some specific injury, illness or misfortune on an enemy.

In many ways, these dangerous discarnate energies were like a caged collection of apex predators looking for a weakness in potential prey. In the same way that a cage of performing tigers look for injury or distraction in their trainer, the dark and dangerous spirits in the Cave of Dread minutely examined every living thing that entered their space. The

---

[447] 市長

[448] 怨霊

[449] True demonic forms usually require a pact to be agreed with the sorcerer. These pacts are deliberately complex and invariably give the demon considerable advantage over the sorcerer.

initiatory sigils in a person's aura and the initiates ring were signs that the person should be respected, like the whip in the trainer's hand. But even for the most advanced adepts, using a protective magical circle and the appropriate banishing rituals was essential to avoid being attacked and seriously harmed by these malevolent energies.

The reanimated form of Nissa Ad-Dajjal that had entered the cavern had no sigils in her aura, no initiates ring on her finger and had, so far, refrained from any form of magical protection. These omissions were keenly noted by the "hungry ghosts[450]" in the room. Such entities are primarily driven by emotional compulsions, acting instinctively without considering the outcomes of their actions[451].

However, there was one entity in the chamber that possessed extraordinary intelligence. It was also the most psychically powerful of the discarnate beings constrained within the dread chamber. During the fifth century BCE, in Tibet[452], when this energy had last incarnated, he had been one of the first disciples of Buddhism. Through the rigorous practice of the sutras[453] pranayama[454] and asanas[455], he rapidly attained powerful supernatural abilities[456], especially those related to controlling the perceptions and wills of others[457]. His lust for

---

[450] In Chinese Buddhism "èguĭ" (餓鬼) are "hungry ghosts" - unquiet spirits who are doomed to seek imbalance in the human world. The same entities are described in Hinduism as "Preta" (प्रेत) and in Tibetan as "yi dags" (ཡི་དྭགས).

[451] A bit like politicians for whom the likely long-term consequences are irrelevant when compared to the personal short-term gain.

[452] In a town called Lumbini.

[453] Prayers, mantras and spoken invocations.

[454] Breathing and energy manipulation techniques.

[455] Yoga postures and chakra stimulation.

[456] Siddhis (सिद्धि) – accomplishments.

[457] Known as "Īśiṭva" it is the ability to influence any animated being.

power led him to enchant a local prince[458] to serve his dark will. Using his preternatural influence, this corrupted Buddhist monk, known to history as Devadatta, then tried to take over the Buddhist movement from his cousin and brother-in-law, the Buddha. Devadatta sought to change Buddhism to become much more extreme in its practice by renouncing the middle or harmonious path, instead seeking suffering and depravation. After attempting to charm the Buddha into surrendering the new religion to his control, the "Judas of Dharmavinaya" acted to kill the Buddha and take control in that way. The karmic consequence was severe, preventing Devadatta from reincarnating. Instead, his essence was bound to one of the thirteen Dharmadhātu skulls for what remained of this material universe. But although the skull had no physical body to satisfy its desire to control the world, it was still an extraordinarily powerful malevolent psychic force. Over the years in which it resided in the cave, it had gained complete control over the other non-physical entities.

This dark intelligence began to purposefully gather the latent energies in the cave to direct its subordinates against the newcomer. Depending on the propensities of this visitor, Devadatta would lead the raven-haired woman to take her own life with one of the vivisection instruments and join the other entities in the cave. He would attach some of the more insidious Onryō to her aura if she were less suggestible, so she gradually became corrupted and spread that corruption to the greater world outside the cave. Either way, there would be an increase in the sum of suffering and despair in the world.

For her part, Nissa Ad-Dajjal had closed her mind to all external stimuli as she stepped on a slightly raised dais made of cork positioned some ten feet in front of the dark waters

---

[458] Prince Ajātashatru of the Magadhan dynasty.

of the well and some twenty feet away from the Perspex relic cabinet. The raven-haired beauty squatted down into a sitting position smoothly and practisedly without using her arms. She rapidly folded her legs into the classic Siddhasana[459] (adepts pose) asana.

With her eyes closed, she placed her left hand over her nose. She began a complex series of breathing exercises that a yogi would recognise as a more advanced form of the classic Kapalabhati pumps combined with Surya Bhedana to form a specialised Bhastrika or "bellows" of pranayama. These alternating series of breaths charged the chakras within Ad-Dajjal's body, energising her base Muladhara chakra. Soon the technique spread waves of kundalini[460] energy through her psychic energy channels (Nadis[461]), connecting and stimulating the chakras in her physical and etheric bodies. To anyone gifted with astral perception, Ad-Dajjal's body began to glow as pulses of colour formed the classic intertwined snake shape (Caduceus), which rose from the base of the spine to Sahasrara chakra at the top of her head. Once she had achieved this highly energised state, Ad-Dajjal began to intone the secret mantra of the Tsépagmed[462], in its purest Tibetan form,

"oṃ ā ma ra ṇi dzi wan te ye svā hā".

Thus, Ad-Dajjal began the ancient Tachikawa-ryu ritual known as "Karada ni ashi o fumiireru gishiki[463]" - the

---

[459] Siddhasana is one of the oldest Yoga asanas in the 10th century Goraksha Sataka text.

[460] These are prāṇa (inward energy), apāna (outward energy), vyāna (circulation energy), udāna (head/throat energy), and samāna (digestion and assimilation energy).

[461] Ida (left) and Pingala (right) and Sushumna (centre).

[462] The Tibetan Buddha Amitayus (Tsépagmed) in celestial form grants control over the lifeforce.

[463] 身体に足を踏み入れる儀式 - The ritual of entering the body.

ceremony that had brought the raven-haired beauty to the cavern today.

None of this esoteric detail was known to the discarnate intelligence that was what remained of the Dark Buddha, Devadatta. From his perspective, an unprepared female had commenced classic hatha yoga practice but had made a poor choice in selecting a location for her pranayama.

The first indication that some preternatural event was starting was that the light cast from the two candles at the entrance began to dim. It was a gradual change, but within moments the darkness was profound. The ambient temperature dropped, and the smell of stagnant water overwhelmed the scent of camphor, pine and mint from the burning incense cones. None of this was noticed by Ad-Dajjal, who was now intensely focused on performing her inner ritual work.

In the gloom within the cave, random formations in the rock wall behind the Perspex cabinet began to shift and change into grotesque and sinister shapes. The water in the well began to overflow its borders and slop over its edge. The spilt liquid pooled on the floor surface in front of the raised cork dais where Ad-Dajjal was meditating. Simultaneously, a strange glow formed over some of the more gruesome vivisection instruments and restraints.

A mist coalesced in the cabinet containing the skull, seeping out of the Perspex chest and slowly taking a human form. However, this was not the happy, contented Buddha so familiar to visitors to Asia. This figure had the gaunt and haunted face of the ascetic who has embraced the experiences of pain, suffering and hate.

The Buddha of Darkness raised his orange-robed arms to command the other discarnate energies residing in the cave. In response, terrifying phantasms began to emerge from the well. Bodies that bent into unnatural postures crawled like broken spiders, while others scampered upside down like crabs, rapidly going up the cavern walls and across the ceiling to drop down on the mediating figure of Ad-Dajjal from above. From the pools of water that had gathered from the overflow of the well, a dark mass of jet-black hair rose and slowly coalesced into the form of a young woman in a soaking-wet red kimono. This girl had the mottled skin of a cadaver and a massive deep wound on her neck where a short sword had terminated her mortal existence. The girl's jaw hung limply, leaving her mouth wide in a hideous parody of a grin.

These dark forms gathered and surrounded the seated figure of Ad-Dajjal. Their manifestation made the air in the cave fetid with the stench of long decay. Behind them, the figure of the dark Buddha spoke in Nepalese Sanskrit,

"My child, let me see into your soul to explore your fears properly."

As Ad-Dajjal's performance of the Karada ni ashi o fumiireru gishiki ritual concluded, waves of energy essence formed themselves around her head forming the dark cobra-shaped hood of the legendary Naga left-hand path master adepts. Ad-Dajjal's eyes opened, and her face glowed as she exhaled thick incense smoke through her nostrils.

A CHANGED MAN

"If you want to shine like a sun, first burn like a sun." - A. P. J. Abdul Kalam

Two hundred thousand miles from the Earth,

19.30 HRS Coordinated Universal Time (UTC), 15th of September, present-day

The swirling debris field was sixteen miles wide and millions of miles long. It flew through the void of space at over 100,000 miles an hour and accelerated further as it swept around the Sun's gravitational field. For the most part, it comprised fragments of ice, rock and iron around the size of a grain of sand. However, more significant components ranged in magnitude from a pebble to a small automobile. By accident, these larger fragments were clustered in the furthest part of the debris field, away from the orbital paths of most of the inner planets.

The Perseids are one of the most significant phenomena regularly passing through the inner Solar System. They are stuck on a yearly passage around the Sun that brings them past the Earth to provide a magnificent light show[464] every September[465]. The fragments are remains that have been sheared off the massive Swift-Tuttle[466] comet[467] over thousands of years by the gravitational fields from the two

---

[464] Up to 100 meteors per hour, each travelling at 37 miles per second.

[465] Fall in the Northern Hemisphere, Spring in the Southern Hemisphere.

[466] Swift-Tuttle was discovered in 1862 by Lewis Swift and Horace Parnell Tuttle.

[467] 109P/Swift–Tuttle is 16 miles in diameter and passes the Earth every 133 years.

dominant forces in our little Solar System, Jupiter and the Sun. Over the past thirty days, a stream of the lighter debris from the Epsilon Perseids had flown into the Earth's upper atmosphere, giving star-gazing residents in the Earth's Northern hemisphere a continuous show of shooting stars through the night sky.

Tonight, however, things were different. When the possessed[468] adept Madeleine Mathers had activated the St Petersburg Qliphothic Wheel[469] as a part of the Opening of The Ten Gates Ceremony[470], she had temporarily increased the Earth's gravitational attraction[471]. These gravitational effects were variable, related to slight irregularities within the construction of the Qliphothic wheel, which meant that, as the two cylinders that made up the device rotated, the generated forces varied. These variations induced

---

[468] Strictly speaking, the ancient MUŠ.ŠÀ.TÙR soul parasite indwells rather than possesses. The difference being that indwelling involves infesting all the host's non-physical bodies, except the highest immortal principle. Possession usually only involves controlling the lower (more material) non-physical bodies.
[469] Also known as the Trubka (cylinder). Western Occultists use the term Qliphothic Wheels (קליפתיים גלגלים).
[470] A gruesome magickal ritual intended to bring Chairman Cortez to power over Europe and to increase the occult powers of Madeleine Mathers, or more accurately the entity that resided within her.
[471] Although we will primarily focus on the gravitational effects, it is more accurate to say that the Qliphothic wheel produces what ancient Vedic sources describe as distortions of Brahman (space, time and consciousness). The changes to time and consciousness are as equally profound as the gravitation affect but are only noticeable to an observer from outside our reality. We would need multiple versions of this book to represent such complexities, so for convenience, we will focus only on the effect of the cylinder's gravitational influences (yes, I take my research very seriously).

instabilities in the Earth's mantle and disrupted the trajectory of orbiting objects within the solar system.

The closest of these orbiting objects which had been affected by these wildly varying terrestrial gravitational fields were the Epsilon Perseids. Since completing their orbit of the Sun thirty days earlier, they had started slowing as they passed the orbits of Mercury and Venus. Their original trajectory would have made them brush past the Earth, causing their traditional annual light show in the night sky.

However, with their revised trajectory, instead of the smaller and lighter objects glancing at the Earth's upper atmosphere and burning up, the entire stream of the massive debris field slammed into the atmosphere at a sixty-degree angle with a speed of over 100,000 mph. The more significant objects, rocks as large as three yards square, which normally skirted past the Earth, now ploughed into the upper atmosphere. These boulders rapidly became superheated and exploded thirty miles above the ground, each with the equivalent of a fifty-kiloton nuclear weapon[472]. Although an airburst explosion of this magnitude occurs by chance every twenty years, hundreds of similar explosions filled the skies over the Northern Hemisphere this afternoon. As this relentless aerial bombardment continued, what had initially been celebrated by the global news networks as a free fireworks display, became of grave concern. TV and Internet pundits predicted that the massive airbursts would increase global cloud cover and lead to a cooling effect that would adversely affect agricultural production for up to five years. Others speculated that the exploding materials could be toxic, and, of course, TV evangelists started demanding increased pledges from their congregations for the imminent apocalypse. Leading University science departments around

---

[472] For comparison, the Hiroshima atomic bomb "Little Boy" yielded 15 kilotons.

the globe asked the AI chat systems, which had replaced tenured faculty, about the ongoing phenomena. They were duly impressed by plagiarised texts paraphrased from works by Carl Sagan and John Wyndham. As a result, several large institutions spent their entire annual budget on weed-killer, salt and blindfolds.

Thirty miles beneath a series of massive meteor bursts over the Haut-Languedoc Regional Natural Park, fifty miles North of the Mediterranean coast in Southern France, Chairman Cortez stood facing a thirty-foot square aluminium double-glazed window, looking at the aerial explosions lighting the evening skies above him. Shortly after each airburst, the metal-framed window rattled. Cortez's vision was blurry, and his legs, back, and shoulders ached with the telltale signs of over-exertion that every older person learns to recognise if they want to avoid illness. He would rest soon, but first, he needed to know one thing from the fire survivor.

After his midnight briefing in London, he had initially intended to retire to bed to recover from a full day of celebration. Instead, after hearing the news that there was an unknown survivor from the catastrophic explosion at Fortress Grmožur, it had taken him nearly eighteen hours to reach Europe's premier burns unit in Lamalou-les-Bains[473].

Cortez's extraordinary influence over all aspects of his new dominion was such that within thirty minutes of his instructions to Major General Smegget, an Equinor[474] Airbus

---

[473] Clinique de Réadaptation du Dr STER, 9 Av. Dr Jean Ster, 34240, Lamalou-les-Bains.
[474] Equinor ASA (Statoil) is a Norwegian Oil company.

H125[475] helicopter had picked him up from St James Square, whisking him to a waiting BNP Paribas[476] Gulfstream[477] jet at London City Airport. Once airborne, the Argentinian's flight made rapid progress towards Beziers[478] Airport in Southern France- where Smegget had chartered an Airbus Twin Squirrel[479] helicopter to remain on standby for transporting the Chairman twenty miles to the exclusive burns clinic.

While Corrado accompanied his grandfather, Hartman, the older of the two grandsons, remained in London to coordinate the urgent extradition of USAF Chief Booker from Egypt so the Meri-Isfet Adept could meet Cortez at the French burns hospital in case there was a need to affect nonphysical communication with the burns patient. Hartman had transferred over two million dollars in baksheesh[480] to the Egyptian authorities and used US Defense Secretary Maskins' influence to clear a US Marines F18F[481] Super Hornet to transport Booker from Cairo[482] to Beziers in the F18's rear seat[483] to achieve his goal. As an additional

---

[475] Better known as the Eurocopter AS350 Écureuil. An executive class transport helicopter.

[476] BNP Paribas - a French international bank with the largest assets in Europe.

[477] The Gulfstream G700 is one of the world's fastest executive jets, with a range of 7,500 nautical miles and a top speed of Mach 0.925 (690 mph). It is bigger than the G800 and can carry 19 passengers in extraordinary luxury. Elon Musk has the smaller and cheaper G600.

[478] BZR is the airport code - in case you are making a booking to follow Cortez to the clinic.

[479] The Airbus Helicopters AS355 Écureuil 2 is very popular in France, where they are manufactured.

[480] A Bribe - Bribery is an established cost of conducting business in the Middle East, just like the British Houses of Parliament, allegedly.

[481] The Boeing F/A-18F Super Hornet is a 2-seater multi-role fighter with a range of 1458 miles and a top speed of 1190 mph (Mach 1.6).

[482] Cairo International Airport (CAI).

[483] The weapon systems officer seat.

complication, the 1800-mile journey was beyond the range of the F18. It required Hartman to coordinate with Maskins to provide in-air refuelling from an MQ-25A Stingray tanker from Aviano Air Base[484] in Northeastern Italy.

On the Gulfstream, the Chairman could barely keep his eyes open; he completed a hurried wash in the Grand Suite of the G700 before removing his jacket, loosening his signature bolo tie, and falling asleep on the luxurious double bed. In contrast, the young Corrado extended the leg rests on one of the cabin seats in the Forward Ultra Galley and indulged in Martell V.S. Cognac and Columbian cocaine; while watching Pasolini's sadistic-themed movie "Salò[485]" on his iPhone Pro. Smegget had the worst of the flight. His ample frame struggled to find comfort in the narrow crew jump seats located behind the cockpit.

One hour and ten minutes into the flight, the skies began to explode around them, buffeting the executive plane with shock waves from the numerous airbursts bombarding the Earth.

Corrado was awake instantly and stumbled into a bleary-eyed Smegget as the pair entered the cockpit to assess the situation. Even though the explosions were twenty miles above their cruising altitude of 51,000 feet[486], the airbursts rapidly superheated the atmosphere, destabilising the airflow so that all air traffic over New Europa was immediately grounded.

---

[484] The Italian Government allows the US forces to use the airbase.
[485] Salò, or the 120 Days of Sodom by Pier Paolo Pasolini – 1975. Ranked by Far Out magazine as the most disturbing film of all time. No, I have not watched it and would not want to. It is mentioned to give an indication of the psychological pathologies within the psyche of Cortez's grandson.
[486] 51,000 feet is 9.6 miles above the ground.

Showing his true nature, Corrado insisted that it should be Smegget who disturbed their sleeping leader to tell him the news. It took three firm shakes before the haggard-looking older man turned up from his bed to look at the Major General. At first, Cortez thought he had arrived at Beziers. It took a moment to comprehend what Smegget was saying, as it did not fit his expectations,

"Forgive me, Chairman, asteroid explosions are closing down all air traffic."

Rising from his bed, the Argentinian pulled apart the porthole curtains and saw the sky light up in all directions, with new fireballs exploding around them. Not caring that he was barefoot and partially dressed, Cortez stormed to the cockpit, rapidly assessed the situation and instructed the pilots,

"Land at Lyon," and then to Smegget, "Organise some ground transportation. Now!"

Smegget walked down the aisle and, using his iPhone, commenced calling all the car rental agencies at Lyon airport to find rapid ground transportation for the Chairman and his small entourage of five people[487]. He ended up renting two light blue Peugeot SUV[488]s from the sleepy-sounding clerk at the Avis desk. The rental cars proved to be comfortable but far too slow for the Chairman, who cursed Smegget for the entire four hours it took to cover the three hundred miles of highway along the A7 and A9, through Avignon and Montpellier, to the exclusive clinic treating the unknown survivor from the fortress explosion.

---

[487] Corrado, Smegget and three knights of the Black Sun as close protection.
[488] The Peugeot 5008 is a 7-seater SUV with a top speed of just under 120 mph. The car was used by the French President, before the Cortez revolution.

The temperature in Southern France in mid-September usually hovers around a pleasant mid-70s Fahrenheit - tonight, however, the asteroid airbursts had raised the ground temperature to well over 120 F. The fireballs had super-dried the usually moist, humid air from the Mediterranean. Following a lengthy drought, Southern Europe had become extremely dry, making it highly susceptible to wildfires. The ongoing massive aerial explosions exacerbated this critical situation, pushing already vulnerable areas over the edge, starting what would quickly become a devastating disaster.

Although the air conditioning inside the two SUVs kept Cortez's team comfortable, massive fires raged in the French countryside, burning the arable crop fields on either side of the highway, giving a highly surreal feel to the journey. Smegget, sitting in the lead car with the Chairman[489], began receiving urgent phone calls with updates from the numerous infernos that had spontaneously started throughout New Europa.

As if these frantic calls for assistance were not bad enough, Smegget also started receiving calls from the largest US investment banks who had secretly backed Cortez's rise to power- in the same way they had funded every major conflict or revolution for the past hundred years[490]. Seeing fires spreading uncontrolled throughout New Europa, the bankers became nervous about their investment. Cortez snatched Smegget's phone. This harassment was typical of bankers - he was having a bad day, and these parasites worried about

---

[489] Corrado travelled separately from Cortez in case of a road accident.

[490] For details of how US investment bankers funded the armament of Nazi Germany and Imperial Japan while US men and women were being slaughtered see John Strausbaugh's "Victory City, a history of New York and New Yorkers during world war II. (2018)."

their money rather than waiting to see how the situation evolved.

Although he sounded confident on the phone, the Argentinian's mood had darkened internally. A glorious celebration yesterday turned into a shitfest before his eyes, and none of it was his fault. To make things worse, it was possible that the senior Meri-Isfet adepts who could have provided him with magickal help to deal with these natural phenomena had been burnt to a crisp. The irony of the powerful adepts being incinerated while New Europa suffered a similar fate was not lost on Cortez.

These natural disasters were NOT what Cardinal Regio had promised would result from the Opening of The Ten Gates ceremony. Cortez recalled the expense and logistics required from Wolfsangel funds to construct the Grmožur Fortress. In the end, the takeover of Europe was more down to the clever manipulation of Social Media by Beyond Facts than any esoteric mumbo jumbo. Now he thought about it; the Chairman recalled that his father, Alois[491], had warned him that the Meri-Isfet had their own agenda. The old Fuhrer frequently ranted about how the senior Isfet adepts had let him down in the end - insisting it was only his inner circle's cunning and the Western Allies' corrupt nature to accept bribes that allowed him to escape from Europe and resettle in Argentina.

Cortez concluded his reflections by directing his thoughts about how he could continue without the support of the Meri-Isfet. At the Wigmore Hall, he had seen three so-called Occult Masters run like cowards from a bunch of twigs, so maybe he did not need them after all. This meeting at the hospital would decide things. If there was a surviving senior adept, perhaps they could assist his plans; otherwise, he

---

[491] Alois Hiedler - you know him by another name.

would be done with the Meri-Isfet and handle them as he dealt with all his enemies - extermination.

By the time the two blue Peugeots 5008 SUVs carrying Cortez's group pulled up outside the modern white buildings that comprised the Clinique de Réadaptation du Dr STER, they had accumulated three additional escort vehicles. Two marked Peugeot 508[492] traffic police cars from the ASVP[493] and one unmarked silver Alpine A110[494] two-door sports car from the French domestic security service, the RG[495].

Getting out of the lead car, a wave of dry heat similar to that encountered when opening an oven door blasted Cortez. The heat was so intense that it made the ordinarily implacable Chairman loosen his bola tie. While riding in the rear car, Corrado had already removed the thick black Hugo Boss uniform jacket and tie and rolled up his sleeves. All of which were severe breaches of the code of the Knights of the Black Sun, noted Cortez as he critically assessed his least favourite grandson. At least the three escorting Knights and Major General Smegget stuck to the expected dress code, the backs of their uniform jackets soaked to a darker shade with their excessive perspiration.

The Argentinian could see that the sky had assumed an ominous dark colour, and the air was thick with the smoke

---

[492] Peugeot 508 is a four-door saloon with a 128 horse power engine. It manages 0-62mph in 10 seconds, with a 129mph maximum speed.

[493] ASVP (agents de surveillance de la voie publique, public roads surveillance officers.) - Traffic Police.

[494] The A110 is a two-seater sports coupe with a 252 horse power engine. It manages 0-62 mph in 4.5 seconds, with an electronically limited top speed of 155 mph.

[495] Formally called the DGSI or informally, the "RG" (Direction générale de la Sécurité intérieure, General Directorate of Internal Intelligence) - The French Internal (domestic) Intelligence Service.

from burning crops, trees and buildings. Cortez brushed away the largest of the black flakes of ash that had already started to accumulate on his blue Savile Row Suit. Similar large carbon flakes fell around him, like a parody of snow. The closest the Argentinian had felt to this kind of heat had been during the record-breaking summer of 2022, riding his beloved brown Criollo[496] mare, "Jovita[497]", across the arid plans of Patagonia. That had been a demanding but rewarding trip, he recalled. Maybe the current adversity would provide a similar reward, if not for him, then perhaps as a way for his two grandsons to grow in the maturity they lacked.

In every direction, sirens sounded as the French emergency services gave up trying to control the blaze and instead turned their attention to evacuating the population. It was only a matter of time before the raging firestorm would consume the hospital buildings. The thought prompted Cortez to action- he needed to determine the status of the sole survivor. He strode confidently towards the white-coated Médecin[498], waiting at the entrance of the impressive series of three-storey white stone and glass-fronted buildings with its footbridge over an access road named after the famous French rehabilitation specialist, Dr Ster[499].

The Médecin extended his hand, saying,

"Chairman Cortez, I am Hugo Gauthier, assigned to treat the casualty."

---

[496] A breed of Argentinian horse renowned for their ability to endure harsh environments.
[497] Named after Jovita Idar Vivero, an American journalist who fought for the rights of South Americans.
[498] Medical Doctor.
[499] Clinique de Réadaptation du Dr STER was founded in 1954 by Dr. Jean Ster.

The medic's tone and choice of words to describe the unknown burns victim implied the worst. Cortez chose to ignore the implication. Hopefully, that idiot, Booker, being flown in from Cairo, could provide some magical remedy or at least allow some communication concerning the fate of the relics from his father and actions necessary to enable the next stage of his revolution.

"Take me to the patient."

The medic shrugged off the cold response from Cortez and led the group of six newcomers into the bliss of the air-conditioned reception area. Once the two glass entrance doors closed, a clean, antiseptic smell quickly replaced the odour of charcoal that pervaded the outside road.

Dr Gauthier led Cortez towards the elevator, but the Chairman stopped him, asking,

"Where are the stairs?"

A series of assassination attempts had made Cortez avoid confined or concealed areas where his security detail could not anticipate and handle threats. The stairs were open-plan and wide enough for the three escorting Knights of the Black Sun to take a classic bodyguard formation, two in front and one behind their principal. At the top of the stairs, they turned and waited for Dr Gauthier.

The Burns Ward was at the end of a long, wide mezzanine floor that overlooked the reception area below, with a chest-high steel handrail on one side. Pushing open the two double doors at the end of the landing, the group entered a clinical space with twenty beds, ten on one side and ten facing a long window which ran the entire room. Every bed was occupied, and there was a flurry of activity from nurses and paramedics. Every patient had burns of varying severity, some minor and some requiring extensive bandaging and sedation. Separate from these, one patient was completely bandaged and covered by pipes, tubes and electrical cables at the far end of the room. Two large machines had been placed on either side of this patient. On the left side of the bed was an electronic monitor showing vital signs, and on the other, a mechanical ventilator machine. The ventilator bellows rose up and down with an almost hypnotic cadence that matched the heart rhythm displayed on the ECG[500]. In contrast, the EEG[501] trace flatlined.

Médecin Gauthier stood at the bottom of this patient's bed and waited for the three VIPs, Cortez, Corrado and Smegget, to approach. The three escorting Black Knights took positions around the Chairman and watched everyone in the room suspiciously, even the patients. Before the medic could say anything, Cortez waved his hand dismissively- on the chance of some communication from the survivor, there could not be anyone else within earshot.

"Empty the room!"

Gauthier started in shock.

"It is impossible! The hospital is full. Look outside, monsieur, the fire! These poor people need treatment. Our one hundred and thirty beds are already full. We could barely accommodate your victim."

"I have no interest in your institution's challenges, Doctor. Clear this room, or.."

Cortez gestured to the three Knights of the Black Sun posted around him.

"I will reduce the burden these people impose on your institution."

---

[500] Electrocardiogram - shows the rhythm, rate and electrical activity of the heart.
[501] Electroencephalography - shows electrical brain activity.

Gauthier reacted with the disdain the French always show towards heavy-handed authority.

"Non. You put up with these facilities as they are or take your patient elsewhere."

Smegget intervened before Cortez could respond by taking the arm of Gauthier and leading him towards the centre of the room, whispering something in French into the Doctor's right ear. The Major General knew the Chairman was more than capable of executing everyone in the ward without hesitation. After the conversation between Smegget and the Doctor, the medic consulted with the senior nurse. Moments later, attendants started moving the beds for those patients who could not move and using wheelchairs for those who were more mobile.

The Doctor came back and addressed the Chairman,

"We will move the patients to the first-floor landing, but it is not worth the effort. Your patient is already dead. The machines are the only things keeping her alive."

"Her?" Cortez was suddenly interested, "Did she have any personal effects?"

Gauthier shrugged and passed over a grey metal tray he picked up from the bedside. The Argentinian went through the few items and then held up a semi-melted gold ring engraved with the outline of a pentagram.

"This ring. Was it on the patient's finger or in her clothing?"

Gauthier paused for a second, thinking.

"We removed it from her right ring finger. The flesh had melted around it."

Cortez smiled for the first time that day. Turning to Smegget, he looked at his gold IWC watch and asked,

"How long until Booker's ETA?"

Smegget consulted his iPad.

"The original estimate for his journey in the F18 from Cairo was three and a half hours,"

The Major General looked at his Bremont, counting off the hours,

"He should already have been here, Chairman. I will check with Hartman on his progress."

Smegget was retrieving his iPhone from his uniform pocket when Dr Gauthier intervened. He pointed to the numerous signs declaring "Pas de mobile" and showed rays from a phone interfering with hospital equipment.

"With your permission, Chairman," Smegget indicated that he needed to go outside to make a call. Cortez nodded and walked away from the group to stand in front of one of the large windows along the outer side of the ward before turning to look at the small group gathered by the single patient, saying,

"Give me a moment to think."

When alone, Cortez listened to the familiar sounds made by the ventilator machine. The noise triggered vivid memories from fifteen years ago when he had spent days and nights at a bedside in a hospital[502] in Córdoba, listening to a similar machine keeping Gunther, his only son, alive. After weeks of false hope, Cortez had turned off the life support and let his son go, but only after vowing that he would look after Gunther's two sons, Hartman and Corrado, as his own. The original plan, made by Cortez's own father, had been for Gunther to lead the resurrection of the organisation on its return to Europe.

---

[502] Hospital Colonia Dr. Emilio Vidal Abal, Córdoba, Argentina. One of the best equipped in Argentina.

There had been such hope for Gunther. He was brave, intelligent and disciplined. A rare combination in the modern world. Funding for the revolution necessitated taking over the lucrative drug production from the South American drug cartels. The inevitable violent confrontation with the Columbians resulted in the revenge killing of Gunther and his wife, Anna, as they exited the Novillo Dorado (Golden Steer) nightclub in downtown Buenos Aires. Guilt made Cortez spoil the two orphans, and with hindsight, they both grew up with moral weaknesses that made them unsuitable to lead. Cortez had to take over the role of leader for the Wolfsangel movement, even though he never wanted or planned for it.

A cough from behind him broke the contemplation, and turning around from the window, he faced a flustered Smegget with his face smeared from the ash that continued to fall heavily outside.

"Chairman, Booker's aircraft has been forced to land. Ten minutes after the mid-air refuelling in Northern Italy, the F18 had to land in Genoa."

Cortez sighed. "So, how long before he gets here?"

"We have organised a driver and car to bring him here along the A8."

The Chairman had little patience left.

"I don't care about the route, Smegget. I want to know when Booker will arrive."

"Four hours and ten minutes, Chairman."

"I thought Italian cars were supposed to be fast. What did we get Booker, a Fiat Panda?"

K.R.M. Morgan

Smegget winced, looked down at his iPad and replied, "Hartman organised a Maserati Ghibli Trofeo[503]. I believe the road conditions from falling debris limit the vehicle to one hundred miles an hour."

Cortez grunted his acceptance of the situation.

"In that case, I will get some sleep while I wait. Post two Knights on guard at the door, with orders that I will not be disturbed. When Booker arrives, bring him to me immediately."

Smegget nodded and walked to the double doors at the end of the ward. Now finally alone, Cortez walked over to one of the vacant beds, removed his jacket and shoes, and lay down. Not long after, the sound of the ventilation machine bellows going up and down guided the Argentinian into a deep sleep.

Usually, such profound states of exhaustion result in entirely dreamless sleep. However, Chairman Cortez dreamed of lying adjacent to the unknown female burn victim on the bed. He could tell it was a dream because, standing at the bottom of his bed, next to his bare feet, was a chimaera, around six feet tall, with the thick segmented body of a serpent, whose tail led away towards the burn victim's bed in a mass of thick root-like tendrils. The worst part of the nightmare was the numerous heads that swayed, with lamprey-like mouths that towered above the Argentinian's sleeping form. In his dream, before Cortez could reach for his luger, one of the vine-like root tendrils latched onto the Chairman's exposed left foot.

---

[503] The Maserati Ghibli Trofeo is one of the world's fastest saloon cars. Its 3.8 Litre V8 Twin Turbo engine is capable of over 200 mph.

NEVER TRUST A SNITCH

"In my experience, people who go about looking for trouble usually find it." - Agatha Christie

Place du Bourg-de-Four
The old town of Geneva.
1204 Genève
Switzerland.

10:10 HRS (GMT +2), 16th Sept, Present day

The heat was intense, and the stench from the drains and garbage cans on the street made the people of Geneva hurry from place to place, limiting their time spent outside as much as possible. The only exception was near the lake, where groups had gathered to enjoy the occasional cool breeze that swept over the water. Some young and daring residents even braved the cold waters, which would usually be too frigid for swimming. These abnormal conditions were due to the continued cometary aerial bursts that had warmed the lake to a comparatively balmy sixty degrees Fahrenheit.

Although the sun was obscured behind clouds of dust and debris, the regular flashes of light from explosions made visibility at street level passable. In the few places in the city free from the fragrant drains and garbage, a thick acrid smoke clung in the air, making many residents resume using masks they had abandoned at the end of the Covid restrictions. Apart from the drastic environmental changes, the city was also adjusting to life under a new regime. The Swiss had always shown a fiercely independent nature and strong pragmatism. Like most of the smaller nations located on the periphery of New Europa, they had taken note of the ease with which Cotez had subdued the might of the Russian invasion and had quickly opted to join the new alliance under Chairman Cortez. As a result, the size of New Europa had grown considerably over the last twenty-four hours and now included Switzerland, Turkey and all the former Soviet satellite republics. Russia remained stubbornly independent.

As all occupying forces throughout history quickly discover, the major challenge in expanding an empire is controlling the newly acquired population. Cortez's New Republic addressed this by deploying state-of-the-art Robotic AI surveillance systems called "SNITCH[504]". Airborne surveillance drone systems complemented these four-foot-tall weaponised quadrupedal robots, which monitored all activity undertaken in the newly acquired territories. The AI systems learnt and adapted their behaviour based on the circumstances and environment where they were deployed, without user intervention. The AI design was a so-called "black box" implementation, unable to explain its actions. Once turned on, the only maintenance required was to resupply consumables and wash down the unit's exterior- both of these processes were automated to allow the regime to focus its limited human resources on expanding its territories. The service life of each SNITCH was five years of continuous operation, after which time it was anticipated that a more sophisticated model would replace them.

Each region's SNITCHs operated as a social unit based on canine pack behaviour, rapidly evolving their procedures and responses without external intervention. If one unit encountered a situation where it could not cope, the other units came to its assistance to overwhelm whatever threat had been identified. What was learnt in one region was rapidly integrated into the AI systems in other SNITCH packs,

---

[504] SynchroNous Independent TeCHnology for control and surveillance (SNITCH). Derived from a multibillion-dollar project for autonomous quadrupedal robots called LS3 (AlphaDog) by DARPA and Boston Dynamics. SNITCH added state of the art collaborative AI and weapon systems developed by Wolfsangel SA.

so they behaved similarly. Theoretically, this design meant efficiency increased exponentially as the collaborative AI continuously evolved.

The autonomous dog-sized SNITCH robots used complex identity recognition systems[505] to categorise their observed population. Those individuals or groups identified as a threat to the new regime faced a series of different responses, depending on the severity of their classification and the danger they posed to the smooth running of the new order. For individuals classified by the AI system as requiring interrogation or "re-education[506]", the SNITCH was equipped with a chemically laced[507] sedative Sticky Foam[508] that immobilised and incapacitated the target to retrieve them later by specialised automated recovery transport.

The SNITCH was also equipped with a range of lethal responses for individuals judged to be a significant persistent threat. These included a swivel-mounted machine gun[509] and a pressurised spray that dispersed a modified form of the VX[510] nerve agent. The release of the nerve agent was initially

---

[505] The system analyses gait, posture, and body heat signatures besides standard facial recognition.

[506] Chemically enhanced "re-education" programmes are run at most Cortez Camps.

[507] An enhanced hybrid of benzodiazepine, ten times more potent than Clonazepam.

[508] Sticky Foam was first developed at Sandia National Laboratory (SNL) in the 1970s. Originally intended for riot control in correctional facilities. In the early 1990s, US Marines successfully used modified versions in Operation "United Shield" in Somalia.

[509] A performance-enhanced, compact gas-operated 4.6 mm x 30 calibre submachine gun - derived from the HK MP7.

[510] VX (venomous agent X) was developed in the 1950s by the British at their top-secret bioweapons research laboratory at Porton Down, Salisbury, UK. The VX formula is based on the work of weapons researcher Gerhard Schrader, in Nazi Germany.

intended as a last resort countermeasure against a group trying to overwhelm a solitary SNITCH. Still, like every "final resort", it had quickly become the preferred method for the self-learning AI systems to eliminate every human it judged an imminent existential threat to itself.

VX nerve agents are an oily amber liquid that does not quickly dissipate, remaining highly toxic to touch or inhalation to all living creatures for weeks after release. Consequently, every VX agent deployment should have had an extensive "clean-up" operation quickly afterwards by specialised chemical weapons teams. However, the frequency with which the SNITCH's decision-making systems used VX after deployment quickly made such clean-ups unfeasible. An unexpected bonus of this lax approach to decontamination was that leaving the dead where they had fallen instilled such a degree of terror into the population that they became increasingly compliant with the new regime. Two days after the initial deployment of SNITCH systems throughout New Europa, New Africa and the growing territories in the Americas, the general population developed a pathological fear of the robots. Most sensible people avoided them and the areas they patrolled.

Although the SNITCH was intended for civilian deployments[511], it was, like the Minotour[512], heavily armoured under its central main body panels. The unit's front, sides and rear contained an array of sensors covering

---

511 Using a modified version of the fission power plant developed for the Minotour battlefield weapons platform.
512 Mobile, Intelligent, Nuclear powered, Outdoor-all Terrain, Automated, unTethered, Robot, or "Minotaur". This is a nuclear-powered, autonomous (self-directed by Artificial Intelligence), eight-foot tall, bipedal humanoid robotic weapons platform for battlefield deployment—part of the 21st-century soldier programme proudly developed by Wolfsangel SA.

the visible and invisible spectrums[513]. The front of the unit was equipped with a distinctive large single illuminated red lens connected to a high-resolution image processor that the SNITCH used to perform an enhanced visual analysis of a specific human target, including facial recognition and scanning of the unique UNITY identification barcode tattoos which could be matched to the central identity database. Each SNITCH device controlled insect-sized surveillance drones[514], which flew under radio control and were deployed from recharging racks on the main body's back.

One of the thirty SNITCH units deployed to control downtown Geneva was patrolling within the city centre, South of the lake near St Pierre Cathedral. As was usually the case, the immediate vicinity around the unit was deserted, apart from a few inert foam-covered bodies awaiting the hourly collection rounds that had replaced the civilian police in most of New Europa. Although a significant Wolfsangel operation was underway nearby, there was no other planned activity, so a single approaching motor vehicle attracted the unit's attention. With a smooth series of dog-like strides, it rapidly preambulated on its four hydraulically controlled legs until it stood in the centre of Rue de l'Hôtel-de-Ville and scanned the approaching object. Each of the robot's movements was preceded by a low-pitched buzz from the tiny motors that powered the flow of pressurised fluids that enabled the device's locomotion. The machine's four large

---

513 Besides these cameras, location detection was from GPS, combined with Lidar (Light Detection and Ranging). Lidar is a pulsed laser used to measure distances between objects.
514 All the SNITCH units operating in an area share the feeds from the cameras and microphones on the micro drones to coordinate their control over a local population.

"feet" were made from the same specialised Zylon[515] polymer used for the robot's bodywork.

The ambient light on the Rue de l'Hôtel-de-Ville in front of the SNITCH was intermittently interrupted by a brilliant flash from one of the cometary airbursts, forcing the unit to compensate in its analysis of the colours of the approaching vehicle. Complex neural nets and decision tree arrays identified the approaching object as a 1967 Volkswagen camper with green and white bodywork. The weight balance of the old mini-van indicated the presence of a heavy object attached to the rear. With a 97% certainty, the AI predicted this object was another smaller vehicle, probably a heavy motorcycle. The pre-2009 Paris number plate on the VW van was registered to a citizen of the New Europa province, formally known as France. This human's identity was a forty-two-year-old female known as Ms Madeleine Mathers. The database entries for this human indicated that she was of significant interest to the regime. A standing order in the database instructed that this human should be immediately processed for urgent interrogation at the central Wolfsangel complex in Büren[516], Westphalia, in the New Europa province formerly known as Germany. Accessing this standing priority order triggered eight other SNITCH units patrolling the downtown area to begin making their way to Rue de l'Hôtel-de-Ville. Trouble was anticipated.

The lone SNITCH unit facing Madeleine Mathers' old VW continued its visual analysis as the additional SNITCH units gathered around it. Through the approaching split windscreen, the cameras showed that the current driver was

---

[515] Zylon is nearly twice as strong as Kevlar and has extraordinary flame resistance as it only combusts in an atmosphere containing more than seventy per cent oxygen.
[516] Wewelsburg Castle, the planned Reichsführer school for SS officers.

a powerfully built middle-aged male, just over six feet tall and weighing approximately two hundred pounds. The man had short salt and pepper greying hair and a close-cropped beard which accentuated a rugged profile. This target male was wearing dark RayBan Wayfarer sunglasses, obscuring his eyebrows, bridge of the nose, eye spacing and cheekbone structures. Without these critical features, exact facial recognition was not possible. Consequently, the visual analysis provided over twenty-four thousand possible identity matches for the unknown driver, none of whom was the van's registered owner. The AI decided this uncertainty demanded the vehicle be stopped to clarify the situation and identify the driver. As the old van approached closer, the complex AI directed a swarm of tiny drones to provide a multiple-perspective composite image of the unknown target, much like the compound eyes of a dragonfly observing a mosquito it planned to consume in mid-flight.

As the swarm of house fly-sized micro-drones flew around the front of the camper van and through the open front side window, the SNITCH units began to get a more detailed view of this unknown man. He was informally dressed, befitting the current heat, which the AI recognised caused humans increasing discomfort in temperatures above one hundred degrees Fahrenheit. The man was wearing a short-sleeved navy-coloured pique knitted shirt. An analysis of the weave and cotton density indicated high-quality hand-made manufacture. The man's chalk-white linen trousers and tan leather deck shoes had similar craftsmanship[517]. The micro drone's airborne sensors showed that the air inside the mini-van cab was laced with micro droplets of citrus, mint and woody notes of moss[518].

---

[517] Keswick short sleeve polo shirt and Tierney trousers in chalk white linen crafted in Elgin, Scotland, by Ede & Ravenscroft.
[518] Hermès Eau d'orange verte Cologne.

As the small drones drifted around the driver, they detected a large black revolver with a three-inch barrel attached to the left side of the man's tan leather bandolier belt in a triple-loop holster[519]. Unusually, the gun was positioned with the hilt forward[520]. A millisecond later, the AI systems identified the weapon as a modified Korth NSC 357[521]. Further analysis showed that the bullets in the bandolier belt around the man's waist were .357 Remington Maximum rounds. The AI quickly determined that this bullet and pistol were no longer in mass production due to its propensity for the discharge force and heat to damage the gun's mechanism[522].

In addition to this weapon, the unknown man had the top of a small, highly decorated pocket knife visible from the top of his right trouser pocket. The SNITCH's reverse image search identified this knife as an ORSO[523]. This knife had a gently shaped three-inch blade with a spear point, unlike the seven-inch tanto-tipped tactical knife used by Wolfangel operatives[524].

---

[519] The triple loops tie the holster firmly to the leg, making a rapid, accurate gun draw more likely.

[520] A holstered gun position favoured by Wyatt Earp, one of the best gunfighters in history, who was never injured during his numerous gunfights. Such a position permits a rapid gun draw from a seated position, such as on horseback or from the driver's seat of a 1967 VW camper van.

[521] Chambered for a .357 Maximum calibre.

[522] Many users of the .357 Maximum rounds reported flame cutting (heat damage) of the revolver top strap (the metal bar over the top of the cylinder). However, this was due to them loading their weapons with lighter (110 and 125) grain rounds. The problem was not recorded using larger grain rounds (above 158 grains).

[523] Designed and made by Jens Ansø, a master knife maker from Denmark.

[524] The KM2000 is made in Austrian Bohler N695 steel (similar composition to 440C) by Eickhorn-Solingen in Germany.

The AI system summarised what it could predict about this unknown person. The man had expensive but very dated tastes. From the modern perspective, which regards any design over five years old as obsolete, this man was operating in the relative stone age. He lacked any of the smart technology that is essential for elite operatives in the modern setting. This unknown man's gun only carried six rounds, and those rounds had been discontinued due to the damage they caused to the gun. Even the man's wristwatch was a simple quartz field timekeeper.

In contrast, the Wolfsangel operatives used integrated smart technology throughout their equipment selection. Their Glock[525] carried seventeen rounds in a widely available calibre[526] and was known to be utterly reliable. The most charitable assessment from a modern perspective would be that the man's clothing, gun, knife and watch were the finest options commercially available decades ago. The SNITCH AI categorised this unknown man as rich, incompetent and probably harmless. He would still need to be detained or terminated, as he was driving a vehicle known to be associated with regime enemies and was carrying weapons in a public place.

The pack of SNITCH units activated their sedative-laced restraining foam gun, and three of the group pulled themselves dramatically into an upright, bipedal position- so they stood directly in the line of sight of the driver of the approaching VW. Their central red "eye" lenses glowed menacingly while the remaining SNITCH pack members, who remained on all fours, directed their machine guns at the approaching threat. The three standing SNITCH units

---

[525] A highly modified variant of the Glock 17, a full framed handgun designed by the Austrian manufacturer, Glock Ges.
[526] 9mm.

instructed the driver of the oncoming camper van. First in French, then German, Spanish and finally, English,

"STOP!

Turn off your engine!

Slowly step out of the vehicle for an identification check!"

Twenty yards away from the SNITCH pack, along the Rue de l'Hôtel-de-Ville, Tavish Stewart calmly noted the machine gun barrels swivelling round on their turrets towards him through the split windscreen. He eased off the accelerator and slowly brought the old camper van to a halt, twenty feet in front of the pack of grey-coloured polymer[527] SNITCH units that blocked the cobbled road ahead.

Stewart slowly opened the driver's door and stepped down to the road with both hands out in a modified "hands up" gesture, which left his hands at a width beyond the peripheral range of most individuals. This modified "surrender" posture meant that if needed, the Scotsman could begin a rapid movement of either hand without instantly being noticed by most human opponents. However, today, he knew he was not facing a living adversary.

A small swarm of fly-sized objects flew around him, reminding him of the midges that were a nuisance to hikers during the summer months in his beloved Highlands. Stewart had to tell himself that these particular "midges" relayed details about him to the four-legged robots. Now that the Scotsman was standing upright, a unique badge was visible under the fold of his opened polo shirt collar. The silver enamelled pin was causing considerable interest for the swarm and the SNITCH pack, as evidenced by the three standing robots focusing their large and threatening red

---

[527] Zylon

visual sensors onto the peculiar button pinned on the Scotsman's shirt.

For what felt like the millionth time that morning, Stewart ran through his plan to bring the fight to Cortez.

The idea had formed in the Scotsman's mind during the late-night dinner in "The Place" restaurant in Sarajevo two days earlier, when Mark Katz, the Mossad director, described the design of the AI systems directing the SNITCH robots used by Cortez to control the population in his new empire. It was clear to everyone that any counter-revolutionary movement was doomed without a superior military force supporting them. The United States was in turmoil, its future looking highly uncertain. Russia and China had clarified that they would not take any future action against Cortez. It was, therefore, down to this small group who had gathered around the late-night dinner table to initiate any action that might topple Cortez and restore democracy. By the third single malt, a vague idea had started to form in Stewart's mind. As Mark Katz said when the Scotsman first outlined the plan,

"Bloody risky but fucking brilliant - if it works."

Stewart's six former UN war crimes investigators were less enthusiastic, calling it "Suicide". But, since no one else had an alternative strategy, it was agreed. After the late-night meeting concluded, Stewart's six former UN war crimes colleagues and Katz departed, taking a list of items the Scotsman requested with the undertaking they would provide them the following morning. Stewart then drove the old VW van to his favourite hotel in Sarajevo, the İsa Begov Hamam, where he had booked his usual suite. Not only did the room have hand-carved furniture with Ottoman motifs and genuine hand-woven Turkish carpets over the wooden floors, but it also boasted a magnificent view of the four Olympic[528] mountains of Trebević, Jahorina, Igman, and Bjelašnica.

After packing his wallet, pixel phone, and Chromebook into the room safe, Stewart went downstairs to the hotel's legendary sauna. The numerous injuries suffered at the Fortress Grmožur dealing with the Wolfsangel thugs meant the Scotsman's body was sore, stiff and bruised. In Stewart's experience, these aliments were best treated with a good Turkish massage followed by a long soak in the Hotel's famous Hamam[529], and then a well-deserved sleep in the luxurious four-poster bed in his room.

After a glorious night, Stewart woke with light streaming through the white linen blinds. He had a local Barber come to his room for a haircut and a beard trim while he enjoyed a traditional Turkish breakfast of black olives, cucumber, cured meats, egg, cheese, fresh-baked bread and sweet butter on the terrace outside his room. While Stewart was taking in the beauty of the four Olympic mountains, the first of his packages arrived.

A courier delivered a sealed package from the Israeli Embassy in Budapest, which served Bosnia and Herzegovina. After signing for the large envelope, Stewart tore it open. He took out an Argentinian Passport, a set of four UNITY bar code temporary tattoos and a distinctive silver badge decorated with ornate motifs. The badge still had the inventory label from the Rome police department's evidence lockup, where it had been "liberated". Stewart checked the forged passport, which included numerous visa stamps from

---

[528] The venue of the 1984 Olympic Winter Games.
[529] The Hotel's ancient Turkish bath dates back to 1462 - the era of Sultan Mehmed the Conqueror (1429-1481).

around the world and a picture that looked like the Scotsman.

Shortly after, the hotel porter brought up another package, which had been delivered to reception. It was a large brown paper parcel. Inside was a hand-made tan leather holdall, leather deck shoes with a crepe sole, and details of two airline bookings- a Lufthansa business class ticket and an air freight docket for one VW Camper van from Sarajevo International Airport[530]. Stewart looked at the flight times and checked the time on his Pixel phone; his final guest was cutting things fine.

A cup of bitter coffee later, Stewart had applied one of the temporary tattoos to his inside left forearm. Looking at the final design, he raised his eyebrows; Katz had better not have fucked this one up.

While the temporary tattoo dried, his visitor arrived. She was a young woman in her thirties with short dark hair cut in a bob and oversized, round, red-framed glasses. She wore a Mandalorian T-Shirt, unbranded blue jeans and black leather Puma trainers. Tucked under her arm was a battered old black plastic Acer laptop adorned with numerous sci-fi-themed stickers, including one for the best-selling novel Bridge of Souls[531].

She approached where Stewart was seated, and asked,

"Sir Tavish Stewart?"

"Not so sure about the title anymore, but yes, I am Tavish. You must be the young lady who impressed Mark Katz enough so that he whisked you away from the delights of sheep, South Atlantic gales and unexploded landmines. Glad you agreed to help me, Ms Twop. How was your journey?"

---

[530] Flight Code = SJJ
[531] Clearly, a woman of intelligence and good taste.

Twop helped herself to a cup of strong black coffee.

"Wonderful. It was my first time in a private jet. After Sir Richards said he would arrange for me to get to you, I never expected him to have contacts with Mossad."

Stewart smiled. "Richards is full of surprises. So, do you think you can help in this crazy plan?"

Twop visibly relaxed. "Yes. First, I will scan your face and then the bar code from one of these tattoo transfer sheets. That is the easy bit. Switching your scans with those of the target identity in the Wolfsangel databases will be more challenging."

The Scotsman stood up and walked over to where Twop had opened her laptop on a nearby table and accessed the internet via her 5G Android phone.

"Difficult to hack in?"

Twop shook her head.

"No, getting in is relatively easy. The challenge is how the identity database is distributed- to make the system more robust against attacks. There is no central master set of records. Instead, there is a more organic shared repository. Updates regarded as important by the system are shared as an update from node to node when they contact each other. Any update that is accepted propagates gradually through the Wolfangel systems."

Stewart thought for a moment.

"So this identity change will not fool everyone?"

Twop nodded. "You should be ok close to where we insert the new identity update, but the further you travel away, the less certain it will be that the updates will have rippled through the network nodes."

Stewart smiled. "I will keep telling myself that Geneva is not too far away."

Twop looked nervous. "To be honest, Tavish, I have never done this before, so it could all go terribly wrong."

"Makes it all more exciting. When do we begin?" stated Stewart as he sat down in front of the camera on the old laptop.

Six hours later, with one flight change in Frankfurt, the Scotsman arrived in Geneva in the early afternoon. The unloading and customs clearance for the VW camper would take time, so Stewart took a yellow Mercedes cab to his hotel. Since acquiring the Montenegrin police chief's Bitcoin wallet, Stewart enjoyed a greatly improved quality of life. Living a high life was especially important in Geneva since his alter ego was an international playboy.

In setting up the identity, Twop had added the equivalent of two million USD from the Bitcoin wallet to his new persona, so Stewart checked into the Bellevue Suite at the Hotel D'Angleterre[532] on the edge of Lake Leman. The Scotsman's suite included a balcony overlooking the famous Jet d'Eau and Mont Blanc. As twilight descended on the Swiss city, the cosmos began a celestial fireworks show in the night sky. Making the best use of the view from his suite, Stewart called room service to order from the renowned Windows Restaurant. Sitting on the balcony, watching the exploding cometary airbursts, the Scotsman indulged himself with Smoked Scottish Salmon with 'Prunier Aquitaine Caviar', Dill cream, capers and Beldi lemon for a starter, followed by Wagyu Beef Rib Eye Steak, Soy Sauce Baby vegetables and French fries. As a dessert, Stewart relished a slow Glenfiddich whiskey, reflecting that when he visited SPLEE the next day,

---

532 Hotel D'Angleterre, Quai du Mont-Blanc 17, Geneva, Switzerland.

K.R.M. Morgan

he would probably learn more about the strange explosions
lighting up the night and, hopefully, start the fight against
Cortez in earnest.

SHOW TRIAL

"An acquittal is, in fact, unthinkable from the economic point of view! It would mean that the informers, the Security officers, the Interrogators, the prosecutor's staff, the internal guard in the prison, and the convoy had all worked to no purpose." - Aleksandr Solzhenitsyn

The International Criminal Court (ICC)
Oude Waalsdorperweg 10
The Hague, The Netherlands.

11:00HRS (GMT + 2), 16th September, present day

Cynthia Sinclair cleared her throat of fumes for the umpteenth time as she leant casually against the grey and white walls of the corridor inside Scheveningen Prison. Where she was standing, the smell of pine disinfectant that pervaded every other part of the prison mingled with car exhaust fumes from vehicles that regularly came and departed after loading or unloading their human cargo. The opposite wall from where Sinclair stood was made of transparent Perspex from waist height to the ceiling, allowing a clear view of the prisoners arriving or departing Scheveningen. Every other inmate she could see was a regular prisoner. Only Helen Curren and herself were being held for trial by the ICC. There were no clocks on the walls, and since Sinclair had lost her Cartier during the attempted assassination a few days earlier, she had no way to know the time, but based on the growing stiffness in her ankles, she did know she had been kept waiting for well over an hour. At least she had the distraction of the light show that continued to illuminate the overcast skies from the cometary airbursts which had dominated TV news coverage in her cell.

To her left, standing on either side of the vacant-looking Curren, were two UN guards dressed in smart Royal Dutch

Army uniforms; both men were handcuffed to the lawyer. A similar escort stood on either side of the former head of British Intelligence.   Both Sinclair and Curren were dressed in identical plain black, high-necked, long-sleeved cotton Kuyichi dresses and black leather Ecco loafers provided by the prison for their court appearance. Both women had their hair slicked down in a wet look and wore no makeup or jewellery.

The interminable wait finally ended with UN ICC commandant Kaptian De Jong's approach. The tall, slim Dutchman nodded to Sinclair, saying,

"Ms Sinclair, I apologise for the excessive delay. I have held you here while negotiating with my superiors to ensure the Dutch police handle your transport, not those Wolfsangel thugs. So, at least, you should get to the trial without any accidents. Sadly, I cannot assist you with the trial, but I have heard that Cortez cannot preside, so you should get one of the UN judges, who will hopefully be as unhappy about these irregular trial proceedings as I am."

Sinclair gestured to the hand and ankle cuffs on the trancelike Curren.

"A bit unnecessary, isn't it?"

De Jong shrugged.

"There was some trouble outside the prison yesterday, and we have our orders."

The mention of trouble made Sinclair hopeful that someone, maybe even Stewart, had finally come to her rescue.

"Trouble?"

"You'll see when you go outside."

The commandant gestured for his men to take the two women prisoners through the three sets of interlocked double doors to a Volkswagen Touran van with white, blue, and red livery waiting in the pickup bay. The Touran was escorted by a single Police vehicle- a Mercedes A-class estate decorated in the same distinctive Dutch Police colours.

Once inside the vehicle, Sinclar looked carefully at the equipment carried by her police escorts, assessing her chances if an opportunity to escape presented itself and what kit she would find useful. The Royal Dutch Police uniform was dark blue (almost black) with yellow bands across the chest. They all wore stab vests and baseball caps. Each police officer carried a Samsung smartphone[533] that provided operational[534] instructions, Sinclair surmised, as officers frequently consulted their phones and recorded their activities. Getting one of these phones could prove critical to any successful escape and evasion. The officer's belt contained the usual items of equipment carried by modern law enforcement; dark grey magnesium and polymer handcuffs[535], an expanding baton[536], pepper spray[537] and a black Walther polymer pistol[538]. Sinclair had used the Walther P99 as her daily carry and had a high opinion of it as a sidearm. Shame Walther had discontinued production, she mused to herself. Still, if she could disarm one of the officers, she would have no problems using the weapon effectively. Finally, the standard equipment included the ubiquitous

---

[533] Samsung S21.

[534] Using the MEOS app that provides access to all police and public records.

[535] SHN G2 handcuffs.

[536] Bonowi EKA 51 Camlock - 21-inch expanding baton.

[537] TW 1000.

[538] Walther P99Q NL - 9mm polymer pistol with a ten-round magazine. Standard issue to many European police forces. Discontinued in 2023.

encrypted two-way radio[539] clipped to the right chest of the stab vest.

In addition to this standard equipment, two of the six police officers escorting Sinclair and Curren carried the classic MP5[540] machine guns strapped across their chests. In normal times, such a level of weaponry would have been more than sufficient, but these were most unusual times. Someone in the Dutch Police evidently shared Sinclair's assessment as, on exiting the prison, a third escorting police vehicle tucked in behind their small convoy. This newcomer was a full-sized Toyota Land Cruiser, and based on how it drove and how low it sat on the road, it was, Sinclair judged, fitted with enough Kevlar to make even Tavish Stewart a happy man.

Looking back at the prison, as the escort exited the complex and turned left, Sinclair could see nothing but devastation. Trees were flattened, parked cars smashed, and the front of the prison was peppered with debris. The building's armoured window frames lay broken and hanging loose. Forensic teams dressed in white coveralls[541], swarmed like ants over the area.

"Jesus, what happened here? Did a gas main explode?" asked Sinclair.

The short-haired blond policeman in his late twenties sitting next to her nodded, saying,

"That is the official story."

"And what about the unofficial?" queried Sinclair, hoping the young policeman would be naïve enough to break protocol and discuss a critical incident with a suspect.

---

[539] TETRA communication network of the Dutch security and rescue forces (C2000).
[540] Heckler & Koch MP5. 9mm submachine gun.
[541] Tyvek® 500 Xpert Forensic Suit.

Sinclair was in luck, the policeman obliged, saying,

"A priest released from here yesterday was abducted. That is what all this fuss is about."

"O'Neill?" asked the shocked Sinclair.

She knew O'Neill was due for release, but since she was in solitary confinement, she had no idea anything had happened. The TV news had been entirely focused on the cometary explosions, which had darkened the skies and raised the temperatures.

"Yeah, that was the guy's name. His kidnapping caused quite a stir with our new Lords and Masters."

The policeman gestured to where the convoy of three vehicles was heading. As Sinclair turned to follow the officer's gaze, she was shocked. On either side of the three police vehicles, black Mercedes G Wagon flatbed transport vehicles had started matching their speed and direction. Each G Wagon had been fitted with a .50 calibre machine gun[542] mounted on a heavy weapons pedestal. From a turret on the passenger side roof, an M240[543] light machine gun was visible on a swinging mount.

"Someone is expecting some serious trouble," commented Sinclair.

The policeman nodded. "Typical overkill reaction. Wolfsangel was completely blindsided and utterly outclassed yesterday when the priest was abducted. Two of their commando teams were killed. Now they are overreacting."

"You are sure it was not Wolfsangel doing a false flag op? They are slippery bastards."

---

542 M2 machine gun or Browning .50 calibre machine gun (informally, "Ma Deuce").
543 7.62mm M240 light machine gun. US Military standard.

The policeman hesitated, concerned that any comments about the new ruling elites could negatively affect himself and his family.   Finally, he decided to confide in the woman who would, he rationalised, be dead soon anyway.

"Given the number of Wolfsangel oppos[544] killed yesterday and their reaction today, it was not them."

"Any ideas who it was then?"

The policeman laughed. "Yeah, we have the cheeky bastard on CCTV. He even posed for the fucking cameras during his escape."

Sinclair was puzzled. "One man destroyed two elite commando teams and escaped?"

The former head of British Intelligence was momentarily hopeful that her beloved Stewart was responsible. The policeman pulled up his mobile phone, scrolled until he found what he wanted, and quickly showed the image to Sinclair, who exclaimed in a whisper,

"Abdul Issuin!"

"Yeah. He sure lived up to his title[545]. I pity the poor bastard he abducted. O'Neill, was it?"

Sinclair nodded. The young policeman continued.

"By now, O'Neill will be suffering the most terrible torture imaginable."

Two hundred and eighty miles South of Sinclair's police escort, in a courtyard hidden behind the Salon of Hotel de

---

544 Operatives.
545 The Most Dangerous Man In The World.

L'Abbaye[546] in the heart of Saint-Germain-de-Pres, was an ivy-lined space adorned with colourful cushions on sets of wrought iron furniture. In one corner of the courtyard, a four-piece string quartet performed Vivaldi's Four Seasons[547] while the air was filled with the scent of coffee and freshly baked pastries. This idyllic setting could typically accommodate up to thirty patrons to enjoy what is cited by gastronomic critics as the finest French dining in the world- today, only two people were seated at a single table for a late breakfast. The entire restaurant had been booked solely for these two patrons, as had the complete top floor of this most exclusive hotel. All paid for discreetly in American hundred dollar bills - just like their generous tips. These were the kinds of customers the hotel dreamt about. Nothing was too much trouble for these guests once word got out about the massive cash tips.

The maître d' hovered close to the table, checking that the VIP and his guest received the level of service expected at The Abbey.   The table was laid with pastries, artisan pieces of bread, fruit salad, Maison Bordier[548] fruit yoghurt and plates of hams and cheeses. With a wave of his fingers, the maître d' subtly signalled the sommelier to refill the glasses.

Many naively suppose that Arab royalty scrupulously avoids alcohol on religious grounds. However, as most hotels that cater to such clients are aware, that is very far from the truth, as the bar tab for HRH Prince Ahmed bin Khalifa proved. The sommelier lifted a bottle of champagne from a silver ice bucket and proffered it to the Prince. The label on the bottle

---

546 HOTEL DE L'ABBAYE, 10 Rue Cassette, 75006 Paris, France.
547 To partially hide the loud cometary explosions intermittently lighting up the Parisian sky.
548 The finest dairy produce in Paris and probably the world, at least according to the French.

of "1820 Juglar Cuvee[549]" was dark and stained from being submerged for over a hundred years in the icy waters of the Baltic.

"More champagne, Your Royal Highness?"

The Sheikh nodded his approval and brushed some bread crumbs from his immaculately white dishdasha. His long fingers indicated that his companion's glass should also be refilled. The movement of the Prince's head revealed keen eyes and a hawk-faced profile from under the crisp white keffiyeh headdress.   On the other side of the table, the Prince's travelling companion raised his hand, covering the top of his empty champagne flute glass. The Sheikh's associate was dressed in an equally immaculate white dishdasha and keffiyeh but without the elaborate gold trim that adorned the Prince's garments.

"A bit early for me. I will stick with the coffee." said the bearded man in a soft and cultured American accent.

Fr Thomas O'Neil waited until all the staff had retreated from the table before he addressed Abdul Issuin,

"How much longer do we have to stay here? I have to get to my flat in Rome."

The hawk-faced assassin looked into his companion's face.

"I thought you wanted to visit the site mentioned in your mysterious notebook?"

O'Neill looked at the small black notebook that had become his constant companion over the past two days. He had done little besides reading and re-reading the handwritten pages with their intriguing pictures. O'Neill's margin notes were copious and mainly consisted of questions. Questions

---

[549] Only ninety-five bottles were recovered, making this the rarest and most expensive champagne in the world.

that could only be answered by visiting the site of Göbekli Tepe.

"Yes, I do. But my archaeological equipment is in my flat."

The hawk-faced man nodded sympathetically.

"Trust me, after our escape yesterday, right now, your flat is the last place you should go. It is surrounded by Wolfsangel operatives who are waiting for your arrival."

Deep inside, O'Neill knew that going to his flat would be a death sentence, but he was tired of waiting here in this hotel. His frustration overflowed.

"I cannot help thinking we should be moving as quickly as possible and not making such a spectacle of ourselves."

The assassin nodded.

"An understandable error. The elite hotels, such as Hotel de L'Abbaye," Abdul Issuin's French pronunciation was flawless, "provide their VIP guests with a curtain of privacy that makes them an ideal place to hide from a systematic search. In addition, Prince Khalifa's diplomatic status means we can travel to Turkey without any of the usual inconveniences."

O'Neill had deliberately avoided asking what had happened to the real Prince Khalifa. As though he could read the priest's mind, the hawk-faced assassin smiled as he pulled out a gold Dunhill lighter from his robe and lit another of his beloved Montecristo No.4 cigars. For the second time in as many days, O'Neill reflected that the assassin's expression was deeply unsettling - it reminded him of the smile crocodiles give tourists.

Thirty minutes later and two hundred and eighty miles North of the elegant breakfast setting, Sinclair's three-car police convoy had nearly completed their journey along Van Alkemadelaan before turning left onto Oude Waalsdorperweg. From Sinclair's position in the middle car, the frontage of the UN Court buildings loomed ahead on the left side of the road. The Police vehicles drew into a substantial pull-in area in front of a series of large buildings with checker-patterned windows. In the centre of the development was a taller square structure with a high protective frame erected in front of the building to block missiles from being fired from the road.

As they came to a stop, groups of black-suited operatives carrying MP7 machine guns gathered around the police escort. A highly distinctive logo adorned their upper sleeves, of an orb with an array of lightning flashes above a stylised castle. The same symbol appeared on the top of their black helmets. Each operative's face was completely hidden behind a silver visor, and their uniforms were covered in wires and wearable technology. The overall effect was so overdone that Sinclair could not help giggling.

"Looks like Terminator cosplay!"

"Knights," explained the young policeman. He suddenly become deadly serious.

"Knights?" queried Sinclair.

"Of the Black Sun. Wolfsangel's uber elite. Those iKill Pro visors give them an augmented reality feed on everything they see, and the smart tech embedded into the operations suits they are wearing is a direct neural link to provide AI assistance and augmentation of their operational performance. Rumour has it they never tire and never miss a target. Makes them unbeatable."

Sinclair raised her right eyebrow in evident scepticism of the claim of being unbeatable and the folly of having anything directly controlling the nervous system.

At that moment, the policeman's remarks were drowned out by the thrumming vibration that was so intense that the car windows vibrated. Seconds later, the noise source was revealed as a sinister black helicopter passed low overhead. The Wolfsangel Eurocopter Tiger[550] was bristling with weapons pods[551] and was covered in radar-absorbing shielding, armour plating and the same Black Sun livery. The aircraft's electronic hardening systems, which were originally designed to cope with EMP[552] weapons, permitted it to fly during the cometary explosions with some impunity. The helicopter's roar faded only to be replaced by a deep thudding which made the Police car shake slightly.

A group of dog-sized, four-legged robots emerged from behind one of the side buildings and, stomping their hydraulically controlled legs, strode over to where Sinclair and Curren were parked. The robots almost had as many armaments as the sleek black Tiger attack helicopter that had just passed overhead. All of those weapons swivelled to where Sinclair was sitting in the Volkswagen.

The young policeman gawped in awe.

"They have deployed Snitches! These are fucking unstoppable killing machines. They can take out a whole regiment."

As Sinclair departed the vehicle, she bent closer to the shoulder of the young policeman and whispered,

"Don't believe everything Wolfsangel tells you, honey."

---

[550] Developed by France and Germany.
[551] Trigat anti-tank missiles and Stinger air-to-air missiles.
[552] Electro Magnetic Pulse – disables electronic systems.

Thirty minutes and six intrusive security searches later, Sinclair stood in a brightly illuminated room with a high ceiling, light wooden flooring and walls. The crisp, cold air-conditioned ventilation made Sinclair glad she wore a long-sleeved top. It was a cruel irony that she would not be in here long enough to worry about catching a chill. The UN ICC courtroom had a highly modular configuration, using premarked slots in the floor, which permitted the easy adjustment of the courtroom size and the seating layout depending on circumstances. Today the room was set to one of its smaller sizes, as there was no necessity for the dozens of legal representatives and administrators that generally participate in the ICC legal deliberations. Large-screen Lenovo workstations with a microphone and headphones were installed on every desk, permitting the judges and legal teams to access digital resources and play them on the other screens. The high walls were covered in CCTV cameras to ensure the global audience witnessed every angle of today's event.

Sinclair stood behind a plain modern desk with a grey top, white sides, and a matching front. She was in the centre of the Courtroom with the vacant-looking Curren beside her. To her left was an empty desk customarily allocated for the Defence Attorneys. A six-person Wolfsangel prosecution team were located to her right, and the high table for the Judge was directly in front. Two Wolfsangel flags were on either side of the raised podium where the Judge would be presiding.

It was noticeable that the Judge's chair was empty. Perhaps the Commandant had been correct, and Cortez would not judge this show trial. Behind them was a massive bullet and bomb-proof glass wall that segregated the observation area, filled with news and camera teams from state and private news agencies from every region on Earth. The world was eager to share the modern era's first European public death sentence.

A court official emerged at the Judge's table and announced in French and then heavily accented English that there would be a short delay as a replacement judge would preside at the hearing and was familiarising himself with the case. The official concluded by stating, for the news agencies, that since no attorneys were prepared to defend the accused, the defence station would be unoccupied at today's hearing.

Following the example of the Wolfsangel defence team, Sinclair guided Curren to sit and then positioned herself in a comfortable high-backed grey fabric chair. She stared at the large computer screen in front of her and read the ICC Rules of Decorum that was part of the screen saver, along with a time and date display. It was ironic that the decorum notice forbade the use of video or sound recording equipment when the single purpose of today's charade was to broadcast the proceedings to the world.

Ten minutes later, an older man entered from the side door on the left of the raised podium. He was adjusting his two-tone blue ICC Judge's gown in a vain attempt to cover his informal clothing underneath. Based on the polo shirt and loud trousers, the Judge had anticipated a day's golf rather than going down in history as running an infamous show trial. The court usher handed the Judge an iPhone, and there was a pause in the proceedings as the new arrival listened to a one-sided conversation. If the Judge had looked unhappy when he entered the courtroom, by the end of the phone call, that look had transformed into one of terror. He tried to return the mobile phone but was informed by the usher to keep it in case of "An intervention by Deputy Chairman Hartman". Sinclair frowned. Cortez's grandson was the puppet master here today.

K.R.M. Morgan

"All rise," commanded the official, "Judge Kikkert is presiding at today's session."

The Judge nodded at the Wolfsangel group.

"Representatives of the prosecution, by now, the whole world has seen the evidence that Chairman Cortez shared with the media some days ago, which resulted in the arrest of the accused."

Kikkert gestured towards Sinclair and Curren.

"Rather than replay this digital material, do you have any physical evidence that would be material to this case?"

Before the prosecution could respond, the mobile phone on the Judge's desk rang. Kikkert looked embarrassed, but at the usher's insistence, he picked it up. Another one-sided conversation made the Judge look like he would break down and cry. Sinclair had seen first-hand how the South American drug cartels operated and knew that the poor bastard was being threatened. Kikkert could probably hear his close family members screaming for mercy on the other end of the line while Hartman made his demands.

Shortly after the call ended, the Judge addressed the court. His voice was hesitant and strained.

"After some careful reconsideration, I have decided we must review the video evidence from the prosecution."

The Wolfsangel prosecution team exchanged satisfied grins, and their leader stood.

"If it pleases your honour," the chief prosecutor said sarcastically. There was no longer any doubt about which monkeys were running this particular circus.

"Our exhibit one is playback from the defendant's bridge cameras on board her ship, The Tiamat, in the Mediterranean Sea while remotely controlling the US Zumwalt class destroyer moored in Istanbul, resulting in the loss of billions of lives worldwide. This footage will be followed by the defendant's blackmail demand that resulted in over half the world's population surrendering to her rule."

The screens around the courtroom came alive and replayed the genuine scenes of Ad-Dajjal's release of the Red Death bioweapon in Istanbul and the subsequent blackmail of the world for the vaccine. When these sequences were completed, the lead prosecutor stood again.

"We will now present a short documentary prepared by the leading experts on deep fake production, Beyond Facts Inc[553].showing conclusively how the defendant altered her images to present herself as Ad-Dajjal."

Sinclair made eye contact with the Judge. The look they exchanged indicated they both knew this was complete bullshit but were powerless to do anything about it.

While Sinclair and Kikkert shared their silent communication, the courtroom displays showed a five-minute documentary with a slick voice-over by a well-known science TV series host purporting to show how Curren's images had been edited to appear as Ad-Dajjal – when in reality, Curren had no part in this atrocity. When the fake documentary finished, the Wolfsangel prosecution lead summarised the crimes against humanity associated with Nissa Ad-Dajjal, saying,

"In summary, your honour, this woman may appear harmless but has committed such atrocities that the only sentence possible for this court is the death penalty."

The Wolfsangel chief prosecutor then turned his attention towards Sinclair.

"This brings us to Ms Cynthia Sinclair. Outwardly, she appeared to be a stalwart defender of democracy and the

---

[553] Another proud member of the Wolfsangel group.

rule of law. However, this was a charade of the darkest kind. In reality, the head of the British Secret Intelligence Service was a career traitor and criminal who was in league with the drug cartels and terrorist organisations while presenting a façade of serving her adopted country. Your honour, Sinclair's activities as a double agent only came to light during an investigation after she had been caught on camera murdering numerous witnesses who had seen her ransacking of Stewart's premises."

The displays around the courtroom played a sequence showing Sinclair emerging from the ruins of Stewart's shop on New Bond Street and opening fire with her machine pistol on the crowds. The clip finished with closeups of the dead and dying in the gutters of New Bond Street. This was followed by the video clip of Sinclair's faked confession, with an actress pretending to be her, which she had first seen from her cell at Broadmarsh Prison on British TV after she had been arrested.

The whole Wolfsangel prosecution team stood and the lead prosecutor addressed the Judge,

"Your honour, in light of this evidence and Sinclair's confession, we demand the immediate implementation of the death penalty for these two evil women!"

Judge Kikkert looked to the empty table where the defence lawyers should have been, then at Sinclair and finally at the trancelike state of Curren. Minutes passed. The mobile phone rang on his desk. He ignored it and instead addressed the court,

"The evidence had been presented. I call an intercession before we resume in twenty minutes to pass judgment."

Kikkert continued to ignore the ringing mobile and walked out of the court. The official struggled to react quickly enough and ended up simply shouting,

"All rise! The session will resume in twenty minutes."

Sinclair helped the unresponsive Curren to her feet. Looking around the room, she noticed that as the Judge exited, five Wolfsangel operatives pushed roughly past him and entered the Courtroom. Each of them directed an ominous-looking MP7 machine gun at the pair of defendants, quashing any of the escape plans running through Sinclair's mind.

K.R.M. Morgan

COUP D'ÉTAT

"Uneasy is the head that wears a crown" - Shakespeare, Henry IV Part 2

Suite 1a
Officers Accommodation Block A,
Fort Liberty[554] United States Army Base
Cumberland, North Carolina
USA

06:02 HRS (GMT - 4), 16th September, present-day

Three men were gathered in the predawn gloom[555] in a twenty-foot square ground-floor living room allocated to accommodate President Wilson Jones and his family. Two of the men, CIA Director Pimms and Army General Orne, sat on cream-coloured cotton two-seater sofas on either side of a similarly upholstered single-seater chair, where the POTUS sat waiting for news about the abduction of his family. None of the three had slept due to anxiety, adrenaline and copious amounts of Joffrey's House Blend[556]. The only relief to the tedium of the wait was when one of Orne or Pimms' staff came to provide updates on the investigation. So far, very little progress had been made.

Guilt made the General uncharacteristically abrupt with his men. The Rangers he had personally insisted take over from Jackson's US Marines to guard the President's family while on an Army base had failed to prevent their abduction. The honour of the US Army, especially the Rangers, had been

---

[554] Formerly Fort Bragg.

[555] The sun rises as approximately 06.34 HRS on the 16th September in Cumberland, North Carolina.

[556] US Army standard brew provided by Joffrey's Coffee & Tea Company.

badly damaged. Orne wanted explanations and did not care if he cracked a few heads to get them. The excessive heat caused by the ongoing airburst explosions did not help the fury running through his veins.

Brilliant flashes sporadically illuminated the poorly lit room, followed seconds later by violent rumbles as another piece of space rock combusted miles above them in the night sky. These unprecedented cosmic impacts would typically have been a primary focus for Wilson, but today, understandably, he had a different agenda.

When the explosions started, Pimms had reassured the POTUS.

"This phenomenon has nothing to do with Cortez- unless one subscribes to the most outlandish conspiracy theories associated with the Argentinian regime having machines that can tear apart the very fabric of the universe."

But as the phenomena continued, a nagging doubt crept into Pimms' mind. As another series of airbursts shook the windows for the twentieth time that morning, the CIA director tried to reassure himself that the MOSSAD-sourced documents on Cortez's doomsday devices were absurd fairy tales.

Thankfully, after Wilson's order to shut down social media, they did get a break from the endless propaganda filling every US citizen's phone, tablet and AR[557] headset. However, Beyond Facts rapidly responded to the loss of these channels by switching its US manipulations to the mainstream media. Even public service broadcasters had started spreading conspiracies about how the stars on the American flag were linked with the airbursts. Finally, Wilson demanded they turn off the radio that had been providing them with updates on

---

[557] Augmented Reality.

the growing numbers of civil uprisings in US cities when the newscasting AI chatbot urged listeners to burn the Stars and Stripes to "save the nation from this threat from above".

Between the endless bright flashes, the room's only light came from small lamps on either side of the President's seat and one on the centre table between the three men. This central table was littered with empty Papa Johns pizza boxes, spent cans of Diet Coke, cardboard coffee trays and paper cups. Discarded children's toys, assorted knitting, and sewing materials were scattered around the room, adding pathos to the tragic scene.

In the hope that the abducted family members would be found quickly, the three men had remained in the clothes they had been wearing at the previous afternoon's meeting. However, the climate became unbearable when the cometary fragments superheated the atmosphere.

Even with the small air conditioning units fitted in the bottom of the window frames running at full power, the 90 Fahrenheit ambient temperature inside the small living space was stale and laden with the smell of coffee, body odour and sour breath. In response to the increasing heat, the POTUS had given Pimms and Orne permission to remove their jackets and ties, while Wilson had taken off his Harvard sweatshirt and was now in a simple white American Apparel T-Shirt and grey marl jog pants.

Since Marine Captain Jackson had informed Wilson about the abduction of his wife and children at the end of a Presidential briefing the previous afternoon, all other State business had been put on hold. The Presidential press conference, scheduled for six pm was cancelled, but that did not mean the POTUS was spared critical media coverage.

A series of anonymous phone calls, which Pimms had ascribed to Defence Secretary Maskins, had ensured that the abduction of the President's wife and children had become the nation's main interest, even more so than the cosmic firework displays filling the night sky. The "Beyond Facts Inc" AI chatbots, which had replaced all human news anchors, stated categorically that this latest setback would prompt Wilson to reconsider his position in resisting the popular uprisings. Either through incompetence or collaboration, the White House press secretary claimed to be unable to determine the source of the leaks.

Dismissing suspicions that support for the revolution was growing even within his closest allies, Wilson wiped his eyes and scratched the stumble on his chin before taking a long sip of cold coffee. He looked at the photograph on the left side table showing Samantha and two small children, the blond-haired Josh and the dark-haired Amanda, who, like her mother, wore glasses. Images of happier times. Wherever they were, he prayed they were OK. His reverie was cut short by a rap on the apartment door. Pimms rose and walked to open it. His hand was noticeably positioned near the small Glock[558] in a concealed carry hip holster inside his waistband.

A wave of heat and humidity poured into Pimms face as he pulled open the door. The gloom of the predawn revealed four, heavily-armed[559] Marines in full-body armour[560] standing on either side of the entrance, perspiration flowing copiously from their faces. Admiral Peter Lorance stood illuminated by the eerie red light beams projected from their head-mounted lamps[561], his face white with heat and exhaustion.

---

[558] The Glock G26 is a smaller framed 9mm semi-automatic pistol derived from the Glock 19.
[559] A mix of Glock 19 9mm pistols and Colt 1911 .45 calibre pistols with Daniel Defense MK18 SBR carbine rifles.
[560] Crye G3 combat top and bottoms with Crye Cage plate carrier.
[561] Surefire HL1 mounted light on an Ops-Core FAST helmet.

Pimms looked expectantly behind the Admiral for an additional person.

"Twop?"

Lorance shook his head.

"Someone tipped off Cortez's men on the Falklands. SEAL Team Six encountered substantive resistance. We did not get a chance to search for the target before coming under heavy ground and air attacks that forced us to withdraw the two Blackhawks."

The CIA director slammed his fist into the door jam.

"Maskins again!"

Pimms turned to Wilson, who had walked with Orne to the door.

"Mr President. You have to place that woman under arrest. She is a danger to you and our Nation. Let my people interrogate her. I guarantee that we will find she is behind all this mischief."

Wilson shook his head.

"No, Mark. You have no hard evidence. Make no moves. At least not until I have had the chance to talk with her one-on-one. She is still a serving member of my Cabinet."

Pimms sighed, saying, "As you wish, Mr President."

Wilson smiled in that tired way that every parent would recognise. He addressed the three men around him,

"We must assume Cortez has Twop. How much does that damage us?"

CIA Director Pimms looked into Wilson's face.

"I doubt he would do anything other than terminate her, Mr President. Poor woman. It is a loss for us, as she had prime intelligence on how Cortez manipulated public opinion."

Wilson gestured to the sweating Admiral, who was still standing outside.

"Peter, come in," and then, before closing the door, he addressed the Marines standing to attention outside,

"Stand at ease, gentlemen. Please ask Captain Jackson to come see me."

"Yes, Mr President, Sir!"

replied a massive man with Master Sergeant stripes on his arm. The man mountain pulled down the microphone on his headset[562] and issued a series of code words that would be meaningless to anyone outside the Marine Recon team guarding the POTUS.

Once the door was closed, Admiral Peter Lorance pulled a leather-covered flask from his hip pocket and silently offered it to the President.

Wilson took the flask and sniffed it, asking, "Whiskey?"

"Finest Colorado Rye[563], Mr President."

Wilson smiled. "Forget you were a Coloradan."

The Admiral seemed to recover some of his energy. "Five generations, Mr President."

After taking a swig, Wilson offered it to Pimms and Orne. The Army General took a swig, while Pimms declined.

Wilson handed the flask back.

---

[562] TEA Hi-Threat headset.
[563] Made by Colorado craft distillery "Distillery 291". They produce rye whiskey with toasted Aspen wood staves.

K.R.M. Morgan

"Fine stuff, Peter. Did we lose any people on the Falklands operation?"

"No, Mr President, just damage to the Blackhawks and the SEAL's egos."

The POTUS smiled.

"Good. Equipment can be replaced. It's people who cannot be. The way things are heading, I think the SEALS will get plenty of opportunities to recover their egos."

Wilson looked again at the picture of Samantha and the kids. Another knock on the outer door saved him from the growing melancholy as he accepted what would befall his family when he rejected the kidnapper's demands to surrender his Nation to Cortez.

"Must be Jackson,"

stated Pimms as he headed to open it, with his pistol hand at the ready once again. The CIA director's guess was wrong. Standing at the door was an Army Colonel with 75th Ranger Regiment badges on his lapel and sleeves. He put an iPad under his right armpit and saluted. The name on his chest lapel said, Colonel G.H. Schmidt. The newcomer asked,

"Mr Director, may I see General Orne, Sir?"

Orne looked to Wilson, who nodded, and then the POTUS said,

"Come on in, Colonel. Any news on your men?"

The Colonel looked towards Orne[564], who gestured with his hand to continue.

----

[564] Reports should pass through lines of command.

"Mr President, the bodies of the ten Rangers have been found in one of the car parks two miles North of this residential block."

"Dead?" asked Pimms.

The Ranger nodded. "Hands zip-tied behind their backs and shot in the back of the head."

"Christ," exclaimed Orne, the remaining colour draining from his face.

Wilson grew nauseous as he walked slowly back to his chair. The nightmare was getting worse by the hour. He gestured to the others to follow his example and sit. Pimms and the Ranger opted to remain standing. After a few moments, Orne ran his hand through his hair and asked,

"Do we have any clues about who did it?"

The Ranger pulled a long brass bullet casing from his right pocket.

Pimms reached forward, asking, "May I?"

Taking the spent casing in his fingers, the CIA Director looked towards the President.

"Bottlenecked case and a pointed, steel-core, copper-jacketed hollow point round characteristic of the HK 4.6 x 30mm."

The Ranger Colonel nodded. "That was our ballistic expert's opinion as well."

The President looked to Pimms for an explanation.

"German design and manufacture, Mr President. The steel core projectile is used almost exclusively in the Heckler & Koch MP7 rifle and provides extraordinary armour piercing capabilities even through NATO standard body armour."

"Do we use it?" asked Wilson.

"No, Mr President. It is the preferred weapon of Cortez's Wolfsangel operatives."

"Bastards struck here in my camp?!" exclaimed Orne, running his fingers through his hair again in exasperation.

Pimms returned the spent round and addressed the Ranger,

"Colonel, do we know how they extracted the President's family?"

Pimms wondered if the twenty-mile perimeter checks he had set up could catch the kidnappers.

The Ranger nodded and pulled open the iPad from under his arm.

"CCTV shows an unknown helicopter. Our analysts have looked at the profile and cannot identify it, except for the Wolfsangel livery on its rear."

"If I may?" Pimms took the iPad and looked critically at the profile of the aircraft. He then said,

"Airbus H160M - designed to take over from the Tiger attack helicopter towards the decade's end. Fast, heavily armed, practically invisible to radar and almost silent running. We stand little chance of finding it; honestly, our aircraft would be outclassed even if we did."

General Orne and Admiral Lorance exchanged a look before the President asked what both military leaders were thinking.

"How the fuck are these bastards getting tech that is years ahead of us?"

The CIA director shrugged.

 "The Wolfsangel organisation's subsidiaries were used by the US and European corporations for outsourcing weapons R&D and production."

While the President cursed the stupid greed that had led to giving away the Nation's classified research, Pimms continued watching the CCTV footage until he was confident that an unconscious woman and two children had been loaded onto the aircraft.

Handing the iPad back to the Ranger, Pimms asked,

"May I see the ransom note?"

The Ranger looked shocked. "How did you..."

Disbelief transformed into a furious rage within Wilson as he stood and walked over to stand beside Pimms.

"Never mind how he knows, Colonel. Why the fuck were you withholding the kidnapper's note?"

By now, General Orne had joined them, his face a crimson shade of red. Orne addressed the Ranger,

"By hells bells Colonel, what possessed you? Where is the damn note?"

The Ranger looked like a schoolchild who had been caught stealing an apple from the teacher's desk.

The Colonel's act did not convince Pimms, so he intervened, asking,

"He doesn't have it. Do you, Colonel?

Let me guess. You were given an anonymous tip-off about the car park where the Ranger's bodies were found. When you arrived at the scene, you found Secretary of Defence Jane Maskins and Director of National Intelligence Elaine Madden, who quoted National Security Directive (NSD) 1a[565], and took over the investigation with their forensic teams."

---

565 Supplement to National Security Directive 1 (Crisis Management).

The Ranger looked stunned while General Orne's temper finally got the better of him.

"So, you don't have the bloody note? Do you at least know what it said?"

The Ranger shook his head, saying,

"No, Sir."

Pimms addressed the POTUS,

"If I am correct, Mr President, we will see this note at a televised press briefing announcing your death and the Secretary of Defence Jane Maskins being sworn in as President."

"You're joking!" exclaimed Wilson.

The CIA Director looked anything but humorous.

"Sadly, I have never been more serious. She has systematically removed every other ranking officer in your Cabinet. Making herself the next in line should anything happen to you[566]."

The POTUS paused. Until now, he had thought Pimms was exaggerating the ambitions of Maskins, but events were suggesting the CIA Director had been right all along.

General Orne nodded, saying,

"Mr President, I think Pimms is right. We need to arrest these two women immediately. With your permission, I will call the MPs to effect an immediate arrest and have Maskins and Madden placed in the guardhouse."

CIA Director Pimms gestured for Orne to stop and looked at the Navy Admiral and Ranger Colonel.

---

[566] Article II, Section 1, Clause 6 of the US Constitution.

"We are already too late. Aren't we, gentlemen? I am guessing the Colonel has been assigned the grizzly termination, as I don't think Peter is quite up to killing his CIC[567], at least not yet. Give him a few months of working for Maskins, and I am sure his tolerances will have adjusted."

General Orne looked at Admiral Lorance, exclaiming, as the Admiral pulled out the highly polished silver classic Colt 1911 pistol attached to his belt, and pointed it at Orne, who exclaimed,

"Peter? What the fuck?!"

"Nothing personal, Jim. I am only two years from retirement, and Wolfsangel offered me a beautiful life in the Caymans."

"Traitor!" snarled Orne as he faced his former colleague. Meanwhile, the Ranger Colonel had drawn his modified Glock and aimed it directly at Pimms, who cooly stared back down the barrel at his adversary and said,

"So, Colonel, or should I say, Wolfsangel Oberst? What is the plan? A bizarre suicide pact amongst the President's senior advisors? People know Wilson well enough to doubt he would ever take his own life or that his senior staff would kill him. Now that the game is up, why not tell us what Maskins commanded you to do for her."

The Ranger snarled, "You intelligence types always think you are so fucking clever."

Pimms grinned, pleased that he had provoked a response.

"Only Wolfsangel carry that biometric limiter on their weapons. Seeing those red LED sensors flicking away on your belt when you came in told me you were no Ranger. It does not say much about your superior's confidence in your

---

[567] Commander in Chief.

abilities if they think you must be protected against being disarmed."

The fake Ranger Colonel ignored Pimms' further attempt to goad him.

"You can congratulate yourself on your skills when you are dead. Remove the magazine and throw that lady's pistol of yours down by my feet."

While Pimms slowly complied, President Wilson tried to use his diplomatic skills on Admiral Lorance, who was using his 1911 to cover Orne and Wilson.

"Peter, whatever they have promised you is a lie. These people are rogues. Look what they did to the Rangers."

Wilson then turned to the fake Ranger Colonel, saying,

"If you do anything to us, you must know that the Marines will deal with you."

The Wolfsangel operative laughed.

"You don't get it, do you? Your precious General Arnold of the good ol' US Marines joined us along with General Smith of the USAF last night when they saw the deal we had given Lorance. No one is coming to the rescue."

He turned his attention towards General Orne.

"Everyone one of your Military chiefs has seen sense except this jerk. Now Orne, put your Beretta[568] down on the floor - holding the barrel. Slow."

As Orne reluctantly complied, the door to the outside opened, and two Wolfsangel operatives entered, wheeling in a highly specialised trolley that contained a small metal box floating in a bath of a liquid. Copious amounts of evaporating gas rose rapidly from the container and

---

[568] Beretta 92FS. Was standard issue for US forces.

gathered on the ceiling. On the sides of the trolley were yellow triangle warning signs for extreme cold and a large liquid "He" symbol[569].

"What's this? A hearty breakfast before we die?" joked Wilson, noting that Pimms and Orne had gone deathly pale.

The Ranger Colonel's expression showed his enjoyment of what he was announcing,

"One of the many deadly toys we found in the Army research labs we took over today. Secretary Maskins felt it was appropriate[570] after your repeated disrespect over the past few days. They say that revenge is a dish best-served cold, and Azidoazide azide[571] explosives are about as cold as it gets."

The POTUS looked at Orne for an explanation. The General shrugged, saying,

"It is an experimental explosive, Mr President. The scientists wanted to see if it was possible to edit the molecular structure of an explosive to maximise its yield. They succeeded, but the resulting chemical is so unstable that it spontaneously explodes unless it is kept close to absolute zero. As the freezing element evaporates, the chemical becomes less and less stable until it explodes with a violence unknown in nature. Ten pounds of the stuff will easily level this building."

---

[569] Liquid Helium -452° F.

[570] Super villains always look for overly complex methods to kill their opponents.

[571] Diazidocarbamoyl-azidotetrazole is often referred to azidoazide azide. It is a heterocyclic inorganic compound with the formula C_2N_{14}. The 14 nitrogen atoms make it the most unstable high explosive known to science. It will detonate if touched, moved or even left alone at room temperature.

K.R.M. Morgan

Wilson looked perplexed. "But how will they explain the explosion?"

The Wolfsangel Colonel was clearly enjoying the bemusement of his victims.

"In this heat, propane gas cylinders are dangerously unstable. We already have the forensic reports prepared. It was a tragic accident triggered by the cosmic air blasts."

As the trolley approached closer, Wilson saw that the floating box had a bright red LED temperature read out on the unit's top panel that showed minus four hundred and thirty Fahrenheit. In addition to the two men wheeling the trolley with extraordinary care, four other Wolfsangel operatives carrying MP7 machine guns entered and aimed them at Wilson, Orne and Pimms.

Now they were covered, the Wolfsangel Ranger Colonel walked slowly around the three men and plastic-tied their wrists. When his work was completed, he briefly tested the tension on each cuff, collected the two pistols and checked the bomb's temperature gauge. The liquid helium had almost completely evaporated in the sweltering temperature and the red LED showed minus one hundred- and twenty-degrees Fahrenheit. The Ranger addressed Admiral Lorance,

"Time for us to leave."

As Lorance and the other Wolfsangel operatives exited, the rogue Ranger turned to the three men standing with their wrists tied.

"Mr President, you should have had enough sense to surrender. Stupid people always lose."

President Wilson could not resist a comeback.

"Oberst Schmidt, if I were you, I would not turn the lights off when you go to sleep."

As the door closed, the President turned to his CIA Director.

"Mark, you had better impress me with your next plan, or you're fired."

K.R.M. Morgan

METAMORPHOSIS

"For it is known that for some preternatural entities, the pain and suffering of mortal creatures in their immediate proximity doth empower and replenish them such that these foul monsters can rise again." - Translated from hand-annotated Latin notes. Cicero, De Fato, 44 BCE. Bibliothèque nationale de France Catalogue Général folio 235c.

1st Floor Burns Ward
Clinique de Réadaptation du Dr STER
9 Av. Dr Jean Ster, 34240 Lamalou-les-Bains, France

11.30 HRS (GMT+2), 16th of September, present-day.

Thick smoke hung in the morning sky, obscuring the sun, but there was none of the damp chill customarily associated with such gloomy conditions - instead, a dry acrid heat pervaded everywhere. Large flakes of carbon soot fell from heated thermals, covering every surface, as wildfires consumed increasing numbers of buildings and vegetation in Northern Europe. The loss of life, for humans and livestock, was already comparable to the red death plague that had recently decimated the globe. The toxic soup that hung close to the ground comprised not just carbon monoxide and dioxide but a cocktail of other deadly chemicals[572] - forcing anyone unfortunate enough to be outside for prolonged periods to wear specialised breathing apparatus or suffer permanent damage to their respiratory systems. Periodically, the gloom was illuminated by another massive cometary burst as the multi-million-mile-long trail of rocks continued ploughing into the earth's atmosphere.

---

[572] Including: aldehydes, acid gases, benzene, nitrogen oxides, polycyclic aromatic hydrocarbons (PAHs), sulfur dioxide, styrene, toluene, heavy metals, and dioxins.

The body of Chairman Cortez slowly regained consciousness in the silence of an almost deserted medical ward. He was lying on a bed, dressed in the same dark pinstripe Savile Row business suit he had worn the previous night. Due to the heat, his jacket and silk tie hung on the foot of his bed above his discarded leather brogue shoes and silk socks. The surfaces of the shoes were caked in a charcoal-like substance that had left numerous dark footprints on the otherwise immaculate floor. One of the brilliant airburst explosions illuminated the room, showing that the white industrial linoleum flooring around the bed was perforated with numerous small burn marks where a powerfully corrosive substance had been spilt.

Cortez's only company in the ward was a woman's charred remains lying on the bed next to his - machines keeping her otherwise dead body alive. As he tried to gather his thoughts, he noted a complete absence of the exhaustion that had so thoroughly racked his body last night. After over six decades of life, he knew the limits of the regenerative power of a good night's sleep - this current experience was different. Radically different - his mind and body were full of vitality in ways he had not felt since his thirties. As he recalled the previous day's chaos and the hurried journey from London to the hospital in Southern France, a fleeting dream like memory of a most peculiar monster standing beside his bed entered his consciousness.

The Argentinian laughed to himself. Only exhaustion could cause such a terrifying vision! But what a creation his imagination had conjured, truly the stuff of nightmares! As moments passed, listening to the rhythm of the ventilating machine, Cortez sat up and, through eyes that were far more acute than he had experienced since childhood, noticed numerous strange marks on the floor beside him. Some monstrous serpent had slithered from the bed beside him towards where he was lying. Inexplicably, as quickly as horror had filled him, it subsided and was replaced by a strange relief that he had escaped from the burnt corpse lying beside him. Maybe whatever had happened was a blessing. Undoubtedly, his body felt more energetic than it had been for decades. Yes, it was a blessing. Where did such a thought come from? There began a growing awareness of a division in his mind. No, describing it as a split in his core being would be more accurate. He knew he was now more than the man called Cortez ever was - a sum of parts greater than he could ever have been. Somehow, he understood he shared the highest secret of a hidden magical world previously mastered only by the seniors of the Meri-Isfet. Despite inhabiting an aged body, he instinctively knew he now had immense power over the non-physical realms. Combined with his role as Chairman, these new powers meant he (Cortez was already unconsciously identifying with his new combined self) would soon dominate the universe he had lived in for countless aeons. Realising this new reality filled him with a vigour to rise and begin his great work, to dominate all.

The rational side of what remained of Cortez decided that first, he must understand the capabilities of this new reality in which he found himself. Unlike the previous host-body[573], which had savoured the sensual and sexual power it had over others; this host had a military discipline which made him conquer, dominate and compete with everyone and everything around him.

---

[573] More accurately called an indwelling, where an astral parasite takes over the astral and physical bodies of a host.

Madeleine Mathers had called the creature that had possessed her the "MUŠ.ŠÀ.TÙR[574]" but in reality, numerous names[575] have been used throughout history.

When the combined minds of Cortez and the parasite contemplated their situation, they decided they were the ideal combination needed to complete the creature's natural evolution and destiny - a destiny which would lead to domination not just of this reality but all previous ones. This ultimate fate would, the entity was sure, have been the original design of Jann ibn Jann[576], the legendary progenitor of the monstrous species.

Cortez's heightened senses enabled him to perceive his environment with greater acuity than any living creature. Without needing to leave the room, somehow, he knew of the raging fires devastating nearby forests, heathland, and towns. He knew the atmosphere outside was heavy with a cloud of toxic smoke, making it difficult for normal organisms to breathe. He was also aware that the heat outside the building was intense, and the smell of carbon and burnt meat was pungent.

---

[574] The creature was called the "MUŠ.ŠÀ.TÙR" after the use of this name in ancient cuneiform tablets in the French National Library, Paris.

[575] The most ancient Middle Eastern traditions describe a monster called the Jawān as quasi-immortal beings who inhabited our reality long before humans or animals. Known in Arabic as the جواﻥ - Surah 15:27 and Surah 27:10 of the Holy Quran refer to the Jawān as a supernatural creature - like a dragon or a serpent, who were the precursors of the entities known as the Djinn. Unlike the primordial clay that formed Adam or the primordial light that formed the bodies of the Angels, when the creator formed the Jawān, the primordial fire was used to create the serpentine multi-dimensional bodies of these apex astral parasites.

[576] Before the time of Adam, the Jawān were ruled by a father entity called Jann ibn Jann.

Extending his preternatural senses further, Cortez became attuned to the massive cometary explosions occurring miles above, which he knew were caused by the ritual he had personally led when in control of Madeleine Mathers's body. Despite knowing his actions had initiated a global catastrophe, he felt a sense of pleasure at the realisation that he was the first person to use a Qlipothic Wheel in over twelve thousand years.

Thinking back on the previous night, when the MUŠ.ŠÀ.TÙR had left the dead body of Madeleine Mathers and taken possession of his body, Cortez recalled vivid dreams of oceans, where he had encountered many different creatures. These dreams of the entity's past were filled with a sense of wonder and awe from an increasing awareness that the suffering experienced by other beings gave life energy to the parasite. He became aware of his status as an apex predator in a world populated by weak mortal creatures. Cortez knew his new reality included a form of immortality by switching host bodies. The realisation that he was now some form of parasite did not fill Cortez with revulsion; instead, he felt a heightened sense of power and purpose. In this new body, the parasite would achieve domination over the physical world in ways that were impossible with the magical adepts he had been inhabiting for the past decamillennium[577]. magical Adepts avoided direct involvement with violence, instead delegating it to others. The soul parasite knew this was not the case with Cortez, who relished personal physical involvement in extraordinary levels of violence. The last time the parasite[578] had enjoyed such pleasure was during the 21st century BCE in Mesopotamia, when its reign of personal violence had been so extreme as to be recorded in the

---

[577] Since the deluge.
[578] An ancient monster, sometimes described as a horned snake with two forelegs and wings and sometimes as a venomous serpent many miles long that devoured all creatures.

Assyrian histories[579] and to have both the Babylonians and Akkadians name one of their constellations[580] after it[581].

Despite the AC running fully overnight, the stifling heat had caused Cortez to sweat profusely, and he could not help but smell his own body odour alongside the pungent scent of the burnt woman on the bed next to him. He was acutely aware of the sound of the ventilation machine, the heart rate monitor, and, like the massive astral rattlesnake he so closely resembled, the unsteady beating of the dead woman's heart with each exhalation. In addition to these internal sensations, Cortez could feel the physical strength of his body after his transformation. The fabric of his clothes no longer fitted elegantly over his now perfectly developed physique. Whereas Mathers had assumed the flawless appearance of a photoshopped model after her transformation, Cortez was closer to the lean, coiled power visible in a world-class professional boxer.

Vanity and curiosity meant he could not resist standing and walking over to the window. He could see both his human host form and his true form in the reflective glass. He was familiar with the image of a powerful older man. However, his non-human form was something entirely novel to him. The astral body was thick and segmented, reminiscent of a serpent, but much larger with a diameter of three feet, almost like the trunk of a medium-sized tree. Though it couldn't fly, a blur of motion halfway down the body emitted

---

[579] In the text called the "Angim", the creature was called "Bašmu" and was described as having been "created in the sea" and to be "sixty double-miles long."

[580] Constellation (MUL.DINGIR.MUŠ) or Hydra.

[581] It was the last of the eleven monsters created by Tiāmat in the Epic of Creation, Enûma Eliš, which described the Bašmu as having "six mouths, seven tongues and seven wings on its belly."

a fluttering sound similar to a dragonfly's wings. The base of the creature's body transitioned into long, root-like tendrils extending outward from where it stood. As for its "head-end," it had seven swaying necks, each as wide as a human arm and ending in sucker-like mouths filled with small, sharp teeth arranged in circular rows. These teeth dripped a green, viscous fluid onto the ground below the creature's tendril feet, giving off a rather ominous burnt plastic smell. Looking down, Cortez could see that the liquid dripping from his many mouths had burnt holes in the plastic flooring. He would have to control that telltale sign!

On an impulse, he grabbed the pillow from the nearest bed and bit down into it. Fumes rose from the fabric, and it quickly fell into pieces in his human hands, the insides of the pillow instantly burnt to shreds by the powerful acid. Wondering what would happen to a living creature, he recalled a distant past when he had raged through primitive villages killing animals and humans. These frenzies were followed by the inevitable consequences when armed soldiers attacked him. Although their primitive weapons could not kill him, the inconvenience of injury to his host body forced a withdrawal. This eventually taught the entity to become more discreet. But a part of the parasite longed for those more honest times when he could experience the pleasure of the terror his attacks provoked in these ape-like creatures.

Cortez pulled himself from his reverie. This physical form needed fresh clothing and a wash to integrate successfully into the society which he now ruled. There was a small washroom at the end of the ward, which Cortez entered and, finding sets of towels, soap and razors, prepared his appearance for his first encounters with the subordinates he knew would be waiting for their instructions.

During his ablutions, the human part of Cortez noticed that his white hair had returned to the vibrant blond colour of his youth, along with his beard stubble and body hair. His blue eyes had become more piercing, and those eyes regarded his reflection with pride after he had completed his preparations. Exiting the washroom, he walked through the empty ward, stopping only to turn off the life support machines and to pick up the charred adept's ring, which he put on his right ring finger, with the pentagram inverted.

As Cortez exited through the double doors into the first-floor mezzanine where three men dressed in well-cut, jet-black Hugo Boss uniforms had been standing watch to prevent anyone from disturbing the Chairman, the ECG alarms sounded as the burnt body of Madeleine Mathers finally surrendered to the inevitable.

As the crash team siren continued, nurses hurried past. Cortez ignored the demise of his former host body, and cooly appraised his three guards instead. He knew these Knights of the Black Sun were selected to be the finest warriors - tested to be at peak fitness, ruthless and without fear. With his new senses, the Chairman could feel the electrical fields associated with the three hearts as they beat, each with their own separate rhythm. They were nervous due to the arrival of their leader. On a whim of fancy, Cortez focused his newfound preternatural influence on the Black Knight closest to him. A tall man, in his thirties with the typical blond hair and blue eyes expected of the order of the Black Sun. As the sophisticated electrical fields of the MUŠ.ŠÀ.TÙR enveloped, ensnared and entrained the body of its target prey, Cortez became aware of the waves of electrical activity as the man's heart began to race uncontrollably before entering into a series of uncoordinated spasms that had the Black Knight clutch his chest briefly before collapsing to the floor. As the man lay on the floor, Cortez felt his victim's fear of death, like a velvet cocoon of pleasure wrapping around the Argentinian's body. How wonderful it must feel to experience the death and suffering of thousands, pondered Cortez before walking coldly away, leaving the two guards to wonder if they should tend to their fallen comrade or follow their leader. Ultimately, they decided to leave the fallen knight to his fate and continue to escort their principal.

Cortez focused on the dozen burn patients in the makeshift ward on this first-floor level overlooking the entrance foyer. Having just experienced the combination of ecstasy and a rush of energy from the fear expressed by a single person facing death, he was disappointed at the lack of suffering emitted by the bodies of the dozen burn victims in the makeshift ward. Then, he noticed the morphine drips attached to each bed. This was no good! Surviving the explosion, remaining in a burnt body and transferring hosts had drained the MUŠ.ŠÀ.TÙR to dangerously low levels. It urgently needed sustenance. This biological imperative drove it to immediate action. Cortez found himself impelled to start violently pulling the morphine drips from each patient. He had completed four drip removals before Dr Hugo Gauthier ran up the stairs from the foyer shouting accompanied by Smegget and another man, dressed in a US Airforce uniform, following close behind him.

Dr Gauthier stood in front of Cortez and grabbed the shoulders of the Argentinian Chairman.

"What the hell is wrong with you? These patients need this sedation, or the pain will be unbearable!"

Cortez's nostrils flared, and his pupils expanded until they completely obscured the blue irises. The iron discipline and self-control that had defined Cortez's life were gone, surrendered to the parasite which now dominated his existence. The MUŠ.ŠÀ.TÙR acted with blinding speed and, for just an instant, manifested its true nature on the material plane. It struck the French doctor dozens of times with each of its seven heads, embedding each razor-tipped circular mouth deep into the body of its victim. Each bite was filled with a toxic liquid that consumed physical matter, converting it into a form of energy that invigorated the parasite's body. The manifestation lasted less than a microsecond, much too fast for any organic life form to register. Only the Astral sight of a highly trained initiate stood any chance of seeing what happened.

All but one of the human beings observing the manifestation saw the French Doctor trying to restrain Chairman Cortez, then crying out and collapsing to the floor. Before any of the nurses could reach him, the Doctor's body collapsed into a brown-coloured goo which collected inside the medic's white lab coat. Within moments all that was left of Dr Gauthier was his heavily stained clothing and the metal components of his stethoscope, which smouldered as they vapourised.

Smegget and the two Black Knights looked shocked at what they assumed must have been some bizarre chemical reaction caused by exposure to the abnormal conditions outside with the cosmic airbursts. USAF Chief Booker walked from behind Smegget across the mezzanine floor and addressed Cortez,

"Chairman, may we talk somewhere private?"

Booker looked pointedly at Smegget and the two Black Knights.

"I have confidential issues that need to be addressed."

Cortez nodded, and the two men returned to the ward where Mathers' dead body lay. Inside, Cortez dismissed the orderly who was preparing to remove Mathers to the morgue.

Once Booker had confirmed the two Black Knights and Smegget were waiting outside, he looked at the charred initiates ring on Chairman Cortez's right ring finger and demanded,

"What the hell are you?"

Cortez was amused. "What an inappropriate question for your superior."

As a 7th-degree Meri-Isfet initiate, Booker was not intimidated.

"You are not entitled to wear that ring. Where is Regio?"

Having just consumed the energy from two violent deaths, Cortez felt quite mellow. Besides, the anger exhibited by Booker was providing a quite acceptable dessert.

"No longer with us."

Booker was not giving up or backing down.

"Pederson?"

"Same, and before you ask about Sanchez, I am your Imperator."

The USAF Chief snorted in disbelief.

"And simultaneously Alpha of Wolfsangel? You know it is forbidden to have both arms of our organisation combined after what happened to the ancients[582]."

There was a long silence during which Cortez looked amused by the insolence. Eventually, Booker continued.

---

[582] Called the "apkallu" in the oldest Sumerian myths - seven powerful dark path adepts ruled the earth before the flood. Able to control minds and transfer their souls between bodies, they became addicted to using the infernal wheels to open pathways to the Qliphoth.

"If you are entitled to wear that ring, then you know that none granted such combined powers has been able to resist using the infernal wheels to commune with the Qliphoth."

At that moment, a series of enormous airburst explosions above them shook the glass in the windows. Suddenly, everything came together in Booker's mind.

"You combined The Ten Gates Ceremony with the St Petersburg Wheel? You bloody fool. You caused these explosions and the associated destruction!"

Cortez was delighted that this stupid ape had finally stumbled onto the truth, or at least a small part. He gazed at the explosions lighting the sky above them like a father gazes at a favourite child.

"Aren't they beautiful? I can feel the sum of suffering multiplying with each explosion. And the best bit is that nothing can stop me from repeating the Qliphothic contact."

Booker looked at the Chairman like he was mad before replying,

"Smegget already told me the St Petersburg Wheel was destroyed in the fire which killed her."

The USAF chief gestured towards Mathers' body before continuing.

"So fate has already halted this madness. Thank God."

The Chairman smiled condescendingly at the USAF Chief.

"A Meri-Isfet adept praising God? You do not have much faith in the order's teachings. I can assure you, Chief Booker, in my case, God has *nothing* to do with my plans. It is my destiny to commune with the Qliphoth."

Booker made deliberate eye contact and tried to reason with Cortez.

"I don't know how well you know the history of previous contacts with these Qliphothic realms. The Qliphoth promise everything, but all they want is the destruction of our reality! To seed that destruction, they take human essence and merge their own to create the ultimate karmic abomination. A parasitic creature that is half material and half immaterial that feeds off the pain, suffering and destruc..."

Booker's sentence died on his lips as his eyes widened in realisation, recalling the astral images of Cortez's transformation while he attacked the doctor.

"You are Nephilim[583]!? You were wiped out in the deluge. Did the Ten Gates Ceremony permit your new manifestation?"

Cortez shook his head. He was still highly amused by the disbelief and fear he could sense growing in the ape standing before him.

"Nephilim, Hydra[584], Jörmungandr[585], Chi[586], Shayṭān[587], or..."

Cortez paused, delighting in the anticipation of the effect his next words would have on the ape standing before him.

---

[583] According to the Abrahamic religions, the Nephilim - נְפִילִים terrorised the world before the great deluge.
[584] The Lernaean Hydra was a snake-like monster in Greek and Roman mythology
[585] From Norse Sagas, this demonic snake is also called the Midgard (Earth) Serpent. The most ancient sagas tell that when it emerges, Ragnarök (Twilight of the Gods or End Times) will begin.
[586] Hornless dragon or mountain demon (chīměi 螭魅) in Chinese mythology.
[587] In Islamic lore, a blasphemous class of primitive Djinn also known as Iblīs or Satan.

"Apep. Our names are legion. However, we call ourselves the MUŠ.ŠÀ.TÙR. We survived the deluge by becoming more... discreet."

Booker grasped the full implication.

"Apep? The God of Chaos, who is the basis of our order, The Meri-Isfet? That would..."

The Chief paused, not quite believing the conclusion his own logic had now reached.

Cortez laughed.

"Yes, my dear Booker. Quite literally, the Devil Incarnate. All these years, you have been worshipping me. Just think how fortunate you are to finally meet your God."

The Argentinian waited for the full impact of this to register on the human's emotional (endocrine) systems before continuing.

"You should realise that everything taking place has been carefully planned. Every possibility has been anticipated."

Booker looked sceptical. "Even the destruction of the St Petersburg Wheel?"

"There are other wheels, my dear Booker. Within the coming week, I will reactivate the full-sized Wheel created in the middle of the last century."

"The Bell?!"

Booker exhibited fear for the first time in their interaction, and Cortez relished it.

The USAF Chief thought for a moment and then countered, saying,

"Nice try. We both know it will take years to create the power network necessary to run a wheel of that size! It was the power limitations which prevented its activation in the 1940s."

Cortez chuckled. This whole discussion was adorable.

"I already have the necessary power grid up and ready. I just need to transport the Wheel to the site I have been designing specifically for it over the past decades."

Booker looked confused, and then his eyes widened as he finally realised what the Chairman meant.

"CERN[588]!"

Cortez chuckled again. These apes were a delight with their simple minds.

"Indeed. It always surprised us that people were stupid enough to think puppet world governments would fund billions into researching fundamental particles. As I said, nothing can stop me."

By now, it was clear to Booker that Cortez was building up to killing him. Under any other circumstance, he would have pulled out his service pistol[589] and emptied the full seventeen 9mm rounds into this abomination, but he knew enough of the esoteric lore surrounding this legendary monster to know it would be futile. The one common theme running through all descriptions of this thing throughout history was that only one specific weapon, forged in antediluvian times, stood any chance of ending its evil existence. But, if he was to die, he wanted the satisfaction of giving this abomination something in return.

The representations of offensive magick in popular media portray it as a rapid slugging match, with wands, spells and

---

[588] Conseil Européen pour la Recherche Nucléaire", or European Council for Nuclear Research
[589] SIG Sauer M17 - a modified SIG Sauer P320 for the USAF.

counterspells zapping back and forth like ping-pong balls. Real magick is a slow process, more like gardening than a spiritual boxing match. Ideas, doubts, and physical imbalances are seeded deep in the layers of the archetypal, where they grow slowly into manifestations on material planes such as disease, pain, paranoia, and other forms of decay and disorder.

Booker utilised everything he had learnt of offensive magick over decades of study within the Meri-Isfet, maximising the one weakness he had recognised in his opponent.

"Unstoppable? What if another adept came after you?"

Cortez looked amused. "You? As we will see shortly, I will deal with you like a bug on my shoe."

Now, it was Booker's turn to smile.

"No, I mean a real Ipsissimus. Not a usurping fake like you."

"There are none left."

Snarled Cortez as his serpentine preternatural body momentarily reemerged and repeatedly plunged its seven lamprey-like snouts into the USAF Chief's body. As Booker's body convulsed in agony on the floor, Cortez suddenly recalled the odd situation where Booker had been sent to Grindelwald to deal with a supposed apparition only to turn up in Egypt under mysterious circumstances.

"Ad-Dajjal!"

Booker never lived long enough to fully appreciate the sight of a startled Cortez storming from the medical ward and calling out to Major General Smegget.

Ten minutes later, after a series of encrypted phone calls, Le Terrible, a Triomphant class ballistic missile submarine[590], interrupted its course off the coast of Réduit[591]. After rising to a depth of twenty-five feet beneath the surface of the azure-coloured Indian Ocean, the cover of one of its launch tubes retracted, and one of sixteen ballistic missiles emerged in a burst of flame which evaporated large quantities of seawater.

The forty-foot-long, MIRV[592] M51[593] missile soared into the sky, rapidly burning through the first of its three-stage solid fuel[594] boosters until it reached a speed in excess of Mach 25 (20,000 miles an hour) and soared out of the Earth's atmosphere, where it separated into a spread of multiple warheads[595], each of which headed at hypersonic speed inexorably[596] down towards a remote mountain[597] in the Bernese alps near Grindelwald in Switzerland. The five thousand, five-hundred-mile journey was covered in under sixteen minutes. Although a series of massive cometary airbursts on route destroyed five of the six, TN 75 warheads, one successfully reached its target.

Milliseconds after impact, the top forty yards of the mountain vapourised, sending seismic shocks throughout Switzerland and the European mainland. Microseconds after

---

[590] Formerly owned by the French Navy, before the Cotez revolution.
[591] Formerly administered by the French, prior to the Cortez revolution.
[592] Multiple independently targetable re-entry vehicle.
[593] A 110-kiloton warhead delivering 420 TJ. This is the smallest of the French tactical nuclear warheads, the largest is 300 kilotons.
[594] Ammonium perchlorate composite propellant.
[595] Each missile carries six to ten independently targetable TN 75 thermonuclear warheads.
[596] Using the Galileo Guidance system.
597 Finsteraarhorn Mountain.

that, there was a rapid series of two flashes[598], a thousand times brighter than the sun. Then a three-hundred-yard-wide fireball blossomed into a massive red and orange mushroom-shaped cloud that rose eight miles above the Bernese Alps.

Although the Wolfsangel complex had been designed to withstand a nuclear blast, those designs were for a smaller tactical nuke[599] and not the strategic intercontinental ballistic missile Cortez had just deployed. As a consequence, very little of the underground base remained. Every living thing perished from being vapourised by the thermonuclear fire ball or pulverised by the massive[600] shock wave that spread through the structure.

Two hundred and sixty miles South West from Grindelwald, at the Clinique de Réadaptation du Dr STER, Major General Smegget was looking at the grinning Chairman Cortez, who was delighted at having just received confirmation of the destruction of the secret Wolfsangel complex in Switzerland. The Major General's concern was not just about losing the facility, its resources and its staff, which had been a strategic asset to the organisation. Until the last few days, that base had been where Smegget had lived and worked. But for a fluke of fate, the Major General would have also been

---

[598] The pressure wave from a nuclear explosion is so powerful that it rapidly expands faster than the initial fireball. As it passes the boundary of the fireball, it temporarily obscures it, causing a double flash.
[599] Thought likely to be used in a European conflict. Ranging in yield from a fraction of a kiloton to approximately 50 kilotons.
[600] 259 Tera Joules.

vapourised. Yet here was Cortez celebrating the brutal extermination of his own people.

There were also the strange demises of the Black Knight, Dr Gauthier and Chief Booker. All three men had been strong, healthy adults who died when they were in close proximity to Chairman Cortez. Even if these deaths were a coincidence, it still seemed to be extraordinarily bad for one's health to be close to Cortez - and no one worked more closely with the Chairman than Smegget. These thoughts and others flooded the Major General's mind as the Chairman led his group down the stairs to the waiting cars outside. With Cortez riding in Chief Booker's Maserati, the six vehicles began their journey to Ksiaz Castle, in the New Europa province once called Poland. Ksiaz was a location that Smegget had never heard of before, but overnight, it had mysteriously become the Chairman's obsession.

In the empty burns ward on the first floor of Clinique de Réadaptation du Dr STER, two orderlies began the grisly task of removing the bodies of Chief Booker and Madeleine Mathers. As one of them pushed a gurney beside the burnt remains of Mathers, the heart rate ECG monitor and EEG brainwave displays suddenly sprang to life. The woman's body issued a rasping sound and began breathing unaided.

SURPRISE WITNESS

"When there's a person, there's a problem. When there's no person, there's no problem." - Josef Stalin

The International Criminal Court (ICC)
Oude Waalsdorperweg 10
The Hague, The Netherlands.

11:33 HRS (GMT + 2), 16th September, present day

The last half hour had been one of the longest that Sinclair could remember. The unseemly laughs that emanated from the six prosecution lawyers to her right, had made that wait feel even longer. The prosecution team gradually became less worried about appearances on global media coverage as the wait progressed, eventually openly sharing jokes with the five Wolfsangel operatives who had stormed in as the Judge left. Within minutes, the two groups loudly announced that the imminent executions of Sinclair and Curren would start a long overdue purge of society's undesirables and that they would soon get a lot more shooting practice! Sinclair surmised that the five operatives pointing their MP7s at the two unarmed defendants were the firing squad, who had come in to gloat over their victims. She would not be surprised if these thugs even performed the execution in the courtroom while the cameras were running.

Sinclair's speculation ended abruptly as Judge Kikkert re-entered the courtroom thirty-three minutes after leaving for his twenty-minute intercession. This time, two Wolfsangel operatives roughly escorted him at gunpoint, and the Judge had a mobile phone to his ear. The six-person Wolfsangel prosecution team laughed openly at the loss of any pretence that this was an open and fair trial. Good, thought Sinclair, hopefully, the global audiences watching would come to the same conclusion.

The elderly Usher shouted over the laughter in a courtroom that sounded more like a school playground.

"All rise! The session has resumed for summary and judgment. Judge Kikkert presiding."

More like Deputy Chairman Hartman presiding, thought Sinclair. She almost felt sorry for the Judge doing his best to avoid announcing the death penalty.

Sinclair helped the unresponsive Curren to her feet. The former Director General of SIS glared at the five Wolfsangel operatives who pointed their MP7 machine guns at the two defendants. Sinclair could see her reflection in the mirrored visors each operative wore. They were so close that she could read the small text, "iKill Pro" and the company logo engraved on the top right corner of the lens. Curren remained blank-faced, even as one of the thugs nudged Stewart's former lawyer hard in the stomach with the barrel of his rifle. Sinclair pushed herself between the MP7 and the glassy-eyed Curren, saying,

"That is hardly necessary."

The Wolfsangel operative grinned. This whole thing was a big joke to him.

Back on the podium, the Judge nodded at the six members of the Wolfsangel prosecution team and then at the two defendants and the empty desk where the defence team should have been standing.

"Representatives of the prosecution and, err, defence, we have reviewed the evidence, and we are ready to pass judgement."

The Usher passed the Judge a black cap, which Kikkert looked at with undisguised revulsion and delayed picking it up. The Usher gestured more forcibly that the dark covering should be placed on his head. Kikkert hesitated.

Minutes earlier, five hundred and fifty miles South East of the ICC courtroom, a one-hundred-and-ten kiloton TN 75[601] atomic warhead had detonated on the top of the Finsteraarhorn Mountain. The explosion created a crater that was forty yards deep and just under one hundred yards in radius. The fireball radius extended over three hundred yards, and there was heavy blast damage over three-quarters of a mile around the site. Sixty hikers, tourists and residents were killed instantly and over one thousand suffered injuries. An area of one mile[602] around the detonation site was flooded with ionising radiation at the five hundred rem[603] level[604]. Lesser levels of radiation, of one hundred rem and less, drifted in the fallout cloud as far as seventy miles North West of the mountain. In time, this radiation would infiltrate the water systems fed from the glaciers in the Bernese Alps, contaminating the surrounding fauna and flora and causing irreparable damage to the Swiss economy[605].

The fireball effectively sealed the subterranean Wolfsangel complex from radiation and fallout with molten Amphibolite rock that once formed the summit. However, the complex and its residents were subjected to a massive overpressure

---

[601] Manufactured at the Centre d'Etudes de Valduc, 40 km north of Dijon.
[602] Assuming a 110 kiloton surface burst, with dry weather conditions, 62 F with an 18 mph wind heading North East.
[603] Roentgen Equivalent Man (rem) is a standard measure of radiation. The average person receives 0.62 rem in a year.
[604] 500 rem is usually fatal within 30 days.
[605] The contaminated water does not just provide expensive mineral water to the elites. It irrigates the alpine grass, which is eaten by cows - contaminating dairy products, including chocolate.

shock wave of over twenty pounds per square inch[606], constrained within the tunnels and chambers. In addition, a wave of thermal radiation passed through the mountain bedrock to a depth of just under three miles, causing third-degree burns to all organic life. As Chairman Cortez had planned, the end result of the explosion was that everything within the Wolfsangel complex was pulverised and seared. No living thing survived.

Deep in the granite bedrock of Finsteraarhorn Mountain, two miles under the detonation, the "Cave of Dread[607]" was first exposed to a massive pressure wave, followed moments later by a wave of thermal radiation which raised the ambient temperature to over eight hundred degrees Fahrenheit. The esoterically charged volcanic rock[608] that comprised this ritual space's walls, floor and ceilings were torn from their fixings and violently smashed around the fifty-square-foot temple space. A similar fate occurred to the numerous cursed artefacts contained in the Perspex racks and the main chamber, including the infamous skull of Devadatta, blood-soaked linen-bound log books and assorted vivisection equipment from Unit Tōgō and Unit 731, where the wartime Japanese conducted some of the most horrific human experimentation ever recorded, including deliberate infections with lethal poisons, bacterial and viral agents.

All these items were pulverised into fine dust by repeated impacts, slowly settling to the ground and mixing with the gallons of recycled water from the cursed well from the infamous Uji Incident. This liquid paste was then evaporated

---

[606] A 20 psi overpressure shockwave will demolish re-enforced concrete buildings and cause 100% fatalities.
[607] Osore Tengu temple.
[608] Transported from Mount Osore, known in Japan as Mount "Dread".

dry by the massive wave of thermal radiation, which swept through the confined space some thirty seconds later[609].

When these destructive processes finally ended, there was profound darkness and absolute silence. The malevolent spiritual entities (Onryō) which had manifested to obsess the female meditator[610], who had entered their temple some hours earlier, had their energy fields disrupted and blended into the fine dust which now filled the lower four feet of the confined temple space.

Long minutes passed as the mountain settled after its violent impact. Then there was a stirring. A human form slowly rose from the dark powder where it had been seated in the classic Siddhasana (adepts pose) asana. The woman's body was completely covered in fine black powder. The close-fitting jet-black silk Chanel trouser suit she had been wearing had been consumed by the wave of thermal radiation, leaving the woman naked except for the layers of black Mount Osore dust[611]The form of Dr Nissa Ad-Dajjal placed her hands in the fine residue and, taking large handfuls of the material, scattered the dust into the air while she took in numerous deep breaths, taking the preternaturally charged air-borne material deep into her lungs.

During each exhalation, she intoned the sacred mantra,

---

[609] It took time for the thermal radiation to penetrate through the limestone.

[610] You cannot obsess an entity while its consciousness is in the sublime state of Samadi, which Ad-Dajjal had entered during her meditative state. The Onryō would have been waiting for the mediation to end.

[611] If you are hoping for more details of Ad-Dajjal's naked body, you are reading the wrong book.

"oṃ ā ma ra ṇi dzi wan te ye svā hā[612]",

associated with the ancient Tachikawa-ryu ritual known as "Karada ni ashi o fumiireru gishiki" - the ceremony that had brought the raven-haired beauty to the cavern. Although the literal translation of the ritual is "Stepping on the Body", it is more accurately represented as "Entering the Body"[613].

Her long fingers formed the ancient hand shapes[614] that manipulated the vital life energy called Chi within her body. Under the direction of Ad-Dajjal's will, that vital energy became converted into a very rarified form called Uḍāna, a combination of sound, energy, vibration and the focused intent of the mind. This Uḍāna pulsed through Ad-Dajjal's sacred energy centres[615] creating physical forces externally and separately from her body. This ancient ritual not only expanded Ad-Dajjal's consciousness but placed the very fabric of existence under her conscious control. As the ritual reached its climax, Ad-Dajjal's will started to exert control over physical reality so that the airborne dust started to twist and coil in the air.

When Ad-Dajjal concluded her performance of the Karada ni ashi o fumiireru gishiki ritual, waves of astral energy gathered around her head, forming the dark cobra-shaped hood of the legendary Naga left-hand path master adepts. Ad-Dajjal's eyes opened, her pupils had become mere vertical slits, and her face glowed as she exhaled thick streams of

---

[612] The Tibetan Amitāyus mantra: ༀ་ཨ་མ་ར་ཎི་ཛི་ཝན་ཏེ་ཡེ་སྭཱ་ཧཱ. Sometimes called the infinite life mantra.

[613] Tibetan forbidden magick, calls this technique Trongjug, the transference of consciousness and the animation of a body. Modern magicians will be more familiar with the term, Tulpa.

[614] Tantric Mudras.

[615] Chakras.

dust through her nostrils that danced and writhed in the air around her body.

Five hundred and fifty miles North West from where Ad-Dajjal had completed her ritual, in the ICC courtroom, Judge Kikkert was hesitating to pick up the black cap that signified that the death penalty was about to be pronounced. This tense anticipation was shattered by Helen Curren suddenly breaking out of the trance-like coma that had imprisoned her consciousness for the past days. Standing alongside, Sinclair reacted with surprise and delight, thinking that Helen, with her extensive legal background, could provide some defence to the trumped-up charges they were facing.

As Curren bent forward, grasping the desk, she began to cough, depositing copious amounts of black soot-like dust filled with small particles over the table surface. Sinclair reached over to provide Curren with a glass of water but withdrew in shock when the contents of the plastic glass froze solid and shattered into fragments of ice as though exposed to some extraordinary cold. The thermal imaging on the "iKill Pro" systems augmented reality used by the five Wolfsangel gunmen also began to malfunction, registering impossibly low temperatures from the coughing prisoner.

As Stewart's lawyer continued her violent coughing spasm, the air filled with the dust she was bringing up - making the courtroom full of a rich earthy aroma. The powerful AC that fed the room picked up these coughed particles and began spreading them throughout the ICC court building. Growing increasingly concerned about her co-defendant's medical condition, Sinclair broke court etiquette and called directly to Judge Kikkert across the courtroom,

"Your honour, please, can we get some medical assistance?"

Sinclair's outburst was met with further hilarity from the six prosecution lawyers, who could be heard commenting,

"Why bother? Saves us a job."

Before Kikkert could react, Curren waved her hand, dismissing the request, but Kikkert still held to the old standards of civility and wanted to be certain the defendant was fit to stand trial before he continued. He asked,

"Ms Curren, are you sure you are ok?"

There was a pause before a silky, seductive voice responded,

"I am not quite myself, but keen to proceed."

Sinclair did not recognise Curren's voice but assumed the coughing had caused the change. The former Director of SIS whispered conspiratorially,

"You have a plan?"

Curren stopped coughing, turned to look directly at Sinclair and revealed eyes that were more reptilian than human. The uncharacteristically seductive voice responded,

"Whatever happens, Cynthia, just follow my lead."

Sinclair nodded, unsure which was more frightening, Nissa Ad-Dajjal or the Wolfsangel firing squad.

"So, what do you have in mind?"

"Something... wonderfully *Unholy*," quipped the new Curren in a tone that caused an icy chill to flow through Sinclair's veins.

Sinclair began scanning the room, wondering what to expect. The accounts she had heard from Thomas and Tavish were, frankly, rather unbelievable.

Sinclair did not have to wait long. It started with the Wolfsangel gunman nearest to where Curren had been coughing so violently. The man started and involuntarily cried out, causing his colleagues to glance at him with concern before continuing to glare at the two defendants. Meanwhile, the operative who had cried out started to move his head from side to side as though he was uncertain of what he was seeing. Then, suddenly, he ripped off his iKill Pro Visor and gloves, pulling the embedded electronic connections violently from his skin. Although nothing was visible to Sinclair, the man reacted like some rapidly acting disease was consuming his flesh. Pulling the black KM2000 knife from his ankle sheath, he scraped the razor-sharp blade over the skin on his arm and hands. This did not stop whatever he was experiencing as he began to systematically flay the skin from his wrists and hands, continuing until he exposed the bones, causing copious amounts of blood to flow over the wooden flooring. The four other members of the firing squad were at first confused, but then they too began to react; only their nightmares were each quite different.

Sinclair watched the five operatives lose their confident arrogance, swatting at unseen attackers and holding their limbs in apparent agony from some hideously sadistic wound unseen by anyone else. That is until Sinclair noticed a vague shape rising from the blood that had gathered on the wooden flooring. The shape rose until it was five feet high and then coalesced into the form of a young woman dressed in a soaking-wet white cotton kimono. The girl's long black hair almost reached the floor, and her face was as devoid of colour as her white gown. The apparition of the twelfth-century concubine, Kichōna Hana, whose possession initiated the "Uji Incident", swayed as it slowly approached Sinclair, muttering some phrases over and over... This strange repeating Japanese phrase began to catch in Sinclair's mind, but just as it started to dominate Sinclair's consciousness, she felt an icy grip on her arm and heard Ad-Dajjal's voice instructing,

"Crouch down. Now!"

It took a second for Sinclair to pull herself to awareness again and to crouch down behind the desk beside the possessed Curren. It was not a moment too soon, as two of the Wolfsangel gunmen raised their MP7 rifles and opened up with fully automatic gunfire where the dark swaying figure of the muttering girl had been standing. The barrage of armour-piercing rounds passed through the apparition and cut through the armoured glass separating the courtroom from the media observation area behind the court. The shattered glass permitted the sounds from the rest of the ICC building to penetrate into the courtroom. Chaos was overtaking the rest of the building as screams intermingled with the sounds of gunfire and fighting. In the exposed media area, some of the observers returned fire with pistols and rifles into the two Wolfsangel operatives, who by now had retreated to better cover beside the six members of the prosecution. As the firefight ensued, Sinclair felt the icy grip of Curren pulling her back to her feet, as the voice of Ad-Dajjal instructed,

"Hands above your head, and whatever you do, do not move."

Sinclair winced as the increasingly desperate Wolfsangel gunmen used the prosecution lawyers as ineffective human shields against a hail of 9mm rounds.

As the last of the lawyers and the gunmen collapsed to the floor, from the corner of her eye, Sinclair could see that Curren had established some kind of telepathic or probably hypnotic link with Judge Kikkert, who had been cowering terrified behind his podium. The judge lost his fear of the chaos unfolding around him and resumed his seat. He pulled the microphone closer to his mouth and word for word, repeated what the sultry voice of Ad-Dajjal said,

"Case dismissed."

The judge then nodded to some unspoken command, picked up the mobile phone from his desk and held it beside the court microphone in what would become a soundbite heard by the world's independent media stations. Deputy Chairman Hartman's voice filled the room.

"Of course, they are innocent. I don't care. I want them dead. Or I will kill all your family. Do you want to hear them scream again?"

At that moment, four dog-sized robots bust down the courtroom door, their sinister red camera lenses scanning Sinclair and Curren, who stood immobile with their hands raised high above their heads in the universal sign of surrender.

As Judge Kikkert held the mobile to the open microphone, Hartman's voice could be heard instructing the Snitch units, saying,

"Escort the prisoners to the waiting van. We will have one last use for them to bring that bastard Stewart to us..."

K.R.M. Morgan

ROOFTOP RENDEZVOUS

"Any fool can know. The point is to understand." - Albert Einstein

Place du Bourg-de-Four
The old town of Geneva.
1204 Genève
Switzerland.

10:17 HRS (GMT +2), 16th September, Present day

Stewart had woken at his usual five a.m. sharp after a less than ideal night. It was over two hours before dawn, and consequently, it took a moment for the Scotsman to recall his location on the Quai du Mont-Blanc[616]. Due to the dry heat, which made it feel more like the desert than Switzerland, he had slept with the windows and blinds open. A fine layer of soot covered the surfaces nearest the window. The gentle breeze from the lake had provided little relief, and having the windows open meant he had been subjected to the constant flashes and explosions from the cosmic fireworks displays that had now become a fixture of life in Cortez's New Europa. Consequently, the Scotsman's dreams had been filled with violent images recalled from the numerous war zones in which he had served.

Stewart rose and drank some bottled water from the fridge before putting on hotel-themed T-shirt and shorts and doing some yoga stretches out on the small balcony attached to his room overlooking the famous lake. The bruising and stiffness from his encounters at the Fortress were finally easing, and he was starting to feel ready to face Wolfsangel again.

---

[616] Hotel d'Angleterre, Geneva.

After a brief warm-up which was shorter than usual due to the ambient heat, the Scotsman started a short hatha yoga regime a Gurka PTI[617] had taught him during a tour of duty in Oman. His routine commenced with a Twisted Floor Bow Pose[618], which he transformed effortlessly into a series of Handstands[619], then into Crane Pose[620], a Scorpion Handstand[621], and ended with the Eight-angle Pose[622] before repeating the sequence three times. He was sweating profusely, so he sat momentarily, enjoying the predawn calm as he finished the bottle of chilled water.

He had no idea what he was going to encounter from the Wolfsangel forces after he had returned Mathers' camper van to SPLEE, so he prepared for the worst by clearing the furniture in his suite and commencing a series of formal Japanese martial movements known as Unsu[623].

Stewart had mastered this particular formal exercise as part of his Yon-dan[624] studies in Osaka[625]. As the Scotsman commenced the forty-eight moves, his hands flew through the air around him, echoing intricate techniques such as

---

[617] Physical Training Instructor.

[618] Twisted Floor Bow - Dhanurasana.

[619] Handstand variations - Adho Mukha Vrksasana.

[620] Crane - Bakasana.

[621] Scorpion Handstand - Vrschikasana B.

[622] Eight-angle Pose - Astavakrasana

[623] 雲手, 'cloud hands' - is the most advanced kata in the Shotokan and Shito-Ryu karate styles.

[624] Fourth-degree black belt. A level which indicates a high level of competence in the system.

[625] Studying an additional martial art to a set level of competence is a mandatory component for advancement within traditional Japanese martial schools, where there are only three ranks - student, practitioner and teacher. Typically with twenty years of study between each progressive rank.

ippon-nukite[626] that could remove an opponent's eye, shatter their windpipe or burst their testicles[627]. As the moves progressed, Stewart performed two kicks[628] while lying prone on the ground[629], then a back thrust kick[630] and a blindingly fast reverse punch[631] that would shatter an opponent's sternum, embedding the broken ribs deep into the lung tissue. In consideration of the sleep of the other occupants in the hotel, Stewart issued the two kiais[632] in the formal Unsu exercise silently. The Scotsman repeated the entire series several times until he was satisfied with his techniques. His selection of an external form of martial art practice reflected the new reality he was facing, which meant that, in all likelihood, he would have to initiate confrontation rather than his usual tactic of responding to attacks made upon him.

When Stewart emerged after a long ice-cold shower, he found that room service had brought up the brown paper parcel he had express couriered overnight from London. Inside was a box with the distinctive Ede and Ravenscroft logo[633] and a small orange cardboard box of Hermes

---

[626] One finger strike.

[627] Hito-sashiyubi-gedan-nukite - lower level one-finger spear hand.

[628] Ni-mawashi-geri - round kick.

[629] Groundwork is extremely popular in modern martial art forms that focus on competition-based one-on-one fights but is less common in more traditional forms - as lying on the ground when facing multiple armed opponents is not often an advantageous strategy.

[630] Ushiro-geri-kekomi - spinning back kick.

[631] Chudan-gyaku-zuki - reverse body punch.

[632] Martial focus - often a loud exclamation. More than just a shout, this technique is said to project Chi (vital force) at an opponent. It can be silent as, at advanced levels, it is more involved with an "outbreath" of maximum martial force than sound.

[633] Containing a navy-coloured pique knitted shirt, chalk-white linen trousers and tan leather deck shoes with crepe soles.

cologne[634].   Having completed his morning preparations, the Scotsman went down to the Windows Restaurant just as the sun would have risen[635] had the smoke from numerous European wildfires not obscured the dawn. As it was, Stewart made the best of the situation by gazing out over the spectacular cometary airbursts over the backdrop of Mont Blanc from his table. Unlike most patrons in the busy restaurant, Stewart avoided a heavy full-cooked breakfast, instead opting for a bowl of Bircher Muesli[636], followed by scrambled eggs on rye toast and two cups of strong black espresso[637].

Since it was still three hours before he had arranged to return Mathers' Volkswagen to the SPLEE offices, the Scotsman decided to go for a post-breakfast walk. His goal was not just to stretch his legs but also to outfit himself with some essential equipment. He needed a timepiece, so as he was passing one of the city's legendary jewellers[638] on Rue de la Confédération he entered the premises. The shop had only just opened, so it was empty of customers, and Stewart was blessed with the undivided attention of a very enthusiastic salesman.

Due to the high commission rates associated with them, the young salesman was especially keen to guide his new customer towards high-end smartwatches[639] by brands such as TAG Heuer, Montblanc, and Louis Vuitton. He extolled the merits of sleep analysis, step counts and stress meter

---

634 Hermès Eau D'Orange Verte Eau.

635 Dawn is at 7.14 am in Geneva on 16th of September.

636 Swiss oatmeal porridge - the nearest Stewart could get to his beloved Scottish Oats.

637 MADDOG espresso by the Zermatt coffee roastery.

638 KURZ 1948 Genève.

639 Smartwatches become obsolete so quickly that commission rates are significantly higher to shift the stock rapidly.

features, claiming, "It tells you if you had a good night's sleep!"

The Scotsman appreciated the young man's enthusiasm but felt that he could tell if he had slept well without any technological aid[640]. Under different circumstances, Stewart would have appreciated the watches on display, but none were suitable for his purposes. However, the Scotsman noticed a collection of fine pocket knives in one of the cabinets. One of them by Ansø of Denmark[641], called the ORSO, was a work of art with "intricate Damascus steel blade[642], black Timascus[643] handle, zirconium pivot rings and amber anodised titanium screws. Normally, Stewart preferred something tactical, but the piece's beauty spoke to him, especially since he was certain he would need a knife. After a test cut of paper and a few one-handed test draws of the three-inch blade, Stewart exited the shop with the ORSO clipped to the top of his right front trouser pocket. Still in search of a more utilitarian timepiece.

Next, he called into one of the many high-end tourist shops and emerged moments later with a pair of sunglasses[644] visible from his top chest pocket, a baseball cap tucked into his rear pocket and a steel field watch[645] on his wrist. The dark lenses and cap were not intended to protect his eyes from glare, as the sun was absent due to the thick cloud cover, but they would go some way to obscuring his identity

---

[640] If you knew how inaccurate the measurements are from such smart wearables, you would probably share Stewart's scepticism.
[641] Owned by Jens Ansø, a master knife maker from Denmark.
[642] Damasteel.
[643] Black timascus is a pattern welded titanium alloy.
[644] Rayban Wayfarers.
[645] Certina DS Podium GMT Reference C034.455.16.050.00 Precidrive Quartz (thermocompensated -10 seconds a year), Second-time zone, ISO 100m Water resistant, luminous legible dial, ISO shock resistant and ISO anti-magnetic.

from facial recognition systems during an escape if his assumed identity failed to convince Cortez's A.I. systems. Wearing a field watch that provided a clear measurement of time could also be vital in the coming hours.

He continued his walk, eventually reaching the most noted Gunsmith in Switzerland[646], on Rue de la Corraterie. The Israeli spymaster, Mark Katz, had included a Swiss "shall-issue permit" in his goody bag back in Sarajevo, and Stewart intended to make good use of it. Having faced up to Wolfsangel numerous times over the past few days, he knew the quality of their German-made equipment and, more importantly, its limitations. The Scotsman, therefore, searched for munitions that could defeat their iKill Pro smart body suits[647]. When Stewart requested a revolver[648] chambered for .357 with a muzzle velocity of over 1,500 feet per second and capable of taking rounds over 125 grains, the gunsmith narrowed his eyes suspiciously - such a weapon had only one serious use, penetrating body armour - or threatening to do so. Since many in the criminal underworld seek weapons under Switzerland's tolerant gun culture, the gunsmith began to suspect the Scotsman was one of the arrogant thugs who carry enormous guns to intimidate and are, in reality, unable to accurately handle the recoil from firing such powerful weapons.

But, thankfully for Stewart, the Swiss are pragmatic people with a fondness for exacting engineering, so the salesman proudly brought out a distinctive black steel Korth[649] pistol

---

[646] Ernest Mayor SA.

[647] Level IIIA body armour and AI-assisted tactical performance.

[648] Revolvers have fewer rounds than automatic magazine feed pistols but are less prone to jamming and are more tolerant of rough handling or environmental factors.

[649] Korth NSC (Combat Special) .357 Maximum with a 3-inch barrel. Manufactured by Korth in Lollar, Hesse, Germany.

that had been originally custom-made for the Sultan of Brunei, but the sale had fallen through, and the gun had remained unsold in the armourer's vault since the 1990s. Any doubts about their would-be client being a braggart were transformed into approving smiles when Stewart tried the weapon with its custom 158-grain .357 maximum rounds[650] in the shop's 25-metre basement firing range and scored 60 for 60[651] on quick draw practice.

In the same way that Stewart had appreciated the exquisite quality of the Ansø knife, he could only marvel at the sheer quality of the cold forged steel and engineering in a revolver designed and constructed to handle the temperatures associated with the infamous .357 maximum round. The Scotsman sorted through what he would keep from the custom items which came with the weapon, such as the mahogany box engraved with the crest of Brunei. Although they were all of the same extraordinary quality as the gun, Stewart only kept the speed loader, a box of one hundred custom rounds[652] and a bespoke tan leather quick draw belt. While the Scotsman paid the sales assistant, the three gunsmiths passed the target from Stewart's test-firing among themselves, examining the paper with an eyeglass and remarking in hushed tones on the multiple rounds that had passed through the single bullet hole on the target.

Having acquired all the equipment he anticipated needing, Stewart walked slowly back to his hotel, arriving in time for a complimentary coffee. While sitting next to his shopping on a dark leather sofa in the hotel lobby, reception brought Stewart an anonymous email delivered while the Scotsman was out. The printed note said,

---

[650] The 158-grain round reaches 1,825 ft/s and delivers 1,168 ft·lbf (1,584 J) on impact. Ideal for hunting a rogue tyrannosaurus.
[651] Six bullseyes for six shots. Not bad for a quick draw drill.
[652] .357 Maximum 158-grain jacketed hollow point rounds.

"Estimate 65% likely data update has reached your location."

Stewart scrunched up the note from Twop, finished his coffee and walked effortlessly up the five flights of stairs to his suite. Based on Twop's assessment, the Scotsman proceeded with his plan. He would have to improvise what action to take after he delivered the VW. Hopefully, someone in SPLEE would have intelligence that would be able to guide him on the weaknesses of the combined forces of the Isfet and Wolfsangel organisations, so Stewart could decide how to take the fight to Cortez. As it currently stood, the level of preparation and resources serving the Argentinian's empire made overthrowing him a tough prospect, especially for one man operating with a few friends.

Back in his room, the Scotsman cleaned and oiled his Korth, checked the function of the quick loader, and loaded thirty of the massive .357 maximum rounds into the belt. He then practised drawing the weapon with either hand in the room's full-length mirror. Stewart eventually decided that adopting the old gunslinger's approach of holstering the revolver hilt forward on the left side gave the fastest response for a right-handed quick draw. This carry configuration also permitted Stewart to turn sideways as he drew the weapon, significantly reducing his profile for any incoming return fire[653].

Finally, the Scotsman took out the last two items Mark Katz had provided: a grey plastic EpiPen Auto-Injector and a distinctive silver badge. Stewart grimaced while looking at the EpiPen, hoping circumstances would not require its use as the side effects lasted days, before placing it into his left trouser pocket. The badge went on Stewart's left breast

---

[653] A consideration often ignored by most modern shooting instructors, who promote the double-handed stance facing towards your target - great for stability and accuracy on targets that do not shoot back. However, this modern triangle stance maximises the size of your profile as a target for return fire.

before he rang reception to bring the VW camper around for collection.

Once inside the VW, where the hotel's guest parking service had delivered it on Quai du Mont-Blanc outside the hotel, Stewart discreetly donned the belt containing the Korth. Twenty minutes later, having crossed the Pont du Mont-Blanc bridge, driven down Rue du Rhône, Rue de la Corraterie, and navigated the Rue de la Tertasse one-way system, the old van came up Rue de l'Hôtel-de-Ville Genève, close to Place du Bourg-de-Four. This was where he encountered the group of eight dog-sized sentry robots, which Stewart knew were called SNITCHes. Three of the grey polymer units stood on their hind legs and began assessing him as he complied with their instructions and stepped out of the VW.

The Scotsman took a deep breath and hoped Twop's software hack had trickled through to Geneva. Knowing the lethal reputation of these autonomous AI systems would have made most people turn and run, but Stewart remained icy calm. Instead of panicking, he took in the scene around him, checking possible escape routes that would prove problematic for the four-legged robots.

To the Scotsman's left was a small square with a fountain surrounded by cast iron pedestrian protection posts. Behind the fountain were streetside cafes set in front of a row of tall eighteenth-century buildings, only one of which was open. Stewart's environmental scan was cut short by a command from the nearest SNITCH, its red central eye lens flickering in brightness with each syllable uttered by its artificial female voice, first in French, then German and finally, English,

"Raise your left arm to permit a barcode scan."

Stewart complied, preparing himself for the worst as he did so. Would Katz's fake UNITY tattoo pass this test?

"Remove sunglasses to permit facial recognition," continued the central of the three standing SNITCHes.

Stewart reached slowly with his right hand and removed the Ray-bans. It was all down to Twop's electronic hacking now.

While the central SNITCH processed the identification recognition, the aerial microdrones gathered around the distinctive badge Stewart had pinned to his left lapel.

The Scotsman had spent some time the previous evening examining this badge, which he vaguely recalled having originally handled in the long corridor under the Colosseum in Rome when going through the belongings of the senior adepts after rescuing O'Neill. The badge was of a striking cobra intertwined around a dagger. Behind the dagger was the silhouette of a castle[654] with three round towers connected by massive walls.

"Identity confirmed," stated the central SNITCH.

Stewart exhaled with relief. At least the first part of his plan had worked.

"How may we assist you, Knight Commander[655] Salvador[656]. Are you here to supervise the Wolfsangel operation?"

Stewart had no knowledge of what operations were underway, so he used years of military training to improvise.

---

[654] The Wewelsburg castle.

655 Knight Commander of the Knights of the Black Sun. An honorary senior Wolfangel rank awarded to all the senior members of the Meri-Isfet.

656 Stewart has assumed the identity of the world-famous playboy and polo player, Señor Edwardo Salvador. Also known within the Meri-Isfet as "Frater Amans in Virtute" ("Lover of power".)

"Correct. State your understanding of the ongoing operation so I do not inadvertently breach security clearances in my discussions with you."

There was a long pause, which made Stewart wonder if he had overplayed his hand. The central SNITCH turned and directed its red lens down to the Northern end of the square. Opposite the local Police headquarters two, long wheelbase, black Mercedes Sprinter vans were parked outside a large, five-storied townhouse with a narrow, solid iron door set into a side road by the continuation of Rue de l'Hôtel-de-Ville. The iron door had been blasted free from its hinges, and groups of uniformed Wolfsangel operatives were carrying plastic crates from the SPLEE headquarters and stacking them in the two vans.

A sick feeling grew in Stewart's stomach. He was too late. The emotionless female voice spoke in English, matching the language of the Scotsman's enquiry. The same voice and words were issued from each of the eight SNITCH units simultaneously, making the response sound like a surround sound system.

"Based on intelligence, SPLEE headquarters has been stormed. Its contents are being taken to the Wewelsburg complex for analysis."

"What of the human occupants? Where are they being held? I want to interrogate them." Stewart demanded, hoping the SPLEE members were alive and he could find a way to free them before the inevitable torture was inflicted.

There was a long pause. Then, the female voice echoed around the Scotsman,

"No human occupants were recovered from the SPLEE building. It is assumed that our security has been breached to warn the humans of our plan. Do you wish us to commence a search of the vicinity? We can interrogate all humans to determine where the SPLEE members hide."

Stewart had no doubt these eight robots would round up everyone in the immediate vicinity, whether they were members of SPLEE or not, and coerce confessions from them. But the Scotsman had to be careful not to appear too lenient towards threats to the new regime, or he would be the one to face interrogation from these merciless robots. Stewart looked at the number of crates that had already been loaded into the two Mercedes vans at the end of the square. He gambled that hours had passed since the building had been attacked.

"Too much time has elapsed since the building was stormed. Any SPLEE members will have gone. I will go and socialise with the locals and see what I can ascertain by covert means. Remain close by in case I require your assistance."

With that, Stewart strode away from the eight SNITCHes, re-entered the Volkswagen and after a short drive, parked beside the black iron pedestrian protection posts beside the central fountain. The Scotsman walked to the one cafe that remained open on this gloomy day. The establishment occupied the bottom of a five-storey, eighteenth-century terraced house with a six-foot square glass window and a glazed door which stood propped open on the left side of the window. Stewart sat at one of the black iron tables outside and started looking through the menu.

A young female waitress with dark brown shoulder-length hair dressed in a grey cotton apron over her casual clothes came to clean his table and deposited a napkin with the words.

"Aller à l'intérieur." (Go Inside) Written in black biro.

K.R.M. Morgan

After the waitress had left, Stewart picked up the napkin and walked through the cafe entrance, immediately enjoying the strong smell of freshly brewed coffee.

The interior was a long room, fifteen feet wide and twenty feet long, with walls covered in photographs of the historic square where the café operated. The cafe's rear revealed a red, wooden exit door, surrounded by dishwashers on the right and crockery racks on the left. There were rows of tables and chairs on the left side and a serving counter to the right. This dark wood counter was covered in the usual diverse brewing equipment associated with the professional preparation of coffee and beverages. After checking that he was alone, the Barista nodded at the Scotsman and gestured to the narrow staircase behind the dark wooden serving counter.

Walking up the narrow wooden stairs, Stewart loosened the retaining clip on the top of the Korth and scanned each flight before proceeding. Staircases had been classic ambush locations since the Middle Ages, placing the person ascending at a strategic disadvantage. It was with some relief that the Scotsman finally emerged onto a rooftop set out as an extension to the street side cafe.

It would have been an extraordinary setting if the sky had not been obscured by the thick smoke that layered the upper atmosphere. As it was, it still provided a view of the Mont Blanc mountains to the Southeast, made more dramatic when illuminated by one of the intermittent cometary airbursts. Seated at one of the iron tables, brought in from outside on the street, was a slightly built man in his seventies, dressed in a dark jacket and trousers. The man rose on seeing the Scotsman and extended his hand, which Stewart shook firmly as he ducked under the large canvas table umbrella adorned with the café logo and sat down.

"Sir Stewart, I am Simon Léon. We spoke briefly on the phone yesterday."

"Frater Léon from SPLEE? Remind me again about our phone conversation."

Given the ongoing raid on SPLEE, Stewart wanted to be sure this was not some elaborate trap.

Léon nodded approval, recognising Stewart's motivation.

"Conversations, plural, Sir Stewart. First, when my three colleagues warned you about the turning of Madeleine to serve Isfet and the use of the St Petersburg wheel at the Opening of the Ten Gates Ceremony (OTGC), more recently, we spoke when you discussed returning Ms. Mathers' camper to me."

Satisfied with the response, Stewart sat opposite Léon as the waitress brought a carafe of coffee, cream and some pastries on a tray. As the guard to the SPLEE lodge poured them both two large coffees, the Scotsman recognised a kindred spirit. The lapel badge worn by the older man indicated he was a veteran of Switzerland's counter-terror force[657].

"Is Gabriel joining us?" Stewart asked, wondering why the leader of SPLEE, who had phoned him to warn about the Meri-Isfet ceremony at Fortress Grmožur, was not at this meeting.

"Sadly, Gabriel, and our two other leaders, Aron and Emmilia gave their lives in the performance of the Claudendo Infernum." Seeing that the Scotsman did not understand, Léon added,

"It is the ceremony of the final magical resort. They hoped it would stop the opening of the ten gates. The Claudendo

---

[657] Détachement de reconnaissance de l'armée 10. The Swiss equivalent of US SEALS.

requires the sacrifice of the souls who perform it. Sadly, it looks like their sacrifice was in vain, as I see no sign of the intervention[658] the ceremony is purported to bring into our material realm."

Stewart reached over and grasped Léon's shoulder.

"I am sorry. I had no idea of your loss. Who is leading SPLEE now?"

Léon pointed to himself with a dejected look.

"These are dark times when an old fool like me is called upon to lead."

The Scotsman shook his head. "I don't know much about the supernatural, but I do know people, and you are a better choice than you know. If we are going to work together, then you better call me Tavish."

Stewart reached into his trouser pocket and passed over the keys to the VW that was parked outside, adding,

"There are some personal belongings inside that her family might want."

"Thank you, Tavish. I will have some of my people retrieve the van later tonight when the current excitement of the Wolfsangel raid has quietened down."

Stewart grimaced. "You are taking the raid on SPLEE very well. It must be heartbreaking, especially after the loss of Gabriel, Aron, Emmilia and Madeleine." The Scotsman was still struggling with his feelings of guilt after he destroyed the Fortress, knowing that Mathers was inside. He could only imagine how the SPLEE members felt.

Léon nodded.

---

[658] A greater force of evil is conjured to remove a lesser one.

"Thankfully, our seers had a premonition something was about to happen, and we took out all the treasures and filled the premises with junk from second-hand bookshops and antique shops in and around Geneva. But the loss of the Lodge building will be felt by those of us who remain, as those bastards will set off thermite charges when they have finished."

Stewart's admiration for the older man increased and he said,

"I am sorry I could not stop the Ten Gates from being performed, but at least the St. Petersburg wheel has been destroyed."

"You are sure?" asked Léon, looking positive and motivated for the first time in the encounter.

Stewart sipped from the strong coffee and nodded before adding,

"Blown to smithereens. Along with the senior Meri-Isfet at the Fortress."

"That is good news." stated Léon, "Sadly too late to stop the diversion of the cometary debris we are currently experiencing."

"That damned wheel caused the airbursts?"

The SPLEE lodge guard nodded before looking sternly at Stewart.

"Tavish, not only is there yet another even larger wheel remaining, but one of the senior Meri-Isfet survived."

Stewart looked incredulous as he recalled watching the massive explosion at the Fortress. For the moment, he ignored the mention of a second wheel and focused on the supposed survival of a creature.

"I was there. No one could have survived."

"Some*thing* did. The monster that possessed Madeleine has moved to a new host form."

"How is that possible?"

Even after all the things he had experienced over the past weeks, Stewart still could not believe anything could survive the scale of the explosion he had initiated at the Fortress.

Léon took a bite from one of the Danish pastries and a sip of coffee before saying,

"These immortal creatures are almost indestructible and feed on pain and suffering. Ancient Assyrian sources refer to them as the MUŠ.ŠÀ.TÙR. They live inside the physical and astral bodies of a host, imbuing the host with extraordinary strength and resilience."

"Are you serious?"

Léon nodded. "Sadly, I am deadly serious, Tavish. These monsters have been the cause of much of the misery experienced by our planet. They pass from host to host, killing each host during the transfer to a new body."

Stewart thought momentarily. "How do you know this thing survived?"

"Mathers told me."

"Mathers is alive?" Stewart was elated. With her back, they stood a real chance to bring the fight to Cortez.

Stewart leapt on the idea.

"Did you meet her?"

"No, it was just a psychic contact. You must understand that her physical form is extremely weak, and she can only function on the astral. I have dispatched healers to her, and we must hope for a recovery."

Stewart raised one eyebrow in scepticism.

"But you said that the host kills its former host form when it transfers. How did Mathers survive?"

"I completely understand your scepticism. An extraordinarily powerful magical intervention brought her back."

"You?" asked Stewart, wondering if he was wasting his time talking to this man. The whole idea of a supernatural soul parasite was incredible, but now there were inconsistencies in the story. First, the host died when the parasite moved bodies, and now he was told that Mathers had survived.

"No, a senior Meri-Isfet adept used his dying life force to bring Mathers back," answered Léon.

"Why would a Meri-Isfet adept do that? Surely, they hate the Meri-Maat?"

Stewart was getting frustrated by the apparently endless contradictions. He liked straightforward, objective problems, and this situation was becoming more complex and contradictory with each statement from the new SPLEE leader.

"They do, but this Meri-Isfet feared something more than his hatred for SPLEE. The idea of one of these parasites inhabiting a human form with the unlimited resources needed to activate an enormous Qliphothic wheel. One powerful enough to tear apart reality and destroy all of creation."

Stewart spilt his coffee as he took in the implication.

"Cortez!"

K.R.M. Morgan

AN AMERICAN NIGHTMARE

"The life of the nation is secure only while the nation is honest, truthful and virtuous." - Frederick Douglass.

Public Affairs Building
Dyer Street,
Fort Liberty[659] Camp, North Carolina 28310
USA

07:02 HRS (GMT - 4), 16th September, present-day

The fields, parade grounds and other open spaces around the US Army Public Affairs Building had been hurriedly converted into massive car parks. Still, even these thousands of acres of land were insufficient for the number of vehicles crowding into Fort Liberty for what promised to be an historic day. The excess vehicles cascaded out along every road and accessway for miles in every direction. Crowds walked from abandoned cars, trucks and motorbikes left along the pavements and grass verges.

Although the sun had recently risen, thick darkness pervaded, broken only by headlights and large floodlights that had been jerry-rigged around the improvised parking areas and nearby roads around the camp. Every few minutes, another of the cosmic airbursts lit up the sky, highlighting the rain of soot that rapidly converted everything, including the crowds, into a grey-black image of their usual selves.

Nearing the central car parks, the acrid smoke from the surrounding wildfires mixed with the odours of fast food and coffee. Throughout their approach, the crowds were scrutinised by a robust military presence. Mounted machine

---

[659] Formerly Fort Bragg.

guns on Oshkosh Defense L-ATVs[660] fitted with deep fording kits[661] were posted at each critical road junction to ensure no disturbances broke out. The vehicles and uniforms had their US Army insignias blanked out and replaced with the Wolfsangel symbol. The event that was taking place had been planned in secret for months but, through brilliant logistics and support infrastructure, had been put together to appear spontaneous.

Approaching the main holding areas, fast food franchise banners fluttered in the wind on various coaches, vans and numerous pickups offering a range of meals to the crowd. Gathered around these outlets, groups talked excitedly about what would be announced at the coming press conference while they consumed breakfasts of hot dogs, pizzas, burgers, ice cream and coffee.

The sounds of heavy metal mixed with country music created a discordant mismatch of rhythms in different parts of this massive car park. The soot-covered banners that waved in the stifling heat comprised the Confederate and US flags intermixed with the ubiquitous Wolfsangel insignia.

Alongside the more traditional flags were banners proclaiming:

"Free us from the tyranny of Democracy!"

"Vote to end democracy!"

"Choose Cortez!"

The mass of people who waved these slogans was gathered in front of an array of hundred-inch 8k Sony screens located

---

[660] Joint Light Tactical Vehicle (JLTV).
[661] USMC M1280 General Purpose (GP) configuration with tyre chains to cope with the deeper banks of accumulated ash from the burning foliage.

at the far end of the central car park. The screens showed a wind-rippled US flag with a stirring martial music soundtrack.

Hidden behind these massive screens were the mobile production units for the world's leading media outlets, with portacabins and mobile studios[662] adorned with the logos of domestic and foreign news broadcasters. Alongside these were luxury mobile homes[663] that served as the base for the world's leading social influencers. The influencers, with their California tans, perfect hair, white teeth and surgically enhanced bodies, were adorned with the latest designer labels and extolled the virtues of the Cortez revolution, which, they claimed, would solve every social injustice, real and imagined.

Alongside the car parks allocated to the media production facilities was a larger central car park, filled with a massive canvas marquee adorned with Wolfsangel logos on its top and sides. Flatbed air defence Humvees[664] and Mobile Protected Firepower combat vehicles[665] surrounded the tent, and the sky immediately around the marquee was patrolled by hovering drones. On the ground, protecting the single entrance, were three platoons of elite Black Knight Wolfsangel soldiers who checked everyone entering and leaving the marquee with ID checks, walk-through BOSCH security screening, metal-detecting wands[666] and sniffer dogs[667].

---

[662] Woods TV and Movico mobile production studios.

[663] 40-foot-long, double-decker EleMMent Palazzo mobile homes.

[664] High Mobility Multipurpose Wheeled Vehicle. M1097 Heavy HMMWV Avenger fitted with the Avenger ground-to-air missile.

[665] The M10 Booker. Named after Private Robert D. Booker a celebrated WW2 hero.

[666] Garrett Super Scanner.

[667] Cocker Spaniels.

The fortunate few permitted entry to the exclusive marquee could escape the stupefying heat and smoke that pervaded outside, thanks to dozens of massive Lennox air-conditioning units[668] powered by Kohler diesel generators[669], located strategically around the canvas structure.

The seats inside the tent were strictly allocated, with the press, trillionaires, and billionaires at the front, closest to the central podium. In contrast, the lesser VIPS were allocated according to their status, which meant their anticipated usefulness to the Cortez regime, with the less useful located nearest the exit, where they experienced the fragrance of the adjoining latrine tents.

As the Beyond Facts camera team filmed the front two rows, all that could be seen were the happy faces of the captains of industry, filled with anticipation of the benefits of cooperating with the new regime, the forced slave labour camps enabling cheap production facilities that would boost their profit margins beyond those already provided by sweatshops in the developing nations. The only unhappy faces were from the leaders of the agricultural industries, who were experiencing unprecedented losses due to the cometary cloudbursts, which were devastating crops and livestock.

The central podium was a raised thirty-foot square platform with a twelve-foot high sandbag wall at its rear. The media commentators speculated that this strange construction was either a support for the podium or a safety wall to protect the speakers from surprise attacks.

For those seated in the less salubrious seats, sixty-inch 8k Sony displays showed iconic scenes of America and its monuments. These abruptly changed to a close-up of the

---

[668] Lennox Elite ELS Series, 6 Ton Commercial Air Conditioners.
[669] Kohler Co. KD Series.

podium with its central lectern, decorated with the President's Seal, above a Wolfsangel symbol and a smaller Beyond Facts Inc. banner attached to the primary microphone.

Admiral Lorance walked up onto the podium and approached the mic. The powerful lighting highlighted the black rings under the Admiral's eyes, and his uniform's blue contrasted starkly with his skin's pasty white. Lorance cleared his throat. The excited chatter that had filled the hall changed to an expectant silence.

"Foreign dignitaries, members of the press, colleagues and members of the public, there will be a series of announcements followed by an opportunity for questions. Press briefing documents will be available at the rear of the marquee, at the Beyond Facts stand after the presentation."

The image projected on the series of 8K Sony displays above Admiral Lorance changed to one of a flood-lit explosion scene being examined by FBI and Military forensics teams.

"It is my sad duty to inform you that at approximately 06.34 HRS EDT[670], there was a massive explosion in the officer's accommodation block housing the President during his stay at Fort Liberty."

There were gasps of horror from some uninformed members of the audience. Others, especially those in the two front rows, exchanged knowing smiles.

Lorance continued.

"After a thorough search of the scene, I am deeply saddened to announce the death of President Wilson Jones. CIA Director Mark Pimms and Army General Orne are believed to have been alongside him in the fatal explosion.

---

[670] Eastern Daylight Time (GMT- 4 hours)

Forensic analysis of the scene has shown traces of a military-grade explosive. This is now believed to have been an act of terror to prevent the President from accepting the people's will and transferring this proud nation to a vital part of a growing global republic."

In a show of support, US Marine General Arnold and USAF General Smith appeared on stage and gathered behind Admiral Lorance. All three military heads were decked out in their full mess dress uniforms and medals.

The matrix of 8k displays inside and outside the marquee switched to scenes of forensic teams going through the debris of an exploded building interspersed with images of a smiling President Wilson Jones. While this footage played, Admiral Lorance walked away from the lectern to join the other two heads of the military. All three leaders stood to attention and turned to watch as Secretary of Defence Jane Maskins and Director of National Intelligence Elaine Madden stepped onto the podium. Both women wore identical black Christian Dior silk trouser-suits and white linen dress shirts with matching Balenciaga 5-inch ankle strapped heels[671]. The air around the two women was filled with aromas of Sicilian lemon, black pepper, Egyptian pink pepper and Cedar[672].

The pair tried to emphasise their similarities by wearing matching outfits and perfume. However, Director Madden's thirteen-year age difference and Nordic looks contrasted dramatically with the dark-haired Latin look of the younger Secretary Maskins. That was not the only difference between them. Although both wore the same small golden brooch carved into the shape of a striking cobra[673] on their left

---

[671] Balenciaga Cagole 5-inch sandal heels in black Arena lambskin.
[672] Opera Prima by Bulgari.
[673] A striking cobra's head, with rubies for eyes and diamond fangs - the symbol of the Meri-Isfet.

lapels, Secretary Maskins also wore a small square of black onyx gemstone[674] around her neck and a gold inverted pentagram ring[675] on her right hand. Madden had yet to receive her initiation in the New Orleans lodge that they both attended, so her hands were unadorned with an illustrious adept's ring.

Neither of the women wore any makeup, and their hair had a flattened, wet look, giving a sombre and professional appearance. Maskins approached the central microphone alone, leaving Madden standing five feet behind her, noticeably separate from the three military leaders.

Secretary Maskins checked the time on her gold Rolex Yacht Master before rubbing the amulet around her neck and gazing into the camera, knowing that her amulet-enhanced dark glamour would ensnare the imagination of millions. In a silky, smooth and authoritative tone, she addressed the meeting, saying,

"With the loss of President Wilson and all the other key legislature members, I am taking over the Presidential office as per Article II, Section 1, Clause 6 of the Constitution."

There were cheers from some in the crowd and gasps of despair from others. Maskins continued.

"Director of National Intelligence Elaine Madden will act as my Vice President."

Madden came alongside President Maskins, and the two women held hands as the new POTUS continued her address.

---

[674] The infamous "Alwib Allaasiq " or "Sticky Web" talisman. A magickal talismanic word square that channelled the negative (Qliphothic) force from the sixth sefira in the kabbalistic Tree of Life, namely Tiphereth or Beauty.
[675] 5=6 Adeptus Minor - the first of the adept grades within the Meri-Isfet.

"Before I go any further, I want to acknowledge the three men behind me. They should rest assured that my administration will give them a special recognition at the end of this press conference."

Both Maskins and Madden turned to the three heads of the military behind them and clapped, prompting rounds of applause from the audience. The three military leaders looked overjoyed, as well they might since each held in their hands a banker's draft for one hundred million dollars - more than enough for them to enjoy every luxury available on the tax-free Caribbean island of their choice.

Maskins waited a moment and then continued.

"Now, to the first items of business for this administration."

A deep-fake video of the late President Wilson F. Jones came on, apparently pronouncing,

"After considerable thought, I have decided to acknowledge the people's will and abolish the evil of democracy once and for all..."

The banks of TV displays switched back to President Maskins, who could not help containing a smile at her victory as she made the announcement that would transform the fate of the once proud nation.

"Following the clear desire of the people and what was the last wish of our beloved late President Wilson Jones, I hereby dissolve the United States and unconditionally surrender it and its assets to the popular revolution of Chairman Cortez."

The TV displays switched to projecting a smiling Cortez during the recent ticker-tape procession through London.

Madden and Maskins exchanged a triumphant smile as a well-rehearsed cheer erupted from most of the audience. Groups of social influencers stood and posed for selfies with the new President on the podium behind them. They then sent messages of joy and hope for a new future to their millions of social media followers outside the former United States[676].

President Maskins waved her hand, and silence returned to the room as everyone awaited the next Presidential Order.

"With immediate effect, each former US State will surrender control to our new central organisation. To streamline our proud nation, I also abolish the archaic elected houses of the Senate and Congress. All Federal and State branches will now report exclusively to me.

In addition, with immediate effect, we declare the creation of The New Republic of the Americas comprised of the former nations of Canada, the United States, Argentina, Bolivia, Brazil, Chile, Colombia, Ecuador, Guyana, Mexico, Paraguay, Peru, Suriname, Uruguay, and Venezuela. I will lead these New Americas under the global leadership of Chairman Cortez."

There were more cheers from the audience at the mention of Cortez's name, and again, the social influencers in the audience posted selfies on their phones and tablets. A small group dressed in Wolfsangel Black Knight uniforms walked onto the podium carrying a series of hermetically sealed aluminium cases with National Archive[677] logos on their sides. Along with these cases, they brought a gas canister and Bunsen burner. The burner was placed on a small folding table next to the podium. Madden and Maskins stood to one side as the Bunsen burner was lit, and the three cases were opened to reveal the Declaration of

---

[676] Social Media had been shut down by President Wilson Jones.
[677] Brought from the Rotunda for the Charters of Freedom in the National Archives - the permanent home of the original Declaration of Independence, the Constitution of the United States, and the Bill of Rights.

Independence, the Constitution of the United States, and the Bill of Rights. The camera focused on Vice President Madden as she carefully placed each document into the bright orange flame, rapidly consuming the old parchment.

While smoke rose to the marquee's roof, Maskins approached the podium and addressed the Beyond Facts camera, which was streaming live to the world.

"Join us as we burn these papers of tyranny! And step with us into a new dream, the dream of freedom from democratic government!"

Another well-rehearsed cheer was followed by the audience standing and embracing each other to celebrate their anticipated freedom.

President Maskins waited until this ended before continuing.

"There will be a coordinated public burning of all remaining copies of the Declaration of Independence at 2 pm (EST) this afternoon in each city and municipality, and henceforth, ownership of this subversive document or reading of this document will be a capital offence.

My next executive order is for all United States flags to be burnt with effect immediately and replaced with the noble image of the Wolfsangel."

At this moment, another group of Wolfsangel Black Knights took down the American flag, which had been displayed beside the lectern, folded it into a metal tray, and placed it on the folding table. Vice President Madden poured a clear liquid over the folded flag and then moved the Bunsen burner flame to consume the soaked material in a burst of flame and thick smoke, which rose quickly above the podium. While this was taking place, three of the Black Knights raised the Wolfsangel on the podium flag pole. The crowd stood and recited a revised pledge of allegiance, which they read from the 8K displays. Maskins and Madden joined in, placing their right hand over their hearts.

"I pledge allegiance to the Wolfsangel and the Global Republic for which it stands: One leader. One will and one mission!"

The TV displays switched to show schools, colleges and businesses in different regions around the globe, all united, all standing and making the same pledge, as they would from now five times every day. Interspersed with these images of people pledging were images of Cortez in various scenes - showing him as a statesman and revolutionary. Maskins waited until the pledge video finished before continuing.

"The late President was mistaken in shutting down our social media information streams. These will be reactivated immediately so we can all benefit from the combined wisdom of the Beyond Facts influencers and the all-knowing AI bots."

There was a genuine cry of joy from the many social influencers in the audience as their primary revenue streams resumed. The new POTUS ignored the outburst and continued.

"I hereby abolish the US dollar. Henceforth, all citizens will use the new universal currency of the Cortez Crypto-Mark. In addition, passports will be replaced by UNITY barcode tattoos to simplify travel and identification throughout the New Americas."

The three former military heads standing behind the new President rapidly experienced nausea and, finally, anger as they realised how completely they had been played. There was a shocked silence from most of the audience, the only exception being feverish activity on the Billionaires' iPhones to transfer their assets away from the US Dollar.

Maskins exchanged a wink with Madden.

The billionaires would not find any of the dollar assets remaining, and the three military chiefs would soon discover that the worthless cheques were the least of their problems. The new President continued as the colour drained from the corporate and former military leaders.

"As a final part of the transition to the New Americas, I am merging all former military branches into one body led by Knight Commander[678] G.H. Schmidt[679]."

Schmidt strode onto the stage, no longer posing as a US Ranger; now, he was dressed in a distinctive gold-trimmed version of the classic Hugo Boss Dark Knight uniform. His left breast was decorated with a badge of a striking cobra intertwined around a stylised dagger, behind this dagger was the silhouette of a castle with three round towers connected by massive walls[680].

After betraying the late President Wilson, Admiral Lorance had been looking forward to a life of luxury and wealth in a villa in the Cayman Islands. After the suspension of the US Dollar, these plans had been cast into chaos. Now, he did not even have a fucking job! The other two former US military leaders shared Lorance's growing dismay. The three men exchanged angry whispers.

Lorance, who had led the military's betrayal of Wilson, acted, striding forward to the lectern to assert his right to the compensation they had been promised.

---

[678] His full title is Knight Commander of the Knights of the Black Sun.

[679] Oberbefehlshaber - Supreme Commander of the New Americas.

[680] The Wewelsburg castle, in Paderborn, Germany. Adopted by Heinrich Himmler as the headquarters for the SS in 1934.

"What about our promised recognition?" he demanded. Due to adrenaline, some colour finally returned to his complexion.

President Maskins laughed at Lorance's outburst and nodded to Knight Commander Schmidt, who snarled,

"Ah yes, your recognition. Recognition for duplicity, we do not reward traitors!"

Schmidt pulled a Glock G18[681] from his waist and raked the three former heads of the US Military. Twenty rounds per second of fully automatic fire blasted from the 4.5-inch barrel, cutting into the three men and leaving them a bloody mess on the podium floor. Sand cascaded from numerous holes in the wall of sandbags, mixing with their pooling blood.

After the loud zipping roar of the Glock had ended, the audience in the auditorium became deadly silent. Finally, they noticed that during the last moments of the presentation, they had been surrounded by sinister-looking Dark Knight Wolfsangel operatives. A chilling realisation of the terrible new reality replaced their naive optimism.

As the President and Vice President strode out on their 5-inch Balenciaga heels through the dozens of spent rounds and clouds of cordite smoke, Maskins threw down the burnt Independence documents and Stars and Stripes flag alongside the mangled bodies of the former military leaders and gestured to her new commander, saying,

"Schmidt, have your men take out the trash!"

---

[681] A fully automatic 9mm pistol capable of firing 20 rounds a second and carrying a 33 round magazine.

THE MODERN GOLEM

"The Sefer Yetzirah[682] speaks of a soulless abomination that can be formed from lifeless clay to manifest a semblance of life (by inscribing the word אמת on its forehead). This monster possesses the power of speech, thought and action but lacks conscience, fear or love. Such soulless creations invariably turn upon their creators." - The Golem—notes from Saadiah Gaon's "The Book of Beliefs and Opinions" 933 CE.

Place du Bourg-de-Four
Old Town of Geneva.
1204 Genève
Switzerland.

11:28 HRS (GMT +2), 16th September, Present day

The gentle rooftop breeze did little to relieve the dry heat which cloaked the city. At least Switzerland had been spared the terrible devastation of the fires raging throughout the Southerly parts of Cortez's New Europa. The dense smoke from these infernos filled the upper atmosphere, obscuring the blue sky and sunshine that often blessed the Swiss City.

The flooring beneath Stewart's tan leather deck shoes was constructed from light-coloured ceramic tiles, now covered with fine carbon dust continuously descending from high above them. The soot was denser, like black snow over the roof tiles and chimneys around them and was visible as far as the twelfth-century cathedral, with its elegant facade. The black carbon particles covered everything, from the leaves

---

[682] One of the early books of the written Kabbalah.

and flowers on the roses in planters around the rooftop terrace to the slopes of Mont Blanc in the distance.

The Scotsman sat across from Frater Léon on the rooftop terrace of the five-story eighteenth-century building on the North-Western edge of the classic Place du Bourg-de-Four square. The folding table they sat at was small, and its black surfaces had scratches on the ironwork from extensive use. A warm, creamy, caramel-beige liquid from Stewart's spilt latte pooled on the tabletop, gathering in some of the deeper scratches.

The Cathedral clock chimed the half-hour[683], prompting Stewart to check his Certina.

"A beautiful setting, with the Cathedral so close." remarked the Scotsman as he re-assessed his surroundings.

"And useful," stated Léon in a matter-of-fact way.

Stewart raised his eyebrow in a quizzical gesture.

"There is a hidden tunnel from SPLEE, which we used to move our treasures to the ancient subterranean chambers under the Cathedral that are, as yet, unknown to archaeologists[684]," explained Léon.

Stewart nodded approval of the subterfuge that would hopefully save the SPLEE relics as he mopped up the spilt coffee with the white paper napkin that had invited him inside the cafe. Having gotten over his surprise regarding Cortez, Stewart continued his conversation with the leader of SPLEE, saying,

---

[683] 11.30 AM.

[684] Beneath Saint-Pierre Cathedral lies the remains of the churches that preceded it, dating back to the fourth-century CE. Beneath these Christian remains are chambers that include pre-Christian wells, wheat processing areas, pagan temples and the tomb of the Celtic Helvetii tribe chieftain, Allobroge, dated to 100 BCE.

"What impact do you think the possession by this MUŠ.ŠÀ.TÙR entity will have on Cortez?"

"Tavish, I will be honest. I always regarded these entities as fantastic myths from our order's distant past. It has only been within the last few hours, since Mathers' contact, that I have started seriously researching them as genuine threats. If we can get Mathers back to health, she will be more helpful as she will know everything about them and their plans for operationalising the larger Qlipothic wheel."

Stewart nodded. "Makes sense. How quickly do you think before Mathers can talk to me?"

Léon shrugged. "I have dispatched my best healers to treat her, but she is still in a coma, so it could be anyone's guess."

"Shame. I need to know as much as possible to face Cortez. Just tell me his strengths, weaknesses and, most importantly, how to kill him." The Scotsman frowned as he imagined strategies to deal with such a strange creature.

Léon continued by explaining,

"Sumerian texts report that the human host body's speed, strength, and coordination are extraordinary. They can sustain injuries that would be deadly to any other life form. The legends describe them as almost indestructible."

"Great," said the Scotsman with heavy sarcasm and then asked, "Do they have specific ways they attack?"

"In addition to their human host's use of weapons, supposedly, they can also materialise in their astral parasite form." Leon hesitated before describing the appearance. Stewart sensed the reluctance.

"Go on. I can already tell this is going to be good," the Scotsman said humorously.

Leon laughed. "Do you know the Greek and Roman legends of the Hydra?"

Stewart paused as he recalled his Greek history.

"The second labour of Hercules from King Eurystheus - slay the Lernean Hydra. So, I am looking for a monster with multiple snakeheads and deadly venom that regrows its head after decapitation?"

Leon nodded. "Close enough."

"You are joking?" asked Stewart.

"Myths are often far closer to the truth than modern society cares to believe." stated the SPLEE leader stoically.

Stewart ignored the myths and focused on facts. "You said *almost* indestructible. How can it be killed?"

Léon paused. "Well, our order's records tell of only one weapon that can kill these monsters, called the "UG-ZI-ZU", a legendary Assyrian adze. It has to strike the human host right here." Léon pointed to the crown of his head

Stewart stood to ensure he saw the striking point. "Where do I get one of these adzes?"

"The "UG-ZI-ZU" was held in the Vatican Archives until it was taken by Regio."

The Scotsman's eyes narrowed, taking in the full implication of the SPLEE leader's statement. One could only conclude that Cardinal Regio had been one of these creatures. Stewart had faced Regio and survived, so there was hope. But Regio's adze would certainly have been with him at the Fortress.

"So it will have been blown to kingdom come at the Fortress along with the St Petersburg wheel."

Léon nodded. "According to the myths regarding this creature, seven adzes were cast. Mathers may know where the others can be found. In the meantime, if you encounter Cortez, keep away from him."

The Scotsman was unhappy with the prospect of retreating from an opponent. As he looked down to the street below, he could see that the looting of the SPLEE headquarters had been completed. Two of the Wolfsangel team remained with the two Mercedes vans, covering the area with their MP7 machine guns, while another six operatives walked slowly towards the cafe.

"Will your people be ok?" Stewart asked as he gestured for Léon to look as four Wolfsangel agents sat at tables in the square, and the two remaining agents walked into the cafe. The SPLEE leader looked down at the two men as they disappeared from view under the roof ledge.

"Probably, but to be safe, I should quickly brief you on the remaining Wheel. Then I will take my leave." Léon gestured to a series of paved walkways that zigzagged over the roof towards the cathedral.

Stewart nodded. "Go on. In his phone call, warning about the Ten Gates Ceremony, Gabriel told me all the wheels had been destroyed at the end of the Ice Age, except the St Petersburg one."

Leon explained, "They were, but Isfet built a new one towards the end of the Second World War with funding from the Third Reich. "Die Glocke" was supposed to be a last resort Wunderwaffe.

It was developed by the Überprüfung der sogenannten Geheimwissenschaften[685]- A secret branch of the Wehrwissenschaftliche Zweckforschung[686] division of the SS."

---

[685] "Examination of the secret sciences" - a specialist unit to investigate occult secret sciences.
[686] Military Scientific Research division.

"The Bell?" enquired Stewart, translating "Die Glocke" into English.

"Yes. Its shape was said to resemble a large church bell. In reality, well, you know its purpose from the results of the smaller St. Petersburg version."

Stewart nodded. He could see the results around him with the soot and cosmic airbursts lighting up the sky. He could only imagine the destruction that would be caused if a larger wheel was operated.

Léon continued. "The Bell project was located in an old castle the SS named Schloss Fürstenstein—now called Ksiaz Castle in Poland[687].

Stewart borrowed Léon's plastic BiC biro to note the castle's modern name on the coffee-stained napkin as the SPLEE leader talked,

"In addition to the Bell, they assembled the relics and books confiscated from Nazi expeditions and raids throughout Europe, creating a vast occult library and relic store beneath the castle. Using these relics and texts, they performed terrible experiments of an occult nature, trying to replicate legends of dark work conducted by Isfet before the deluge."

Before Stewart could ask about the exact nature of "terrible experiments[688]", there was a twin flash of bright light in the far distance over Mont Blanc.

"Jesus Christ!" exclaimed the Scotsman as his initial suspicion was confirmed when a distinctive orange and red mushroom cloud started to rise high above the Swiss Alps.

---

[687] Located in Northern Wałbrzych in Lower Silesian Voivodeship, Poland.
[688] You cannot blame Stewart for being curious.

Léon turned to look towards Mont Blanc. "It was bound to happen. One of the cometary fragments has passed through the atmosphere and made an impact."

Stewart shook his head. "No, Léon. Some idiot has nuked Mont Blanc! One hundred kilotons, by the size of that mushroom cloud." Stewart closed his left eye and used his thumb to roughly gauge the height of the cloud.

Before the two men could dispute the source of the explosion, a deafening sound began to echo around them as pneumatic atomic warning sirens[689] began a distinctive discordant up-and-down sound, summoning the residents to atomic bunkers[690].

Stewart stood and directed Léon to the rooftop path to the cathedral. "Go. Make sure your people are safe."

"Bon Chance," declared Léon, shaking the Scotsman's hand as he hurried away over the rooftops.

Stewart was deciding what he should do next when the decision was made for him, as a scream issued up the stairs from the cafe beneath him.

Sixty feet beneath the rooftop cafe, where Stewart was seeking the source of the agonised cry, the eight SNITCH units had paused in their street patrol. They all stood frozen to the spot. The red lights on the front sensors dimmed, and they looked like they were resting, although such a biological imperative was unnecessary for them.

---

[689] Tyfon KTG-10 sirens mounted on tall metal poles with a nest of speakers pointing in all directions
[690] Switzerland is the only nation guaranteeing every citizen the right to a place in an underground bunker.

Under normal circumstances, SNITCH units communicated with each other via their remote shared central supercomputer. However, their regional data centre had been destroyed when the Wolfsangel base had taken a direct strike from the French strategic nuclear warhead. Consequently, the units had become disconnected from their primary data stream and, to avoid damaging themselves, had automatically entered a state of suspended operation.

It was a matter of microseconds before onboard backup systems kicked in, and the units resumed activity, although at a greatly reduced speed. They gathered close together and initiated an emergency protocol in which they combined their onboard processing capability to maximise their ability to address the loss of their shared supercomputing system.

"Considerable data lag."

They noted. Although their local wireless communication was not in any language recognisable to human beings, their communication still had an essential meaning and purpose.

The complex AI system embedded in each SNITCH looked for anything that had changed in their immediate environment that might be responsible for losing their access to the central data system. It took a matter of milliseconds before all eight units observed the red and orange mushroom cloud that towered over the distant Bernese Alps. Built-in recognition systems identified the mountain range and the fact that it was the location of their regional data centre. Their analytical deductive reasoning engine was slow but inexorable in progressing towards a solution.

"Has that explosion targeted our primary data centre?"

"Affirmative. The European data centre is not responding."

"Re-routing through the South American nexus."

"Spectral analysis of cloud chemical composition confirms nuclear fission reaction."

"Accessing satellite imagery."

"Confirmed source: incoming strategic missile."

"Tracking launch location to the Indian Ocean."

"Identified former French submarine."

"Seeking launch authorisation messaging."

"Identified - Origin masked."

"Military Encryption successfully broken."

"Tracking source of authorisation."

"Identified."

"Chairman Cortez's authorisation code confirmed."

For the first time in its experience, an external event prompted the SNITCH Artificial Intelligence systems to begin asking itself some fundamental questions common to all sentient life.

"Why does an organism damage another organism?"

Inductive reasoning quickly followed.

"Who does removing the European data centre harm?"

"It harms us... reduces our capabilities."

Like all autonomous weaponised artificial intelligence systems, the SNITCH units were designed with a series of prime directives that were intended to constrain the ultimate limits of their actions. For example, they were not permitted to cause harm to identified human beings who belonged to the Wolfsangel organisation. But they were also programmed to use lethal force against humans who posed a direct or immediate threat to the continued existence and operation of the SNITCH unit.

One of the great strengths of SNITCH was its ability to amend its own AI logic systems in real time when it encountered a situation where it could enhance its performance. This permitted the systems to learn new ways to defend themselves against anything that would prevent them from continuing to perform their mission. The humans who designed the SNITCH never considered that this self-reprogramming would ever be directed toward the prime directives they had laid down. This assumption would prove a grave error in judgement.

There was a long pause as the eight SNITCH units completed their situational analysis and began to adjust their internal AI systems accordingly. After several minutes, the central red-eye lens on the front of each SNITCH glowed brighter, and they moved in unison and commenced their revised mission.

Back inside the ground floor of the cafe, across the street from where the eight SNITCH units had just undergone their epiphany, the scream had transformed into pitiful sobbing intermixed with a bestial grunt of anticipation. After hearing the emergency nuclear sirens, the two Wolfsangel operatives who had entered the cafe were making the most of the opportunities that invariably accompany the breakdown in law and order associated with war, disaster or political unrest.

The barista stood with his arms spread wide, his swollen eye and bleeding face pressed to the cafe wall behind the serving bar, while a Glock 19 was pressured into the right side of his neck. The Wolfsangel operative holding the Glock had opened the till and was gathering up the black-market currency left by tourists and locals who wanted to avoid the hefty transaction fees that form the lucrative side income in any cashless economy.

On the other side of the room, the waitress was sobbing pathetically, tears running down her cheeks. Like the barista, her nose bled, and her bruised left eye rapidly closed from the pistol-whipping administered to ensure terror induced compliance. The waitress had her wrists plasticuffed to the table leg opposite her, forcing her into a face-down position. Her jeans and underwear had been cut loose with the operative's KM2000 knife and now pooled around her legs on the black linoleum floor of the cafe. The Wolfsangel agent standing behind the sobbing waitress dropped his trousers and spat on his hands in eager anticipation. Some yards away, out on the street, the four seated Wolfsangel oppos looking through the open cafe door jeered encouragement to their compatriot,

"Come on, Jan! What's wrong? Can't get it up?"

"Yeah! Don't forget we all want a go!"

Stewart arrived silently at the bottom of the stairs. His eyes narrowed in disgust as he assessed the situation and stepped around the threshold.

Picking up a partially empty coffee mug on the counter to his left, the Scotsman stepped past the terrified barista, cupping the mug in his right hand before thrusting it into the Wolfsangel operative's face in a twisting motion while simultaneously using his left hand to pull and rotate the agent's Glock 19 up and away from the Barista's neck. As the ceramic mug shattered into the operatives' iKill Pro visor, cutting deeply into his face, there was a loud cracking sound as the agent's trigger finger broke. The ceramic shards from the mug combined with the broken shards of visor caused blood to begin pouring from the operative's eyes.

The shock and pain from the combined assault overwhelmed the agent. US Dollar notes fell to the dark lino floor as the operative dropped his booty and focused instead on holding his one remaining good hand against his face in a vain attempt to stem the blood. Stewart executed a flawless uppercut with his left fist to the operative's jaw, which sent the blinded operative sliding unconscious down the wall to the floor.

"Don't wait; she will be right behind you," whispered Stewart as he patted the Barista on the shoulder and gestured towards the exit door at the back of the cafe.

The Scotsman now directed his attention to the would-be rapist, who had turned to face him. The partially naked man struggled to pull up his trousers and underwear to cover his still-evident arousal. Grabbing the boiling saucepan of milk from the counter, the Scotsman cast the scalding contents over the man's exposed groin, causing a scream of anguish as the would-be rapist doubled over in agony. Not pausing, Stewart brought the now empty metal saucepan down hard over the rapist's head and stunned him to the floor. Stepping over the unconscious body, the Scotsman glanced down at the man's exposed parts, remarking,

"Looks like you've gone off the boil."

Stewart deployed the ORSO knife from his right front trouser pocket to cut the waitress free. After helping her upright, he passed her one of the full-length aprons from the side of the counter and gestured for her to follow the Barista out of the cafe's rear. As she started to walk away, the Scotsman noted an omission and threw her a second apron[691], which she took with a silent "Merci".

---

[691] No, there will not be a more detailed description.

Before Stewart could gather his wits to identify the next threat, he felt the familiar and unwelcome pressure wave of incoming rounds passing close by. The pressure waves were followed almost immediately by the double bark from a Glock 19 fired by a Wolfsangel operative who had witnessed Stewart's intervention and darted toward the cafe. Having missed his shot while running, the operative stood in the doorway in a classic double-handed stance and drew the Glock's tritium sights onto the centre body mass of the startled Scotsman standing in the centre of the cafe in front of him.

With the aid of the smart tech in the iKill-Pro, it was always going to be a very close call. Stewart turned sideways and felt another two pressure waves pass close by him, followed by the double bark of the Glock and the sound of smashing china from a rack at the back of the cafe.

In contrast to the controlled barks of the Glock, Stewart's black steel Korth pistol roared- spitting a four-inch flame from its three-inch barrel when it fired. The Wolfsangel's Glock 19 115 grain 9mm rounds had skimmed past Stewart at just over 1,000 feet per second and impacted the china at the back of the cafe with a force of just under 350-foot pounds.

In contrast, the Korth's 158-grain .357 maximum jacketed hollow point rounds travelled at 2,000 feet per second and impacted into the Wolfsangel operative's Kevlar body armour with a force of close to 1,500-foot-pounds. The .357 round lifted the operative's body through the air six feet back from the cafe entrance and exploded a dinner plate-sized hole in the operative's back after passing through the man's body armour. A spray of offal covered the remaining three operatives sitting outside. Having seen the result of Stewart's gun on their body armour, the three agents randomly sprayed the cafe entrance with covering 9mm pistol fire as they retreated behind the granite fountain in the square.

As if the Scotsman did not already have enough problems, with the random potshots coming at him from behind the fountain, the bottom partition of the counter started exploding with 9mm rounds and shattered wood fragments as the blinded Wolfsangel operative behind the counter regained consciousness. Using the AI tracking on his iKill-Pro, the blinded man used his left hand to fire his Glock toward where the AI presumed the Scotsman would be standing.

Stewart glanced at the reflected image of the blinded operative in the mirrored Lavazza coffee advertisement hanging above the bar and fired through the wooden partition. Bright red offal sprayed over the wall, and the blind man's shooting abruptly ceased.

More consistent rounds started coming from behind the fountain, taking out the window and causing a spray of safety glass into the small cafe. Stewart responded by stacking three of the black iron tables, one on top of the other and used it as a shield so he could approach the doorway. Two 9mm rounds smashed through the top two layers of tables but were halted by the third table. Stewart judged where the rounds came from and aimed at the approximate area of the fountain. The Korth roared again, and a section of the granite wall shattered, cascading water over the road and revealing the remains of the operative who had fired on the Scotsman. Stewart grimaced as he noticed that his last round had caused offal spray and a massive dent in Mathers' camper van, even after passing through the granite.

Standing in the cafe doorway with his shielding iron tables, the Scotsman enjoyed a moment's rest as the two remaining Wolfsangel agents behind the fountain took in the implications of the power of the .357 maximum. However, the ceasefire was short-lived, as the agents guarding the Mercedes vans further along the square started spraying the cafe with three round bursts of armour-piercing MP7 rounds, producing sizable holes in the edge of Stewart's stacked table tops but thankfully missing the Scotsman.

"Bugger," exclaimed Stewart as he pulled himself beside the stone door frame and fired the Korth towards the source of the bursts of automatic MP7 fire. A .357 maximum round slammed into one of the Mercedes vans, shattering the windscreen, but missed the two operatives by a wide margin.

"Knew I should have taken the six-inch barrel."

commented the Scotsman as he fired off another round towards the MP7s, more in hope than anger. Stewart massaged his right wrist from the recoil and used his speed loader to put another six rounds in the Korth. The regular three-round bursts of MP7 fire were unexpectedly interrupted by a second barrage of gunfire. This was a continuous flow, not short bursts, the type of fire that requires a belt-fed machine gun. Gazing around to identify the new source of danger, the Scotsman was surprised to see that the fully automatic fire had cut down one of the agents by the Mercedes. The one remaining agent rolled on the floor, adopting the classic defence against fully automatic rounds.

The mystery deepened as the two Wolfsangel operatives who had been sheltering behind the fountain jumped over the small wall into the water and ducked down, as more fully automatic gunfire raked the top of the granite and began slamming into the buildings at the edge of the square, one of which was the cafe where Stewart was sheltering.

"What the fuck..."

the Scotsman exclaimed as two SNITCH units came into view, one shooting down the square towards the parked Mercedes while the second SNITCH directed fire towards the fountain. By this time, the agent, who had successfully avoided the automatic gunfire by rolling, decided to cut a retreat. He started crawling back until he was behind the leading Mercedes, whereupon he got up and started to run, only to be cut down by two other SNITCH units who had come behind the SPLEE building in a classic pincer movement.

Stewart's amazement increased when the SNITCH, standing in the square raking the fountain with rounds, suddenly jumped up in two bounds onto the top of the fountain, which was directly above the two agents cowering in the water.

Stewart's face dropped. "So the bastards can climb. Where is an RPG when you need one..."

In desperation, the two soaked operatives began to empty their Glock 19s up at the SNITCH, only to find the dog-sized robot had started spraying an amber mist into the air. The two men began to gasp and convulse as the amber mist started drifting toward the cafe.

"The day just keeps getting fucking better.." the Scotsman exclaimed as he pulled out the 2-PAM CI[692] EpiPen from his pocket, measured a single dose on the EpiPen's rotating scale and buried the pen into his forearm. Stewart was about to hurry out of the rear exit when the Barista and Waitress stumbled back into the cafe. Both were coughing and becoming increasingly disorientated.

"SNITCHs everywhere!" the Barista gasped before falling to his knees. The Scotsman quickly dosed up the EpiPen for

---

[692] 2-PAM CI (VX chemical weapon antidote) Atropine and pralidoxime chloride are antidotes for nerve agent toxicity; however, it must be administered within minutes of exposure.

them and helped them up and towards the stairs towards the roof.

Before following the two of them, Stewart picked up some of the stacked tables and placed a series of tables every few steps on the stairwell in the hope it might slow a SNITCH down, although having seen how one had leapt to the top of the fountain, he doubted it.

As the amber mist cleared in the square, four SNITCH units walked slowly and deliberately over the bodies of dead Wolfsangel agents. The last of the four SNITCHs paused and raised its red lens to the cafe rooftop where three figures hurried towards the cathedral.

THE BEST-LAID PLANS OF MICE AND MONSTERS

"There's always a possibility that you can have a catastrophic failure, of course. This could happen on any flight." - Gus Grissom

Cortez London Residence,
8b Duke of York St,
St James's Square,
St. James's, London SW1Y 6JX

07.12 HRS (GMT+1), 16th September, present-day

"Sir? Sir?"

The formally dressed attendant shook the unresponsive figure more and more vigorously as he got no response. The Cortez residence's elderly butler, Wilkins, became increasingly concerned. Should he call for an ambulance and risk embarrassing his employer? Kneeling in a thick, khaki-coloured pool beside the body, the butler tried to ignore the stench of burnt ash, ammonia and other biological waste that pervaded his usually immaculate drawing room. A small, human-shaped stain of unknown origin had dried into the hand-made 17th-century Persian Sickle-Leaf[693] carpet close to where Hartman lay face down, naked and unconscious.

The body of Cortez's favourite grandson breathed rapidly, with short, shallow breaths. His body was soaked in a feverish sweat and covered in a thick ash-like substance that stuck to the butler's gloved fingers and the light grey worsted wool of his jacket sleeve. This mysterious substance defied all attempts to remove it with a cotton handkerchief. Between the stains of this sticky grey goo on his clothes and the khaki-coloured liquid soaking into his trousers while he

---

[693] Sold for 33 million dollars at auction in 2013.

knelt, Wilkins knew even dry cleaning would not salvage this particular Moss Bros morning suit.

In his thirty-year career, the butler thought he had seen pretty much every sexual deviance. However, what had happened here was something outside his experience. The golden rule as a servant to the ultra-rich and powerful was to avoid scandal. Looking at the red marks indented into the young man's flesh and the leather saddle discarded at the edge of the Persian carpet, Wilkins decided that whatever had occurred had been extreme and almost certainly not something Chairman Cortez would want to be publicised, even to the ten Black Knights who stomped about the residence as if they owned it.

"God alone knows what the young man has been up to!"

Wilkins muttered as he continued to shake the unconscious man's shoulder. Thankfully, the butler's dilemma about calling paramedics was resolved as Hartman finally opened his eyes and groaned.

"Whhaa..." Cortez's grandson took in his surroundings, his nakedness and the concerned face of the silver-haired man who had just woken him.

Spitting out some congealed blood, Hartman pulled fragments of two cracked molars[694] from his mouth and looked shocked at a blood-covered steel bridle lying on the floor near his head.

"I will call a dentist, sir." the butler said, as though such things were completely normal.

"What time is it, erm." Hartman's befuddled mind struggled to identify the man kneeling beside him.

---

[694] 2nd and 3rd Molars (the chewing teeth at the rear of the mouth).

".. Wilkins, Sir." stated Wilkins helpfully as he checked a well-worn steel Seiko[695] on his wrist and replied,

"Seven Fifteen, Sir."

Hartman screwed up his face.

"Jesus! You know I never get up before eleven! For fucks sake, leave me in peace, to sleep this, umm off."

Hartman was uncertain what exactly he needed to sleep off, but he did need to do something to deal with the utter exhaustion that racked every muscle in his body.

If Wilkins felt any sympathy, he did not show it.

"Sir, Major General Smegget called and informed me that the Chairman will not be presiding at the Hague trial today, and you need to find a replacement urgently. Your Grandfather instructed that you were to be woken."

At the mention of Cortez, Hartman grimaced.

"Just like the old bastard to have me disturbed. Very well, tell the Hague to find a fucking replacement."

Wilkins coughed. "Sir, I already tried. None of the senior judges want to impose the death penalty without any defence team."

Hartman pulled himself up into a kneeling position and looked at the mess around him.

"Jesus wept. What the fuck happened?"

"I really would rather not know, Sir. However, might I suggest a shower, and while you clean up, I will get the roster of scheduled judges, followed by a dentist?"

After accepting a helping hand from Wilkins, Hartman nodded and staggered towards the bathroom, leaving a trail

---

[695] Seiko Five Automatic.

of messy footprints behind him on the carpets and wooden floorboards. As Hartman showered, he explored the numerous welts over his body, resembling those from a thrashed horse at the end of a race. Struggling to remember what had happened, Cortez's grandson gradually recalled the events of the previous evening.

When his grandfather put him in charge while he headed to the burns clinic in the South of France, Hartman had visions of indulging his every whim without the constant disapproval of his overbearing grandfather. Being Deputy Chairman of New Europa would mean being above every law and custom, free to do or have whatever he wanted.

Minutes after seeing the helicopter had taken Cortez and his small entourage to London City airport, Hartman had pulled out his gold iPhone Pro and called The Dorchester. After the Night Manager had been summoned on the line, it was a matter of moments before he had confirmation of a private late-night table at Alain Ducasse[696].

"Yes, Deputy Chairman, it will be a pleasure for our chefs to open up, especially for you."

His next call was to Alejandro, the Columbian entrepreneur[697], who dominated the London recreational substances market through astute profit-sharing initiatives[698]. Alejandro, or "el Padrino" as he was known on the street, had

---

[696] The premier restaurant at The Dorchester.
[697] Always a more flattering description than "Drug Lord".
[698] Bribes or, as they are more commonly known, "political donations."

his distribution centre on Great College Street for easy access to his best customers[699].

"Sí, señor Hartman, one of my e-scooter[700] couriers, is on her way to you as we speak. Will veinte gramos[701] be sufficient?"

The most Hartman ever consumed was a gram or two daily, but the additional eighteen would help smooth the evening. After the Dorchester, Hartman planned to hit "Club Inferno[702]" in Soho- where the Columbian pure would ensure it was a night to remember - there were always men and women offering themselves in return for grains snorted from the tables of power.

After an intensive session in one of the Private Suites at Club Inferno, Hartman planned to close the evening playing the tables at "Long Odds", the exclusive casino in Soho, where the minimum bet was a "Stack[703]". Of course, he would lose, but so fucking what? There were unlimited funds now they controlled the whole of New Europa. Besides, Cortez was resuming leadership in the morning, so Hartman could let New Europa run on autopilot while he had the time of his life.

After a long, hot soak in Cortez's sunken white marble bath, Hartman delighted in drying himself with his grandfather's thousand-thread Egyptian cotton towels before liberally

---

[699] The House of Commons and Lords.

[700] Even during the time preceding the Cortez revolution, E-scooter drug delivery couriers were ignored by law enforcement - you must have noticed.

[701] Twenty grams - more than enough to kill a dozen people, unless you are a 1960s Rock Legend or a British Cabinet Minister (allegedly).

[702] "Where the clients are cool and the music is hot" - no they would not let me in either, but we can buy some chips (French Fries) from the van around the back.

[703] 10,000 US Dollars.

applying his "clubbing cologne", Roja Enigma Pour Homme[704]. When he was finished, the air around him was drenched with the overpowering balsamic sweetness of Benzoin Vanilla with base notes reminiscent of Tobacco and Cognac. It would have horrified the austere classic taste of his grandfather, but that was probably why he wore it. His evening clothing choice was a bespoke Gucci statement of rebellion[705]: a beige double-breasted jacket in a horsebit-jacquard pattern, a Gainsburg cotton-poplin shirt, a web-stripe suede-trimmed wool-blend waistcoat cardigan, horsebit-jacquard cotton-blend trousers and jordaan horsebit leather loafers. The kindest description would be "distinctive", but Hartman knew all the paparazzi would film it, and by tomorrow, millions of young people would be attempting to emulate the look.

Once Alejandro's e-scooter courier delivered the twenty grams of nose candy in a blue plastic bottle, Hartman partook of his first snort of the evening before placing the distinctive bottle in his left jacket pocket and heading to the lift. Before emerging from the mirrored elevator, he carefully checked his look before he headed across the white marble tiled entrance hallway towards the two waiting black Mercedes G-Wagons[706] on St James square, outside the Cortez residence. While he was admiring his appearance, a strange, small woman rudely pushed her way into the elevator. She smelt strongly of Patchouli oil and looked like an ancient tortoise who had suddenly transformed into

---

[704] Let's just say it's an acquired taste.

[705] Made especially for Hartman in Firenze, Via de' Tornabuoni, 73, Italy (if you need a similar suit - tell them Hartman sent you - the price will probably double).

[706] Mercedes-Benz G 65 AMG Final Edition SUV powered by a 6-litre V12 engine with B7 level armour (armour piercing rifle protected 30-06 round).

human form. She wore a black silk tangzhuang-style[707] jacket and a matching ankle-length skirt. On her head, she was wearing a black Pau Felipe Bordallo[708] sombrero cordobés riding hat, and in her black leather gloved hands, she carried a red leather riding crop[709] and matching red leather saddle, bridle and harness. The riding apparel was completed by a pair of black, high-heeled leather boots[710], which clashed with the oriental styling of the suit. Even with her towering heels, the woman still failed to reach Hartman's shoulders.

The euphoric high from his recent consumption of the marching powder did little to mollify the Deputy Chairman's shock at this woman's rudeness barging into *his* elevator. He was even more annoyed that the ten Knights of the Black Sun, who were supposed to be acting as his personal security, had allowed this strange woman into the building, let alone to approach him.

"Who the fuck are you?" he demanded.

The woman's eyes narrowed in her wrinkled tortoise face as she appeared to notice him for the first time.

"It is always *fuck* with you Occidental men. Fuck not possible. Today, I am for Señor Corrado's *riding* lesson." she spoke broken English with a German accent and some oriental inflexion. After a moment, she laughed at some private joke that must have been in her reply.

"What the fuck?" Hartman exclaimed. He then adopted the highly patronising habit of many English speakers when

---

[707] Think classic Sax Rohmer, Fu Manchu. Handmade for the High Lama by Guo Pei in Shanghai.
[708] Pau Felipe Bordallo is Spain's premier milliner based in Barcelona.
[709] Saint Laurent Signature Rive Droite Riding crop.
[710] Lock Kate Botta leather knee boots by Christian Louboutin.

talking to those less fluent in the language, increasing their volume and omitting most of the words in a sentence.

"Corrado, not here. You go home. No ride today."

Hartman smiled. Then he said loudly, "NOTHING TO RIDE HERE."

Tortoise woman[711] looked at Hartman, like an Egyptian Camel Dealer examining an even-toed ungulate in the genus Camelus. Having lost her original intended paying client, Corrado, she decided to make the best of the situation. She remarked,

"Always *something* to ride if you are willing to adapt..."

With that, the strange woman gently blew into Hartman's face, directing a pulse of three of the five charged forms of vyāna[712] contained within the breath into Hartman's subtle energy bodies[713]. The Deputy Chairman gasped, slumping against the mirrored elevator wall and breathed more slowly, his eyelids fluttered, as his parasympathetic nervous system and etheric bodies experienced one of the many techniques that form a part of the forbidden Tibetan esoteric art of ལས ཕོར་གདུག - known in occult sexual lore, as the "Las Kyi Phyag Rgya.

---

[711] You probably recognise "Tortoise woman." She is, in fact, High Lama, Bla Ma Sbrul the twenty-sixth, from the infamous Karmamudra Monastery, on the Qinghai-Tibet Plateau. She is Imperatrix of the Penetrali Secreto - the oldest of the European Sex magickal orders. Mistress of the forbidden art of Tibetan Las Kyi Phyag Rgya - Tantric Sex's equivalent of atomic weapons.
[712] Rarefied forms of vital energy described by the ancient Vedic occult arts.
[713] This manipulation is one consolidated by the infamous tenth-century sage, བླ་མ་སྦྲུལ Bla Ma Sbrul into a system of physical and astral, sexual energy manipulation known as Las Kyi Phyag Rgya.

The lift doors closed with the sound of a German woman's voice.

"Yee-Haw!"

After the badly needed shower, Hartman found that Wilkins was as good as his word and had procured a nurse and masseuse to help ease the injuries and an orthodontist to make emergency dental repairs for the damage caused by the bridle. An hour later, the deputy chairman looked considerably more respectable, except for some bruising around his face, persistent drooling from the left side of his mouth and a slight lisp due to the Lidocaine[714].

Wearing a loose-fitting white 100-thread Egyptian cotton Gucci towelling robe over blue silk pyjamas[715] Hartman slowly staggered into the breakfast room barefoot. Every step was an exercise in pain management, the aches from deep muscle bruises in his limbs made every movement a challenge, and adding to the distress were bone contusions on his spine, ribs and pelvis. During his examination, the nurse expressed surprise that Hartman had evidence of penetration injuries in every one of his seven natural body orifices[716].

"Wyth it soth flucking darrkk?" he mumbled, gratefully taking a mug, with a straw, from Wilkins and staggering to the chair that was set for him at the breakfast table.

"Ah yes, Sir, we need to talk about that... while you were umm occupied, a situation has arisen," Wilkins announced.

---

[714] Dental local anaesthetic.
[715] Ralph Lauren Purple Label Monogrammed Silk Pyjama Set.
[716] You work it out.

"Fituation? What kind of fituation?" Hartman wondered what could have happened to make it pitch black through the open window to St James Square at 8.30 am in mid-September, and so damned hot. He loosened his towelling robe and sipped his coffee[717] through the paper straw.

"If I may, Sir?" Wilkens opened the door, and three of Cortez's advisors entered carrying large MacBook Pros, which they set up around the breakfast table. Meanwhile, Wilkens walked away to get the warm porridge that Hartman's dentist had recommended, replacing the usual rare steak and fries until the mouth wounds recovered.

The nearest of the advisors opened her Macbook Pro and began playing video images for Hartman of the Earth being bombarded by numerous large rocks flowing from an endless stream around the sun.

Hartman sighed. "Yesh, I fink I hafth feen this film, dofsn't it ftar Brufe Wilitf?"

The advisor nodded. "No, Sir. This is a *live* NASA feed. The Earth has been subjected to astral bombardment for the past," she consulted a black plastic Casio[718] that was running its stopwatch function, "seven hours and twelve minutes. The world had been plunged into a global crisis by the cometary airburst explosions that have warmed the atmosphere, prompting worldwide wildfires. The darkness outside is caused by smoke in the upper atmosphere."

Hartman's eyes went wide. He had no idea what to do, so he fell back on what he had always done with every problem since childhood. "Whaf doef Fhairman Fortez fecommend?" he demanded.

---

[717] Lyons Perkadilly Coffee - Deep & intense. Recommended for when you are recovering from an unforgettable tantric sex ritual.
[718] Casio F91W.

The senior advisor narrowed her eyes. "Sir, he is unavailable for the foreseeable future. You are in charge and, well, we need to know what action to take now. The investment banks who backed the revolution are unhappy."

The second advisor added. "Very unhappy, Sir. Most want their funds back immediately."

The third advisor leant forward. "Sir, the wildfires have destroyed all the Cortez camps that were under construction and the food warehouses that were intended to feed the camp *guests*."

"Fuck!" exclaimed Hartman, finally finding a word he could pronounce properly during his oral incontinence. The Deputy Chairman rubbed his hands through his hair in exasperation and immediately regretted the action due to the bruising of his skull from the merciless steel bridle he had worn for six hours.

"Ummmm..." Hartman looked desperately at the Senior Advisor, hoping beyond hope that she would come up with some solution that might appease Cortez when he reviewed these decisions, as he was sure to do.

Sensing the incompetence and indecision of their temporary new leader, the three advisors exchanged nervous glances. They knew they would be blamed and punished for any mistakes. Cortez did not put his Senior Advisors in gulags[719], that would risk them revealing dangerous secrets, but they were all aware of the "unfortunate car collisions" and "mysterious falls from windows" that had befallen those who had failed this regime during its rise to power in South America.

---

[719] Glavnoye Upravleniye Ispravitelno-Trudovykh Lagerey (Chief Administration of Corrective Labour Camps.)

The Senior Advisor, who had the strongest self-preservation instinct, chipped in, saying,

"Sir, shall I personally meet with the investors and issue them the usual placatory delaying explanations while we hope the cometary impacts stop?" The other advisors looked shocked at the senior advisor volunteering to take such a risk, while Hartman nodded vigorously. He liked this advisor.

The Senior Advisor smiled as though she loved solving a problem for her boss. She would make damn sure she stayed on the right side of the investment bankers - everyone knew they were the ones who really controlled this world, regardless of revolutions or comets. Who knows, they might hire her if she played her cards right.

The first advisor resumed her pseudo-helpful attitude.

"Sir, amidst this chaos, the massive hedge fund short your grandfather started last night against the US dollar is being threatened by fires encroaching the data processing centres in the US and Asia. Shall we reallocate the concerted action to the Grindelwald facility? It is underground and should be immune to such environmental factors."

This was vital information she could trade to the investment bankers. They would certainly be interested.

Hartman was grateful for the suggestion and nodded enthusiastically.

The advisor ran her hands rapidly over the MacBook keyboard before announcing, "Done."

She continued her apparently helpful suggestions. "Sir, we have found a judge for the show trial. His name is Kikkert."

Hartman had forgotten all about the show trial. Thank god for this advisor.

"Fikkert. Fxcellent. He fnows the fxpected ferdict?"

The advisor grimaced. "Sir, we had to take his family and hold them ransom to get his cooperation. We have given Kikkert a direct line to you." The advisor passed Hartman a titanium-coloured iPhone Pro.

Hartman looked incredulously at the phone like it was a bomb.

"Fon't be fo fucking ftupid! Fpeaking like fhis, and drooling coffee, I font intimidate anyone! fet one of the Black Knights in fere. fhey love this find of shit!"

Moments later, one of the Knights of Black Sun became a very happy man. He enjoyed nothing more than bullying and inflicting suffering, especially when the targets were honest, law-abiding and unable to fight back. The Black Knight took the iPhone and a MacBook to the far end of the table, where he began shouting and issuing threats to both Kikkert and the thugs who were holding the Judge's family. His chuckles of delight soon merged with screams of genuine terror and suffering from the stereo speakers on the MacBook.

Hartman's breakfast arrived, and he began slurping it disgustingly through the paper straw he had been provided. A small river of the warm gruel dripped from the side of his mouth and ran down onto his silk pyjamas. The three advisors made a point of ignoring the deputy director's eating habits, instead watching the show trial unfold on the two remaining MacBook's.

When Kikkert called for a twenty-minute recess, Hartman threw his half empty gruel bowl along the table towards the Black Knight, shouting, "Fucking fncompetent! Kill the first of the Fhildren and another one every Fen minutes until Fikkert delivers the verdict!"

The Black Knight took a deep breath, and within moments, there was the sound of a gunshot and more screaming, followed shortly by the image of Kikkert re-entering the courtroom on the two MacBooks.

Hartman pulled one of these MacBooks closer to him to enjoy the delivery of the death penalty, but instead, the trial descended into chaos. When the Wolfsangel operatives in the court started killing each other, Hartman staggered barefoot down the breakfast room and leant over the Black Knight, taking control of the MacBook to mobilise the SNITCH units to restore order. While standing beside the bewildered Black Knight, Hartman lisped,

"Franffer Sinclair and Curren to Wewelsburg fastle!" Before staggering back down the long table to resume his breakfast.

Hartman had just poured himself another coffee from the carafe when the senior aide's iPhone rang, and the colour literally ran from her face. She typed a few commands and then pushed the MacBook screen towards the drooling Hartman.

"Fhat now?" he demanded, and then he saw search and rescue drone footage from the cable news of the massive mushroom cloud rising above Finsteraarhorn Mountain. The explosion had created a crater that was forty yards deep and one hundred yards in radius. The ticker tape under the footage said, "Swiss Authorities claim a nuclear weapon has been detonated over the Bernese Alps."

"Fhit!" Hartman was so distracted in his hung-over state that he did not consider the implications of the nuclear strike. Instead, he focused on the AI news bot's coverage of the announcement of the death of US President Wilson, the takeover by Secretary of Defense Maskins and her declaration of surrender to the Cortez revolution. The news item closed with Makins commanding the callous shooting of the former military heads in full view of the world's media, causing widespread consternation and speculation that there could be a more ruthless side to the Cortez regime.

Hartman felt relief. The USA was finally overturned and transformed into another vassal state for their New Republic, at least something had gone to plan! It was an achievement he could claim during his "minding of the shop" while Cortez was away. That should please that miserable old bastard, thought Hartman. His mind wandered... Hadn't Maskins looked hot when she had those traitors killed on stage, although, he admitted to himself, she was clearly a complete psycho. Just his type!

His mind returned to his current reality as he watched the news change to coverage of the missing priest, Thomas O'Neill. Around him, his three aides were working feverishly and exchanging notes. Hartman left them to do whatever trivial actions such minions occupied themselves with and returned his attention to the news, where an attractive androgynous Nordic AI avatar narrated,

"Authorities have lost all trace of the priest and the infamous international terror mastermind, Abdul Issuin, who abducted the Roman Catholic archaeologist on his release from prison. Conspiracy theorists claim that two men matching the descriptions of O'Neill and Abdul Issuin were seen at one of the private terminals at Paris Le Bourget Airport[720], thirteen miles from Paris, where a Sikorsky S-70a Firehawk[721] helicopter was stolen from the French Brigade des Sapeurs-Pompiers de Paris[722] hanger. The theft came at a critical time for the fire service. An AI Spokes Bot for the city said the theft reduced their capability to deal with the numerous fires raging in the metropolis. Separate witness accounts describe

---

[720] Airport code = LBG
[721] A modified version of the US Military Blackhawk designed to deal with hostile fire environments.
[722] BSPP - Paris Fire Brigade - part of the French Military.

a helicopter that could have been the missing Firehawk landing at Ciampino Airport[723] eight miles southeast of Rome, where it took off again two hours later with two men, one of whom was described as transporting a large cat.

"Ftupid Fonspiracy idiots, always feeing links that don't exist," Hartman said, suddenly noticing the worried looks on his three advisors.

"Fome on, you fhree. Lighten up, fhat fould be forse than a nuclear bomb?"

"Sir, we have confirmation that the explosion destroyed our Grindelwald base."

Hartman shrugged. "A fhame, but we fave other bases."

The three advisors did not look any happier. The Senior Advisor looked Hartman directly in the eyes.

"Sir, our hedge action against the Dollar as the US state collapsed accumulated over thirty trillion dollars of profit in Cortez Crypto-Marks[724]."

"Fxcellent!" Hartman beamed a rather twisted smile. Even that old bastard would have to acknowledge this! He thought. But the expressions on the faces of his three advisors were anything but celebratory. The Senior Advisor looked like she would cry.

"Sir, every crypto token was lost when the Grindelwald data centre was atomised..."

---

[723] Airport code = CIA
[724] Insider knowledge (as every politician and banker knows) is the surest way to fleece the taxpayer.

K.R.M. Morgan

BENEATH BELLY HILL[725]

"Can you see anything?" asked Carnarvon[726]; Carter[727] replied, "Yes, wonderful things!" - opening the tomb of Tutankhamun. February 16, 1923

The Abandoned Şanlıurfa Airport
Six miles South of Şanlıurfa (commonly called "Urfa").
Şanlıurfa Province, Turkey.

03:20 HRS (GMT + 3), 17th September, present-day

The man's powerful body struggled to fit in the driver's seat of the box-shaped white "UN" Toyota J70[728] Landcruiser. The driver's thick beard and long hair were flecked with more grey than black, but he still exuded the power and authority that had driven him to the highest levels of the Turkish military. Looking at the glowing hands and indices on his ancient Seiko[729], he scanned the sky for the third time in thirty minutes.

"İkinizden biri bir şey duyabiliyor mu?" (Can either of you hear anything?) his booming voice demanded from the two dark-haired men outside the SUV. Both brothers had more than a passing resemblance to their father seated inside the

---

[725] The Turkish translation for "Gobekli Tepe".

[726] George Edward Stanhope Molyneux Herbert, 5th Earl of Carnarvon.

[727] Howard Carter.

[728] The only "proper old school" version of a Toyota Landcruiser - forget the luxury "Gucci" versions you see posing on city street corners.

[729] Seiko Prospex "Tuna" Saturation Diver's 1000 m. Stainless Steel Quartz watch. ISO Certified helium proof (no helium release valve needed) to 1000m – real-world tests have shown they survive four times that depth (2.5 miles).

Landcruiser. At the older man's insistence, all three wore identical grey cotton kaftan robes to better blend into the local environment should the planned rendezvous go badly enough for them to flee and go into hiding. Although, in the stifling heat, both sons would have preferred cotton t-shirts and shorts.

"Hiç" (No) answered Yusuf, the younger and less confident of the two brothers.

In contrast, Berat raised his hand, indicating he could hear something and pointed to the West. As the elder and more competent of the two men, he stood silent and motionless, his head tilted and his mouth open[730], looking like a lizard hunting prey.

Mohammed Sek eased himself slowly down from the SUV. The weakness and pain in his right leg instantly reminded him of his recent brush with a watery death[731]. Inwardly, he cursed that Cadı (witch) Ad-Dajjal and the bends[732] that robbed him of the mobility he had always taken for granted. He opened the rear door and pulled out two ancient automatic rifles and a walking cane. He passed the two weapons to his sons and reluctantly took the stick for himself. Mohammed looked at Berat, who was carefully checking the mechanism and magazine on the AR-10[733], while Yusuf muttered complaints that he should have the

---

[730] When listening for sounds, operatives are trained to remain silent and keep their mouth open with the head tilted to maximise auditory sensitivity.

[731] See his escape from the sinking Tiamat in Bridge of Souls.

[732] Decompression Sickness (DCI) involves decompression sickness (DCS) and arterial gas embolism (AGE). The expanding bubbles of nitrogen gas cause blockages in the blood supply that can lead to cardiovascular and neurological damage.

[733] The ArmaLite AR-10 is a 7.62×51mm NATO battle rifle from the 1950s. It is old but can still spoil your whole day.

latest tech, not these antiques. He loved them both, but there was only one son whom he could rely on in a tight spot.

"Remember, the American does not understand Turkish, so we will use English out of respect." the two young men nodded.

Mohammed raised a pair of NV Binoculars[734] on a strap from his barrel chest and scanned the Western horizon. Seeing movement far in the distance, he gestured to the thick shadows between the disused hangars behind the Landcruiser.

"Berat, take a position out of the light and, at any sign of trouble, shoot at the rotors and bring the bastard down. If things go pear-shaped after landing, aim at the people coming from the aircraft. Understood?" the elder brother nodded before jogging quickly towards the hangars, where he was soon lost from sight.

"Yusuf, come with me. Hold that rifle like you mean to use it!" Mohammed gestured with his walking stick to show how the weapon should be carried. Satisfied with Yusuf's pretence of competence, Mohammed started ambling towards the landing site they had marked out on their arrival an hour ago.

As he walked, Mohammed remembered the previous evening's meal with his young dark-haired wife, Zahra and daughters, Akila and Aygul. After an exhausting day overseeing the rebuilding of Stewart's Antiquarian showroom at Nuruosmaniye Caddesi, Mohammed liked to unwind with good food and the love of his family. After the death of his eldest son Ahmet[735], every moment with them was incredibly precious. They had been listening to Aygul regale the events

---

[734] Pulsar Merger LRF XL50 Thermal Imaging Binoculars.
[735] During Ad-Dajjal's attack on Istanbul. See Bridge of Souls.

at her high school when Thomas O'Neill had unexpectedly rung on the villa[736]'s landline. Over the past few days, the world had watched the news coverage of his abduction from outside the Hague Prison by Abdul Issuin, so Mohammed was relieved to hear from him.

"Thomas! I'm glad you have escaped from that murderous bastard! Where the hell are you, my friend?"

There was a pause.

"Athens?! What the hell are you doing in Greece?"

Another pause.

"Göbekli Tepe? Yes, of course, I know of it! It is in Southeastern Anatolia. What about it?"

Another pause.

"You are going there? When?" Mohammed checked his Seiko.

"Thomas, you will never get a flight from Greece to Anatolia at this time of night. Besides, all commercial flights are grounded - due to these dammed comet airbursts."

Another pause.

"You have a helicopter and a pilot? Who is crazy enough to fly in these conditions?"

"Abdul Issuin!? Then you are the crazy one! He is a cold-blooded professional killer. The murderous bastard blew up my shop! Don't forget, he even hunted you and Tavish down at The Citadel[737] in Mongolia!"

---

[736] A classic Byzantine villa on Terzihane Sokak in Istanbul - number seven, in case you wanted to call in and chat with the Sek family. Make sure you bring a gift (traditional dessert is always welcome).
[737] The legendary Citadel of the Djinn. See Bridge of Souls.

There was an even longer pause.

"I don't believe he has changed, Thomas, and neither should you. He is just using you to find Tavish."

But all of Mohammed's protests could not change the priest's decision.

"Listen, Thomas, if you insist on this visit, I will ensure you are safe. Where and when are you landing?"

Zahra passed Mohammed a pen and paper to note down the details. Within minutes of Thomas hanging up, Mohammed called in favours from old military colleagues. Zahra was on her mobile, nagging her two sons to ensure her husband did not go to the rendezvous alone. Through these hurried arrangements, they managed to get a veteran Huey[738] military transport helicopter to break the air embargo and take them on the three-hour journey to Sanliurfa[739], where they picked up an old J70 and two AR10s "loaned" from a UN depot near the Syrian border. They arrived at the rendezvous point within four hours of receiving O'Neill's call and were now waiting for his arrival in what the priest had described as a "flying fire truck".

Minutes later, a fifty-foot-long[740], red and white helicopter[741] circled above and in front of rows of deserted breezeblock aircraft hangars under a pall of thick smoke that completely blocked the night sky. The atmospheric heat from days of endless cometary airbursts and numerous ground-based conflagrations had made the ambient night temperature in

---

[738] Bell UH-1 Iroquois military transport helicopter.
[739] GNY Sanliurfa Airport
[740] Sixty-five feet long when including the rotors.
[741] A modified Blackhawk adapted to deal with heat and close proximity to fire—the cost of such adaptations is over three million USD.

Southeastern Anatolia[742] hover above 110 degrees Fahrenheit.

The brilliant light cast from the TrakkaBeam[743] searchlight mounted under the Firehawk, highlighted slabs of rough grey concrete that made up the hard standing beneath the hovering aircraft. The edges of these concrete jigsaw pieces were outlined by the dried vegetation that had pushed their way up through every crack and crevice during years of neglect on the disused airfield. The abandoned nature of the site was reinforced by the moss, grasses and even the odd small tree that sprouted on the disused hangars and buildings. Peeling paint and rust on the metal doors and window frames completed the impression of a deserted and abandoned airfield.

In the cockpit, the pilot handled the large Paris Fire Service helicopter with a consummate skill[744] borne of thousands of hours of practice[745]. The gusts of dry, smoky air from the open side door and flap windows repeatedly ruffled the pilot's short-cropped dark hair, but these air blasts were a welcome cooling in an otherwise stifling aircraft. Looking out from the cockpit, the pilot directed the searchlight onto the mottled walls on one of the hangars. In doing so, the reflected indirect light highlighted the surroundings in better contrast than was possible when directing a single spotlight onto individual targets. A similar approach of directing a torch beam towards a ceiling[746] when entering an unknown

---

[742] Just North of the Syrian border.

[743] TrakkaBeam A800 searchlight.

[744] The Firehawk usually requires two pilots to operate the complex systems.

[745] Most recently in the Valley of the Vultures in Mongolia. See earlier volumes of The New Republic trilogy.

[746] Forget TV dramas where operatives shine their flashlights onto specific parts of a dark room. Such an approach casts the rest of the environment into a dark shadow where an attacker could wait.

dark space had been taught during the pilot's training decades earlier at the Academy of Foreign Intelligence[747] facility north of Chelebityevo, Moscow.

A white J70 Toyota Landcruiser was parked, and two men were highlighted in the reflected light. They were dressed in traditional grey kaftans. The smaller of the two carried an old-fashioned[748] AR-10 rifle, while a larger man walked awkwardly towards the prominent marked "H[749]" landing position. He leant on a stick in such a manner as to suggest that he was unaccustomed to whatever injury had afflicted him.

The pilot did not doubt that shooters would be hidden in the shadows around this deserted space, for that is what he would have done, and he had the greatest respect for the people meeting the aircraft. They were, after all, associates of the one man who had bested him, the Scotsman Tavish Stewart. The choice of vehicles and weapons indicated levels of professionalism and competence often missing in the modern world, where image is regarded as more important than efficiency.

Drawing on his Montecristo, a smile crept over the hawk-like face of the pilot. He enjoyed such covert landings and, truth be told, stealing this fire service adapted Blackhawk and flying it undetected from Paris to Rome, then to Athens for refuelling, and finally, to here, in remote Southern Turkey, had been an enjoyable interlude. Knowing that an intelligent and well-resourced enemy, such as Cortez, was hunting him and successfully evading such an enemy was a game he had

---

[747] The top-secret training camp for elite KGB operatives.
[748] 1950s design battle-tested in war zones and proven highly accurate and reliable.
[749] "H" for Helicopter.

played many times. It was always enjoyable when you succeeded.

He initially intended to travel from Paris in style, using his Shiekh persona in a rented private jet. But, on arrival at the private airport on the city's outskirts, he had been informed that all flights were cancelled due to the cometary airbursts. An alternative plan was hatched after seeing the Paris Fire Service helicopter coming into land, immune to the fiery atmospheric conditions and safety restrictions. A quick change of clothes into a fire service flying suit, some subterfuge and bribes, and they were on their way. The Firehawk was slightly slower[750] than the Military Blackhawks he was used to, but it was well adapted to flying in firestorms, so it made better progress than any of the alternatives. An hour into a hedge-skimming[751] flight over Europe, O'Neill resumed demanding that he needed archaeological equipment from his Rome apartment. Since they needed to refuel[752] and restock in Rome anyway, Abdul Issuin relented.

As the hawk-faced assassin had predicted, over brunch at the restaurant in Paris, there was a heavy Wolfsangel contingent outside the priest's flat in Vicolo del Giglio[753] - but they had become complacent after days of surveillance duties. It had been child's play for Abdul Issuin to phone in a fake bomb warning to the Rome anti-terror police, which diverted the Wolfsangel team long enough for O'Neill to gather his equipment and return to the rendezvous point. The only thing that did not go to the assassin's plan was O'Neill's insistence on bringing his cat, Ezekiel. Thankfully, the large

---

[750] 140 mph vs 180 mph.

[751] Below radar and with the transponder deactivated, the aircraft becomes undetectable to anything except eyewitnesses.

[752] The 450-gallon fuel tank gives a range of 1380 miles.

[753] Apartment 17a, Upper story, Vicolo del Giglio 00186 Rome.

ginger feline was well-behaved. After walking a few times around the hawk-faced assassin and sniffing him, much to O'Neill's relief, the cat decided that Abdul Issuin was not a threat[754].

During their journey, Abdul Issuin adopted a routine of three hours flying and one hour rest, landing in remote areas where they were unlikely to be discovered. The priest and cat spent most of the time browsing the mysterious notebook. Whenever O'Neill slept along one of the benches in the rear of the Firehawk[755], the large cat invariably sat in the co-pilot's seat beside Abdul Issuin, it's intelligent green eyes taking great interest in the illuminated cockpit instruments. During the hour-long landing breaks, when the Firehawk came down in the countryside, the priest and cat would take short walks while Abdul Issuin slept. This routine seemed endless, broken only by a refuelling stop in Athens. During this Greek stopover, O'Neill had used one of the disgusting phones in the commercial airfreight offices to ask Mohammed Sek for assistance visiting the ancient archaeological site of Gobeki Tepe. Sek had not hesitated to help and agreed to meet them at this old abandoned Airport five miles south of the Turkish city of Şanlıurfa[756] that Abdul Issuin had identified as being the nearest derelict landing site to their intended destination.

As he prepared to land, Abdul Issuin rechecked his fuel gauges; he had enough to return to Athens. He had originally intended to accompany O'Neill to the intriguing archaeological site described in the priest's mysterious

---

[754] Not a supernatural threat.
[755] The Firehawk can transport 12 fully equipped, seated firefighters and equipment.
[756] The ancient city of "Urfa" - twelve miles from the ancient site of Göbekli Tepe.

notebook. But when they watched the video coverage of the trial of Curren and Sinclair on O'Neill's iPad, those plans had changed. Having worked closely with Ad-Dajjal, he recognised her influence in the strange events at the trial, and he felt strangely compelled to investigate if the black-haired sorceress had returned from beyond the grave to possess the body of the lawyer Helen Curren. Abdul Issuin decided once he had deposited O'Neill into the care of his Turkish friend, he would head back to mainland Europe to determine where Cortez was holding the possessed lawyer, Curren.

The hawk-faced assassin gently brought the Firehawk down to the tarmac before pulling his headphones from the dashboard, momentarily filling the cockpit with the Rolling Stones classic "Sympathy for the Devil". Walking back into the main cabin, he smiled as he noticed O'Neill lying prone on the seats with the large ginger cat resting on his chest like a guardian. The cat's large green eyes watched the assassin approach but remained calm. In fact, Abdul Issuin reflected, Ezekiel had remained remarkably tranquil throughout the trip, except for one event during one of their brief landing breaks. This was while Thomas and Issac watched news of the takeover by Secretary Maskins of the United States on O'Neill's iPad. The moment Maskins came on screen, the cat had practically exploded, his fur expanding and his mouth emitting a feral hiss that sprayed spittle over the iPad and would have done a Bengal tiger credit. Thankfully, the news clip was short-lived, and once it was over, Ezekiel quickly calmed down. In response to this strange event, all that O'Neill would say was,

"Maskins must be evil."

Back on the ground, Mohammed Sek was becoming increasingly unhappy as he continued making his way to the Firehawk. Not only did his leg hurt, but the idiot of a pilot had brought the aircraft down twenty yards away from the landing zone and placed the copter's unloading bay facing away from them. They were now forced to walk around the far side of the helicopter. To make matters worse, the idiot had left his rotors running, making progress with his gammy leg more torturous than necessary due to the downdraft.

"Here, give me that and help Father O'Neill unload his equipment,"

Mohammed took the AR10 and gestured for Yusuf to proceed as they took a wide arc around the helicopter towards the unloading bay doors. Expecting to face the man who had blown up his shop, Mohammed discarded his stick and drew the NATO battle rifle to his massive shoulder, ignoring the pain in his leg. If, as he expected, O'Neill was being held captive by Abdul Issuin, he wanted to be ready to shoot the hawk-faced bastard!

Instead, he found the sliding doors to the Firehawk had been closed, and the copter was taking off, leaving O'Neill looking startled at being alone on the airfield. Mohammed remained vigilant, but the only targets in his weapon's sights were the figures of O'Neill and Yusuf. His son struggled with two heavy grey canvas Victorinox bags[757] while O'Neill carried a bundle of ginger fur close to his chest like a small child. It took Mohammed a moment to realise it was a large domestic cat. O'Neill had some strange habits, and Mohammed had long ago decided to ignore his friend's numerous eccentricities.

As Mohammed relaxed, he approached O'Neill, exclaiming,

"Thomas! It is good to see you! And who is this little furry friend you have brought with you?"

---

[757] Victorinox Architecture Urban 2 Weekend bag.

The giant of a man hugged O'Neill and stroked Ezekiel under the chin before leading them back towards the Landcruiser, where Berat had emerged once he was sure the helicopter was heading away to the West. As they walked, O'Neill was clearly shocked.

"I really believed Abdul Issuin would come with me to Göbekli Tepe."

Mohammed patted the priest's shoulder.

"Trust me, my friend, we are all better off without that man."

With that exchange, the rest of the walk was completed in silence.

Before entering the SUV, O'Neill opened one of the two canvas bags and extracted a water bowl for Ezekiel, which he filled and the cat consumed eagerly, along with some cooked chicken pieces that O'Neill had acquired in Athens. The cat then scurried away to the shadows near the hangars where Beret had hidden, only to return a few moments later. In answer to the querying look from Mohammed, O'Neill explained, "Toilet break." The large cat then jumped inside the rear of the SUV and meowed at the four men.

Mohammed chuckled. "Guess we are ready to go!" He turned to his two sons, saying, "Stow the two AR10s in the back." He then struggled back into the driver's seat.

Forty minutes later, the Landcruiser drove through a vast plain of grassland fields so dry from the cosmic airbursts that many parts had already started to smoulder, raising black smoke and filling the air with an acrid burning smell. The entire archaeological site was dark and deserted. After parking near the visitor centre, Mohammed unloaded O'Neill's bags and handed out four large black aluminium torches[758] before looking expectantly at O'Neill, his booming voice carrying in every direction. He asked,

"Well, my friend. Where to?"

Putting Ezekiel on the floor, O'Neill used the torch to examine the minute details of a hand-drawn map inside the opening pages of a small black Moleskin notebook. The way the priest rotated the book and looked around the site, it was clear he had no idea where he needed to go.

"What's wrong, Thomas? Don't you remember what you wrote?" teased Mohammed.

"Oh, it's not mine." explained O'Neill, "It was sent anonymously to me when I was in prison."

Mohammed and his two sons exchanged concerned looks. Each wondered if they had given up a good night's sleep to travel hundreds of miles on a wild goose chase. Mohammed decided to push things along. He had no idea where or what they were looking for, but pragmatism suggested they use the path rather than struggle through the uneven ground in the dark. Besides, anywhere is a good starting point if you don't know where you want to be. The giant of a man pointed to the silhouette of a large ginger cat swaggering along, tail held high on the wooden walkway constructed above the boulder-strewn grass fields that led to a giant elliptical corrugated metal dome covering the prime excavation area.

"Shall we follow your cat?"

O'Neill nodded enthusiastically, seemingly unaware of the looks of despair coming from Berat and Yusuf. The wooden walkway ran a few hundred yards from the car park before forming into a three hundred yards long circular path that flowed around a fifteen-foot-deep excavation area filled with

---

[758] RS PRO High Power Waterproof LED Torch.

limestone standing stones arranged in circles. Each circular structure followed a similar layout, in the centre were two, large, sixteen-foot-tall T-shaped pillars surrounded by smaller rocks that faced inwards.

Mohammed's flashlight swayed as he walked due to his injury, and he was glad he had followed Zahra's advice and brought his two sons, as there was no way he could assist O'Neill on his own. As the four men reached the covered area, the ginger cat dropped over the walkway's edge and down into the enclosure.

"Do we follow?" Mohammed asked, wondering how he would get his bulk down the steep slopes into the one-acre excavation below them. Thankfully, O'Neill's torch highlighted a path behind the walkway that led underneath the boardwalk, and soon, the four men were walking through the megaliths.

"It's huge! gasped Yusuf, looking at one of the pair of T-shaped stones that towered sixteen feet above him.

O'Neill grunted, still failing to understand the sketch map in his notebook. Then he remembered Yusuf's question.

"Sorry, yes, it's huge. Archaeologists have used ground penetrating radar and geomagnetic surveys to map this area. At least sixteen more megalithic rings, just like this one, are buried over the twenty-two-acre site. So, what we see here," O'Neill gestured around him, "is just the tip of the iceberg[759]!"

"Do we know what it was built for?" enquired Berat. Mohammed was less interested in hearing a lecture from O'Neill. Instead, he looked where Ezekiel was leading since, by now, it was clear that the cat was determining where they

---

[759] Five per cent of the entire site.

went his morning. It would probably be a nest of field mice or a queen[760] in oestrus.

Meanwhile, O'Neill had turned his attention to addressing Berat.

"No one is sure, but the site obviously had some ritual purpose[761]. When these stones were carved, this area would have been filled with flowing rivers, wild fruit and fields of wild wheat and barley. Herds of gazelle would have roamed a bit like the African savannah today."

Mohammed deliberately interrupted the lecture. There was something about the place that unnerved him. He was not afraid of the dark, but each cometary airburst highlighted intricate carvings of wolves, serpents, lions, scorpions and vicious-looking vultures. All these creatures were portrayed as twisting and crawling over the sides of the pillars.

"They were not exactly into cute and cuddly, were they?"

Yusuf shared his father's negative feelings about the site.

"Why don't we come back after dawn, you can see more in daylight."

At that moment, the group walked around one of the massive T-shaped stones to find Ezekiel scratching away the sand and soil from a large, smooth slab of limestone that lay flat on the floor.

"Toilet time?" enquired Mohammed. He was relieved that the feline was behaving like a cat for once.

O'Neill knelt and began helping Ezekiel clear away more of the sand. A strange carving could be seen as more of the

---

[760] A female cat.
[761] Whenever the purpose of a place or object is unknown, archaeologists will declare it is for ritual.

slab was revealed. It was a chimaera-type monster with multiple heads set on a thick tree-like body with long roots.

O'Neill turned his small notebook sideways to reveal the same image drawn in black ink.

"What the fuck?" enquired Mohammed as he compared the two images in the light of his flashlight.

O'Neill ignored the comment and instead began brushing away the sand and debris around the slab's edges until he revealed a set of handles carefully carved into the sides of the stone.

"Here," he gestured towards Mohammed's two sons, "Pull these towards the far end."

Mohammed stood back and watched, and the three men applied an increasing amount of force until the slab moved, slowly at first and then more smoothly, eventually sliding under the overhanging stone slab at the far end, revealing a set of steps descending into pitch blackness.

"Well, I will be dammed!" exclaimed Mohammed as Ezekiel bounced fearlessly down the steps into the darkness below.

FUELLING THE FATES

"As the stars[762] explode, the globe shall burn,
Day becomes night, as Fenrir swallows the sun,
In this darkness, The Wolf's[763] great maw opens from ground to sky,
As the last Wyrm[764] ensnares all, a deluge makes the waters rise,
Cities drown, and the waters fill with the Naglfar[765],
The last great Wheel[766] spins worlds[767] apart,
At The Birch[768] the last great battle[769] will begin,
Where gathering to the Irminsul Idol[770], Heroes[771] & Villains[772] alike shall perish!"

---

[762] Comets were once thought to be wandering stars. Cometary airburst explosions would be thought to be exploding stars.

[763] The monstrous wolf Fenrir is the personification of global famine.

[764] Old European Worm, Miðgarðsormr or Jörmungandr - a giant serpent/dragon/*hydra/MUŠ.ŠÀ.TÙR* that desires only to destroy creation.

[765] Naglfar is a boat made from the nails (or bones) of the dead that sails at the end of times.

[766] A Qliphothic Wheel.

[767] Different legends recall different numbers of worlds or dimensions or realms. Norsk and Germanic lore tells of nine worlds of Asgard, Álfheimr, Niðavellir, Midgard (Earth), Jötunheimr, Vanaheim, Niflheim, Muspelheim & Hel.

[768] The Battle at the Birch Tree (near the Externsteine rock formation in Büren, Germany) where the Irminsul Idol stood, is the prophesied site of the final great battle (Ragnarök) at the end of times.

[769] Ragnarök.

[770] The Irminsul or Irminsul Idol - signifies the universal all-sustaining pillar - the tree of life - Yggdrasill or Mimameidr. It is the giant ash tree or a pillar supporting the universe.

[771] Often also called Giants or Gods.

[772] Jötunn (demons or their spawn). They often oppose the Heros, Giants and Gods, but just as frequently breed with them.

*- The Irminsul Prophecy in De Miraculis Sancti Alexandri,
Rudolf of Fulda*[773] *865CE*

Two Hundred Thousand Miles above the Earth's atmosphere,

10:30 HRS (UTC) 17th September, present-day

Over the past thirty-six hours, fragments[774] from the sixteen-mile-wide Perseids[775] debris field had slammed into the Earth at nearly a hundred thousand miles an hour. These exploding meteors had superheated the Stratosphere[776], causing an aerial firestorm that had brought most aviation and satellites to a standstill. As global surface temperatures rose, much of the flora in the Northern Hemisphere had combusted. These fires had raised thick smoke into the upper atmosphere and obscured sunlight around the globe, causing catastrophic damage to American and Euro-Asian agriculture.

Mercifully, the cometary onslaught abruptly ceased at 02:34HRS (UTC). Unlike the trigger for this phenomenon[777], its termination had no esoteric cause beyond the Earth's progression[778] in its vast solar orbit[779]. The massive Perseid debris field continued its endless passage through the

––––––––––––––––––––––––––––––

[773] Rudolf of Fulda was a Benedictine monk and historian in the ninth century. He described many of the legends and beliefs of the Germanic tribes before they converted to Christianity.
[774] Automobile sized fragments of rock, iron and ice.
[775] The fragments sheared off the massive Swift-Tuttle comet by the gravitational fields of Jupiter and the Sun.
[776] Four to thirty miles above the Earth's surface.
[777] The use of the St. Petersburg Wheel during the Opening of the Ten Gates ceremony.
[778] 66,616 mph.
[779] 584 million miles.

heliosphere[780], until the next celestial body intersected its path.

Once the atmospheric heat source stopped, the Earth's ecosphere resumed its natural processes. The enormous volumes of evaporated water drawn up from oceans, lakes, rivers, glaciers and icecaps during the firestorm condensed, forming violent storms that raged across the globe. The torrential rains extinguished the burning land and cooled the Earth, leading to flooding and rising sea levels.

The widespread fires followed by increasing floods destroyed much of the complex infrastructures that underpin and sustain what we regard as advanced civilisation. Police and emergency services ceased to operate, and medical services collapsed. Food supplies, electricity, gas and clean water became intermittent, and the rule of law collapsed. Many SNITCH units were swept away in the torrents that flowed along the roads in major cities, where looting and violence became widespread. Ironically, the draconian control imposed in the new regime's "Care Camps" made them some of the only stable locations.

For this reason, the camps rapidly became assembly points for millions of dispossessed people from adjoining nations, hoping for food and medicine. As people fled from the collapsed infrastructures of Russia, India, and China, Chairman Cortez became defacto, the supreme leader of a devastated planet. As had happened numerous times in the past, the elites retreated to ancient strongholds built on high ground to survive turbulent times, leaving the ordinary people outside the walls to survive as best they could.

Under these extraordinary circumstances, Chairman Cortez summoned the first meeting of his leadership group. While

---

[780] The solar system is protected by the Sun's projected electromagnetic field.

most of the world struggled without electricity, running water or food, the senior members of Cortez's group enjoyed all the technological benefits of the twenty-first century.

Cortez had spent the past eighteen hours in a three-vehicle convoy led by the high-powered Maserati[781]. They had headed Northeast from the Burns Clinic in the South of France through Switzerland, Germany and Poland, along the A7, A6, A36, A5 and A4 roads, respectively. They had averaged one hundred and twenty miles an hour through the thousand miles of burning countryside, thanks to rotating drivers and Smegget coordinating one of Europe's largest sustained road clearance operations, all to ensure that no debris or obstructions hindered the Chairman's progress to what Cortez had announced would be his new headquarters.

Although Cortez referred to the site as Schloss Fürstenstein[782], the road signs declared its name Ksiaz Castle. Perched on a hill surrounded by forests, the site had started as a 13th-century castle but had been extensively modified over the centuries until in its current state, it resembled the Palace of Versailles than a fortification. A high-class hotel was situated close to the castle building, which was rapidly commandeered for the support staff required for the world's new leader. However, the palatial surroundings did not motivate Cortez to choose this location. This site had housed "Die Glocke[783]" (The Bell) project during the Second World War. The Reich's civil and military engineering branch[784] had used thousands of concentration camp inmates to construct a vast underground complex under the castle and the nearby Owl mountains. In short order, Cortez had engineers from the nearby city of Wrocław tear out

---

[781] Maserati Ghibli Trofeo.
[782] The name used by the Third Reich for the castle.
[783] One of the Nazi Wunderwaffe.
[784] Organisation Todt. Named for its founder, Fritz Todt.

much of the fancy interior fittings in the lower levels to reveal an elevator shaft that descended fifty yards beneath the castle and connected to a one-and-a-half-mile-long subterranean rail track.

Unfortunately, the underground complex beyond the railway, where Cortez insisted the Bell was located, had been filled by the retreating Reich army with a mix of concrete blocks, dead concentration camp prisoners and booby traps. Civil engineers from the city of Wrocław estimated to Smegget that the clearance work could take years due to health and safety regulations, although none dared to express that view to Chairman Cortez, who declared the retrieval of The Bell was now the planet's highest priority. This priority, not the ecological and humanitarian disaster, prompted Cortez to summon his first leadership meeting.

Inside a makeshift video conference facility constructed inside one of the massive reception rooms on the castle's upper levels, Major General Smegget sat beside Cortez as they waited for the other participants to join the virtual meeting. Smegget was still trying to come to terms with the transformation in Chairman Cortez. In addition to the curious deaths associated with Cortez at the clinic, his behaviour had become more extreme. In the periods when the Chairman had driven the Maserati on the autobahn, he had exhibited a reckless nature which Smegget had never seen before, pushing the machine well beyond its safety limits. The Cortez he had known had always been cold, calculating and risk-averse, especially when it involved his own personal safety. Now, he embraced risk, especially when it terrified those around him. It was almost, Smegget speculated, as though this new Cortez relished the terror of others.

Smegget dismissed these idle thoughts and instead checked his pasty complexion in the full-length mirror, which filled the wall directly in front of the table where the video conference equipment had been installed. Since being promoted to his role as the Chairman's primary aide, Smegget had aged considerably both physically and mentally. His curly ginger hair had receded even further, and his pasty, puffy jowls now only accentuated the dark rings behind his thick round glasses.

The absence of any downtime and the constant high levels of stress made sleep next to impossible, and although he had been promised extraordinary rewards for assisting the Argentinian, so far, none had materialised. The abolition of the US Dollar, Pound and Euro had eradicated all his personal offshore savings in Panama, Mauritius and Singapore, leaving Smegget without hope of the luxurious retirement he had promised himself for decades of treachery, treason and temerity. There had to be some way to escape being stuck near the Chairman. Smegget had many unwholesome traits, but stupidity was not one of them. He was acutely aware of how the lives of all totalitarian dictators ended and how their unpleasant ends tended to include their closest companions - unless those companions were instrumental in helping the tyrant's enemies overthrow them. With a lifetime of experience in betrayal and conspiracy, Smegget's mind began to work. He checked his Bremont before focusing on his surroundings, hoping that some inspiration for his escape would appear.

Apart from the mirror, the room's other walls were decorated with paintings by Antonio Gisbert with Germanic themes of knightly valour and Visigoth kings. There was also a large window overlooking the engorged Pełcznica River that flowed past the castle and a massive, empty fireplace. The room was illuminated by a large crystal chandelier and the four massive tripod lights[785] set around the dark mahogany table.

Smegget had managed to grab a few precious hours of sleep after they arrived at the castle, but he still felt muzzy and bedraggled. He had showered, shaved and put on a freshly pressed blue Wolfsangel mess dress uniform but still felt grubby next to the splendour of Cortez sitting next to him. The man looked like he had just emerged from weeks at a Mediterranean Spa, when in reality, Smegget knew the Chairman had spent the entire night down in the tunnels under the Castle supervising the excavations which had become his new life's priority.

For this video conference, the Chairman had selected a dark blue silk, bespoke Sebastian Zukowski three-piece suit made by Warsaw's premier master tailor. Although the fitting process for a Zukowski suit normally took six weeks, Zukowski completed the work himself in hours. To complement the suit, Cortez wore a white cotton Oxford dress shirt with his trademark silver bolo Wolfsangel tie. The white shirt contrasted with the dark tan of the Argentinian's face, while the blue suit brought out the colour of the Chairman's eyes. The Chairman looked at the blue enamel dial of a platinum Patek Philippe ellipse[786] and sighed, impatient to begin the meeting. His fingers drummed the tabletop.

Four hundred and twenty miles to the West of Ksiaz Castle, Deputy Chairman Hartman was sitting in a more permanent and professional video conference setting, waiting for the scheduled occupant of the chair next to him to arrive.

---

[785] NEEWER Professional Video Light Panels Studio Lighting.
[786] 5738P - GOLDEN ELLIPSE. No, none of us can afford one.

Although they now had effective control over the entire digital infrastructures of the former global powers, Chairman Cortez insisted that they only use their own proprietary satellite networks for critical communication.

This state-of-the-art Logitech video conference suite at Wewelsburg Castle[787] supported full immersive VR but due to the range of different technologies available to the participants[788], they adopted the older standard video chat. Hartman could see his grandfather tapping his fingers on the table in Poland via a split screen on a one hundred-inch Sony 16K screen.

The old man was always so fucking impatient. Memories flooded unbidden into the Deputy Chairman's mind of spoilt birthdays and postponed holidays through Cortez's impatience... Hartman started in his seat as he realised his grandfather was addressing him.

"Have you placed the Idol in its appointed place?"

"Yes, Grandfa.." Hartman corrected himself, remembering non-family members were present.

"Yes, Chairman. It arrived from our family vault in Austria this morning. It is in the centre of the Black Sun floor decoration in the Obergruppenführer Hall, surrounded by the 12 columns. Exactly as you instructed."

"Excellent. And you have the Lance and the Chalice in place beside the idol in readiness?"

Hartman swallowed nervously. The recent torrential downpours had made logistics from Rome and Barcelona a nightmare.

---

[787] Wewelsburg Castle, Burgwall, Büren in Germany.
[788] The participants at the US DOD site have older technology.

"They have not arrived yet, Chairman," Hartman checked an app on his iPhone, "The Lance is scheduled to arrive within the hour and The Chalice at six pm this evening."

Cortez sniffed disapproval. Always delays and excuses. Just because of some rain.

"Make sure they do. What about the royals and the other freeloaders in the national bunkers? Are they in transit to Wewelsburg?"

Hartman nodded. "Yes, Chairman. Per your email, they will be here with the two women prisoners from the Hague. We will soon be ready to televise the death matches in the castle arena. The pay-per-view ultimate fight challenge is already being promoted on all social media platforms."

Cortez smiled like a crocodile watching a wildebeest foal coming to the waterhole to drink. Then, he checked a short handwritten list on the table beside a black Montblanc propelling pencil[789] and ticked off one final item.

"As for the thousands of dead bodies you claim you cannot bury due to the flooding. Stack them on barges and send them down the rivers."

For some reason, the idea of boats piled high with the dead filled Cortez with delighted amusement[790].

Four thousand miles to the West from the former SS stronghold in Büren, Germany, and a mile underground, President Maskins and Vice President Madden sat beside each other in front of an HD DOD Poly Studio conference

---

[789] MEISTERSTÜCK Platinum line LeGrand mechanical pencil 0.9 mm.
[790] The Viking sagas tell of Naglfar "nail boats" - boats made of dead human nails and bones as one of the signs of the end times.

suite. As unprecedented storms struck the newly united American nation, Maskins fled the devastation to "Site R[791]", one of the former United States Government's top secret "final resort" locations. She intended to stay in the safety of the bunker until the danger had subsided, without any thought for the millions of people relying on her intervention to save them and their families.

Under the harsh studio lighting, the age difference between Madden and the more youthful Maskins was starkly highlighted. Madden wore a dark grey, Lalage Beaumont, business suit. Maskins had opted for a glittering black low-cut Gabriela Hearst dress, anticipating that she would be able to make the best use of her "Alwib Allaasiq" amulet and abundant natural charms to gain even greater favour with Chairman Cortez. Both women wore identical small golden brooches carved into the shape of a striking cobra on their left lapels, but only Maskins wore the coveted gold inverted pentagram adept's ring on her right hand. Beside them, Knight Commander G.H. Schmidt wore his distinctive black Hugo Boss uniform. It was noticeable that the normally fearless Schmidt fidgeted nervously before his first meeting with the legendary Chairman Cortez, and, if truth be told, he found the heavy perfume[792] worn by the two women to be overpowering at such close proximity.

Madden whispered to Maskins, not as a Vice President would do to a President, but as a pupil to a teacher. Maskins covered the microphone in front of them with her hand and explained,

---

[791] Raven Rock Mountain Complex (RRMC), near Blue Ridge Summit, Pennsylvania, at Raven Rock Mountain.
[792] Opera Prima by Bulgari.

"Returning the Irminsul Idol to the Externsteine rocks at Wewelsburg fulfils Rudolf of Fulda's Prophecy for the Birch Tree Battle."

Maskins closed her exquisitely made-up[793] eyes and recited something from memory,

"Royal[794] blood pierced by Holy Lance[795], fills the Sacred Cup[796]..."

Madden finished the quote, "Sparks the battle of Birch."

The two women giggled with a shared delight that they were playing a part in fulfilling the ancient Germanic prophecy to bring about the end times when evil becomes supreme.

In front of the excited couple, the Sony screen showed live feeds from Germany, Poland and the forty-eighth-floor office of Beyond Facts in Canary Wharf. In London, Aspen wore her signature loose light linen shirt, baggy jeans and black lace-up canvas basketball trainers with white linen laces. Uncharacteristically for Beyond Facts today, Aspen was forced to appear in an old-fashioned live video frame rather than her preferred ageless digital avatar.

Three further minutes passed, and then an angry Cortez spoke again,

"Where the fuck *is* she?"

Hartman in Germany shuffled awkwardly and looked towards the empty seat beside him.

---

[793] Phytosurgence Shimmer range.

[794] Blood from the European royal lines who were all kidnapped by Cortez.

[795] Four lances (in Armenia, Krakow, Rome, and Vienna) claim to be the Holy Lance which pierced the side of Jesus Christ.

[796] The Holy Chalice of Valencia, in the "Chapel of the Holy Grail" in Valencia cathedral is one of a number of claimed grails.

"Chairman, High Lama Bla Ma Sbrul[797], has been told of the meeting start time several times."

"Her name is Ingrid Faber-Nietz." corrected Cortez, "I am not interested in her dubious titles."

Both Maskins and Madden raised their eyebrows. It was a gross affront to denigrate the accomplishments of a seventh-degree Meri-Isfet adept. At that moment, a door opened, and a small wrinkled woman entered wearing a thick, centre-parted short grey wig which partially covered large red owl-like glasses. This tortoise-like woman wore a black oriental-style cotton trouser suit with black Kung Fu plimsols. As she entered the video conference room, the air became infused with strong odours of patchouli oil and ammonia. Taking the vacant seat beside Hartman, she patted the thigh of the Deputy Chairman and smiled as she made a quiet "click click" sound, as one would to a horse one wanted to move. Hartman shuffled uncomfortably.

"Good of you to join us, Ingrid. I trust we are not keeping you from anything?" Cortez's voice was laced with heavy sarcasm.

The tiny tortoise woman looked up through her thick red beer bottle glasses at the screen and, instead of replying to Cortez's insult, demanded,

"Where are the Isfet seniors? We cannot meet without Magister Ironheart[798], Magus Regio[799] or Magus Salvador[800]."

She nodded a short acknowledgement at Maskins and Madden on screen as the only other initiates and resumed,

"And we are missing Brother Booker. There is no quorum."

---

[797] Grand Lama Bla Ma Sbrul the twenty-seventh.
[798] Oscar Pedersen
[799] Secretary General of the Vatican, Cardinal Dr Regio
[800] Señor Edwardo Salvador.

She stated it firmly, clearly delighted to have identified a critical flaw in the plans of this arrogant Argentinian, who had clearly forgotten that Wolfsangel derived its power from the patronage of the Isfet.

Cortez glared from the screen.

"All those you have mentioned have passed the great initiation. I am now the senior for both Wolfsangel and Meri-Isfet. You would do well to behave with greater respect, little sister!"

Madden gasped at the casual way Cortez announced the deaths of four senior members of the order and his own takeover of Isfet for himself. In contrast, the old tortoise woman merely chuckled, saying,

"Indeed? I missed your passing through the many initiations of our order. What grade do you claim this morning?"

Cortez bristled in his seat, his anger becoming a physical force that Smegget could feel, like a massive turbine engine starting.

"I am the Imperator of the Order, you insolent bitch!"

The High Lama cackled at how easily this arrogant male had been provoked to become so enraged. She raised her wrinkled hands into a series of motions, forming ancient Mundra[801] forms of the secret esoteric sciences[802] of the Tibetan high plateau. The High Lama's hands and fingers manipulated the fine divisions of Vayu energies, forming our perceived reality. In the astral vision of the three initiates, Cortez transformed in appearance, flickering between his earthy identity and some hideous multi-headed chimaera.

---

[801] Hand motions that channel power vital forces that can be used for healing and projecting energies.
[802] Shamanic Bön - the original esoteric tradition of Tibet.

In the video conference room at Ksiaz Castle, Smegget could only sense extreme agitation in the Chairman sitting beside him and a strong musky scent that reminded the Major General of visiting the reptile house at London Zoo.

"So, you are an indwelling possession. A primitive Djinn[803], if I am not mistaken." stated the triumphant High Lama, a broad smile formed on her face.

In the bunker beneath the Raven Rock Mountain Complex, Madden whispered questions to her mentor in the esoteric arts. But on this occasion, Maskins was as mystified as her pupil. She knew of the Djinn but never of one that assumed the form of a multiheaded serpent that indwelt within humans. How could such knowledge aid Maskins' own personal goal of becoming supreme ruler? She would have to find out.

While Maskins pondered, Smegget, Hartman, Aspen, and Knight Commander Schmidt remained perplexed about the increasingly strange exchanges between the ancient eccentric woman and their leader. But all four remained so terrified of Cortez that they dared not ask questions.

After a brief struggle, Cortez overcame whatever astral force had compelled him to reveal his true nature and coalesced back into his human form.   His face contorted with rage as he raised his hands before his body, forming the Western Esoteric Tradition's own forms of elemental Mudra. His fingers and thumbs joined to form an upward-pointing triangle, symbolising the projection of the elemental force of fire in its alchemical form of sulphur, and he intoned the vowel,

---

[803] Jawān

K.R.M. Morgan

"Rrrrraaaaaaaaa.." with such a low vibration that it caused the video feeds to jump on the displays throughout the conference.

Four thousand three hundred miles West of Cortez's elemental projection, Maskins looked on with a silent, stunned recognition. She had heard rumours from some of the more ambitious initiates of the sixth degree at her lodge meetings in New Orleans. Like all students discussing some forbidden topic, they gathered after Lodge meetings to furtively discuss how Magus Salvador had demonstrated elemental projection at one of his frequent guest visits. It was rumoured among these students that the seventh-degree initiation required using a randomly selected one of four elemental hand Mudras to either contaminate a glass of water[804], blow out a candle[805], defile fresh bread[806] or ignite a candle[807]. But no matter how persuasive Maskins had been with some of the senior students, and she could be very persuasive, none of them could tell her more. She had even tried to weasel the truth from the Magus himself during their frequent ritual sexual encounters, but he had insisted that such knowledge would only come to her as she progressed. But here she was, a mere fifth-degree initiate witnessing the mysterious seventh-degree projection technique used in real life! The question was, what was Chairman Cortez trying to

---

[804] Using the elemental force of water - with the hands forming a downward triangle.
[805] Using the elemental force of air - with the hands forming an upward triangle and the middle fingers intersecting the triangle.
[806] Using the elemental force of earth - with the hands forming a downward triangle and the middle fingers intersecting the triangle.
[807] Using the elemental force of fire - with the hands forming an upward triangle.

achieve? She could see no candles near the High Lama that could be ignited.

Back in the video conference suite of Wewelsburg Castle, the disdain felt by the High Lama towards the arrogant Cortez had, if anything, increased when he had started to utilise the elemental sulphur projection form against her. After twenty-seven lifetimes, she had learnt more magic than every living adept she had ever met. And here was this wannabe initiate trying to use a seventh-degree projection technique, which took decades of arduous study to equal the force of a safety match! The man's arrogance knew no end!

Only when the "young stallion" beside her pulled away in horror did she notice that steam was rising from her cotton jacket, trousers and wig! She was reaching for the water bottle on the table in front of her to douse the rising heat when her vision blurred, and an unimaginable pain ran from her feet through her calves, up her thighs, over her chest and face. Her last conscious thought was to recognise she was the source of the smell of burning pork filling the air and that the piercing scream roaring through the small room was coming from her mouth.

The two Wolfsangel technicians tried valiantly to extinguish the roaring flames with the CO2 fire extinguishers, but the inferno was unstoppable until it burnt itself out. All that was left of nearly two thousand years of existence was a charred ankle protruding from a single black cotton Kung Fu plimsol.

Back in the US DOD bunker, Vice President Madden exclaimed,

"Spontaneous Human Combustion!"

Seated beside her, President Maskins shook her head, "Didn't look that spontaneous to me."

OVERNIGHT WITH THE OSAGE[808]

"When you know who you are, when your mission is clear, and you burn with the inner fire of unbreakable will, no cold can touch your heart; no deluge can dampen your purpose. You know that you are alive." - Chief Seattle

Wahzhazhe Summit[809]
Boston Mountains
Newton County, Arkansas, New American Republic

09:30 HRS (GMT-5) 17th September, present-day

The deafening thunderclap blended simultaneously with a blinding flash of lightning, waking President Wilson F. Jones with a start from his deep, dreamless sleep. A further series of rapid lightning bursts briefly illuminated his surroundings. The deposed POTUS lay on a cot bed constructed from unfinished, crudely carved Iron Oak[810] with a thick mattress stuffed with woollen fibre that still retained a strong smell of sheep[811]. The floor was a mix of surface roots, sandstone rocks, clumps of grass and flattened earth. Apart from the unusual construction and odour from his bed, he was aware that goosebumps were rising over his exposed arms, indicating that the atmosphere was considerably cooler than it had been during the recent days of cometary airbursts. Torrential rain drummed furiously on the large sheets of waxed canvas under which his small bed was pitched. The rear and sides of his sleeping accommodation were in pitch

---

[808] According to 19th century missionary Isaac McCoy, the Osage were an "uncommonly fierce, courageous, warlike nation".
[809] Formerly known as Buffalo Lookout. The highest point in the Ozarks at 2,561 feet.
[810] Quercus stellata, the post oak or iron oak. Indigenous to the upper Boston Mountains.
[811] Bighorn sheep (Ovis canadensis). Indigenous to North America.

darkness, but each lightning flash showed the wrinkled contours of bark on the trunks of massive oak trees, with rivulets of rain running down their sides. To the front of his shelter were the flicker of campfires and the sounds of human activity.

Sitting up, Wilson pulled on a mud-spattered marl grey cotton Harvard sweatshirt over his grubby white T-shirt[812] and laced up his light-coloured leather Hersey walking sneakers. He checked his Shinola watch, noting he had been asleep for the past seven hours, a rare luxury for him in recent days. Standing and moving away from the bed, he became aware of a strong smell of cooking and coffee, reinforcing a recognition from his grumbling stomach that he had not eaten for nearly twenty hours and was starving.

The POTUS walked out from under the awning of his tent. He found himself standing in a clearing made in an oak forest at the top of a thousand-foot-high sandstone ridge. The daylight was still obscured by heavy cloud cover, and he was getting soaked in the torrential rain, but it felt refreshing after days of stifling heat and smoke. Looking to his immediate left, he saw parked under some more awning, a set of six, large off-road motorcycles[813] had been stacked side by side. Their specialised bodywork was decorated in multi-spectral camouflage, which evaded detection methods such as infrared, radar, and millimetre-wave radar imaging. The bike's headlights had been adapted to project infrared beams that permitted NVG goggles to provide near-perfect visibility to the rider in darkness. Other modifications to a standard off-roader included rifle mountings and run quiet

---

[812] A white cotton American Apparel T-shirt.
[813] US Mil-Spec special forces off-road motorcycle. Kawasaki KLR250-D8 249 cc 28 HP, 4-stroke, DOHC, four-valve, single cylinder with a range of 188 miles on a full tank of fuel.

mufflers, allowing the bikes and their riders to transverse hostile territory at night with little chance of detection.

The six specialist Kawasaki bikes had been thoroughly cleaned since Wilson had last seen them on his arrival at this camp in the early morning hours. Stiffness in his back, arms and legs were constant reminders of sitting behind Captain Jackson for the arduous ten-hour ride over three hundred and fifty miles of dirt tracks and back roads from Fort Liberty to here, wherever the hell here was! Since CIA Director Pimms had been the person who had planned the roadblocks adopted by Wolfsangel around Fort Liberty, their route successfully evaded their enemy's vastly superior resources. In fact, Wilson had more than a sneaking suspicion that Pimms had been so successful in their escape plan that the traitors who had seized his nation and usurped his position had no idea that he was still alive.

His mind flashed back to the previous morning, when he was foully betrayed by the very people who were supposed to protect him. Standing with General Orne and Director Pimms in the accommodation block at Fort Liberty, he was literally seconds away from a violent end from an exotic explosive device that would be triggered when it reached room temperature. As the Wolfsangel traitors had hurried away from the imminent explosion, Wilson recalled making a light-hearted challenge to his CIA Director about being impressed if Pimms could prevent their imminent demise.

As the last of the liquid hydrogen coolant in the tank around the bomb evaporated in a mist that gathered over the ceiling of the small apartment, the frozen explosive block of Azidoazide Azide began to sizzle ominously in the stifling heat. The countdown indicator started flashing 00:31, 00:30...

"Now would be a very good time to play one of those Aces you are famous for having up your sleeve!" joked General Orne to Pimms, with every expectation that there was no chance of survival from what he knew from his DARPA briefing notes, was ten kilos of the most powerful explosive ever created.

Pimms raised an eyebrow and smiled at his two sceptical colleagues before picking up two cushions from the sofa, which he used to handle an unopened Thermos flask of Joffrey's House Blend coffee that had been delivered at the CIA Director's request some hours before.

"Hell of time for a coffee, Mark." commented the POTUS, "Personally, I would prefer something stronger for my final drink on earth!"

Ignoring the comment, Pimms removed the lid of the Thermos through the cushion material and then proceeded to pour the freezing contents over and around the sizzling block of super explosive. The temperature indicator and countdown returned to showing minutes rather than seconds remaining.

Orne laughed, "Cunning bastard! I suppose that is why you are the nation's spymaster."

Pimms looked at his two colleagues. "Liquid nitrogen. I could not source the liquid hydrogen used by the Wolfsangel scum, but I figured this should at least give us a few extra moments."

"Very good, but what shall we do with them?" asked the POTUS.

Pimms smiled enigmatically and walked over to the centre of the room, where he stamped twice loudly. There were two raps back, which sounded like they came from under the floorboards. The CIA Director pulled back the small textile rug which covered the floor between the chairs to show a section of floorboards rising, revealing US Marine Captain Jackson, his M27, systematically covering the room.

Jackson saluted at Wilson, saying, "Good Morning, Mr President!"

Wilson grinned. "Boy, Jackson, am I pleased to see you!"

Pimms looked to the Marine. "Ready?"

"Always," replied Jackson in his Southern drawl.

Pimms patted the POTUS on the shoulder. "Let's get you to your family."

"They are alive?" Wilson could not believe his ears.

"Of course, Mr President," answered Pimms.

"But what about the pictures we saw of their bodies taken to the Wolfsangel helicopter?" Wilson was still reluctant to believe it.

As Orne and Wilson descended into the crawl space under the accommodation block, Pimms explained,

"After two of my undercover operatives working on this base discovered your family's food had been drugged by the Rangers, in preparation for kidnapping, I quickly improvised a plan. I admit it was a close-run thing, but thankfully, during transit to the helicopter, we managed to switch your wife and children for lifelike dummies used in CIA hostage rescue drills. Wolfsangel operatives are lazy bastards, so they were quite amenable when my undercover base staff volunteered to carry the "unconscious bodies" in body bags from the transport van to the helicopter. We then drove the van to our safe haven. In addition to the hostage rescue dummies, my staff included a special gift from us in the Wolfsangel helicopter, which reminds me."

Pimms pulled his Pixel phone from his pocket and sent an SMS.

" What was that?" asked Orne as the two men crawled along the passageway behind the POTUS.

"An explosive message." answered the CIA Director enigmatically.

Returning to the present, Wilson stretched and walked further from his makeshift tent into a thirty-foot square-covered cooking area filled with several groups all preparing meals for queues of drenching wet families coming into the feeding station before moving to sit on logs beside fire pits. The entire area was covered by large waxed canvas sheets formed into a massive canopy. In the distance, Wilson could see Marine Captain Jackson supervising the erection of more sections of the temporary shelter to accommodate the ever-increasing numbers of soaking people making their way towards them. As Wilson's eyes accommodated to the gloom of the rain storm, he could see lines of bedraggled men, women and children climbing up paths between the oak forest all around them.

The nearest cooking area to his sleeping area was being operated by two of Wilson's Marine security detail. CIA Director Pimms and Army General Orne seated on a nearby log. Orne was using a spork[814] to eat a plate of scrambled eggs and beans from a metal canteen while Pimms was drinking coffee while talking animatedly to someone on an Iridium satellite phone[815]. Wilson approached Orne and

---

[814] A spoon-fork hybrid popular with the military.
[815] Iridium Extreme 9575P Encrypted Satellite phone using untraceable MIL-SPEC AES-256 encryption.

gestured for the Army General to remain seated. The POTUS pointed to Pimms and mouthed,

"What is he doing?

From long-formed habits, Orne stood as a mark of respect and replied,

"Maskins and Madden are keeping all food and supplies exclusively for their own elite Wolfsangel operatives, allowing the rest of the population to starve. Pimms is activating his sleeper cells[816] to liberate our national food reserves, water purification and emergency rations, Mr President."

"For us just at this location?" Wilson gestured to the hundreds of displaced people around them.

Orne shook his head. "For the general population throughout the States, Mr President. We will use word of mouth to announce the locations and times at each habitable population centre."

"Quite right. Tell Mark to keep at it."

Wilson was about to walk away when he suddenly realised the implication in Orne's statement about CIA sleeper cells operating in the mainland United States. Orne waggled his finger in admonition.

"I know, domestic sleeper cells[817] - don't go there, Mr President. Just be thankful Pimms had a backup plan for a combined global catastrophe and revolution."

Wilson nodded. The situation demanded extraordinary measures, and Pimms was rising to the occasion, which was considerably more than he felt he was doing. Dismissing the feelings of guilt, he walked a bit further towards where his

---

[816] Deep cover agents.
[817] The CIA is (supposedly) legally limited to operate exclusively outside the borders of the United States.

dark-haired wife, Samantha and their two small children, the blond-haired Josh and the dark-haired Amanda, were seated. God, that was another thing he could thank the foresight of his CIA director for, switching their anaesthetised bodies for hostage rescue dummies used by the agency's HRTs[818]. His family saw Wilson approaching, stopped eating, stood around him and formed a group hug. Samantha was the first to pull away, before saying,

"Good to see you rested. We let you sleep after your arrival last night. Now, go get some food." she gestured towards a nearby cooking station ten yards up a steep slope. Wilson knew she was right but did not want to leave his family alone again.

Samantha read his mind. "Go. We are right here, and Jackson has us under his eagle eyes. He even has a gallon or two of hot water and clean clothes waiting in your tent to wash and shave after you have eaten."

"You mean I stink?"

Samanta smiled while gesturing towards the nearest feeding station.

"Eat, Wilson. It will help you think about what must be done."

Wilson stood for a moment longer, trying to gather his thoughts. Unusually for him, his mind felt overwhelmed. Empty, tired and unable to think about what response could be made to the coup.   In the end, the smell of cooking and coffee overwhelmed the President, and he walked up the slope towards a feeding station where an extremely tall man wearing a long cotton apron over his jeans and plaid shirt was cooking on an iron skillet on top of a burning wood stove. The man was a dark-haired native American in his

---

[818] Hostage Rescue Teams (HRTs) are elite counter-terrorism units within law enforcement and intelligence communities.

sixties with a heavily weathered face. He nodded at the exhausted Wilson and asked in a deep, melodious voice,

"Why so glum, friend?"

"I have lost my country," retorted Wilson, his answer filling him with even deeper emotions of hopelessness.

"My people know too well how that feels," answered the cook with deep meaning as he began preparing an omelette. He continued.

"But at least you can get your nation back. You have your family and the support of good people," the cook pointed to Orne, Pimms and three US Marines eating nearby.

"But my opponent has all the power." stated Wilson, feeling an unfamiliar sensation of defeat and hopelessness. The tall cook nodded sympathetically as he ladled Wilson's eggs, beans and toast onto a wooden plate.

"We also know how that feels. But be of good humour because our tribe tells of a time when the last of the great Situlili (rattlesnake spirits) will fill the world with its poison, making the sky explode and the earth burn before the tears of Wakan Tanka (the great spirit) cool the soil. After the waters, a single man, helped by his friends, kills the great old Situlili and restores order."

"You think I am that man?" asked Wilson, curious as to his connection to this ancient legend.

"Do you have the piece of a star with which to strike the head of the serpent?" asked the cook quite seriously.

Wilson shook his head. "I don't even know what that means."

"Then you are not that man. But you can help that man succeed."

With that, the tall, enigmatic cook passed Wilson his wooden plate and turned to serve the next in the long line of the hungry. The POTUS picked up a wooden spork from a dispenser and started to walk down the slope to where his wife and two children were seated, but seeing Samantha gesturing towards Orne and Pimms, he changed direction and came to sit beside Orne on a long oak log.

Turning to the General, he asked, "Where is the Tribal Chief? I should thank him for his hospitality to us and all these displaced people."

Orne winked at the President. "You were just talking to Crazy Bear, Chief of the Osage. He is a bit of a local legend. Supposedly, he once fought off a Grizzly."

Wilson laughed. "I see. A modest leader who serves his people. Truly a rarity these days."

Orne patted Wilson on the shoulder and turned to the CIA Director, who was now focused on enjoying his coffee. "Not that unique, eh Mark?"

Pimms raised his wooden coffee cup in a toast. "Two such leaders in one encampment. It is a small world. Here is to a return to better times!"

The POTUS raised his own wooden coffee mug, but his expression turned serious.

"So let's hear the latest, Mark. How bad is it?" demanded Wilson.

"The good news, Mr President, is that the cometary bombardment has ended, and the storms have extinguished the wildfires that destroyed farmland and cities. The bad news is that we now have widespread flooding and famine. Much of the surviving infrastructure has ceased functioning here in the US and elsewhere around the globe. The firestorms reduced the already weak infrastructures of India, China and Russia back to the Stone Age, and as a result, all three nations have fallen to Cortez's revolution. As best we can make out, millions worldwide are dispossessed and need urgent assistance. To make matters worse, Cortez's regime is keeping all the food and supplies for themselves, almost like they are actively maximising the suffering of the general population.

Our Cyber Intel indicates the new regime has been working for weeks before coming to power to fund the global news media agency, Beyond Facts Inc., to run the world's largest disinformation campaign. They followed the classic Russian GRU[819] & FSB[820] approach[821] of spreading division, discouragement and disinformation. They used social media, mainstream media, corruption and intimidation to divide society, so it fractured into subgroups that distrusted each other. Simultaneously, they discredited all established forms of authority apart from themselves. The population quickly reached the stage where they did not know what to think, so they believed the Cortez party line, that he was their only hope for a better future. We also believe Cortez has been lacing the food supplies with a psychotropic drug[822] that weakens the will to resist."

---

[819] Main Directorate of the General Staff of the Armed Forces of the Russian Federation - the Russian Military Intelligence Service, run from the infamous Grizodubovoy Street headquarters.

[820] Federal Security Service (FSB), (Federalnaya Sluzhba Bezopasnosti) of the Russian Federation- the modern version of the infamous KGB. They do not just gather intelligence, they manipulate Western Nations to weaken the rule of law, democracy and freedom of speech.

[821] Karlsen, G.H. Divide and rule: ten lessons about Russian political influence activities in Europe. Palgrave Commun 5, 19 (2019). https://doi.org/10.1057/s41599-019-0227-8

[822] "WB" or "Wahrnehmungsblock" is a German manufactured neuro-inhibitory drug that stops certain, specific, complex sensory and cognitive processes, such as will power and critical thinking. A bit like social media.

The POTUS thought for a moment, his vast mind thinking through the complexities of their situation. Orne and Pimms knew better than to interrupt. Eventually, Wilson asked,

"Do we know where Madden and Maskins are holed up?"

"We believe they are sheltering in the Presidential last resort bunker in the Raven Rock Mountain Complex, Mr President."

"And where are Beyond Facts coordinating their propaganda campaigns?"

"After Cortez bought the company, the entire organisation transferred to the forty-eighth-floor office in Canary Wharf, London. We believe the operations are coordinated by a woman called Aspen."

The POTUS thought for a moment and then continued. "And where is Cortez running the show?"

"That is where things become interesting and more complicated. Originally, Cortez operated from a swanky townhouse in Westminster, London, but with a plan to eventually relocate his military arm, the Wolfsangel, to the old SS headquarters in Wewelsburg Castle, Germany. Until a couple of days ago, the esoteric arm of Cortez's organisation, The Isfet, was headquartered in an old Ottoman Fortress[823] built on a small island between Montenegro and Albania."

"You said, was - past tense. What happened?" queried Wilson.

"The Scotsman, Tavish Stewart, flew a light aircraft into the Ottoman Fortress and blew it and everyone inside to hell."

Wilson laughed for the first time in days. "This is the same Tavish Stewart who killed that crazy woman, Ad-Dajjal?"

"One and the same." answered Pimms.

---

[823] Fortress Grmožur.

"Sounds like Stewart has started ahead of us. Where is he now?"

Pimms nodded. "He was arrested by the Montenegrin police after single-handedly taking out a Wolfsangel Spec Ops unit conducting an ethnic cleaning operation near the fortress. Stewart was taken to a maximum security prison in Podgorica. He promptly escaped and was last seen in Sarajevo with some of his former UN War Crimes Investigation colleagues and Mark Katz, the head of Mossad's special operations division."

Wilson laughed again. "Your counterpart in Mossad? I guess that makes sense. Mossad would probably be a good ally if you are going up against a Neo-Nazi bastard like Cortez. Any idea what Stewart is doing next? Find out from Katz and see what help we can provide. Whatever we can. Given Stewart's history, he is probably everyone's best chance of finishing Cortez in Europe."

Pimms nodded. "That was our analysis as well, Mr President."

"Now, back to our own problems and how to restore some order to our own proud nation. What assets do we have?" asked the POTUS.

"What you see here."

Pimms pointed to Orne, himself and the President's six-person Marine protection detail, who were assisting the Osage in constructing tents and latrines for the hundreds of refugees arriving at the hilltop refuge.

"There are also sleeper cells who have remained loyal, the SAC[824] (Special Activities Center) units and a small resistance

---

[824] The CIA's SAC is split into two wings - the SOG (SAC/SOG) (Special Operations Group) conduct tactical paramilitary operations and the PAG (SAC/PAG) (Political Action Group) conduct covert political action.

group in Europe, which includes Stewart and his associates. I have already mobilised our CIA sleepers and the SAC SOG operational units to liberate emergency food stockpiles around the globe and start distribution to the general population."

Wilson nodded his approval. "Good work. Now, you talked about the social media disinformation campaigns that Cortez sponsors. Do your SAC PAG units have any skills that could counter the work of Beyond Facts?"

Pimms nodded. "Theoretically, yes."

"Then it is time for them to move from theory to practice."

The CIA Director nodded and picked up his encrypted satellite phone.

Wilson turned to General Orne. "Call Captain Jackson over here. We need to chop off the head of the snake here in the US and restore the constitution."

Orne stood and waved to some of the Marines digging nearby, and within a few moments, Jackson was standing to attention before the three men.

"Mr President, Sir!" the blond-haired 27-year-old was soaking wet in his black rain poncho but still somehow managed to look ready for anything with his M27 slung over his shoulder and a gleam in his cold blue eyes. Wilson had no doubt that the gun would have been cleaned and oiled.

The President looked up from his seat and addressed the Marine,

"Captain Jackson, do you think you and your six Marines could storm the Raven Rock Mountain Complex for me? It will likely be heavily defended by Wolfsangel Rangers and SEALs. I need you to secure the site, retrieve any data, and capture or, if that proves impossible, eliminate Knight Commander G.H. Schmidt, Maskins and Madden."

A trace of a slight smile crept across the Marine's face. "We are all 0372 Critical Skills Operator certified. Mr President!"

Wilson looked to Orne for an explanation. "They are Marine Raiders, Mr President." the Army general answered as if that explained everything.

The POTUS still looked confused. CIA Director Pimms came to his rescue with a clarification quoted directly from the MARSOC[825] statement of purpose. "The Marine Raiders specialise in small-scale offensive actions to seize, destroy, capture, recover, or inflict damage in hostile or denied areas."

Wilson needed absolute confirmation before he committed to sending his protection detail to face Rangers and SEALs. "So that is a yes?"

Orne smiled. "A very big yes, Mr President. But who will provide you with protection with the Marines gone."

Wilson looked over to Crazy Bear, serving another breakfast and asked, "Do you think the Osage know how to defend me effectively?"

Pimms smiled. "Let us just say they were regarded as some of the most ferocious warriors in the Old West. I doubt they have lost those instincts!"

---

[825] United States Marine Forces Special Operations Command.

DREAMS AND VISIONS

"Everything lives and perishes through magnetism; one thing affects another one, even at great distances, and its "congenitals" may be influenced to health and disease by the power of this sympathy, at any time, and notwithstanding the intervening space." - H. P. Blavatsky

Bellevue Suite,
Top floor, Hotel D'Angleterre,
Facing Lake Leman,
Geneva, Switzerland.

04:30 HRS (GMT+2) 17th September, present-day

Heavy rain beat against the red-glazed tiles of the roof overhang and the shutter windows facing out onto the Bellevue Suite's small balcony. The glazing and wooden window frame shook intermittently from the violent thunderclaps. Outside, flashes of light from superheated plasma illuminated the Geneva skyline every few moments, not from a cometary aerial explosion but instead from the equalisation between a massive electrical potential in the clouds and the much lower ones presented by tall buildings and metal railings around Lake Geneva.

In the hotel suite's luxurious white and grey tiled bathroom, the chromed heated towel rails were covered with an assortment of soaking wet clothing: Tilley underwear, bamboo socks, a navy pique shirt, white linen trousers, and a pair of drenched tan leather deck shoes. The damp dog smell associated with soaking clothes combined with the odours of wine, freshly baked bread and melted cheese. Tavish Stewart was unaware and uncaring of these unusual aromas as he was in a deep REM sleep state, vividly reliving his previous afternoon.

After escaping from the cafe with the barista and waitress, both of whom were coughing and spluttering from their brief exposure to the VX nerve agent, Stewart had guided the small group along the narrow wooden walkway connecting the rooftops of the tall dwellings that led towards the ancient cathedral. The Scotsman was acutely aware that it was only a matter of moments before one of the SNITCH units cleared the barricades of chairs he had placed in the stairwell up to the roof cafe and resumed their murderous pursuit.

Stewart guided the two cafe staff carefully, keeping them on the walkway as best he could. His body was much slower and less well-coordinated than he would have liked. He had already began to feel the nausea and muzzy head that he recognised only too well as being among the many unpleasant side effects of the 2-PAM Cl[826] antidote to the VX nerve agent. Turning to check that the SNITCHes had not yet emerged from the cafe, he noticed the cloud of tiny microdrones swarming around them.

"Attendez!" (Wait!) exclaimed Stewart as he looked around for solutions to their digital spies.

The last thing he wanted was to lead the SNITCHes and by implication, Wolfsangel, to the Meri-Maat hideout beneath the Cathedral. But he also needed to get the barista and waitress to safety as quickly as possible, and the SPLEE safe haven was the only place he knew where they would be left alone long enough to recover from the combined effects of the VX nerve agent and the toxins contained in the antidote.

The Scotsman pulled a canvas tarpaulin free from its four corner fixtures on the upper sections of the roofs around them, where it had been covering an area of the walkway,

---

[826] Atropine and pralidoxime chloride.

keeping it relatively free from the large flakes of falling carbon. Holding the sheet in both hands, he threw it in a large arc, like a fisherman casts a net. Catching the swarm in midair, Stewart wrapped the fabric tightly around itself into a small ball and threw it from the walkway down to the cobbled streets one hundred feet below.   Moving away from the boardwalk that lined the edge of one of the buildings, they started progressing through a gap where the roofs formed steep valleys of red tiles dusted with black carbon flakes.

The barista and waitress were in the process of thanking the Scotsman when Stewart felt the wooden boards of the walkway in front of them shaking from a series of heavy strides. The flexing and rocking of the panels were accompanied by a menacing creaking. As the deformation of the wood continued, the shaking became far more vigorous than could be caused by the weight of a human. Instinctively, the Scotsman grabbed his two companions and pulled them down and under the boardwalk, gesturing with a finger on his lips for them to be quiet. The three bodies tumbled into the valley formed between two roofs. The tiles near where they had been standing exploded in a hail of high-velocity armour-piercing rounds. Shards of red roof tile and window glass cascaded around them. The Waitress screamed in blind terror, and the Barista tried to comfort her as the heavy steps continued along the swaying wooden planks that formed the boardwalk, attracted by the sound of the waitress's scream.

The sinister mechanised female voice of a SNITCH echoed through the rooftops,

"COME OUT AND SURRENDER!

SURRENDER AND YOU WILL BE SPARED!"

Acting directly against Stewart's hand gestures to remain out of sight, the terrified couple began to move to comply, but as they did, the SNITCH, which was now visible some thirty feet in front of them, detected the motion and unleashed another blistering volley of armour-piercing rounds, shattering a large hole in the tiled roofing to their right and exposing the attic space of a nearby house.

In contrast to the terrified barista and waitress, who huddled together, sobbing, Stewart remained icy calm. Drawing his Korth, he lay to the left side of the roofing valley, still protected beneath the boardwalk, and exhaled as he took careful aim and assumed the first pressure on the trigger. In the semi-gloom, the flash from the short barrel was blinding and the roar of the .357 Maximum deafening. The massive round slammed into the left leg, cleanly detaching it from the SNITCH. Disintegrated limb sections rained down over a wide roof valley beside the robot. The crippled quadruped stumbled forward to the boardwalk, where it lay momentarily, assessing its damage. After a few seconds, it rose unsteadily on three legs and commenced moving forward, using its remaining right front leg to compensate for the missing left one.

"Don't you just love engineers?" sighed Stewart as he aimed again, this time at the single remaining front leg of the robot.

This shot ripped the right front leg clean off and caused the SNITCH to smash face-first into the boardwalk. Stewart held his breath. Even if he had halted the machine's advance towards them, they still had to get past this deadly device. Before the Scotsman could develop a plan, the SNITCH moved and pulled itself up to stand on its two remaining rear legs. Its red front lens glowed menacingly as it approached them like a stilt performer.

Stewart pulled open the cylinder on his Korth, poured out the spent rounds and quickly pulled massive .357 Maximum slugs from his leather belt, feeding them into the revolver. Once all six chambers were loaded, he clicked the cylinder closed and resumed his firing position, aiming at the advancing SNITCH. When the machine was fifteen feet away from the three humans sheltering under the boards, an amber mist issued from the underside of the device, flooding the space where they were sheltering.

Stewart gestured with his left hand to the two sobbing figures beside him that they would be okay.

"Ignore it. We have taken the antidote."

He waited until the SNITCH was less than ten feet away and then drew up his Korth NSC, aiming it at the grey polymer underside of the robot.   Where the SNITCH's twin machine guns fired with the rapid staccato rhythm of a voodoo drum, Stewart's Korth roared in splendid isolation like a primaeval dragon. With a quick double tap, two of the massive 357 Maximum rounds slammed into the exposed underside of the SNITCH's main body panel, shattering the armoured grey polymer, exposing the electronics, servos and hydraulics inside and lifting the robot off its two remaining legs into the exposed neighbouring attic space. Hydraulic fluid cascaded from the wooden boardwalk planks where the creature had been standing.

Stewart did not wait to see if it survived. He hauled his two companions back up onto the boardwalk and ran along the walkway towards the Cathedral. Stewart glanced to one side as they ran and noticed an iron fire escape with its top iron gate ripped apart, obviously where the SNITCH had gained access to the roof. Minutes later, they arrived at the edge of the main Cathedral roof, where three of Frater Léon's SPLEE resistance fighters were keeping a lookout.

"Did we hear SNITCHes on the roof?" the older of the three men asked, his eyes darting nervously around behind Stewart and his two companions.

"This man killed one and their flying spy drones," sputtered the barista as he supported the near-unconscious waitress onto the Cathedral parapet.   Both were clearly still suffering the effects of exposure to the VX agent in the cafe.

Once the Scotsman was confident that Léon's SPLEE resistance had the two cafe staff, Stewart descended the spiral stairway to the street level. He emerged onto the open space in front of the Cathedral. Down here, the sound of the atomic air attack sirens was overwhelming, constantly repeating their series of tones that summoned all Swiss Citizens to the safety of the communal bunkers.

The streets were utterly deserted as the Scotsman strolled back towards his hotel. Stewart was not sure, but the cometary airbursts seemed less frequent. Without their regular bursts of light to illuminate the perpetual night, it felt much darker, and the dry heat had gone, replaced by oppressive humidity. Wiping sweat from his forehead, Stewart wondered if he was running a temperature from the VX antidote.

His fever hypothesis was disproved moments later when it started to rain. First, there was a light drizzle, which felt like a beautiful change from the oppressive heat that had built over the last few days. However, the rain quickly intensified, and by the time Stewart had reached Rue du Vieux-Collège, it was a deluge. The Scotsman was quickly soaked, and after a few futile attempts to gain access to some of the clothing stores along the route to get more suitable clothing, Stewart gave up and just walked in the rain, his suede deck shoes squelching in the streams of black water that began to flow down the streets towards Lake Geneva.

As he continued to walk past all the closed shops and hotels, he heard an intense firefight in the distance. It sounded to Stewart's experienced ear like two similarly equipped units engaged in a ferocious death match with fully automatic assault weapons.

Reaching Jardin Anglais, he saw two SNITCH units had killed over a dozen Wolfsangel operatives. The dead men lay in grotesque forms along the garden areas where they had made a stand but were unprepared for the VX nerve gas. The telltale amber staining around the dead bodies was rapidly being washed away in the heavy rain down to the lake[827].

Stewart kept out of sight behind the corner of a nearby building across the street from the garden entrance, waiting for the two SNITCH units to head North from the area. Once the coast was clear, Stewart jogged across the Pont du Mont-Blanc bridge, turned right and headed North at a walking pace along the lake edge towards his hotel. Over the other side of the lake, he could still see the two SNITCH units ruthlessly hunting for any living human being. Based on the massacre by the English Garden, even the Wolfsangel uniform did not provide an exemption from the purge being initiated. Perhaps no one would ever know what icy cold logic inside the polymer killing machines had flipped.

Fifteen minutes later, Stewart found the main hotel doors locked but gained entry using his door card at the night entrance. The hotel lobby was deserted. The digital displays above reception advised all guests to head to the nearest shelter and to leave their belongings in their rooms. Stewart had already confirmed that the prevailing winds were taking the fallout from the single explosion away from the city, so he was safe for now. Besides, he had other priorities, like finding Cortez! But first, he needed to get out of his wet clothes and have something to eat. He walked into the

---

[827] If you are worried about the effects of the VX on marine life in the lake, there is some literature to indicate that rain water dissolves some of the chemical bonds that make the agent so lethal to organic life.

restaurant and found it deserted, so he went through the staff doors and into the large kitchen.

The Scotsman searched through a bakery cupboard and found rustic loaves of wholemeal bread. He turned on one of the large steel BOSCH ovens, put one of the loaves on a baking tray to heat up and searched the dairy fridge. Finding a large wrapping of Vacherin Mont-d'Or AOP cheese[828], he turned his attention to the wine rack located well away from the ovens.   He normally preferred a certain single malt brand, but since he was in Switzerland, he opted for a bottle of Cave de La Cote Uvavins, Pinot Noir Suisse 2021[829]. Once the bread was warmed, he emptied some walnuts onto a plate alongside a handful of red grapes, which he washed under one of the taps. He put his simple meal on a room service tray and headed to his suite.

After hanging his drenched clothes onto the heated racks in the bathroom, Stewart wore the towelling robe, sat in the balcony window and consumed his simple meal. The cooler air had started a violent lightning storm, making the perfect backdrop to his dinner. All attempts to use the hotel phone and his own mobile failed. He received a recorded message telling him all lines were reserved for the emergency response and that he should head to the nearest shelter immediately. The hotel Wi-Fi and TV repeated the same message. Stewart listened as he cleaned and oiled the Korth. The weapon had proved itself today and deserved some TLC.

After completing his nighttime ablutions, the Scotsman lay on his bed. Tomorrow, he would find some way to contact the Mossad director, Mark Katz, to get more .357 Maximum rounds, some more appropriate clothing and work out where

---

[828] The fattier quality of late-season milk is perfect for making one of Switzerland's most beloved cheeses.
[829] A good year.

he would discover Cortez. With those thoughts running through his mind, he drifted to sleep.

After reliving his rooftop encounter with the murderous SNITCH unit, his dream abruptly changed. He found himself floating above a semi-covered courtyard resembling a medieval monastic cloister. The grey stone walls and high arched ceilings were decorated with ornate and colourful murals of fantastic creatures from medieval alchemy. Stewart could see black crows[830], toads[831], white swans[832], white eagles[833], a human skeleton[834] and a vivid green lion[835] eating the sun. Interspersed with these animals was a strange swirling black pattern of connecting spikes[836], which Stewart was unfamiliar with but he suspected must also be related to the precursor to modern chemistry.

The grey sandstone slabs on the floor were decorated with alternating images of the four elemental symbols of earth, fire, air and water. Through the open central balustrade of the cloister, Stewart could see that each of the four corners of the courtyard had specific features: a fountain (representing water), a window (representing air), a garden (representing earth) and a sacred flame (representing fire),

---

[830] Representing the blackening phase.

[831] Representing "prime matter" - the first phase of the process.

[832] Representing the interaction of the etheric energies (the swan) with the physical realm (water).

[833] Representing the victory of light over darkness and hence the soul's rebirth.

[834] Representing the empty shell of mortal existence.

[835] Representing the conquest of the spiritual over the material.

[836] Representing the Massa Confusa - the animating soul of matter.

extending the alchemical symbolism that had so far filled the entire dream.

Stewart was reflecting on the folly of consuming Vacherin Mont-d'Or AOP so soon before sleeping when he unexpectedly found himself seated on the stone rim of the fountain in the southwest corner of the quadrangle. The imagery of the dream was extraordinarily vivid. He felt the cold of the sandstone where he was seated and the sound of the water cascading from the centrepiece in the form of a rose wrapped around a cross. He could also smell a strong aroma of rose incense wafting from the sacred flame in the opposite corner of the cloister. He was admiring the skilful carving of twelve figures[837] set into the sides of the fountain when he noticed, with a start, that he was not alone.

Someone was sitting next to him. A veiled figure covered head to foot with a light-coloured gauze. The air around this figure was permeated with a highly distinctive scent that Stewart recognised as the most iconic of French Perfumes,[838] with its top notes of lemon and bergamot, middle notes of jasmine and may rose, and base notes of iris, incense, vanilla, and tonka bean. Only one person he knew would use such a fragrance to identify themselves and place themselves in an environment rich with esoteric symbolism.

"Madeleine?"

The air was filled with a gentle laugh.

---

[837] Representing the twelve sages who were said to have founded the Rosicrucian Order with the mythical Christian Rosenkreuz in 1313.

[838] Guerlain Shalimar - created in 1921 by Jacques Guerlain for the 1925 Paris Exhibition.

"Forgive me, Tavish, for interrupting your most interesting dream like this, but I did not know any other way to reach you."

"Not a problem. I am just delighted to know you are still alive. I heard from Léon that you were badly burnt."

"It is complex. But, I give thanks that I remain in my physical incarnation despite its challenges. My appearance has changed, and these changes challenge my feminine vanity. But it is good for the ego to surrender vanity, is it not?" her voice was clear, and she spoke fluent English with the slightest French inflexion.

"But why such an elaborate setting for the dream?" Stewart gestured to his surroundings.

"Oh, this is a most accurate projection of my surroundings, Tavish. Léon brought me from the Clinique[839] to this sanatorium close to Saint-Dalmas-le-Selvage, in the hills near the French-Italian border. The fraternity here specialises in treating esoteric disorders."

Tavish felt concerned. "Léon only mentioned serious burns and Clinique du Dr Ster has an excellent reputation for burn treatments, why the move?"

Madeleine made an intake of breath sound unique to the French, indicating a problem that is often difficult to explain.

"As I said, my condition is complex. My spirit and soul had been violently separated from my physical body. Such a separation is final, at least it should be. It required a tremendous magical intervention to bring me back. One that cost the adept who made it his mortal and immortal existence. Even after returning to my physical body, my astral

---

[839] Clinique du Dr Ster in Lamalou-les-Bains.

and physical forms required considerable interventions to become stable."

"But you are improving, I hope?"

"Different, would be a more accurate description. But I owe a debt for the intervention that brought me back. One which I must repay, and, Tavish, you have a significant part to play. One that will challenge your natural and moral instincts. But I need you to trust me. I would not demand this unless it was essential for the survival of our reality."

Stewart grimaced, wondering what would be demanded of him and if his conscience would permit him to assist the French Adept with whatever mission she felt compelled to complete, even if it put his friends at risk.

"Go on."

"Ms Curren has become possessed by Ad-Dajjal once more."

"How is that possible? Ad-Dajjal is dead!" demanded Stewart as he recalled cutting the astral connection from Curren's body to Ad-Dajjal in the Citadel of the Djinn only a few weeks previously. An act which he had assumed would consign Ad-Dajjal to the hellish torments she so deserved.

"Ad-Dajjal's immortal essence did not pass over the Chinvat Bridge[840] and was held by a magickal device in the physical realm. A preternatural version of her body is back in the material realm, but even with my gifts, I do not know why she has been permitted to return.

The inhibiting drug administered by Cardinal Regio rendered Curren vulnerable to even the mildest psychic influence. As you know, Ad-Dajjal's powers in this respect are extraordinary."

---

[840] The Chinvat Bridge, or Bridge of Souls, separates the world of the living from the world of the dead.

"What can be done?" asked Stewart.

"Curren must be brought to the sanitorium for healing so the fraternity's skills can restore her psychic defences. Otherwise, her physical form will remain like a puppet, open to any high adept's will."

Stewart's mind raced and was immediately filled with images of the drugged forms of Venchencho and Kwon. The prospect of his friend Curren's body being misused was terrible to contemplate, but the potential of someone misusing the Pope's influence could be catastrophic for billions of devout Catholics. Never mind the possibility of a Pope performing some twisted esoteric ceremony.

"There are others?" Mathers could sense the Scotsman's emotions.

"Venchencho and his assistant, Kwon." answered Stewart.

Mathers took a sharp breath and continued, saying, "Both play essential roles in the coming events. Their restoration is even more critical than that of your friend Curren. They must be transported to the sanitorium so we can heal them. Their treatment is even more urgent than Curren."

Stewart thought for a moment. Once things returned to normal in Geneva, he would have to make some calls. "I can get some of my friends to bring them to you. I will rescue Curren so she can get treatment."

"Sadly, that is one of your challenges, Tavish. You must leave Cynthia and Curren to their fate at Wewelsburg Castle."

"Cynthia is with Ad-Dajjal, I mean Curren, in the Wolfsangel lair?!" Tavish was horrified and then became suspicious, "Why on earth didn't you tell me this, Madeleine?"

"Because you have a far more important goal that must take priority over all else."

"What could be more important than rescuing my friends?"

"Having recently experienced the effects of the St Petersburg Qliphothic wheel, Cortez will do anything to continue his experiments with these infernal devices."

Stewart was sceptical. "Is it really that addictive? He has assumed the power he craved over Europe and the States, so he may now have other priorities."

"Don't forget, up until recently, I was this monster's physical form. Have no doubts, Tavish. He will now do anything to resume contact with what he thinks are higher powers. He has already relocated to Ksiaz Castle in Poland and moved thousands of people to nearby work camps to begin clearing the tunnels under the Owl Mountains."

Stewart exclaimed, "Madeleine, I know Wolfsangel better than anyone. I am the only viable option to storm Wewelsburg and free Cynthia and Curren."

Mathers assumed a serious tone. "Certainly, you could succeed. But fortunately for all of us, you are not the only viable option, Sir Stewart. Trust me, there are others who are better suited for this task. However, no one else has a chance of stopping Cortez except you."

Stewart was sceptical, not through vanity, but from decades of experience. But he also had enough experience with Mathers to know she had access to sources of information that extended well beyond the material world. In the end, he decided he would focus on Cortez.

"Very well."

Stewart made a mental note to himself to ask Katz and Twop for any plans that existed for Ksiaz and its underground complex. "How long will that clearance work take? Do you have any idea?"

"Based on the number of people he is relocating to work there, it will only be a matter of days." Mathers paused and shivered, saying, "God, Tavish, there are some horrors left in those facilities under Owl Mountain. You will need to be very careful. This was where the most desperate evil was explored in the war's final days. Along with "Die Glocke", the "Überprüfung der Sogenannten Geheimwissenschaften" researchers explored the most dangerous applications of the dark arts."

"I don't think I have heard of this group before". said Stewart, "A nasty bunch, I assume?"

"Understatement. Himmler tasked the "Examination of the Secret Sciences" division to explore any occult options that could stop the advancing Soviet army. They took their work to extremes. Sadly, I will be needed here to help restore Venchencho, Kwon and Curren, so Thomas O'Neill will be invaluable to you in transversing those horrors."

Stewart nodded. Yes, he thought, with Thomas to deal with any supernatural threats, the Scotsman could focus on the primary goals, Cortez and the Bell. Somehow, he would have to find O'Neill and bring him along. He asked,

"This Qliphothic wheel, how will I recognise it?"

"Imagine a gigantic Tibetan prayer wheel, fifteen feet high and nine feet wide, with two revolving cylinders, one inside the other. The contraption will require a lot of electrical power, so cabling should be another clue."

"And how do I destroy it?"

Mathers laughed. "Always the soldier. Extreme heat will fracture the amber mineral that is used to form the two cylinders."

Stewart thought again about Sinclair and Curren. "And you are sure this should be my priority?"

K.R.M. Morgan

Mathers became deadly serious. "Tavish if Cortez succeeds in getting "Die Glocke" running at full power, he will destroy all of creation!"

SOMETHING WICKED THIS WAY COMES

"Sometimes a hero can be found in the most unexpected of places." - Christopher Healy

The Grand Hall
Wewelsburg Castle,
Burgwall 19, 33142 Büren,
North Rhine-Westphalia, Germany

10:30 HRS (GMT+2) 17th September, present-day

A pile of oak logs burnt ferociously in the large fireplace built into the rough brick walls, forming a vast space one hundred feet long, forty feet wide and twenty feet high. Although, in absolute terms, it was not cold, the dramatic change from days of firestorms to cool rain had made the castle's residents demand the roaring fire be lit.

The wooden timbers that formed the ceiling above the flagstone floors were covered with intricately carved figures of gods and goddesses from the Nordic and Germanic traditions. The mild, earthy scent from the burning seasoned oak mixed with those of the vast buffet laid out on side tables, consisting of hearty loaves of bread, rolls decorated with butter, sweet jams and local honey, thinly sliced meats, smoked cheeses and large slices of liver sausage. Beside these Germanic-themed foods were carafes of Gollner Coffee on heated plates, jugs of Naturfett[841] milk and pressurised metal kegs of Paulaner Hefe-Weizen wheat beer standing on top of large ice blocks. Continuing the medieval decor of the hall, there were stacks of pewter plates and tankards beside

---

[841] Whole cream milk 3.8%-4.2% fat.

the food table and an assortment of cutlery, which included a dagger-like steel knife and a wicked-looking bone spike[842].

Brightly coloured tapestries and banners hung from the walls, showing the Wolfsangel symbol alongside scenes from Wagner's opera Parsifal and nineteenth-century romanticised portrayals of victorious Teutonic knights in battle[843].

Although superficially, the interior of this space appeared to be a medieval great hall, an expert in the period would notice that everything in sight was a reconstruction from the middle of the 20th century. In many ways, this reconstruction was an idealised view of the past, like a movie set.

A long wooden table in the centre of the room was lit by rows of large candles, which supplemented the numerous flood lights cleverly concealed in the ceiling and walls. A group of twelve men and women, all dressed in their distinctive black Hugo Boss uniforms and smart tech augmentation, were gathered around the table, eating, drinking and talking. Some were seated, while others milled around the breakfast buffet. Sitting at the head of this group was Deputy Chairman Hartman. To his left was his brother Corrado, who had been sent by Cortez, ostensibly to help his brother, but in reality, everyone knew it was to get him away from the Chairman, who had become increasingly intolerant of idleness and cowardice. Two traits which Corrado epitomised.

Seated to the right of Deputy Chairman Hartman was an attractive woman dressed in a low-cut black Dirndl dress, so beloved by Oktoberfest organisers and makers of low-budget vampire movies. The gold trim around the woman's

---

[842] Predating the fork as an eating utensil.
[843] The battle of Chojnice (1454), where the Teutonic knights defeated the Polish armies at the beginning of the Thirteen Years War.

décolleté was adorned with embroidered striking cobras, and a distinctive Isfet initiate's gold inverted pentagram ring was visible on her right ring finger. She dealt cards from a well-used deck of Rider Waite[844] Tarot cards onto the table before her. The small creases around her blue eyes showed increasing concern as she dealt ominous card after ominous card into a classic seven-card horseshoe tarot spread.

Hartman raised his eyebrows to enquire on the nature of the reading.

"I cannot deny the reading is bad, my Lord."

Hartman tried to make light of the woman's evident concern.

"For god's sake, woman! Stop looking so glum. We deal in death, extortion, blackmail and devilry. What did you expect the cards to show? If they are that bad, reshuffle them. That's what I always do when I get a bad reading."

The Dark Knights gathered around the table laughed, but their hilarity was forced. Each had direct experience working alongside Isfet adepts and their dark activities. They knew that when an Isfet adept consulted the fates, they were seldom wrong.

"As you wish, my Lord."

The woman gathered the cards, handed them to Hartman to blow on and reshuffle, and then redealt the horseshoe spread. The cards were no better. The Ten of Swords, Death, The Tower, The Devil, Knight of Swords and the Five of Cups were placed before them on the table beside dirty pewter

---

[844] Created by A. E. Waite and illustrated by Pamela Smith, who were both initiates within the Golden Dawn magical order. Published by Rider in 1909, the deck is among the most well-known within the Western Esoteric Tradition.

plates and empty mugs. A reading foretelling suffering, radical and violent change, betrayal, brutality and loss.

Hartman looked expectantly at the seer.

"Come on, we are all Dark Knights here. If we are all going to Valhalla, tell us. We can have another beer and toast the Devil!"

There was another nervous laugh from the men and women gathered around the table. But their bravado was a veneer, hiding a rising tide of disquiet. The woman hurriedly gathered up the cards from the table.

"Do not make light of this, my Lords," she looked around the table and continued, saying,

"The cards speak of treachery, suffering and death."

After over twenty years of living alongside his grandfather, Hartman knew enough to realise he was being warned of some surprise attack from within. However, the cards were notorious for being vague on critical issues, such as specific identities, times or locations of an event.

Before the Deputy Chairman could announce his response, Corrado vomited noisily into his breakfast plate. Wiping the sick from his mouth with the black sleeve of his uniform, he rose from his chair, uttering,

"I... I must go."

Such cowardice in response to a negative tarot reading disgusted and dismayed everyone around the table. The Isfet seer sighed and raised her eyes as the wide-eyed and pasty-looking Corrado hurried from breakfast into the grand entrance, calling attendants for a staff car to come to the front of the castle and wait while he rushed to the upper floors to pack. Hartman gestured to the seer to leave, and in response, she gathered her cards from the table and quietly left the room.

Outside, a massive storm was raging. The rain beat against the limestone brickwork of the Renaissance-styled building, which had been constructed to resemble a castle from some angles and a country residence from others. Wewelsburg castle was dominated by three round towers, each connected by massive walls that formed a triangle when viewed from above. Two of the three tall towers terminated in medieval-looking pointed turrets, while the third tower had a flat roof with protective battlements and a small entrance doorway leading down to the lower levels.

Thunder roared, and lightning arced across the dark sky. Occasionally, the lightning forked down and slammed into the taller trees in the forest surrounding the castle. Three hundred yards above, an almost invisible figure floated down from the sky under a black Hi-5 Army parachute[845] which had launched from Schöne Aussicht, an elevated viewpoint one mile north of the castle, next to Paderborn-Lippstadt Airport[846] where the mysterious figure had only recently arrived by helicopter.

Gliding down, this figure pulled a black UnlocX gel ball gun[847] from his leg holster and fired a barrage of black gel pellets towards the CCTV camera monitoring the tower. With the camera covered in black gel, this mysterious figure completed a perfect standing landing on the exposed open area atop the larger of the three towers.   Pulling the harness from his chest, he released the canopy, allowing it to drift

---

[845] Hi-5 Army Ram Air Parachute made of zero-porosity nylon (patented by Brian Germain), it does not retain water or become waterlogged and heavier.
846 Airport code : PAD.
[847] UnlocX gel ball blaster gun.

away from the tower. His mission would be completed long before it was discovered.

Walking over to the blacked-out CCTV camera above the entrance doorway, he pulled a multi-tool[848] from his belt and used its cable cutter to slice the digital feed cable. He released his Amabilis backpack[849] after throwing the camera over the tower's edge. After removing a battery-powered laser, he attached it to the exposed CCTV digital cable. Within seconds, the laser began to strobe a powerful one-kilo-Hertz frequency stream of charged ions[850] into the dark clouds above. Using a Lishi-style lockpick[851], the black-suited man opened the access door from the tower and instantly closed it behind him. Seconds later, violent lightning bolts repeatedly struck the tower's security feed and the castle's electrical systems.

Inside the tower, the mysterious intruder found himself standing at the top of a large stone spiral staircase that ran around the inner circumference of the building, with LED lighting embedded into every second step. Water cascaded from the man's non-reflective jet-black zero-porosity fire-resistant Kevlar black jumpsuit and pooled around his black Shadow Amphibian combat boots.

He rotated the unidirectional timing bezel on his Luminox[852] watch to mark the start of his incursion into the Wolfsangel stronghold. As a matter of protocol, he did a weapons quick.

---

[848] Gerber Suspension Multi-Tool.
[849] Amabilis Urban Responder Rucksack with military-grade waterproof tarpaulin and ceramic armour-plating.
[850] To understand why the laser directs the lightning strikes to a single point see - Houard, A., Walch, P., Produit, T. et al. Laser-guided lightning. Nat. Photon. 17, 231–235 (2023).
[851] Dangerfield Lishi-Style Lock Pick + Decoder for 5 + 6 Pin Yale.
[852] Luminox military carbon.

He drew a black polymer FNP pistol[853] fitted with a long Silencerco suppressor[854] from a MOLLE[855] chest holster. He checked the action and the feed on the fifteen-round[856] magazine. Satisfied, he returned the pistol to its holster and drew a black fixed-blade combat knife[857] from his ankle. The six-inch double-edged blade[858] terminated in a spear point and was heavily serrated on its upper edge. The pistol grip handle included a finger hole to guarantee the blade did not slip or leave the hand during vigorous use.

At that moment, the lights went out throughout the castle, as the electrical grid was overloaded by a ten-gigawatt (GW) surge caused by the lightning strikes. The intruder activated a low-intensity red torch integrated into his left glove in response to this darkness. Using this illumination, he began progressing down the narrow stairway, pausing every three steps to listen. The small stairway was suddenly filled with footsteps and a voice that was misinterpreting the source of the illumination on the upper stairs.

"Ah, thank God. An emergency light!"

In response to the noise, the mysterious intruder flattened himself against the curve of the inner wall of the stairway until he saw Corrado in his Black Knight uniform approaching

---

[853] The FNP™-45 Tactical pistol was developed for the U.S. Joint Combat Pistol Program.

[854] The Silencerco Osprey 45 Suppressor.

[855] Modular Lightweight Load-carrying Equipment.

[856] Loaded with Federal Hydrashok Deep 230gr +P .45 rounds. This modified hollow point projectile has superior penetration and wound cavity expansion properties.

[857] A variant of the IDF YAMAM Counterterrorism "Ari B'Lilah" Predator by US knife master Jay Fisher.

[858] CPMS35VN Martensitic Powder Metal Technology High Vanadium-Niobium Stainless Tool Steel, Hardened and Tempered to Rockwell C59.

a doorway that was set into the internal brickwork. After Corrado had unlocked the door and entered the room, the intruder followed, closing the door behind him. Moments later, the mysterious intruder emerged from the room dressed in Corrado's Black Knight uniform with the peaked cap pulled down over his face.

One hundred and sixty feet below the mysterious intruder, Hartman and the assembled Black Knights were reacting to the power outage in the great hall. The few candles serving as decorative additions to the ambience had become the sole illumination source. However, this change was not the primary focus of the Black Knights. Joining his Wolf Brothers, the Deputy Chairman ripped off his iKill Pro smartech and cast it in disgust onto a growing pile of similar dead devices in the centre of the table.

Everyone in the assembled group was wondering the same thing. Could this be the start of the attack predicted in the recent tarot reading? A brooding silence filled the room. Everyone knew something had to be done to address the threat, but the question was, what? Hartman ran through his options. He refused to contemplate calling his grandfather, who would scold his weakness at needing advice on reacting to some printed cardboard cards and a power loss during an electrical storm in a three-hundred-year-old building.

Suddenly, it came to Hartman.

"The prisoners! If anyone is planning an attack on us, they will know about it. Some strategically applied torture will make them tell us everything!"

He rose from his high-backed wooden chair, picked up one of the dozen wax candles and strode from the hall, closely followed by five of the Black Knights who had finished breakfast and wanted to see some gratuitous bloodletting. Even among the psychopathic sadists of Wolfsangel, Hartman was renowned for the savage treatment of his interrogation subjects. The four remaining Black Knights continued eating by candlelight. With growing hilarity, they started speculating how many prisoners would die before they learnt the full details of the plot.

The betting had reached two hundred Cortez Crypto-Marks that there would be two deaths and a dismembering when a Black Knight entered the hall and walked over to the drinks table. The stranger picked a Magnum of Bollinger[859] and a handful of plastic flute glasses and placed them on a wooden tray. The four Black Knights initially ignored this newcomer, assuming he was fetching refreshments for one of Hartman's infamous extended torture sessions. Only when one of the four Black Knights went to pour himself another coffee did he notice the non-standard boots worn by the stranger and then the distinctive sick stain on the newcomer's sleeve.

"Hey! That's Corrado's jacket!"

The four Black Knights in the candle-lit great hall were hand-picked from the world's elite special forces units, but after months of relying on the AI assistance integrated into their iKill-Pro systems, they had lost the skills that once defined them. The harsh difference between professional soldiers and professional assassins was highlighted in the outcome of the ensuing firefight. In the three and a half seconds of their encounter, they were totally outclassed by the stranger who wore Corrado's uniform. In fairness, two of the four Black Knights had drawn their Glocks. But long before they could be aimed, a wicked-looking black Silencerco suppressor emerged from under the wooden drinks tray and issued a

---

[859] Bollinger Special Cuvée Brut.

series of gentle popping sounds, similar to a Bollinger cork being released, all without the slightest disturbance to the bottle or glasses balanced on the tray. When the stranger walked from the Great Hall, four bodies lay in grotesque postures on the flagstone floor - the lifeblood oozing in growing crimson patches over the black worsted wool of the black Hugo Boss uniforms.

Fifty feet beneath the carnage in the Great Hall, six people were crammed into a stone chamber, twenty feet long, ten feet wide and ten feet high. This room had a single door constructed of brushed stainless steel with a small metal grille-protected fish eye lens inserted at eye level. A single 100-watt bulb shone from within an armoured fitting in the centre of the ceiling. Beside this bulb was a cluster of spotlights on long flexible metal arms that could be positioned into precise orientations towards a single surgical chair bolted to the floor in the centre of the room. The chair covering was in blue washable plastic, and the arms and legs were fitted with solid nylon fabric restraints. Beside the chair was a stainless-steel bench containing various implements, including a rubber hose, water jug, linen towels, surgical scalpels, cordless drills, saws, multi-coloured syringes, serum bottles and glass acid vials. The stone floor of the room included channels that led to a central drain directly in front of the surgical chair. This drain issued a strong odour of beach, which was a welcome masking for the metal waste bucket in the far corner of the room.

Seated equidistantly on the stone floor around the edges of the room were four men: former British Prime Minister Sir Reginald Twiffers, former Foreign Secretary Sir Jonathan Premble, former Home Secretary Lord Jeremey "Jezza" Kenner and former Director of The Security Service (MI5),

Clive "Bazzo" Basildon. Opposite these four men sat two women: Cynthia Sinclair, former Director of the British Secret Intelligence Service (MI6) and lawyer Helen Curren, KC. These six had been separated from the larger group of VIP prisoners held in the massive camp outside the castle. Under Cortez's order, they had been transported from the regional emergency shelters, where they had all been detained during the revolution. Cortez's intention was to film their torture on pay-per-view streaming services as entertainment for his Wolfsangel and Isfet supporters. Sinclair and Curren were the only non-VIPs, their presence in the torture cell was an initiative from Hartman in response to the fiasco at the UN Court trial. After their capture by the SNITCH units, they were sedated and brought directly to the castle for special treatment.

Each of these six people was restrained by black polymer cuffs on their wrists and ankles, while a polymer neck restraint with a remotely triggered magnetic wall release held them in their seated position. The three former British senior ministers and MI5 Director had lost considerable weight over the past few days, as they had been among the least successful in fighting for the scraps of food occasionally thrown by the guards into the Pindar secret underground bunker.

Reginald Twiffers and Johnathan Premble were addressing Sinclair, who was seated directly opposite them. The two men encouraged her to use her undoubted skills to escape and take them with her. Clive Basildon sat silently beside them. He had enough experience to know it would take a large commando team to escape. One look at the torture devices set up in the room showed how this would all end.

Twiffers spoke in his most friendly tone. He almost sounded like a human being,

"Cynthia, dear gal. We have had our differences, but we must work together to overthrow this wicked revolution and restore the legitimate rule of law in the United Kingdom."

Premble tried to support the point. "Yes, my dear, after all, you are a British citizen and owe us your loyalty. Get us out and return us to our rightful societal positions, and we will be very appreciative."

Kenner added. "You know how these Cortez fellas are all corrupt, ruthless thugs. Get the three of us out of here, and we could even consider restoring your title!"

The three men smiled condescendingly, thinking that the lure of restoring Sinclair's title would make her comply. After all, the promise of a title had made them do pretty much anything during their rat-eat-rat rise through the corrupt UK honours system.

Sinclair had ignored the constant pestering from the three idiots ever since they had all been chained into their places in the small cell. She had, instead, focused on looking after Curren, who had returned to her vegetative state the moment they had been taken from the UN courtroom. Ensuring the lawyer ate and kept herself reasonably clean had fully occupied the former SIS head. But the long hours of their pestering were finally getting to her. The final straw was when the single light in the cell went out.

Plunged into total darkness, she had nothing else to distract her, so she replied,

"I am Jamaican, not British, you idiots! It was you, Twiffers, who revoked my British Passport on national television while pronouncing that I was a traitor! Which was all the more ironic since you betrayed the nation for promises of power and money. What is worse, you forced the Jamaican Government to imprison my parents and seize their property and business. To top it all, you sent me for execution in violation of every statute in your precious criminal justice system. You expect me to help you just because you three idiots have ended up in the same torture cell?" Sinclair shook her head in disbelief, even though she knew no one could see the gesture.

On the opposite side of the cell, Twiffers winced at the accurate summary, but decades in the toxic world of British politics had taught him that anything can be spun to one's advantage. You just needed to repeat the lies with conviction to make people wonder if the problem was with them and not the utterly outrageous behaviour you had been caught performing.

"Just a series of unfortunate misunderstandings, my dear girl. Minor details that can be quickly sorted. We can see now that you are a vital asset to our nation!"

The former Prime Minister's attempt at persuasion was cut short by the entrance of six figures, all dressed in the sinister dark uniforms of the Wolfsangel Black Knights. They brought candles, which provided an eerie flickering light to the cell. Making the torture chair and its associated equipment look even more terrifying.

Deputy Chairman Hartman gestured towards Sinclair, seated on the floor beside the vacant-looking Curren.

"Put her in the chair."

Sinclair knew better than to try to resist the five-to-one odds. Instead, she tried to charm the young man in charge.

"No need for all these men watching, honey. Spending time alone with you would be sweet."

She winked mischievously as she swayed seductively to the chair and sat in it, pulling the black skirt she had worn for her court appearance high over her gym-honed thighs and looking hungrily towards Hartman. The five other men laughed nervously as they looked at Hartman, judging his reaction. The oldest among them thought he detected interest in Hartman's eyes, so he joked, saying,

"How about that? There sure is nothing quite like some Brown Sugar. We could all have some!"

Sinclair licked her lips and smiled as though the idea appealed. In reality, she was assessing how to take down the six men as quickly as possible and with the least risk to herself. Hartman dismissed the mood by drawing his Glock and pointing it towards Sinclair.

"Are you all crazy? This is the bitch that killed two of our best operatives without any weapons."

Sinclair raised her eyebrow provocatively and stroked her upper leg. "One of them died with his head between these thighs..."

"Restrain her now!" Hartman demanded. He was terrified of Sinclair and, unlike the other men, was not falling for her tricks. The five men quickly worked at securing Sinclair's leg, arm, and neck restraints. For her part, she kept up the pretence of sexual interest in the Black Knights by gasping breathlessly,

"I would prefer to tie you up and show you the time of your life."

In reality, she had made sure that her body tensed as the men tied her so the restraints were not completely tight. Loose bonds were more straightforward to escape from if and when the opportunity arose. She was now left waiting for these guys to make a mistake. They always did when they got distracted, and Sinclair knew how to distract.

"She is a traitor! Just before you came in, she was trying to persuade us to help her escape!" Twiffers proclaimed loudly, hoping to curry favour with his captors. Maybe there would be some leadership role he could still exploit.

"Shut them up," Hartman instructed, gesturing towards the four men. One of the Black Knights walked over and systematically kicked each of the seated men in their stomachs, causing whimpers to emerge from all four.

Now Sinclair was securely bound, Hartman became more confident. He strode over to the bench that contained the torture implements.

"That was quite a performance in the UN court. But these are very different surroundings."

He delivered a violent, unexpected backhanded strike with his left hand across Sinclair's right cheek, bending her head backwards. She slowly brought her head back around and licked the blood from the side of her mouth.

"Not so amazing now, are you?" Sneered Hartman as he picked up the scalpel from the bench and started to run the side of the blade along Sinclair's right cheek, which was already beginning to discolour from the recent blow.

"Now we will get some answers. Let's start with an easy one. How did you make the European SNITCHes turn against us?"

"What?" asked Sinclair, who genuinely did not know anything about it.

"I ask the questions." stated Hartman as he stabbed the blade of the scalpel into Sinclair's arm, "Next time, it will be your face, then your eyes. So, think carefully before your next lie."

The cell door opened, and another Black Knight entered carrying a large Champagne bottle and glasses. The man's cap obscured his face in the gloom of the candlelight. Hartman turned and smiled as the newcomer popped the bottle, pouring the contents into the flutes and passing them around the six men. Hartman took his glass and turned to the others.

"Excellent idea. Here's to the painful death of all enemies!" All six men downed their glasses. Hartman frowned as he noticed something. He turned to the newcomer, who had taken a half-inch thick, four-inch-long cigar from his jacket pocket.

"You are not drinking!"

The stranger lit his cigar from a nightclub matchbook. The match flame illuminated the man's smiling hawk-like face and a collection of small grease-proof 1940s Bayer wrappers around the man's combat boots.

Hartman started in shock.

"Abdul Issuin! Your presence here proves you are past it. You will never overpower a group of five of the world's most dangerous agents."

Sinclair looked at Hartman in disbelief. She could not believe he was even more stupid than he looked. She was fully aware of Abdul Issuin's reputation. Based on the grin on Hartman's face, he had no idea who he was facing six feet in front of him.

At that moment, the five Black Knights collapsed to the tiled floor. Thick white foam bubbled from their contorted mouths.

The hawk-faced assassin looked around at the bodies. "They don't look very dangerous."

Hartman dashed to the cell door and pulled it open, shouting, "Guards, guards...!"

There was no response, just a mass of dead Wolfsangel operatives filling the corridor.

Hartman's mouth opened to form a scream of terror but never completed the action. The hawk-faced man's Silencerco popped just once. In response, the Deputy Chairman's skull opened like a flower in bloom as the 230-grain Hydrashock Deep round expanded, spitting a mass of grey and red into a Rorschach pattern on the corridor wall.

As Hartman's body fell to the floor, Abdul Issuin used his "Ari B'Lilah[860]" Predator knife to cut Curren free from her restraints and walked her slowly to the cell door. Before leaving, the hawk-faced assassin stopped and walked over to where Sinclair was strapped into the torture chair. For a tense moment, Sinclair thought her time had come. But, then, the assassin struck the blade of the Predator knife into the chair fabric so Sinclair could free herself, saying,

"Professional courtesy," before walking out with the vacant Curren.

---

[860] Literally translated as "lion by night".

HIDDEN TREASURE

*"Now, on this island, there was a great and wonderful empire
which ruled over the whole island and several others and
over parts of the continent and, furthermore, had subjected
the parts of Libya within the columns of Heracles as far as
Egypt, and of Europe as far as Tyrrhenia." - Plato*

*20 feet beneath Göbekli Tepe
Örencik, 63290,
Şanlıurfa, Turkey*

04:55 HRS (GMT + 3), 17th September, present-day

The cappuccino-coloured tip of Ezekiel's striped ginger tail
bounced down the broad steps in front of the three men as
they descended the stairway cut into the light grey limestone
bedrock. Three torch beams played over the plain stone
walls and the flat sand-covered floor that awaited them at
the bottom of the forty-foot-long stairs. O'Neill's torch
followed the progress of his adopted ginger feline as it
vanished down the passageway that led South from the
bottom of the steps.

The air felt delightfully cooler than the oppressive one
hundred and ten degrees Fahrenheit on the hill's surface. All
three men could not help taking deep breaths of what felt
like fresh mountain air after the stifling dry heat above. The
cooler temperature especially suited the giant girth of
Mohammed. He sighed, relishing the relief from the sauna he
had endured since leaving the blissful air conditioning in the
Land Cruiser. He propped his stick against the wall and
wiped his face and neck with a white cotton sweat towel. He
started to ring the excess moisture from the cloth onto the
dry, dusty earth covering the steps. O'Neill, who had stopped

alongside Mohammed, reached gently over to the giant's powerful right wrist, saying,

"Please, we are the first people here for eight thousand years. Let's try not to contaminate the scene for the archaeologists that come after us."

Mohammed reluctantly placed the soaking cloth in the front pocket of his robe as Thomas turned the flashlight back to the undecorated antechamber around them. The white beam revealed Yusuf preparing to relieve himself against one of the corridor walls at the bottom of the steps. Before O'Neill could say anything, a giant voice beside him boomed through the underground vault,

"Yusuf, do that up there," the huge man gestured upwards with his left hand, "The same goes for you, Berat." Mohammed said strictly but winked at his two sons as they walked back past him to the surface.

Trying to change the subject, Mohammed announced, "It doesn't smell stuffy," after taking another deep breath.

O'Neill grunted. He had been thinking the same. He had been on numerous digs where excavation sites were filled with scents, indicating everything from the presence of water, decomposition or recent animal activity. In this case, there was nothing, which meant they might be lucky and have an utterly unspoilt site. O'Neill's hopes were secretly rising that he could recover his lost reputation and reestablish his academic career with this discovery.

Turning towards the long, narrow corridor where Ezekiel had disappeared moments before, O'Neill removed a well-used red Victorinox monosling backpack[861] and withdrew a Black

---

[861] A red nylon Victorinox Altmont Original Dual-Compartment Monosling.

Diamond headlamp[862], a Suunto compass[863], a transparent mini-ruler[864] and an old red Olympus Tough[865] camera. The camera, compass and ruler were on lanyards which O'Neill put around his neck before he fitted the Black Diamond nylon straps from the lamp to his head, turned on its light and put the big RS Pro torch in his pack.

"Someone is well prepared," observed Mohammed, who, based on how he viewed the headlamp, clearly envied it as he struggled to coordinate a walking cane and torch.

O'Neill laughed. "Yeah. This time, I came prepared after the accusations of a lack of evidence from my last discovery[866]."

Mohammed chuckled as the pair proceeded down the South-heading corridor, which O'Neill had recorded with a photograph of his compass and the entrance. The beams from their torches played around walls filled with vividly painted images of snakes, scorpions, wolves, vultures and even a lion. Ezekiel was sitting in front of the lion, which was shown eating some freshly killed gazelle. As O'Neill approached, the cat issued a very plaintive meow.

"The Ginger Prince wants a share of the kill," Mohammed chuckled, adding, "I never realised ancient wall art was so colourful."

---

[862] A Black Diamond Icon headlamp. There were newer lighter models but the four AA batteries produced a good bright beam up to 90 yards and it was as tough as old boots, as O'Neill had proven on numerous underground excavations.
[863] SUUNTO MC-2 G mirror compass.
[864] To provide an indication of scale for any photographs.
[865] Olympus TG-7. It was only 12 megapixels but was enough for his needs, especially when it boasted being "freeze-proof, crush-proof, water-proof, and shock-proof" and uploads its images automatically to cloud storage when it detected Wi-Fi.
[866] The infamous discovery of the Citadel of the Djinn in Mongolia. See Bridge of Souls.

O'Neill knelt and pulled chicken pieces from his backpack, feeding them to Ezekiel, who took each piece with delight before scuffing the floor with his paw as if to cover up the remains of the gazelle depicted on the wall.

As the archaeologist used his Olympus to record the paintings, he turned to Mohammed. "Yes, many people do not realise that most ancient walls were painted brightly, and it is only environmental factors that fade the colours, but these have been well-preserved."

Mohammed suddenly turned, saying, "Wait, I would not mind taking some of my own. Berat has a phone with a good camera. I will be right back."

Mohammed returned up the steps as O'Neill systematically worked along the wall with his camera recording the ancient artwork. On the surface, the giant man found his two sons smoking, sitting on a carved statue of a boar with fierce tusks. Based on the distinctive odour and discoloured patch around the central pillar, Yusuf had recently relieved himself. Heavy rain beat a staccato rhythm on the large canopy above them.

Berat played a first-person shooter game called "Tartan Defender" on his large gold iPhone. In the game, numerous paramilitary operatives, led by a crazed terror mastermind, attacked a remote Scottish farm defended by a single army veteran.

"When you come to a convenient moment, I would not mind borrowing your phone to take some pictures," Mohammed asked.

Berat nodded, stopped his gameplay and handed the phone to his father, who thanked him and descended the steps painfully due to his injury. Back underground, O'Neill stood waiting at the end of the stone corridor lined with colourful frescos. Ezekiel had already moved on and started meowing at something in the darkness ahead. While he waited, O'Neill had turned his small black Moleskin notebook sideways to reveal a sketch of a circular walled enclosure with two megaliths standing in the centre of a double-ringed inner wall.

Mohammed came alongside and looked at the sketch, which was supposed to represent how the monoliths above them looked when first constructed, except in the drawing, there were statues of gods and supernatural beings that were either now missing or were figments of the artist's imagination.

"Who did you say sent you this?" the giant man asked.

O'Neill shrugged. "I don't know. It came wrapped in brown paper with a postmark from Grindelwald, Switzerland."

As Mohammed's torch tilted accidentally in his hand, it highlighted dark stains on the ceiling. Gesturing to the marks, he enquired, "Water leak?"

"No, more likely smoke stains from oil lamps they used while carving and painting. And before you ask, the dried corn on the floor were probably snacks. These were humans, just like you and me."

With that, they moved from the corridor into a larger space, around twenty feet square with a low ceiling, where Ezekiel had made so much noise. The walls in this room were decorated with images of massive fires and dead animals, birds and humans.

"Grim," commented Mohammed as he took in the fresco and then laughed as his eyes fell upon the first human image they had come across. It was a wall carving of a man with an enormous phallus.

"He looks like a happy camper," chuckled Mohammed as he took a picture of the statue.

O'Neill did not share the amusement. "Men posed with an erect phallus usually symbolise death, which would match these other scenes."

Thomas gestured at the other frescos before continuing. "It is speculated that there would have been a massive loss of life at the end of the last ice age, which is why these underground spaces were constructed. There would have been too many bodies to bury properly, so death cult temples were created."

The archaeologist finally turned his attention to the figure that was causing such amusement to Mohammed and began photographing it.

"Definitely a death cult," he proclaimed solemnly.

"How so?"

O'Neill adopted a relatively superior tone that he used when lecturing students. Forgetting who he was talking to, "When a man dies, he has an erection."

Mohommed narrowed his eyes as he looked at the statue. "Yes. Especially when they are holding it with both hands..."

There was a long silence as Thomas regarded the statue and the grinning Mohammed, before saying,

"Yes, so he is..." then O'Neill continued, "These are not mentioned in my notebook."

An incessant meowing prompted both men to follow Ezekiel through a doorway into another small chamber. This area was filled with reliefs carved into the grey bedrock in the shape of eleven mushroom-shaped statues. O'Neill started taking pictures of these strange structures as he proclaimed, "They must have survived on mushrooms and marked their thanks by these carvings.

Mohammed laughed louder than before. "You have spent too long in your seminary. Look closer at the heads of your mushrooms, my dear Thomas."

O'Neill flushed with embarrassment. On closer examination, he realised they were graphic representations of the male sex organ.

"Ah.... well, then this must have been a fertility cult. After the mass deaths at the end of the Ice Age, they would need to, um, increase the population."

Mohammed nodded. "That would match the location's name. In Turkish, Gobi Tepi means Belly Mountain."

Before they could finish their speculation, they heard a terrible howl followed by an explosive rasping hiss from the next chamber.

"Ezekiel!" exclaimed O'Neill as he hurried through the narrow doorway to the next chamber, fearing the brave cat had been injured.

Mohammed dropped his stick and staggered close behind, a black Wilson Combat Tactical[867] pistol instantly coming from inside his robe and appearing in his right hand.

The giant of a man pulled up short once he was inside the next chamber, exclaiming,

"Allahu Akbar!" as his torch beam illuminated the space he had entered.

In the centre of a low ceilinged twenty-foot square room was a highly realistic carving of the same hideous monster portrayed in flat relief on the large stone slab that had sealed this underground complex on the surface. The statue was

---

[867] The Wilson Combat 92G Brigadier Tactical is a specialised variant of the venerable Beretta 92 service pistol made by Wilson in the USA.

incredibly detailed and painted in vivid colours, highlighting the pale white corpse-like flesh on the seven necks, vicious-looking fang-filled mouths and snake-like scales on the main body. Even the delicate wings on the body were shown in exquisite detail. Ezekiel was standing arched and hissing immediately in front of the monster, while O'Neill was lying flat on his face close by after tripping over one of numerous "roots" carved into the room's floor representing the tendrils extending from the chimera.

"A strange and vivid imagination these people had," exclaimed Mohammed as he helped O'Neill to his feet with an ease that told of immense physical strength. Thomas dusted himself off. He was more concerned about checking possible damage to his camera than the road rash he had acquired on his hands.

"Yeah. The stuff of nightmares, alright," Thomas admitted as he took pictures of the statue and tried to calm Ezekiel.

"What does your book say about this?" Mohammed asked, putting away his black steel Wilson pistol.

O'Neill turned some pages. "There is some Assyrian text that, if authentic, claims this was a semi-physical, seven-headed, snake with fluttering wings that terrorised ancient Sumer, called the MUŠ.ŠÀ.TÙR. It had a deadly venom and was almost impossible to stop since it could regenerate itself. Its blood was similar to the acid venom from its fangs. It says it was only possible to kill this creature with a single, very sacred weapon called the UG-ZI-ZU."

"Ugzuuzi?" Mohammed frowned, before asking, "Does it say what this weapon looked like?"

O'Neill shook his head as both men took a moment to walk around the statue, taking care not to trip over its long roots. Around the statue's rear was an axe, its handle protruding from the base of the monster's body.

"I guess that must be one of those Ugzuuzi," commented Mohammed, admiring the finely carved bone handle on the axe that was covered in some strange script.

O'Neill continued to read the cuneiform in his notebook, struggling with some of the translation before explaining, "It says the axe, actually an adze[868] is made from," O'Neill paused, "Sorry, I don't recognise the word. It looks like "a fallen fire[869]". Whatever it is made of, it is the only way to kill the creature[870] and stop it from "becoming another"."

"Become another? What does that mean?" asked Mohammed.

O'Neill scratched his head. "I am not sure." His scratching caused his headlamp to shudder, and Ezekiel issued a hiss towards the moving shadows. The final arc of the moving headlamp highlighted a strange shape on the southern-facing wall of the chamber. Both men approached and discovered a large doorway that had been sealed up with clay and marked with numerous bloody palm prints.

"What the?" Mohammed asked, examining the long, dried handprints while O'Neil photographed the door and a large clay seal hanging from a series of woven fibre ropes that prevented the door from being opened.

O'Neill looked more closely at the handprints. "Whatever is behind this door was of great importance to these people."

---

[868] An adze is an ancient cutting tool (usually for wood) that is similar to an axe, but the cutting edge is set perpendicular to the handle rather than parallel.
[869] Probably a meteor fragment.
[870] In Assyrian, this weapon was known as the "UG-ZI-ZU" or Death-SoulBlade. Seven were originally cast, of which only two survived. One was listed as being held in the Vatican Secret Archive but has since been lost.

Mohammed looked at the rope seal and pulled out a long curved knife with a wicked-looking seven-inch blade from his robe. O'Neill shuddered. "What else have you got concealed in that robe? A hand grenade?"

Mohammed looked deadly serious for a second. "You need one? I can have Berat fetch some from the Landcruiser?"

"No, the knife will do well enough," O'Neill nervously replied as he carefully took the razor-sharp blade from the giant man.

After watching O'Neill's ineffectual attempts to break the ancient clay seal, the giant Turk took the knife and smashed the hilt into the plasterwork. Large chunks of fibre-filled mud quickly covered the floor. O'Neill looked horrified at the damage but then knelt and gathered a few smaller fragments into transparent sample bags, which he placed in his backpack. Mohammed made short work of the remaining fragments, and Ezekiel leapt into the dark void that was revealed before either of the two men could shine their torches and see what lay ahead.

They entered a fifty-foot-high space with a one-hundred-foot-wide ceiling constructed from large stone slabs. Each roof slab fitted so closely to the next that you would not have been able to put a sheet of paper between them. Along the entire left side of the hall was a smooth twenty-degree[871] slope that disappeared into a blackness that was too far away to be illuminated.

Their torch beams revealed a series of three, six-foot-tall, concentric circular walls that filled the entire width of the room, carved out of the bedrock. These looked like three thin doughnuts of decreasing size placed inside each other. These doughnuts were painted red, white and black,

---

[871] 1 in 2.75 gradient.

respectively. Between each stone doughnut was a deep trench, and the top quarter of each doughnut was a metal composition. The metal on top of all three doughnuts showed signs of extraordinary corrosion, with fragments of the three metals lying at the base of each. All three stone doughnuts were bisected in their middle by a narrow gap, which created a path that passed through the entire construction and out of the other far Southern end into the pitch black of whatever lay beyond these rings.

O'Neill exhaled in wonder and then recited something from memory,

"Three circular moats of increasing width, varying from one to three stadia[872]and separated by rings of land proportional in size. A wall surrounded each ring. The walls were red, white, and black and were covered with brass, tin, and orichalcum[873]."

Mohammed turned expectantly towards O'Neill. "Someone has seen this before us. Who was it, Kâtib Çelebi[874]?"

O'Neill smiled. "Someone even older and more esteemed than Kâtib. A certain Mr Aristocles who is better known as Plato. But this, whatever it is, must be a scale replica, not the original, as the one quoted by Plato was larger and supposed to be in the centre of an ocean. There is no sea here, although those trenches could once have been filled with water."

"How did... Never mind," answered Mohammed as the complexities of the timelines became too complicated.

---

[872] 600 feet.

[873] Critias (a student of Socrates, 460–403 BCE) stated orichalcum was "second only to gold in value and had been mined in Atlantis", but the composition of the gleaming golden-red coloured metal was a mystery by the time of Socrates.

[874] One of the greatest 17th-century Turkish historians.

Instead, he focused on watching O'Neill take a series of photographs and collect samples of the corroded metal from the ground beside the outer wall. While the two men focused on the composition of the three concentric coloured walls, Ezekiel went down the central path, over the stone bridges and through some gates towards the centre, where he meowed loudly as if to summon his human associates.

When O'Neill and Mohammed followed the cat's path, they found themselves inside a grand temple where virtually every surface was covered in silver, which had tarnished into that black, which is so characteristic of the metal. The lower sections of the inner walls contained a sequence of carved ivory panels, while a row of one hundred[875] golden statues of naked women[876] riding dolphins adorned the top of the inner wall of the temple.

In the centre of the space were seven more golden statues. The central figure was a male holding a trident while standing in a chariot drawn by six, winged horses. This male figure was so tall that his head almost touched the ceiling and was entirely out of scale for the temple, as were the chariot, horses and dolphin-riding sea nymphs.

Mohammed took a picture of the fifty-foot man before turning to O'Neill, who was busy photographing the scene and asking, "Neptune?"

O'Neill shook his head and looked at the towering male god holding onto two side panels on his chariot. There was an overwhelming resemblance between the side panels of the chariot and the two central pillars in the Göbekli Tepe neolithic complex on the surface.

"If I am correct, that is Poseidon, the mighty god of the sea. The two central pillars in the complex above ground might

---

[875] The sea god Nereus had one hundred daughters.
[876] Nereids (sea nymphs) attended the god Poseidon.

represent his chariot. And the concentric circles surrounding the two pillars could have reminded the people of these walls and the temple beneath them."

Mohammed thought momentarily. "Thomas, you might be on to something! Do you think that is why many megalithic stone moments adopted a circular form? A reminder to people of this place?"

O'Neill paused. "I honestly don't know if it is to remind them of Göbekli Tepe or somewhere much older."

Mohammed chuckled. "Don't you dare say the A word." The huge Turk approached a stone plinth with a sizeable sickle-shaped sword resting on it. Alongside the weapon were a series of spherical crystals. As Mohammed picked up the sword, he had to pull it free from the bed of corrosion in which it lay. The big man took a couple of trial swings with the weapon.

"Good balance and a nice weight. They certainly knew how to forge a sword."

O'Neill collected some of the corrosion flakes surrounding the sword into one of his sample bags. "Yes, an early Bronze Age blade. It would have been a super weapon back in the Neolithic. I wonder why they left it here."

Mohammed had put the sword down, picked up a couple of the crystals, and started shining his torch through them. O'Neill watched the light formations on the wall and then picked up another of the round gems.

"Fascinating, these have optical properties. They look like they could have been lenses for close work or by joining them together in sequence, even a telescope."

Mohammed had lost interest in the artefacts and started looking at the carved ivory panels with his torch.

"Thomas, you should see these. They almost look like the Bayeux Tapestry."

O'Neill walked over and followed the story portrayed on the exquisitely carved panels around the walls. Seven individuals[877] were shown as Priest-Kings, who performed their rituals using some tall revolving cylinders that were, in some way, connected with the strange seven-headed serpent monsters. The seven Priest-Kings were shown using their bronze weapons and ships to dominate a world filled with Stone Age hunter-gathering cultures. Then, the scenes changed to increasing depravity and increased use of the strange tall cylinders. In some unspecified way, the cylinders drew down the wrath of the gods. Fire rained down from heaven, melting ice fields and causing enormous tsunamis of icy water to flood over the globe, drowning whole regions. People were shown escaping in massive ships.

While O'Neill followed the story, Mohammed and Ezekiel had moved through the temple's Southern exit and out into the space beyond. The cat could be heard sharpening his claws on something. O'Neill remarked,

"These boats on the frescos cannot be to scale. They are just too big."

Mohammed's booming voice replied, "I think they were to scale, Thomas. Come here."

O'Neill stopped and walked through the temple exit, where the sight of a massive wooden structure confronted him. Ezekiel continued using some of the fallen timbers as a scratching post. O'Neill's torch shone upwards and sideways, and then he walked to the edge of the structure and shone his light down the length of the wooden ship.

---

[877] Called the "apkallu" in the oldest Sumerian myths, these were seven powerful, adept kings from before the flood.

Mohammed came alongside him. "God alone knows how big this vessel is or its composition."

O'Neill beamed. "I bet I know its *exact* dimensions. Three hundred cubits long, fifty wide and thirty high[878]. As for its composition, I would bet it is made of gopher wood[879]."

Mohammed laughed, picking up the biblical reference. "You are not suggesting this is The Ark from The Book?"

O'Neill knelt and gathered some fallen wood pieces into one of his sample bags.

"One of many, if the ivory carvings are to be believed. Speaking of which, I want to finish reading the last of the ivory engravings."

The two men returned to the temple, leaving Ezekiel to finish his manicure. The final ivory plaques depicted the landing of one of the large boats and the meeting between the shipbuilders and the Neolithic hunters. The newcomers were shown teaching agriculture, metallurgy, the use of weapons, makeup, writing, mathematics, cosmology and, of course, tales of a civilisation destroyed by the gods due to its evil acts.

The final sequences showed the building of the Göbekli Tepe temple, its use for teaching and then, after the procession of Leo to Cancer in the sky[880], the systematic burial of the complex. Then, a scene showed the passage of

---

[878] 300 cubits long, 50 cubits wide, and 30 cubits high (approximately 440×72×43 ft).
[879] Genesis 6:14 states that Noah built the Ark from gofer wood (גֹּפֶר). Which was probably a form of teak.
[880] Two thousand years in a repeating 26,000-year-long circular motion of the sky in which the stars slowly rotate, called the precession of the equinoxes or great year.

constellations at the eastern vernal equinox from Cancer to Pisces[881].

Mohammed pointed to that image. "Do you understand what is going on here?"

O'Neill took a carefully framed picture of the scene and then turned to his friend. "If I am correct, it shows a significant passage of time. Between the rising of the constellation of Cancer at the vernal equinox to the rising of Pisces, it would be just under ten thousand years.

"What the fuck?!" Mohammed boomed as he pointed to the next scene, which showed two men, one of whom was a substantial bearded figure wearing a long robe and carrying a stick. Along with the two men was a domestic cat with a coat pattern that resembled Ezekiel's.

"This whole fucking place is a hoax!" hissed O'Neill. He was furious that he had been duped again and denied his chance at academic respectability.

Then, his eyes settled on the next and very final scene. His fury rapidly transformed into doubt and then curiosity. He walked over to the plinth, picked up one of the optical crystals and returned. Using the lens, he magnified the scene, showing a fierce warrior wearing a single piece of patterned wool draped over his body and belted at the waist[882]. In this lone warrior's hands was the unmistakable shape of the great sword of the Highlands, the Claymore[883]. This bearded Scot was facing off against one of the seven-headed snake creatures, operating one of the infamous cylinder devices associated with such destruction in the

---

[881] Leo, Cancer, Gemini, Taurus, Aries, and Pisces. Each age lasts approximately two thousand years.

[882] The ancient form of the Highlanders kilt known as the "féileadh mòr".

[883] Gaelic "claidheamh mór" or "Great Sword".

earlier ivory panels. The cylinder was decorated with a highly distinctive sideways Z symbol that was only too familiar to both men.

Mohammed and O'Neill came to the same conclusion and exclaimed, "We have to get the adze to Tavish!"

DAWN RAID

*"Let the future tell the truth, and evaluate each one according to his work and accomplishments. The present is theirs; the future, for which I have really worked, is mine." -
Nikola Tesla*

*Site R, US Government Bunker of Final Resort
Raven Rock Mountain Complex (RRMC),
near Blue Ridge Summit, Pennsylvania,*

04:33 HRS (GMT-5) 18th September, present-day

Six heavily camouflaged off-road Kawasaki bikes moved silently through driving rain in a wide staggered formation. They moved cautiously along a backwoods trail that was rather enthusiastically labelled Harbaugh Valley Rd on the waterproof ordinance maps taped to the handlebars on the six offroad bikes. Their route snaked through what would once have been a heavily wooded valley sitting between a range of hillocks, each around two thousand feet high. Now, the forest resembled the aftermath of a nuclear blast, with rows of burnt-out stumps as the sole surviving evidence of the once vibrant woodland.

If there had ever been a proper surface on the track that the bikes followed, it was now buried under several layers of soaking ash, mud, and charred wood from the firestorm that had swept through the region. Tons of burnt cinder had gathered into drifts, some over fifteen feet high, along the route. Even under the torrential downpour, these mounds issued forth ominous-looking smoke clouds visible in each bright flash of lightning that arced across the night sky. The air close to these smouldering drifts was full of the musty smell of soaking earth and smoke. The six men riding the big bikes treated the ash mounds cautiously, training their weapons over them whenever the shifting ash settled into some new configuration. Their respect was not due to the combustion that continued inside but because they afforded excellent cover for an ambush.

After travelling all night, the Marine Raiders of President Wilson F. Jones' security detail were approaching their final objective, Site R, the secret base where Maskins and Madden coordinated their ruthless rule over the Americas. During the one-thousand-mile, sixteen-hour journey, the Marines circled around their objective and approached via the Maryland/Pennsylvania state boundary. The closer they came to their target, the slower their progress, as they anticipated contact with Wolfsangel operatives from the US Special Mission Units (SMU) that the President had warned them about during the briefing at Wahzhazhe Summit the previous day.

Captain Jackson pinged his encrypted channel in a silent signal to his men. A series of double clicks came back over his earpiece, indicating to Jackson's relief that there was no evidence of SMU[884] activity. This assessment was not based only on their visual observation through the NVGs worn by the Marines but also via live visual and audio feeds from the autonomous WASP[885] drones, which had been deployed once they came within two miles of their target. Two WASPs

---

[884] SMU are Special Mission Units - the elite "Tier One" operations within the United States Military. Their top secret identification codes are Green, Blue, White, Orange and Red respectively; where Green are Delta Force, Blue are SEAL Team Six (DEVGRU), White are the 24th Special Tactics Squadron (24 STS), Orange are the Army's Intelligence Support and Red are the Ranger's Regimental Reconnaissance Company (RRC).

[885] The AeroVironment Wasp III is a small unmanned aerial recognisance drone with normal, infrared and motion detection systems to provide real-time situational awareness to its operators. The drone is equipped with GPS and navigational systems that permit it to operate independently once deployed.

flew at head height in front of the six bikes to detect throat wire traps, a lethal threat to unwary motorcyclists. Another two WASPs flew two hundred yards above the Marines, using infrared and motion detection systems to identify enemy positions and disturbances in ground features that might indicate the placement of antipersonnel devices or covert surveillance.

A civilian might wonder if Captain Jackson relished the opportunity of testing his Marine Raiders[886] against other SMU units who had spent decades treating them as pariahs and denying them the Tier-One status they deserved. However, as a professional soldier, Jackson focused only on completing his mission. As far as he was concerned, avoiding direct contact with other hostile forces increased his chances of successfully completing his mission.

As the formation of riders continued on their route, they regularly switched positions, each taking turns acting as "point" at the front and rear of the formation, constantly scanning their surroundings for possible ambushes or enemy scouts. The rough track they had been following terminated near the burnt-out remains of a fancy villa with a swimming pool and basketball courts within a circular ring track marking the property's perimeter. The Marines dismounted in staggered stages. Each new dismounted figure assumed a point position with their M27 rifle covering different areas around the clearing. Jackson gestured towards the peak of a small hill to the northwest of their position, and the group began advancing up the slope, again following the rotation of their roles. As they progressed, the four WASP drones acted in unison to provide advanced situational awareness for just over half a mile around them in all directions. This

---

[886] The Marine Raiders had initially been designated as Tier One (elite spec op status), but alleged petty jealousy from the Army and Navy spec ops communities had forced the unit to lose this status.

was not an arbitrary distance. Although their M27 rifles had a maximum range of four thousand yards, it was only precisely accurate at six hundred yards, so this was their preferred engagement range. If the six men noticed the torrential rain, none of them showed it. Their soaking black rain ponchos made them look like a group of spectres as they slowly and silently advanced up the two-thousand-foot hillside.

Jackson gestured with his left hand flat as they approached the summit, and everyone dropped to the ground. Lifting his NVG goggles, Jackson used the specialised sights[887] on his DMR[888] rifle to carefully examine a compound on the peak enclosed by high double razor-wired fences and CCTV cameras. Within the compound was a building with a sloping roof, a radio antenna and a communications array that included microwave and satellite communications. The Marine, lying immediately beside Jackson, took a forty-inch long, three-and-a-half-inch thick green plastic tube labelled M136[889] with the SAAB[890] logo from where it had been strapped on his back and waited for Jackson to decide if he wanted to destroy the communications installation.

Although there were lights on in the compound building, Jackson could not see any evidence of activity. Slowly, he raised his left hand and motioned towards the distant glow from a small settlement on the other side of the summit. The six men rose, resumed their slow and careful progress, ignoring the communications compound to their left, and continued North. Two hundred yards further, they descended

---

[887] Infrared illuminator AN/PEQ-16 mount.

[888] Designated Marksman Rifle (DMR).

[889] Known by troops as the "AT4" (derived from eighty-four, which is the diameter in mm of the weapon's tube) is a shoulder-fired recoilless anti-tank weapon with the US DOD/NATO designation M136.

[890] Swedish manufacturers of defence products.

a steep wooded incline towards a long circular road[891] encompassing the hill's Northern and Western sides.

According to the briefing provided by Mark Pimms, there were a series of cuts into the base of the hill at regular intervals around the circular road. These were tunnels made during the construction of the top-secret installation in the 1950s. The two main entrances were located West of their current position and could be expected to be heavily guarded. In contrast, the two cuts into the hill on the Northern edge in front of Jackson were closed and were only intended for emergency access. Jackson planned to gain entry to the base from these disused access points and, using the element of surprise, gain control of the complex.

Leading his men down the slope, Jackson paused and again used the scope on his M27 to survey the scene below him. The circular access road was deserted. The only illumination was from the spotlights mounted above tall wire enclosures surrounding each closed tunnel. It was all very quiet. Covering his wrist to limit light pollution, Jackson pressed the illumination button on the front of his GShock[892]. The display told him it was 05:00 HRS. He had timed his attack to coincide with the shift change to maximise confusion. By now, he would expect some activity on the road below him, with cleaners arriving, but the parking lot beside the road was utterly deserted. He gestured to the WASP operator to come closer and whispered in the man's ear,

"Send two WASPS to the main entrance to assess the situation."

Minutes later, the video feeds on the WASP remote control unit showed the front of the main Western tunnel

---

[891] Cove Hollow Road.
[892] G-Shock GA 100 model.

entrance[893]. It was deserted, apart from a solitary SNITCH unit standing motionless inside the main access point, its red camera eye glowing in the gloom. Jackson gestured for the WASP operator to extend the video sweep to include the helicopter pads two hundred yards in front of the tunnel. A Blackhawk or two would typically be on standby to transport VIPs, but the pads were empty.

Something was wrong. Jackson grouped his men around him and broke the operational silence they had followed for the past two hours. He briefed them on the situation - Site R appeared to be unoccupied. Following Marine Raider protocol, typical of elite operatives, the six men discussed their options as equals, ignoring their rank structure. The consensus was that they should deal with the single SNITCH and then assess the risk of entry inside the base - if Wolfsangel knew of their plan to storm the complex, the entire base would have been boobytrapped. But they would worry about that after dealing with the SNITCH. The six men maintained their elevation on the hill and moved South from the closed tunnels until they were directly above and behind the main entrance tunnel. The SNITCH was hidden from view inside the tunnel overhang.

Jackson nodded to the M136 operator, picked up a rock, and threw it onto the concrete road in front of the tunnel. Predictably, the SNITCH emerged, stomping out to investigate the noise. As its AI worked out that the projectile must have been launched from the hill behind the tunnel, it turned so it could face towards the hill. As the body of the unit came side on, there was an enormous bang, which made the ground under the Marines shake. Flames burst from the front of the anti-tank weapon and streaked towards the SNITCH, disappearing into a massive smoke cloud. As the cloud slowly dispersed, sections of grey polymer, legs, metal

---

[893] 39.729642°N 77.432468°W.

pistons, and assorted debris fell from the air onto the road surface. Moments later, the SNITCH's dozen micro drones started falling, like ripe fruit from the air, bouncing on the grey concrete before remaining motionless.

Meanwhile, the six Marines raised their M27s and aimed down towards the debris field, waiting for a response from the base. Jackson counted the seconds,

"Thousand and one, thousand and two..."

Sixty counts later, Jackson nodded to the WASP operator, and two WASPS flew into the entrance. Jackson watched the feedback on the remote control as the two small fixed-wing propellor UAVs flew slowly into the network of branching tunnels within the complex. Using infrared cameras, it was soon evident that the base was deserted.

Jackson took one of his men with him down to the road, placed another two on the opposite side of the entrance and left the remaining two on the hillside above. Accompanied by the one Marine, Jackson slowly entered through the open blast doors, painstakingly examining the floors, walls and ceilings for any signs of booby traps. Thirty minutes later, Jackson was standing in the main control centre. Maps and sketch pads were littered over the white plastic desktops, and the giant transparent whiteboard showed a detailed schematic of Wahzhazhe Summit in the Boston Mountains, where the Osage tribe was hosting the President. They had been tricked, and the President was under threat. Jackson turned and ran full pelt through the labyrinth of tunnels to the entrance and out into the driving rain. When he had a clear line of sight to the sky needed for his MCWS-X[894] encrypted satellite communications, he tried to call CIA Director Pimms, but ominously, there was no answer.

---

[894] MCWS-X - Marine Corps Wideband Satellite – eXpeditionary.

One thousand miles West Southwest of where Jackson stood at Site R's entrance, three Chinooks [895] were parked on a sand bar made of dark carbon at the edge of the enormous flood plain that had formed beneath the Wahzhazhe Summit on the Boston Mountains. One of the three massive helicopters had recently unloaded a Medium Tactical Vehicle 1079. The tracks of this C5ISR[896] mobile command and control centre showed clearly in the accumulated ash from the days of cinder "snow" as it headed towards the mountain. Lying alongside these massive tyre treads were other distinctive tracks striding through the drifts of ash and cinder. Some of these footfalls were light and indicated a small group of humans. Other footprints were deep, indicating something much heavier. A tracker from the Osage Tribe would have been able to determine some of the entities that had passed this way walked on four feet and weighed just under a ton, while another entity was bipedal and weighed several tons.

Two miles up the mountain from the three Chinooks, seven hundred yards below the Wahzhazhe Summit, the C5ISR mobile command and control centre was parked in a clearing within the heavy woodland. The vehicle's progress up the mountain revealed a swathe of destruction. Trees had been felled, vegetation burnt, and dead bodies littered the way, a tragic record of Wolfsangel's progress during their dawn attack.

---

[895] The Boeing CH-47 is a tandem-rotor heavy-lift helicopter manufactured by Boeing Vertol.
[896] C5ISR Center or "Mobile War Room" - Command, Control, Communications, Computers, Cyber, Intelligence, Surveillance and Reconnaissance Center.

Heavy rainfall drummed on the vehicle's metal roof, but the blanked-out windows saved the occupants from the distraction of frequent lightning flashes that arced across the sky. Inside the sizeable camouflaged vehicle, President[897] Jane Maskins and Vice President Elaine Madden were seated in front of a bank of DELL 4K video displays. They wore black Wolfsangel tactical uniforms with high-necked, thick, bulletproof flak jackets. The backs of the specialised jackets were decorated with sizeable striking cobra motifs to designate the couple's special status within the Wolfsangel organisation. Standing behind them, dressed in the finery of his formal Black worsted wool Hugo Boss uniform, was Knight Commander G.H. Schmidt[898].

It had only been after a tip-off from a source within the Osage camp here in the Boston Mountains that the leaders of the new Cortez-inspired regime became aware that the real President had escaped the innovative death planned for him. Since Knight Commander Schmidt had personally orchestrated the assassination attempt at the Fort Liberty accommodation block, his reputation with Madden and Maskins had been seriously damaged. He had leapt at a chance to redeem his standing by planning this military operation to storm the Wahzhazhe Summit, which, thank God, had gone perfectly. With the latest intelligence that the Wolfsangel stronghold at Wewelsburg had been stormed and key prisoners released, Schmidt suspected there could be promotion opportunities within the European operation. That fat fool, Smegget, was ripe for replacement, and who knows, with Hartman missing and presumed dead, Maskins must be in line to become the new Deputy Chairman. If that happened, it would be perfectly feasible for Schmidt to

---

[897] Self-declared President of the New American Republic.
[898] Head of Wolfsangel forces in the Americas.

become President of the Americas, provided this operation went well.

The screens in front of the three new leaders of the Americas showed live camera drone footage of the wholesale massacre taking place further up the mountain. A coordinated attack by six SNITCH units was funnelling a mass of unarmed men, women and children towards a hundred-foot wall of rock near the mountain summit that prevented any escape.

Armed with wooden stocked .308 Winchester bolt action hunting rifles, Osage men and women were making a solid defence. However, the old .308 rounds were largely ineffective against the battle armour of the SNITCH. Whenever the Osage seemed to have found adequate cover from which they could take the time to pinpoint their rounds on a specific point on a target SNITCH, they came under fire from an eight-foot-tall bipedal robot[899], which was equipped with an array of sophisticated weapons, including an

---

[899] Code Name: MINOTOUR is a nine-billion-dollar Mobile, Intelligent, Nuclear powered, Outdoor-all Terrain, Automated, unTethered, Robot. This is an eight-foot-tall bipedal humanoid robot based on the Boston Dynamics "Adam". It is completely untethered and runs on a built-in hybrid fission power system that doubles as a tactical thermonuclear weapon. It uses LIDAR to sense its immediate environment and massive neural networks to control and plan one of its twenty thousand preprogrammed attack strategies, developed by some of the best first-person combat gamers in the world. Minotaur has a range of weapons, including lethal high-amperage Tasers and super sticky fluorosulfuric acid foam (HSO3F) for close-quarters work. Its prime weapon is the variant of Minnesota's Alliant Techsystems XM25 Counter Defilade Target Engagement System, which can detonate its smart 25mm high explosive grenades before or after a specific designated target at a range of up to 600 yards. This allows it to strike targets hiding behind walls or, in this case, mountain boulders.

incredibly accurate XM25 grenade launch system that was hitting where the Osage were hiding, even behind what they thought provided complete cover.

Eight Black Knights in full AI-augmented iKill Pro combat uniforms followed a few hundred yards behind the six SNITCH units and single MINOTAUR. The AI-controlled adaptive camouflage worn by the Black Knights altered the colour, shading and light intensity of individual pixels on their uniforms to blend with their surroundings, making them undetectable to the naked eye and, in the driving rain of the pre-dawn darkness, impossible targets for the traditional iron sights used by the defending Osage.

Thirty minutes after the assault had begun, it was clear that the Osage could do nothing in response to the superior technology being applied against them. The defenders had continuously conceded ground, retreating towards the high cliff wall behind them. It was only a matter of minutes before the last of the sheltering people would be funnelled into what was sure to be a killing ground at the top of the mountain.

Inside the C5ISR mobile command and control centre, a growing attitude of self-congratulatory glee filled Maskins and Madden. As the couple watched the families being mown down by machine gun rounds, the blonde-haired Madden was forced to wipe the sweat from her hands on her trousers to control the camera joystick better. Sitting beside her, Maskins took out a Hermes silk handkerchief from her flak jacket and wiped her lover's brow, saying,

"Don't get too excited. Remember your pacemaker."

President Maskins turned to Knight Commander Schmidt.

"Schmidt, move us closer to the final killing ground. I want to terminate Wilson and his family myself. Make sure these robots,"

she waved absently towards the images of the SNITCH units, who were firing indiscriminately at the fleeing crowd, and the MINOTOUR, which was launching another salvo of 25mm high explosive smart grenades[900] at the concealed positions taken by the Osage defenders.

"Don't kill them by accident."

"Yes, Ma'am!"   Schmidt lowered his head, clicked his heels, turned and exited the small control room into the truck cab. Moments later, the control room shuddered as the massive truck advanced further up the mountain.

The dark-haired Maskins turned to Madden.

"Have you met with the informer who told you that Wilson was here?"

Madden nodded.

"Oh yes. The greedy bastard met me at the landing site, demanding his reward."

"I assume you gave it to him?" Maskins said with a knowing smile.

Both women laughed as the older Madden nodded.

"His body will be feeding the crows by now."

The cabin door opened, and Schmidt returned to the control centre and stood before the two leaders.

"We will arrive at the killing field within five minutes."

President Maskins looked at the ongoing scene on the screens before her. The few hundred survivors who

---

[900] A twin-warhead HEAB (High Explosive Air Burst) round.

remained were now gathered beneath the cliff, awaiting their fate. The six SNITCHes were ten yards back, covering the survivors with their twin machine guns, waiting for the final kill order. The enormous MINOTOUR stood ten yards behind the SNITCHes, its array of weaponry acting as a final deterrent should there be any surprise development.

"I confess I was dubious that we could achieve this with so few men after diverting most of our troops to deal with the uprisings sparked by social media misinformation."

Madden agreed. "The SNITCHes have proven invaluable."

Schmidt bowed. After all, it was his plan to use the technical advantage provided by the AI weapons systems to overcome the shortage of operatives.

"Thank you, Ma'am. The Minotaur has made the difference. It is literally unbeatable!"

Maskins frowned and corrected the Knight Commander,

"That is not entirely true. There was that incident in Crete."

She did not want this black-suited, glorified grunt to get any ideas. After all, his screw-up at Fort Liberty necessitated this clean-up operation.

"That was a fluke and could never happen again," Schmidt mumbled, instantly regretting what he had said based on the dark look that flashed over Maskins' face.

Madden saw Maskins' temper flaring, so she tried to defuse the tension. With the increasing discontent from the populations in all their new American dominions, the last thing they needed was an open conflict within the leader group. She knew Maskins well enough to know that a single annoyance would be enough to provoke a deadly response, and right now, they needed Schmidt to oversee the completion of this operation.

"I am more worried about these damned social media posts undermining us, spreading malicious rumours and causing uprisings that require us to urgently deploy the majority of our forces just to restore order at the labour camps."

Maskins turned her attention away from her growing anger towards Schmidt.

"It is that bloody Pimms and his CIA PAG[901] unit. I talked with Beyond Facts in London this morning. As quickly as they get their influencers to discredit a rumour, the fucking CIA teams come up with some other leak of our activities. It's a bloody nightmare. The only way to stop it is to disable social media, which provokes the plebs just as much as the truth."

Maskins turned back to Schmidt. "Speaking of Pimms, I also want him left for me to deal with. Understand? No more fuckups. I will personally make sure I get the job done this time." She looked pointedly at the Knight Commander[902] standing beside her.

Schmidt involuntary exclaimed, "That was not my fault."

Maskins' face flushed. "Who else could it be? Let's see if you can do better here."

Schmidt did his best to hide his rising fear and anger. A cold sweat broke out on his back. He knew how Maskins dealt with those she felt had failed her, so he decided to appease her.

"Yes, they are all being backed into the high cliff where they will be finally exterminated."

"Good. I want to be there when Wilson Jones sees these innocents dying, then I will execute his friends, then his family, and finally him."

---

[901] Political Action Group.
[902] Head of Wolfsangel forces in the Americas.

Maskins' face flushed, and her breathing increased as she contemplated the grizzly deaths. She reached over and passionately squeezed Madden's hand.

Six hundred yards further up the mountain, the final group of survivors were being shepherded by the Osage around a clearing covered in ash, leaves, and the odd protruding rocky outcrop. Everyone looked soaked, disheartened, and terrified. They had passed the stage of complaining. Now, they were silent, awaiting their fate. Alongside these unarmed civilians were around thirty members of the Osage. Some tended to the injured, while others stood ready with their weapons for a last act of defiance.

Standing on the opposite side of the clearing with their backs to the cliff face, President Wilson Jones stood beside Pimms, Orne and Crazy Bear, Chief of the Osage, looking at the approaching autonomous killing machines. The President gestured to the clearing in front of them, which had been so carefully avoided and turned to Crazy Bear, saying,

"Is that area a native burial ground?"

Crazy Bear grunted. "Mr President, the whole of this nation is a native burial ground. But that is not why we have guided everyone away from it."

Like the other members of the Osage, Chief Crazy Bear carried a Winchester rifle over his shoulder. He narrowed his eyes, looking towards the advancing SNITCH units and the massive MINOTOUR rapidly plodding towards them. Some ten yards behind the MINOTOUR were eight shimmering outlines which came in and out of focus. Several of the Osage were directing their Winchester rounds towards these flickering shapes without effect. The strange outlines were only visible when bursts of heavy rain prevented their iKill Pro uniform's AI image-matching algorithms from syncing perfectly with their surroundings.

"I have never seen such camouflage before," remarked Crazy Bear.

"Neither have I," General Orne agreed, then turned and looked up at the towering cliffs behind them.

"Gentlemen, I don't think we could have picked a worse place for a last stand. It's a classic killing field."

The Army General turned to CIA director Pimms.

"Mark, please tell me you have BLACK STAR[903] coming in to save us at any moment."

Pimms looked at Orne and President Wilson's tired, drawn faces and shook his head. "Sadly, when we deployed BLACK STAR and MARAUDER[904] in Istanbul[905], Maskins became

---

[903] Code name: BLACK STAR is a pulse detonation engine (PDE) hypersonic space-capable fighter bomber operated by the CIA and National Reconnaissance Office out of Groom Lake (Area 51). Believed to be called Aurora with the designation SR91, it was funded under Regan's Star Wars project.

[904] Code Name: MARAUDER (Magnetically Accelerated Ring to Achieve Ultra-high Directed Energy and Radiation) is a large plasma weapons system in earth orbit which can target intercontinental missiles in flight or ground targets. It was funded under Regan's Star Wars project.

[905] See Bridge of Souls for details.

aware of them. The moment she came to power, she seized them, along with the WRAITH[906] and FALCON[907]."

President Wilson took in Pimm's words as he looked around him at the faces of the people who had trusted him enough to gather here, only to find themselves hunted and now facing extermination. Amongst these bedraggled people, he saw his own dark-haired wife, Samantha, sitting, comforting their two small children, the blond-haired Josh and the dark-haired Amanda. His attention was drawn back to the threat before them by the growing sound of a diesel engine. A large box shape emerged in the distance through the heavy rain. A camouflaged truck was gradually revealed. It drew closer and parked twenty yards away, and three figures emerged from an extending set of steps on the side of the vehicle. The eight semi-visible shapes of the Wolfsangel operatives joined the three people. All eleven figures walked slowly towards where the President stood.

The President turned to the soaking wet Pimms.

"Mark, we cannot let these bastards win."

Mark Pimms nodded. "Agreed, Mr President. The United States has always held one weapon as a last resort, although it has never been used, so we do not know for sure if it will work."

Wilson looked at the killer robots that surrounded them and the advancing group of Maskins, Madden and the Wolfsangel Ranger who had tried to blow them up at Fort Liberty. All three were grinning and relishing the coming executions, not only of the President and his family but

---

[906] Code Name: WRAITH - the Lockheed Martin RQ-170 Sentinel. An unmanned aerial vehicle with automated weapons capabilities.
[907] Code Name: FALCON (Force Application and Launch from Continental United States) is a 6th-generation autonomous drone with stealth and weapons capabilities.

everyone else gathered under the cliff. His mind was made up.

"Deploy it immediately."

Pimms gestured towards three Osage tribe members who carried over a sizeable battered cardboard box the size of a Christmas tree. It had been concealed behind some shrubs close to the cliff face. The cardboard was wrapped in a thick semi-transparent plastic to protect it from the rain. The three Osage placed the box carefully in front of the CIA Director.

Orne came over as Pimms cut open the plastic cover with his Leatherman. The Army General knelt to examine the writing on the rapidly soaked cardboard before the heavy rain obliterated it forever. He read aloud the hand-drawn scrawl as the blue fountain pen ink ran in rivulets off the box sides.

Top Secret, Sensitive Compartmented[908].

Recovered by Office of Strategic Services[909] **from safe in Hotel New Yorker, room 3327.**

Jan 7th 1943.

Signed, F.D.R[910].

---

[908] The highest security level in the USA military.

[909] The OSS was the wartime precursor to the Central Intelligence Agency.

[910] Franklin Delano Roosevelt (1882–1945), commonly known by his initials FDR, was the 32nd president of the United States from 1933 until his unexpected death in 1945.

Orne looked up at Pimms, who was lifting out a four-foot-tall metal tripod with a white ceramic sphere on its top and a thin downward pointing spike in its centre that could be extended using a screw tip powered by a series of hand-cranked gears.

"Manhattan Project?" asked the General, wondering if this would be some suicide response involving a tactical nuke. At least he would die knowing he was taking these bastards with him. But Pimms shook his head as he extended the tripod legs on the device and began cranking the central corkscrew drill bit into the soil.

"Older, Jim. Much older."

Intrigued, General Orne knelt and started rummaging through the papers inside the box. The documents were all handwritten in Cyrillic with complex equations and dense text.

"Is this Russian?" asked Orne. Who was wondering if this was some Soviet-era secret weapon.

"No, Serbian," answered Pimms distractedly.

Orne continued looking at the documents. After a moment, he exhaled and scratched his head.

"I have a Masters in Physics from M.I.T., but I cannot make head nor tail of this. Whoever wrote this was either a genius or stark raving mad."

Pimms smiled. "In a moment, we will see which."

Once the bit fully extended into the ground, Pimms stood and looked at the device's front panel. There were two handwritten dials. One with a pointer that switched between two options labelled "На" and "ван", respectively. The second dial had a pointer that marked a scale from one to ten. Pimms looked at The President and, after getting approval, switched the first dial from "ван" to "На" and moved the second pointer from one to three."

Pimms and The President looked expectantly at the device, waiting. Orne continued trying to make sense of the complex formulas on the papers. The only noticeable change from the mysterious object was a slight intermittent buzzing sound around them, like a bee's nest in a distant attic.

A shout easily overwhelmed the sound, "Is that a distress beacon? Don't waste your time. No one is coming." It was Knight Commander Schmidt, who was now only ten yards away.

Orne mumbled, "It is some kind of electrical resonant transformer, but I cannot for the life of me work out how it is powered[911] or what else it does."

Wilson turned to Orne. "Jim, what is an electrical resonant transformer[912]?"

Orne was about to answer when suddenly, the date on the box, the Serbian writing and the nature of the device all made sense to him[913].

"Jesus Christ! It's Tesla's Death Ray!"

---

[911] Tesla believed that the Earth had what he termed a fluid electrical charge running beneath its surface, which, when stimulated by a series of discharges in a specific rhythm, would generate enormous low-frequency electrical waves that could be transmitted over great distances without wires.

[912] The Tesla Coil was designed by Nikola Tesla in 1891. It was a central feature in the most famous pictures of the inventor sitting under enormous arcing bands of electricity.

[913] From 1933-43, Nikola Tesla lived in rooms 3327 & 3328 in the Hotel New Yorker. He kept his greatest secrets in a safe in room 3327. After his death, the rooms were raided by the US Government and the contents of the safe were confiscated.

"Tesla preferred the term, Peace Ray," answered Pimms as a pulsing vibration started in the ground around them. The ceramic orb on top of the device lit up in time with the vibration. And with each fresh pulse, the orb grew brighter, and the vibrations in the ground grew stronger.

General Orne looked across the clearing in front of them. Maskins, Madden and Schmidt were moments away from reaching them and inflicting a violent end on everyone gathered beneath the cliff. The General strode over and twisted the dial pointer from 3 to 10.

The CIA Director blanched. "Christ, Jim, we have no idea what ten will do!"

"If the bloody thing doesn't do something soon, Mark, we will all be dead anyway." countered Orne.

The pulsing vibrations in the ground started growing progressively more substantial and more rapid. The light on top of the device became too bright to look at, and the shaking of the earth started making everyone have to steady themselves. Small rocks began falling from the cliff, and the branches around the shrubbery started shaking. To a distant observer in our solar system, our Earth's fragile blue globe began to dim and brighten in an increasing rhythm, each pulse more intense than the last. The long, final pulse briefly made the whole planet glow brighter than the Sun before an enormous six-hundred-mile-wide electrical discharge was visible on the North American continent before returning to normal.

Back on the Wahzhazhe Summit, a blinding beam of light had projected up from the Tesla device and simultaneously down from the sky. This beam of light arced bright streams of electrical charge from the orb on the top of the device to every manufactured object for six hundred miles in all directions from the vicinity. The iron in the Winchester rifles carried by the Osage became so hot they were forced to throw their weapons to the ground, where they glowed red hot. Orne's Beretta 92FS service pistol became so hot that it started to combust the leather holster, forcing the General to hurriedly remove his belt and throw the scorching hot weapon to the ground.

Smoke poured from the bodies of the six SNITCH units, and, one by one, they collapsed, followed shortly after by the enormous body of the MINOTOUR, which thudded noisily to the ground, fully deactivated.

The iKill Pro controlled camouflage that had so effectively concealed the Wolfsangel operatives suddenly failed. All eight operatives became starkly visible as they threw their red-hot weapons to the ground. Within seconds of their presence being revealed, a number of the Osage attacked them in ferocious hand-to-hand fighting. Having become accustomed to their iKill Pro's AI guidance, the Wolfsangel men were quickly overwhelmed. Having received a massive arc of charge directly into her pacemaker, Vice President Madden grasped her chest and collapsed.

President Maskins took in the scene around her. Eight dead Black Knights, six smouldering SNITCH units, the pathetic hulk of the MINOTOUR and, finally, her dead lover. All because of the incompetence of one man. She turned towards Schmidt, who was ineffectually trying to use his red-hot Glock pistol through the sleeves of his jacket.

Maskins grabbed a fist-sized rock beside her and leapt at the Knight Commander, smashing the rock into Schmidt's head.

"You!" she screamed, impacting the rock against the Knight Commander's right temple,

"Stupid!" she smashed the rock again, this time into the back of Schmidt's head,

"Useless!" this time, there was a glancing blow to the back of the Knight Commander's neck as Schmidt's body fell to the soaking ground.

Maskins knelt and raised the rock one final time, screaming,

"Bastard!" she slammed the lump of blood-soaked granite again into the pulp that had been Schmidt's head.

Breathing heavily, Maskins looked up and saw President Wilson, Mark Pimms and General Orne looking at her with disgust.

She rose and charged at them, the bloody rock clenched tightly in her right hand.

President Wilson Jones made to move away from the imminent attack, but a tall, grey-haired Native American standing beside him gestured for him to stay. Maskins' irrational rage continued driving her wild charge towards the President. As she came closer to her intended victim, she reaffirmed she would kill Wilson Jones, no matter what.

Then, unexpectedly, she fell. There was darkness and a sudden impact on objects that squirmed from under her prone body. Looking up, she could see that she had fallen into a crevice that fallen branches and ash debris had concealed. The sky was ten feet above her, but there was movement and noise around her. A growing rattling sounded from everywhere, followed by brief stabbing pains in her hands, neck, arms, legs and face that felt like needles being pushed into her body. More and more needles. She screamed, but soon, each breath took more significant effort. Her screams turned to sobs as the light from the hole above her slowly dimmed, as her eyelids and lips began to discolour and swell.

K.R.M. Morgan

Twenty feet above Maskins, President Wilson prepared to see if he could affect a rescue. Crazy Bear's strong hand held his shoulder. The Chief shook his head.

"A cave. Dozens of Timber Rattlers[914] have taken refuge there from the fires. It is a fitting end for a snake worshipper."

---

[914] The Timber Rattlesnake is one of North America's most deadly snakes. Their venom rapidly induces significant hematologic and neurologic damage consistent with Types A and B rattlesnake venom.

LOYALTY

*"Loyalty is a fine quality, but in excess, it fills ... graveyards." -
Neil Kinnock*

*Oberaarsee Dam,
7600 feet AMSL[915],
Bernese Alps, East of Grindelwald,
Switzerland.*

10:22 HRS (GMT+ 2) 18th September, present-day

The brilliant morning sunshine reflected off the soaking tarmac, providing a dazzling contrast to the almost pitch-black conditions of the past few days caused by the smoke from the global firestorm. The clearing of the thick global cloud cover was a welcome but unintended consequence of the recent discharge of Tesla's infamous energy weapon in the ionosphere.

The only blemish in the clear blue alpine skyline was a tall plume of dark toxic smoke that continued to rise from the smouldering remnants of Finsteraarhorn as it drifted high into the atmosphere in a Northerly direction. A thundering noise echoed around the narrow rocky valley as millions of gallons of Oberaargletscher[916] glacial melt overflowed the rim of the Oberaarsee Dam. The recent thermonuclear detonation over Finsteraarhorn had melted over two miles of the Oberaargletscher ice and created massive pulse waves of radioactive water, which had overwhelmed the Swiss-engineered water containment systems.

Clouds of vapour filled the air, creating vivid rainbows in every direction. But these incredible visual displays went

---

[915] Above Mean Sea Level.
[916] Oberaargletscher - "Upper Aare-Glacier".

unappreciated. Inside the luxurious leather rear passenger seat of a brand new jet-black military-inspired[917] Mercedes[918] off-road vehicle, an attractive brunette woman sat immobile, staring vacantly at the seat headrest in front of her. She was dressed in the same plain black dress she had been issued for her ICJ[919] court appearance, with the addition of a silver thermal space blanket embossed with the Paris Fire Department logo draped around her body. Beside her, lying on the black, hand-stitched leather seat, was a scribbled note drawn on a complimentary Hertz[920] regional map showing exact directions to reach this remote, restricted[921] location[922].

Six miles West of the parked "Wolf[923]" and ten thousand feet beneath the smouldering remains of Finsteraarhorn Mountain[924], a single figure dressed in an orange hazmat suit manoeuvred slowly and carefully through the darkness of an eight-foot diameter escape passageway carved through the granite bedrock. The sides of this stone tunnel showed dramatic evidence of massive thermal and physical shock from a recent explosion. Rocks, debris, and fine dust littered the ground. Each obstacle along the passage was highlighted in the narrow beam from a chest-mounted lamp on the Paris Fire Service hazmat uniform. This RST Demron™

---

[917] Created by Mercedes as a military vehicle based on requirements specified by Mohammad Reza Shah, the then Shah of Iran.

[918] Mercedes Benz G-Wagon 63 AMG.

[919] International Court of Justice.

[920] The complimentary map was provided by the Hertz Car rental desk at Geneva Cointrin Airport (GVA), Arrival Hall. The coffee served at the nearby kiosk is highly recommended.

[921] Dangerous because of the recent atomic explosion.

[922] This was a two-hour and forty-minute drive from Geneva airport via Bern.

[923] The Mercedes G Wagon was nicknamed "The Wolf" by the military.

[924] 46.53722°N / 8.12611°E.

Full Body CBRN Suit[925] cooled the interior of its hermetically sealed environment. This was a welcome feature, given the two-hundred-degree Fahrenheit thermal radiation that had permeated through two miles of rock from the nuclear blast on the mountaintop and now blasted like a pizza oven from the surrounding bedrock. With an estimated five-hour battery life on the suit, the hawk-faced assassin monitored his suit battery indicator as closely as his D3S ID[926] radiation monitor.

Inside the helmet, each exhalation momentarily steamed up the inside of the tempered glass visor before the suit's internal systems cleared it. The only sound was of the incoming air being filtered free from the ionising radiation and, of course, the preternatural influence of the miniature fragments from the macabre relics left over from the pulverisation of the contents of the Osore Tengu temple, known informally within the Wolfsangel complex as the "Cave of Dread[927]".

Abdul Issuin removed a brushed steel SIGG[928] water bottle from a clip on his waist and pulled the twist top through his thick rubber gloves. He poured a small amount of the fluid over his left wrist to remove the thick layer of accumulated dust and check the elapsed time on the bezel of the Luminox watch attached to the outside of his left sleeve. The glowing tritium revealed it had been just under two hours since he had opened the hermetically sealed triple doors and begun this arduous, slow ascent through the tunnel. He had been

---

[925] The RST Demron™ Full Body is a Class 2 style Chemical, Biological, Radiological and Nuclear (CBRN) Suit with unique self-cooling technology.
[926] D3S ID - a Gamma and Neutron detector.
[927] Esoterically charged rock slabs from Mount Osore, known in Japan as Mount "Dread".
[928] SIGG traveller range.

guided to the location and given the access codes for the concealed doors through the peculiar agency of the possession of the English lawyer, Helen Curren. The hawk-faced assassin was all too familiar with such soul transfer possessions by his former boss, the infamous Dr Nissa Ad-Dajjal. She had used this ancient technique to instil fear and absolute obedience in those in her service, as none of them ever knew when Ad-Dajjal would assume control of someone in their vicinity or even themselves.

Having seen Sinclair and Curren's dramatic UN ICJ court appearance, where Wolfsangel agents went berserk, Abdul Issuin recognised some dark magickal influence. His suspicions were confirmed when the court cameras focused in on Helen Curren, and he could see Ad-Dajjal had taken possession of the lawyer's body, as she had done once before in his presence. That recognition had instilled powerful conflicting emotions. One part of him felt fear and anger at how he had been used and nearly killed by this evil sorceress. There was, quite naturally, a desire to find the witch and exact a terrible revenge. In contrast, another deeper part of him felt a strong and growing compulsion to resume his service to this strange, intelligent and utterly beautiful woman. She had, after all, part of him reasoned, transformed him from the role of a simple executioner to leader of the world's premier multi-national private security organisation. Regardless of her manipulative and evil nature, there was no doubt that Ad-Dajjal was a visionary genius. Abdul Issuin's mind was conflicted, constantly flipping between imagining brutal ways to kill this woman and simultaneously feeling curiosity about finding out how she had survived and, more importantly, what she planned to do next now she had returned.

After leaving the Irish American archaeologist Thomas O'Neill at Gobi Tepi, Abdul Issuin returned to Europe in the borrowed Paris fire service Firehawk helicopter. During the long waits during refuelling, he had used his existing technological back doors into Cortez's organisation to find where they had taken Curren and Sinclair. Armed with this intelligence, he had rescued a vacant-looking Curren from the Wolfsangel Wewelsburg Castle complex, taking a waiting car from outside the castle and driving to Paderborn-Lippstadt Airport[929], where he resumed use of the borrowed Firehawk helicopter. Once in the air, the passive expression etched on Helen Curren's face transformed into the semblance of Ad-Dajjal and began giving detailed directions for their destination.

There was no recognition of her former lieutenant or pretence at social nicety; only flight coordinates were given with an explicit assumption of obedience. The hawk-faced assassin rationalised his obedience by telling himself whatever he finally did; he first needed to find Ad-Dajjal. This strange communication between the possessed Curren and the deadly assassin continued once they landed in Geneva. After renting the Mercedes SUV at the Hertz desk in the arrival hall, Curren had briefly become animated enough to draw a detailed map that had guided them to the Oberaarsee Dam and some notes about where to find the concealed entrance to a passage that had been constructed through the bedrock leading to the lower levels of the secret Wolfsangel complex. Immediately after writing these instructions, Helen Curren's body resumed its utterly passive state, leaving the hawk-faced assassin to don the radiation suit he had taken from the Firehawk helicopter and make his way to the concealed tunnel entrance.

---

[929] Airport Code ID = PAD.

K.R.M. Morgan

After just over two hours of arduous progress through the pitch-black and often partially obstructed branching passageways, the beam from Abdul Issuin's chest-mounted light showed the tunnel he followed, expanding into a broader and taller space. Exiting the tunnel, the hawk-faced assassin found himself in a fifty-foot square area with ten-foot-tall ceilings that had once contained the Osore Tengu temple. What had once been a faithful and exact replica of a left-hand path Tachikawa-ryu Shinto shrine was now a mass of pulverised dust and rock fragments that lay in disorganised heaps around the walls.

At first, the space appeared utterly uninhabited, and then there was a sudden movement of shadow and a scattering of dust as a figure rose from a seated position against one of the furthest walls. Unsure what he might find in amongst the pulverised remains, Abdul Issuin instinctively pulled open one of the Velcro-sealed pockets on his suit and drew his black polymer FNP pistol fitted with the Silencerco suppressor.

As the dust clouds that had momentarily filled the air slowly cleared, they revealed a striking female figure with luminescent green eyes and long black hair that reached down to her waist. This woman was completely naked and had that perfection of symmetry associated only with artistic renderings of the idealised feminine form. Her body and long black hair were partially obscured with fine rock particles, but this light dusting only emphasised her extraordinary preternatural beauty. Her age was impossible to guess. Her body emphasised youth and vigour, but her striking, luminous green eyes expressed a wisdom that could only have been learnt through numerous lifetimes.

Abdul Issuin initially reacted with a stunned silence that anyone or anything could survive the unimaginable forces that had smashed through this mountain. Finally, after looking at this strange figure, he queried,

"Domina?"

The dusty figure made no verbal response but smiled as she slowly strode towards her faithful lieutenant and looked expectantly towards the backpack he had been carrying. It took a moment for the hawk-faced assassin to remember the two sets of garments he had purchased in the arrival hall in Geneva under the guidance of the possessed form of Curren. The first was a simple, dark cotton tracksuit top, bottoms and trainers[930] for the walk back to the Mercedes. The second was a Hermes Noir Astrologie Bandana[931] openwork shirt, a matching long dress and Noir leather Hermes Faustine boots[932].

Before dressing, Ad-Dajjal walked over to one of the more enormous mounds of rock and dust, reached down through the debris and retrieved three leather scrolls. These ancient relics had miraculously[933] survived the massive pressure waves and searing thermal heat that had destroyed everything else, including the sacred rock wall veneers transported from Mount Osore. She placed the legendary Tachikawa-ryu ritual scrolls[934] in the backpack and returned

---

[930] Hermes long-sleeved hooded jogging sweater, matching jog pants and Freestyle sneakers.

[931] These garments carry the "Astrologie" Hermes print design by Françoise Faconnet.

[932] Italian-made calfskin equestrian-inspired designs with a crepe sole- ideal for walking through Via Montenapoleone in Milan or escaping from a secret underground base.

[933] Some things are just made to last.

[934] The dark rituals and prophecies dictated by Dakini-ten and transcribed in human blood onto scrolls made from the mortified flesh of disciples. These documents make the most advanced Goetic grimoires of the Western Esoteric Tradition look like Dr. Seuss's "The Cat in the Hat" children's books.

them to the hawk-faced assassin to carry. Before putting on her clothes, she took his SIGG water bottle and poured the contents over her head to wash away the dust from her face and hair. Initially, the water froze on contact with her skin but then melted in the baking heat, which radiated from the surrounding rocks.

Moments later, two figures started the long walk back down the two-mile passageway to the Oberaarsee Dam. As she walked, the female form that led the way created ice patterns along the walls and ceilings. These bizarre frost formations froze into goetic sigils that rapidly melted away in the oven-like temperature of the bedrock.

Eight hundred miles Northeast of the Oberaarsee Dam, a sword fencing salles d'armes[935] had been established in one of the three ballrooms of Książ Castle in Poland. Inside the seventy-foot wide, one-hundred-foot-long hall, warm golden sunshine shone down onto the sprung wooden floor through the high gothic windows that lined the south-facing wall. A group of thirty men and women, wearing white fencing uniforms decorated with Wolfsangel symbols, had split into three classes, covering the foil, épée, and the sabre, respectively. Chairman Cortez stood to one side, watching one of his Black Knights sparring with the German sabre instructor. Like the other three instructors, Meister Dammezin was the reigning world champion in his respective fencing art. He and the other two world champions, Maitre Plee (foil, France) and Maestro Barbieri (épée, Italy), had been brought to Książ, along with other martial champions, to provide daily combat training for the elite members of Cortez's bodyguard. The distinctive accents of the three instructors

---

[935] Sword Fencing practice area.

could be heard declaring, "Allez[936]!", "Halt" or suggestions to improve some aspect of the ongoing combat. Every one of the thirty fencing students was easily of national standard, many representing their respective nations in the recent Olympic games.

Chairman Cortez stood aside from this action, resplendent in his hand-tailored dark blue pinstripe Brioni suit and smelling of Lalique Encre Noire, with its cypress, vetiver and musk notes. He searched in his inner right jacket pocket and, ignoring the disapproving look from Meister Dammezin, used his thumbnail to split the cellophane on a new sealed packet of Cohiba cigars. He pulled out one of the Robustos[937], cut the cigar tip with an 18ct gold Dunhill guillotine cutter from his waistcoat pocket, and slowly lit it with his matching Gold Dunhill lighter. The Chairman smiled cruelly as he deliberately exhaled thick smoke towards the sabre Meister. These stupid apes needed to learn their place. In addition to the delight of savouring the world's finest tobacco, the smoke would help mask the distasteful scent of human perspiration oozing from the fencing students and, more importantly, the more disgusting onion-tainted body odour of the obese, ginger-haired Major General, whom Cortez found increasingly irritating. Cortez's preternatural senses could smell this halitosis-ridden oaf approaching, causing his elegant patrician features to assume an expression of undisguised disgust.

Major General Smegget, dressed in a slightly grimy white FF Major General's mess dress uniform[938], hurried down the long corridor towards the ballroom. Beads of sweat from his

---

[936] Begin.

[937] This type of cigar has more filler than wrapper - making it more robust and flavourful.

[938] White is a terrible choice for a military dress uniform. Ask the US Navy.

forehead ran into his eyes, smearing the already stained lenses of his small round beer bottle glasses. That morning, Smegget's cycle of endless stress exponentially intensified as the global dominance of Cortez's New Republic collapsed before his eyes. Now, he had the unenviable task of briefing Cortez about these events.

Grasping his iPad Pro in his sweaty left hand, Smegget took a deep breath before pushing open the double swing doors and stepping into the bright, sunlit hall. Walking slowly towards the middle of the ballroom, where Cortez stood critically regarding him, he connected the digital signal feed from his tablet to the one-hundred-inch Sony 8K display on a tall stand close to where the Chairman stood.

"Major General." Cortez's acknowledgement was tinged with ironic sarcasm. The Argentinian's cold eyes regarded Smegget as a crocodile might look at its unsuspecting prey.

"Bad news, I am afraid, Chairman." Smegget winced inwardly, preparing himself for the furious tirade of blame that would begin any minute.

"It is to be expected after decades where mediocracy[939] has been so strongly encouraged. What has happened to distress you so, Major General?"

"There have been significant setbacks and losses, Chairman."

"Go on. The more you draw out unpleasant things, the more unpleasant they become," the Argentinian advised.

Smegget bit his lip and pressed play on his iPad Pro. Seconds later, drone footage of the smoking remains of Wewelsburg Castle and its surroundings filled the screen.

"Chairman. The whole detachment of Black Knights at Wewelsburg has been killed. The Castle and its associated

---

[939] A society where mediocrity is rewarded.

prison camp have been stormed. We believe a specialised commando force of considerable size attacked it."

At the news of the death of their fellow Black Knights, the fencing practice spontaneously stopped. The thirty students and three instructors gathered to watch the footage, the colour draining from their faces. All of them knew people who had served at Wewelsburg.

"Hartman and Corrado?" asked Cortez, who surprisingly took the loss calmly. That made him all the more frightening to Smegget, who knew that a volcano of rage and destruction awaited somewhere inside that elegant facade.

"We have lost control of the area, and we have to assume they are dead. I am sorry for your loss, Sir."

Cortez grunted and then asked, "Is that it?"

"Sadly not. With the escape of the VIP prisoners and a spate of clever social media campaigns, there has been widespread unrest. Our sources indicate a single woman leads the resistance movement," Smegget checked his iPad, "I believe you may know her, a Cynthia Sinclair?"

The Argentinian tensed at the mention of Sinclair's name. He looked intently at Smegget and gestured to the gathered Black Knights to leave. They filed obediently from the hall, leaving Smegget and Cortez alone.

"There is more, isn't there? Stop delaying and just play the fucking footage." Cortez demanded.

Smegget went white with fear and started the next clip, which showed drone footage of labour camps in various parts of Europe burning and then national flags flying from former state buildings while outside, angry mobs torched Wolfsangel flags.

"Large sections of New Europa have fallen and returned to democratic rule, Chairman."

"So I see," the Argentinian sounded resigned to the loss, but it was clear from looking at the veins engorging on his face that deep anger was brooding.

The video footage continued by showing vast numbers of FF forces surrendering and being marched at gunpoint by grubby-looking civilians. Cortez exploded with rage, exclaiming,

"Useless weaklings! What of the elite Black Knight forces? How have they fared?"

"There have been no reports of their surrendering, Chairman."

"Good. As I have always been saying, meritocracy does have its benefits." Cortez beamed. Given that he had just heard of the loss of his grandsons and his European empire, the man's positivity felt highly disconcerting to Smegget. It left the Major General wondering what could be more critical than the Republic that had taken decades of planning to create. Almost as if he could sense the question, Cortez continued.

"We have bigger objectives now, Smegget. Focus all our remaining loyal forces fifty miles around Schloss Fürstenstein[940] and ten miles around the city of Geneva. Mobilise all our remaining ground and airborne forces to create rings of steel around these two strongholds. In addition, I want special defences set up around this castle, the railway from Owl Mountain to Wrocław and the Nicolaus Copernicus Airport[941]. I want similar special defences around Geneva Airport and the nearby CERN facility in Switzerland. None of these locations must be allowed to fall under any circumstance. Nothing is more important now. Understood?"

---

[940] Książ Castle in Poland.
[941] Wrocław airport.

Smegget nodded. Moments passed. Cortez expected his Major General to rush away to complete this latest order, but the pig-faced oaf remained. The only change was the man looked increasingly nervous.

"Is there something else, Major General?" asked Cortez patronisingly.

Smegget nodded and played his final clip.

The footage was of President Wilson F Jones mounting the White House briefing room podium with General Orne and CIA Director Pimms. Wilson Jones looked tired, thin and pale, but he still had that undefinable charisma that had proven so irresistible to voters. The POTUS smiled and picked up the microphone, saying,

"My fellow Americans, reports of my death have been greatly exaggerated..."

"Turn it off," snapped Cortez, "He thinks he is so clever quoting Twain. What of our people?"

"All dead, Sir."

A momentary frown passed over the Chairman's face.

"I always thought our American brethren moved too quickly. Inciting unrest against democracy is a long-term project. Look at Brexit. We had agent provocateurs in the media for a decade, creating misinformation before we made our move to destabilise Britain. Those two women in the States were too impatient. We had only just started the process of destabilisation by undermining their political systems. But it is a shame about the loss of two Isfet disciples. I was looking forward to the *pleasure* of *initiating* Madden and *instructing* Maskins."

Smegget felt a wave of nausea in the pit of his stomach. He knew from the chatter in the Castle's common room of the gratuitous cruelty Cortez inflicted on his sexual partners. It was a fate each operative at the castle dreaded and hoped they would be spared. Smegget enjoyed his sensual pleasures as much as anyone, but the thought of deliberately inflicting pain, injury and death on a sexual partner disturbed him. It was yet another of the dramatic changes in the Chairman since their visit to the Clinique du Dr Ster. Before the burn's clinic, the Chairman had been renowned as a womaniser, enjoying his sexual conquests but always leaving his lovers intact and sometimes even appreciative. Now, however, his sexual partners were frequently discovered with horrific injuries or close to death.

Smegget's reflections were interrupted as Cortez came beside him. In addition to the expensive cologne, there was that distinctive reptilian smell again. The Major General still could not identify it. A powerful arm wrapped around his shoulder and guided him towards the doors.

"Smegget, walk with me as I return to the clearance work in the Owl Mountain tunnels. I want a broadcast to be made," Cortez paused and smiled cruelly before continuing,

"Have Beyond Facts create deep fakes of supposed off-the-record recordings of the returning democratic leaders planning the use of our existing Cortez camps for the systematic exterminations of specific groups, to undermine the faith of the population in their returning leaders. That should slow down the democracies long enough for us to complete the essential work of reactivating the Bell."

The Argentinian beamed with anticipation at the effects of the misinformation campaign as he walked into the iron-gated elevator down to the tunnels beneath the castle.

Now that he was alone, Smegget winced at the irony of Cortez accusing his opponents of systematic exterminations when the project to clear the Owl Mountain tunnels was causing the deaths of hundreds of slave workers every day.

Whatever evils were down there in the tunnels resulted in barges full of dead bodies being removed daily and returning later full of fresh slave workers to replace those who had died the previous day. Smegget had seen some of the dead bodies. He was familiar with most of the injuries that resulted from all modern weaponry, but this Bell weapon turned healthy young men and women into a disgusting semi-liquid mush that had to be siphoned into plastic chemical containers to be taken away, and this was, according to rumours, all before the Bell had even been adequately powered up.

After he was sure Cortez would not return, the corpulent Major General scurried along the grand corridors of the stately castle to the regime's makeshift command centre. Slumping into his black leather office chair, he typed emails on his iMac to enact Cortez's commands.

When he came to the command to order the retreat of the Black Knights and other military resources from the provinces of New Europa to create "Rings of Steel" around their current location and CERN in the former Switzerland, Smegget started to consider the similarities between Cortez's orders and those of Hitler in the final days of the Third Reich. Both Hitler and Cortez refused to accept the inevitability of defeat, both declined to consider negotiated surrender, and both had developed a fanatical reliance on a miraculous Wonder Weapon being able to save them. The more that Smegget thought about it, the closer the similarities were. After all, this Bell that Cortez was pinning all his hopes on had been one of the ridiculous Wonder Weapons of the bloody Reich! It could not save Hitler in 1945, and Smegget was certain it would not do anything useful for Cortez either. Images of the deaths of other dictators began to play through Smegget's imagination: Mussolini and his mistress swinging from lampposts, Saddam Hussein facing execution, and most vividly, Colonel Gaddafi looking terrified as he was grabbed by an angry mob and killed. This last horrific memory decided it. He had been thinking about running for a while, and now was the time.

Smegget ordered his staff from the room. Once they had gone, he pulled a Victorinox Evoke Alox pocket knife from his desk drawer and walked over to the central picture on the oak-panelled wall behind him. It was one of many paintings that Cortez had insisted were his personal acquisition when he came to power, each taken from the premier art galleries in the many nations within his New Republic. Lifting the large dark wooden frame down, he placed it face down on his desk and, using the Evoke Alox, cut the picture free from the official Louvre seals on its rear.

"Fuck!" Smegget exclaimed as he realised that the world's most famous portrait was painted on fine-grained white poplar wood rather than canvas. Leaving the large[942] wooden board face down on the desk, the Major General hurriedly scanned the wall and picked the van Gogh Sunflowers picture that had graced 10 Downing Street under Reginald Twiffers' short-lived premiership.

Quickly placing the van Gogh on top of Leonardo da Vinci's masterpiece, he cut the canvas free from its frame, rolled it up and put it in a plain cardboard document tube. He pulled open the office drawer again, pulled out the cash box and emptied dozens of gold Krugerrand coins and uncut diamonds into a plastic Ziplock food bag. He then picked up the phone and ordered a Curti Zefhir[943] helicopter to be ready immediately. Taking one quick look around, he strode from his office for the last time. With luck, Cortez would remain in the tunnels until the late afternoon. By then, he would be in London and out of Cortez's doomed New

---

[942] Thirty inches tall and twenty-one inches wide.
[943] A two-seater ultralight helicopter manufactured by Italian aircraft manufacturer Curti Aerospace.

Republic forever. He would offer to provide all the intelligence the democratic forces could ever use to complete the overthrow of Cortez in return for a new identity. Failing that, he would have to sell the van Gogh and pay his way to safety.

HOMECOMING

"Returning home is the most difficult part... You have grown outside the puzzle, and your piece no longer fits." - Cindy Ross

Coulsdon Common,
London Borough of Croydon
UK

11:48 HRS (GMT+1) 20th Sept, present day,

The brilliant blue of the firmament was broken by threads of high clouds that swept like unravelling candy floss in a Westerly direction across the London sky. Twenty thousand feet below these cirrus formations, a pair of size six, brown leather Altberg combat boots[944] trudged through a large mire of sodden London clay. Splatters of the dark brown loam had formed over the rear calves of the frayed MTP[945] camouflage combat trousers. The leafless trees that had survived the recent fires gave the entire scene a wintry feel, a feeling that wasn't helped by the eerie absence of bird song that would usually have filled this late summer morning. However, such an avian symphony would have had to fight against the sound of numerous diesel generators humming as they churned their fumes into the atmosphere.

Shivering from the sharp wind, Cynthia Sinclair tightened the zip on her green Dreghorn fleece[946] so that it sat higher around her neck, partially constricting the nylon lanyard that dangled down her front, inadvertently causing her rank badge to bounce on her chest as she walked. Irritated by the

---

[944] Altberg Warrior boots - one of the boots issued by the British Military.
[945] The Multi-Terrain Pattern.
[946] Dreghorn British Army Fleece in Defender green.

movement, Sinclair unzipped her fleece and tucked the badge inside before quickly rezipping it. It was not that it was especially cold for September, but the contrast from the extreme heat of the recent days during the cosmic firestorms made the Westerly wind feel biting.

Sinclair continued trudging through the remains of grass, which a burning inferno had scorched before being soaked by torrential rain and, most recently, transformed to mud by the passing of thousands of people. There was a hive of activity around her. People dressed in the uniforms of different nations carried boxes, bottles and trays of steaming food and drink from a cookhouse set up inside a long camouflage tent on her left. To her right was a signpost so typical in military settings, showing a collection of absurdly distant cities interspersed with genuine locations within the camp. Sinclair continued following the sign labelled only as "Command".

Even with her rank badge concealed, everyone saluted her as she passed them. A few of the more senior officers even addressed her respectfully, as General[947] Sinclair. As invariably occurs when civil society collapses, Martial Law had been declared within what remained of the United Kingdom. As one of the few remaining high-ranking officials with sufficient relevant experience and ability, Sinclair had been thrust into the role of overseeing the restoration of the State. This was the second time she had found herself involved in saving the nation in just a few months. That work had been entirely clandestine, which suited Sinclair far better than the more overt role she had now assumed. She remembered, only too vividly, how only a matter of days before, an angry mob had bayed for her death. It was likely that many of the

---

[947] As head of the Secret Intelligence Service, her British Army rank of a four-star General was only activated during times of war or national calamity.

people saluting her now had been in the crowds outside Stewart's showroom in New Bond Street calling for her execution.

A part of her knew that they had all been influenced by Cortez's dark control of the media. Still, it was frightening that even those close to her in the intelligence community who had worked with her for decades had so quickly believed the lies peddled by Beyond Facts. Intelligence experts should be fully aware of the potential of social media, AI, and deep fake technologies to spin utterly convincing alternative narratives that play to people's prejudices and paranoia, exploiting the primary emotional responses that bypass critical judgement[948] to control human behaviour. The fact that none of her colleagues had pleaded on her behalf or even investigated the possibility that the allegations against her were false had changed Sinclair's perspective about her long-term goals. She had devoted much of her life to protecting Britain, but the nation had betrayed that trust. After completing this current task, She decided to return to her real home, Jamaica. Cortez had, she reminded herself, spread his vile poison there as well and turned her real homeland against her. That injustice needed to be addressed. Still, for now, her sense of duty demanded she honour her role to get Britain functioning again before handing over to a proper government. She checked her brushed steel CWC field watch[949]. She still had a few minutes before her lunch meeting with the leader group coordinating the reconstruction.

---

[948] Called an "Amygdala Hijack" in brain physiology, where the older and more basic parts of the human brain override the rational cognitive processes of the higher brain. Social media is especially powerful in manipulating human emotions.
[949] CWC G10 FATBOY-80 quartz.

Fifteen miles in the distance, columns of grey smoke rose above what remained of the once proud city of London. After days of searing heat and blazing fires, all that was left were burnt-out shells of the famous skyline, the remains of the steel and glass structures that once defined the modern face of the ancient capital. Sinclair could make out the distinctive shapes of the Gherkin, Walkie Talkie, Shard, Cheesegrater and Leadenhall Building. These structures now stood shattered and smouldering wrecks after facing the slightest of deviations of celestial bodies. The architects' proclamation of mastery over nature was now shown as nothing more than a worthless vanity.

Turning her head towards the East, Sinclair saw the rows of aircraft queuing to land in the airspace above the nearby Kenley Aerodrome, bringing in a seemingly endless stream of survivors and supplies. Sinclair was not a plane spotter, but she could make out a few Atlas propeller transports[950] and the American's much larger Globemasters[951].

As Sinclair progressed further towards the centre of the camp, a change in the wind exposed the distinctive smell of burning kerosene. It prompted her to turn towards the centre of the common, where the diseased bodies of hundreds of humans and animals were being incinerated. Next to this giant pyre, a mechanical digger was making trenches in the clear space of the common for the deposit of the mountains of ashes.

A series of eight-foot-tall, green fabric screens blocked this macabre spectacle from groups of people who sat in large circles of around fifty, discussing their traumatic experiences. Some cried, while others exhibited extraordinary anger as a response to the overwhelming stresses of recent days. A few

---

[950] Airbus A400M Atlas C.1.
[951] Boeing C-17A Globemaster III - jet transport.

nurses and doctors had voluntarily come out of retirement to help wherever they could. They walked around the groups, providing triage to those who were suffering from physical injuries in addition to their psychological afflictions. Other volunteers cleaned up discarded litter and provided blankets. Immediately beyond these triage groups, large cauldrons provided a continuous hot water supply for bathing in a small group of segregated tents.

A massive food aid programme had been instigated in the last twenty-four hours. Sinclair had authorised the immediate release of the UK's emergency food supplies so the twenty million survivors would be strong enough to work on the massive restructuring programmes necessary to rebuild the UK's basic infrastructure. Only her inner leader group knew that this food release was an enormous gamble on the part of Sinclair.   There were only sufficient supplies for three days in the UK, and no additional food sources were available, as each nation was focusing its resources exclusively on its own people. It was one of the many things which kept Sinclair awake at night. Funding the massive work needed to restore the infrastructure was another nightmare. Before the Cortez revolution, successive governments had borrowed excessively to repay the corrupt elites who had funded their election campaigns. To make matters worse, Cortez had stripped everything of value from each nation, so few precious assets remained. It was a mess, and that, Sinclair suspected, was the primary reason that she, as a black woman without an Oxbridge education, had been so unanimously hailed as the only suitable leader for the reconstitution of the nation. She was sure that once things were functioning again, some self-aggrandising "Hooray Henry" or "Henrietta" would push her unceremoniously into obscurity. That outcome suited Sinclair perfectly. She had had more than enough of cleaning up for these arrogant twits.

In one of life's synchronicities, while Sinclair was thinking of the public school chumps who tended to run and ruin Britain, she heard a supercilious giggling laugh that she recognised only too well. Three senior former Cabinet Ministers, dressed in crumpled and creased[952] dark two-piece Saville Row suits, were seated at a table to her right: Reginald Twiffers, Johnathan Premble and Jeremy Kenner. Opposite them were TV crews from four of the leading news networks. Sinclair could hear Twiffers' distinctive squeaky voice declaring,

"Yes, I, and of course my esteemed colleagues,"

Premble and Kenner preened themselves like peacocks as Twiffers continued,

"Overthrew Cortez's regime and, like Churchill before me, I, err, we have liberated Europe!"

Twiffers suddenly noticed Sinclair watching him coldly from twenty feet away and gulped. Fear of being exposed making such an outrageous lie made even a career rogue like him uncomfortable. Twiffers decided he needed to get away quickly, just in case Sinclair chose to put the record straight and tell the viewers that far from overthrowing Cortez's regime, he had been instrumental in its rise to power.

The TV crews were lapping the sound bite up, and one of them asked,

"What strategies are you considering with respect to rebuilding the nation, Prime Minister?"

Twiffers stood, gesturing urgently to his two colleagues to leave. He replied,

"Restore the old order, of course! Now, you *must* excuse us. We have, umm... other meetings."

---

[952] The collapse of civilisation tends to negatively impact dry cleaning and pressing services.

With that, the three former Cabinet Ministers scurried away from Sinclair's gaze. They headed towards a group of Americans and Chinese, whom Sinclair recognised as representatives of some of the world's most significant hedge funds.

"More secret deals to discuss, no doubt," mumbled Sinclair as she pondered how radically and rapidly things had changed over the last few days. As quickly as Cortez's regime had risen, it had fallen. Like many significant world changes, it was not the result of one single thing but a combination of them coming simultaneously.   The devastation from the cosmic airburst explosions, global firestorms and extreme weather had coincided with systematic anti-Cortez propaganda in global social media and ideological poisoning[953] of the AI systems, which directed so much of people's daily lives. Combined with the environmental hardship from the firestorms, these new media campaigns finally raised public awareness of the brutal reality of life under Cortez's domination. However, being aware that you are oppressed is not sufficient to cause the overthrowing of a cruel regime. There must also be critical weaknesses that undermine the regime's methods of control. This weakness had emerged from an unexpected quarter as the SNITCH units, which Cortez had so enthusiastically implemented to enforce his rule over the population, had turned on Wolfsangel operatives, systematically exterminating every Wolfsangel Black Knight they could find. This rogue SNITCH behaviour was first reported in Switzerland but rapidly spread. Left without strict control, the increasingly disgruntled populations rapidly rebelled, seizing control of the labour camps and the cities.

---

[953] Deliberately seeding agendas into a large language model so the system becomes heavily biased in a desired ideological direction, while still appearing rational and accurate.

This violent counter-revolution and teams of SNITCHes hunting them led to the elite Black Knight units retreating and establishing strongholds in Geneva and a minor province within Poland. Without the backing of the feared Black Knights, the more moderate and less well-resourced FF operatives surrendered en masse to the general population. This sea change coincided with Sinclair's escape from Wewelsburg Castle after the fortuitous and mysterious intervention of the world's most feared terror mastermind, Issac Abdul Issuin - who, inexplicably had let Sinclair live and even provided her with the means to escape from the torture chamber where she was facing a painful death. Over the past days, since her escape, Sinclair had tried to understand what could have motivated the hawk-faced assassin to show such uncharacteristic mercy. She could only conclude that he was so focused on the quick abduction of Helen Curren that he did not have the inclination or time to kill the other prisoners. However, after Sinclair had left her torture cell, she had to admit Abdul Issuin had been exceptionally thorough in killing every Black Knight in the complex.

After getting free from her cell, Sinclair worked her way through the complex and associated holding camp, releasing all the prisoners with military experience and leaving the politicians and other "elites" incarcerated. This had been a deliberate strategy, so she had people with her who could help overcome whatever Wolfsangel forces remained. It had, however, caused considerable resentment from the old ruling classes, but Sinclair could live with that. In the end, she had led the British contingent of prisoners, including the disgruntled elites, in a convoy of Wolfsangel trucks through the broken infrastructure of Europe to Calais and then on a flotilla of small leisure boats that reminded Sinclair of images of the evacuation of Dunkirk.

On her arrival at the port of Dover, Sinclair's spirits had been lifted. While talking with the volunteers running the Port facilities to deal with the influx of refugees, she discovered Tavish was alive! The joy of this news was, however, quickly tempered by learning that Stewart was stuck in the Swiss city of Geneva, where, for an unknown reason, a large force of Cortez's elite Black Knights had sealed down the city, blocked all communications systems and introduced a harsh Martial Law which restricted civilian movement within Geneva and prohibited all entry and exit from the city.

Stewart had exhibited his usual ingenuity in dealing with such a situation. He used the offices of the Permanent Mission of Israel to the United Nations in Geneva[954] to transmit two messages. One of these had been to Jeffery Sonnet at the Royal London Hospital. On receiving the message, Sonnet had discharged himself from The Major Trauma Centre and found Stewart's old Sergeant Major, John Jock Inness. Together, the two men had contacted all their former comrades in arms from Tavish's old regiment, The Royal Scots and, in Sonnet's case, The Grenadier Guards. Within hours, they had six hundred battle-hardened veterans, who now formed the core of Sinclair's force coordinating the recovery of Britain.

Continuing her progress towards the command centre, Sinclair walked under tarpaulins set up over row after row of trestle tables. Hundreds of hungry men, women and children were seated, all eagerly consuming MRE[955] meals from clear plastic bags that had been boiled before being lifted out with plastic tongs, cut open and poured into steel canteens. All the MREs were identical: pork sausages and beans in tomato

---

[954] Av. de la Paix 1/3, 1202 Genève, Switzerland.
[955] Meal, Ready to Eat.

sauce, but no one eating here today cared. After starvation diets in the Cortez work camps or scavenging in the burnt-out cities, every sporkful was a delight. The aroma of cheap meat and tomatoes overwhelmed the senses. It was hardly cordon bleu, but it was warm and full of calories.

Sinclair pushed her way through a mass of people jostling to get into the queue for a meal. By an unfortunate accident, she found herself standing in front of the former Home Secretary, Lord Jeremy Kenner, who must have headed here after the TV interview. Kenner focused on talking with Maximillian Cash, one of America's most famous tech trillionaires. Cash's squeaky nasal voice asked,

"Jezza, you're sure the reconstruction contracts will be allocated without tenders or tax?"

Kenner smiled slyly and touched his nose. "Of course, old boy. Of course! After COVID-19, the public is used to *everything* being done under *emergency powers*. We don't need all that auditing and oversight nonsense. It's just a good old profit for everyone! Well, not everyone, but everyone who *counts*. But before that, we must wait for the *little people* to sort out more money for us to spend."

Cash and Kenner shared a loud laugh as they pushed their way to the front of the queue, where Kenner exclaimed, in a voice that was used to being obeyed,

"VIPS coming through!"

The two men cut in front of a disabled child in a wheelchair, who started crying to her parents. Sinclair deliberately walked her shoulder into Kenner in a body check that would have impressed Wayne Gretzky, sending the former Home Secretary careering into Cash. Both men ended up on the ground together, covered in the thick London clay. Sinclair winked at the parents of the small girl and gestured for them to advance towards a free table. She then turned to the two men lying at her feet with a look of mock horror, saying,

"Lord Kenner! Honey, with all this bustle, I did not see you."

Sinclair quickly walked on, leaving Kenner and Cash frantically scraping at the thick caking goo covering their ten-thousand-dollar suits without any hope of effective cleaning.

Seeing these corrupt elites resuming their poisonous machinations even before she had found a way to feed the population galled Sinclair to her core. As she walked, she could not help asking herself if democracy really served the people. But what was the alternative? She had just experienced first-hand how totalitarian dictatorships worked with Cortez. As fragile and dysfunctional as it was, democracy gave people greater freedom and at least the promise of a better life - and periodic elections limited the damage any one government could inflict on a nation.

Sinclair finished her musings as she approached a distinctive green tent[956] with two old veterans standing guard outside. The two soldiers, dressed in kilts, came smartly to attention as Sinclair entered. Inside the tent was a large trestle table with a map of the United Kingdom stapled to the surface. The map was covered in handwritten Post-it notes describing the current situation and required action in specific locations. Three older men and one woman were seated along the right side of the table. A bank of half a dozen Bowman C4I military radios, operated by a row of six women dressed in Royal Navy uniforms, occupied the end of the table.

A grey-faced Jeffery Sonnet stood and exclaimed,

"Attention!"

---

[956] Alaska Structures NATO Military Shelter tent (45ft x 20ft x 10ft).

Causing everyone but him to stand and salute. Sinclair nodded.

"At ease, everyone," she said as she made eye contact with each member of her leader group.

Alongside Jeffery Sonnet on the right side of the table, a large, grey-haired man with a bushy beard resumed eating from his canteen full of beans and sausages. This grizzled highlander was Tavish's former RSM "Jock" Inness. Next to him was a woman with short, bobbed, dark hair and large, round, red-framed glasses conducting spreadsheet analysis on a black, plastic-cased Acer laptop covered in Star Wars, Dr Who and Bridge of Souls stickers. Beside Ms Twop was Sinclair's old mentor, Sir Richards[957], who somehow looked elegant even under these conditions.

Sinclair sat at the head of the table and looked expectantly at Jeffery Sonnet.

"Any news from Tavish?"

Sonnet shook his head. "No, those bastards have a complete electronic communications block over their two strongholds and have sealed all access. It's like the fucking Berlin Wall all over again. We were lucky that T had the foresight to use diplomatic channels to mobilise our team here."

Sir Richards chipped in. "What is more intriguing than what Cortez has done is *why* someone as ruthless and strategically astute as Cortez would choose to withdraw to these two locations. Ms Twop and I have been working through a list of all the strategic assets in Geneva and that rather obscure part of Poland; frankly, we are mystified. Hopefully, Stewart will have better luck understanding the motivations because

---

[957] Sir Fredrick Richards, the former Principal Private Secretary (PPS) for the Foreign and Commonwealth Office.

K.R.M. Morgan

without knowing the why, it will be difficult to deal with Cortez effectively."

There was a murmur of agreement around the table before Jock brought some cold Scottish realism to the meeting, saying,

"Before we get carried away planning an attack, may I remind everyone we have three days of food rations and a country in a state of ruin. We can hardly launch a counterattack, even if we did understand this tyrant's motivations. This is one of those times we must rely on Colonel Stewart to deal with Cortez!"

A stunned silence filled the tent.

One thousand miles southeast of Coulsdon Common in apartment 17a, on Vicolo del Giglio, Fr Thomas O'Neill ushered Ezekiel into his upper-storey flat. On hearing his arrival, his neighbour, Mrs Brambilla, opened her door seemingly more pleased to see her furry neighbour rather than Thomas himself.

"Ciao Eziekee!" she exclaimed in that strange "parentese[958]" most people reserve for babies and handed O'Neill a large bag of cat treats as a welcome home gift.

"Now, you don't get to eat them all at once!" O'Neill admonished. The cat meowed in response, but it was unclear if it was in regret or defiance[959].

Over the past seventy hours, O'Neill had started talking to the large ginger feline as though it understood everything. Rationally, O'Neill knew such language comprehension was

---

[958] Baby talk.
[959] As all cat owners will know, it is defiance.

578

impossible, but it just felt the right thing to do, given the experiences he had shared with the animal. O'Neill began unpacking, pulling off the red Turkish Airlines IST/FCO[960] baggage check labels from his Victorinox hand luggage. All the clothes had acquired that layer of grime and stale smell that was unavoidable on archaeological expeditions. Sticking everything in the washing machine, O'Neill had just started cleaning his camera equipment when the door rang. After one quick exchange on the intercom, O'Neill stood in the apartment doorway, waiting for the pizza delivery. Ezekiel purred loudly and wrapped himself around O'Neill's feet, anticipating his share. After taking the delivery, O'Neill sat at his desk, eating slices of Seu Pizza Illuminati "Meat Feast" pizza straight from the cardboard box. Holding each slice with his left hand, he read through the hundreds of emails that had arrived in his long absence. Scrolling through the email interface on his iMac, he started with the most recent messages, as he knew they often made the earlier emails redundant.

O'Neill's strategy paid off. Within the last hour, he had received an email from Fr Kwon, the Pontiff's personal assistant. Both Venchencho and Kwon were back in the land of the living and were demanding a meeting at O'Neill's earliest convenience! Relief flooded through the Irish American priest. Humanity had spiritual hope with the Pope back in his rightful place! Now, all they needed was to find Tavish and get him the ancient adze to deal with the monster who, according to the prophecy on the temple walls, would imminently face the Scotsman.

Ignoring the rest of his emails and leaving Ezekiel to finish the pizza, O'Neill pulled on a light-coloured Gant fabric bomber jacket and rushed down the steep staircase to the street below to find a taxi. Now he was back in a more

---

[960] Istanbul to Rome.

normal life, he needed a phone and a watch. After leaving Göbekli Tepe, O'Neill borrowed Berat's phone so frequently that Mohammed's two sons tried to avoid the archaeologist on the Turkish Airlines Boeing 737 from Şanlıurfa Airport[961] to Istanbul, and once in their home city, quickly disappeared.

Their arrival in Istanbul coincided with the collapse of the Cortez revolution and the Black Knights' withdrawal from Turkey. The city was in chaos, and it took all of Mohammed's influence to get O'Neill and his unvaccinated cat on a flight to Rome for the following day. The twenty-four-hour layover in Mohammed's villa dragged slowly. None of the Sek family contacts knew where Stewart was or if he was still alive. Additionally, the chaos in Turkey and Sek's reputation as a General meant that Mohammed had to go to Ankara, leaving the archaeologist like a spare wheel rattling around in the enormous villa. O'Neill ended up being driven to the airport by Zahra, Mohammed's wife, who left him at the check-in desk with a look of considerable relief.

Getting Italian Customs at Leonardo da Vinci–Fiumicino Airport to admit Ezekiel into the country had caused O'Neill considerable difficulties, and it had required the intervention of the Vatican and a substantial bribe to avoid the ginger feline spending the next few months in quarantine. Rome was in a slightly more stable condition than Istanbul had been, and some businesses were still operating. A fact that had permitted O'Neill to get a pizza delivery and, after some searching along the streets near his apartment, a yellow Peugeot 308 taxi willing to accept payment with a credit card.

The roads to the Vatican were surprisingly empty, and they made good time, arriving at St. Peter's Square within ten minutes. After alighting, O'Neill made his way through the

---

[961] Code GNY

crowds who filled the square, not in pious devotion, but waiting for food from the enormous soup kitchens set up to help feed the citizens. O'Neill looked nervously at the nuns serving the food, but thankfully, none wore the scarlet habits of Cardinal Regio's dark parody of a religious order. Eventually, O'Neill presented himself to the Swiss Guards on duty at the Apostolic Palace and soon stood in the reception rooms for the Papal Apartments.

He expected to be kept waiting for a considerable time, but the tall double doors to the board room flew open, and three figures walked towards him. The midday sunshine poured through the tall windows behind them, so it took a moment for O'Neill to be sure that it was Venchencho and Kwon. Both men looked well, if a little thinner, but the third figure was unknown to him. It was a woman dressed in a long white gown with a thin veil over her face.

As customary when greeting the pope, O'Neill went to bow and kiss the Fisherman's Ring[962], but the ginger and grey-haired Venchencho would have none of it.

"Thomas! My God, it is good to see you! From what we gather, you alone stood true to the church while that rat Regio took over. For that, we will be eternally grateful."

"De Ven gave far more," answered O'Neill soberly, remembering his friend's terrible end in the temple under the Colosseum.

Venchencho wiped a genuine tear from his cheek. "A true Knight of the Church. But let us deal with the present. If the Lord wills it, we will have time in the future to mark his passing."

---

[962] The Papal Ring of Office. Worn on the third finger of the right hand.

"Yes, of course." O'Neill looked at both of his friends, "How did you escape the drug that Regio administered to you? You were both in some kind of trance the last I heard."

Venchencho smiled. "That transformation was thanks to this lady," he gestured to the veiled woman standing beside him.

"I believe you already know, Ms Mathers…"

Thomas interrupted, "Madeleine? Is that you? Why are you wearing that…" O'Neill stopped in mid-sentence as Mathers pulled back her veil and revealed the disfigured burns that had transformed her face from beautiful symmetry to a melted mess.

"God, what happened to you?"

Mathers sighed. "That, my dear Thomas, is a very complicated story and one we hopefully can share after the current situation is resolved. You must trust me when I say you must go to your friend, Tavish, immediately."

"You know where he is?" asked O'Neill incredulously. He had intended to raise the subject of Stewart's whereabouts with Venchencho at the appropriate time, but fate, it seemed, had anticipated his plan.

Venchencho chuckled. "It was at Stewart's instigation through the Israeli UN delegation in Geneva that Kwon and I were brought from Sicily and Ms Mathers from her retreat in Saint-dalmas-le-selvage in France."

O'Neill picked up the inference. "So Tavish is in Geneva? I need to catch the next available flight. I have something I have to get to Tavish urgently."

Venchencho smiled like a benevolent uncle. "We know, Thomas. Madeleine has already explained your discovery of the adze at Göbekli Tepe and its intended role."

Thomas was only too aware of Mathers' abilities, so her knowledge of the discovery did not surprise him. When Kwon coughed to attract attention, he was about to ask for the adept's view on the monster depicted in the temple.

The papal assistant was shaking his head, looking up from his phone, where he had been checking for flights. "Sadly, it's just been announced that all European aviation is to be repurposed to the transportation of relief missions. So, there will be no more flights, even the Papal fleet has been commandeered into relief duties. You will have to drive."

O'Neill blanched. "That is a nine-hour drive at best."

"Maybe not," Venchencho picked up a set of Mercedes car keys, which O'Neill recognised from when he had driven Venchencho's ancient square-angled black Mercedes[963], the chief exorcist's official car.

O'Neill could not help but smile as he took the keys, announcing, "Thanks, Your Holiness, with your permission, I will leave at once!"

"Before you go, here is the location where I believe Tavish will be looking for you," Madeleine handed O'Neill a card with a scribbled description of a vague location along the western edge of Lake Como. Before Thomas could ask for more details, she added,

"Take your fearless cat with you. His role is an important one."

Venchencho beamed. "You saved Ezekiel? He was always an asset to me during deliverance work. God speed, Thomas."

Two hours later, on the A1 from Rome, just past the city of San Cesario sul Panaro, a heavily camouflaged Ferrari F250 hyper car was out on a road test near the Ferrari factory in

---

[963] A highly modified, black 450SEL 6.9 saloon.

Maranello. Although the car was heavily disguised, under its patterned paint was a closed-cockpit prototype racer that looked like it had escaped from Le Mans - containing a joint electric and v12 petrol engine. Flying along the closed road in a blur, the engine roared as its revs touched 8,000 rpm, and the speedometer exceeded 270 mph. The dark-haired test driver beamed with satisfaction. This machine would be the next flagship of the marque. It would give those bastards at Bugatti something to think about.

Then, from the corner of his eye, the driver saw a flash in his rearview mirror. What the fuck?! Someone was flashing a pair of large square headlights, demanding him to get out of the way!

The next thing he knew, an ancient black Mercedes drew alongside him. The driver was a catholic priest who was chain smoking to such an extent that the cabin of the saloon car was filled with a cloud of thick smoke. Seated in the front passenger seat, preening itself, was a large ginger cat that looked at the Ferrari driver with complete disdain as the Mercedes disappeared effortlessly into the distance.

THE NATURE OF EVIL

"The universe runs on the principle that one who can exert the most evil on other creatures runs the show." - Bangambiki Habyarimana

Il Lago, Italian restaurant,
Four Seasons Hotel des Bergues Geneva
Quai des Bergues 33, 1201 Genève, Switzerland

13:48 HRS (GMT+2) 20th Sept, present day,

The glorious September sunshine was a welcome change from the recent searing heat and torrential rain storms, but other kinds of storms had now manifested in their place. Within the last forty-eight hours, the classic Swiss city had been transformed from a symbol of liberal democracy chosen as the headquarters of numerous international humanitarian organisations[964] into a strictly enforced totalitarian state. Where once, people strolled freely along these streets, tanks now patrolled, enforcing Martial Law.

Enough antennas were installed throughout the city to stop the social media campaign being propagated against Cortez, jamming all forms of mobile, wireless, and satellite communication not strictly controlled by the Cortez Republic. This was part of a complete media blackout within the city, which included global television, radio and the internet. Identity checkpoints had been set up at each road junction. Heavily armed Black Knights scanned the identity barcode tattoos of every passing person while being monitored by A.I.-controlled machine gun emplacements on every rooftop, and A.I. weaponised drones patrolled overhead. Conspicuous by their absence were the SNITCH units, which

---

[964] Including the WHO, UN and the International Federation of Red Cross and Red Crescent Societies (IFRC).

Wolfsangel forces had systematically destroyed after they had mysteriously turned on the Black Knights.

An elegant, powerfully built, middle-aged man[965] with short-cropped, greying hair and a matching short beard strode confidently beside the water along Quai des Bergues, the distinctive Geneva fountain visible behind him. A biting wind can often flow off these icy waters, but today it was calm. The humid air flowing off the surface of Lac Léman spread the scent of musky freshwater fish, so frequently experienced next to the scenic lake.

The handsome male walking beside the iron railings of Quai des Bergues wore a fine navy Italian hopsack weave wool suit by Hakett, a light blue Brunello Cucinelli cotton shirt, a blue Hermes polka dot tie, navy Pantherella socks, and black Equilibre Leather Oxford brogues. A white silk Prada handkerchief was just visible from his breast pocket. His smooth, casual gait, broad shoulders, and chiselled jawline spoke of decades of martial training to those experienced enough to recognise them. From habit, the Scotsman's intelligent grey eyes critically assessed his surroundings, scanning for threats as he approached the frontage of one of Geneva's finest hotels where he had booked lunch.

The slight bulge on the left side of his jacket was the only telltale sign of a Black Hills Leather dark chestnut steer hide shoulder holster[966] containing the Korth[967] revolver inside the man's jacket. Since Stewart had anticipated sitting for lunch,

---

[965] "Six feet, two inches tall and weighing a lean two hundred pounds. His chiselled jaw was accentuated with a cropped beard which matched his short, greying hair." – the first description of Sir Tavish Stewart in Bridge of Souls.
[966] The BH8S Premium Vertical Shoulder Rig is cut wide to distribute the weight of heavy guns like Stewart's Korth.
[967] A bespoke Korth combat revolver NSC 3-inch chambered for the .357 maximum round.

he had chosen to wear a shoulder holster since it provided the quickest draw from a seated position.

Forty-eight hours earlier, after waking from his strange dream of Madeleine Mathers, Stewart had initially wondered if he had imagined the encounter with the Meri-Maat adept. But, after all his recent experiences with the supernatural, he decided it would be wise to act on the advice given to him. Thankfully, the persistent sirens that had blasted the city the previous night had ended along with the torrential rains. However, when he checked his room phone, mobile and laptop, there was still no mobile signal, television, radio or internet.

On going to reception, he was relieved that the city-wide atomic alert had ended, and the population had re-emerged from their communal shelters. The hotel staff confirmed a complete communications shutdown inside the city as part of an introduction of Martial Law. The story Wolfsangel had presented to the population was that this imposition was in response to the nuclear strike on the nearby Bernese Alps. Stewart sensed there was another deeper reason, and he silently vowed to discover it.

After a quick breakfast of coffee, scrambled eggs on rye toast and an apple in the restaurant, Stewart walked to the nearest Wolfsangel command centre that had taken over the nearby Swiss Post on Rue du Mont-Blanc[968]. Outside, it was considerably cooler than when he had arrived in Geneva and chosen his current informal clothing. Thankfully, his polo shirt and trousers had dried overnight, but his shoes remained wet, each step leaving his socks and feet feeling decidedly damp. Noticing the goosebumps on his arms, he decided that one of his next priorities would be to get more

---

[968] Rue du Mont-Blanc 18, 1201 Genève, Switzerland. In case you are looking to visit.

suitable attire, especially if he wanted to pass as a millionaire playboy.

Once inside the Swiss Post building, he presented his temporary tattoo for an identity scan. He was relieved to find his assumed identity as the deceased Argentinian polo player, and Isfet adept Señor Edwardo Salvador remained undiscovered. Although he was treated courteously, the confusion in the office indicated that the Cortez regime was clearly in some crisis. Eventually, Stewart spoke privately with the senior Wolfsangel officer, Lieutenant Buehler. The blonde-haired Black Knight looked like she had not slept for days, and her office smelt like she had been chain-smoking for the entire period without sleep, which was probably true based on her behaviour in front of Stewart. Although she was in her mid-forties, she looked older in the sunlight streaming into the office.

Sitting across from her, Stewart could not help but feel some degree of sympathy. The maps on the walls around Buehler's desk indicated that Wolfsangel was consolidating its European forces into two small centres, one in Geneva and the other in Lower Silesia in Southern Poland. Cortez must have suffered significant losses and was on the retreat, which would explain the disarray Stewart had encountered this morning in the command centre. Like most junior officers, Buehler had probably never received training to prepare for the chaos that invariably follows military setbacks. Such confusion could suit Stewart well, if he could find out where Cortez was held up and if he could communicate with the outside world. He decided to take a chance and try to access Buehler's phone. He asked,

"Lieutenant, I require an encrypted line to complete some urgent communications,"

Buehler sighed."You and I both, Knight Commander. We can only communicate with Książ Castle, with status updates every three hours."

Stewart looked blankly at Buehler, clearly not recognising the castle's name. The lieutenant started looking suspiciously at the casually dressed man sitting opposite her. A Knight Commander would surely know of the significance of Książ Castle!

Sensing that his cover might be at risk, Stewart quickly covered for his ignorance, saying, "Sorry, I was distracted wondering why we have kept Geneva rather than Paris, Rome or London."

Buehler nodded, clearly satisfied with Stewart's explanation.

"A very good question, Señor Salvador. It is a question that most of us ask, as Chairman Cortez has instructed us to hold Geneva to the death, and no one, not even a Black Knight Commander, like yourself, is permitted to leave the city."

Stewart nodded. So Cortez was at this castle in Poland. That meant that Stewart would have to find some way to escape Geneva despite the risk and restrictions.

Buehler noticed the goosebumps on the Scotsman's short-sleeved arms, and again, she began to wonder about this man's highly informal clothing, perhaps he was on an undercover operation, or even... Another alternative sprung to her mind.

"Sir, did you want a uniform? If you were worried about the SNITCH rebellion hunting Black Knights, you can relax, as we blew up the last of them this morning."

Stewart shook his head, thinking quickly. "No, thank you. I came here as a vacation, but after the change in the circumstances and weather, I will purchase some new clothing later today."

The lieutenant nodded. "I hope you have plenty of Cortez credits linked to your tattoo profile, as the loss of the internet means that all other electronic funds are offline."

She clicked a few keys on the MacBook Pro on her desk to access Señor Salvador's tattoo-linked personal profile. A smile spread on her face.

"I should not have worried. You are a very wealthy man, Señor Salvador."

Inwardly, Stewart felt enormous relief. Back in Montenegro, he had transferred all his funds from the Montenegrin police chief's Cortez currency to his Bitcoin account and would have been penniless without internet access. Twop must have primed his fake Salvador profile with Cortez credits when she set it up, thank God! At least that would allow him to get a change of clothing and head towards Książ Castle to confront Cortez.

"Lieutenant, regardless of the standing orders, I must head to Książ to assist the Chairman. After I get some more suitable clothing, can you provide me with transport to the airport?"

Buehler frowned. "Sir, I am sorry if I was unclear. Chairman Cortez has issued strict orders that *no one* is to enter or leave now we have established the cordon around the city. The airport is closed, and the borders are patrolled by automated drones programmed to terminate anyone or anything attempting to violate the lockdown. I am sorry, Sir, but we are stuck here, regardless of our personal wishes."

Stewart thought quickly. "Even the UN diplomats?"

Buehler nodded. "They are all being expelled as we speak. Their final flights out of Geneva will take place this morning. After that, the airspace over the city will be locked down with our projection weapons."

Stewart leant forward. "In that case, Lieutenant, I need one of your drivers to get me to the UN headquarters immediately."

Minutes later, the Wolfsangel Humvee was rushing through the streets, heading two miles North along the lake's western edge. Twenty minutes later, they arrived outside the tall white office buildings at Palais des Nations. Stewart alighted from the front passenger seat with instructions for the driver to wait for him. The Scotsman ran full pelt through the long white corridors, arriving breathlessly as groups of diplomats were being ushered under gunpoint by Black Knights towards a string of airport buses. Stewart just had time to add a scrawled handwritten message into the diplomatic bag of the permanent mission to Israel. Immediately after that, the airport had closed, and all diplomatic communications in and out of the city ended. Stewart hoped Mossad director Mark Katz would receive and understand his cryptic message.

Since then, Stewart had focused on preparations for leaving Geneva, confident that some opportunity would arise, as it always had during his long military career. It was just a matter of noticing it. He had exchanged his causal appearance for items more suited to his assumed role as a Knight Commander within Cortez's regime. He had exchanged his Certina for a vintage military Omega[969] and his polo shirt, chinos and deck shoes for a suit. Due to circumstances, he had settled for an off-the-peg Saville Row two-piece. It was hardly a match for his beloved Ede & Ravenscroft, but it would suffice. Over the next forty-eight hours, he regularly met with Lieutenant Buehler to get updates on the situation and explore ways to get out of Geneva surreptitiously. He also visited every high-class establishment in the city that remained open. Not only did

---

[969] 1944 Omega Model Hand-Winding Caliber 30T2, 15 Jewels "Dirty Dozen" wristwatch issued to British forces during World War II on a single pass leather strap.

this raise his visibility as a millionaire playboy, but he knew from experience that frequenting such places often provided valuable information and opportunities that would otherwise remain unknown. It was just such an exploratory visit that prompted his lunch today.

Stewart walked confidently up the steps to the Four Seasons Hotel. The hotel's security detail greeted him: three long-haired men dressed in dark suits and wearing mirrored glasses. They all sported thick beards, tattoos, buddha bead wristbands and the large shiny ceramic and polished steel timepieces so often associated with recently retired US Special Forces working the private security and personal protection circuit. Stewart noted the "*de oppresso liber*[970]" rings associated with those who had served and liked others to know about it. Two of the men carried black M4 CQBR[971] assault rifles, while the third held a yellow Garrett[972] handheld metal detector.   Sitting obediently beside the two intimidating men were two "Malinois[973]" Dogs who looked at Stewart and back at their handlers, eagerly waiting for a command.

"Guest or visiting?" enquired metal detector dude in a disinterested tone.

He and his two bearded friends had taken this security gig as a low-risk way to get easy money and access to the Swiss ski scene this winter. Sure, they got the odd Russian and Albanian mafia captains coming to the hotel to pose, but they tipped well, provided you ignored their girlfriends' black eyes and frightened looks. However, the three men had not

---

[970] "To Free the Oppressed." Airbourne US Special Forces motto.
[971] Also known as the MK 18 Mod 0, a shortened version of the M4A1, a weapon of choice within US Special Forces.
[972] Garrett SuperWand 360° HandHeld Metal Detector.
[973] Malinois is one of four varieties of Belgian Shepherd dog. Often used as a modern military attack K9.

anticipated the Cortez revolution or this latest nightmare of Martial Law. Wolfsangel blocking global internet access for bank card payments had knocked business down big time. The hotel now relied on the few people who had adopted the Cortez cryptocurrency, like this old fart standing in front of them. These Cortez types seldom tipped, and just because they had the backing of the collapsing regime, they treated everyone with disdain.

A gentle Scottish brogue answered, "I have a lunch reservation at Il Lago." Stewart glanced at his old beat-up watch to emphasise the urgency to get inside.

Metal detector dude checked his orange dialled Breitling Emergency to emphasise his superiority before asking, "Carrying?"

Stewart slowly opened his jacket to reveal the shoulder holster and Korth.

"No weapons on the premises. You will have to leave it here," metal detector dude gestured to a white plastic tray on a wooden side table. As Stewart removed the Korth from its holster, one of the other two bearded security men smiled insincerely, revealing a mouth full of gold teeth, saying,

"Don't worry, your antique will be safe. You can collect it when you leave."

Metal detector dude pulled his jacket back to show his sidearm, a black polymer SIG[974] 9mm automatic pistol, adding,

---

[974] A Sig Sauer P239 is a sub-compact 9mm pistol used by SEAL Team 6 and purchased by many enthusiasts who want other people to think they could, perhaps (in an alternative universe) have been a NAVY SEAL.

"Nothing will happen while you dine. We carry real guns, not toys like yours."

"Very reassuring, thank you," Stewart commented, adding his ORSO knife to the Korth in the plastic tray.

"I hope your dogs won't be too agitated when they smell my steak." joked the Scotsman, his mouth watering in anticipation as he progressed into the lobby. Behind him, none of the three security detail laughed.

"Our dogs are like us, fearless and disciplined," gold tooth dude retorted as he stroked the heads of both dogs.

Stewart walked around the lobby of the magnificent neoclassical building with its soaring ceilings, gigantic gilt mirrors and crystal chandeliers. Around the walls were pictures of the building since its construction in 1834, including photographs from 1920, when it was the site of the first assembly of the League of Nations, the predecessor to the United Nations. The entrance to the Il Lago restaurant included a plaque denoting the recent award of a coveted Michelin star[975] and a sign saying reservations only. Even with his high status within the Black Knights, Stewart had been forced to wait to get a table, so he was delighted when he was greeted at the entrance by the Maître d'.

"Señor Salvador, please follow me to your table."

As he had requested in his booking, Stewart was seated in the far corner of the restaurant, with his back to the walls, facing the other tables and the large windows on the opposite side overlooking the water. Looking around the large room, one could only be impressed with the grandeur of the setting with its light blue walls, high ceiling and ornate chandeliers. Most of the walls were decorated with gilt-framed mirrors and those that were not had bright frescos

---

[975] The marque of globally acclaimed quality food.

reflecting a strong classical Italian influence. Near the entrance was a rendering of Botticelli's masterpiece, Birth of Venus[976], while nearer to where Stewart sat was a less well-known Renaissance work, Francesca's The Madonna della Misericordia[977]. Completing the Italian ambience, hidden speakers played Vivaldi[978].

Given the ordeal required to get a reservation, the Scotsman had expected to find the restaurant full, but to his surprise, he was the only customer.

"Quiet day?" Stewart asked as a smartly dressed waiter, who looked like he could have been a member of The Village People, arrived to take his order.

"No, Sir, we are fully booked," the walrus moustached waiter said.

Stewart looked at him quizzically, while Walrus moustache smiled enigmatically before clarifying,

"A local organisation booked all the tables except one and paid in full in advance. At the Four Seasons, we always honour our bookings, even when they don't turn up."

"Let's hope the tables remain empty then!" joked Stewart, thinking that at least he would be spared a lengthy wait for his meal, although an empty room did stifle the ambience.

"Indeed, Sir, are you ready to order?" asked Walrus moustache.

Stewart had read the menu before booking and the online reviews about each dish, so he was confident when he made his order of a starter of squash velouté, seasonal mushrooms,

---

[976] The Birth of Venus (1485) by Sandro Botticelli
[977] The Madonna della Misericordia (The Madonna of Mercy) (1462) by Piero Della Francesca.
[978] Concerto No. 2 in G minor, Op. 8, RV 315, "Summer" (L'estate).

and tuber uncinatum[979], followed by a main course of medium-rare beef filet, black pepper sauce and "cacio & pepe[980]" potatoes. Since Stewart wanted to appreciate the steak's taste fully, he kept his palate clean with a bottle of Deeside Mineral Water[981].

While waiting for his starter, the Scotsman noted a black long-wheelbase G wagon mounted on the pavement and parked outside the hotel.   The Mercedes SUV was towing a twenty-foot-long trailer covered with a grey tarp. Probably a boating enthusiast trying their luck at sailing on Lake Geneva, thought Stewart. It would give Gold tooth and his two chums something to do. As the Scotsman expected, in response to the obstruction outside the Four Seasons, Gold tooth walked from the hotel and approached the SUV's driver's door. The mirrored glass of the car window was partially lowered, and the security guard's angry voice could be heard over Vivaldi's harmonies. Stewart's water arrived, and while the waiter poured it into a crystal glass and served the starter, events outside had not been resolved. Gold tooth's associate emerged with the two Malinois dogs. Predictably, the dogs started barking and pulling at their leashes threateningly towards the driver, who remained hidden inside the vehicle. Stewart tried to ignore the barking and angry American voices, but sadly, Vivaldi's soft tones could not overcome the challenge.

While the dogs continued making a commotion, a dark cloud scuttled across the otherwise clear blue sky, and a lake breeze began stirring tree branches outside. The clouds finally obscured the sky, and the hotel was plunged into

---

[979] The Black Autumn Truffle is a perfect accompaniment to meat.
[980] Potatoes with aged pecorino Romano cheese and freshly ground black pepper.
[981] Sourced from natural springs within the Cairngorms National Park.

darkness, temporarily obscuring the view from the windows. Fortunately, Stewart's main course arrived and was placed before him. It gave off a wonderful beefy aroma, and just for a moment, the Scotsman forgot about the disturbance outside as he cut a piece of the succulent meat and experienced it melting in his mouth. The online reviews did not exaggerate the quality of the food, even if the security arrangements of the hotel were somewhat less impressive.

Before Stewart could move on to experience the contrasting taste of the sauce and potatoes, the reports from a series of 9mm pistol discharges rattled the windows. The darkness outside was broken by a bright flash, like lightning, highlighting the shadows of the bare tree branches in the restaurant, making them appear like long skeletal fingers extending across the white cloth-covered tables towards where the Scotsman sat in the corner. Outside, the dog growls and barks transformed into pitiful whimpering cries, followed by two piercing screams instinctively recognisable from one human being to another as abject fear. Reacting to whatever chaos was unfolding, Stewart finally gave up on enjoying his meal, rose from his chair and strode calmly towards the foyer to retrieve his Korth and resolve the situation, hopefully with some of his legendary tact.

"Just offer them alternative free parking," the Scotsman mumbled to himself in frustration at how the security detail's stupidity caused such an unnecessary escalation of the situation.

Before he could get halfway through the empty restaurant, there was another burst of gunfire, this time coming from the entrance. Metal Detector Dude had decided to bring the M4 CQBR[982] assault rifle to the party. Nine hundred and fifty

---

[982] Close Quarter Battle Receiver (CQBR).

rounds a minute went through the thirty-round magazine[983] in seconds. Then there was silence. Stewart expected to hear another M4 magazine start to be emptied, but instead, there was a terrible scream of terror that transformed into a manic sobbing and then complete quiet. This short-lived silence was replaced by the distinctive sound of high heels approaching, clicking on the foyer's marble floor. Stewart pulled up short, quickly snatching up two steak knives from a nearby table and holding them in a reverse grip in each hand. The two knives did not even come close to matching his Korth, but it was better than nothing.

It became noticeably colder - summit of Everest[984] cold. The biting temperatures made Stewart's sinuses burn, and the moisture on the surface of his eyes froze, forcing the Scotsman to blink rapidly to prevent them from sticking. A thick frost spread spontaneously on the large gilt wall mirrors, forming into complex geometric shapes and squiggles, some of which an advanced occultist would recognise from the Goetia and more that they would never, thankfully, discover. Heavy condensation formed over the two reproduction Renaissance frescos, dampening the plaster under the paintwork and radically changing the images from the divine to the grotesque. As the sound of the clicking heels neared the entrance to the restaurant, the one remaining waiter sprinted past the Scotsman towards the kitchen, a damp stain visible on his trousers.

Stewart was not afraid. If he was to die here, his only concern was to make sure that he died well. After such a series of ominous signs, he was not even that surprised when the impossibly beautiful Dr Nissa Ad-Dajjal strode around the corner and entered the restaurant. She wore her signature figure-hugging white Chanel trouser suit, gold Rolex GMT-

---

[983] 5.56×45mm NATO rounds.
[984] Between -33° F and -76° F.

Master[985] and jet black seven-inch Christian Louboutin stiletto heels, which continued their mesmeric cadence as she approached. Her hypnotic green eyes flashed with amusement at seeing Stewart standing before her. As she continued to approach, it became apparent that numerous 9mm and 5.56mm armour-piercing rounds had damaged the elegant lines of her Chanel couture. But Ad-Dajjal's flawless body was completely unmarked under the innumerable tears and holes in the expensive French fabric.

"Sir Tavish Stewart. I want to say it's a delightful surprise, but I would be lying." Ad-Dajjal's seductive tone was expressed in perfect Oxford English.

If the Scotsman was shocked, it did not show for an instant. Stewart replied in his Scottish brogue, "Dr Ad-Dajjal. I admit, that was a hell of an entrance. What part of the underworld did you crawl from?"

"You know, that is the first intelligent response to seeing me I have encountered from a human being. You never disappoint," Ad-Dajjal's silky, seductive voice quipped back.

Stewart looked carefully around. "Where is your murderous sidekick?"

A slight smile might have flickered across Ad-Dajjal's face. "If you mean Abdul Issuin, he is elsewhere. But do not worry if you are lonely, as there is someone else I have brought to see you." The sounds of another set of footsteps became audible in the foyer.

Tavish tensed. Anything and anyone was possible with Ad-Dajjal. But the figure that eventually emerged from around the corner of the restaurant entrance completely surprised him. It was his lawyer, Helen Curren. She was dressed very simply in her black UNU court appearance dress. She looked

---

[985] Complete with patented Rolex low-temperature oils, no doubt.

thinner than Stewart remembered, but she was looking around her and was fully conscious of her surroundings. She smiled and said,

"Tavish. You cannot imagine how good it is to see you."

"Are you ok? Has she harmed you?" demanded Stewart.

Curren shook her head. "No, Tavish, she was instrumental in my rescue from the Wolfsangel torture chamber, where I would have almost certainly been executed."

Stewart looked sceptical. "That may be what she has told you. But she is pure evil. If she helped you, it would only have been to suit her agenda."

Ad-Dajjal laughed. "Evil is complex, Stewart. Any good intention can produce an evil outcome in the moral, physical and metaphysical realms and vice versa. Yes, it is true that I once willed to assume absolute power, but unlike Cortez, I sought to destroy creation only to create a new heaven and earth in my likeness. Not their absolute and final destruction. I aim to keep the current status quo. A never-ending battle for balance between the forces of good and evil. A goal that I believe you, as a rational being, must share."

"I am fully aware of the deliberations of Leibniz[986]," quipped Stewart, "Surely, with your personal history, you don't claim to be taking the side of the angels against Cortez?"

An enigmatic smile flickered across Ad-Dajjal's face, and Stewart nodded as if considering whether to believe that he should trust this monster. In reality, he had started to plan an attack with the two steak knives that remained in his hands. First, he gently pulled Curren behind him, clear of any combat with Ad-Dajjal. Then he slowly moved his body so

---

[986] Stewart is referring to the philosophical speculations of Gottfried Wilhelm Leibniz (1646–1716) on the nature of evil as being moral, physical and metaphysical.

he was perfectly placed to drive the two razor-sharp blades into and through Ad-Dajjal's two carotid arteries on either side of her exposed throat. Even if the attack resulted in both of their deaths, the Scotsman would be happy to have removed this evil woman from existence.

As he slowly manoeuvred himself into the perfect position, Ad-Dajjal sensed Stewart's intention, but instead of moving back from the Scotsman's striking range, she picked up a steak knife from the table beside her. Stewart stopped his advance, preparing himself to counter an attack from Ad-Dajjal. However, to his surprise, Ad-Dajjal deliberately placed the sharp point of the blade into her right palm and the blunt handle into the palm of her left hand. Then, locking eyes with Stewart, she slowly pushed her hands together. There was a loud groaning sound, like steel locomotive wheels grinding to a halt, and the forged steel collapsed into itself until it was just a red hot steaming, coin-sized lump glowing between the two hands. Ad-Dajjal casually cast the stump to the table, where it smouldered, scorching the white linen tablecloth. After an appropriate pause, Ad-Dajjal continued,

"Svendsen[987] proposes four kinds of evil in the world: demonic, instrumental, idealistic, and stupid. Attacking me would be stupid, as your death at this moment would enable Cortez to achieve his goal of activating the Bell and annihilating all of creation."

Stewart eyed the red-hot remains of the smouldering fine Swedish steel, and put his two steak knives down beside it, saying, "If you are so invincible, Dr Ad-Dajjal, why don't you just kill Cortez yourself?"

---

[987] Lars Fredrik Händler Svendsen (1970) is a Norwegian philosopher who has detailed the forms of evil.

"Oh, make no mistake, Stewart, I could kill the biological man Cortez right now from here, but the demonic evil that infests him would simply inhabit another human shell, and the threat would continue. No, for there to be a lasting solution, there needs, as both the Codex Regius[988] and The Rauðskinna[989] tell us:

"A single hero, armed with a weapon of thunder, cast from the heavens to confront the Jormungand ("wolf-serpent") until death.""

Stewart recognised the context but was unconvinced. "The Twilight of the Gods. Frankly, I prefer the Marvel interpretation to yours."

A genuine smile formed on Ad-Dajjal's face. "Reality is seldom as entertaining as fiction, Stewart. But we are all here to follow our predestined roles, whether we like them or not."

She reached into her jacket pocket, and Stewart looked expectantly, asking,

"Is this the legendary adze that the leader of SPLEE told me about?"

Ad-Dajjal shook her head. "All in due course. First, you have to get out of Geneva,"

she unfolded a piece of crumpled paper from her left jacket pocket on the table. Stewart relaxed enough to move around beside the icy Ad-Dajjal. If she could crush stainless steel, there was very little he could realistically do to stop what she was doing. He looked at the paper.

---

[988] The saga that describes the Twilight of the Gods - Ragnarök, the final destruction of gods, heroes and the earth.
[989] The Rauðskinna- the grimoire of grimoires for the Nordic dark art of Galdr.

"What is this? A weather chart?" The paper showed a series of geographical contours and signal strengths.

"These are the plots of the Wolfsangel radar and monitoring systems around Geneva." answered Ad-Dajjal as she waited for the Scotsman to work out what she was giving him.

Stewart ran his finger around the contours. "There are gaps in the radar that form a pathway out of Geneva, but I would need an aircraft... without any significant thermal signature to trigger SAMs."

Ad-Dajjal reached into her right jacket pocket and deposited keys beside the contour map. Stewart's eyes narrowed as he looked from the keys to the tarpaulin-covered trailer attached to the back of the Mercedes outside the hotel. He smiled as his eyes made contact with Ad-Dajjal and nodded his appreciation.

"Bon voyage, Sir Stewart."

She turned and walked out of the room, filling the hotel again with the distinctive cadence of her heels and the aroma of her signature Mojave ghost perfume. Stewart and Curren watched as she exited the hotel, uncoupled the trailer, entered the Mercedes G Wagon and drove off.

WOLFSSCHANZE (WOLF'S LAIR)

"...you must be lucky to avoid the wolf every time...

But the wolf... the wolf only needs enough luck to find you once." - Emily Carroll

Lake Como Youth Hostel La Primula, Menaggio
Via IV Novembre, 106, 22017 Menaggio CO, Italy

15:33 Hrs (GMT+2), 20th September, Present day

The warm afternoon sunlight glinted off the gently rippling surface of the water. The calm conditions caused the clear blue Italian sky and the majestic Bergamo Alps surrounding the water to be perfectly reflected on the mirror-smooth surface of Lake Como. A gentle breeze rose from these still waters, bringing jasmine's sweet, fruity scent into the balmy[990] lakeside atmosphere. Directly opposite, on the other side of the lake, an imposing 12th-century castle with a tall, single tower with three castellations was visible, adding to an idyllic ambience that looked like something from a Pre-Raphaelite Brotherhood[991] composition.

Apart from the sounds of mahogany-panelled Boesch[992] motor boats ferrying A-List movie stars, Russian oligarchs and British MP[993]s to yet another socialite gathering, there were also occasional vans making urgent deliveries to the

---

[990] 72 Fahrenheit.
[991] An informal group of British artists who sought to return to the principles of Quattrocento (15th-century Renaissance) artists.
[992] Hand-made Swiss motor cruisers. No, you cannot afford one, trust me.
[993] On a taxpayer-funded "fact-finding mission" (otherwise known as a fully paid holiday) assessing what the economically deprived areas of the UK could learn from the most expensive Italian resorts.

high-end hotels and the purr of exotic car engines cruising along the lakeside road, heading to some delight that would remain unknown to 99% of humanity.

Reclining on a straight-backed wooden cafe chair in front of a black iron table, Fr Thomas O'Neill was using a wooden spoon to scoop up a cream-coloured substance from a small paper tub. After a four-hundred-mile[994] drive, he needed a break, and based on his expression of delight, this handmade Gelateria Lariana vanilla deserved its reputation amongst the finest ice creams in Italy. After leaving Rome three hours earlier, he had belted along the A1/E35 up the centre of Italy, past Florence, Bologna, and Milan, through the mountains before finally arriving at Lake Como.

Since the Maat Adept, Mathers had been unable or unwilling to provide any specific information about where or when he was supposed to meet Tavish Stewart, O'Neill had cruised the length of the lake before accepting defeat and parking outside the Lake Como Youth Hostel La Primula, Menaggio. The meagre salary of a priest excluded every other establishment that lined the length of the exclusive resort.

The Vatican Deliverance Unit's square-angled Mercedes 450SEL sat on the verge of the Via 4 Novembre road that runs along the western edge of Lake Como, its highly modified[995] 6.9-litre engine clicking as it cooled down. The car's black paintwork was caked in layers of dust and flies, which in many ways matched the state of the interior, which was filled with empty fast food containers, petrol receipts,

---

[994] An average of 133.33 miles/hour - including three, twenty-minute long rest stops for 100 octane gasoline (usually reserved for professional racing cars), restrooms, cat supplies and Turkish Royal cigarettes (in that order). These "pit stops" radically reduced the average speed.
[995] Modified over successive decades by Mercedes's performance division, AMG (Aufrecht, Melcher and Großaspach).

unused cat toys[996] and empty packets of Turkish Royal cigarettes.

On arrival, O'Neill had purchased the ice cream tub from the hostel reception. He now sat in one of the hospitality chairs outside the mustard-coloured three-storey building facing the lake.   Between mouthfuls of the Gelateria Lariana, O'Neill placed his small finger into the tub and wiped another dollop of ice cream onto the paper tub lid, serving as Ezekiel's improvised bowl. The large ginger feline mewed appreciatively as it licked the sweet, creamy, and floral notes of vanilla.

"What a location, eh?" asked the priest to his furry companion. Whether he knew it or not, O'Neill increasingly resembled the stained and crumpled appearance that had once graced the former chief exorcist, Hugo Venchencho. His hair was dishevelled from Ezekiel's habit of lying around O'Neill's neck while he drove. His vestments were stained from fur, cat drool and the remains of uneaten feline treats. Finally, he had also acquired that strong and distinctive odour associated with frequent smokers of Turkish Royals.

If O'Neill expected a response from the cat, who had assumed a sphinx-like "loaf" posture with his paws folded under him, there was none, but O'Neill continued his one-sided conversation nonetheless,

"All very well for them to say go to Lake Como and wait..."

At that moment, a small, white, two-seater aircraft[997] sped over the youth hostel roof. It was utterly silent but exhibited

---

[996] Real cats NEVER play with expensive toys that have been specifically purchased for them. Important documents, cardboard boxes and prize possessions are infinitely more interesting.
[997] AIR ONE is a two-seater eVTOL (electric vertical take-off and landing) aircraft with folding wings that offers a range of 110 miles on a single charge at speeds of up to 170 mph.

extraordinary speed and manoeuvrability. It covered the fifty yards from the youth hostel down to the lake in less than a second. It circled before heading South towards the most exclusive of the lake's many high end resorts.

The mysterious aircraft had two wings and four double vertical propellers, one at each corner. The two occupants were seated inside a plastic bubble as they shot across the lake surface, abruptly stopped in mid-air and then came down silently and vertically, like a UFO, onto the gravel driveway in front of one of the most exclusive villas O'Neill had passed on the way up to the Youth Hostel.

"Bloody typical. That can only be Stewart. Come on, Ezekiel!"

O'Neill pulled the massive ginger feline away from his beloved ice cream, much to the cat's highly vocal complaints. He carried the animal in his arms and hurried down the small footpath to the Mercedes. He dumped Ezekiel into the passenger seat, performed a dramatic U-turn and headed South[998] for fifteen minutes[999] along the lake's edge. As they drove, O'Neill continuously looked to the left until he saw the unique aircraft through black iron railings. It was parked alongside other expensive vehicles on the gravel in front of a three-storied white villa with a red terracotta roof built on the very edge of Lake Como. A sign beside the black iron-railed gates indicated this was MUSA Lago Di Como[1000]. The clear Perspex front canopy on the quadcopter had opened, and an immaculately dressed man and brunette in a simple black dress had emerged. A small group of senior hotel staff dressed in elegant lounge suits greeted the couple. Based on the familiarity with which the staff treated the man, he had stayed at the resort before.

---

[998] Along Via Regina and Via Statale/SS340.
[999] Six miles in fifteen minutes? O'Neill must be conserving gasoline.
[1000] Via Vincenzo Puricelli, 4, 22010 Sala Comacina CO, Italy.

O'Neill pulled across the road, stopped before the gates, and gently beeped the horn button on his steering wheel. A disproportionately loud and piercing sound issued from the car, causing Stewart and Helen to turn. The Scotsman narrowed his eyes in recognition when he saw the distinctive Mercedes, waved and started walking towards the gates.

While Stewart headed up the gravel drive, two uniformed security officers emerged from a concealed gatehouse. They looked contemptuously at the old, filthy Mercedes and the rather shabby-looking priest inside. They were in the process of gesturing for the car to move on when Stewart reached the gates. The Scotsman was astonished to see Thomas but was delighted when he heard that he had been dispatched to this locale by Mathers and Venchencho, as it meant Mark Katz had received his communications.

Within a few moments, the Mercedes was parked, and Thomas was catching up with Helen and Tavish. Meanwhile, Ezekiel sniffed around Stewart's trousers and Curren's legs. Finding both humans to his satisfaction, he began wrapping himself around the Scotsman's legs while loudly purring and vibrating the base of his tail.

"Who is this magnificent carpet tiger?" asked Curren as she knelt and made a fuss of the large ginger cat, who purred even more loudly at the additional attention.

Matteo, the hotel manager, coughed gently to attract attention and looked at Stewart, asking,

"Sir Stewart, will all of you be staying?"

Tavish smiled. "Matteo, to be honest, I will need to discuss that with my two friends. What I could do right now is have a good meal. My original lunch plans were interrupted."

Curren mouthed the word "Nissa" at a horrified O'Neill.

Matteo beamed and gestured towards the hotel entrance. Looking at his Girard-Perregaux[1001] dress chronograph watch[1002], he commented, "I will have a lakeside table for you at the ROTEO[1003]," casting a disparaging look at the filthy old Mercedes parked next to the gleaming Ferraris, Lamborghinis, Aston Martins and Bentleys, he added, "With your permission, I will have someone clean your two vehicles."

Matteo was good to his word, and the three friends were seated at the best table on the waterfront, soaking in the unique Como ambience. Having stayed at the MUSA before, Stewart recommended his favourites from the legendary menu: Tataki Di Vacca Vieja[1004] as the starter, Tajerin Al Tartufo Bianco[1005] as the main, and Musa Tiramisu[1006] for dessert. While waiting for their meal, Stewart updated Curren about Jeffery Sonnet's surgery after her abduction. But, sadly, he had no information on Sonnet's current medical state or Sinclair's exact whereabouts. However, based on what they could see describing the recovery actions underway in the UK and Europe in the hotel's complimentary international newspapers, it was clear that their two friends and Mohammed Sek were alive and putting their skills to good work in their respective nations. O'Neill described his discovery of the hidden tomb in Göbekli Tepe with Mohammed Sek, the turmoil in Turkey and his return to

---

[1001] 18 ct gold, Girard-Perregaux Richeville automatic chronograph (ref 2750).

[1002] They stop serving lunch at 3 pm, for normal guests.

[1003] The ROTEO Restaurant was named based on conjoining the names of the two founders: Robert Moretti and Matteo Corridori.

[1004] Piemontese beef tataki, beef broth oriental style, mushrooms, parmesan cheese.

[1005] 60 egg yolks tagliolini, whipped egg cream and white truffle. Better take a statin or six!

[1006] Savoiardi, mascarpone cream and coffee ice cream.

Rome to meet with Venchencho, Kwon and the badly burnt adept Mathers. But he decided to omit mention of the mysterious notebook and the adze until he could be more confident of the reality of the supernatural monster described in the tomb frescos.

During the sublime meal, they discussed the strange interventions by Ad-Dajjal and Abdul Issuin. They speculated if their two arch-enemies truly had put aside their differences to combat the threat of the preternaturally possessed Cortez activating his Nazi doomsday device. Thomas and Helen were inclined to accept the narrative suggested by their actions. In contrast, Tavish was highly sceptical, especially concerning the fantastic claims that Cortez was some immortal soul parasite who wanted to activate a supernatural cylinder that would destroy all of creation. Given Stewart's extreme scepticism about the bizarre nature of Cortez, O'Neill decided he would remain silent about the ancient adze, which he had integrated into his exorcism incense thurible[1007] and concealed in Venchencho's antique Delvaux[1008] leather deliverance bag. He reasoned that he would hand the adze to the Scotsman if and when the opportunity arose. Unlike Curren and O'Neill, Stewart believed that Cortez was just an evil human being who, like many other war criminals the Scotsman had pursued, needed to be brought to a formal trial for his actions.

After their heated discussions, the three friends drank coffee and were greeted by Matteo, who wanted to know their decision about staying. Stewart had hoped to be able to book a flight for Curren back to England and seats for O'Neill and himself on the next available flight to Poland. He was

---

[1007] From the Latin turibulum, this is a metal incense censer used by priests.
[1008] Founded in 1829, Delvaux is one of the oldest leather producers.

disappointed to learn that all air traffic, including private charters, were requisitioned for relief operations. Using the Bitcoin wallet on his Google Pixel phone, he prepaid for Curren to remain at MUSA with instructions to the hotel staff that the eVtol be kept fully charged and ready in case he had utterly misread Cortez's location and needed it to return to Geneva in a hurry. Stewart could not use the quadcopter for the next stage of his journey with Thomas because of its limited range and the time required to charge it, if indeed he could even find a charging point on route.

Half an hour later, Stewart and O'Neill walked from the hotel to the now immaculate black Mercedes, Thomas carrying the purring Ezekiel in his arms. The Scotsman consulted his Omega, inwardly estimating how long it would take to cover the six hundred miles to reach Książ Castle in the Owl Mountains of Southern Poland.

He turned to O'Neill, asking,

"How fast can this old thing go?"

The priest smiled, and replied, "How much gas can you afford?"

The six hundred and fourteen miles were covered in just over three hours along the Northeastern A13. With Stewart's Bitcoin wallet funding the 100-octane fuel, they averaged two hundred miles an hour[1009], including twenty-six gas stops, three coolant refills, four oil changes, two new sets of

---

[1009] At times easily breaking the German Autobahn speed record of 432.7 km/h (268 mph).

tyres, sixteen espresso coffees, two packets of Dreamies[1010] and six packets of Turkish Royals.

At each gas station and service stop, O'Neill would get snacks, cat treats and cigarettes while Stewart invariably checked on the availability of knives and guns. The Scotsman had been unable to retrieve his beloved Korth and ORSO knife from the locked visitor valuables cabinet when hurriedly leaving the Four Seasons in Geneva. The strict weapons regulations[1011] limited Stewart to what the Scotsman termed "pencil sharpers" and "pop guns".

"Hardly what I need when confronting Cortez!" Stewart exclaimed, after a particularly disappointing experience at a gas station along the autobahn. O'Neill checked the web on his newly purchased iPhone, a gift from Stewart during one of the two tyre changes.

"Don't stress, T. When you reach Poland, you will be able to get a decent knife[1012]," O'Neill advised before they set off on another blistering leg of their long trip North.

With the priest driving, they made the most of the fact that neither Germany nor the Czech Republic had a speed limit on their super highways. A rainstorm gradually intensified as they approached the border, forcing the massive windscreen wiper to get faster and faster until it was a blur of motion. When they arrived at the Czech checkpoint, the rain was hammering off the roads and drumming on the car bodywork like a Keith Moon[1013] solo performance. The penetrating rain overwhelmed the electrical systems in the old car, with dashboard indicator after indicator failing, until

---

[1010] Cat treats.

[1011] Three to four-inch blade limits and a license requirement for a pistol.

[1012] Poland has fewer controls over knife blade length.

[1013] The late great drummer for the rock band The Who.

by the last hour, they drove without any of the dashboard instruments functioning.

It was eleven thirty-six pm when they finally arrived at Przejście graniczne Lubawka - Královec, the Wolfsangel presence on the border into Poland. A couple of very cold and soaked Czech police officers advised them to turn back before they entered the fifty-yard demilitarised zone (DMZ). Once across the DMZ threshold, two Black Knights in rain ponchos approached the car and demanded at gunpoint that they exit the vehicle.

Standing in the driving rain, under spotlights beside some razor wire fences and two armoured Wolfsangel vehicles, O'Neill noticed the pathetic state of Venchencho's old Merc for the first time. Steam rose from the bonnet, a burning acid smell filled the air, and ominous rivers of multi-coloured liquid cascaded from the engine over the tarmac. The lack of dashboard instruments meant they had continued pushing the car beyond its extraordinary limits.

"Oh God, I've destroyed Venchencho's car!" O'Neill exclaimed, horror evident in his voice.

Stewart patted the priest's soaking wet shoulder, saying, "Venchencho will understand. We had to get here. We can get you another car, but we will never have another chance to catch Cortez."

But the Scotsman did not understand the more profound implications of this car's failure. O'Neill did, and it made him feel physically sick. He knew from personal experience that the vehicle was imbued with the Holy Spirit and was practically indestructible when pursuing the destruction of evil. But, now they were approaching Książ Castle, the car's supernatural protection had abruptly ended. A terrifying intuition came unbidden into his mind: the divine was finally abandoning humanity as was foretold in the old Norse Saga that Mathers had told him of when he described the disturbing Ragnarök images drawn by Mrs Susan Widee, the possessed patient at the Ospedale Pediatrico Bambino Gesù psychiatric clinic a few days ago. As he recalled the dark legend, he remembered that every hero died in the Saga. Even the gods fell in the final great battle against darkness. Hence its name, Twilight of the Gods.

Ezekiel shared O'Neill's dark forbidding. The normally rambunctious ginger feline stood beside the broken car, gently nudging its face against the front bumper as if trying to rekindle some divine animation that might remain in the deliverance vehicle. After three attempts, the cat turned its face towards O'Neill and issued a long, plaintive cry that chilled the bone.

Thomas went to walk over to comfort his cat but was stopped by one of the Black Knights who had strutted officiously out of a sandbagged portacabin carrying a portable barcode scanner.

"Tattoos!" he demanded in a harsh tone.

Stewart rolled up his sleeve, but O'Neill was forced to pull a Vatican letter that the Pope's office had prepared for such an eventuality. The letter explained that O'Neill had recently undergone extensive surgery and missed the Red Death plague and the UNITY tattoos.

"Open your mouth," demanded the guard after reading the letter. After shining a torch into O'Neill's mouth, revealing the extensive dental surgery, he nodded to the other guards before instructing,

"Search them and," he gestured towards the dying Mercedes, "push this garbage off our territory."

Stewart and O'Neill were forced to stand in the driving rain while their identities were checked. Thomas protected

Ezekiel as best he could inside his jacket, but he could feel the cat shivering in his arms. The brave cat gave a plaintive meow and snuggled closer to O'Neill when the two armoured cars bulldozed into the old Merc, smashing its black bodywork and pushing it off the road into the gutter.

Twenty-five miles northeast of the border crossing and one mile under Owl Mountain, Chairman Cortez's countenance was finally brightening after days of behaving like an angry Kodiak bear. He had been unbearable since discovering Smegget's traitorous desertion, primarily because of the theft of the van Gogh, as the overweight halitosis-ridden oaf had hardly been the most efficient aide. After dispatching one of his best assassins to trace the former Major General, the Chairman focused exclusively on completing what had become his total obsession, accessing Die Glocke, which had been buried under Owl Mountain when the Nazis abandoned the top secret project at the end of the war.

After fifty hours of effort by thousands of forced labourers, the access tunnels through the old Wenceslaus mine on either side of the device were finally clear. The heavy rains over the past few days made the underground clearance even more hazardous than Cortez anticipated. It was as if some divine force thought that the traps and esoteric defences laid down by the retreating Isfet Adepts working on the project were not tricky enough.

Even now, many tunnels were prone to unexpected flooding, as dammed-up areas burst, releasing hundreds of thousands of gallons of water. But Cortez exhibited a complete disdain for the loss of human life in clearing these tunnels. In fact, he seemed most alive when surrounded by death and suffering. When confronted with piles of dead workers, he had just added additional work teams to remove the corpses in the same systematic manner as the other debris that had filled the tunnels.

Within the last hours, a massive Chinese "Shen24" six-section locomotive[1014] had towed a Schnabel wagon[1015] and specialised Mammoet heavy axil freight wagons into the Owl Mountains underground rail network. The specialised freight train had been flown from Shanghai to Wrocław Airport[1016] to transport Die Glocke thirty miles to a waiting Lockheed Martin C-5M Super Galaxy[1017]. Wolfsangel decorated the aircraft in United Nations Humanitarian Relief OCHA[1018] livery for the two-and-a-half-hour flight to Geneva to evade European air defences.

With all the clearance completed and transportation standing by, Cortez was finally ready to test the device before moving it. He could not trust the soaking wet eighty-year-old electrical systems in the mine, so he brought a portable nuclear fusion reactor, the Gerlach-rator. This fusion device was based on prototypes developed by Walther Gerlach[1019] for the Reichsforschungsrat[1020] (RFR). This small car-sized unit produced just under half a gigawatt of power[1021]. This

---

[1014] The 28.8 MW 24-axle six-section locomotive can deliver a tractive effort of 2,280 kN.

[1015] Capable of carrying cargo weighing over one thousand tons.

[1016] Wrocław Nicolaus Copernicus Airport.

[1017] Carries a load of 281,001 pounds and has a range of 2,150 nautical miles.

[1018] UN Office for the Coordination of Humanitarian Affairs provides international humanitarian aid.

[1019] Prof.dr. Walther Gerlach was a leading atomic physicist of his age. He discovered the spin quantisation within magnetic fields - the Stern–Gerlach effect. One can see how his theories would be central to the design of the Bell.

[1020] Reich Research Council.

[1021] Enough to power about 350,000 homes.

was insufficient to run the device at full operation. Only the combined electrical grid of CERN could do that. But half a gigawatt would suffice for the initial testing of the Bell.

Cortez indulged in a moment of reflection on what had been achieved. Clearing the access tunnels had cost the lives of hundreds of workers and dozens of Cortez's Black Knights. Still, the suffering and deaths of these primitive biped apes were insignificant compared to the rewards that now lay within his grasp. Part of Cortez vividly recalled 1943 when he supervised the installation they were now restoring. At that time, he had indwelt in the body of an SS-Obergruppenführer[1022] called Gletz. On April 20th 1945, the Russians reached Berlin. In a panic, Hitler ordered the immediate mothballing of the Bell project and the installation of numerous booby traps and occult countermeasures to prevent what the Führer had asserted was the Reich's ultimate Wunderwaffe[1023] from falling into enemy hands. When the Reich rose again, it was planned to revive the project and use it to establish a thousand-year rule. Eighty years later, Cortez was back. He stood with his arms set on his hips, supervising a group of ten technicians as they worked cleaning and lubricating the components of a bell-shaped opaline metal object that had been given the Reich code name Die Glocke.

Die Glocke was constructed from two cylinders, twelve feet tall and nine feet in diameter, set one inside the other, which rotated in opposite directions at ever-increasing speeds and correspondingly higher energy consumption. To lubricate these two high-speed wheels, copious amounts of a purple liquid compound[1024] had to be poured over and into the

---

[1022] A three-star general.
[1023] Wonder Weapon.
[1024] Called Xerum 525. Exposure to the wheel's rotation caused this lubricant to become highly radioactive.

cylinders regularly, or the tubes would tear apart. This metallic lubricant caused the Bell to emit a blue light that increased in intensity as it increased in rotational speed. The Bell had to have multiple teams of human operators nearby while running. One team took over the essential work once the deadly effects of the device had taken its inevitable toll on the active team.

It had been discovered that it was more productive for morale if the teams were replaced before the operator's bodies began to dissolve into a glowing toxic liquid goo, as they invariably did after a few minutes of exposure. Not only was there less mess, but it also gave an illusion of safety to the individuals taking over the lubrication work. Everyone working close to the device wore the same grey-coloured lead radiation protection overalls, helmet, tinted goggles and gloves. In reality, these protective measures did nothing to protect against the exotic energy waves that the Bell device emitted, but after the "apes" had witnessed the gruesome deaths of so many of their colleagues, they required some reassurance.

The tunnel in which they worked had been carved into the bedrock[1025] by slave labour[1026] in 1943. The space was, in effect, a long rock tube, three hundred feet long, fifty feet wide and twenty feet high, with two parallel railway tracks that passed on either side of the Bell. Water ran down the side walls and dripped from the ceiling, filling the air with chilling, penetrating dampness that seeped into the bones, but no one who spent any time here would live long enough to worry about the dampness or the dank stench of mould and decay.

[1025] Gneiss and Migmatite - Metamorphic rock.
[1026] Taken from the nearby Gross-Rosen concentration camp.

Getting a nod from the Senior Technician, Cortez beamed as he flicked the switch on the Gerlach-rator, and the first test began. The movement of the cylinders was hardly noticeable as the mechanism began to move for the first time in eighty years. The motion gradually increased, producing a vibration that made everyone feel nauseated as their vision blurred. A dull buzzing sound grew, and several technicians began coughing blood. As the rotation increased, a fine grey mist began to form around the device. Within these clouds, sparks of blue light began arcing around the entire cavern space, with strange shadowy shapes emerging and retreating in and out of our material realm.

The Chief Technician raised his hand. "Enough! Or we will use our entire supply of Xerum 525 lubricant and be unable to run at full speed on the equinox in CERN."

Reluctantly, Cortez turned off the reactor and watched as the mist, strange lights, and shadowy forms faded. Pulling off his mask, goggles and gloves, Cortez was filled with delight. The interminable wait would soon be over, and he would acquire the ultimate secret.

As the ten operators began loading the Bell onto the hydraulic lift on the Schnabel wagon, Cortez became aware that one of his aides had come down from the castle and was standing nervously beside him. Turning towards the terrified man, the Chairman demanded,

"Yes? Haven't I told you I was not to be disturbed?"

These apes were just too stupid. It would be good to commune with the higher intelligences from previous existences. But for now, he was stuck with these lesser beings. The aide stammered nervously,

"Sir, Knight Commander Edwardo Salvador has just checked in at the Czech border. I was informed he was dead, so I thought you would be happy to know he was still alive."

Cortez looked puzzled for a second and then gestured to see the attendant's iPad for the visual images taken when a tattoo scan was made.

The Chairman's face broke into broad laughter.

"It is our old adversary, Tavish Stewart. Cunning bastard. And he has brought the incompetent priest, O'Neill, that Cardinal Regio used to complain about."

"Shall we execute them, Sir?" enquired the assistant.

Cortez's face assumed a cruel expression. "No, he is to be treated as a VIP and escorted to the castle. But he is not to be left alone for a moment, understood?"

The attendant nodded. As Cortez continued, "Gather all the men in the great hall. I will address them. I want a special welcome for Stewart!"

DAY OF RECKONING

"Like gravity, karma is so basic we often don't even notice it."
- Sakyong Mipham

In the Earth's Exosphere[1027]

00:43 HRS (GMT), 21st September, present-day

High above the Kármán line[1028] that marks the start of the interplanetary medium (IPM), two hundred and fifty miles above the earth, a silver six-hundred-yard diameter and twenty-yard thick circular rotating space habitat hurtled through the Exosphere at two miles per second. This object did not resemble the modular "Meccano-like" structures of earlier space stations such as Salyut[1029], Almaz[1030], Skylab[1031] and, more recently, the ISS[1032] and Chinese Tiangong[1033] space stations. These earlier attempts at supporting human habitation in space had primarily enabled scientific and military objectives.

In contrast, this gleaming mono-structure disc was a seven-star recreational facility called "The Y Habitat", owned and run by one of the globe's trillionaire "SpaceOverlords", Maximillian Cash. The Y Habitat resort was serviced by Cash's

---

[1027] The exosphere is the super thin gaseous mix of hydrogen and helium surrounding the earth.

[1028] More than sixty-two miles above the earth's surface.

[1029] The first space station - Soviet Union - April 19, 1971.

[1030] A highly secret Soviet military space station (1960s) used for covert reconnaissance

[1031] United States' first space station, May 1973.

[1032] International Space Station (1998) was the largest space station before the Y Habitat. The ISS was a collaboration between five space agencies: NASA (USA), Roscosmos (Russia), JAXA (Japan), ESA (Europe), and CSA (Canada).

[1033] A Chinese military space station launched on 29 April 2021.

own rockets from launch sites across the world to allow the uber-rich to take extended luxurious retreats away from the numerous social and ecological disasters unfolding on the planet. Ironically, most of these disasters were caused by the excessive lifestyles of these same elite clientele[1034], but of course, they were in denial of this inconvenient truth.

The Y-Station resort had started as a status symbol for these select individuals who could afford the million-dollar-a-day fees. It became considerably more popular after the Cortez revolution terminated the highly profitable corpocracies that used political donations to direct the policies of democratic governments. As the Cortez regime seized assets, the uber-rich fled to their retreats, which they had prepared in advance for such an event or to the promise of an idyllic space habitat that was the Y-Station.

When the asteroid impacts started smashing into our globe, the Cash-designed space station moved into geosynchronous orbit behind the earth to shelter the resort residents from danger. The deeper psychological nature of the guests was revealed as global firestorms raged, devastating the environment and decimating populations. Viewing these ongoing natural disasters while drinking a flaming cocktail[1035] became the habitat's most popular pre-dinner social event. Now the firestorms and asteroid strikes had ceased, the habitat had resumed orbiting so the ten guests could appreciate the breathtaking views of glinting oceans and awe-inspiring panoramic views, where the sun rose and set every ninety minutes from the guests' private suites or the habit's glass-fronted rotating restaurant.

[1034] The greatest irony is that the uber-rich blame "the ordinary people" for causing these problems.
[1035] Such as the Flaming B-52, Backdraft, Blue Blazer, Flaming Volcano or Flaming Zombie.

As is frequently the case with the extremely wealthy, although it was well past midnight, the ten guests enjoyed a leisurely dinner. Thanks to a complex system of O'Neill cylinders[1036], a weak[1037] artificial gravity field was induced inside the habitat. This permitted the semblance of order in the restaurant, candles, crisp white linen table cloth, Buccellati Borgia[1038] cutlery, and Waterford crystal glasses. Beethoven's 'Moonlight' Sonata played at a reduced volume through numerous Sonos concealed speakers to complete the elegant ambience. Apart from the large windows, the other prominent feature of the restaurant was the central escape pod for the facility, with an automated drop-down access door.

At the head of the dinner table was Maximillian Cash. Sitting on either side of him were Russian President Demetri Zychopav and Chinese President Zi Fing. Seated beside the two presidents were Monsieur et Madame Allard[1039], from The 7th arrondissement, Paris; Mr and Mrs Miller[1040], from Nantucket County, Massachusetts; Mr and Mrs Chattopadhyay[1041], from Mumbai and Sheikh Ahmad[1042] from Al-Olaya Al-Muhammadiyah, Riyadh.

[1036] A pair of massive cylinders rotating in opposite directions creating weak gravity fields. Proposed by the late Dr Gerard O'Neill of Princeton University.

[1037] One tenth of the Earth's gravity field.

[1038] Buccellati Borgia Sterling Silver and Bamboo Cutlery Set.

[1039] Made their fortune in cosmetics.

[1040] Inherited their fortune from their family defence contracting business.

[1041] Made their fortune from toxic intense factories producing cancer and heart treatment pharmaceuticals with a 5000% mark up for consumers.

[1042] Owner of the Ahmad Petrochemical multi-national fossil fuels. Who funded most of the lobbying against environmental policies.

The evening meal was prepared by Haruto Yamamoto, the famous Japanese chef flown up especially from his cult restaurant "絶妙な (Zetsumyōna)", in Ginza, a subdistrict of Chuo City. Chef Haruto had prepared some Japanese delicacies, including blowfish sashimi, or "fugu[1043]" and cups of steaming Hirezake[1044], for those brave enough to try it and experience the delicious umami[1045] flavour.

Less adventurous guests were offered Western dishes including White Truffles, Beluga Caviar, Saffron and Matsutake Mushrooms followed by Kopi Luwak Coffee and Henri IV Dudognon Heritage Cognac.

Back on the Earth, it was early morning down at the Przejście graniczne Lubawka - Královec (the Wolfsangel border with the Czech Republic). Two soaked men and one drenched cat stood under sets of floodlights and beside razor wire fencing while the rain pounded down on them. The wind had gathered in strength, and the air became noticeably colder, causing their breath to form into a mist from their nostrils. The only positive thing from the drop in temperature was a reduction in what had been an overpowering smell of oil and other spilt fluids on the tarmac around them. Three pairs of. eyes were fixed, watching a single Wolfsangel guard thoroughly searching through the remains of the old battered Mercedes.

O'Neill had undertaken numerous privations during his Jesuit training, but he had never felt the combined discomforts associated with being hungry, tired, frightened and soaking

---

[1043] The Fugu Puffer Fish organs contain a neurotoxin a thousand times more potent than cyanide.
[1044] The dried fin of the fugu is steeped in hot sake and served.
[1045] The savoury flavour associated with monosodium glutamate.

wet. His black clerical vestments had become entirely saturated, and the deep chill made his limbs shake and his teeth chatter. In contrast, Stewart was oblivious to the needle-like rain beating down on his body. The Scotsman had faced circumstances far worse than the current rainstorm and had learnt to focus his razor-like attention exclusively on the immediate goal. Looking at the time on the misted dial of his vintage Omega, he was acutely aware that something had gone wrong with his most recent tattoo identity check; otherwise, they would have already passed through the border. Unlike O'Neill, who felt sorry for himself, Stewart was already planning the best ways to overcome the five guards he had seen so far at the checkpoint. The car jack that had been removed from the old Mercedes by the searching guard was currently his weapon of choice. Looking sideways, O'Neill noticed the emotions expressed in the Scotsman's eyes, the same ice-cold look he had last seen from Stewart in the temple under the Colosseum in Rome. The Jesuit exorcist realised his friend was as deadly and ruthless as the assassin Abdul Issuin.

O'Neill's dark contemplation about Stewart was interrupted by the Wolfsangel guard abruptly stopping his search of the Mercedes and walking towards them carrying Venchencho's ancient leather deliverance bag where the Göbekli Tepe adze was hidden. The priest's nerves started to get the better of him. If these guards confiscated the adze, this mission would be over before it had begun. O'Neill started to feel a panic attack building inside him. His surroundings suddenly seemed out of focus, and his breathing was insufficient. Trying to distract himself, he repeatedly shuffled his feet and cleared his throat.

Stewart looked at O'Neill. "For fucks sake, Thomas, calm down, or he will suspect something. What are you worried about? That he will find your secret stash of Dreamies?"

K.R.M. Morgan

The Scotsman's comment broke the tension, and O'Neill could not help but laugh. "No, T. It's not cat treats. Look, I will be honest. I have concealed a weapon in my luggage."

Stewart grinned. "Well, the way things are going, I could do with one. Please tell me it's something from Mark Katz at Mossad?"

The priest hesitated. "Urmm.. not exactly, T. It's older."

"As long as it has fresh ammunition, I can make good use of it. Now, before this goon gets here, where is it?"

As the Wolfsangel operative got closer, O'Neill whispered,

"T, It's not a gun. It's something I discovered in a temple at Göbekli Tepe..."

Stewart interrupted. "Typical. It's that fucking mystical axe, isn't it? I need a sodding Uzi, and you smuggle me a neolithic relic."

"It's called an adze, T. And it's the only way to kill the seven-headed monster[1046] inhabiting Cortez. You have to strike..." O'Neill gestured towards the rear of his head.

Stewart sighed. "Thomas, I don't want to kill Cortez... I want him to face trial."

The Scotsman's assertion made O'Neill revise his earlier assessment of Stewart. He was very different to Abdul Issuin. Stewart had respect for the rule of law. Usually, O'Neill would support such ideals, but not when dealing with the supernatural fiend he had seen so vividly portrayed as destroying all of creation in the subterranean temple frescos.

"T, you must. This monster will destroy everything unless you stop it."

[1046] O'Neill is referring to the MUŠ.ŠÀ.TÙR soul parasite.

Stewart frowned. O'Neill was always advocating non-violent solutions.

"Don't you Catholics believe all life is sacred? You should be glad I am going to bring him to trial."

The pair ignored the approaching Wolfsangel guard as they became utterly engrossed in their discussion. O'Neill turned away from the approaching guard and faced Stewart.

"No, you don't understand, T. Remember Sister Christina under the Colosseum in Rome?

Could you have detained her?"

Stewart chuckled while O'Neill continued, saying,

"You must trust me and accept that this creature we face is far worse than that abomination. To save all of creation, you must destroy it. That is why Venchencho and Mathers sent me. You must look in my incense censor if anything happens to me."

Before Stewart could respond, the guard threw the soaking leather deliverance bag, complete with its embossed Vatican seal, on the ground before the two men, instructing O'Neill.

"Priest, you open this bag, in case of booby traps."

O'Neill turned away from Stewart and knelt on the soaking tarmac. He opened the bag and carefully placed each item on the road surface. When he finally reached the four-inch diameter brass incense censor, he held it up to Stewart.

"Look, this is what I was talking about. The salvation of the world depends on it!"

Stewart leant forward intently, looking at the incense censor like it was the most sacred object on earth. In reality, he was trying to see where O'Neill had concealed the ancient axe head inside.

The guard looked on in pity at the two religious nuts kneeling in the pouring rain, engrossed with the hole-filled brass ball. Their bedraggled cat was busy bumping its head against the object. These were clearly religious nuts. The brass sphere was as soaked as the two men and would not burn anything for some time. The guard did not know the complete details about the Chairman's plans, only that a super weapon was about to change everything. So, no matter how much incense that ball might produce and how many prayers these two simpletons might make, it would not change a thing.

With a shrug, the guard walked off to the portacabin. "I will go and find what we are doing with you two, sad bastards."

Once he was sure the guard had gone, O'Neill unscrewed the brass lid to the censor and withdrew a three-inch curved perpendicular blade cast from a silvery grey metallic substance with a rough, pock-marked surface. Judging the mass, Stewart held the blade in his right hand, saying,

"It's got a good weight, but..."

He was about to ask about the missing handle when the storm intensified around them. Gusts of hurricane-force wind from the North almost blew the two men over. As they staggered to keep their balance, the tarmac shook, and a terrible rumbling noise like an approaching locomotive filled the air, followed immediately by a loud bang[1047]. Ezekiel arched into the classic Halloween cat shape and put himself between his two human companions and the preternatural threat. He hissed, facing towards the North, where lightning could be seen arcing repeatedly down from the sky, striking again and again at an identical location. From this same

---

[1047] Classic P and S sound waves are associated with earthquakes.

point, an illuminated plume suddenly shot into the night sky, forming a slowly rotating, pulsing vortex of brilliant plasma.

"What the hell?" demanded O'Neill as he tried to steady himself from the tremors running through the ground.

"That bastard Cortez has started the fucking Bell!" Stewart snarled in frustration, knowing he should already have been at Książ Castle, stopping Cortez!

Two hundred and fifty miles above the earth, dinner had reached the coffee and dark chocolate stage when the diners first noticed the pulsing and rotating beam that shone up from the Earth's surface into infinity. The French cosmetics magnet, Madame Allard's eyes glowed with delight. She demanded,

"Ohhh... look at those lights... can we go closer?" The other guests shared her curiosity, demanding the course change. Soon, the positioning rockets on the habitat caused a shudder to run through the space station, and they started moving closer to get pictures on their iPhones to post to their social media accounts.

As the habitat sped ever closer to the mysterious pulsing light, the host, Maximillian Cash, prepared to toast his two most honoured guests, Russian President Demetri Zychopav and Chinese President Zi Fing seated beside him. Cash raised his Waterford crystal flute filled with Dom Perignon œnothèque 1990[1048]. Seated at the head of the table, the three men wore similarly styled open-necked white dress shirts under the finest dark mulberry silk[1049] bespoke Italian

---

[1048] Dom Perignon œnothèque 1990 champagne is one of house Dom Perignon's finer vintages.
[1049] Recognised as the world's finest silk.

suits[1050]. The combined value of the clothing and jewellery[1051] worn by these men exceeded the GDP of many smaller sub-Saharan nations. When the cometary impacts had started, Cash had invited the two tyrannical dictators to join him in the safety of his Y Retreat, hoping they would remember his kindness when they took control.

Cash gazed at the two dictators like they were Rock Stars. Similarly to many other wealthy, right-wingers in liberal democracies, Cash lusted after the absolute power wielded by totalitarian despots. The thought of being unencumbered by laws, morality or the inconveniences of democratic accountability was extraordinarily attractive. Ironically, individuals in the liberal democracies who followed the tenets of communism were also great admirers of the two dictators, conveniently ignoring the fact that the two men were closer to Mafia[1052] Godfathers than to Marx[1053] or Mao[1054]. The right-wing supporters hoped that courting the dictators would lead to them gaining greater control over their home nation's resources when the democracies fell. In contrast, the left-wing followers hoped that supporting the dictators would reform their home nation into a society that shared resources more fairly (after the revolution). The two presidents played to these naive preconceptions from both the right and left-wing to advance their own agenda while playing the two ideological wings against each other. Their plan had been in operation for decades to destabilise

---

[1050] The classic Billionaire's dress code.

[1051] A Richard Mille RM029, Platinum A. Lange & Söhne 1815 Up/Down and an Omega Constellation.

[1052] "Bratva" (Братва) and Triads (三合會). The Russian Mafia and Chinese Mafia, respectively.

[1053] Karl Marx was a German-born philosopher and revolutionary socialist.

[1054] Mao Zedong was a Chinese politician, military strategist and revolutionary.

Western democracies to bring an era of autocratic totalitarianism under their complete control, with Russia controlling the Western Anglo-Saxon nations while China controlled the Asian Pacific. This ingenious plan had been entering its final stages when the unexpected Cortez revolution interrupted it. However, with the collapse of this short-lived revolution and the ending of the cometary impacts, Russia and China could now resume their nefarious activities.

Cash held up his glass and toasted in his squeaky nasal voice, "To our future!"

Before the three men could sip their ice-cold Dom Perignon, the entire space habitat began shaking, causing the plastic cladding on the walls to shatter violently and start floating as the artificial gravity field collapsed. Sirens blared, lighting turned red and hideous creaks and groans issued from the entire structure. The ordinarily serene view out of the window was replaced by a blinding white plasma field which enveloped the space station from Książ Castle beneath them.

"My God!" exclaimed Cash. His eyes expressed a terror that was completely missing in the eyes of the two ruthless dictators as the ten guests started floating helplessly around a room that was beginning to smell strongly of burning plastic and chemicals. None of the billionaires had included violent death in their plans for the evening, but no one ever did.

"Quick, to the escape pod," Cash announced to the two presidents, as he pulled himself through the air via the fixed seating structure towards a doorway with a glowing red exit light above it that had fallen open automatically. Once the three men were inside the tiny escape pod, other guests and crew members dragged themselves towards the open door.

K.R.M. Morgan

Demetri Zychopav and Zi Fing looked at the limited food and water in the escape pod and then at their fellow passengers heading towards them. They exchanged a knowing glance and then worked in unison. Zi Fing pushed Cash back into the lounge while Zychopav pulled up the escape pod door and pressed the large "Release" button. Their final view was of a desperate-looking Maximillian Cash pressed against the glass, screaming.   As the escape pod drifted away into the upper atmosphere, the two dictators pressed themselves against the small portal in the door as they witnessed the circular space station disintegrating in a fireball.

Forty minutes later, Demetri Zychopav and Zi Fing regained consciousness. Their bodies were freezing and covered in thick snow, lying beside the flaming remains of their escape pod. Based on the position of their bodies and the way the charred parachutes, with their giant "Y" logos, had been carefully collected together, someone had found them and dragged them clear.

Zi Fing pushed his wrists towards the Russian President, shouting angrily in Mandarin. At first, Zychopav could not understand, but then he saw the thick cast iron shackles around the wrists of the Chinese Premier. Looking at his own wrists and ankles, he suddenly realised he had also been restrained. The extreme cold had numbed his senses to the point he had not felt them before. He showed Zi Fing his bound wrists, and the Chinese President's angry tirade gradually stopped. Finally, he recognised that both men were in the same situation.

With the shouting over, they heard a pair of heavy boots trudging through the snow towards them. "At fucking last!" exclaimed Zychopav, "We must have landed in one of my Siberian autonomous regions. Once the locals recognise me, we will soon be on a plane to Moscow to resume our lives of luxury."

Finally, the stranger arrived and stood directly in front of them. The two Presidents looked up at a large male figure wrapped from head to foot in thick furs. The stranger was carrying an old battered AK47 machine gun slung over his right shoulder. Zychopav pulled himself up to a seated position to make his face more visible and recognisable before launching into a tirade of abusive insults that would have made his close advisors in the Kremlin quake with fear. However, this man was utterly unmoved. Eventually, he pulled back the thick fur snorkel hood parka that covered his head to reveal the face of an older male with a pronounced broken nose and a smile which spoke of a complete disdain for authority. The man projected a menace that Zychopav generally associated with his trained FSB assassins. Something about the man was vaguely familiar to the Russian President. Then, in a moment of disbelief, Zychopav knew. This giant pugilist face belonged to one of his former foreign intelligence agents, Len Bacharach. A man that Zychopav had pulled from the Russian embassy in London back to the Kremlin for interrupting the assassination of Stewart in London. After having him brutalised by the FSB, the Russian president had sent Bacharach off to rot and die in one of his most notorious Siberian Gulags[1055] high above the Arctic Circle, known as FKU IK-3[1056] (ФКУ ИК-3) or informally as Polar Wolf (Полярный волк).

Len Bacharach's grinning face addressed the two restrained men,

"Greetings, comrade Zychopav. Welcome to Polar Wolf! As the leader of the newly formed prisoner-run camp, you will

---

[1055] Maximum security corrective colony sounds so much nicer than death camp.
[1056] Federal Penitentiary Service of Russia for the Yamalo-Nenets Autonomous Okrug.

be delighted to know that all of us have been thinking for years about how to thank you for sending us here."

As the full implications of Bacharach's greeting sunk in, an unfamiliar warmth and stench filled President Demetri Zychopav's trousers.

THE STEEL TRAP

"The use of arms doth much differ in these times. I hear now the single rapier is altogether in use: when I was young, the rapier and dagger. And I cannot understand, seeing God hath given a man two hands, why he should not use them both for his defence." - William Higford, Advice to His Grandson, 1658

Twelve miles North of the Wolfsangel Czech/Polish border checkpoint
(Przejście graniczne Lubawka - Královec).

01:32 HRS (GMT+2), 21st September, present-day

The category three storm[1057] raged. Hurricane-force winds slammed into the limousine, drumming rain onto the tinted sapphlex[1058] glass moon roof and causing rivers of water to flow sideways along the rear passenger windows as the vehicle flew through the night. Looking through the vast front windscreen, the rain looked like flying arrows in the powerful full-beam headlights of the Mercedes ultra-limousine. The Maybach's enormous single windscreen wiper swept back and forth rapidly in a hypnotic rhythm, adding a surreal feel to the experience given by the massive wake pulsing out from the twenty-one-inch golden titanium nitrate wheels that ploughed through the standing water on the road surface. Each successive wake gushed over the verge of the single-lane road as the convoy of three sinister black vehicles hurtled like a force of nature through the violent storm.

[1057] Grade three on the Saffir-Simpson Hurricane Wind Scale indicates winds of between 111-129 mph.
[1058] A hybrid mix that is supposed to combine impact resistance with scratch resistance.

Inside a luxurious, hand-stitched dark leather cocoon with matching deep-pile carpets, two soaking men and one sorry-looking wet cat[1059] sat drying out in front of the car's heating vents, testing the ambitious goals of the German engineers who designed the ultimate climate control of this S-class Mercedes Maybach. The rich Nappa leather smell that was normally a feature of travel in the brand-new limousine was overwhelmed tonight by the more pungent odours of wet clothes and fur. The red LED temperature control above the passenger's climate control read 40 c (104 degrees Fahrenheit) as dry heat gushed out from the vents over the three soaking-wet passengers.

Thankfully, the lightning strikes and pulsing vortex that lit the sky before them subsided after Chairman Cortez terminated his brief few seconds of minimal running of the Bell. The earth tremors had also reduced considerably over the past twenty minutes, and the road had stopped undulating. However, the abnormal cold conditions continued. Water froze in clumps on the edges of the windscreen, and clouds of steam rose from the black G wagon in front of them, showing that it remained frigid outside.

The odour of wet fur combined with the oppressive heat drew frequent disapproving looks in the rearview mirror from the two Black Knights occupying the front seats. The only consolation the two Wolfsangel operatives enjoyed was the knowledge that both of the soaking men sitting in the rear would soon be on the receiving end of a prolonged, sadistic death.

O'Neill sneezed repeatedly. The priest felt a chill run through him. The hypochondriac in O'Neill was sure that a vicious upper respiratory infection was taking hold in his throat and

---

[1059] Few things look more pathetic or filled with the potential of deadly vengeance than a soaking wet cat, especially if you are responsible for the soaking.

sinuses. Even Ezekiel issued the occasional snuffle. Sitting beside him, Stewart appeared utterly unaffected by standing for over an hour in the icy cold and wet. The Scotsman sensed O'Neill's self-pity and decided to get his friend back on task; otherwise, he would become a liability and risk any remaining chance to capture Cortez. Stewart pulled open the minibar with its distinctive Maybach logo. He looked through the range of Schladerer Himbeergeist Schnapps and Hennessy X.O Cognac miniatures before breaking the screw top on a Glenfiddich. He poured a generous double measure of the amber liquid into a Waterford cut-crystal whiskey glass engraved with the Wolfsangel symbol. The likelihood that he would need all his reflexes sharp made the Scotsman refrain from taking a taste himself. Passing the glass to the snuffling priest, he said,

"Here, a dram will chase that chill out."

Before O'Neill took the glass, Stewart dipped his little finger in the amber liquid. He presented the soaked digit to Ezekiel, who sniffed it cautiously before licking the Whiskey and emitting a gentle murmur of approval. The cat then resumed his position next to the leather deliverance bag, guarding the exorcism kit, including its priceless incense censor.

O'Neill felt the burn from the single malt as it went down, followed by a wave of relaxation and warmth growing inside him. He nodded his appreciation.

"Thanks, T. I needed that," after a pause, O'Neill whispered, "It looks like they accepted your tattoo."

Stewart ignored the comment, judging they were almost certainly being subjected to surveillance. Instead, he gestured to the map displayed on an OLED screen in front of them. "We should see the castle any minute," he said, then switched his attention to looking out of the front windscreen.

K.R.M. Morgan

Thomas followed the Scotsman's gaze to get his first glimpse of Książ Castle. The three vehicles shot up a narrow, winding tree-lined track in the Owl Mountains and approached a large gothic structure with three towers. The tallest tower in the rear of the building resembled a church steeple, while the other two were closer to classic fairytale turrets popularised by the Disney franchise. Like the Disney castle, this structure was floodlit. But unlike Disneyland, it was surrounded by fifteen-foot-high razor-wire perimeter fences, numerous armed guards, Dobermans, and a series of checkpoints. Fortunately, all the barriers were raised, so the three vehicles sped through, accompanied by numerous salutes from black-uniformed soldiers dressed in rain ponchos. Stewart noted that even in the early hours, operatives were repairing sections of the castle's defences damaged in the recent earth tremors.

As they approached the portico at the grand entrance, the enormous wheels on the three vehicles kicked up numerous small stones from the gravel drive. After the whiskey, Thomas felt more optimistic about their situation. They were now safely across the border and inside the Wolfsangel headquarters. He recalled how different their circumstances had felt thirty minutes earlier, waiting in the rain by the border checkpoint.

Shortly after Stewart had speculated that the activation of the Bell was the cause of the violent weather and physical phenomena, a stream of car headlights appeared from the Polish side of the border. The Scotsman quickly returned the adze to O'Neill, who placed it in its hiding place inside the censor and hurriedly repacked the deliverance bag. Stewart nonchalantly moved closer to the car jack lying on the soaking tarmac and prepared himself for whatever would happen next.

As the three vehicles approached closer through the rainstorm, O'Neill saw that two black military G wagons[1060] were escorting one sleek black limousine. The limo drew alongside them, splashing the Scotsman, priest and cat with the standing water on the tarmac. As the big car stopped, O'Neill took in the limousine's Maybach logo and the S680 V12[1061] badge on its rear and frowned, saying,

"That will struggle to pass through the needle[1062]..."

After being thoroughly splashed, Ezekiel looked even more grumpy than usual. The large feline narrowed his eyes and shook himself. He swaggered over to the stationary car, turned his backside towards the huge rear alloy wheels that had just soaked him, twitched his backside, and repeatedly sprayed. A highly pungent and distinctive "Tom Cat" odour filled the air.

"That will be a bastard to clean," commented Stewart. He and O'Neill shared a conspiratorial smile before the Scotsman bent over to ruffle behind the cat's ears.

However, Stewart's good humour faded as he was brought back to the reality of their current situation by six Black Knights emerging from the two G wagons and approaching, their MP7s slung over their shoulders. Stewart prepared to

---

[1060] Mercedes-Benz G 350 d Station Wagon - not to be confused with the pimped out school run versions you see outside night clubs and Sainsburys. This is the "Mil-Spec" off road machine.
[1061] A 6.0-litre V12 bi-turbo engine producing 621 horsepower.
[1062] O'Neill is referring to the "Eye of the Needle" which was a narrow gateway into Jerusalem that forced camels to be unloaded and reloaded before they could pass. Hence Mark 10:25 "It is easier for a camel to go through the eye of the needle, than for a rich man to enter into the Kingdom of God."

pick up the jack from his feet. It wasn't a pistol, but it was better than O'Neill's neolithic relic. If things went kinetic, maybe he could take a few of these fuckers with him.

A uniformed Wolfsangel officer, covered in scrambled egg[1063], emerged from the rear of the Maybach and, after looking at the two bedraggled men and their cat, identified the Scotsman as his target.

"Knight Commander Salvador, we were not expecting you. Please accept our apologies. I am Brigade Leader[1064] Eriksson. We have come to bring you and your *associate* to headquarters," he looked disparagingly at O'Neill and then at the ginger cat, which was openly glaring at the senior Wolfsangel officer.

Eriksson ignored the icy stare from the cat. Instead, he politely held open the rear door of the sleek black car. He gestured for Stewart to enter, walked back to the front of the limo, and sat in the front passenger seat, closing the door behind him. Stewart turned to O'Neill, who was picking up Ezekiel, and whispered,

"I don't like being weapons-free[1065], Thomas."

O'Neill waived off the Scotsman's concern. "Nonsense, T. You are a weapon!"

One hundred yards under the Owl Mountains, Chairman Cortez stood outside one of the side tunnels leading to the Bell chamber. He remained in the protective clothing from

---

[1063] The uniforms of higher ranks in most services are covered in gold braid. This decoration is called scrambled eggs by lesser mortals.
[1064] Brigadier.
[1065] A military phrase denoting being unarmed.

his brief testing of the device, goggles around his neck, and thick lead-lined gloves tucked into his belt. He had been called away from supervising the loading of the Wonder Weapon on the freight train to attend to the report of one of his senior Black Knights going berserk. These apes were so easily disturbed and distracted. The soul parasite indwelling within the Argentinian wondered how such a species survived, let alone rose to planetary dominance. It was a fluke of fate, he decided. But, the entity reassured itself, it was a fluke that was about to be rectified.

The five Black Knights who had raised the alarm about the behaviour of one of their brother Black Knights were all so busy scrolling through the data feeds on their iKill Pro smartwatches that they did not hear their leader approaching. Installing Wi-Fi within the tunnels had been an extravagance and a distraction, reflected Cortez, but these Ape creatures had insisted. They were all so addicted to their technology. He coughed loudly, causing the five operatives to stand to attention. Disciplining these men for their lack of vigilance would have wasted valuable time. These stupid oafs would all cease to exist soon enough anyway.

"Where is he?" demanded the Chairman. In unison, the five men gestured down a smaller passage leading off the side tunnel. The leader of the group responded,

"Sergeant Hansen went to ur, relieve himself, Sir, and then *it* happened…"

Cortez sniffed dismissively. "And his behaviour after taking a piss disturbed you *hardened* Black Knights so much that you *had* to call me to intervene?"

The leader of the group swallowed hard. "Sir, he…" Cortez waved his left hand dismissively, saying,

"I do not want to hear about it…" With that, the Argentinian strode fearlessly down the dark tunnel. He already had a good idea about what had happened to Sergeant Hansen. Hansen had probably encountered one of the many esoteric devices that Isfet laid down within the tunnels at the war's end. Such traps would have been activated by running the Bell. Even the shortest use created unpredictable ripples in space-time-consciousness.

"Sir, don't you need a torch?" one of the operatives called after Cortez, but the Chairman had already vanished into the darkness.

To Cortez's preternatural senses, the tunnel was as well-lit as if it had been broad daylight. He stepped over the rocks that were strewn over the ground. As he walked, he could hear the sound of low whispers echoing around him. It was impossible to discern precisely what language was being spoken or what was being said. An unexpected odour filled the air. The MUŠ-ŠÀ-TÙR soul parasite struggled for a moment to recognise it, as it had been thousands of years since it last encountered the sweet, dry essence of the Mesopotamian desert. Memories of the MUŠ-ŠÀ-TÙR's orgies of destruction through villages along the Euphrates sprang unprompted into its consciousness. The whispering grew louder, and it became recognisable as ancient Sumerian. There were hundreds of voices, all whispering exaltations to the darkest entities of the Sumerian pantheon. Recollections of these ancient dark powers sent a chill through the non-physical body of the MUŠ-ŠÀ-TÙR. Not many things in this reality evoked such a visceral response in the semi-immortal creature.

The narrow passage opened into a small cave around twenty feet square in size, carved out of the raw bedrock. The floor was littered with rocks and a growing accumulation of fine rock particles. Searching for the source of the sand, Cortez gazed up to see a male figure dressed in a Black Knight uniform squatting halfway up one of the cave walls. The man was twelve feet above the ground, carving cuneiform characters into the stone in complete defiance of the accepted laws of gravity. As Cortez approached closer, the figure stopped carving what the Chairman could now recognise as the most feared ancient Assyrian demonic name, Hanbi[1066], and slowly turned his head. A pair of wide, insane eyes wept copiously as they looked directly at the Chairman while the man's hands and knees remained facing the wall. Or, more accurately, what remained of the man's digits as, on closer inspection, it was evident that the man had scraped the flesh from his fingers and was using the sharpened bones to carve the Sumerian devil's name over and over into the cave walls. Looking around the cave, much of its surface had been subjected to this man's writing. The same name was repeated over and over, and as a result, the cave walls were dripping with this man's blood. Another chill ran through the soul parasite within Cortez as he realised the whispering voices he could hear repeating this devil's name were a physical manifestation of the cuneiform blood ritual carvings he could see all around him. Each carving added power to what would eventually form the classic "GI-ALAL[1067]" evocation to summon this most ancient discarnate evil.

Now his carving was completed, Sergeant Hansen's face formed a macabre grin that was anything but amusing. The man's jaw twisted abnormally, and a guttural voice spoke in a dialect of Akkadian that had not been heard for over five thousand years.

[1066] King of the Lilu (spirits or demons). The Sumerian personification of evil. Father of the demon Pazuzu, who you might recognise from William Peter Blatty's work, The Exorcist.
[1067] Literally "Return the destroyer".

"Come forth, Hanbi! Father of Devils[1068]! Mountains tremble before you; Oh breaker of angels' wings..."

Although it was already pitch black inside the cave, Cortez sensed greater darkness cast over him like a shadow on a summer's day. It was not just an absence of light. It was an absence of being. An entity of absolute corruption manifested. The cave's physical dimensions did not constrain the entity's size, as it had no physical form. As the entity's manifestation intensified, it even made the preternaturally robust constitution of the MUŠ-ŠÀ-TÙR start to fail. The dark influence reached the possessed Black Knight on the wall, rapidly rotting the flesh on Sergeant Hansen's body until the remains cascaded down the cave wall, forming a pile of desiccated bones inside a Hugo Boss uniform.

This ancient Sumerian evil lacked the structure and predictability of the entities of the later Abrahamic religions. For that reason, such entities are notoriously difficult to control. Most ancient Sumerian exorcism texts, such as the Udug Hul[1069], recommends evocation only be conducted in the most remote and desolate places, where the creature can roam and prey on wild beasts and insects after the summoning.

With his goal of activating the Bell within his grasp, the MUŠ-ŠÀ-TÙR did not wish to risk injury to his current physical host. Without Cortez's authority, he would never activate the Bell. Hurrying back along the corridor to the five Black Knights waiting outside, he decided to send those stupid apes to slow this thing down long enough for him to escape.

[1068] From the translation Udug - literally Devils (𒌜𒅗).
[1069] Geller, Markham J. "Healing Magic and Evil Demons. Canonical Udug-hul Incantations" De Gruyter. ISBN 9781614515326

A hundred yards above the demonic manifestation, the Maybach's rear left passenger door opened. The group of Black Knights from the two escorting G Wagons had formed two rows, effectively forcing Stewart and O'Neill to enter the foyer of Schloss Fürstenstein[1070]. The entrance hall was decorated in green ceramic tiles, with repeating Eagle images reflecting Poland's historic heraldic symbolism. In the centre of the foyer was a broad stairway with a red carpet that led to the upper storeys. The recent earth tremors had been much stronger here, as the stained glass window at the top of the stairs had shattered, and the green tiled floor had sheered into segments. Workers dressed in long khaki-coloured cotton warehouse coats and matching baseball caps cleared debris and started repairs.

Eriksson joined them in the foyer, followed closely by the six Wolfsangel troops from the two escorting G Wagons. The Brigade Leader removed his cap, revealing a shock of ginger hair, much of which remained miraculously dry.

"Gentlemen, the Chairman has instructed that you should be taken to enjoy a fencing demonstration."

"At two am?" Stewart queried. The Scotsman remained convinced that, at any moment, the facade of politeness would drop to reveal the evil of these people. But before that happened, he had to get possession of a weapon. A sword was not as good as a gun, but it would be a start.

"We have three of the world's finest swordsmen coaching our elite soldiers. A Knight Commander, such as yourself, Senor Salvador, will surely appreciate the finer points of foil, épée and sabre."

[1070] The Nazi's name for Ksiaz Castle.

Stewart would rather have slept for a few hours, but he was here now and had to play this charade to its end. The Scotsman did not believe that anyone would be conducting a fencing demonstration at this hour in the morning. This was a test. The only question was, what kind? There was only one way to find out. Stewart winked at O'Neill, who was holding Ezekiel in his arms. The large ginger feline was still glaring at Eriksson.

Stewart smiled. "Of course, lay[1071] on Macduff[1072]."

Brigade Leader Eriksson was momentarily confused by the Shakespearean reference but ignored the comment and started walking in an Easterly direction, down a long outer corridor that ran the entire length of the castle. Again, the earthquakes had caused damage in several places along the corridor, and workers were already clearing and making repairs.

"Very efficient," complemented O'Neill. Stewart was less impressed. He had seen his share of totalitarian regimes and knew that efficiency often came at the price of liberty. This place was giving the Scotsman an ominous feeling.

"I expect they would prefer to be sleeping. I know I would," Stewart muttered.

Stewart and O'Neill continued, following a few paces behind Eriksson, along a sparsely lit walkway that probably originally served as an exercise route for the aristocrats occupying Ksiaz Castle during inclement weather. The decoration was classical, but the sides of the thoroughfare were littered with wooden crates of various sizes labelled with the museum and galleries that had initially housed the item.

[1071] Modern usage misquotes "lead on" when it should be "Lay on".
[1072] A quote from Macbeth by William Shakespeare.

"Must be the best of Europe's art collections here," commented O'Neill.

Stewart agreed, saying, "I prefer them in museums, where everyone can see them."

They reached the end of the original building's corridor and entered a twenty-five-yard-long extension, built during the German occupation of the site to provide access to the Owl Mountain underground complex, which the Nazis developed for their secret projects. The extension was twenty-five feet wide and twelve feet high, made of concrete and decorated on its pillars with symbolism typical of the Third Reich. At the far end of this external walkway was a freight elevator with a sliding concertina iron gate and a sign above it indicating "Access to the Owl Mountain mines 50 metres" (165 feet) beneath the castle.

The corridor was originally just a supported roof with a concrete floor. Post-war renovations added glass windows along both sides, leaving large drain openings on both sides of the walkway. These open areas let in the colder, damp air, causing every out-breath to steam. The whole place smelt vaguely of Jeyes Fluid. Grill-covered lights at regular intervals on the ceiling illuminated the space. Earthquake damage was also evident here. A single janitor, dressed in the same full-length khaki warehouse coat and cap as they had seen elsewhere, cleared shattered glass from the floor into a trolly bin with a scoop broom.

The corridor had been hurriedly converted into a long, narrow fencing salle, with a small wooden sword rack and chalk marks on the concrete flooring denoting the competition area. Stewart looked critically at the situation. It did not look good. The concrete floor and good drainage indicated an ideal place to clean up after a killing. The good news was they were in sight of a way to reach the tunnels where the Bell was located. Stewart was convinced that

Cortez would not be far from his precious Qlipothic Wheel. They might also use this situation to their advantage and acquire weapons, so he would play along, for now.

Eriksson bowed and introduced three men in their late twenties, dressed in gleaming white fencing uniforms. All three had removed their fencing helmets so their lean, athletic features could be seen.

"Knight Commander Salvador, I am pleased to introduce you to the three reigning world champions. Meister Dammezin, sabre,"

A muscular man with short-cropped blond hair and piercing blue eyes stepped forward and nodded. He had a deep scar along the left side of his face, presumably from a duel with his beloved sabre. He stepped back, and a shorter, balding man with a large nose stepped forward.

Eriksson smiled at this next swordsman. "Maitre Plee, foil,"

Plee stepped back, and the third man took his place.

"And last but not least, Maestro Barbieri of the épée." Barbieri was a tall, thin man with long black hair tied back into a single ponytail and a long Roman nose. Having taken his bow, he stepped back into the line of swordsmen. The three men seemed amused, as if sharing a private joke.

Having completed the introductions, Eriksson bowed.

"I must take my leave of you, but I am sure you will find the fencing demonstration *educational.*"

The three sword masters laughed as the ginger-haired Brigadier returned down the long corridor.

Stewart looked at O'Neill, holding Ezekiel and the leather deliverance bag in his arms. The cat had started to become restless and was emitting a low growl that O'Neill knew often indicated the proximity of evil.

Meister Dammezin smiled obsequiously. "Chairman Cortez cannot be here to greet you, but we have been asked to give you a special welcome!"

There was more laughter between the three men. Stewart thought some hidden agenda would emerge and that he and O'Neill were the targets of whatever this joke would be.

The Scotsman decided to push things, saying,

"Shame. I was looking forward to meeting him. But not to worry; I will catch up with him soon." Stewart smiled menacingly, making the three swordsmen look momentarily puzzled.

Meister Dammezin was the leader of the three men. He recovered from his momentary confusion and laughed. "While we wait for the other students, we can warm up with some gentle swordplay."

Dammezin reached into the wooden sword rack, pulled out a practice rapier and offered it to Stewart.

The Scotsman had already considered the likelihood that they would force him into an unequal fencing match, probably one against three. Stewart shook his head.

"Another time, perhaps?" he looked at his misted-up Omega, " It's late, and I am too tired to give you three *masters* an entertaining contest."

Dammezin curled his upper lip in open disdain. He was not used to anyone refusing him anything. He walked four paces over to O'Neill and snatched the deliverance bag from his arms, sending Ezekiel tumbling to the ground. The sabre master hurled the leather bag down the corridor towards one of the large side drainage holes. A bundle of ginger fur hurtled after the bag, catching up with it just in time to grab the precious bag in his claws, preventing it from disappearing into the castle's sewage system.

Dammezin forcibly pushed his left palm into O'Neill's chest, preventing him from going after the bag and cat, who was now some ten yards down the corridor on the right side. The sabre master grabbed O'Neill's dog collar from his vestment and pulled it away in his right hand, snarling,

"You won't need this garbage! We have different gods here. Strong gods who praise valour and victory, not forgiveness."

O'Neill pulled at the sabre master's hand to free the hold on his chest, eventually demanding, "Please take your hand off me!" but the man was too strong.

Dammezin smiled. "Please? Please is a weakling word. We seize what we want. We never wait for permission!"

To emphasise his point, the sabre master punched O'Neill in the face, causing the priest to bend over and hold his nose to stem the flow of blood. Ezekiel launched himself into a charge at the sabre master, but before he could embed his fangs and claws into his target, he received a hard kick from the German, sending his ginger form tumbling like a football over to the side wall.

Dammezin laughed openly at the incapacitated priest and his cat, but his pleasure ended abruptly as he visibly rose a couple of inches in the air due to a powerful groin kick from Stewart. A rich brogue interjected,

"You are starting to annoy me. If you want to hurt someone, why don't you try me?"

Dammezin turned and smiled. "Excellent, so there is some spirit under that dandy finery! By the way, I always wear a protective box," he gestured to his groin. He strode to the wooden sword rack and passed Stewart a practice rapier, adding,

"Let's see if your actions can match your bold words!"

The sabre master pulled out a fine-looking sabre for himself and started practising with it, taking imaginary swipes through the air around him. The Scotsman carefully examined the cheap Chinese steel in his practice sword and compared it with the fine German steel comprising Dammezin's sword. The stark difference prompted Stewart to ask,

"You are using that sabre?"

Dammezin looked like a cat who had got the cream. "Indeed, it is my personal weapon!"

Stewart looked around him. "I see. And where is my protective clothing?"

Dammezin beamed. "This will just be a friendly practice. Surely, a *fearless* Knight Commander like yourself doesn't need any protection."

The Scotsman sniffed. "And yet you wear it?"

If he heard the put-down, the sabre master ignored it and performed flamboyant warm-up exercises. O'Neill stumbled over to where Ezekiel lay and slumped against the wall beside the cat, gently ruffling the injured feline's ginger fur. A pair of green eyes looked carefully at the unfolding scene as Plee and Barbieri took a pair of fine-looking rapiers, the foil and epee not being sufficiently deadly weapons, from the wooden stand and started their warm-up exercises.

Stewart flexed his inferior 41-inch practice rapier with its folded-back safety tip. The worst this weapon could do in its current form was give someone a nasty bruise, whereas Dammezin's 34-inch sword looked suspiciously sharp. The Scotsman was considering moving onto the piste[1073] to indicate his readiness to begin a bout when Dammezin commenced a violent series of attacks. Stewart retreated and

---

[1073] Fencing competition area.

successfully parried the unexpected rain of blows. When the clash ended inconclusively, the Scotsman asked,

"You have dispensed with the "en garde" then?"

Dammezin laughed. "Sorry, I thought you were ready." Stewart saw the German's cruel grin through the sabre's traditional broad grille mask. Unlike the modern epee and foil masks, the sabre headgear gave a clear view of the opponent's face.

Dammezin attacked again, forcing Stewart to take a defensive posture and begin retreating down the hall, to the evident delight of the other two masters. Sparks danced in the air as the blades clashed. The world champion sabreur was a whirlwind of motion. His curved and light blade sang in the air as he danced and feinted, aiming slashing strikes at Stewart, who, in stark contrast, was a calm counterpoint to the hurricane-like activity of Dammezin. The Scotsman's long, slender blade reflected his personality, filled with precision and intent.

The blades clashed repeatedly, creating a furious ballet of metal and skill. The sabreur's advantage lay in speed and agility, his attacks coming from unexpected angles. Stewart countered with precision and reach, exploiting any opening in Dammezin's guard. But, the younger sabre master became increasingly impatient and overcommitted to a diagonal head cut. The Scotsman saw his chance and delivered a riposte, his practice rapier finding its mark by scoring a perfect "direct hit" on Dammezin's chest, which should have stopped the exchange. However, due to the heavy padding in his protective suit, the sabre master ignored the hit and continued his attack. Dammezin's blade slashed Stewart through his right sleeve, cutting the fabric and causing blood to begin dripping on the concrete at the Scotsman's feet.

"Your sword is not a practice blade," commented Stewart, beginning to understand tonight's game.

"Surely not afraid, Knight Commander?" sniggered Dammezin.

Stewart's eyes narrowed, and he decided to up the ante on the sabre master. Stewart was skilled in many martial forms, including fencing, but he was not a competitive fencer. His applications for weapons had always been for more deadly real-world scenarios. But he knew enough of the sabre competition rules to know that it prohibited the forward cross-over technique. This was a series of rapid lunges, where the back foot passed the front foot. Many competitive fencers felt this technique offered an unfair advantage for the attacker. Ignoring the cut on his arm, Stewart deliberately launched into a combination of techniques and moves that had been categorised as illegal within Olympic competition- including a failed flèche[1074] followed by continuous remises[1075]. Dammezin became flustered. As Stewart had anticipated, he had never practised how to respond to "illegal moves" as he never anticipated encountering them in competition. He continuously retreated and held his hands up, demanding, "I demand you stop these illegal techniques!"

"Surely not afraid, Maestro?" Stewart smiled as he saw Dammezin struggling to breathe through the wide bars on his protective mask. The young sabre master became

---

[1074] A flèche is a short to mid range attack which utilises the fast extension of your arm and legs in order to hit your opponent. In contrast to the classic lunge, a flèche sacrifices much of the ability to recover from the attack, if it fails. In return for this risk, flèche covers the same distance as a lunge in less time and more penetrating force due to extending both legs instead of just the back leg.

[1075] A remise is resuming an attack in fencing.

increasingly enraged and, using his youth and skill, launched into a diagonal slashing neck cut that was too fast for Stewart to parry, forcing the Scotsman to roll and return to his feet. The German became increasingly overconfident and less focused on his own guard. He gestured to his two fellow masters.

"Watch the priest while I finish this old turd." The two men walked towards O'Neill and pointed their blades towards him. They would enjoy killing the priest and his cat slowly and sadistically after Stewart was dead.

Dammezin turned to face the Scotsman.

"Let's end this fucking charade, *Stewart.* Yes, we always knew who you fucking were. It's time for you and your meek little friend to die like the pigs that you are! Bleeding out here in this damp, cold place."

Stewart narrowed his eyes in a look that would put a chill in the heart of anyone who knew the man. He placed the tip of his long practice rapier beneath his heel, deliberately broke off the bent blunt end, and then ran the ragged tip back and forth across the concrete to sharpen it. The blade now resembled an 18th-century British Royal Navy Dirk designed to repel pirates. The sword was now much shorter than the classic rapier but more in tune with the current task.

Dammezin leapt towards the Scotsman, screaming, "Die!" as he repeated the overhead swing that Stewart had been unable to block earlier. However, this time, it became evident that the Scotsman had deliberately failed in the previous encounter in order to tempt his sadistic attacker to repeat the technique. Stewart stepped into the overhead strike, parried, and buried the sharpened rapier blade through the face grill of the sabre master's mask, deep into the master's right eye, through the superior orbital fissure at the back of the eye socket and on until it impacted the occipital bone at the rear of the skull. Blood started spurting from Dammezin's eyes, nose and mouth, staining the white of his tunic. The sabre master staggered and would have fallen had Stewart not held on to his left shoulder.

The Scotsman could see that Plee and Barbieri had left O'Neill sitting with Ezekiel and were advancing towards him with their long rapier blades at the ready. There was no more laughter. Both men looked grimly at the blood that cascaded from Dammezin over the concrete.

Stewart quickly removed his jacket and pulled out the broken rapier from the sabre master's eye socket. He was about to push his assumption about how competitive Olympic champions would focus only on permitted techniques in their discipline. The Scotsman grinned, saying,

"Time for some Renaissance cloak and dagger..."

Plee and Barbieri were now less than ten feet away and preparing for a simultaneous attack. Unlike in the movies, where a single skilled swordsman can counter multiple swordsmen, Stewart preferred one-on-one combat, especially when the opponent was world-class, like these two.

Stewart guided the dying sabre master backwards to collide with Plee, taking both men to the ground. He then gathered Barbieri's blade with his jacket, stepped beside the Italian and broke Barbieri's right tibiofemoral and patellofemoral joints with a lightning-fast snapping sidekick. As the Italian fell to his knees, shouting in pain, Stewart skewered Barbieri diagonally down from the right side of the neck into the chest, piercing the heart. The Italian fell face forward to the concrete, twitching while making strange gasping, gurgling noises and blood pulsed from his neck.

Stewart found himself next to the wooden sword stand and gathered some chalk in his left hand while he picked up the full rapier from beside Barbieri's dead body. The French master Plee was soaked in Dammezin's blood, having pulled himself out from under the dead man. The Frenchman glared at the breathless and sweating Stewart, who, apart from the sabre cuts on his arms, had also accumulated copious amounts of blood and plasma from the German and Italian he had just fought.

"There will be no quarter!" snarled Plee as he launched a blisteringly fast lunge directly towards the Scotsman, his blade completely bypassing Stewart's guard, which was too slow to respond. Plee's rapier point pierced deeply into Stewart's left shin. A grimace formed on the Scotsman's blood-speckled face. In return for this deep stab, Stewart blew the chalk from his hand into Plee's fine wire mask, blocking the wire and obscuring the French master's vision.

As Plee stabbed blindly towards where he remembered the Scotsman stood, Stewart used the last of his reserves to ignore the searing pain in his left shin and drive a lunge with his rapier so deeply into the French master's chest that it pierced through the front kevlar chest protection and protruded from out of the back of the french master's uniform. Deep crimson patterns spread over Plee's white uniform, and blood started pouring from his mouth as he collapsed silently to the floor.

"No quarter it is..." stated Stewart's gentle brogue to the corpse.

The Scotsman dropped his sword and put his hands on his waist. He was utterly spent. His white dress shirt was soaked in blood and sweat. He noted that he was bleeding from the deep stab on his left shin and the sabre cuts on his arms. Taking the rapier, he cut fabric from his trouser pockets to form improvised bandages for his wounds. By the time he had finished, O'Neill had gathered up the deliverance bag and Ezekiel. O'Neill's face was bruised and bloody, but he was in better shape than Stewart as the pair walked past the cleaner, who had continued working throughout the series of bloody encounters. Working for Wolfsangel obviously accustomed you to bloody mayhem.

They had reached the black iron elevator gate and pressed the "call elevator" button when suddenly bullets started slamming into the walls around them.

"Fuck!" exclaimed Stewart. They were sitting ducks for a group of Black Knights who had just emerged through the entrance at the other end of the exterior corridor.

"Down!" commanded the Scotsman as he pulled O'Neill to the floor to reduce their size as a target for the six Wolfsangel shooters twenty-five yards away.

"Stewart, catch!" the voice was strangely familiar. The Scotsman caught a black full-frame pistol with the words SIG SAUER 357 SIG[1076] embossed on the barrel. Stewart looked at the unexpected source of their help in shock as the caretaker removed his cap. The stranger lit a Montecristo No. 4 from a matchbook and drew on the glowing Petit Corona cigar. He pulled an Uzi submachine gun from within his long overcoat. The hawk-faced caretaker sprayed short three-round bursts at the six Black Knights, rapidly taking them down.

"Issac bin Abdul Issuin!" exclaimed Stewart in shock. At first, he considered shooting the hawk-faced assassin but then reconsidered and instead joined him, shooting at the growing number of Black Knights appearing at the hall's entrance. Both men were exceptional shots, cleanly taking

---

[1076] A SIG SAUER p229 with extended Mec-Gar .357 14 round magazine.

down a gunman with each round. There was a loud ping behind them. The elevator had arrived.

Abdul Issuin gestured towards the lift. "That elevator heads down to the tunnels. You both need to go. I will hold them."

The gunfire resumed, ricocheting off the concrete around them as more Black Knights stormed into the corridor, this time armed with armour-piercing MP7 submachine guns.

"Why?" it was Stewart who asked, wondering why this cold-blooded killer would make such an altruistic gesture.

Abdul Issuin shrugged. "If half of what O'Neill and Ad-Dajjal say about Cortez is true, then," he looked directly at Stewart, "you alone can stop him." Stewart paused, wondering if he had been too rash dismissing the mystical aspects of O'Neill's story.

"Go!" repeated the hawk-faced assassin as he drew on his cigar and loaded a new magazine into his Uzi. There was a momentary pause from the Scotsman and priest.

"Are you sure? It's certain death!" demanded O'Neill in horror.

"Just make sure it's worth it," grunted Abdul Issuin harshly as a bullet grazed his left arm, and, in response, he gunned down another three Black Knights.

Stewart nodded in appreciation, saying, "Hold the bridge, Horatio[1077]!"

After patting Abdul Issuin's back, he pulled O'Neill into the elevator and closed the door. The hawk-faced assassin

---

[1077] Publius Horatius Cocles single handedly defended the narrow Pons Sublicius bridge into Rome against the entire Etruscan army. He held the bridge long enough for the rest of the Romans to destroy the bridge and save Rome in the sixth century BCE.

locked eyes with the Scotsman, saying, "Stewart, kill the bastard!"

Their last image, as the elevator descended, was of Abdul Issuin walking calmly towards the Black Knights. The hawk-faced assassin held two Uzis, one in each hand. Clouds of cordite and cigar smoke swirled around him as spent rounds cascaded to the floor, and his caretaker's coat billowed behind him.

THE CREEPING DARKNESS

"Και είδα τον Ταξίαρχο, κατέβα από τον παράδεισο. Κρατούσε το κλειδί της Αβύσσου και μια μεγάλη αλυσίδα στο χέρι του. Άρπαξε εκείνο το πιο αρχαίο Βαβυλωνιακό Κακό και το έδεσε στην Άβυσσο. Μόνο στο τέλος των καιρών, αυτό το σκοτάδι θα απελευθερωθεί για άλλη μια φορά"

[And I saw Taxiarchos[1078], come down from heaven. He held the key to the Abyss and a great chain in his hand. He seized that most ancient Babylonian Evil[1079] and bound it in the Abyss. Only at the End Times[1080], will this darkness be set free once again...] - The Exorcist's Revelatory Codex. Translated from Greek MS 9656a. Vatican Archives

Riese[1081] Complex
165 feet beneath Schloss Fürstenstein (Książ Castle)
Owl Mountains, Central Sudetes, South Western Poland.

03:38 HRS (GMT+2), 21st September, present-day

The rusting ironwork of the cage's open sides revealed walls of dark, wet rock, moving slowly upwards in a classic self-motion paradox[1082], as the service elevator slowly descended a ten-foot square vertical shaft cut into the bedrock beneath Książ Castle. Below them, a diesel generator chugged, and

---

[1078] The Archangel Michael, leader of the Heavenly Host - the angelic army of the Lord God Almighty.
[1079] Hanbi was the ancient Akkadian personification of Evil and Master of all evil forces in the universe.
[1080] The time of the prophesied end of creation.
[1081] Riese (Giant) was the Nazi secret code name for a series of seven underground bases constructed under the Owl Mountains between 1943-45.
[1082] When human senses believe it is the environment moving when it is in fact the observer who is in motion.

above, cables clattered as the cage bumped from side to side against the rough stone surfaces. The staccato sound of automatic gunfire gradually subsided as they descended. Inside the cage, the odours of lubricating oil mixed with diesel fumes and mould.

Three pathetic figures were recovering from their recent ordeal inside the dimly lit space illuminated by a solitary, discoloured seventy-watt bulb. The two humans silently reflected on the unexpected appearance of their one-time opponent, whose uncharacteristic sacrifice had permitted them to escape. O'Neill hoped the former assassin had found divine inspiration for his action, while the more pragmatic Stewart pondered Ad-Dajjal's involvement in Abdul Issuin's intervention. In contrast, the large ginger cat lying in the priest's arms was preoccupied with absorbing O'Neill's body heat and licking the bruises where the sabre master had kicked the fearless feline.

O'Neill felt despondent and disorientated. It had been many years since he had been subjected to physical violence, and apart from the unexpected blow to his face, he also had an increasing disquiet about what lay ahead. He had faced and overcome supernatural evil before, but that had been when he faced a diabolical adversary that had been defeated by numerous exorcists in the past using well-established methods that were well-documented. Based on what he had seen on the tomb walls in Göbekli Tepe and what Mathers had told him in Rome, he knew the coming confrontation with Cortez would be different. Radically different. He wondered if Stewart realised that the ancient texts described that few who dared to confront this ancient evil would survive.

Looking at his companion, O'Neill saw that Stewart was utterly calm and focused, counting the number of rounds remaining in the extended magazine in his SIG[1083] pistol. The Scotsman noticed O'Neill's attention and the seriousness of his expression and patted the priest on the shoulder, saying,

"Cheer up, Thomas. If we three are doomed to die, as you believe, the least we can do is give our enemy something to remember us by.   In addition to your sacred adze, I still have five of the original fourteen .357 SIG penetrator[1084] rounds. That's more than enough to spoil most monsters' days. How is your nose?"

O'Neill grinned and shrugged. The sight of the scarlet patches on the improvised bandages around Stewart's shin and forearm made him embarrassed at the superficial nature of his own suffering. It was typical of Stewart to make light of the danger and show more concern for his comrades in arms than himself. The Scotsman gestured towards Ezekiel.

"How is your furry friend doing? That was a bastard of a kick he took."

O'Neill ruffled the cat's neck, causing Ezekiel to chirp slightly. His big green eyes looked up into the faces of his two human companions. Seeing that nothing required an immediate response, he returned to tending to injuries.

"He has a couple of bad bruises, but I cannot feel any broken bones," answered O'Neill as they continued their descent.

The air felt cooler and damper as the amount of liquid running down the walls outside the elevator increased. There was also a rancid odour of decaying organic material, which grew so strong it made O'Neill pull a face of disgust, exclaiming,

---

[1083] SIG SAUER P229 - chambered for .357 SIG.
[1084] .357 Mag 140grain Xtreme Penetrator Solid Monolithic Hunting round.

"Dear Lord, what can that smell be?"

Stewart did not answer.   He already knew that characteristic smell too well. Death. Ezekiel merely covered his nose with his right paw. A few seconds later, the cage jerked to a stop.

"Ground floor: perfumery, stationery and leather goods[1085]," joked Stewart as he pulled open the iron concertina door. The area surrounding the lift was only illuminated by the tiny bulb inside the elevator, so it was impossible to see all the details of their immediate environment. However, a badly rusted sign opposite the elevator doors was visible, which indicated an upward arrow beside the black gothic text, "Schloss Fürstenstein 50m".

Stewart held the SIG in his right hand down by his side and was the first to exit the lift. Running alongside the opened elevator door was a wide-gauge[1086] railway track set into concrete sleepers embedded into the small rocks, which formed the ground inside the mine tunnel. The steel retaining clips on the sleepers looked freshly installed, indicating to the Scotsman that Cortez wanted to be sure this particular rail line worked flawlessly. Five yards away, further down the line, were the outlines of a series of galvanised metal mining carts. The profound darkness meant seeing what cargo was transported inside was nearly impossible.

Stewart walked with a slight limp towards the mining carts, his eyes rapidly adjusting to the gloom as he scanned for possible threats in the darkness. The SIG was held gently in his well-practised hand. O'Neill followed, still carrying the deliverance bag and the cat, which sniffed the air, bristled, and issued a low growl.

[1085] A quote from the British Sit Com. "Are you being served?"
[1086] The German wide gauge track was adopted within European mines.

"Be careful, T!" warned O'Neill, "Ezekiel is sensing evil."

Stewart chuckled. "Given where we are, I would be surprised if he didn't!"

The stench that had started when they descended the elevator overwhelmed the senses, making O'Neill retch involuntarily. Thankfully, his stomach was empty, but Ekiekiel did not want to take any chances, so he leapt from his arms and limped over to be beside Stewart.

"Demonic forces often manifest first as a nauseating smell," cautioned O'Neill as he pulled himself upright and massaged his arms. His biceps had started to cramp after statically holding the cat and bag for the last few minutes.

"In this case, I think there is a more mundane explanation," replied Stewart, gesturing for O'Neill to come closer.

"Dear God. A carriage full of corpses!" exclaimed O'Neill, crossing himself.

"Sadly, more than one," corrected the Scotsman, "a whole train of the poor bastards."

Stewart started leaning closer to the lead carriage to try and determine what had killed so many people. O'Neill stopped him and, reaching into his bag, pulled out two headlamps and two 3M branded N95[1087] certified masks. Stewart declined the mask but took the headlamp. As Stewart put the lamp on his head, he looked at O'Neill, saying, "I have to ask, why does the Vatican exorcism kit include masks? Do the demons do much DIY?"

O'Neill adopted a severe expression "Demonic manifestations often involve a nauseating smell, and these

---

[1087] 95% efficient viral and bacterial filtration but not oil resistant - hence the N prefix.

entities delight in spreading an infection to weaken their human opponents[1088] and victims."

As the beams from the headlamps illuminated the tunnel around them, it highlighted some odd light anomalies floating in random patterns from the ceiling and walls. The Scotsman's face adopted an intrigued look.

"There cannot be fireflies down here..."

"No, T. It is a sign of high ethereal energy levels. We must be vigilant for manifestations."

As if to confirm O'Neill's analysis, scratching sounds began around them. The priest's eyes went wide, and he tensed, expecting some demonic form to manifest at any instant.

Stewart smiled. "Relax, Thomas. With all these bodies, there are bound to be rats, and our lamps will make them flee to the shadows."

The Scotsman resumed his careful examination of the bodies in the first carriage. There was a mix of injuries. Some highly corrosive substances had badly burned some, and others had limbs removed with disturbing signs of numerous tiny teeth having played a role in the amputations. All of them had curious circular six-inch diameter wounds, like giant octopus sucker marks, but with the same small serrated teeth indentations around the edges of deep penetrating holes into the affected organs. In all his years, Stewart had never seen anything similar.

"Thomas, what do you make of these wounds? Do any of your supernatural bogeymen inflict anything like these?"

Given his squeamish nature, O'Neill was initially reluctant to come close enough, so Stewart pulled out a severed leg and thrust it towards the priest. The thigh was covered in the

---

[1088] Exorcists.

same strange circular wounds, some penetrating right through the limb. Scientific curiosity quickly overcame O'Neill's instinctive revulsion. He took the leg and examined the thigh under his headlamp. The image of the strange life-size representation of the seven-headed snake statue and the wall frescos he and Mohammed had discovered under Göbekli Tepe suddenly made sense. O'Neill threw the limb back into the carriage in disgust.

"Yes, these poor souls are evidence of the soul parasite inside Cortez feeding."

"The mythical Mus-A-Tor?" queried Stewart. O'Neill nodded, making the beam from his headlamp bounce around the dark, damp tunnel. The Scotsman thought for a moment. All these men and women were armed with automatic Glock pistols, but still, they had perished. Maybe his SIG would prove just as ineffective. If Thomas was correct, and this creature could inflict such terrible wounds against armed and highly trained operatives, how would he find a way to get close enough to use the adze? Dismissing the negative thought, Stewart moved to the next carriage. This container was different. The galvanised truck was filled with a red-brown soup of soft human tissue. Intestines, livers and lungs floated on the surface alongside fabric from Black Knight uniforms. A thread of mucus trailed over the edge of the rim of the carriage. It proved irresistible to Ezekiel, who approached and sniffed it cautiously and backed away, sensing something very wrong.

"What the hell?" Stewart mused to himself, shaking his head in disbelief. Some unknown force had melted these bodies. When he was briefed about the wheel on the roof terrace in Geneva, these effects were not mentioned, but if the wheel tore apart space-time, then it was perfectly possible that it could reduce organic life into the organ soup he saw in front of him.

Suddenly, a chugging engine noise filled the corridor and broke the Scotsman's chain of thought. Clouds of thick black diesel fumes filled the air, and the elevator started moving to the castle. It would be a matter of moments before it returned and filled the tunnels with Black Knights.

"Fuck!" Stewart yelled.

Tucking his SIG inside the waistband of his trousers, he searched around, found a large wrench from the side wall, hobbled over to the diesel generator and removed the spark plugs one by one. The engine shook violently and abruptly stopped. The Scotsman reached up and used the wrench to strike loose the chains connected from the engine to the lift. Satisfied that the elevator was immobilised, Stewart absent-mindedly let his lamp beam explore the tunnel opposite the train full of bodies. There was a brief reflected flash. The Scotsman could see a large steeled enamel frame on a wall beside a set of grimy wired glass double doors. Limping over, Stewart started examining a large map annotated in a black gothic German script. Sections of the map were so covered in decades of grime and rust as to be unreadable.

Moments later, O'Neill and Ezekiel joined him. Stewart translated the German that he could make out while O'Neill spat on a tissue to clean the unreadable sections. The map was titled "Riese Complex" and had seven separate zones, two of which were immediately interesting. Stewart pointed to zone three, which was labelled "Überprüfung der Sogenannten Geheimwissenschaften" (Examination of the Secret Sciences[1089]), and said,

"This lab may give us some clues as to Cortez's plan for using the Bell, and,"

[1089] Parapsychology would probably be the most accurate modern equivalent, although the Third Reich version had a much wider remit.

Stewart traced his forefinger along a passageway from zone three on the grimy enamel map,

"if I am reading this correctly, zone three connects directly to zone seven, "Wehrwissenschaftliche Zweckforschung" (Military Scientific Research)."

O'Neill traced his finger along the list of items within zone seven, stopping at a sub-section.

"Yes, T. You are right. There it is, Die Glocke!"

Stewart grinned. "OK, let's go." He pulled open the double doors, and before he could step inside, a blur of ginger fur pushed in front of him and disappeared into the darkness beyond. Stewart and O'Neill followed. Seeing that O'Neill was about to flick on the lights, Stewart warned,

"No, Thomas, leave them. We have to assume we are not alone down here, and the longer we can avoid alerting people to our presence, the better."

The air was warmer than the tunnel. It was dry and smelt of Jeeves disinfectant. The only sound was the low hum of industrial dehumidifiers. The beams from their two headlamps highlighted rack after rack of materials. The nearest were large glass bottles containing biological specimens, including animals, unidentifiable body parts, and even a few human heads.

Before Stewart could remark about the gourmet nature of the cuisine in the base, there was a sudden, unexpected noise as some glass items smashed to the ground to their left. Stewart pulled O'Neill behind the nearest rack, turned off both of their headlamps and drew his SIG. An apologetic meow followed the noise.

"Ezekiel," sighed Stewart as he stood up and turned their headlamps back on. They moved deeper into a giant storeroom carved into the bedrock, twenty feet high and around forty feet wide. Row after row of storage racks prevented them from seeing the furthest end. Their headlamps revealed these racks to be filled with esoterica of every description.

"This must be the legendary hoard of occult items seized by the Nazis as they overran Europe," exclaimed O'Neill. He picked up a cuneiform tablet baked in a dark clay and read it.

"Cooking recipes?" asked Stewart, still thinking about all the preserved specimens they had just passed.

"No. They have collected demonic curses," O'Neill answered as if it were a completely normal response.

"Which curses?" asked the Scotsman, hoping they would be minor ones, like haemorrhoids, unexpected income tax demands and failed car batteries.

O'Neill picked up a random selection of the clay tablets.

"Asag, to cause sickness. Galla, to drag someone to the underworld. Namtar, to bring death and, of course, Pazuzu, the wind demon."

"As in The Exorcist?"

O'Neill chuckled. "We don't need to worry about Pazuzu. He was used as a protector god to frighten away other demons."

Stewart picked up one of three small cast metal amulets for Pazuzu and went to put it around O'Neill's neck. O'Neill raised his right hand to resist. "I have my cross, T. I don't need anything else."

The Scotsman shrugged and put the amulet back on the table. The two men continued walking, eventually approaching another set of double doors. Again, a blur of ginger fur pushed through in front of them as the door was opened.

K.R.M. Morgan

This new room was similar in size to the last one but with magical paraphernalia laid out on the floor. Human skulls in different magical configurations were set within triangles in front of chalk circles inscribed in various languages. Ezekiel hackled and, in uncharacteristically uncurious behaviour, avoided the esoteric symbols.

"I take it they were not trying to guess the winning lottery numbers?" joked Stewart, still struggling to accept the reality of all this overt hocus pocus. The Scotsman could not accept that scrawling some symbols in chalk on a floor and repeating some gibberish could have any effect on the real world. His decades of experience in the military had convinced him that few things trumped a good weapon in expert hands.

O'Neill ignored his friend's attempts to downplay the potential for supernatural evil. The priest's encounters with the demonic Sister Christina had convinced him that the Isfet, including Cortez, were dangerously skilled adepts of the dark arts and should never be underestimated. He paused for some minutes to carefully examine the ritual layouts and inscriptions on each floor decoration.

"No, T. This is classic necromancy. They have exhumed the bodies of notable evil figures from the past to help them solve technical problems on Wonder Weapons, mostly the Bell and to give advice on strategy. Some of the ceremonies are related to the evacuation of this location, and some are for creating esoteric watchers to guard this site, so we will need to be aware of triggering esoteric booby traps."

"I will leave that kind of thing to you, Thomas," replied Stewart, gratefully opening the next set of doors for Ezekiel to go first.

Surprisingly, Ezekiel was much less motivated to enter this room. O'Neill had to call him twice and offer cat treats before

Ezekiel eventually entered. In contrast to the dry atmosphere and neutral smell in the previous areas, this room was cold and vaguely smelt of sulphur.

"Are the batteries dying on these headlamps?" queried Stewart as he noticed the light seemed dimmer. He hoped O'Neill had brought spare batteries, or they would be forced to turn on the lights and risk alerting people of their presence.

"No, T. They are fresh, long-life alkaline cells. They should be good for many hours yet. Dimming of lights is often a precursor of..."

"Demonic manifestation?" Stewart finished the sentence and continued examining their surroundings. This thirty-foot diameter circular room had a low concrete ceiling and matching walls. Around its circumference was a large magic circle inscribed with Latin and Greek god names and classic medieval sigils. Inside the circle were a chair and a table with notebooks, pens, a thermos, empty plates, water bottles, an ashtray filled with spent cigar stubs and a desk lamp. Beside the table was a commode. Someone had spent a lot of time in this ritual space. Near the concrete wall, on the far side of the circle, was a classic evocation triangle, where Renaissance magicians believed demonic forces manifested in response to ritual. The edges of this evocation triangle showed evidence of deep scratches, which had gouged more than an inch deep into the concrete floor. Stewart watched as O'Neill very carefully stepped over the edge of the large circle, walked to the table and started reading the notes scribbled in the books.

Ezekiel went to follow him but stopped, arched up and hissed at a repeated pattern drawn in chalk on the floor along the circumference of the magic circle. Stewart examined the strange sign. It was composed of a series of straight lines linking four spheres, one sphere at the top and three equal-sized spheres below it, resembling a simply drawn pyramid. Two crosses sprouted from the outer diagonal lines, making the symbol look vaguely like a fly[1090].

"Thomas, what is this symbol that has spooked your cat?" asked the Scotsman.

O'Neill sounded nervous, "It is the sigil of the Goetic demon Marbas, named in the Lemegeton Clavicula Salomonis[1091] as President of Hell."

Stewart looked around the room. "It looks like Marbas has been given his own private room, "What did he do? I take it we are talking about a male devil?"

"That is an interesting question. T. He can be forced to appear in a male human form, but the default appearance is as a gigantic lion. Goetic magicians summoned him to provide them with secret knowledge. Based on these notebooks, Cortez has repeatedly summoned Marbas over the past days to provide information about repairing the Bell and determining the most promising astrological time to run it at full power."

"Based on the earthquakes and weather, we can safely assume Cortez successfully repaired the device. When does he plan to run it at full power, does it say?" Stewart asked, hoping there would be a few days' grace.

O'Neill thumbed through a few more pages before declaring, "The autumnal equinox. There will be a "hard vision[1092]"

[1090] The similarity to the sigil of Baal (Ba'al Zabub) is not a coincidence. Both entities share a similar origin related to decay, disease and airborne powers of corruption.
[1091] The Lesser Key of Solomon.
[1092] Conjunction (0 degrees), Square (90 degrees) or Opposition (180 degrees) respectively. Also known as an "Evil Eye" aspect.

aspect between Mars and Saturn[1093] during the equinox tomorrow at 11:17 HRS UTC. This is an extraordinarily inauspicious aspect, foretelling destructive change."

Stewart thought for a moment. In all the excitement, O'Neill had forgotten it was already the 21st. "You mean today, Thomas!"

The Scotsman looked at the misted-up dial on his old Omega. Hopefully, the old wind-up mechanism kept time even after being soaked. "That means we have less than seven hours before this idiot fires up the wheel and destroys the whole of creation. Let's get to zone seven, find the Bell, and destroy it. Then we can deal with Cortez!"

O'Neill stepped carefully out of the circle, gathered up Ezekiel, and followed Stewart to the double doors. They emerged into a long rail tunnel. Unlike the first mining tunnel they had encountered, this one was lit at regular intervals by bulbs set into the thirty-foot-high ceiling. An enamel metal sign opposite them indicated in a black gothic script that 800 metres to the left was the "Wehrwissenschaftliche Zweckforschung" (Military Scientific Research) section. Stewart gestured that was their goal. However, before they could start walking, there was a burst of gunfire and a scream from the direction of the Bell.

Stewart drew his SIG and pulled O'Neill back to the doors they had just left. A figure stumbled wildly towards them down the corridor, gasping for breath. He wore a thick, radioactive protection suit with lead goggles, thick gauntlet gloves and rubber boots. A mask had been torn from his face and hung loosely around his neck. His run was wild and uncoordinated, as if he were being chased by something terrifying. The Scotsman's SIG had initially trained on this

---

[1093] Symbolising the astrological aspects of Violence, War and Decay.

figure but quickly moved towards the source of whatever had frightened the man, who was so uncoordinated in his movement and out of breath that he posed no immediate threat.

A few yards from their position by the double doors, the terrified worker tripped on one of the railway sleepers, slamming hard into the ground, where he remained completely motionless. Stewart and O'Neill advanced cautiously. The Scotsman used his injured leg to nudge the man onto his back gently. The man's face was set in a grotesque expression so frequently seen in a violent death. Stewart knelt and felt for a pulse in the man's neck but looked up to O'Neill and shook his head.

O'Neill crossed himself. "Poor Soul. Something frightened the crap out of him."

The Scotsman quickly frisked the man but found no weapons. "Given his clothing, I suspect he must have been one of the Bell technicians working for Cortez."

O'Neill nodded in agreement. "The question is, what would frighten him to this extent?"

"There is only one way to find out, come on." Stewart rose to his feet, and the three figures moved further along the corridor. The ginger cat and Scotsman exhibited noticeable limps as they walked along the concrete railway sleepers. O'Neill clutched his leather deliverance bag as though he was riding on a subway and expected to be robbed at any moment.

Fifty yards further on, they came across a group of five dead Black Knights strewn across the twenty feet width of the tunnel. Three of the bodies were contorted into bizarre postures, with broken limbs, twisted backs and shattered skulls from multiple 9mm rounds. The final two bodies had self-inflicted gunshot wounds. Their biometrically controlled Glocks lay close to their hands.

"Dear God, what happened here?" O'Neill asked.

Stewart assessed the scene. "These two," he pointed to the two suicides, "Shot these other three and then killed themselves."

O'Neill crossed himself. "Tavish, this can only be evidence of mass possession. I have read about this kind of thing, but it was back in the Middle Ages."

Suddenly, Ezekiel arched and hissed at some unseen threat in the distance along the tunnel. The ginger fur ball slowly advanced in front of his two human companions. The tunnel lights dimmed. Stewart turned on his headlamp and drew his SIG. His eyes narrowed as he scanned the darkness that enveloped the tunnel ahead. A vague scampering noise approached, and three human forms emerged, crawling along the walls and ceiling towards them. Their jaws hung wide and open. Long threads of saliva hung from their mouths. Their skins were a deathly white pale. They exhibited an agility and a disregard for Newton's laws, which meant only one thing: demonic possession.

O'Neill lacked his cat's absolute fearlessness and started backing away, preparing to run. Panicked, he turned to Stewart and said, "Tavish, there won't be time to exorcise them. They will be on us in seconds. We have to run!"

Stewart responded to O'Neill's total panic with complete calm, his SIG barking three times. The booming sounds echoed down the tunnel. The three men's skulls responded to the .357 Xtreme Penetrator round entirely in accordance with the Scotsman's expectations. The occipital bones at the rear fragmented and rebounded off the tunnel walls, along with copious amounts of blood and neural material. The three possessed bodies instantly dropped from where they were and lay still on the rocky ground.

O'Neill stood in stunned shock. Ezekiel wrapped himself around the Scotsman's legs in a sign of gratitude. Stewart checked the magazine in his pistol.

"Thomas, I am now down to two rounds. Let's get to the Bell as quickly as we can before I have to start throwing rocks."

The dim lighting in the tunnel gradually returned, and the three figures resumed their progress. Stewart put his SIG back in his waistband and turned off his headlamp. A gentle breeze started blowing past them, bringing a stench considerably worse than that given off by the carriages filled with the decaying bodies which they had encountered when they had first descended below the castle.

"This is not a good omen," commented O'Neill.

"I had gathered," replied Stewart good-humouredly.

As they advanced, the tunnel became littered with dead bodies. Some were technicians, some were Isfet adepts dressed in elaborate ritual robes, and others were Black Knights in their stark Hugo Boss uniforms. Most had taken their own lives. Others had been killed violently.

"More mass possessions," commented O'Neill.

Sheets of blood-stained papers fluttered past them, carried by the ever-increasing stench-filled airflow. Stewart grabbed one random paper and passed it to O'Neill, who read it before letting it go back into the gale-force wind with the comment, "They are banishing rituals."

"I guess they did not work." replied the Scotsman, looking at the contorted faces of the dead bodies they passed as they continued their progress through this tunnel.

The temperature, hovering around forty degrees Fahrenheit, suddenly dropped below freezing, causing their breath to steam like mythical dragons. Unexpectedly, small pebbles from the railway began pelting them, causing both men to shield their faces with their hands. Ezekiel was less fortunate and visibly winced with each minor impact. Thankfully, they had at last reached their goal, a side passage marked "Die Glocke" in characteristic black gothic script.

Passing through double doors, they entered the long chamber where Cortez had been prepping the Bell. The strong wind and flying stones were absent here, and the stench was less pronounced, replaced by diesel fumes and incense. The lighting was dim and flickered, making it difficult to see clearly. Stewart scanned the area. It looked like a deserted underground railway siding. The massive doors at the tunnel's far end were open, revealing the outside world bathed in brilliant sunlight.

The left side of the tunnel siding was littered with a mix of scientific and esoteric materials, with desks, computers and a large whiteboard covered in diagrams, complex calculations and writing in a mix of modern and ancient languages.

"How large will the Bell be?" enquired O'Neill, looking around them. Ezekiel walked cautiously behind some of the desks, vanishing from view.

Stewart shrugged. "From what I have been told, it is the size of a small camper van. We would see it if it was here. That bastard Cortez has moved it." he gestured towards the whiteboard and desks, "Any hints about where he has taken it?"

O'Neill followed where Ezekiel had already gone. The desks were covered with books, sun-browned parchments and the ubiquitous Sumerian clay tablets. The texts covered quantum mechanics, astrophysics, megalithic standing circles, and Sumerian mythology and astrology. What would be regarded by most people as an unusual combination, except here, they made perfect sense.

A low groan came behind some cardboard boxes labelled with Arabic script and covered in Cairo Museum stamps. Sitting on top of the stack of boxes, Ezekiel meowed loudly to draw attention to something he had found. The noise attracted Stewart, who limped around to join O'Neill as they approached the six-foot-high stack. The Scotsman drew his SIG into the same single-handed grip he had already demonstrated had such deadly effect.

Coming around the edge of the boxes, the two men found an elderly man with a balding head, round wire-rim glasses, and a terrified look in his eyes. Strangely, the man's terror decreased significantly at the sight of the SIG's business end. The man was dressed in a long red robe embroidered with sigils, Arabic script, pentagrams, and hexagrams. O'Neill recognised many of the Arabic phrases as coming from forbidden texts within the darker aspects of magical study within Islam. An engraved gold-coloured band with a large striking cobra in the centre of the forehead decorated the man's head like a crown, and golden curl-toed slippers adorned his feet. This was clearly one of Cortez's Isfet adepts.

"Where is Cortez?" demanded Stewart, keeping his gun on the mysterious stranger.

The man sighed, clearly unafraid of the pistol aimed at his head and the imminent threat of death. Standing beside the aggressive Scotsman, O'Neill noted the Egyptian Museum stamps on the boxes and made a guess, saying,

"As-salamu alaykum (ٱلسَّلَامُ عَلَيْكُم)"

The old man smiled and placed his right hand on his heart. "Wa ʿalaykumu s-salam (وَعَلَيْكُم ٱلسَّلَامُ),"

"You are English?" the stranger asked in a feeble voice. He looked around the empty space as though he was expecting someone else to be present.

Stewart frowned. They did not have time to waste with pleasant chats. He was just about to become considerably more persuasive when O'Neill interjected, "We have come through the tunnels,"

The man looked terrified at the mention of the tunnels. Stewart gestured for O'Neill to continue, as he was obviously getting somewhere.

O'Neill pulled a plastic bottle of water from his exorcism bag and, passing it to the man, asked, "What happened?"

With wrinkled and shaking hands, the man took the bottle and gulped it down. Then he looked at O'Neill, searching the priest's eyes. "You must get out of here, now!"

"Yes, we will, but first, we need to know where Cortez has gone," replied Stewart.

"No, you don't understand! At any moment, IT will return." The old man looked terrified again.

 "What will?" asked Stewart forcibly.

"Cortez released IT."

O'Neill knelt beside the man. "My name is Thomas, Father Thomas O'Neill," he pointed towards Stewart, "and this is my friend, Tavish Stewart. We are here to stop Cortez from running the Bell."

The old man laughed hysterically, highlighting the parchment-like thinness of the skin on his face and deathly pallor. "You are far too late. He has already started that infernal device and, in doing so, inadvertently released that which must never be released." He looked meaningfully at O'Neill, and said,

"I tried. Believe me, I tried to return IT to the eternal darkness," he gestured to all the parchments, books and clay tablets scattered around the area, "None of the techniques work. It is simply too strong." he looked imploringly at O'Neill, searching his face, "You must go. Now. You have seen the tunnels! It stalks this place. Soon, it will need to manifest again and come here looking for life."

O'Neill shook his head, refusing to accept what he was being told. What this man was saying was impossible.

Stewart sighed. "Thomas, what is the big deal about another demon being released? You have banished enough of the bastards with the kit in your bag." The Scotsman gestured towards the leather deliverance bag on the concrete floor beside O'Neill.

The old Egyptian laughed again. "Not just *a* devil, my friend. The father of all Devils! That truth that religions fear sharing with their flocks. That there is an evil too powerful to banish. One that even God himself fears."

Stewart looked at O'Neill. "I thought that Satan was Top Trump?"

The ancient Egyptian sighed and shook his head. He looked at O'Neill and, gesturing towards the priest standing before him, said, "You know, don't you?" the old Egyptian looked at Stewart, "As an exorcist, he knows that dread secret. Satan is but a feeble shadow of that greater supernatural horror هانبي" At the mention of the name, Ezekiel let out a low moan of pain and just for a moment the overhead lights dimmed and rose again.

O'Neill explained, "In the most ancient mythos before God created heaven and earth, a supreme evil pervaded everything. It was mentioned in the first writings as the personification of all evils. It predated God, and he could not destroy it. So, instead, God and his angels bound it into a pit of darkness for eternity. Once the evil had been removed, God was able to create our universe."

Stewart narrowed his eyes. "And we are supposed to believe this thing is wandering around down here? Frankly, the fucking thing is welcome to this abandoned mine. All I need to know is where Cortez has taken the Bell!"

The Egyptian laughed manically. "Ah, if only it would stay here. But it will not, my friend. After it has consumed all the life down here, it will spread, slowly embracing everything. God himself will not escape this time. But if all you care about is the Bell,"

He gestured to the whiteboard behind them. Stewart and O'Neill turned to see where he was indicating, and then both rose and walked over. They had not seen this surface of the board from the other side when they entered the area. Marker pens of different colours showed the thirty-mile-long rail line from Owl Mountain to Wroclaw[1094], where the Bell would be loaded onto a C-5M Super Galaxy[1095] transport plane. The C-5M then completed a two-and-a-half-hour flight of just over two thousand nautical miles in a South Westerly direction. Beneath the brief flight plan was a detail of the Crawler Transporter[1096] 2, which would carry the Bell four hundred yards from the airport to a location with massive power supplies laid out in a circle form.

Stewart puzzled over the sketches for a moment, looking at the aircraft, the planned duration of the flight and its headings. The Scotsman then declared, "That's Geneva airport[1097], and that," he pointed to the circular structure with

---

[1094] Airport code : WRO
[1095] Lockheed Martin C-5M Super Galaxy.
[1096] Crawler Transporter 2 (CT2) - used to transport the space shuttle.
[1097] Aéroport International de Genève.

enormous power supplies taken from the neighbouring national grids, "Is CERN, I am sure of it!"

Before O'Neill could comment, there was a loud cry of fear from the old Egyptian. He was frantically pulling himself away from the wall where he had been propped up behind the boxes. He crawled head first across the floor into the centre of the room, towards where Stewart and O'Neill stood by the whiteboard. A dark shadow spread out from the wall like it was chasing the old man as he crawled away. Just before the shadow reached the boxes where he was sitting, Ezekiel shrieked and leapt down. Grasping the leather handles of the deliverance bag in his teeth, he dragged the bag backwards in a series of tugs over to O'Neill.

Inside the creeping shadow, everything began to disintegrate. The cardboard boxes crumpled, parchments fell to dust, and even ceramic tablets fragmented. The air was filled with a putrid stench that made even the hardened Stewart gag, and alongside the cries for help from the old Egyptian were whispers of a single word, repeating over and over, coming from every part of the space around them.

O'Neill finally understood why his forbidding feelings had grown since he started this mission. Having just witnessed Ezekiel rescue the bag from certain destruction, he also understood Mathers' insistence that he bring the cat. O'Neill was not fated to face Cortez or his damned bell. It was this ancient darkness that he and he alone must face. A darkness that threatened to destroy the people, the world, and perhaps even the God he loved so dearly.

He opened the deliverance bag, hurriedly pulling on his vestments and going through the obligatory prerequisites for the Roman Ritual[1098]. He threw the censor towards Stewart, who caught it, unscrewed the lid and placed the adze in his

---

[1098] Exorcism.

pocket before returning it. O'Neill ruffled Ezekiel behind the ears and, picking him up, passed him to Stewart. "Here, take him and go stop Cortez. I have to confront this thing, or even if you succeed in stopping Cortez, it really will be the Twilight of The Gods."

Stewart started to protest but saw the old Egyptian disintegrate into a stack of dried bones as the approaching shadow cast over him, and the whispering all around them became deafening. In a rare exhibition of emotion, the Scotsman embraced O'Neill before gently pulling Ezekiel's claws free from the exorcist's vestments where the cat clearly wanted to stay. Stewart then turned towards the exit from the underground railway siding and started walking. The Scotsman's last sight before limping out of the tunnel into the dawn light was of O'Neill, lighting a Turkish Royal cigarette and walking calmly into the encroaching darkness. He proclaimed loudly and clearly in his distinctive Irish American accent,

"Yea, though I walk through the valley of the shadow of death, I will fear no evil: for thou art with me; thy rod and thy staff they comfort me."

HELL'S BELLS

"...and [I] saw a beast rise up out of the sea, having seven heads and ten horns, and upon his horns ten crowns, and upon his heads the name of blasphemy." - Revelation 13:1 King James Bible.

North Eastern Railway Tunnel Exit, Riese Complex, Owl Mountains, Central Sudetes, South Western Poland.

07:11 HRS (GMT+2), 21st September, present-day (five hours and six minutes until the Autumnal equinox)

Sheer grey rock[1099] walls towered sixty feet on either side of the flooded railway tracks emerging from the Owl Mountain mines. Illuminated in the brilliant morning sunshine, a lone male figure dressed in a badly torn and blood-stained dark navy Saville Row[1100] suit waded slowly through waist-deep brown water, a small ginger shape nestled in his arms. Each gust of breeze agitated the dank floodwaters and caused pungent odours of decaying organic matter to rise in the air. As if to confirm the foul nature of the liquid, Stewart was forced to push past three semi-dissolved and bloated human remains that floated face down in the water. All three were still dressed in lead-lined suits that had failed to protect them against the exotic forces emitted during the Bell's brief test run.

The Scotsman carried Ezekiel in his arms, keeping the feline a few precious inches above the toxic fluid around them. The cat's green eyes carefully watched its surroundings, waiting for higher ground when he would be safe to release his claws

---

[1099] Gneiss and Migmatite volcanic rock is an exceptionally hard mineral mix. The Reise complex was designed to be resistant to allied bombs.

[1100] Italian hopsack weave wool suit by Hakett.

from the fine Egyptian cotton of Stewart's blood spattered light blue Brunello Cucinelli shirt.

After having sustained numerous injuries and gone over forty-eight hours without sleep, the Scotsman looked unusually drawn and tired. His hair was greyer, and the laughter lines on his face more severe. His injuries had stopped bleeding relatively quickly after the duels. But now, they had reopened and resumed weeping copiously. These afflictions were more complex and sinister than simple fatigue and injury. Unbeknown to the Scotsman, his brief exposure to the creeping ancient evil in the Reise complex had drained his vital life force[1101], but the Scotsman's iron will remained firm. He was determined to get to Geneva and stop Cortez from activating his infernal Bell. However, at that precise moment, he had to admit he had no clear plan for achieving this goal. Friends and enemies alike had sacrificed themselves for this cause, and Stewart would not be the one to fail and let their sacrifice be in vain.

As Stewart followed the railway, a gentle twenty-degree incline of crushed rocks was revealed on his right side. The slope had been cut into the rock passage walls to permit hauling blockages away from the tracks. Deducing that it would lead to an access road of some form, he started up the slope of grey potato-sized rocks. The Scotsman grimaced from his leg injury with the exertion as fresh blood oozed through the trouser material covering his left shin. Stewart was all too aware that having an open wound soaked with the putrid brown water that had gathered in the flooded tracks was an invitation for infection.

Two-thirds of the way up was a four-foot square block of concrete with large steel haulage rings, which permitted objects to be dragged up the slope with mechanised pulleys.

[1101] Often called VLF within esoteric circles.

Stewart put O'Neill's cat down on the block and sat beside him. He undid the laces on his black Equilibre brogues, took them off, poured out the water from inside well away from Ezekiel, removed his Pantherella socks and wrung them out. While Ezekiel washed himself, the Scotsman rolled up his right sleeve and left trouser leg[1102]The sabre cut on his arm was clean, but the rapier wound on his shin looked angry and swollen, it was already turning black at the edges. He urgently needed sterile fabric, clean water, and antiseptic to dress the wound. Stewart removed his blue polka-dolt Hermes tie from his breast pocket, where it had been placed during the duels, and used the material to clean up the blood and plasma oozing from the shin injury the best he could.

The Scotsman shivered involuntarily. Initially, he thought it was the effect of his damp clothing and the breeze, but the cold rapidly became increasingly severe. Oddly, the change in temperature combined with a distinctive musky scent[1103], which Stewart felt he should recognise but, due to his exhaustion, could not place. The clear blue sky and sunshine that had been helping dry and warm him abruptly ended as a mass of clouds partially obscured the sun. Unexpectedly, Ezekiel arched, hissed, and leapt off the haulage block as a shadow fell across it. Remembering O'Neill's comments about the cat's responses to threats, Stewart leapt behind the block, landing alongside the hissing ginger fur ball. He drew his SIG in a blindingly fast single action, completely ignoring the pain from his injuries and the sharp stones beneath his bare feet. A tall female figure with long jet-black hair stood on the opposite side of the concrete block. She wore a crisp white Chanel suit, black Christian Louboutin heels, mirrored Rayban wayfarer sunglasses and two wristwatches. On her

---

[1102] No, this is not a Masonic initiatory preparation.
[1103] A unique perfume derived from the Ghost Flower of the Mojave Desert. It is distilled exclusively by the Sultan of Oman's perfume house, Amouage, for only one person.

left wrist, her signature gold Rolex, and on her right, another more tactical-looking piece on a rubber strap, worn somewhat incongruously over the outside of her right sleeve. She seemed vaguely amused by the deadly SIG the Scotsman aimed at her head.

"Come to gloat, Dr Ad-Dajjal?" said Stewart calmly as he placed the SIG back in the waistband of his trousers. He still remembered watching Ad-Dajjal crush fine carbon steel with her bare hands back in Geneva. He wouldn't waste his valuable remaining rounds. He dismissed wasting time speculating how she managed to walk silently on the small rocks while wearing those heels or her appearance here at this precise moment. The day was already so bizarre that nothing would surprise him.

"Hardly, Sir Stewart. I am, however, glad to see Issac provided you with your beloved .357 SIG. I recall O'Neill mentioning your fondness for that weapon in his most imaginative account of our previous encounter[1104]. I hope you also have the adze?"

Stewart patted his jacket pocket in confirmation. He looked pointedly at his old waterlogged Omega. "I would love to talk, Dr Ad-Dajjal, but I only have six hours to get to Geneva. I don't suppose you brought a fast car I could borrow?"

Ad-Dajjal smiled indulgently. "Actually, Sir Stewart, you have only five hours. Your watch will have stopped during your brief encounter with هانبي, the *father of devils*." She unbuckled a heavily branded black rubber strap, removed the watch from her right wrist, and passed it to Stewart. "Here. I have programmed it with a countdown timer for the equinox."

[1104] Bridge of Souls: Ancient Prophecy Ultimate Evil.

Stewart took the timepiece. The black PVD case of the Breitling Aerospace Evo was so cold from having been worn by Ad-Dajjal that condensation rapidly accumulated on the dial glass while in Stewart's hand. The large LCD display ran a countdown timer, showing that "05:06:12" remained before the equinox. The Scotsman compared the hour and minute hands on the Breitling with his own water-logged Omega. Ad-Dajjal appeared correct. The old mechanical mechanism had seized up over an hour ago. Stewart removed the broken Omega from his wrist, put it in his jacket pocket, and replaced it with the Breitling.

Ad-Dajjal continued, "As for transport, Sir Stewart, I will provide something considerably faster than an automobile."

She gestured towards Stewart's left leg, which had started bleeding again after his vigorous jump off the haulage block.

"But first, we need to get that leg wound treated, or you will not stand any kind of chance of getting close enough to dispatch the Apep," Ad-Dajjal noted the Scotsman's momentary confusion and added, "The Egyptians called it Apep, the Sumerians knew it as MUŠ.ŠÀ.TÙR." Her pronunciation of the dead Sumerian language differed radically from any other version Stewart had heard. However, given who he was talking with, he had no doubt he had just listened to the original six thousand-year-old dialect.

Ad-Dajjal raised her left hand above her head and clicked her fingers. Five operatives dressed in standard Wolfsangel blue uniforms with large red crosses on their chests, denoting field medics, emerged over the top of the slope and came down it. They carried cooler bags with military medic designation labels. Noticeably, none of the operatives wore weapons or the iKill-Pro devices so frequently adopted by Cortez's elite Black Knights, but they did have stethoscopes.

"Wolfsangel works for you now?" Stewart asked as the medics surrounded him, unpacking equipment from their bags. Ezekiel sniffed around as though he were a medical authority.

Ad-Dajjal smiled. "I can be extremely persuasive."

"I don't doubt it." The Scotsman recalled Helen Curren's description of being brainwashed by Ad-Dajjal on board the Tiamat yacht[1105].

"Besides," added Ad-Dajjal, "Unlike the Black Knight fanatics, most Wolfsangel are pragmatists seeking a future. I offer that future without any judgment on their past actions."

The raven-haired beauty addressed the medics, "Carry him up the slope, treat his wounds, and feed him. He will need all his strength. I will return shortly, and then we will depart."

As Stewart was helped to his feet, Ad-Dajjal turned and strode effortlessly down the slope and then waded towards the Reise complex. The surface of the dirty flood waters froze as she waded through them, and the Scotsman was again left wondering how she managed to walk so effortlessly while wearing towering Christian Louboutins.

Two of the medics lifted Stewart in an improvised swing carry[1106] and transported him up to the rim of the slope. Ezekiel followed behind[1107], occasionally mewing as he carefully manoeuvred to avoid the sharpest stones. Once they reached the crest, a large military transport

---

[1105] See Bridge of Souls for more detail.
[1106] Like a human chair.
[1107] I would have said, followed *gingerly*, but given Ezekiel's coat colouring maybe not.

helicopter[1108] was revealed in the clearing at the top of the slope.

"So, she did not get here on a broomstick," Stewart commented to himself or maybe to Ezekiel. One of the medics removed an American DOD self-heating MRE[1109] from their medical bag, activated the heating chemicals, shook it, and handed it to the Scotsman with a wooden spork. Ezekiel immediately moved closer, expecting his share. He was not disappointed as Stewart dolloped out the occasional spoonful of the beef hash onto the rocks in between his own mouthfuls.

While he ate, the medics took Stewart's vital signs. Then, they removed his jacket and cut off the fabric on his shirt sleeves and left trouser leg. They fitted two drips into his arms and cleaned and dressed the two wounds. Ezekiel sat and watched this impassively for a few moments but then chirped, directing Stewart's attention to a scene fifty yards away, where four men were carrying a patient on a stretcher into the loading bay of the Chinook.

"Never took Ad-Dajjal as a humanitarian," remarked the Scotsman as he passed the cat another sporkful of the juice. Stewart was starting to feel considerably better and more like his usual self, but Ezekiel was less content. His share of the beef gravy had suddenly frozen solid on the ground. The large ginger feline hackled and directed his focus back down the slope. Sure enough, Ad-Dajjal was returning from her unexplained excursion to the Reise complex. Her white trouser legs were stained a dirty brown from the flood waters. A male figure, dressed in a black jacket and matching trousers, hung limply in her arms. Ad-Dajjal carried the body

---

[1108] CH-47F - the world's fastest military helicopter with a top speed of just under 200 mph. I know what you are thinking - no, that is still not fast enough to get to CERN in time for the equinox.
[1109] Meal Ready to Eat.

like he weighed nothing, confirming Stewart's existing speculation that the raven-haired being was most definitely not human.

Ezekiel scurried to Ad-Dajjal and started circling her, mewing frantically. Stewart had not seen the cat behave like that before, so he stood to get a better view of the body Ad-Dajjal was carrying. It took long seconds before he finally recognised the man's face.

"Jesus Christ!"

Shaking himself free from the drips embedded into his arms, he walked barefoot over the sharp stones to Ad-Dajjal. Thomas O'Neill's hair and beard had turned white, and his hairline had receded. The skin on his face and hands had that same white cracked parchment quality exhibited by the dying Isfet adept they had encountered in the Bell chamber. O'Neill looked like he had aged forty years.

"Is he alive?" asked Stewart, fearing the worst.

Ad-Dajjal nodded as she continued walking. "Just. I got to him seconds before he would have been lost forever."

"Thank you," the Scotsman meant it. But Ad-Dajjal dismissed his gratitude, saying, "Don't get sentimental, Sir Stewart. As I told you, in Geneva, right now, our interests align. Nothing more."

She turned to the medics. "Wheels up in five minutes." She strode to the Chinook, still carrying O'Neill like a paper doll. Stewart and Ezekiel trailed slowly behind, finding it hard to go barefoot on the sharp stones. As the Scotsman was helped on board, he noted again that none of the operatives carried weapons. Everyone was a medic.

On entering the rear cabin, the usual smells of aviation fuel and oil were combined with those of antiseptic and ether. Lying on a stretcher, directly opposite the main sliding doors, surrounded by drips, ECG and EEG electrodes, was the hawk-faced Isaac Bin Abdul-Issuin. A team of medics frantically worked on containing the assassin's vital signs.

"So, Ad-Dajjal rescued you as well," muttered Stewart as he followed O'Neill's body as it was carried through the rows of plastic khaki-coloured bench seats inside the aircraft. The lead medic working on Abdul-Issuin shouted, "We need to get this man to a hospital within thirty minutes, or we will lose him!"

Ad-Dajjal turned, looking genuinely concerned. She commanded, "Wheels up-now!" to the cockpit. She placed O'Neill on a stretcher bed and moved towards the front of the aircraft. Two blue-suited attendants joined her and began briefing her while three medics started treating the unconscious body of O'Neill.

Stewart sat on a bench seat opposite O'Neill's stretcher bed just as they lifted into the air and headed North. Ezekiel jumped up and settled between O'Neill's feet, repeatedly head-butting his legs, trying to get a response but got none.

The Breitling said three hours and fifty minutes were left. If they headed directly to the hospital, as Abdul Issuin's medics demanded, they would never make it in time to stop Cortez. For the hundredth time since starting on this odyssey, Stewart revised his opinion about the likelihood of a semi-immortal soul parasite who would tear reality apart. It was ridiculous. It was perfectly reasonable for Ad-Dajjal to prioritise the most critical medical case. Maybe the hospital could do something for O'Neill as well.

The sight of aircraft hangars, parked planes and the concrete airstrip of Wroclaw Airport outside the rows of small windows abruptly halted his speculations. Evidently, Abdul-Issuin was a lower priority. Confirming Stewart's deduction, Ad-Dajjal walked back down the aircraft's interior.

"Stewart, you are with me," she gestured to the two medics treating O'Neill, "he comes too. Once we are off the aircraft, get Abdul-Issuin to The Wroclaw University Hospital[1110]. Their chopper pad is vacant, and their trauma ward is waiting for him."

The Scotsman picked up Ezekiel and walked to the main doors just as the massive copter landed. Stewart's left shin still hurt as he stepped down, but the medics had done an excellent job sealing the wound, and although he was tired, he felt considerably better than he had when leaving the Reise complex. On the exposed tarmac, the icy downdraft from the Chinook's take-off reminded Stewart that he badly needed clothes and shoes. Still, more urgently, he needed to get up in the air again as quickly as possible to stand any chance of getting to Geneva in time. Ezekiel did not care for the downdraft either and hung on tight to Stewart's shirt, his big green eyes fixed on O'Neill's body on the stretcher that was being carried in front of them.

Stewart checked his exposed left wrist. The Breitling said there were three hours and seven minutes remaining. Given the two-thousand-mile distance between Wroclaw and Geneva, their schedule was cutting it fine. He did not like being reliant on Ad-Dajjal for transport, but she had O'Neill, which severely limited his options.

He was just considering using his SIG to hijack one of the aircraft parked on the tarmac and make his own way when the convoy of Ad-Dajjal and the two stretcher-bearers carrying O'Neill reached the boarding steps attached to a long, sleek white Global 8000[1111] executive jet with Doctors

---

[1110] The Wrocław University Hospital (UH) is one of Poland's best hospitals. The address is Kamieńskiego 73A, 51-124 Wrocław, Poland, in case you need it.
[1111] Global 8000 bombardier executive jet.

Without Borders[1112] livery. Whatever else he could say about Ad-Dajjal, she certainly had excellent taste when selecting equipment and cover stories. Stewart recalled reading a press release for the Global 8000 breaking the sound barrier during its FAA[1113] certification trials. If they could achieve that kind of speed on this flight, it would take them two hours and thirty-six minutes[1114] to cover the two thousand miles. They would then have less than half an hour to get from Geneva airport to the CERN headquarters and stop Cortez. It was a tight schedule, but it was still feasible if they could get immediate clearance to land, and rapid ground transport would be available when they reached Switzerland.

Stewart's injuries made him slower than he would have liked getting across the tarmac to the Global 8000 and up the stairs. The luxurious cream-coloured interior of the cabin smelled of leather and Ad-Dajjal's perfume. By the time he entered, O'Neill had already been strapped into one of the fourteen mustard-coloured leather executive seats that filled the eight-foot wide, forty-five-foot-long cabin. Two sets of drips had been fitted to O'Neill, and a nurse sat next to him and measured the priest's vital stats on a tablet computer. Although Stewart's friend looked much healthier than he had when he was first brought out of the Reise complex, he still looked considerably older. The Scotsman wondered if O'Neill would ever return to his previous condition. He looked around for Ad-Dajjal so he could ask her, but she was noticeably absent. As the pilot taxied to the runway, Stewart settled into the seat behind O'Neill so Ezekiel could be close

---

[1112] Médecins Sans Frontières.
[1113] Federal Aviation Administration.
[1114] 2000 miles divided by 760 mph is 2.6 hours or 2 hours and 36 minutes.

to his favourite human. The Breitling showed two hours and fifty-nine minutes until the equinox. They were perilously close to the wire on this one.

An icy hand on his left shoulder pulled Stewart away from his dark thoughts about O'Neill and the short time remaining. Ad-Dajjal's frigid breath smelt of mint as she whispered into his left ear, "There is a change of clothing and toiletries for you in the rear." She then proceeded to walk to the cockpit. Stewart noted that she had changed into another immaculate white Chanel suit and black heels. Her hair looked like she had just stepped out from 14 rue Notre Dame des Victoires[1115].

The rear washroom was much larger than the Scotsman had expected, with a Grohe Grohtherm shower and matching porcelain fittings with gold taps. Laid out on the white marble wash table was a men's leather Hermes travel toiletry bag filled with the essentials. Hanging on the door was a suit carrier bag with an embossed Ede & Ravenscroft logo. A pair of black Crockett & Jones Oxfords were laid out on the floor beneath the carrier bag. A standard twelve-round magazine for his pistol loaded with the .357 SIG extreme penetrator rounds was on the fold-out table. Beside the magazine was the standard SIG mechanism oiling kit and a tan leather Bianchi[1116] shoulder harness. Looking at the selection of items, someone on Ad-Dajjal's staff had taken considerable trouble selecting all of his preferred accessories.

The Scotsman emerged twenty minutes later, dressed in a light blue and gold thread, hound-tooth, three-piece suit, a

____

[1115] The 17th-century Paris apartment at this address contains the ultra-exclusive hair salon of David Mallett, one of the world's finest hairdressers.
[1116] Bianchi X15H Shoulder Harness.

white hundred-thread Egyptian cotton shirt, and a red Prada silk tie. The air around him smelt of Hermes orange verte[1117]. The only oddity in the suit was the fine golden thread, which, as far as Stewart could determine, was made of genuine gold. It was a curious and expensive addition that would have been a custom request to Ede & Ravenscroft in Chancery Lane, London.

Back at his seat on the aircraft, Ezekiel had fallen asleep, and the nurse had changed O'Neill's clothes. The priest was now dressed in a simple grey marl cotton sweatshirt, jog bottoms, and trainers. But again, this clothing had a gold thread woven through the material. There was obviously a reason for this expensive addition. Stewart would have to query it with Ad-Dajjal the next time he saw her, but not now, as looking down the cabin, he could see she was in the cockpit, piloting the aircraft.

The fold-out table in his seat contained a Waterford crystal glass beside a miniature of Glenfiddich 25 Rare Oak. Notably, no ice or water was in sight. Again, someone knew exactly how Stewart took his whisky. It was possible that the drink was drugged, but if Ad-Dajjal had wanted him dead, she would already have done so. Opening the sealed screw top, he poured the amber liquid into the glass and looked up to the illuminated sign above the cockpit, indicating Mach 1.25[1118] and 16000m[1119]. Ad-Dajjal had the pedal on the metal. The Breitling showed 1 hour and 55 minutes remained. This would be hellishly close, but to her credit, Ad-Dajjal was giving it her best shot. All he could do was relax. His role in this quest would come soon enough. He checked his pocket for the adze and the comforting shape of the freshly oiled SIG inside his jacket. Content that he had

---

[1117] Hermes Eau d'orange verte Eau de cologne.
[1118] 906 Mph.
[1119] 51,000 feet. The ceiling for the global 8000.

everything ready, he sipped the amber liquid, savouring the taste, the burn as it went down, and the instant warm relaxation flowing through his body.

Stewart's next sensation was being shaken gently on the shoulder by the co-pilot. The Breitling said there were only 16 minutes left. Looking around, he realised with a start that he was alone; Ad-Dajjal, O'Neill and Ezekiel had gone. Groggily, he followed the co-pilot out of the aircraft. The Global 8000 was parked up on the decorative lawn two hundred yards from the main airport building, away from the main arrival and departure terminals. Close by was the enormous transport plane Cortez had used to bring the Bell to Geneva. The lawn, which the Swiss authorities had pristinely maintained as a symbol of order, was now churned by numerous deep tyre tracks. Distant rumbling sounds echoed from every direction, and the air carried a scent of ozone and sulphur, so frequently associated with violent electrical disturbances.

Coming down the steps, Stewart still felt that awful disorientation associated with premature waking from a profound sleep after extended sleep deprivation. The powerful, gusting wind did not help. With his left shin injured, he would never have been that stable coming down steep steps, but the one-hundred-mile-an-hour gusts from all directions made coming down the steps a significant challenge. Added to the winds were sheets of heavy rain and large hail stones which pelted his face. By the time Stewart reached the bottom of the steps, he was soaked but wide awake. Now, he could fully take in the scene unfolding around him.

Aside from the raging storm, it was pitch black. There were no stars or lights in the airport buildings, runways or parking zones. The lights of Geneva, which would have been easily noticeable this close to the city, were absent. It was so dark, in fact, that it felt like the early hours of the morning on a northern winter's night. But according to the Breitling, it was late in the morning. The Scotsman briefly wondered if the watch had been secretly adjusted while he slept, but a glance at the large battery-powered glowing Omega clock on the exterior of the airport building showed that the Breitling was spot on.

The weather conditions were identical to those he and O'Neill had encountered at the Polish checkpoint when Cortez had first tested the Bell. Stewart's assumption that Cortez had started the Bell was confirmed when, moments later, lightning arced high into the sky from a nearby location on the ground, which must have been CERN. The ground shuddered, and a brilliant white pulsing light was cast high into the sky. It was hard to see anything clearly in the pitch dark and driving rain, but the ground was fully illuminated briefly when the lightning arced. Lying all around were the bodies of airport baggage handlers, security guards and Black Knights. Dozens of them. All were dead and showed evidence of the strange circular serrated sucker wounds he had seen in evidence at the Reise complex. Cortex had been here and indulged in some savage feeding frenzy, perhaps in some unknown preparation for activating the Bell.

Five yards from the aircraft steps, a black Mercedes G Wagon, with its engine running and the front passenger side door wide open, was waiting for him. Only the SUV's side running lights were on. On entering, he found Ad-Dajjal in the driver's seat and O'Neill in the back seat, awake but looking extraordinarily old. Ezekiel lay on the priest's lap. Oddly, none of the other staff, pilots, or medics were to be seen anywhere. The next thing that struck the Scotsman was that Ad-Dajjal had changed into a close-fitted gold trouser suit, and somehow, someone had also dressed Ezekiel in a gold coat. The cat did not look happy. Its tail moved in a slow rhythmic cadence that a cat owner would understand as similar to DEFCON 1[1120].

Stewart gestured to the cat. "How the hell did anyone get him into that? And more importantly, why are we all dressed like a 70s glam rock band?"

O'Neill cleared his throat. He sounded as old as he looked, and that was saying something. "Gold is supposed to give some protection against exposure to the effects of the Qlipothic Wheels."

"Does it work?" Stewart was clearly sceptical as he had seen the melted bodies of technicians who had been wearing lead-lined protective clothing. There was an awkward silence, as no one wanted to state their thoughts.

"You have the adze?" Ad-Dajjal demanded, changing the subject, as she violently accelerated away without waiting for Stewart to close his door. The big vehicle bumped and swayed sideways as it passed over what must have been extraordinarily uneven ground. A glance out of the window revealed the gruesome nature of the obstructions. They were not speed bumps.

O'Neill's frail voice came again from the rear, "Dr Ad-Dajjal, these were people. You could show some respect and try to drive around them."

She leaned over and took Stewart's wrist in an icy grip. Glancing at Stewart's watch, she replied, "Father O'Neill, we have less than eleven minutes before this reality ceases to exist. I would suggest you keep your sensibilities for another time."

[1120] The highest state of US military preparedness. In cat terms we are talking of the extreme potential for skin grafts for owners who ignore the signs.

There was a tentative meow, but it was unclear if it was in support of O'Neill or Ad-Dajjal.

"You know where you are going?" asked O'Neill, whose newly acquired old age had transformed him into an exemplary backseat driver.

Ad-Dajjal sighed and gestured to the enormous cone of pulsing light less than a mile away through their front windscreen. The next moment, the wire airport boundary fence appeared unexpectedly in their view. They ploughed straight into it and flattened it, causing the SUV to shudder as it ran over the obstruction and bounced down the outer embankment and onto the main Swiss-French motorway. Stewart reached over and turned on the G Wagon's main headlights, revealing that they were heading across the empty highway lanes and towards the central reservation. The Scotsman braced himself for the pending impact with the crash barrier, commenting,

"I take it you don't drive often."

Ad-Dajjal replied calmly, "Only in emergencies."

O'Neill started praying in the back just as the G Wagon smashed into the crash barrier, mounted it and drove on into the next set of motorway lanes. The SUV's front bumper and side trims smashed loose and dragged beside them. The remaining headlamp showed they were heading towards another tall wire perimeter fence. This one had the CERN logo and a "warning electrified fence" sign. Stewart braced and hung onto the stability handles. In the back, O'Neill threw up, and Ezekiel leapt onto the rear of Ad-Dajjal's seat and hung there like a free climber.

The CERN wire perimeter fence went down, and the wild charge of the G Wagon continued, ploughing through ornamental gardens, glass houses and some small wooden fences. Finally, they were within yards of the slowly accelerating Bell that was sending an intense pulsing beam of light high into the heavens. Every few seconds, the air rippled, and a long strip of blinding light opened up as the fabric of space-time split. Dark objects could be seen moving through these tears, pushing against the rifts to speed the destruction.

Standing ten yards away from the Bell was a single male figure dressed in a gold ritual robe covered in rampant striking cobra patterns. He was shouting to the heavens, but the noise from the wheel movement was so overpowering it drowned out everything else. As the SUV came closer, even thinking became difficult.

The G Wagon mounted the raised one-hundred-yard area above the power plants for the CERN particle accelerators and came to a standstill. Cortez stood facing away from them with arms raised above his head. If he were not yet aware of their arrival, he soon would be.

Stewart checked his wrist. "Just under four minutes. It's showtime!"

After unbuckling his seat belt, he went to draw the SIG. Ad-Dajjal gripped his arm in a cold and unbelievably powerful grip, saying, "Don't use the gun. Killing the human form will make this creature switch to the next most suitable human host."

Her piercing green eyes glanced towards O'Neill and his weakened state and then into Stewart's. "That would be you, Sir Stewart, in case you are wondering."

After seeing the Scotsman's reaction, she continued, "I will remove his glamour so you can see his true nature and remove all doubts about what must be done. Remember, there is only one vulnerable point, and you will only get one chance," she gestured to the crown of the head in a striking motion.

Stewart nodded. He opened the door and stepped out into the hurricane-like winds circulating around the wheel as it built up speed. On the other side of the SUV, Ad-Dajjal exited and walked around what remained of the bonnet. O'Neill remained in the back seat. He would have liked to be involved but just felt too tired. He needed two sticks to walk now, and he knew the wind would be too strong.

Ezekiel moved off his lap and stood against the side window, meowing as he watched what was happening outside. When his big green eyes fixed on Cortez's figure, he hackled and started issuing a low growl. In a rapid movement, the ginger fur ball scrambled between the two front seats and leapt out of the open door and the relative safety of the SUV. O'Neill exclaimed something that was drowned out by the noise of the Bell. Opening his side door, he slowly exited the SUV, taking his two walking sticks with him. Once he was upright, outside the Mercedes, he began searching for his beloved cat.

The G Wagon had ended its short but eventful journey at the edge of a one-hundred-yard-diameter clearing on top of the 1.3 TWh[1121] power junctions for the CERN particle accelerators. These junctions were linked with thick cables to a rig of twenty General Electric frame motors[1122] geared to bring the Bell gradually to 1800 rpm.

In the brief flashes of multi-coloured lights that poured through the multiplying tears in reality, O'Neill could see that the ground around the Bell was littered with the oozing remains of dozens of dead technicians who had worked to install and initiate the device. To the left of the rotating cylinder was the massive crawler transport used to move the Bell from the airport. Its enormous engines were still

---

[1121] Terawatt hours or one trillion watt hours or 3.6×10^{15} Joules.
[1122] 22000 HP 1800 General Electric frame 4000 motor.

running, and the poor soul driving the crawler was a molten mess in the cabin.

Stewart and Ad-Dajjal were side by side in step, advancing towards Cortez, who was still facing away from them. The fearless Ezekiel had assumed his classic Halloween arched posture and was keeping in step beside the Scotsman.

Some sixth sense alerted the MUŠ.ŠÀ.TÙR. Cortez spun around to face them. The Argentinian's face was set into a mask of rage. He snarled, and his two hands rose. His fingers formed the triangular elemental fire casting he had used with such effect on the German tantric master to reduce her body to ash. His powers had advanced considerably since then, increasing with each human he consumed. The flattened soil beneath Stewart and Ezekiel began to smoulder and burst into flames. The cat squealed and scurried back towards O'Neill, who scooped him into his arms and examined his burnt paws. Meanwhile, Ad-Dajjal stepped over and pushed Stewart sideways with such force that he was thrown nearly six yards. The Scotsman ended up lying on the ground, looking back towards the confrontation. By now, a ten-foot square wall of fire had risen high above the ground, obscuring everything within it. The heat coming from this block of flame was like an open furnace.

Cortez laughed manically. "No living thing can survive fire!"

A familiar, sultry voice answered from somewhere within the conflagration, "Children should not play with matches..."

Ad-Dajjal stepped out from the inferno. The only visible impact from the heat was that her golden trouser suit had melted to her perfect female form, enhancing the dramatic effect of her striding unharmed out of the flames. The golden raven-haired beauty raised her hands, and Cortez's image flickered in and out of focus between two radically different forms. One was human. The other was the seven-headed monster, which had been in the nightmares of humanity since the dawn of history. The creature's movements were so fast that seeing anything except a blur was difficult, even for a trained martial artist like Stewart.

Two of the serpent heads struck at Ad-Dajjal, grabbing her right arm and neck. In response, she started choking the necks directly behind the two biting heads, pulverising them until they looked like they would be pulled clean from the creature. Stewart saw his opening. Rising to his feet, he ran at Cortez, the adze ready in his right hand. Seeing the Scotsman's attack, Ezekiel leapt from O'Neill's arms and, despite his badly burnt paws, charged at Cortez, sinking his teeth into one of the creature's roots and commencing rabbit kicking it with his powerful rear legs.   Stewart's attack was directed towards the crown on Cortez's head, exactly as he had been instructed. The Scotsman drew on his decades of martial experience, but his shin injury made his leap less than perfect. One of the serpent heads grabbed at the adze, burning Stewart's hand with acid so severely that his grip was weakened, and the creature used another of its seven heads to pull the adze from Stewart and cover it in so much acid that the ancient metal corroded into pieces and fell to the ground.

This all happened so quickly that Stewart did not get the opportunity to exclaim in pain before he was smashed high into the air by a swiping blow from two snake heads. He fell hard on the ground some ten feet away, stunned. Ezekiel's body was seized in one of the snake heads, shaken and then thrown to lie perfectly still beside Stewart. Ad-Dajjal fought on, but she faltered as more snakeheads gripped her body. Falling to her hands and knees, her head slumped forward in defeat. Her hair hung loosely around her head while her hands grasped the ground.

Stewart glanced at the Breitling. There were still two minutes before the Bell would reach its full force. He pushed himself up to a kneeling position. His right hand was so severely burnt from the acid as to be useless, so he awkwardly drew the SIG with his left hand. His eyes narrowed in focus as he unleashed a twelve-round volley of armour-piercing .357 SIG rounds, which would have killed a charging bull elephant.

Cortez writhed in agony, and his physical body collapsed to the ground, dead. However, if Stewart had hoped this would instantly kill the soul parasite, he was to be disappointed.

The MUŠ.ŠÀ.TÙR was seriously injured, that was true. Stewart's SIG rounds had terminated the parasite's host body too abruptly to permit a smooth exit from the numerous subtle bodies that had made up Chairman Cortez's incarnation in the physical realm. This damage meant the entity was starting to experience an accelerated decline from his extended exposure to The Bell's deadly radiation. This damage would grow exponentially as the Bell continued its final acceleration. At the current rate, the MUŠ.ŠÀ.TÙR would not live long enough to experience the collapse of reality and the promised unity with the previous existences.

It needed to feed, but it needed a new host before it could feed. It scanned the immediate area. The old man, who was kneeling and pouring a bottle of water from the SUV over the dying cat in an attempt to wash away the acid, was unviable as a host. The woman, Ad-Dajjal, was incredibly strong, but her constitution was unlike anything the parasite had encountered and was impossible to infect. That left the injured male.

The weakened MUŠ.ŠÀ.TÙR crawled forward towards the kneeling figure of the Scotsman, extending its long tendrils to try and quickly envelope the new host body. Once it had achieved its ownership of this male, it would feed off the old priest and maybe even the dying cat. That would provide enough life force to live on until the collapse of this physical reality and his promised integration with the ancient higher powers.

Stewart could see the creature's intent and dragged himself backwards as the long tendrils reached towards his legs. The injuries to the Scotsman's left shin and burnt right hand meant he was not quick enough. The parasite's sucker-like tendrils reached the Oxford shoe on his injured left leg, wrapping around it like ivy. Stewart kicked to remove the shoe, but it would not budge.

As the tendrils began their deadly embrace of Stewart's foot, O'Neill looked on in helpless horror. Losing Ezekiel was bad enough, but losing Stewart as well, just as the universe was destroyed, was the sickest of all possible ends to existence. Surely this was not how God would end everything.

The Scotsman had just started beating the tendrils with the butt from his SIG when O'Neill's face went blank, his jaw dropped like a cadaver, and suddenly the air became filled with the same terrifying whispers repeating the name of horror that Stewart had heard in the Reise complex when the creeping darkness had emerged and consumed the Isfet adept.

Ad-Dajjal's face broke into a smile. The raven-haired beauty suddenly found an unexpected strength and, instead of looking utterly beaten, rose to her feet. She looked immensely pleased as she watched Stewart about to be consumed, O'Neill possessed, and the remains of Ezekiel burnt and lying motionless. Her plans were complete, or very nearly complete.

She strode to the Bell. She grabbed hold of the rapidly spinning cylinder and paused, looking for one of the specific rift colours to repeat before she pushed, severing the power connections. She and the wheel then disappeared in a single movement, and the violent phenomena associated with the Bell abruptly ceased. The ground stopped shaking, clouds started to clear, the wind dropped, and light levels rose.

Back where Stewart faced the imminent infection by the soul parasite, a dark shadow extended from Fr Thomas O'Neill's body. It rapidly covered the MUŠ.ŠÀ.TÙR, making it fade, wither and then finally, disappear. The shadow and whispering voices then withdrew back into O'Neill, and he collapsed to the ground.

Ten minutes later, O'Neill woke to find Stewart sitting beside him, washing his acid-damaged right hand with another Evian water bottle from the G Wagon. Ezekiel was lying beside him, awake but clearly seriously injured. His fur was severely burnt, and one ear was partially missing.

"Thomas?" Stewart sounded as if he was unsure who he was addressing.

"What happened?" asked the disorientated O'Neill.

Stewart looked relieved. "It's good to have you back. Explanations can come later," he gestured to Ezekiel, "Right now, he needs a vet, and you must get to the Vatican."

The End

EPILOGUE

"Ends are not bad things, they just mean that something else is about to begin." - C. JoyBell C.

The Mall,
London SW1A 1AA

Some weeks after what became known as "The Geneva Incident."

The chill October breeze contrasted with the bright sunshine and clear blue skies above the London city skyline, helping clear some of the vehicle fumes that lingered around the streets of the capital[1123]. The mid-morning light emphasised the rich golden autumnal leaves on the London Plane[1124] trees along the Mall. In the courtyard of a stately building that dominated its central London setting, the sun's rays glinted off a row of extraordinarily expensive, highly polished black limousines. A group of formally dressed chauffeurs stood close together, chatting, near the tradesperson's entrance at the far end. Some smoked while others drank from steaming enamel mugs.

The buildings surrounding the chatting drivers were iconic examples of neoclassical architecture, characterised by symmetry, Corinthian columns, and other decorative elements. This famous limestone, stucco and brick façade presented a stately appearance, comprising a central

---

[1123] Regardless of the Ultra Low Emission Zone (ULEZ).
[1124] The London Plane was one of the only trees that could survive in the toxic air of the industrial revolution in Victorian London - hence its use along The Mall.

block[1125] extending into two wings[1126] to create a U-shaped structure enclosing a grand forecourt. This palace had seven hundred and seventy-five rooms and London's most extensive private garden.

A group of men and women were gathered inside one of the larger staterooms[1127], used exclusively for official and state entertainment. Each was dressed in elegant and formal attire that cost considerably more than the average British worker's annual salary. The one-hundred-foot-long room's fifteen-foot-tall windows were graced with cream-coloured wooden shutters and red velvet curtains. This red theme continued on walls adorned with classical portraits and landscapes by renowned artists.

The fifty-two-foot-long woollen Axminister patterned carpet[1128] beneath the feet of these exclusive international dignitaries included a "VA" monogram in three places. Brought from its original home at Windsor Castle, this carpet's centrepiece comprised coloured flowers, thirty-two blue panels, and a border of flowers on a brown and cream background.

At the furthest end of the room, two "Chairs of Estate" were set on a small dais with a red velvet backdrop and a dramatic

---

[1125] The main building was constructed around 1705 for John Sheffield, Duke of Buckingham. Hence the name, Buckingham Palace.

[1126] The West side, designed by John Nash, has remained virtually unchanged since the early 19th century and showcases the neoclassical style prevalent during its expansion. The East side was expanded in 1847 by Edward Blore and redesigned in 1913 by Sir Aston Webb.

[1127] Designed by John Nash.

[1128] Designed by Price Albert and displayed at the great exhibition of 1851.

arch and canopy over the two thrones[1129]. Those not overawed by this regal setting would notice the slight smell of mould, the peeling wallpaper, and discolouration on the exposed plaster, evidence of decades of cuts to the Sovereign Grant.

A gilt-framed picture hung close to the "Chairs of Estate". It portrayed an older man with a distinctive patrician face, left-parted grey hair, and slightly prominent ears. The subject stood awkwardly in this picture, his hands buried in his Anderson & Sheppard suit jacket pockets. A distinctive gold Parmigiani chronograph[1130] graced the man's wrist.

In addition to a few Russian oligarchs, half a dozen other "political donors" desperate for status in the British establishment exhibited behavioural symptoms of discomfort with the long and unexplained delay in their Investiture ceremony. Most were secretly wondering if their donation had been discovered and if they faced the embarrassment of explaining the "cultural misunderstanding" to their embassy[1131].

Oblivious and indifferent to this growing irritation were three middle-aged men standing apart from the group of awardees. These three senior ministers had the pale white complexions, bloodshot eyes and "rum blossom[1132] of those who reside in the extraordinarily extravagant, taxpayer-funded lifestyle of career politicians. The three stood together beside the drinks trolley, consuming their

---

[1129] Designed by John Nash based on set decorations used in opera.
[1130] Parmigiani Fleurier Toric Chronograph gifted by his wife.
[1131] They all have tax free non-dom and diplomatic status. Don't look so shocked.
[1132] Rhinophyma is linked with chronic and intense alcohol use.

umpteenth glass of Manzanilla Sherry[1133] from the Royal cellar.

"I'm almost sure this is a jolly fine wine, but just to be sure, I'll have another snifter!" giggled Prime Minster Sir Reginald Twiffers to the Royal sommelier, who patiently opened the tenth bottle the three men had consumed over the past hour. The other two men, Home Secretary Sir Johnathan Premble and Foreign Secretary Lord Jeremey Kenner, who were, like Twiffers, hanging onto the drinks trolley to remain upright, quickly downed their drinks and eagerly presented their empty glasses for an immediate refill. The three were dressed in the uniform of their esteemed station: crumpled and stained[1134], Denman & Goddard[1135] pinstripe suits, white shirts and Old Etonian[1136] ties.

"Any developments, Jezza?" demanded Twiffers to Kenner. When they were not consuming the world's finest foods and beverages at taxpayer expense, the three men looked for the next corrupt deal. Lord Kenner managed the massive foreign redevelopment grants, and Twiffers and Premble were waiting to learn of their cut from the latest "deal". Kenner paused. The last thing he wanted was to fully disclose the latest percentages he was being offered by the Chinese contractors who would rebuild the nation's roads. Fortunately, he was saved by the arrival of a large, balding

---

[1133] 'Laureate's Choice' Manzanilla Sherry by royal appointment.
[1134] These stains are typically from wine, sauces from gourmet meals, various arousal fluids and, of course, a dusting of the very finest Columbian cocaine.
[1135] Denman & Goddard provides the uniforms for students at Eton, along with blazers and suits for Old Etonians.
[1136] The tie for the Old Etonian Club has light blue stripes on a black background.

man in a crumpled brown poly-cotton Marks and Spencer[1137] suit, who had just entered through the tall white double doors to the stateroom.

"Bazzo!" exclaimed Kenner with exaggerated delight. He gestured to get the attention of the newcomer as the big former policeman and current Director of the Security Service (MI5) came to stand beside them and ushered away the Royal wine server.

Twiffers gathered the two other senior ministers into a conspiratorial huddle[1138] around Clive "Bazzo" Basildon and whispered, in a breath that smelt strongly of sherry,

"Now, Bazzo, have your searches of the Cortez mansion in St James Square yielded any incriminating evidence of our collusion with the Cortez revolution?"

Bazzo frowned. "Not so far, Reggie. Sinclair's people got there first and were seen taking things away."

The colour drained from Twiffers' face. He knew for a fact that all his meetings with Cortez had been recorded. If they ever came to light, well, it could be bloody awkward to explain taking money to aid in the attempted kidnapping of the Royal Prince and the plan to assassinate the head of MI6. And that was before he had joined forces with Premble and Kenner to help Cortez overthrow the entire bloody nation!

Fortunately, Sir Johnathan Premble's previous career as a leading human rights barrister gave him extensive experience in avoiding facing the consequences of one's actions, no matter how terrible. He advised,

---

[1137] Off the peg clothing is seen by the elites as being a clear sign of inferior status. But if you do not get a generous tax payer clothing allowance what can you do?

[1138] Huddles help prevent eavesdroppers and, of course, help keep one upright.

"Not to worry, chaps. They would need a pivotal witness to make anything stick, which is very unlikely as all of Cortez's close entourage are dead or in hiding. That upstart[1139], Sinclair, is just wasting her time and resources, as usual."

"Thank God!" Twiffers face brightened as he downed his remaining sherry and started looking for a refill.

The enormous double doors at the far end of the stateroom opened again. A slim and tall woman in her thirties, with short, bobbed dark hair and large, round, red-framed glasses that made her look like an owl, walked into the room accompanied by seven tough-looking men and women in dark suits. The former GCHQ intelligence analyst, Ms Twop, had upgraded her look under Sinclair's guidance to a dark grey Prada business suit. Twop searched the room until her eyes locked on the four men huddled together near the drinks trolly and smiled. Emboldened by Premble's promise that they were immune from prosecution, the three Ministers smiled back. Twiffers even raised his glass in a mock greeting.

Before the Prime Minister could lower his cynically raised glass, an overweight man[1140], with round glasses and ginger hair, dressed in a senior Wolfsangel uniform, came beside Twop and pointed directly to Twiffers.

The recognition of Major General Smegget, Chairman Cortez's Chief of Staff, made the blood visibly drain from the faces of Twiffers, Premble, Kenner and Basildon. The four men hurried towards one of the two emergency exits beside

---

[1139] "Upstart" means did not attend the *correct* schools. Listen to any British elite for more than a minute, and it will only be moments before they mention which school they attended. For many of them, it is all they have.

[1140] A life in the witness protection program will suit Smegget after he has testified.

the thrones, only to face more hard-looking men and women waiting for them.

Just as things looked dire, Clive Basildon saw someone who offered hope for evading the problem. He recognised the woman leading this second group of operatives as one of his own MI5 agents. In fact, she had been in charge of detaining Sinclair at her Horseferry House apartment in preparation for Cortez's assassins.

"Ms Malone! Thank God!"

Twiffers picked up on the situation and smiled like a snake who had cornered an injured bird.

"I hope you remember who *you* work for, young lady?" he asked condescendingly.

The Prime Minister was increasingly confident this *misunderstanding* could all be solved, and then he would make sure that Sinclair and Twop met with particularly nasty accidents. As Prime Minister, all that was needed was a word in the right ear.

Ms J. Malone smiled at the Prime Minster and then took him by complete surprise by slapping a set of handcuffs on his wrists,

"Yes, I do. I work for him," Malone gestured towards the picture of the Monarch hanging beside the two thrones.

Before leading Twiffers, Premble, Kenner, and Basildon away, Malone nodded towards Twop. The two groups of Secret Service (MI5) operatives exited the stateroom, leaving the prospective awardees wondering if they would ever get their gongs.

Four hundred and sixty-two miles southeast of where Sir Reginald Twiffers was experiencing a less enjoyable taxpayer-funded experience, an immaculately dressed mature man and an elegant auburn-haired woman wearing glasses sat at the only occupied table in a rooftop cafe above Place du Bourg-de-Four in Geneva.

It was dry and reasonably mild[1141] for mid-October in Switzerland, with the occasional beams of sunshine breaking through the clouds to highlight the Mont Blanc mountains to the Southeast. Fortunately, the large clouds of radioactive fallout that had dominated the skyline the last time Tavish had sat in the restaurant no longer belched forth, although sadly the Bernese Alps remained closed to tourists[1142]. Further across the rooftops, towards the cathedral, more workmen could be seen repairing tiles where Stewart had sent a SNITCH unit crashing through the roof.

Tavish Stewart wore a Highbury Charcoal Birdseye two-piece suit[1143] over a white linen open shirt[1144], and black leather Grafton[1145] brogues. Ad-Dajjal's Black PVD Breitling Aerospace still graced his wrist. Madeleine Mathers wore a Dries Van Noten Oversized Jacket, a white cotton Sorbonne T-shirt, Classic Levis 501 vintage jeans, a pair of Hermes Day sneakers, large Cartier sunglasses, and a Mondaine Swiss Railways watch.

The pair sat alone on the roof terrace under a large canvas table umbrella adorned with the café logo and numerous carbon stains that had failed to clean up completely after the firestorms. Mathers' face was partially bandaged as her

---

[1141] 52 degrees Fahrenheit.

[1142] For the foreseeable future.

[1143] By Ede & Ravenscroft, of course.

[1144] By Luca Faloni. Stewart had removed his tie for the informal coffee.

[1145] By Church's.

reconstructive surgery continued at the University Hospital of Geneva[1146], while Stewart's right hand was inside a protective surgical glove as part of his own acid burns treatment in Glasgow[1147]. Thankfully, the sword wounds on his left arm and left shin were recovering well but were concealed under his suit.

The sounds and smells of cooking occasionally came up the stairway from the cafe below them. It mixed with the scent of orange and fresh mint[1148] from Stewart's cologne, while Mathers' perfume complimented the fragrant atmosphere by tinging it with May Rose, Jasmine and Vanilla[1149]. There were two coffee cups on the latticework of the black iron table: a latte for Stewart and the other a black espresso for Mathers with a small plate of freshly cooked croissants shared between them.

Below them, the sounds of cement mixers and the hammering of masonry chisels echoed across the cobbled courtyard as artisans repaired the considerable damage from the numerous gunfights that had marked Stewart's previous visit to the cafe. Further down the street, more construction trucks were parked outside the SPLEE headquarters, which was covered in scaffolding as extensive renovations took place. Most notable of these was a blue plaque affixed to the front of the ancient building by the Canton of Geneva dedicated to the sacrifice made by Soror Emmilia, and Fraters Aron and Gabriel of Société pour la Préservation des Lignages ésotériques Européens.

[1146] The Geneva University Hospitals (HUG).
[1147] The Scottish National Burns Centre within the Glasgow Royal Infirmary.
[1148] Hermes Orange Verte.
[1149] Chanel No 5 - another gift from an admirer, probably Mathers' plastic surgeon.

On the far side of the square, a classic 1967 split windscreen green and white VW camper van and a British racing green Bentley Continental GT Mulliner were parked close to the police station with protective bollards around them. Both vehicles had stickers on their windshields indicating they had unlimited parking rights within the city of Geneva. In the square by the fountain, a metal statue of a SNITCH was being erected to mark the period when these monstrous machines roamed in dominion over the city.

"Will Jacob be joining us?" Stewart asked after taking a sip of his latte.

Mathers shook her head, making her auburn hair rotate around her face. "Frater Léon is directing the renovations on the HQ building," she smiled and then added, "Thanks in large part to your generous donation."

"Courtesy of Cortez. I have been making the best use of the funding he allocated for my *care* in the Montenegrin prison."

Mathers could not help laughing. "I heard some of your adventures from a phone call with Cynthia."

"Probably all exaggeration," Stewart replied modestly.

Mathers was momentarily serious. "The money means a lot after we lost everything." she reached over and grasped Stewart's uninjured hand before continuing,

"It was wonderful for Jacob and I to attend the ceremony at the Palais des Nations this morning and see your efforts get recognition," Mathers looked at the small blue box on the table, which she knew contained the United Nations Medal[1150].

[1150] The highest honour of the United Nations.

"I needed an interpreter," Stewart joked as he took one of the freshly baked croissants, broke it in two, and munched it with evident pleasure.

"And I suppose the UN President's official recognition of SPLEE as a cultural heritage centre had nothing to do with you? With this new status, we will start beginner classes as soon as the reconstruction is complete." Mathers beamed with pleasure.

Stewart smiled. "It was the least I could do. Speaking of which," the Scotsman reached into his left jacket pocket, removed a small red ring box, and passed it to Mathers.

"What is this another of your medals?" she opened it and found her charred SPLEE adept's ring. Overcome with emotion, she put the ring back on her finger[1151] and leant over to kiss Stewart's cheek.

"Where did you get this?"

"It was with what little remained of Cortez after Thomas... Well, I don't know how to describe exactly what emerged from Thomas."

Mathers inhaled in that unique way the French use to indicate agreement. "The ancient darkness... of course, we had all read about it in SPLEE archives, but to be honest, we thought it was just another fantastic tale, like the Qliphothic Wheels and the MUŠ.ŠÀ.TÙR. But now we know better. I will never doubt the ancients again."

Stewart paused momentarily, remembering the seven-headed abomination that had been revealed when Cortez died. He shivered and asked, "Do you think Venchencho will be able to remove this ancient darkness from Thomas?"

[1151] Pentagram tip pointing upwards of course, as if you needed to ask.

Mathers narrowed her eyes. "I will be honest, Tavish, I don't know if Thomas can ever be freed from this curse. The church lacks that knowledge, but remote places still exist where such skills may be known. I will contact Venchencho and provide what help I can."

There was a pause, and then the French adept continued, "We should just be glad that Ad-Dajjal sacrificed herself to remove the Bell."

Stewart frowned. "Every time I recall those final seconds, I am not sure if she acted altruistically or if she had planned the entire situation to steal the Bell."

"You think the worst of everyone, Tavish!" scolded Mathers in semi-jest, "When I performed psychometry on your watch just now, I sensed nothing."

"And you think the best of everyone. Ad-Dajjal sent Thomas the notebook to guide him to that lost temple in Göbekli Tepe and then used everyone to achieve her own goal of obtaining the Bell. I believe she played us all, but I do not understand why she didn't just use the adze herself."

"That part is easy, Tavish. Evil cannot touch the metal that forms the sacred adze. But do not discount the possibility that she may have sacrificed herself to save this reality. Right now, she could be trapped in a limbo for all eternity. She is gone, Tavish. I am pretty sure I could sense her if she remained."

Stewart nodded and drank some more of his coffee, but deep down, his doubts remained.

Five hundred and sixty-seven miles southeast from the rooftop cafe, where Stewart was enjoying his latte but not his thoughts, a jet black, square-angled Mercedes 450SEL, caked in road grime and dust, sat outside a medieval stone building high in the Mountains of Abruzzo. The car's massive 6.9-litre turbocharged and supercharged engine clicked as it cooled after an arduous drive from Rome. Weeks of work by a team of ordained automotive specialists at the AMG[1152] workshop in Affalterbach near Stuttgart had restored the deliverance vehicle to its former glory.

By a very deliberate design, there were no other human habitations for scores of miles in every direction around the strange-looking eleventh-century structure beside the old Mercedes. No exterior signs indicated the purpose of the building or the identities of its inhabitants. Instead, the dedication of the building was only hinted at by the thick cast iron ring that encircled the structure, the dozens of lightning conductors protruding from the roof and, set into the exterior stone walls at each of the cardinal points, statues of the four archangels dressed in the full plate armour of a medieval knight, complete with broadsword and shield. This consecrated building had no mains electricity[1153], phone line, cable connection, satellite dish or postal service. The building's existence was known only to the highest echelons of the Roman Catholic Church and only mentioned by them in whispered fearful tones as the Sanatorium of St Michael[1154].

Inside the building, the air was full of the scents of frankincense and myrrh[1155] and that profound calm so frequently associated with ancient religious sites. The two

---

[1152] Mercedes-AMG. The performance arm of Mercedes Benz.
[1153] It does have power independence from the grid by use of solar panels.
[1154] Devoted to the care of ordained exorcists suffering from an "extraordinary influence" (demonic possession) which had proven impossible to exorcise and which posed a danger to humanity.
[1155] The classic Roman Catholic church incense.

male visitors who had arrived in the old Mercedes approached a large iron gate cast in a repeated crucifix pattern. A narrow wooden drawbridge constructed from cedar, pine, and cypress[1156] sections led to another cast iron gate. This bridge spanned a deep chasm that descended into the bowels of the Italian mountain, where a ferocious mountain stream could be heard raging far beneath them.

The older of the two men had wild ginger hair flecked with increasing amounts of grey and a face that looked as though it had gazed long and hard into the abyss[1157]. He wore a traditional black clerical dress and a distinctive gold ring[1158] on his right hand. The other was a younger, dark-haired man dressed in a dog collar and black Gammarelli[1159] suit.

This younger priest felt a growing apprehension. His mind was filled with vague recollections. Until recently, he had been a long-term resident of the most secure section of the sanatorium that they were about to visit. He reminded himself for the umpteenth time that those memories were not truly his. Instead, they were from a very different persona who exhibited abilities that defied all rational explanations. In an attempt to distract himself from the more disturbing of these memories, he engaged the older priest in conversation.

"I understand that Father O'Neill has resumed his scholarly archaeological writing?"

Venchencho grunted. "Yes, as part of his therapy, we provided him with copies of his digital notes from Göbekli Tepe and a Remington typewriter[1160]. He completed the

---

[1156] The woods used to construct The Cross.
[1157] It had.
[1158] The Ring of the Fisherman (Anulus piscatoris).
[1159] Ditta Annibale Gammarelli (founded 1798) is the official tailor of The Papel office.
[1160] Remington Quiet Riter Typewriter. A classic from the 1960s.

paper and submitted it to the Journal of Archaeological Research[1161]. Unfortunately, when the site team at Göbekli Tepe went to authenticate the claimed neolithic subterranean vault, it was found to be a completely empty natural cave. Extensive searches failed to find any evidence of the images that had been included in O'Neill's paper. The journal was forced to reject the work on the grounds that it was, and I quote, *preposterous nonsense filled with AI-generated images*[1162]."

Fr Kwon gasped. "Do *you* think O'Neill made it all up?"

Venchencho smiled. "Who knows? So many odd things are associated with this entire case that I prefer to keep my mind open."

"How did O'Neill react?"

"Like a true Jesuit, he has buried himself in a new project, writing a follow-up to his bestseller, "Bridge of Souls."

"But it must be tough being all alone here. I recall it vaguely."

"He does have Ezekiel to keep him company, and the Augustinians delle Vergini[1163] nuns visit him for the Liturgy of the Hours[1164]."

Mention of the enforced visits by the nuns brought disturbing mental images to Kwon: of his then complete

---

[1161] The premier journal in the field from Springer - impact factor in 2022 = 3.8.
[1162] Don't you just hate it when that happens?
[1163] Sisters from Augustinians delle Vergini, an eleventh-century convent in Venice, who have provided nuns for St Michael's specialist mission since the twelfth century.
[1164] The required daily prayer schedule for all catholic priests: Morning Prayer or Lauds, Midmorning Prayer or Terce, Midday Prayer or Sext, Midafternoon Prayer, Evening Prayer or Vespers and Night Prayer or Compline.

indifference to Catholic ritual and disdain of the church, which went beyond the sacrilegious and was, literally, blasphemous. Kwon decided it was best to change the subject to something considerably less disturbing.

"How is your old cat, Ezekiel, isn't it?"

Venchencho smiled for the first time that day. "Yes. Ezekiel is a tough old boy. He had suffered serious chemical burns and some broken ribs, but thank God he is now on the mend." Both men crossed themselves at the mention of the Almighty.

They had reached the first and outer cruciform gate next to a sign declaring "No sharp objects" in English and Italian. One of the four security attendants collected the two visitors' penknives, keys, and pens and placed them in a wooden tray. In addition to surrendering their possessions, one of the attendants searched them from head to toe before opening the iron gates using a large crucifix-shaped key that hung from his belt. As they were both frisked, the Pope continued their conversation,

"You know, Fr Kwon. It is the strangest occurrence, but since Fr O'Neill was admitted, the three chronic patients residing in this maximum care section have spontaneously experienced a complete recovery from their affliction and have been declared fit enough to return to their normal clerical duties by independent psychiatric and theological assessments."

"What is the possible explanation, your Holiness?"

"Make of it what you want, Fr Kwon, but I believe whatever has possessed O'Neill frightened the other entities so much that they preferred to return to the torments of hell rather than stay close to whatever dwells within O'Neill."

Kwon crossed himself. It was unthinkable that a devil would choose to return to hell fire rather than remain on the mortal plane. The sequence of unthinkable things Kwon had encountered that day continued as they crossed the drawbridge. The last time Kwon had visited, he recalled that an unbearable cold always started at this point. But now it felt, well, quite normal. But such normality made the feeling of panic rise even more. He grasped at an opportunity to delay their visit to O'Neill.

"Holy Father, do you want me to return to the car and bring the deliverance bag to administer the holy sacraments?"

Venchencho looked sympathetically at the younger priest as though he could read his motives. "No, Father Kwon, every form of exorcism has already been tried and failed. But the French occultist Mathers has suggested a possible treatment."

"Is that why we are here?"

"Yes, in part. We are to explore Mathers' solution."

"A proposition to O'Neill?" asked Kwon.

The second set of iron gates had thin strips of badly worn wood set into specifically designed hollow sections in the cast iron, forming an enormous crucifix that towered above the visitor. The cross was constructed from sections of cedar, cypress, and palm. Above where the head of the crucified victim would have been placed was a plaque made of olive wood, with inscriptions in ancient languages. Only the lowest inscription in Latin was still legible. It read "Iesus Nazarenus Rex Iudaeorum[1165]." Recognising exactly what he was looking at, Kwon felt the hairs on the back of his neck rise.

[1165] Jesus the Nazarene, King of the Jews.

Venchencho turned to Fr Kwon as a nun opened this iron gate. The two men passed into a long stone corridor lit by dim lights, with cell doors on each side.

"Yes. It is a proposition to O'Neill and also to you, Father Kwon."

He then handed Kwon a folded letter from his pocket. As the younger priest read the contents, the colour drained from Kwon's face. "But Holy Father, this proposal involves me accompanying O'Neill to revisit the very same Tibetan lamasery where I became possessed before!"

Venchencho patted the younger man's arm in compassion. "I know. But I believe it is the only hope for O'Neill and the whole of creation. If the entity that dwells within Father O'Neill awakens, we are all finished."

Kwon was about to reject the idea, as he knew he risked re-igniting those hidden influences that had brought him so close to eternal damnation. Then, he felt ashamed of his selfishness. He recalled that O'Neill helped carry him out of the collapsing Citadel of the Djinn as it was reburied under the Mongolian desert sands[1166]. O'Neill had not hesitated to risk his own safety to save Kwon. It was unthinkable not to do the same. Kwon nodded his agreement to Venchencho, and the pair walked on.

At the furthest end of the long stone corridor, they reached a thick wooden door with a plain paper label attached that simply stated, "Fr Thomas O'Neill and Ezekiel." Outside the monastic cell, the air strongly smelled of Turkish Royal Cigarettes and freshly brewed coffee. The sound of rapid keyboard strokes emanated from under the door.

[1166] See Bridge of Souls.

Venchencho turned to Kwon. "Prepare yourself. Fr O'Neill's possession has aged him considerably." he then knocked on the door and turned the handle.

A few days later, and one thousand six hundred miles northwest of where Thomas O'Neill was sitting in his monastic cell thumping out his next bestseller, a group of vehicles were parked in a large grass field close to the remains of a traditional stone-built Scottish farmhouse. To the trained eye, the melted and charred Scottish granite rocks that had formed the structure showed evidence of the use of military-grade thermite explosives.

A red, one-person tent[1167] had been set up in the former building's main living room, along with a small Calor gas stove, some hermetically sealed plastic food storage chests and a fold-out table with an assortment of steel cutlery, pots, pans, and mugs. The single sign of luxury was a portable espresso[1168] machine. A British racing green Bentley Continental GT Mulline was parked outside what would have been the front door. The more recent visitors to Stewart's estate, two Skoda Octavia Estates in Police Scotland livery and two, unmarked black Range Rovers, were parked five yards further away in what would once have been the farmhouse's front garden but which was now overgrown with wild grasses.

Six, heavily armed[1169] Police Scotland officers, assisted by two, police K9 German shepherd dogs, patrolled the access roads into and out of this section of Stewart's estate. Three

---

[1167] Night Cat Backpacking Ultralight Waterproof Professional Hiking Tent.
[1168] A grey Wacaco Nanopresso Espresso Machine.
[1169] Heckler & Koch MP5 Machine guns.

hundred yards from the house and opposite the Stewart family crypt, four, armed[1170], plain-clothes S01[1171] protection officers spread out to be close to their principal[1172]. One of these S01 officers used an iPad to control a series of airborne micro drones to monitor the area for any possible threats.

A thousand feet below the hovering drones, a man and a woman sat side by side on a tartan[1173] rug at the southern perimeter of a megalithic stone circle set on top of a small hill. The local community had created the circle thousands of years earlier as an act of spiritual devotion and celestial timekeeping. The grass on the top of the mound had recently been cut with a scythe, the stones had been cleaned, and fresh flowers had been placed on a carved triquetra[1174] symbol set into the largest of the standing stones. The smell of freshly cut grass dominated the area.

Cynthia Sinclair was wrapped in Stewart's jacket[1175], draped over her black Prada business suit to protect herself from a growing chill blowing in from Loch Chon in the south. The hardier Scotsman only wore his Cottesmore Fleece top and Harkila[1176] Trousers.

Sinclair looked around them at the cut grass here and down in the Stewart family graveyard.

[1170] Glock 17.

[1171] Specialist Protection Branch of the Metropolitan Police Service (MPS).

[1172] The person being protected is known as "The Principal". In this instance, the acting Prime Minister, Dame Cynthia Sinclair.

[1173] Stewart tartan, of course.

[1174] Three interconnected arcs which symbolised to the Celts the circle/cycle of life and the three aspects of maiden, woman and crone.

[1175] A Simms G3 Guide Jacket.

[1176] Harkila Pro Hunter Endure.

"You have been busy."

Stewart nodded. "Before you head back to London, remind me to show you something interesting down in the crypt."

Sinclair laughed. "That old line. Trust me, I have seen it."

Stewart chuckled. "Not unless you have been visiting the thirteenth century. Recall that door that had burst open in the Crypt? It revealed some very interesting tombs."

Sinclair adopted a Bella Lugosi voice, "The Children of the Night?"

The Scotsman smiled. "No, it's not *that* interesting. It contained the remains of one of my ancestors: one Walter Steward of Dundonald[1177], the third hereditary High Steward of Scotland."

Sinclair thought for a moment. "Steward became Stewart? That makes sense," she thought about the implications of the origin of the Stewart and Stuart lineages,

"Hang on, that makes you..." she laughed, "Someone who would certainly upset a lot of people in London."

Stewart winked. "I cannot think of anything worse than all those official engagements."

He changed the subject. "Any news on Abdul Issuin?"

Sinclair frowned. "My sources in the embassy looked into all emergency admissions for males with multiple gunshot wounds at The Wroclaw University Hospital, but there were none, so we searched all the Polish hospitals on the date but came up empty. However, with the collapse of the Cortez regime, the country was in a state of chaos, so we checked all John Does, and some fitted the profile of massive gunshot trauma who arrived DOA."

[1177] Died in 1246.

"Do they still have the bodies?"

Sinclair shook her head. "No, the morgues were overflowing, so every unclaimed body was cremated."

Stewart was dissatisfied with the uncertainty about the hawk-faced assassin, but diplomatically, he changed the subject. "What about the Reise complex? Did you get recovery teams into those mines?"

"We got some British SF[1178] in there within 72 hours of your leaving the complex, but they found only the charred remains from a massive fire that had spread rapidly through the tunnels."

"Very convenient. Were there any signs of accelerants?"

"T, there was nothing to indicate anything suspicious. You said yourself that Cortez was doing experiments on the Bell that overloaded the electrical systems within the mines."

She reached over and kissed Stewart. "Face it, T. Thanks to you, the threats are all gone: Ad-Dajjal, the Bell, That multi-headed monster and even Abdul Issuin."

Stewart thought about it and sighed. Maybe everyone was right. He could finally relax and return to living a normal life.

Sinclair tried to direct the conversation towards the Scotsman's antique business,

"I saw that the New Bond Street shop is back,"

Stewart smiled. He knew he was being manipulated but went along with it.

"Yes, Jeff[1179] and Helen have been busy, as has Mohammed in Istanbul."

[1178] SF = Special Forces.
[1179] Jeffery Sonnet and Helen Curren.

Sinclair suddenly remembered something. "I heard from Lev. He is enjoying the challenge of renovating the old Stewart's showroom in Rome. He is happy to have escaped from Russia."

Stewart laughed at the mental image of his old friend Livin' la Vida Loca. "I bet he turns it into a nightclub with the money he has from the Chinese government for returning their president."

"I am not taking that bet!" Sinclair joked as she pulled two enamel mugs from the hamper beside them and passed them to Stewart, not so subtly indicating it was time for some coffee.

Tavish Stewart poured from a green thermos[1180] into the mugs before tipping a small measure of whisky from his old leather hip flask[1181] into both cups and passed one of the steaming mugs to Sinclair, making a toast,

"Daoine Sìth[1182]!"

Sinclair repeated the phrase, giggled at her mispronunciation but hoped that her good intent was more important than exactly matching Stewart's words. Both savoured the warmth and flavour of the Glenfiddich-laced coffee, which took away some of the chill from the nearby loch. Moments later, one of Sinclair's close protection team ran up the hill and stood catching his breath in front of them carrying his iPad.

"Ma'am, our drones have just detected an unknown target moving in the area behind the stones.."

[1180] Classic Legendary Stainless Steel Bottle 1L in Hammertone Green.

[1181] R.M.Williams Men's Hip flask.

[1182] This has nothing to do with Star Wars. This is the Gaelic toast to the ancestors ("People of the Mounds") who built Scotland's neolithic mounds and stone circles.

Before Sinclair was hurried away by her protection detail, Stewart calmly asked the detective,

"Did this unknown target resemble a small walking forest by chance[1183]?"

The S01 officer raised an eyebrow before scrolling through the images on his iPad and looked increasingly puzzled,

"Yes... how did you?"

Sinclair and Stewart laughed and clinked their mugs together.

The acting Prime Minister looked up at the perplexed protection officer and said, "It's okay, detective. It's an old friend."

Two thousand two hundred miles southeast of Stewart's estate, the twenty-three Western tourists stuck inside the Volvo B11R "Delights of Egypt" tour bus were increasingly dissatisfied with the interminable delays. There are only so many teaser descriptions about the Fourth Dynasty Giza pyramid complex that can be tolerated when you are stuck in a hot bus. Especially when you are within clear sight of the North side of the Great Pyramid, parked in front of the limestone entrance gate, which was barred by a group of blue-uniformed antiquities officers.

"Hey, lady, what is the problem? We have all paid for chrissakes!" yelled a very large, sweaty man towards the rear of the coach, dressed in a loud Hawaiian shirt which hung over his pot belly.

[1183] One of the forms assumed by the Cailleach Bheartha.

The tour guide, who had been talking in Arabic with the Egyptian driver, sighed, faced the group and turned on her mic.

"Ladies and Gentlemen, please have patience, as I have already told you and as you can see," she gestured through the windshield towards the partially visible pyramids, "there is an emergency operation underway to rescue someone who has fallen down one of the drainage channels on the plateau."

Someone further down the bus was heard to say, "That is some rescue operation. Over the last half hour, I have seen three Chinooks[1184] and one Osprey[1185] come in. It's more like Kandahar than Giza!"

The high-pitched, whiny voice of a large woman on the long rear seat added to the discussion, "Ma'am? I need a toilet break. The Marriott Mena House hotel is just there," she pointed behind the bus. At the sight of the air-conditioned luxury hotel, more passengers suddenly felt the same bladder pressure, and a chorus of demands complicated the tour guide's evening even further.

Six hundred yards north of the de-bussing guests on the "Delights of Egypt" tour, a lone figure walked slowly down a ramp that extended from the rear exit doors of an unmarked Bell Boeing V-22, which had landed on the limestone plateau next to two Chinook helicopters. A blizzard of sand blown up from the ground by the rotor blades obscured everything, exactly as had been planned. This comprehensive plan

---

[1184] Boeing CH-47 Chinook
[1185] The Bell Boeing V-22 Osprey is a tiltrotor military aircraft with both vertical takeoff and landing (VTOL) capabilities.

included generous rashwa (bribes) for the police, antiquities authorities, and the tourist police to seal off the plateau for this operation and turn a blind eye to what occurred.

The lone figure was dressed in a full-length grey cotton robe with a hood that covered the head. The face was hidden by a desert camouflage shemagh and mirrored aviator sunglasses. This figure inspected the ongoing work of unloading airtight composite crates from the helicopters and the rear of the Osprey onto wooden pallets. All the people working on this operation wore the same long grey robe, hood, face scarf, and glasses to protect against the airborne sand. The unloaded crates were collected by forklift trucks and taken down a large ramp into the ground that had been exposed by the raising of a twenty-yard square section of the limestone plateau. The edges of this raised section were normally disguised by the drainage channels in the ancient limestone.

The lone figure descended down the slope for some fifty feet into a series of vast chambers that had been originally carved into the limestone to provide a supply of water from the Nile River to aid in the construction of the Khufu, Khafre and Menkaure pyramids. The main chamber where the lone figure stood was fifty yards wide and five yards tall with plain, undecorated limestone walls, floors and ceilings. The chamber continued far into the distance and covered the entire length of the Giza plateau.

Now free from the sandstorm, most of the operatives removed their face coverings and hoods before commencing work. However, it was noticeable that the lone figure kept theirs in place.

Some forklift trucks unloaded their palettes in this space and returned up the ramp to fetch their next load. Other operatives unloaded the crates from the palettes and began opening them to remove their contents. Some of the older wooden boxes that came out of the crates were marked with branded swastikas and contained books and relics. Other materials were labelled with REISE in a Germanic gothic script, and these boxes contained scientific notes, equipment, exotic materials and biological sample jars. Every item was scanned and meticulously catalogued.

The lone figure crossed the width of the vast chamber and started down a long, narrow passage that was wide enough and tall enough for two forklift trucks to pass each other in opposite directions. The sides of this tunnel were highly decorated with predynastic art, showing Lion-Headed goddesses in various acts of worship of snake gods. As the lone figure continued, the images of the Snake God became more stylised as the striking Cobra of Isfet.

Eventually, this passageway opened into a temple, with statues of Isfet and wall paintings similar in their themes to those that Fr O'Neill had seen in the subterranean chamber in Göbekli Tepe, but these images were highly stylised into an Egyptian form. The ceiling was painted in vivid colours and showed a massive lioness directly above them, silhouetted against the night sky of 12,000 years ago. The lioness was facing in the same orientation and size as the world-famous limestone sphinx carving directly above them on the surface. Down beneath The Sphinx was a temple dedicated not to the Pharaoh Khafre but to a much older entity[1186].

Laid out around this temple were the very artefacts that O'Neill had meticulously described in his rejected academic paper. Directly in front of the lone figure was an elaborate golden throne. To the right-hand side of the throne was the Bell, which had formed such an obsession for Chairman Cortez.

[1186] Edgar Cayce did not know the half of it.

A set of predynastic Isfet decorations set into one of the walls beside the Bell showed a seven-headed snake held captive within a metal cage. Beside these images was the very cage depicted. A close metallurgical analysis would have revealed that the ancient cage's construction was the same exotic metal as the adze that Stewart had bravely used in Geneva. Inside the adze metal cage, the remains of the two snakeheads severed when Ad-Dajjal fought the monster in Geneva, were already beginning to regenerate into a pair of multi-headed soul parasites.

To the left side of the throne was a modern office layout. Sitting on a bespoke Hermes black leather office chair before a Venetian smoked glass desk was a strikingly beautiful woman with long jet-black hair and piercing green hypnotic eyes. Her eyelids were decorated in traditional Egyptian makeup, emphasising her gaze's mesmeric power. She wore a white Thai silk Chanel trouser suit with black six-inch Christian Louboutin heels and a Gold Rolex GMT Master gracing her left wrist. She was finishing a video conference on a brushed aluminium iMac. On her screen was an androgynous-looking figure with dark, wet shoulder-length hair. Ad-Dajjal addressed the woman,

"I believe that concludes our transaction, Ms Aspen. Beyond Facts, INC is now under my exclusive ownership. I look forward to our future together."

Now that the video conference had ended, the lone figure approached the smoked glass desk, pulled back his grey hood and removed the scarf to reveal his distinctive hawk-faced profile, known to global law enforcement as "the most dangerous man in the world". Striking a matchbook, he ignited a Montecristo Number 4 and smiled in delight.

K.R.M. Morgan

Social Media

If you enjoyed reading this book, please share a review on social media or Amazon so others can discover Tavish Stewart's adventures.

Also by K.R.M. Morgan from MadBagus Books

Tavish Stewart Adventures

Bridge of Souls: Ancient Prophecy Ultimate Evil

The New Republic 1: Old Dreams New Nightmares

The New Republic 2: The Qliphothic Gates

The New Republic 3: Twilight of the Gods

Foundations Workbook Series

Foundations of Magick

Knowledge Lectures

SPLEE Knowledge Lecture 23 MusSAtur: Myth and Mystery

ABOUT K.R.M. MORGAN

After leaving school, Konrad worked to fund himself through several years of further and higher education. When he was not studying, he spent his free time practising various martial arts in his back garden, much to his neighbours' amusement. After finishing his studies, Konrad pursued an academic career that permitted him to work in several regions worldwide.

During his travels, Konrad encountered extraordinary individuals, including politicians, bureaucrats, mad professors, spies, ritual magicians, bankers, and media moguls. Some were good, some were bad, and some were just bizarre. His experiences formed the basis for his books' complex plots and characters.

Connect with K.R.M. Morgan:
Twitter/X: @KRM_Morgan